THE TIGER THRONE

Preetha Rajah Kannan is the author of *Shiva in the City of Nectar,* an enthralling collection of stories based on the revered Tamil text, *Thiruvilayaadal Puranam*. This was followed by *Son of Shiva*, narrating the exploits of the warrior-god Kartikeya, commander-in-chief of the heavens and epitome of wisdom and valour. Her third book, *Hounds of Shiva*, is a treasure house of tales detailing the impassioned, heroic acts of sacrifice, devotion and service in the life and times of the Saivite saints, the Nayanmars. Her next book is *The Warrior God: Ayyappa of Sabarimalai,* the fascinating story of the renowned Sabarimalai temple. Preetha's fifth book is *Dance of Shiva*, a collection of sthalapuranams, narrating the precious legends behind our temples. She is also the editor of *Navagraha Purana,* a translation of the eponymous Telugu work by V. S. Rao. Kannan has contributed to newspapers and magazines, such as *The New Indian Express* and *The Express School Magazine*. A homemaker and grandmother, she lives with her family in Madurai, Tamil Nadu.

THE
TIGER
THRONE

Kalki's Ponniyin Selvan
Retold

PREETHA RAJAH KANNAN

JAICO PUBLISHING HOUSE

Ahmedabad Bangalore Chennai
Delhi Hyderabad Kolkata Mumbai

Published by Jaico Publishing House
A-2 Jash Chambers, 7-A Sir Phirozshah Mehta Road
Fort, Mumbai - 400 001
jaicopub@jaicobooks.com
www.jaicobooks.com

THE TIGER THRONE
ISBN 978-93-91019-97-6

First Jaico Impression: 2022

Page design and layout: R. Ajith Kumar, Delhi

For Vaanan and Arun

Amma's love and my prayer for you

May you be blessed with
Abiding wisdom, a long life
True friends, perennial prosperity
Constant youthfulness, a healthy body
A steadfast mind, an ever-loving wife
Righteous children, enduring fame
Integrity in speech, large-heartedness in charity
Boundless wealth, unswerving justice
A sorrow-free life and devotion to the divine

From: Abirami Andhadhi

Contents

Author's Note

MY EARLIEST RECOLLECTION of *Ponniyin Selvan* is of five hardbound volumes standing tall in Amma's book collection. To my eternal regret, the convent-educated-English-speaking me had my nose too deep in English novels to explore one of the greatest Tamil novels ever written.

The years passed and I stepped into the courtyard of Thanjavur's 'Big Temple' for the first time. I froze: the towering gopuram drew my eyes like a magnet and automatically lifted my head up to the evening-sun-splashed sky. The huge lingam in the sanctum thrilled my soul with its stark, truly 'god-sized' grandeur. And so, I came to Raja Raja Chola, the emperor who had the audacity to think big and build the Brihadeeshvara Temple on this vast scale.

Ramasamy Aiyar Krishnamurthy (1899–1954), or Kalki, immortalized Emperor Raja Raja Chola as *Ponniyin Selvan*. The novel was serialized weekly during 1950–54 and then published in five volumes. The brilliant Kalki packed dashing warriors and beautiful princesses, secret passages and dark dungeons, sorcerers and spies, vengeance and romance, shipwrecks and quicksand, leopards and assassins into 2000-odd pages of roller-coaster excitement.

Dear readers, I give you *Ponniyin Selvan* as a 673-page, one-volume treat: *The Tiger Throne*. I have tried to remain completely faithful to Kalki: after all, who dares take liberties with a masterpiece which is perfect as it is? I have tried to give you a compact version suited to the 'fast' world today, while retaining the body and soul of Kalki's work.

As always, I hope you will pass on the story to your children and grandchildren. This is not just a book, it is a record of our glorious history and culture ... parting the veil of centuries to give us a glimpse of our roots and the rich lives of our ancestors.

I hope you enjoy *The Tiger Throne* so much that you decide to read the original *Ponniyin Selvan* in Tamil, as I did at: https://www.projectmadurai.org/pm_etexts/utf8/pmuni0169_01_01.html

Happy reading to you all!

Preetha Rajah Kannan

Main Characters

The Cholas

Sundara Chola	the reigning emperor
Vanamadevi	Sundara Chola's wife
Aditya Karikalan	Sundara Chola's eldest son and the crown prince
Arulmozlivarman	Sundara Chola's younger son and the future Emperor Raja Raja Chola
Kundavai	Sundara Chola's daughter
Sembiyan Madevi	the queen mother
Madurandaka	Sundara Chola's cousin
Malayaman	Sundara Chola's father-in-law

The Pazluvur clan

Ambalavan	Pazluvur chieftain
Kalaanthaka	Ambalavan's younger brother
Nandini	Ambalavan's wife

The Kadambur clan

Sambuvaraya	Kadambur chieftain
Kandamaran	Sambuvaraya's son
Manimekalai	Sambuvaraya's daughter

The Kodumbalur clan

Velir	Kodumbalur chieftain
Vanathi	Velir's niece

The Pandian conspirators

Ravidasan   the leader
Devaralan
Soman Sambavan
Idumbankari
Kiramavithan
Rakamma

Others

Aniruddha   the chief minister
Azlvarkkadian   a master spy
Chendan Amudhan   a flower seller
Mandakini   a fisherman's daughter
Parthibendran   a warrior of Pallava lineage
Pinakapani   a doctor's son
Poonkuzlali   a lighthouse keeper's daughter
Vandhiya Devan   a young warrior of noble lineage

PART 1

A NEW TIDE

The *Aadi* Festival

VALLAVARAYA VANDHIYA DEVAN, brave descendent of the Vallam kings, slowed his tired horse to a walk. The young warrior admired the beauty of Veeranam Lake, a vast reservoir on the River Ponni, with seventy-four sluice gates. *What marvels the Chola kings have built! The Cholas are large-hearted, devout and brave. How lucky I am to be Prince Karikalan's friend!*

It was the auspicious day of *Aadi Perukku* in the year 968 AD. Evening revelers crowded the riverbank, dressed in their festive best: singing, dancing, wading in the shallows and picnicking. An old woman called out, "Young man, you look tired. Why don't you have something to eat?"

Devan considered her kind offer–especially as a group of young women stood nearby, giggling and making eyes at his rippling muscles. Just then, a fleet of white-masted boats sailed swiftly down the river. The first boat reached the shore and disgorged a company of strapping soldiers, armed with shining spears. The men charged into the crowd, shouting, "Move! Make way!"

The people hurriedly cleared a path and ran to a safe distance with their belongings.

Devan asked an old man hobbling along with the help of a stick, "Sir, whose boats are these?"

The old man pointed to the flag flying above the mast of the large boat in the center of the fleet. "Only the Pazluvur brothers travel under the banner of the Palm Tree."

"The great Lord Ambalavan himself?!" exclaimed Devan in awe.

The Pazluvur brothers, Ambalavan and Kalaanthaka Kandar, were the most powerful and privileged of all the Chola chieftains, with close ties to the royal family. Their city, Pazluvur, stood on the Ponni's northern bank. Ambalavan, renowned veteran of twenty-four battles, was the Chola kingdom's chancellor and food controller, with the right to levy and collect taxes on behalf of Emperor Sundara Chola.

Devan was eager to see Ambalavan. But even as he craned his neck over the crowd, he remembered Crown Prince Aditya Karikalan's orders: *Vandhiya Devan, the two letters you carry are crucial - one is for my father, the emperor, and the other is for Princess Kundavai, my sister. You must make sure these messages reach them in secret. I hear whispers of treachery in the highest circles of government. Above all, beware of the Pazluvur brothers and my uncle, Madurandaka. They must not know about you or your mission.* The prince had smiled and added, *My friend, don't let anyone provoke you into a fight. There's no need to prove your courage: it's already beyond question.*

Aditya Karikalan, the emperor's eldest son, was the Supreme Commander of the Cholas' northern army, based at Kanchipuram.

There's no time to lose. I must hurry to the emperor's court at Thanjavur and then on to Pazlayarai to meet the princess. Devan spurred his horse on, but the exhausted beast only managed a trot. *I'll spend the night at Sambuvaraya's palace at Kadambur. I'll get a fresh horse there.*

Azlvarkkadian

VANDHIYA DEVAN TURNED his horse southwards, relishing the thought of the adventures ahead of him. What had he to fear when he had his spear, sword and armor … and courage in his heart?

He reached the Veeranam Temple. The Chola kings were renowned for renovating old brick and mortar temples, building magnificent stone edifices in their place. As he crossed the temple which was thronging with devotees, Devan heard angry voices. Curious, he dismounted and pushed his way through the crowd. He found two men arguing furiously, with the spectators cheering and booing them on.

After hundreds of years of Buddhist and Jain dominance, there was a Hindu revival in Tamil Nadu. With their soul-stirring hymns, the

Azlvars and *Nayanmars* lit the fire of devotion to Vishnu and Shiva in the hearts of the people. Vaishnava and Shaiva fanatics often clashed violently, with some arguments even ending in bloodshed. One of the debaters was a short, sturdy young man, armed with a heavy staff. The tuft of hair over his forehead and the sandalwood paste smeared on his body showed he was a Vaishnava. The second man's body was smeared with holy ash: the mark of a Shaiva.

The Shaiva shouted, "Azlvarkkadian, Vishnu and Brahma surrendered to Shiva when they could not find the head or foot of the Pillar of Fire: how then can Vishnu be greater than Shiva?"

Azlvarkkadian retorted, "Shiva Padha Dhuli Bhattar, your Shiva granted Ravana many boons. Yet, Vishnu, as Lord Rama, defeated Ravana. Tell me, how then can Shiva be greater?" The stout Azlvarkkadian shook his stick threateningly at the puny Bhattar. The crowd cheered him on, thirsting for a fight.

Devan intervened. "You two: if you want to fight, why don't you join our army in Sri Lanka?"

On seeing the handsome young warrior, cries of, "Hear, hear!" rose from the spectators.

Enjoying his role of mediator, Devan said mischievously, "I have solid evidence that Vishnu and Shiva are equal. I met them both in Vaikundam. They were seated on chairs of equal height. In fact, both the gods were also of equal height and weight: I measured them with my own hands." The crowd cheered him on as Devan continued. "When I asked them who was greater, they replied, 'We are equal—throw sand in the mouth of anyone who disagrees.'"

Devan held up a fistful of sand; immediately, the crowd began to throw sand at the debaters. The furious Azlvarkkadian cursed them and entered the fray with his stick.

The rhythmic tattoo of drums halted the brawl. A herald cried: "Make way for the honorable Lord Ambalavan!"

A company of soldiers armed with spears marched past, followed by a huge, caparisoned elephant. The dark, well-built Ambalavan sat on its back. Behind the elephant came a palanquin with silk screens. Devan saw a slender, fair arm, wearing bangles, part the screen. He felt a pang of dark premonition as a lovely face looked out at the crowd.

The woman's beautiful eyes stopped at something near Devan: she shrieked and disappeared behind the screen. *What frightened her?* Devan wondered. He followed her line of sight: Azlvarkkadian leaned on a tamarind tree, staring at the palanquin.

Veeranam Temple

AS THE COMPANY MARCHED away, a few ruffians in the tail of the procession spotted Devan's horse. One man tried to climb on the horse, but the animal immediately threw him off. The infuriated man twisted the horse's tail–it neighed in pain and charged wildly into the crowd.

Azlvarkkadian appeared by Devan's side and taunted him. "Where's your courage now? Why don't you fight with those men?"

Devan ignored him. With his mission in mind, he had no intention of quarreling with Ambalavan's men. He found his horse near a thicket of tamarind trees. He rubbed its back to calm it and led it back to the road. To his annoyance, Azlvarkkadian approached him again.

"*Thambi,*" the Vaishnava cajoled in a sweet voice. "I have a favor to ask. If you plan to spend the night at Kadambur Palace, can you take me with you?"

Devan was surprised. "How do you know my plans?"

Azlvarkkadian smiled. "That's easy: everyone is headed there today. Lord Ambalavan and his company are staying there tonight."

"And why should I take you along? Are you planning to pick a quarrel with a Shaiva there?"

"Oh no! I'm not a professional Shaiva baiter. I want to enjoy tonight's feast and entertainment at the palace. Do you have an invitation? I can pose as your servant."

"You can find someone else to be your partner in deceit. Sambuvaraya's son, Kandamaran, is my friend. I have an open invitation to visit Kadambur Palace whenever I come this way."

Azlvarkkadian sniffed in disdain. "I thought you were one of the royal guests with a special invitation. You won't be allowed into the palace tonight."

They walked on in silence.

"Why are you following me?" Devan asked.

"You are following me!" Azlvarkkadian countered. "I'm going to the Veeranam Temple."

"I'll come with you and worship Vishnu," Devan said. To his surprise, when they reached the sanctum, Azlvarkkadian sang the devotional hymns of the *Azlvars* with tears streaming down his face. Devan revised his opinion of the man. "I see you are a true devotee of the Lord, Vaishnava. Please forgive me if I have offended you in any way."

"I forgive you. Now, will you do me a favor? I have a letter. Will you give it secretly to the lady who was in the palanquin?"

Devan was indignant. "Do you think I'm the kind of man who goes about carrying love letters?"

"Okay, okay," Azlvarkkadian pacified him. "Let it be …"

Devan spurred his horse and the animal, rested now, flew into a gallop. He was in Kadambur by nightfall.

Kadambur Palace

SAMBUVARAYA OF KADAMBUR was an eminent Chola chieftain. His fortress-like palace reflected his rank. The entrance was a hive of activity. Servants milled about attending to elephants, horses and bulls, holding flaming torches to light the scene. The open gates were heavily guarded.

Surveying the activity, Devan thought, *Maybe I should visit my friend another day.* But he was curious about the coming events of the night. Assuming a confident air, he tried to gallop past the open gates. The alert guards barred his way with crossed spears. One man held his horse's reins while another examined his face under the light of a torch. Devan shouted in righteous indignation, "Is this how Kadambur welcomes its invited guests?"

The guard captain came to him. There was menace in the man's voice: "Who are you?"

Devan declared defiantly, "I'm Vandhiya Devan of Vallam. Make way!"

The captain stood his ground. "All the invited guests have arrived; we have strict orders to let no one else in."

"Very well," Devan pretended to give in. "Let my horse go." The soldier let go of the horse's reins. Devan immediately spurred the animal forward. As the horse charged into the palace, he unsheathed his sword and waved it threateningly.

The soldiers scattered, shouting, "Catch him!"

The palace gates clanged shut and a war drum beat a warning. In minutes, Devan was surrounded by armed soldiers. As he jumped down from his horse and defended himself with his sword, Devan shouted, "Kandamaran! Kandamaran! Your men are killing me!"

His attackers froze at the name. At the same time, a voice thundered from the balcony above: "What's happening there?" It was Sambuvaraya.

The captain replied, "Lord, a man is trying to enter the palace using the young master's name."

"Kandamaran," Sambuvaraya ordered his son, "Go and see what the fuss is all about."

Kandamaran hurried to the gate. Seeing Devan, he exclaimed, "Is it really you, my dear friend?" and embraced him warmly. Kandamaran angrily scolded and dismissed the soldiers; taking his friend's hand, he escorted him happily into the palace.

Devan was curious. "All this activity ... and security! What's up, Kandamaran?"

Kandamaran smiled. "You have always longed to meet Lord Ambalavan, Mazlavaraya and other great warriors and chieftains. Today's your lucky day—you can see them all." He took Devan to his father and said, "*Appa*, do you remember me talking about my close friend, Vandhiya Devan? Here he is."

Devan stood with his hands folded in respect before the old man.

But Sambuvaraya frowned. "Maybe today's not a good day to pay a visit and cause a ruckus after dark!"

Kandamaran's face fell but he did not argue. He moved to Ambalavan, the night's honored guest, who was seated on a high chair. "Uncle, this is Vandhiya Devan. We were close friends during our tour of duty at the Pennai army camp. He's your admirer: he used to ask, 'Does Lord Ambalavan, the bravest warrior of the Chola kingdom, really have sixty-four battle scars?'"

To the friends' alarm, Ambalavan asked, "Are you questioning my courage?"

Devan quickly said, "Sir, your courage is known throughout the land. Who am I to question it?"

Ambalavan was pleased. "Hmm ... you're a clever young man."

Sambuvaraya took his son aside and said, "Give your friend something to eat and let him go to bed early." His meaning was clear: he did not want Devan to witness the night's events.

Kandamaran then took Devan to the women's quarters and introduced him to his mother. A girl peeped shyly at him from behind the old woman. *That's Kandamaran's sister*, Devan guessed. He was rather disappointed that she did not measure up to Kandamaran's description of her. He wondered which of the women in the room was the beautiful woman in the palanquin.

Kuravai Koothu

AS THE TWO friends left the women's quarters, they heard the buzz of curious voices and loud laughter behind them. Vandhiya Devan flushed in anger and embarrassment. *They are making fun of me.* Kandamaran showed him around Kadambur Palace's vast courtyards, granaries and marble halls. Devan couldn't resist asking, "I heard the women laugh: were they mocking me?"

"Oh no!" his friend exclaimed. "All of them like you. They were discussing Lord Ambalavan's new wife. He recently married a girl young enough to be his daughter. He's besotted with her and takes her with him everywhere in a screened palanquin. He does not let her join the other women." He shrugged. "If an old man makes a fool of himself over a girl, he becomes a laughing stock, however great he may be."

Devan was telling Kandamaran how he had caught a glimpse of Ambalavan's young wife in her palanquin when he was interrupted by the sound of music.

"The entertainment is about to begin," Kandamaran said. "Let's go."

The friends walked to an open-air stadium, encircled by the fortress walls. It was fast filling with people. A raised stage stood in the center, illuminated by oil lamps and torches. The show began with the *Kuravai Koothu,* a dance drama depicting God Muruga's triumph over the demons and his marriage to the hunter princess, Valli. This was followed by the *Velanattam.* A man and a woman, all in red, danced an aggressive duet. With red tongues and eyes, and foreheads smeared with vermilion, they lunged violently at each other, fighting over a spear. Finally, the male dancer grabbed the spear and threw himself into a frenzied solo. At its finale, the orchestra fell silent. As a lone priest beat a hypnotic rhythm on the *udukkai,* the dancer went into convulsions.

Awed whispers ran through the spectators: "He's possessed by God Muruga!"

The priest made an impassioned call: "Great God Muruga! Answer our questions. Will the monsoon be good this year? Will we prosper?"

The dancer roared, "The rains will bless your land. All your wishes will come true. But you have sinned against my mother, Durga. She demands a sacrifice: will you give it to her?"

"We will!" cried the priest.

The dancer's voice echoed eerily through the stadium: "Durga demands blood—royal blood. She wants to drink the blood of a prince descended from a thousand-year lineage of kings!"

The guests exchanged meaningful glances. Sambuvaraya caught the priest's eyes—the drum fell silent. The dancer collapsed on the stage and was carried away; the crowd quietly dispersed.

A jackal howled in the distance. Devan, spellbound by the drama, turned in the direction of the sound and froze in amazement— Azlvarkkadian's head hovered above the fortress wall as though it had been impaled and mounted there. Devan blinked and looked again: the head had vanished. He shook his head in embarrassment: *It must be my imagination ...*

Midnight Conspiracy

KANDAMARAN PROUDLY POINTED out the chieftains and tribal leaders present at the sumptuous dinner. Most of them were battle-hardened veterans with high positions in the Chola kingdom. Even as he looked around in awe, Vandhiya Devan was filled with misgiving: *Why are all these men gathered here tonight?*

After dinner, Kandamaran took him to a terrace and pointed to a corner. "You must be tired. Sleep here. Once I have seen to the other guests, I'll come and sleep beside you."

Devan fell asleep at once. But he was plagued by nightmares. He ran through a dark forest, chased by a horde of howling jackals on one side and a huge pack of bloodhounds on the other. The animals' eyes blazed like burning coals. He ran into a temple and found himself face to face with a huge idol of Kali, her tongue protruding from her open mouth. A priest emerged from behind the idol, armed with a sharp sword.

"Ah, you have come at last," said the priest. "Tell me your lineage."

"My clan ruled Vallam for three centuries. My father lost his kingdom to the Vaidhumbarayas."

"Go!" screamed the priest. "You are not worthy to be sacrificed!"

The statue of Kali vanished. In its place stood an idol of Krishna. To Devan's horror, Azlvarkkadian's dismembered head lay on the sacrificial altar, singing a devotional hymn.

Devan started awake. He opened his eyes and saw Azlvarkkadian's head peering over the fort wall. But, this time, it could not be his imagination—he saw Azlvarkkadian's hands clinging to the wall. Azlvarkkadian's attention was fixed on something inside the palace compound. *Is he a spy? I must warn Kandamaran. Kandamaran is my friend and I have eaten his salt.* Devan jumped up, grabbed his sword and made his way stealthily towards Azlvarkkadian.

He froze at the sound of voices. Hiding behind a pillar, he peeped out cautiously. Below the terrace was a small courtyard, enclosed on three sides by the fortress walls. It was illuminated by the dim light of a single oil lamp. The visiting chieftains were seated there in a close circle. Kandamaran was also there.

It was obvious that Azlvarkkadian was there to spy on the gathering. From his concealed vantage point, Azlvarkkadian could see only a part of the courtyard, but could overhear everything being said. Devan decided to catch the Vaishnava imposter red-handed and drag him before Sambuvaraya. But, to do this, Devan would have to cross the courtyard. If he warned the men, Azlvarkkadian would have time to escape and Devan himself would come under suspicion for wandering around the palace at night. Recalling Sambuvaraya's displeasure at seeing him, Devan decided not to disturb the men. *I'll ask Kandamaran about this tomorrow.*

Just as he turned to leave, he noticed the screened palanquin he had seen in the procession. *Why is the palanquin here? Is Lord Ambalavan so jealous he can't let his young wife out of his sight? Poor old man— enslaved by his passion for a girl at his age. Maybe Azlvarkkadian has some connection with the girl. She may be his sister or his lover. Lord Ambalavan may have abducted her; that ruthless man is capable of anything. Anyway, it's none of my business ...*

As he again turned to leave, Devan heard his own name and quickly moved back to his hiding place.

Ambalavan said, "Sambuvaraya, where's your son's friend? That young man is in Prince Aditya Karikalan's service. No one must hear our plans. If there's the least doubt that the young man has heard something, he must not be allowed to leave the palace alive. Is that clear?"

Devan's blood froze in his veins.

Kandamaran intervened. "Uncle, he's fast asleep on the terrace–he can't hear a single word spoken here. I vouch for him. He won't pry into matters which don't concern him."

"He may be your friend, Kandamaran, but he's a stranger to us: that's why I'm warning you."

Ambalavan turned back to the gathering. "This is our question: who has the right to ascend the Tiger Throne after Sundara Chola's death?"

Laughter and Rage

WHO ARE THESE people to discuss the succession issue? Devan wondered. *I knew there was something suspicious going on. Why bother about Azlvarkkadian? I must get to the root of this mystery. Kandamaran lied to me: he let me sleep and came to attend this secret meeting ...*

Ambalavan continued, "I have important news: Emperor Sundara Chola is dying. I heard it confidentially from the royal physician himself. The astrologers say the same thing."

"Why consult astrologers?" someone asked. "The comet in the night sky is an omen of death."

Ambalavan said, "We must choose the emperor's successor."

"Aditya Karikalan was anointed crown prince two years ago," piped up a voice.

Ambalavan replied angrily, "But we were not consulted! Our clans have served the Cholas for generations. Our ancestors sacrificed their lives to safeguard Chola territory. Even now, our sons fight under the Cholas' Tiger Flag in Sri Lanka. But we were ignored in this crucial matter."

A sarcastic voice remarked, "But you can be sure the emperor consulted the Queen Mother, Sembiyan Madevi, and Princess Kundavai."

This comment was met with a burst of laughter.

Ambalavan was furious. "How can you laugh? My blood boils at this insult! Why do I shamelessly cling to life, paying homage to an emperor who consults the women of his harem on affairs of state?" He stood up and faced the company. "My lineage is more than a thousand years old. Strike me with your swords ...let me be your sacrifice to Durga!"

His outburst was met by a stunned silence, broken only by the rustling of the wind in the trees.

Sambuvaraya quickly pacified Ambalavan. "Lord, forgive us for our foolish laughter. You are our undisputed leader. We are ready to obey you. Just give us your orders."

Ambalavan calmed down. "I too apologize for my outburst. Think of our glorious past. A hundred years ago, King Vijayalaya Chola defeated his enemies and expanded the Chola kingdom, which grew from strength to strength. We now live in the golden age of the Cholas. The Tiger Flag flutters proudly from Kanyakumari in the south to the River Krishna in the north. Numerous kingdoms, including the Pandian and the Chera, accept our sovereignty and pay our levies. It's only Sri Lanka in the south and Kalinga in the north which continue to defy us." He paused meaningfully. "And you all know the reason for that …"

Mazlavaraya declared, "Yes! The princes: Aditya Karikalan and Arulmozli."

"Exactly!" Ambalavan said. "By tradition, only battle-hardened veterans are appointed commanders-in-chief of the army. But Prince Karikalan commands our forces in the north. And, instead of going on the offensive against Kalinga, he sits comfortably in Kanchipuram, building a golden palace! He has plundered the wealth of vassal states to embed precious gems in his palace walls: not a single copper coin has come to the Chola treasury."

"Has the palace been completed?" someone in the gathering asked.

"Yes," declared Ambalavan. "My spies tell me the work is done. And now, Emperor Sundara Chola receives letters from his son urging him to go live in the golden palace."

A worried voice spoke up: "Does the emperor plan to go to Kanchipuram?"

Ambalavan said, "I'll make sure it doesn't happen. Kalaanthaka, my brother, controls Thanjavur Fort. No one enters without his permission. The emperor receives no visitors or messages without my knowledge. I have intercepted three letters from the crown prince."

The assembled chieftains cheered: "Bravo!" "Brilliant thinking!" "Long live Ambalavan!"

Basking in the applause, Ambalavan continued, "Coming to the younger prince, Arulmozli, his behavior is even stranger. Instead of financing the Chola army by plundering enemy country, he insists food and wages for our army must be sent from here. Last year, I sent him ten ship loads of grain from our granaries!"

Angry protests erupted from his audience: "Madness! Down with Arulmozli!"

Ambalavan was pleased. "And how does Arulmozli justify this madness? He says our enemy is the king of Sri Lanka—not its people.

He says we must not loot the country and antagonize the people: only then will they support us after we win the war."

"Does Arulmozli want us to abjectly fall at our enemies' feet?" someone protested.

"His misguided policy is emptying the Chola treasury and granaries," Ambalavan said. "I'm forced to levy heavier taxes on you all. I considered resigning as a mark of protest, but I decided to put the greater good of the kingdom above my personal feelings."

This was met with cries of, "No, no!" "Do not resign!" "You are our only safeguard!"

One chieftain asked, "Have you discussed this with the emperor?"

Ambalavan exclaimed, "The emperor has lost his mind! Whenever I try to discuss important matters with him, he tells me to consult the Queen Mother or Princess Kundavai. Their word is law to him." He snorted in disgust. "After all our years of service to the Cholas, we are reduced to taking orders from women! How long will we put up with this humiliation? Tell me, how do we overthrow this rule which is dominated by women?"

Who's in the Palanquin?

THE GATHERED CHIEFTAINS broke into excited murmurs. Sambuvaraya called them to order: "Come now, we don't have all night. Speak up."

A voice was raised. "I have a question for Ambalavan—I hope he won't be angry."

Ambalavan identified the speaker. "Chieftain Vanangamudi, speak openly."

"You accuse the emperor of being controlled by women but some men accuse you of the same thing. You have married a very young woman ..."

Sambuvaraya rushed to intervene. "Vanangamudi, that's a personal matter. You insult our chief guest by bringing it up here. Apologize!"

Ambalavan was calm. "Sambuvaraya my friend, let him speak." He turned to Vanangamudi. "Yes, even at this age, I admit the desires of the flesh are strong in me. I fell in love with a young girl and married her according to the prescribed rites. What's wrong with that?"

"Nothing," said Vanangamudi. "Most of us here have more than one wife. But I hear you take her with you everywhere and consult her on matters of state."

"I see nothing wrong in taking my wife with me wherever I go. But I assure you I don't let her meddle in the affairs of the kingdom," Ambalavan declared emphatically.

"In that case," Vanangamudi asked, "What's that palanquin doing here?"

Ambalavan said, "I'll explain that soon." He addressed the gathering at large. "I wish the emperor many years of good health. But in case he dies, we must choose his successor now."

"What's your opinion, Lord Ambalavan?" Sambuvaraya asked. "We will all support you."

"Let's trace the Cholas' line of succession in the recent past," Ambalavan said. "Twenty-four years ago, the great warrior and Shiva devotee, King Gandara Aditya, died suddenly. His son, Madurandaka, was only a year old. As the king wished, his younger brother, Arinjaya, succeeded him. Unfortunately, Arinjya's reign was short-lived. After his death, his son, Sundara Chola, became emperor at the age of twenty with our approval. He has been a just and able king and the empire has flourished under him. He consulted us on state matters until a few years ago. But now he's dying. Who should be the next emperor? Madurandaka, Gandara Aditya's son, is intelligent, noble and god-fearing and is worthy of being emperor. Aditya Karikalan, the emperor's eldest son, is the crown prince. Who should we choose? Our age-old dharma is clear: the elder brother's son takes precedence over the younger brother's grandson. The Chola throne belongs to Madurandaka by tradition and by right." He was met with a chorus of approval. "Are you ready to sacrifice your lives to ensure Madurandaka ascends the Tiger Throne? Are you ready to pledge your loyalty to him at Goddess Durga's feet?"

An uneasy silence followed his impassioned call.

Sambuvaraya said, "Before we pledge our support, we have a few questions. Is Madurandaka willing to accept this responsibility? We all know he has embraced spirituality… and Queen Sembiyan Madevi is against her son ascending the throne."

Ambalavan said, "Sembiyan Madevi encouraged her son to become an ascetic because she feared for his life if he became king. But Madurandaka has now decided it's time for him to take his rightful place on the Tiger Throne."

"What proof do we have of this?" Sambuvaraya asked.

"I'll give you proof right now and clear Vanangamudi's earlier doubts too," Ambalavan declared. "If I do that, will you all pledge your allegiance to Madurandaka?"

"Yes!" the assembled chieftains cried.

Ambalavan strode to the palanquin and said respectfully, "Prince Madurandaka, come."

Devan gasped in surprise. The fair hand he had seen that evening again parted the screen… it was adorned, not with bangles, but with the *kangan*, the bracelet worn by male royalty. He watched the graceful figure step out of the palanquin and smile at the gathering. *I assumed only women travel in palanquins, and so, the occupant seemed to be a woman in my eyes! Azlvarkkadian must have also been misled … is he still around?* Devan looked around, but darkness hid the walls.

Jumping to their feet, the conspirators raised their swords and spears and shouted: "Long live Madurandaka!" "Crown Prince Madurandaka!" "Spear of Victory!" "Spear of Valor!"

Devan left his hiding place and quietly ran back to his corner on the terrace.

A Friendly Chat

VANDHIYA DEVAN'S MIND was in a whirl. He had stumbled upon a great conspiracy. The Chola empire was close to defeating its enemies and reaching the pinnacle of glory. But a greater danger now loomed over it: an internal struggle for power. These midnight conspirators were powerful men who wielded enormous influence. Devan had accepted Aditya Karikalan as the rightful heir. He had never considered Madurandaka as a rival claimant to the throne. But now, it seemed as if both of them were entitled to be king. Who would win the throne? And how would this affect his own prospects? He had planned to win Karikalan's favor and rise to a high position in the Chola empire. In fact, he had even dreamt of the Vallam kingdom being restored to him. He tossed and turned, falling asleep only in the early hours of the new day.

When Kandamaran woke him, it was long after sunrise.

"I came here after seeing to the other guests," Kandamaran lied. "You were sleeping like a log."

"It's late! I must leave at once," Devan said. "Please ask your men to bring my horse."

"Nonsense!" Kandamaran protested. "You must stay for at least ten days."

"My dear fellow, my uncle in Thanjavur is on his death bed. I must hurry to him," Devan lied.

"In that case, you must stop here for a few days on your way back," Kandamaran insisted. "Let's have breakfast together; then I'll ride with you up to the banks of the Kollidam. We can chat on the way. I had no time to talk to you last night."

As they rode slowly away from Kadambur Palace, the two friends fondly remembered their days on joint patrol duty in the army.

Devan said, "After hearing so much about your sister, I'm sorry I couldn't meet her. I just caught a glimpse of her hiding behind your mother …"

Kandamaran flushed in embarrassment. "Please forget Manimekalai."

"Why, Kandamaran!" Devan exclaimed. "You said you would be happy if I married your sister."

"My parents have chosen another groom for her …"

Ahah! I bet that groom is none other than Madurandaka. What a brilliant strategist Ambalavan is: this alliance will strengthen his cause. Aloud, Devan said, "I understand. I'm descended from kings, but now I'm just a poor orphan. You must have chosen one of your wealthy guests."

"My friend, my sister's marriage is part of a larger scheme which I can't talk about now. When the time comes, I'll reveal everything to you and we'll stand shoulder to shoulder against a common enemy. Believe me, I'll let nothing come in the way of our friendship." Kandamaran refused to say more.

They reached the banks of the Kollidam, a tributary of the Ponni. The river was in flood. A boat waited for departure at the jetty, with a passenger on board who was obviously a Shaiva.

Kandamaran said, "My friend, take this boat. One of my men will come with you and arrange a horse for you on the other side. I'll take your horse back to Kadambur."

The friends embraced and said goodbye. Just as the boatmen pushed off, another man ran towards the boat, shouting, "Stop, stop!" It was Azlvarkkadian.

Nandini

AS THEY CROSSED the river, Azlvarkkadian got into an argument with the Shaiva about the relative merits of Shiva and Vishnu. The two men came to blows and the boat was in danger of capsizing.

Devan shouted, "Stop it! You two may not mind a direct ticket to heaven by drowning, but I still have a lot to achieve in this world."

One of the boatmen added, "If you fall into the river, whether you end up in heaven or not, you'll definitely end up in a crocodile's mouth."

When they reached the shore, the Shaiva walked away with a final curse. Kandamaran's man went to the nearest town to get a horse. Devan and Azlvarkkadian, each determined to milk the other for information, settled down comfortably under the shade of a peepal tree.

After some casual remarks, Azlvarkkadian asked, "Did you get into Kadambur Palace, *thambi?*" He then bombarded Devan with questions.

Devan gave him evasive answers and concealed the details of the chieftains present, the possessed dancer's predictions and his own knowledge of the midnight conspiracy. Pretending to be completely ignorant of politics, Devan said, "Kandamaran hinted something very important is going to happen soon. Do you know anything about this?"

"About what?" Azlvarkkadian countered.

"Oh, about the rumors flying around the country regarding the succession."

"I don't know anything, *thambi*," Azlvarkkadian said piously. "I'm just a simple Vaishnava who sings the *Azlvars'* hymns." He burst into a hymn.

"Stop, Vaishnava—enough of your hypocrisy! You're a man who lusts after another man's wife. Why else would you ask me to carry a letter to Lord Ambalavan's wife?"

Azlvarkkadian sighed. "Very well, I'll tell you the story behind this …

"I was born in a village near Madurai, on the banks of the Vaigai in the Pandian kingdom. For generations, my family has devotedly served Vishnu. One day, as my father gathered flowers for the temple, he found a beautiful baby girl in the garden. He named her Nandini and brought her up as his daughter. We all showered her with love. I considered her to be my own sister. Nandini was devoted to Vishnu and we thought she would dedicate her life to the Lord. After my father died, she became my ward. We travelled together, singing the *Azlvars'* hymns. One day, leaving Nandini behind, I went on a pilgrimage to Tirupati—and disaster struck.

"The Cholas decisively defeated the Pandians in a battle near Madurai. The Pandian king, Veerapandian, was severely wounded and lay unconscious on the battlefield. That night, his trusted bodyguards secretly carried him to our house which stood nearby. Taking pity on the king, Nandini gave him shelter. But the Cholas got wind of this. Chola soldiers, under Ambalavan, surrounded and stormed the house and killed Veerapandian. Captivated by Nandini's beauty, Ambalavan fell in love with her. He forcibly carried her to his palace." Azlvarkkadian paused. "This happened three years ago. Since then, I have been trying to meet my sister and rescue her from that villain. I have not yet succeeded."

Devan was deeply moved by this story. But he had a lurking suspicion that the cunning Azlvarkkadian might be lying to gain his sympathy. He decided to keep his own counsel. He asked Azlvarkkadian, "And who do you think will succeed the emperor?"

Azlvarkkadian shrugged. "How would I know? Am I the Kudanthai astrologer?"

"Is the Kudanthai astrologer so wise?" Devan asked.

"Yes," Azlvarkkadian replied. "He can predict the future and also read your mind."

Kandamaran's man arrived just then with a horse. Devan said farewell to Azlvarkkadian thinking, *I must meet this astrologer.*

The Astrologer

AT THE SAME time, a swan-shaped boat sailed down the Arasalar, another tributary of the Ponni. Princess Kundavai, glowing with regal beauty, sat in it, surrounded by the daughters of Chola chieftains. These young girls lived with her as her companions at Pazlayarai, the Chola capital.

When they reached the shore, Kundavai said, "Vanathi, come with me; the rest wait here."

Vanathi, a lovely young woman from the Kodumbalur chieftain's family, willingly followed the princess to a waiting chariot. She asked, "*Akka*, where are we going?"

"To consult the astrologer at Kudanthai. I want him to read your horoscope. You have lost weight and tire easily. You never laugh."

Vanathi cried, "*Akka,* I'm fine! Let's go back, please!"

"Okay," said the princess. "I'll ask him about my marriage prospects."

"Why should you consult him, *akka*?" Vanathi said. "You have only to say the word and every king in the country will line up before you, begging for your hand."

Kundavai said seriously, "I'll never leave the Chola kingdom. If I ever marry, I'll choose a Chola warrior who is content to stay here with me in the land where the Ponni flows."

"I'll stay with you, *akka*. I too love the Chola kingdom. I won't get married."

Kundavai's eyes twinkled. "I think the Chola kingdom you love is now in Sri Lanka!"

Vanathi blushed and sighed. "*Akka*, can a little dewdrop dare to love the mighty sun?"

"Why not?" said the princess. "The dewdrop's love can make her fuse with the sun."

The charioteer avoided the city and took a circuitous route to the astrologer's humble house on the outskirts. He parked the chariot under a banyan tree and the princess and Vanathi went in. The astrologer welcomed Kundavai with great respect and ordered his disciple to stand guard outside the door saying, "No one is to be allowed inside—no one, understand?"

The Intruder

ONCE THEY WERE seated, Kundavai said, "I want you to study my friend's horoscope."

The old astrologer studied the palm leaf in amazement. "This is the most auspicious horoscope I have ever seen! It's even better than yours. This girl is destined to marry the King of Kings."

Kundavai smiled. "And where will this great king come from?"

"This mighty warrior belongs here. Right now, he's fighting in an alien land beyond the sea."

Vanathi glowed with happiness.

"Tell me more," Kundavai urged the astrologer. "How will we recognize him?"

"You'll see Vishnu's conch and chakra traced by the lines of his palm. He will be one of the greatest warriors of our time. He will face many enemies and dangers but will ultimately triumph and have a long, glorious reign. You'll find the outline of a peepal leaf on this girl's stomach."

"And what does that signify?" Kundavai was curious.

"This girl will have a son like Lord Vishnu-he who sleeps on the peepal leaf. Her son will plant the Cholas' Tiger Flag wherever he goes. The Goddess of Victory will always be by his side. Under him, the glory of the Chola empire will cover the earth and endure until the end of time."

Kundavai was distracted by a feeble cry: "*Akka* ..." She was just in time to catch Vanathi as she fainted.

"She'll be okay in a few minutes," Kundavai said. "While she's unconscious, tell me this- is some great danger looming over the country? I'm haunted by a vague foreboding ..."

The astrologer quickly said, "My dear lady, I can't foretell the future of a nation."

"Hmm," said Kundavai. "I see you are a cautious man. Very well, tell me what the future holds for my father and my brothers."

"All I can tell you now is the royal family is in danger. You must all be careful. But by the grace of Goddess Durga, all will end well."

Vanathi stirred and sat up. "Did I faint?" she asked.

"That will do for today, astrologer." Kundavai turned to the girl. "Can you walk, Vanathi?"

"Yes, *akka*," the girl replied. As the astrologer put away his palm leaves, Vanathi said, "You have not told us anything about Princess Kundavai. Which great warrior will win her hand? When will he come?"

"He's on his way," the astrologer replied. "He'll arrive very soon."

Just then, they heard the sound of horse's hooves. A loud voice asked, "Is this the Kudanthai astrologer's house? Let me in."

The disciple blocked the way saying, "You can't see the astrologer now. Come later."

The stranger declared, "It's urgent. Get out of my way or I'll kill you."

As the disciple protested and tried to stop him, the intruder forced open the door and barged into the room. It was Vandhiya Devan.

Devan froze at the sight of Kundavai. In a split second, her beauty was etched on his heart: from her slightly parted coral lips and dimpled cheeks, to her wide eyes and shell-smooth neck. Embarrassed, Devan turned on the disciple. "Fool! You didn't tell me there were ladies inside." Roughly pushing the bewildered man ahead of him, he went out.

Kundavai burst into laughter. "Just as we were wondering how my man would come, this man arrives on horseback. Who is he?"

Vanathi joined in her laughter, but the astrologer was thoughtful. "He's a stranger, lady."

The two women took their leave.

Devan, standing outside the house, said, "I'm sorry. This idiot did not tell me you were inside."

Kundavai's beautiful eyes glanced at him as she glided past silently.

Devan said, "Kudanthai women lack courtesy. If a man apologizes, can't they gracefully accept his apology with a few words?"

Still without a word, the two women climbed into the chariot and sped away. Devan stood looking after them until the chariot was out of sight.

The Waxing Moon

THE ASTROLOGER LED Vandhiya Devan into his house. Once they were seated, he enquired, "*Thambi*, who are you? What do you want?"

Devan in turn asked, "Who are the two women who just left your house?"

"My professional code of honor does not allow me to give you details of my clients—just as it will not let me reveal your details to others."

"Okay," Devan paused. "Do you know Azlvarkkadian? He's the one who sent me here."

The astrologer frowned. "Can you describe this man?"

"He's stout and short with sandal paste smeared on his body. He wears his hair in a tuft and is ready to pick up a fight with any Shaiva ..."

"Ah, you're talking about Thirumalai!" the astrologer exclaimed.

"Hmm," said Devan. "Looks like he assumes different identities to suit the circumstances."

"Yes," agreed the astrologer. "He plays many roles. He also lies often."

"Is he a bad man?"

"Only to bad men."

"He suggested I ask you to predict my future. But hurry, I'm on an important mission."

"I need your horoscope, or your name."

"I'm Vandhiya Devan."

"Vallavaraya Vandhiya Devan of Vallam! I collect horoscopes of ancient clans: I have yours."

"My clan is past its glory. I'm not rich or famous. What do the stars and planets predict?"

"You will grow in stature from day to day. You will succeed in any personal quest, as the planets and stars are aligned in your favor. But, if you are on a mission for someone else, your success depends on that person's horoscope."

"Will I be able to meet the emperor in Thanjavur?"

"Only the Pazluvur brothers can predict that," the astrologer smiled.

"Is it true the emperor is very ill? Who will be his successor?"

"It's best to ignore rumors. The succession has nothing to do with you and me."

"What does the future hold for Crown Prince Aditya Karikalan?"

"I need his horoscope to tell you that," the astrologer replied.

"Okay," Devan said. "What about Madurandaka?"

"His horoscope is rather strange: he will always be dominated by others."

"Is it true, as rumored, that Princess Kundavai controls her father and rules by proxy?"

The astrologer froze for an instant. *Did this young man recognize the princess?* "That's a blatant lie! The princess stays in Pazlayarai while the emperor is in Thanjavur. Anyway, all power lies with the Pazluvur brothers."

Devan said earnestly, "Sir, I'm not a spy for the Pazluvur brothers. Just tell me this: what does the future hold for the Chola dynasty?"

"The Chola empire will grow like the waxing moon for many years to come."

"I have always longed to travel overseas. Will my wish come true?"

"Yes. You will always be on the move. You will ride horses and elephants and ships."

"Sir, one last question: what do the stars predict for Prince Arulmozli who is now in Sri Lanka?"

"Prince Arulmozli is the Pole Star—always constant. He is renowned for his righteousness, courage and wisdom. Let him be your guide as you voyage through life," the astrologer advised.

"High praise indeed!" exclaimed Devan.

"*Thambi*," the old man said. "Arulmozli is the darling of all who live in the land of the Ponni."

Devan thanked the astrologer, paid him a generous fee and continued on his journey.

Vanathi's Scheme

KUNDAVAI'S COMPANIONS GOSSIPED about Vanathi as they waited in the boat.

Varini complained, "That lucky Kodumbalur girl: the princess loves her best."

"Hah!" said Niravathi. "Vanathi's scheming to win Prince Arulmozli's heart. Did you see how she dropped the *aarti* plate to catch the prince's attention?"

Tharaka agreed. "Yes, and the little minx also pretended to faint. What an actress!"

"Both the prince and princess fell for it!" exclaimed Senthiru in disgust.

"Come now," said Varini. "It's getting late. Let's carry out the princess's orders."

The girls took out a stuffed crocodile hidden under two loose planks on the boat. They climbed ashore and arranged the crocodile under a large tree with the lower half of its body submerged in the river. The stuffed reptile looked very real.

"Why's the princess doing this?" Niravathi wondered.

"Nowadays, Vanathi's frightened for no reason at all. Maybe the princess is planning to cure her with some kind of shock treatment," suggested Senthiru.

Tharaka said sadly, "I think the princess wants Vanathi to marry the prince."

"No chance!" Varini exclaimed. "When every emperor in the land is lining up to offer his daughter's hand to the prince, why would he even look at Vanathi?"

"Prince Arulmozli has said he'll marry only a Tamil girl," Senthiru reminded them.

"In that case, we'll all try to win his heart. After all, we're as beautiful as Vanathi."

With that, they settled down to wait.

Prince Arulmozli

THE GIRLS WERE referring to Vanathi's behavior a few months before. The Sinhala kings were traditional allies of the Pandians. Whenever the Cholas waged war on the Pandians, the Sri Lankan army came to support the Pandians. Once he had decisively defeated the Pandians, Emperor Sundara Chola decided to invade Sri Lanka. The first Chola army which set out for Sri Lanka was led by Vanathi's father, Chieftain Paranthaka of Kodumbalur. Before the entire Chola army could cross the sea and mobilize, Paranthaka, raring to do battle, went on the offensive. The outnumbered Chola battalion was ambushed by Sena, the Lankan general. Paranthaka put up a brave fight but was defeated and killed.

As Crown Prince Aditya Karikalan was occupied with the northern command, the Chola generals vied with each other to command the Sri Lankan army. The emperor was in a quandary, knowing that choosing any one of them would antagonize the others.

Arulmozli, then nineteen, was the darling of the women in Pazlayarai Palace. But it was Kundavai, his elder sister, who lavished the most affection on him. She would fondly trace the conch and chakra in the lines of his palm. *He's meant for great things. I'll help him achieve his destiny.* Arulmozli returned Kundavai's love and would do anything for his sister.

At Kundavai's suggestion, the handsome prince went to the king and said, "Father, let me lead our army to victory in Sri Lanka."

The emperor dearly loved his only daughter and trusted her wisdom. He appointed Arulmozli commander of the southern army and the prince went to battle in Sri Lanka.

Arulmozli returned to Pazlayarai to discuss arms and supplies for the overseas army. On the eve of his departure for Sri Lanka, Kundavai gave him a grand sendoff. Pazlayarai Palace echoed with cheers and the sound of drums and conches. The queens smeared the prince's forehead with holy ash and blessed him. The young girls gathered at the gate with oil lamps glowing in golden *aarti* plates.

As the prince walked towards them, Vanathi dropped her plate with a loud crash. A whisper ran through the crowd: *An ill omen!* But to everyone's amazement, the lamp on the plate continued burning. *What could be more auspicious than that!* the whispers now went.

Vanathi's mind was in a whirl. *What have I done? Have I brought bad luck to the prince?* As Arulmozli smiled and walked past, Vanathi fainted.

Kundavai ordered her companions to carry the unconscious girl to a nearby room. As she held Vanathi in her arms and tried to revive her, Arulmozli came in. "*Akka,* who's this girl?"

"She's Vanathi, Chieftain Paranthaka's daughter," Kundavai replied.

"Ah! She must be upset because she associates Sri Lanka with her father's death."

Vanathi regained consciousness and blushed in embarrassment. "*Akka,* I'm so sorry to have caused all this trouble."

"Don't worry, Vanathi," Arulmozli comforted her. "We understand."

Vanathi was ecstatic: the prince, who had not so much as looked at any girl in the palace, was talking to her!

"I'll take care of her, *thambi,*" Kundavai said. "May victory be yours in Sri Lanka. I'll be looking forward eagerly to your messages."

"Goodbye, *akka.* You must also send me news from here. Let me know how this poor girl is."

Kundavai and Vanathi became close friends. Vanathi was given to fainting and sudden tears and Kundavai cared for her lovingly. The princess shared her dreams for Arulmozli with Vanathi who was only too eager to hear about him. Kundavai's other companions watched jealously. Kundavai considered Vanathi a good match for her beloved brother. But Arulmozli was the greatest warrior of his age: could the timid Vanathi be the wife he needed? She decided to test the girl's courage with the fake crocodile.

Vanathi passed the test with flying colors. Even as everyone around her shrieked in horror, Vanathi stayed calm. "*Akka,* a crocodile is dangerous only in water. It's harmless on land."

The jealous girls accused Vanathi: "You cheat, you knew it was a fake crocodile."

"Even if it was a real one, I would not have panicked," Vanathi retorted. She added as an afterthought, "I'm scared only of lizards and cockroaches."

Crocodile on the Bank

VANDHIYA DEVAN RODE slowly towards Thanjavur, feasting his eyes on the beautiful Chola landscape which unfolded before him. He passed fields and smithies, ponds and temples, coconut groves and villages with neat houses. But even as he delighted in the sights and sounds and smells around him, his mind was filled with one vivid image: the face of the beautiful woman he has seen at the astrologer's house. *Why was she silent? Am I so ugly?*

Thinking about this and the astrologer's predictions, he came to the bank of the Arasalar. Hearing giggles and the music of women's bangles, he smiled and rode in that direction.

Suddenly, terrified cries of, "Help! Help! Crocodile!" split the air.

Devan spurred his horse and charged forward. He took in the scene at a glance: a group of women, including the two he had seen at the astrologer's house, stood between the river and a clump of trees. A huge crocodile lay partly submerged in the river. Its jaws gaped open, showing cruel teeth. The women were trapped between the monstrous reptile and the trees.

Without a moment's hesitation, Devan jumped off his horse and threw his spear at the beast. Even as the spear pierced the beast's hide, he rushed forward, knife in hand. He froze at a burst of laughter from the women—their eyes sparkled with mischief. *Are they mad?* he wondered.

The woman whose beautiful face filled his thoughts stepped forward. "Stop laughing," she ordered the others. She turned to Devan. "Sir, we don't need your help."

The World Stood Still

THE WORLD STOOD still for Vandhiya Devan when he heard her voice which was sweeter than honey. Thrilled to the core of his being, he was speechless.

She continued: "I apologize for my silence at the astrologer's house. I was worried about my friend who had just recovered from a faint. Please don't think Chola women lack courtesy." She paused. "And your throw: what remarkable marksmanship!"

Another peal of laughter from the women broke the spell.

Devan walked up to the beast; as he retrieved his spear, he realized the crocodile was a fake. He burned with humiliation and hatred for these mocking women. Grabbing his spear, he ran up the bank and jumped on to his horse. Venting his anger on his mount, he cracked his whip. The horse neighed and galloped away.

Kundavai stood looking after the horse. She then turned to her companions and scolded them. "You should not have laughed at that young man. What will he think of Chola women?"

Idumbankari

AZLVARKKADIAN ALIAS THIRUMALAI, stood under the peepal tree, watching Vandhiya Devan ride towards Kudanthai. *That young man is very clever. I couldn't get any information from him. I don't even know whom he is working for. I hope the astrologer manages to learn more.* He was distracted by Kandamaran's servant—the one who had fetched Devan's horse. "What's your name?" Azlvarkkadian asked.

The man hesitated before saying, "I'm Idumbankari." He placed one hand over the other and wiggled his thumbs.

"Is that some signal?" Azlvarkkadian asked. "That's the traditional dance gesture for the fish."

Idumbankari frowned and said innocently, "A signal? No, *swami.* Do you like fish?"

"Don't be a fool!" Azlvarkkadian scolded. "I think I'll follow that Shaiva who was on the boat; I have a few more things to tell him. Where are you going?"

"I must get back to Kadambur or my master will be angry," Idumbankari said.

"Hurry then," Azlvarkkadian urged him. "The boat is about to leave the jetty."

The man rushed towards the boat. In a flash, Azlvarkkadian scrambled up the tree and hid in its thick foliage. He watched as Idumbankari stopped at the jetty and turned back to see whether Azlvarkkadian was in sight.

Azlvarkkadian heard the boatman say, "Climb in. We're leaving."

Idumbankari replied, "I've changed my mind. I'll take the next boat."

I was right, thought Azlvarkkadian. *There's more to this man than meets the eyes. He made the sign of the fish. What does the fish signify? Aha! The Pandian flag carries the fish symbol. Can it be … patience, let me wait and see.*

Idumbankari came and sat under the tree. It was obvious that he was waiting for someone. Azlvarkkadian remained motionless in the tree. An hour passed and his feet went numb. He could not hold on much longer. Just as he considered stunning Idumbankari by jumping on top of him, a stranger walked up to the tree. Placing one hand over the other, he wiggled his thumbs. Idumbankari leapt to his feet and replied with the same gesture.

The stranger said, "I'm Soman Sambavan."

"I'm Idumbankari. I've been waiting for you. Where are we to go?"

"West—to the enemy's war memorial," Sambavan replied.

"To Thirupurambayam?" Idumbankari asked.

"Hush!" the other cautioned.

"There's no one here," Idumbankari assured him.

"I don't know the way," Sambavan said. "You go ahead and I'll follow at a distance. If you see anyone, hide immediately."

The two men set out.

Azlvarkkadian thought, *I must find out what these men are up to. The Thirupurambayam memorial, erected in honor of King Prithvipathi of Kanga, is in the forest, far from habitation. It's clear some meeting's going to take place there. Why did they refer to King Prithvipathi as the enemy? Are my worst fears coming true? I'll go to Thirupurambayam by another route and learn what this is all about.* Azlvarkkadian waited until the two men were out of sight; he jumped down from the tree and set out through the thick forest.

Battlefield in the Forest

A HUNDRED YEARS before, Thirupurambayam was the scene of a historic battle. The once mighty Chola dynasty was in decline. As the dominant Pandians and Pallavas battled for supremacy, the Cholas were often caught in the crossfire. The brave king, Vijayalaya Chola, ruled from Pazlayarai. A battle-hardened veteran, he wore his ninety-six battle scars as badges of honor. The king, with his small army, joined the frequent battles, supporting either the Pandians or the Pallavas. Whatever the outcome, these battles honed the Cholas' fighting skill and war spirit. At a ripe old age, Vijayalaya Chola was succeeded by his son, Aditya Chola.

War again broke out between the Pandians, led by King Vargunavarman, and the Pallavas, led by King Aparajithavarman. Aditya Chola and King Prithvipathi of Kanga allied with the Pallavas.

The final battle was fought at Thirupurambayam, on the banks of the Manni, another tributary of the Ponni. This was Chola territory. Chariots, elephants, cavalry and infantry clashed in a mighty storm which raged for three days. Slowly, the tide of battle turned against the Pallavas and their allies. Facing imminent defeat, they decided to retreat.

Vijayalaya Chola knew that to retreat now would doom the small Chola army. The old lion, both legs useless, went to the battlefield and roared, "Give me an elephant!" He was met by silence: the elephant brigade had been completely destroyed.

"Then give me a horse!" the indomitable old king shouted. Again, an embarrassed silence greeted him. No horses had survived the enemy attack.

The old lion cried, "Then give me two brave Chola warriors!" Not two, but two hundred Chola soldiers stepped forward. "Let two men carry me on their shoulders; if they fall, two others must take their place." With that, Vijayalaya Chola roared, "Forward!" and stormed into the battlefield.

Armed with two long, curved swords, the old king decimated the Pandian army, leaving a trail of corpses in his wake. Inspired by his heroism, the Cholas, followed by the Pallavas and the Kangas, threw themselves into battle again. The Pandians were defeated. But King Prithvipathi was killed in the battle and a memorial was built in his honor at Thirupurambayam. Over the years, it fell into ruin; the forest covered the battlefield and swallowed the memorial too.

Azlvarkkadian reached the ruins at night. He climbed a tree whose branches overhung the memorial and settled down to wait. Eyes peeled to penetrate the darkness, and ears straining to pick up the least sound, he passed the hours pondering on foolish men who shed blood in the name of courage. All he heard was the hoot of owls and the howl of wolves and jackals.

Just as he decided that the Pandian spies had changed their plans, he saw torches flickering in the darkness. Two men went past the memorial and settled down to wait in a clearing just beyond. Soon they were joined by two other men. They conferred in low voices. To Azlvarkkadian's disappointment, he could not make out their words. A little later, two more men arrived. The last man held up a bag and emptied it on the ground. Azlvarkkadian saw the gleam of gold coins under the torch light.

The man laughed and said loudly, "Friends, we are using Chola money to destroy the Cholas. What delicious irony!"

"Ravidasan," one of the others hissed. "Quiet!"

"Who's there to hear?" Ravidasan retorted. "The nocturnal animals are our only witnesses."

But the men again lowered their voices to whispers.

What's the point of sitting on this tree? I can't hear a word or see these conspirators. Azlvarkkadian quietly climbed down from the tree—only to be betrayed by the rustling of leaves.

The conspirators jumped up and shouted, "Who's there?"

Just as Azlvarkkadian decided to make a run for it, even at the cost of certain capture, an owl hooted and took wing from the same tree.

The Arch-Enemy

THE CONSPIRATORS RELAXED. "It's only an owl," one man said.

Azlvarkkadian crept to an ancient Arjuna tree and hid in a gap between its sprawling roots. He was now well placed to hear every word spoken.

Ravidasan continued, "We need not worry about money as long as we have access to the Thanjavur treasury. We must form two teams: one for Kanchipuram and one for Sri Lanka. The safest route to Sri Lanka is across the sea from Sethu to Mathottam. The men in this team must know how to handle a boat and to swim."

Several men in the group volunteered.

"Before executing our plan, we must get King Mahinda's approval. So, at least one man must be fluent in Sinhalese ...." Ravidasan broke off. "Where's Soman Sambavan?"

"Here I am," a voice answered.

Two men joined the circle of conspirators. Azlvarkkadian edged forward and craned his neck. He recognized the newcomers as the men he had eavesdropped on under the peepal tree.

Ravidasan pointed to the heap of coins. "Here's the means to destroy our enemy."

Sambavan examined a coin. "The tiger on one side and the palm tree on the other."

"Yes, the Chola tiger and the Pazluvur palm tree. I have accomplished my mission," Ravidasan boasted. "And what news do you bring?"

Idumbankari spoke up. "I followed your orders and took up service with Sambuvaraya at Kadambur. A secret meeting of Chola chieftains, including Ambalavan and Mazlavaraya, was held last night at the palace. I was posted as sentry and managed to see and hear everything."

"Excellent! What did they discuss?" Ravidasan asked eagerly.

"Ambalavan said the emperor is on his death bed. The chieftains agreed on Madurandaka as his successor. And Madurandaka himself was present—he travels secretly in a palanquin, pretending to be Ambalavan's wife."

The conspirators broke into excited murmurs.

Ravidasan smiled. "Rivalry among the Cholas will help our cause. Did you see anything else?"

"Yes. There was a man clinging to the fortress wall, spying on the midnight gathering: a Vaishnava with a tuft. I thought he might be one of us and didn't raise the alarm."

Ravidasan exclaimed, "A serious mistake! He's Azlvarkkadian alias Thirumalai. He's a dangerous spy."

"I later realized my mistake," Idumbankari was contrite. "I made sure Kandamaran chose me to escort his friend to the Kollidam. There, I met the Vaishnava. He did not recognize our signal."

Ravidasan frowned at him. "Don't use the fish signal on strangers." He turned to the gathering. "This Azlvarkkadian is the greatest danger to our mission. He's determined to kidnap our noble queen. If any of you comes across him, kill him immediately!"

"Who employs him?" one of the men asked curiously.

"I haven't been able to discover that," Ravidasan said. "I first suspected he was either the emperor's man or Prince Aditya Karikalan's. But now, I think he serves Sembiyan Madevi."

"Why would an old lady, devoted to building temples, need a spy?" one of the men asked.

"The old hag only pretends to be devout. She's against her own son, Madurandaka. That's why her brother, Mazlavaraya, has nothing to do with her: he supports Ambalavan."

"Is there anyone else we need to watch out for?" another man asked.

"Yes," said Ravidasan. "There's an astrologer at Kudanthai. I suspect he's working for that pretender who is now waging war in Sri Lanka. But he's harmless compared to Azlvarkkadian. The Vaishnava must be crushed like a scorpion before he destroys our cause."

Azlvarkkadian broke into a sweat at these words. To his horror, just at this point, he was overcome by the uncontrollable urge to sneeze. "Atishoo!"

The conspirators froze.

"There's someone behind the Arjuna tree!" Ravidasan shouted.

A man grabbed a torch and ran to the tree. Azlvarkkadian's heart raced: discovery meant certain death. His eyes fell on a huge bat hanging from the tree. He grabbed the animal and held it in his hands. When the torchbearer was almost on him, Azlvarkkadian flung the bat at the man. The frightened man dropped the torch and stood rooted to the spot. "What is it?" the other men ran towards the tree. "It ... it's ... it's only a bat," the man stammered. Azlvarkkadian made his escape under cover of the commotion.

The Screen Rustles

VANDHIYA DEVAN RODE on towards Thanjavur, his mind in a whirl. *I'll deliver the letter to the emperor: my duty to Karikalan ends with that. What do I care who sits on the throne? And there's no guarantee Karikalan will remain my patron.*

He reminded himself that it was the Cholas who were responsible for his present state. They had allied with the Kangas and the Vaidhumbarayas to defeat his father and annex his fiefdom. *Then again, I must be fair: kings have always battled for supremacy. The loser must submit to the victor. My ancestors, the Vallam kings, also waged wars and annexed their enemies' lands.*

Even as his eyes delighted in the fertile Chola landscape and his mind analyzed political intrigues, Devan's heart was filled with images of the beautiful woman he had seen twice. He saw her radiant face in the flowers and heard her sweet voice in the hum of the bees. *I must be careful: Ambalavan is a laughing stock because of his obsession with a woman.*

His thoughts moved to Madurandaka. *What kind of a man hides himself in a woman's palanquin? A fine king he'll make!! Ambalavan's puppet, I suppose. The emperor is also to blame. Why has he given Ambalavan so much power when he has two brave sons of his own ... and a pearl of a daughter?*

He was struck by a sudden thought: could the lady he had seen at Kudanthai and on the riverbank be Kundavai herself? He shook his head. *No, it can't be. But, if it's true, how can I face her and deliver her brother's letter to her?*

Devan reached Thiruvaiyaru, a pilgrim town. He considered

stopping there for a day to worship at the famous Shiva temple and enjoy the town's renowned dance and music. *Why hurry? It's rumored the emperor is being held hostage by the Pazluvur brothers. If that's true, I doubt I can even see him.*

Just then, a palanquin, escorted by a company of soldiers, came along the riverbank and took the road to Thanjavur. It bore the Pazluvur palm tree emblem. *Ahah!* thought Devan. *They are on their way back from Kadambur.* Instinctively, he followed the palanquin. Maybe they would halt and he would get a chance to see Prince Madurandaka. Perhaps he could even use him to gain entry into Thanjavur Fort. However, the group moved on without stopping. Soon, the walls of the fort loomed in the distance. Once the company entered the fort, Devan would lose his chance. He quickly shortened the distance between himself and the palanquin.

One of the guards challenged him: "You! Who are you? Why are you following us?"

"Why should I follow you?" Devan said indignantly. "I'm going to Thanjavur to see my uncle."

"Why don't you go ahead?" the guard asked suspiciously.

"Can't you see how tired my horse is?" Devan replied. He was now almost alongside the palanquin. In a flash, he urged his horse forward with his legs and, at the same time, pulled on the reins. The horse veered dangerously close to the palanquin, almost colliding with it. Devan shouted, "Help! Help! Lord, your men are attacking my horse!"

The screens of the palanquin rustled and a fair hand parted the curtains.

The *Velakkara Padai*

DEVAN JUMPED OFF his horse and ran to the palanquin. "Prince," he shouted, "your men ..." He stopped in shock—the occupant of the palanquin was a woman! And not just any woman: this was the most beautiful woman he had ever seen. Dazzled by her beauty, Devan stammered, "Sorry ... sorry ..." His wits returning, he cleared his throat and began again. "My humble apologies. You must be Lady Nandini. I've been trying to meet you."

At a look from Nandini, the guards moved aside. Nandini turned to Devan with a bewitching smile. "Yes, I'm Lady Nandini of Pazluvur." Her voice was intoxicating. "And ..." the smile vanished; in its place was an angry scowl. "Why did you deliberately charge into my escort?"

Devan lowered his voice to a conspiratorial whisper. "Azlvarkkadian—I mean Thirumalai, asked me to meet you."

Nandini's eyes mirrored her surprise and suspicion. "Whatever it is, we can't discuss it here in the middle of the road. Come to my palace tomorrow."

"But," Devan quickly pointed out, "how can I enter the fort?"

Nandini gave him a ring from a little silk pouch. "This will let you into the fort and my palace."

Delighted, Devan examined the ivory signet ring: it was etched with the palm tree symbol. He looked up to thank Nandini, but the screen was closed. He heard the honeyed voice warn, "Keep at a distance. It's dangerous to come near me."

Devan obediently fell back as the company moved on. *What a beauty! No wonder old Ambalavan is her slave.*

Devan reached the fort gates at sunset. Thanjavur city sprawled around the fort. Men, women and children lined both sides of the road. There was a buzz of excitement in the air.

A young man stood nearby with baskets of fragrant flowers. He wore *rudraksha* beads around his neck and his forehead was smeared with holy ash. Devan asked him, "*Thambi*, what's everyone waiting for?"

"You're obviously a stranger," the young man said. "Better climb down from your horse."

"Why?" asked Devan.

"The king's bodyguards are due to march from the fort to their city barracks. If they see your horse, they may take it—and you along with it."

"Really?" Devan was amazed. "Does no one protest?"

"The *Velakkara Padai's* word is law; even the Pazluvur brothers don't interfere with them."

Of course, Devan had heard of the *Velakkara Padai*. They were the king's personal bodyguards, fiercely loyal to their master. They took a vow to protect the king with their lives. If they failed in their duty, these men would behead themselves at a Durga temple in atonement.

To loud drumbeats and shouts, the fort gates opened and two horsemen galloped out, holding a banner depicting a crown and a tiger above an altar with a severed head on it. Behind them walked a gigantic bull, carrying a war drum on which two soldiers beat a loud tattoo. Next came fifty drummers and fifty percussionists. A thousand soldiers marched behind the band.

The guards thundered: "Love live Emperor Sundara Chola!" "Victory to the Tiger Flag!" The spectators cheered loudly and watched until the company marched out of sight.

Amudhan's Mother

AS THE BATTALION marched past, one soldier grabbed a basket of sweets from a nearby shop and shared them with his friends. He upended the empty basket on the shop owner's head. To Vandhiya Devan's surprise, the spectators laughed at the soldier's pranks and even cheered him on. It was clear that the people loved the emperor's bodyguards. Devan controlled his anger: *I must keep out of sight.*

He realized that once the *Velakkara Padai* left the fort, trying to enter would look suspicious. He decided to spend the night in the city and enter the fort in the morning. As he walked through the bustling market place, he saw the young man he had met earlier walking ahead of him. Devan dismounted and struck up a conversation with the lad.

"*Thambi*, what's your name? Have you sold all your flowers?"

"I'm Chendan Amudhan. Those flowers were for the Thalikkulathar temple."

"Are you paid for your flowers?"

"No. King Gandara Aditya gave my grandfather a royal grant for this service and my widowed mother and I continue the work."

"Can you suggest a good inn for me to spend the night?"

"There are many inns ..." Amudhan hesitated. "If you want, you can spend the night with me. My house is on the city outskirts."

Devan gladly accepted the offer and went with Amudhan. After half an hour, they came to a modest house in the middle of a fragrant garden. Instructing one of the workers to care for Devan's horse, Amudhan welcomed him into the house and introduced him to his mother. Devan realized that the lady was deaf and dumb. At the same time, he was impressed by the compassion in her face and the intelligence which sparkled in her eyes.

Soon, they sat down to a hearty dinner. As he ate, Devan questioned Amudhan about the fort. He learnt that, in addition to the royal family and the Pazluvur brothers, the fort accommodated the Chola treasury and granary. Government officials, gold and silversmiths, and a division of the Chola army all had their quarters inside. The chief minister, Aniruddha Brahmaraya, also lived inside, although he was now on a voyage. Kalaanthaka Kandar was the fort commander.

"What about Prince Madurandaka?" Devan asked.

"Prince Madurandaka is rarely seen. I hear he's an ascetic. His palace is next to the Pazluvur brothers'. He's married to the commander's daughter."

"Really?" said Devan. "I didn't know that. How come he married so late?"

"Yes, it was a surprise. I hear he has changed a lot since his marriage …" Amudhan broke off. "Anyway, it's better not to discuss such things."

Devan decided it was wiser not ask any more questions. Exhausted by his journey and his sleepless night at Kadambur Palace, he was glad to go to bed. As he fell asleep, he thought of Nandini's radiant beauty. She reminded him of his childhood encounter with a cobra. Mesmerized by the beautiful snake, Devan had stood with his unblinking eyes fixed on its hood, swaying in rhythm to its dance. Fortunately, a mongoose had attacked the snake at that point, breaking the spell and letting him run for his life. *Why am I comparing that innocent beauty to a snake? Ah! I'll see her charming face tomorrow and hear her sweet voice. She's extraordinarily beautiful but so is the woman I saw in Kudanthai. Ambalavan's wife is bewitching, but the other woman is dignified and compassionate.*

I'm Not Worthy of Her

VANDHIYA DEVAN WAS up at sunrise. Amudhan, already bathed and dressed, was gathering flowers, singing *Thevaram* hymns in a divine voice.

Devan wondered, *Why can't I be like this happy boy, content to serve god? Why must I always be on the move, armed with sword and spear, on the alert for enemies?* He shrugged away his doubts. *The world is made up of good and bad men. It needs strong, just rulers to keep the wicked in check. It also needs men like me. I must meet the emperor.* Devan bathed in the pond and dressed in his best clothes. He decided to leave his horse behind. *Better to let it rest. I may need to make a quick getaway later today.*

Devan and Amudhan set out together. "Do you have any other relatives, Amudhan?"

"Yes. My mother's elder sister died long ago, but her elder brother lives in Kodikkarai. He looks after the Kuzlagar temple garden during the day and is the lighthouse keeper at night. He has a son and a daughter ... Poonkuzlali ..."

Something in his voice made Devan say, "A beautiful name!"

Amudhan glowed. "She's as beautiful as her name. She outshines the deer and the peacock."

Ahah! thought Devan. *Amudhan is not devoted only to Shiva.* "So, when's the wedding?" he teased. "After all, you can claim her as your bride by custom: she's your maternal uncle's daughter."

Amudhan sighed. "Living with Poonkuzlali would be heaven on earth. I'm not worthy of her ... but who am I to decide?"

"Why not? Who asks for the girl's consent? Look at Lord Ambalavan—married to a girl young enough to be his daughter! Do you think he married her with her consent?"

Amudhan's voice was grave. "*Anna*, be careful. Don't mention the Pazluvur brothers when you're in the fort. They rule the Chola empire."

"What about the emperor?"

"The emperor is bed-ridden. I hear he gives the Pazluvur brothers a free hand in everything. Their power has increased drastically since the emperor moved from Pazlayarai to Thanjavur."

"And why did he do that?"

"After King Veerapandian was killed in the last war, the Chola army occupied Madurai, the Pandian capital. I hear Veerapandian's bodyguards are determined to avenge his death. The Pazluvur brothers brought the emperor here, as Thanjavur Fort is more secure than Pazlayarai Palace. The royal physician also advised that Thanjavur is better for the emperor's health."

"What exactly is wrong with the emperor?"

"He suffered a stroke and has lost the use of his legs."

"Oh!" Devan exclaimed. "He can't walk?"

"He can't walk or ride. There are rumors he has even lost his mind."

"The poor king!" Devan said.

"Don't show your sympathy, *anna*. The Pazluvur brothers may arrest you for treason."

Devan thought, *The Pazluvur brothers seem to be in absolute control. And now they're plotting against the emperor himself. I must warn the emperor.* Devan left his new friend at the fort gates.

Inside the Fort

VENDORS AND GOVERNMENT officials milled around the gates, clamoring to go in. But when the guards saw the signet ring, they bowed and immediately opened the gates for Vandhiya Devan.

Devan looked around in wonder. Palaces sparkled like jewels in lush gardens. The streets were beehives of activity. Not wanting to draw attention to himself by asking for directions, Devan carefully studied the buildings. The Tiger Flag fluttered high above one of the largest palaces.

That must be the emperor's palace, Devan decided and walked towards it. *It's impossible to see the emperor without the commander's permission. And I must accomplish my task before Lord Ambalavan returns; I can't risk being recognized by him.* Devan walked confidently through groups of tourists gawking at the palace and reached the entrance. Two spears barred his way. Devan casually displayed the signet ring on his palm.

"Let him in," the guard captain barked.

The spears parted and Devan walked into the palace. *What now? How do I meet the commander? And where can I find the emperor?*

Behind him, he heard the captain tell a guard, "These poets have come to see the emperor. Take them to the main hall. The commander is there."

A large group of richly dressed men walk past Devan ... he quickly mingled with them.

Danger!

VANDHIYA DEVAN WALKED into the hall ahead of the poets. Commander Kalaanthaka Kandar sat majestically on a high chair, surrounded by officials and guard captains. Devan, impressed by the authority which radiated from the man, bowed respectfully.

Kalaanthaka, always on the lookout for strong young men to join his guards, smiled warmly. "Come," he said. "What can I do for you?"

Devan took out his message. "Sir, I bring a letter from Prince Aditya Karikalan to his father."

The smile faded from Kalaanthaka's face. "Give it to me," he said abruptly.

"Sir, the message is for the emperor ..."

Kalaanthaka leaned forward, grabbed the cylinder and extracted the palm leaf inside. He handed it to an aide and ordered, "Read it out aloud." Kalaanthaka frowned and listened to the message. "It's nothing new. I'll pass on your message to the emperor." He dismissed Devan.

"Commander, Lord Ambalavan ordered me to personally give the emperor the letter ..."

"And where did you meet my brother?" Kalaanthaka asked suspiciously.

"I was at Kadambur Palace with him. He also gave me this signet ring as a mark of his favor."

Kalaanthaka relaxed. "Ah! And who else was at Kadambur?"

"The chieftains Mazlavaraya, Vanangamudi ..."

"Enough!" Kalaanthaka cut him off. "We'll discuss this later. Go and meet the emperor before the poets begin their long-winded recitations."

Kalaanthaka gestured to one of the guards who escorted Devan into another hall. Emperor Sundara Chola reclined on the throne with Queen Vanamadevi beside him. Devan was moved to tears at the emperor's weak, emaciated state. He touched the emperor's feet in respect. "Your Majesty, I bring a letter from Crown Prince Aditya Karikalan in Kanchipuram."

The emperor opened the letter eagerly. As he read it, his face clouded in disappointment. He turned to the queen. "Devi, my forefathers built a golden roof for the Shiva temple at Chidambaram. Our son has sunk so low that he builds a golden palace for himself."

Devan said, "Your Majesty, the prince sees god in his parents: isn't he right to build a golden palace for you?"

Sundara Chola smiled. "You're a clever young man. Come and see me tomorrow. I'll have a reply for my son."

Devan heard footsteps approaching. He leaned toward the emperor and said urgently, "Your Majesty, the prince asks you to leave Thanjavur at once. You are in danger!" Devan turned to find Kalaanthaka standing right behind him.

The commander's eyes blazed in anger: he had heard Devan's last words.

Iron Hand

KALAANTHAKA WAS ACCOMPANIED by the poets who launched into a chorus of praise of the emperor. The commander tried to cut them short, but Sundara Chola, a great patron of literature, welcomed the poets and said, "I'm eager to hear your poems."

The poets seated themselves on a carpet and Devan quickly sat among them. He felt the commander's cold eyes on him as the poets began their recitations. One poem exaggeratedly praised the emperor, depicting him as the benefactor of the gods themselves. The emperor burst into laughter for the first time after his stroke. To the poets' amazement, Sundara Chola confessed that he himself had composed that poem at his daughter's request.

At the mention of Kundavai, Devan's hands instinctively reached for the little silk package meant for the princess. To his horror, the pouch was missing from his waist! *I must have dropped it when I was with the commander. What if it's in his hands?* Devan mingled with the departing poets, desperate to find the letter. Just as he reached the door, an iron hand caught him by the wrist and held him back—it was the commander.

Our Honored Guest

THE EMPEROR SIGHED. "My forefathers died bravely on the battlefield or while on pilgrimage in search of god. I'm condemned to die on a sick-bed."

Kalaanthaka pushed Devan forward and said, "Lord, the royal physician and the astrologers agree you are out of danger .... but I heard this young man say, 'Danger.'"

"Come, my boy," Sundara Chola said kindly. "What were you saying about danger?"

Devan quickly said, "Your Majesty, I think the commander misheard my words. How can danger lurk near you when the commander, the royal physician and the queen are by your side? Your Majesty, I was asking for your help. I am the last heir to the kingdom of Vallam. I now serve your son. I beg you to grant me at least a small part of my ancestral land."

Compassion glowed in the queen's eyes as she said, "This lad has a silver tongue."

Sundara Chola smiled. "Commander, I like this young man. I think we can grant his request. What do you think?"

Kalaanthaka said, "Sir, we need to know Prince Aditya Karikalan's views on this ..."

Devan complained: "The prince refers me to the Pazluvur brothers and the Pazluvur brothers refer me to the prince. My request is stuck between the two of them!"

"Don't worry, my son," the emperor said. "I'll bring them together for you." He turned to Kalaanthaka. "Commander, my son urges me to go to Kanchipuram ..."

"As you wish, lord," Kalaanthaka murmured.

"But my legs will not cooperate and I won't be carried in a palanquin like a woman. I'll write to my son, asking him to come to Thanjavur instead."

"Sir," Kalaanthaka objected. "The north will be left undefended ..."

"Parthibendran and Malayaman can easily hold the fort until Karikalan returns to Kanchipuram. And," Sundara Chola continued, "another message must be sent to Prince Arulmozli in Sri Lanka: he must also come to Thanjavur. I have important matters to discuss with my sons. You can also tell Arulmozli you object to sending grain from here to Sri Lanka."

Kalaanthaka said hurriedly, "Sir, neither my brother nor I object. It's the people ..."

"Arulmozli would never do anything to harm the people. When will Lord Ambalavan be back?"

"My brother returns tonight, lord," the commander said.

"Very well, let the message to Lanka be sent tomorrow." The emperor turned to Devan. "And let this young man take my letter to Kanchipuram tomorrow."

"He's exhausted by his long travel, lord," the commander said. "Let him rest. We'll send someone else with your letter."

The emperor smiled. "I agree. Let him stay here until Karikalan comes from Kanchipuram."

The queen spoke up, "Treat him as an honored guest, commander."

Kalaanthaka replied, "Yes, Your Majesty." But his eyes glinted dangerously.

The Art Gallery

KALAANTHAKA ACCOMPANIED VANDHIYA Devan to the main hall, his mind a whirl of suspicion: *I swear I heard him say, 'Danger!' But he has my brother's signet ring. I'll keep him under my eye until my brother returns.* Kalaanthaka ordered an attendant, "Take this man to my palace. Treat him as an honored guest."

Devan's eyes frantically searched the hall for the missing letter, but it was nowhere to be seen. He reluctantly left with the attendant.

Even as the commander turned away, another attendant hurried forward with a silk pouch. "This was lying in the passage to the king's hall, sir. It may have been dropped by that young man."

Kalaanthaka grabbed the pouch and eagerly read the message inside. His face paled and his eyes blazed in fury. In his letter to Kundavai, Karikalan wrote: *Sister, the bearer of this letter is a brave and trustworthy warrior. You can confidently trust him with any secret mission.* The commander beckoned to the attendant and whispered to him. The man hurried away.

Meanwhile, Devan received a warm welcome at the commander's palace. He washed, dressed in the rich new robes given to him and enjoyed a sumptuous meal. He was then escorted to the palace's art gallery to enjoy the exhibits, Thanjavur being a center of art. His guards whiled away the time playing dice at the entrance.

Thieves! Thieves!

VANDHIYA DEVAN ADMIRED the paintings which depicted the rich history of the Chola dynasty and detailed the courageous acts of the kings and the highlights of their reigns. One fact stood out: it was always a Pazluvur man who stood by the Chola king, making his victory possible. *I now understand why the emperor has given the Pazluvur brothers so much power. I also sense danger: the commander is suspicious. If I don't escape from the fort before Lord Ambalavan returns, it will be the underground dungeon for me.* He was certain that Karikalan's letter to Kundavai was in Kalaanthaka's hands. *I can still deliver the message to the princess as I have memorized it. She'll have to take my word for it. But how do I get out of the fort?*

Hearing a commotion in the courtyard, he looked down from a window: Kalaanthaka was back. *There's no time to lose,* Devan decided. He walked up to the guards and said, "Friends, I need my old clothes."

"They have been sent to the laundry," one man replied.

"Liar! You stole the gold coins I had in my pocket. Bring my clothes at once or ...."

"Or what?" another guard mocked. "Remember you're in Thanjavur: what can you do?"

Devan charged towards the entrance. The three guards barred his way. Devan punched the first man on the nose, twisted the second's legs and kicked the third man's knees. The guards fell, bleeding and writhing in pain. They jumped up and circled him cautiously. Devan shouted, "Thieves! Thieves! Help!"

Kalaanthaka strode into the room and barked, "What's going on here?"

The Test

VANDHIYA DEVAN EXCLAIMED, "Commander, thank goodness you're here! These rascals have robbed and insulted me—a royal guest and Prince Aditya Karikalan's messenger. In our land, such a crime would merit the death sentence."

Kalaanthaka took in the situation at a glance: *He has single-handedly knocked down three of my best men. What a warrior he is!* He calmed Devan. "*Thambi,* let me make enquiries." Kalaanthaka's eyes blazed in fury as he shouted at his men: "Fools! How dare you lay a finger on a royal guest? Shame on you! Three of you knocked down by one man!" He turned back to Devan. "*Thambi,* what do you want?"

Is this a show put on for my benefit? Devan wondered. He said, "I want my clothes and belongings."

"Why are you so upset? Were you carrying something valuable?"

"Yes," Devan said. "I had some gold coins for my expenses …"

"Don't worry," Kalaanthaka assured him. "I'll give you gold."

Devan said proudly, "I'm the crown prince's messenger. I won't take money from anyone."

"Very well," Kalaanthaka said. "And were you carrying anything else?"

Devan hesitated for a split second and then said, "Yes, I had something very valuable. But I can't tell you, it's confidential."

Kalaanthaka said, "Let me remind you, the prince has no authority in Thanjavur. I'm responsible for the emperor's safety here: so, no secrets from me."

"The nation is grateful to you and your brother for guarding the emperor. Didn't the emperor say even the God of Death would be afraid to enter Thanjavur Fort with you in command?"

Kalaanthaka was pleased. "If we had not brought the emperor here from Pazlayarai, god alone knows what those Pandian conspirators would have done!"

"Ah!" exclaimed Devan. "What I heard is true. There's a conspiracy being hatched against the emperor and his two sons."

Uneasy with the direction in which the conversation was headed, the commander said, "Don't worry, we're here to protect the Chola dynasty. Now, tell me: what were you carrying?"

"A letter from the prince to his sister, Princess Kundavai, at Pazlayarai," Devan said.

"What does it say?" Kalaanthaka asked.

"Commander, I'm not in the habit of reading others' letters," Devan declared loftily. "Of course, I have no objections to you reading the message."

"Wait," Kalaanthaka said. "I'll fetch your belongings."

Devan followed the commander but was stopped by the soldiers. Kalaanthaka soon returned; behind him came a guard with Devan's belongings. Devan found the letter with his clothes. He counted his money: there were extra gold coins. *Is this some kind of a test?*

"Is everything in order?" Kalaanthaka asked.

Devan placed the extra gold coins on a table. "I'm a prince of Vallam. I'm the crown prince's messenger. These coins are not mine."

Kalaanthaka clapped his hands. "I admire your integrity. Please accept these coins for your expenses. Now, do you want to leave or will you stay to meet my brother?"

Pocketing the gold coins, Devan replied, "I must pay my respects to Lord Ambalavan before I go. But I would like to do some sightseeing first."

"These two men will go with you and show you the sights," the commander said. "Please stay inside the fort. If you are outside when the gates are closed, you can come back only tomorrow." Kalaanthaka took the two guards aside and gave them instructions in a low voice.

The Woman in the Tree

AS VANDHIYA DEVAN followed the guards around the fort, his mind was busy with escape plans. *If Lord Ambalavan sees me, I'm doomed. I can easily give these men the slip, but how do I leave the fort? The guards at the gate would definitely have been warned. There must be some secret underground passage from the fort, but whom can I ask for directions?* Devan thought of Nandini. *Maybe the beautiful lady will help me. But how can I find her palace and meet her without the Pazluvur brothers' knowledge?*

He walked on, feigning interest in the fort. He saw many deserted alleys and lush gardens near the busy streets. He could hide there for a few days but Kalaanthaka would find him eventually. Devan heard drumbeats and cheers. He hid a smile and asked his guards, "What's happening?"

"The *Velakkara Padai* is returning to its city barracks," one of the guards replied.

Devan exclaimed: "The *Velakkara Padai!* I have always dreamt of joining it. I must see this." He hurried to the marching battalion. "I must see the drummers," he said and mingled with the soldiers. He joined in their shouts of praise for the emperor and weaved through their ranks.

"Idiot!" one soldier shouted. "He must be drunk."

But no one stopped Devan. His two escorts stayed at a safe distance, keeping him in sight and marching alongside the bodyguards. A woman walked towards the marching soldiers, carrying pots of curds for sale.

One of the soldiers shouted, "Hey, you! I'm thirsty. Give me some curds."

"I'll give you two slaps!" the woman replied defiantly, trying to walk past. The soldier blocked her path. The frightened woman turned and ran. A few soldiers chased her.

Seizing his opportunity, Devan shouted, "Catch her!" and charged behind them.

The woman disappeared into an alley. The soldiers gave up the chase and returned to their battalion. Devan continued running in and out of backstreets and alleys until he lost his guards. As he wandered among the dense foliage and fences, darkness fell. He came to a high wall and sat with his back against it, exhausted after the eventful day. *Let the moon rise. I'll find an exit from the fort. And even if Kalaanthaka launches a manhunt for me, I can easily hide here. I'll find some way— after all, I'm from the Vallam clan ...* Devan fell asleep.

He awoke with a start. A sound had disturbed him. He looked up at the wall in the moonlight and froze: something sat on an overhanging tree branch. *Can it be a ghost?*

"You!" the figure spoke. "How many times must I call you?"

It was a woman. Devan gaped at her.

"Are you asleep?" she scolded. "Here's the ladder. Watch out: if you fall, that will be the end!" She lowered a bamboo ladder. Devan was dazed. But he was not one to miss an opportunity. He grabbed the ladder and began to climb.

"Hurry up!" the woman said. "The lady has been waiting impatiently for you."

Devan almost toppled down the ladder in his excitement. *How is this possible? Have I been mistaken for somebody else?* He reached the top of the wall. The moon shone on the woman's face—it was the curd seller who had run from the soldiers.

"Come on," she urged. "Drop the ladder and jump down." She clambered down the tree.

Devan obeyed and found himself in a large garden. Before him was a palatial mansion with light blazing from its windows. Beside this stood a smaller mansion which was shrouded in darkness. Before he could question the woman, she placed a finger on her lips and gestured to him. Devan followed her along a narrow path between mango trees.

The Garden Pavilion

THE WOMAN STARED at his face. "You look younger—and your large moustache is missing ..."

"In my profession, I must often change my appearance: and the lady's favor keeps me young."

The woman declared, "The lady will soon rule the entire kingdom." She mocked him: "And I suppose you'll take credit for it and say it's because of your magic!"

Ah! Devan thought. *Her mistress is either Nandini or Madurandaka's wife, Kalaanthaka's daughter. And she thinks I'm a sorcerer. How do I deal with this?* Never one to lose heart, he resolved, *Fortune favors the bold. No woman can get the better of me.*

They came to a pavilion standing between the two mansions. The servant gestured, asking him to wait, and entered the small building.

Devan heard a voice: "Send him in at once." It was Nandini.

The servant came out and signaled to him. Devan walked into the pavilion. Nandini lounged on a flower-strewn couch in the light of a fragrant oil lamp. Devan was intoxicated by the bewitching mix of beauty and fragrance. *Careful!* he thought. *I must not let this atmosphere cloud my mind.*

Nandini eyes widened in surprise on seeing him. She ordered the servant: "Vasuki, go stand guard. If anyone comes, slam the door as a signal." Vasuki left. Nandini turned to Devan. "You are indeed a sorcerer—what magic did you use to come here?"

"Only my smile," he replied. "I used the ladder to get here."

"Why didn't you come during the day using my signet ring?"

"I'm hiding from your brother-in-law, the commander. His servants stole my belongings and clothes; I had a difficult time evading them. I was hiding in the alley when your servant lowered the ladder. I now realize it was a case of mistaken identity. I apologize."

Nandini smiled. "Don't apologize. In fact, I summoned the sorcerer to consult him about you."

"Really?" Devan was surprised.

"Do you believe in reincarnation?" Nandini asked. "The bonds we forge with someone in our previous birth instinctively bind us to them in this birth, even when they are strangers to us."

"I did not believe this earlier, but I have changed my mind since yesterday," Devan said, recalling the beautiful woman in Kudanthai.

Nandini smiled, thinking he was referring to their encounter on the road to Thanjavur. She said, "Now, give me your message from Thirumalai."

"I met him at Veeranam. Thirumalai recognized your palanquin. When he knew I was going to Kadambur Palace, he asked me to give you a message. But I did not get a chance to meet you until your palanquin banged into my horse," Devan lied glibly.

Nandini's teasing eyes sparkled at him. "Yes, my palanquin can be very dangerous indeed!"

The Sorcerer

THEY HEARD DRUMS and trumpets, followed by loud cheers and the tramp of horses and elephants.

The terrified Vasuki rushed in. "The master is back!"

Nandini stayed calm. "Go back to your post," she said. She turned to Devan. "The chancellor will pay his respects to the emperor and then meet his brother. Only then will he come here. We have time. Tell me, what did Thirumalai say?"

"I find it hard to believe he's your brother—can a monkey and a parrot have the same mother?"

Nandini laughed. "We grew up together and he loved me as a sister. I have disappointed him."

"Lady, Thirumalai waits eagerly for you to wed Lord Vishnu."

Nandini sighed. "Tell him to forget me. Tell him I'm no Andal."

"Why not, lady? One look at you, and the Lord Himself will rush to be your groom."

Nandini laughed in delight. "You are an expert in the art of flattery. And you have a silver tongue. Who are you?"

"I'm Vandhiya Devan of Vallam."

"Which kingdom do you rule?"

Devan smiled. "The sky and the earth. My kingdom was annexed by the Chola kings."

"Maybe I can return it to you," Nandini said.

"After seeing the emperor, I prefer my independence to his royal life."

"You're right," Nandini said. "Now, why are the commander's men hunting for you?"

"They are suspicious about my identity and how I got the signet ring."

A flash of fear crossed her eyes. "Where's the ring?"

"It's safe with me. I used it to meet the emperor. The commander wanted to know how I got it. I said the chancellor gave it to me."

"Did he believe you?"

"I think he wants to check with the chancellor."

"Don't worry about the chancellor," Nandini said confidently. "I'll take care of him."

"The entire kingdom talks about your hold over Lord Ambalavan, lady. But I need your help to get out of the fort at once."

"Why the hurry?" Nandini asked.

"I must meet your brother," Devan replied. "What shall I tell him?"

"Tell him to forget Nandini."

"That's impossible, lady. I have seen you only twice—and I can never forget you. How can someone who has spent his life with you ever forget you?"

Nandini glowed in pride. "Why did you meet the emperor?"

"I wanted to see the king who is renowned for his beauty."

Nandini sniffed in contempt. "Hah! He's vain about his looks - just like his daughter, that conceited woman in Pazlayarai: Princess

Kundavai." She sat up abruptly. "Let's come to an agreement. I'll help you—and I need something from you in return."

"What can I, a nobody, give the woman who's married to the most powerful man in the Chola empire?"

"Will you be my secret agent?" she asked. "I'll get you a job in this household."

Devan hesitated. "Lady, I serve another. If she dismisses me, I'll be your trusted helper."

"And who's this lady, my rival?" There was ice in Nandini's voice.

"The lady you just mentioned, Princess Kundavai. I carry a letter for her." Devan handed it to her. "It's confidential but many have already read it."

Nandini studied the message. Her face darkened in anger. Again, she reminded him of the beautiful cobra with its forked tongue. Devan suppressed a shiver.

Nandini's voice was harsh. "I'll help you leave the fort. In return, you must promise to show me Kundavai's reply to this letter."

"It will be very risky," Devan said. "What will be my reward?"

Nandini's sensuous look made him giddy. "Reward? I'll give you something for which my husband, the most powerful man in the Chola empire, has been waiting for years …" She stopped short as an owl hooted. She turned in the direction of the sound. The owl hooted again. "The sorcerer is here: he may help you escape from the fort. Hide in the garden. Quick!"

Do You Remember?

NANDINI WENT TO the entrance, clapped softly thrice and went back to her couch.

The sorcerer emerged from the darkness of the trees and entered the pavilion. The lamp light fell on his face: it was Ravidasan, the man who had held the meeting of the Pandian conspirators. Ravidasan's face darkened in anger at the sight of Nandini relaxing on the couch. Sitting on a wooden bench across from her, he chanted, "Aum! Hreem! Chandi …"

Nandini stopped him. "There's no need for all that: by now, the servant would have fallen asleep on the steps. What do you want? Be quick–my husband is back and will soon be here."

"You evil woman!" Ravidasan hissed. "You ungrateful wretch! I must remind you of your past." Nandini sighed and turned away. Ravidasan continued, "Three years ago, in the middle of the night, a small group of men hastily built a funeral pyre on the bank of the River Vaigai in Madurai. They brought a corpse from its hiding place behind a tree and set it to burn on the pyre. Then, they dragged you from the dark forest. You were gagged and bound. Your unkempt hair, now adorned with flowers, trailed in the dust.

"'Let the flames rise higher,' one man said. 'We'll throw her into the pyre.'

"You watched the men form a circle and swear a terrible oath. When they returned, you rolled your eyes and struggled to lift your bound hands.

"'She's trying to say something,' another man said. 'Just throw her into the fire and be done with it.'

"But their leader said, 'Remove the gag: let's hear what she has to say.'"

"And do you remember what you said?" Ravidasan asked. Nandini's face showed revulsion and fear; her eyes filled with tears; she stiffened with resolve. Ravidasan hissed at her: "You're silent. Very well, I'll do the talking. You pleaded with those men to let you share their oath. You insisted you had more reason than they had to take revenge on the enemy. You promised to use your beauty and brains to advance their cause. And you swore that, once their mission was accomplished, you would end your life. No one believed you. But I did … if not for me, your life would have ended on that funeral pyre. Do you remember?"

Nandini whispered, "That night is etched on my heart in letters of fire."

Ravidasan took up the story once more. "One day, our gang ran for cover at the sound of horses' hooves. But you stood your ground and were captured by Ambalavan's men. The chancellor fell in love with you and married you. My men insisted you had cheated me. I followed you for days … and when I had you in my clutches, you begged for your life once more. You said your actions were all part of your plan for the success of our mission. True or not?"

"It's the truth," Nandini said. "I have never denied it. Why are you raking up the past?"

"Because you have forgotten the past," Ravidasan accused. "You have become used to silks and jewelry and ivory palanquins ... or are you so in love with that handsome young man who was here that you have forgotten your oath?"

The shocked Nandini gasped, "That's a lie!"

"Then why was your maid not in her usual place tonight?"

"She was there as usual but another man climbed up the ladder."

Ravidasan was furious. "I narrowly missed being captured by that man's pursuers. I had to stay submerged in a pond to escape."

Nandini tossed her head. "So, you have washed away your sin of doubting my intentions!"

"Tell me," Ravidasan insisted. "Have you fallen for that man's good looks?"

"Nonsense! It's only in this shameless Chola kingdom that a man is admired for his beauty instead of his courage. He's here because Vasuki mistook him for you."

"Why did you give him the signet ring? You have never given me one."

"I plan to use him for our mission."

"You foolish woman! Have you revealed our secrets to him?"

"No, I have ferreted out his secrets: he carries a letter for Princess Kundavai."

"And what is that to us?" Ravidasan asked.

"Haven't we sworn to destroy the Chola dynasty? Who do you think rules the country? Not the bedridden emperor; not his two sons; not my husband, the chancellor: it's that tigress Kundavai who rules in all but name. And I'll use this young man to destroy her."

Ravidasan's anger faded, to be replaced by admiration. "How do I trust you?" he asked.

"Blindfold him and take him out of the fort through the secret passage. Go with him to Pazlayarai and bring him back here with the princess's reply. If he tries to escape, kill him."

Ravidasan shrugged. "No, let him go his way. The commander has launched a manhunt for him. If I'm with him, I share his danger. Let's come to our plans: our men must leave for Sri Lanka soon. We need Sri Lankan currency."

Nandini gave him a bag. "This has Sri Lankan gold coins. Now, go—my husband will be here."

Ravidasan slipped away into the darkness.

She called, "Wait! At least take that man outside the fort. He can go his own way after that." Nandini clapped and called out softly, but Devan was nowhere to be seen.

Clash of Lions

AMBALAVAN ENTERED THANJAVUR Fort with his escort. To his surprise, his brother did not receive him at the gate with the usual fanfare. The worried chancellor hurried to Kalaanthaka's palace. *Is the emperor dead?* he wondered.

Kalaanthaka met his brother at the gate, embraced him and took him to a private room.

The chancellor asked, "What's the matter, *thambi*? Is it the emperor?"

Kalaanthaka replied calmly, "The emperor's condition remains the same, *anna*. This is a different problem. First tell me, how was your trip to Kadambur Palace?"

"Our mission is a success. The hosts, Sambuvaraya and his son, Kandamaran, fully support us. All the invited chieftains were there and accepted our choice of Madurandaka as the next king. Even Mazlavaraya and Vanangamudi have fallen in line. Only three men will oppose us—Malayaman, the emperor's father-in-law, will naturally favor his grandsons; Parthibendran, Karikalan's close friend, will also protest; we can ignore Kodumbalur Velir for now, as he's with the army in Sri Lanka."

"What if the people protest?"

Ambalavan shrugged. "Who cares? The people will accept anyone the emperor chooses. Luckily, Arulmozli is in Sri Lanka. They'll rise only in his support." He laughed. "We can build up Madurandaka's reputation as a Shiva devotee—the public will fall for it: and for his beautiful face!"

"What about the *Velakkara Padai, anna*?"

"They have sworn their oath to the emperor, not to his sons," the chancellor pointed out. "And if they rebel, you have your guards: crush them and throw them into the dungeon."

"I think our greatest danger is from Pazlayarai. We have no idea what the old queen and the princess are up to."

Ambalavan laughed. "Are you afraid of two women? Leave them to me."

"The emperor has ordered his sons to come to Thanjavur," Kalaanthaka informed his brother.

"The princes must not be allowed to return until Madurandaka becomes king. I'll take care of that. Now, tell me, what's happening here?"

"A young man arrived this morning from Kanchipuram with letters to the emperor and Princess Kundavai from the crown prince."

"I hope you took the letters and threw him into the dungeon?"

"No, *anna*. He said he met you at Kadambur and you asked him to meet the emperor ..."

"Fool!" shouted Ambalavan. "There was a suspicious young man at Kadambur—Kandamaran's friend. Did you read the letter before letting him meet the emperor?"

"I did. There was nothing new in it. But I heard him say, 'Danger!' to the emperor."

"Wasn't that enough for you to arrest him?"

"I agreed to let him tour the fort. I assigned two of my best men to guard him but he has given them the slip. We are now combing the fort for him."

"Stupid! I made you the commander of Thanjavur Fort and you have let a young man fool you."

"*Anna*, he had a signet ring with the Pazluvur palm tree emblem. He claimed you gave it to him."

"Why would I give him a ring?!" Ambalavan snorted in disgust.

Kalaanthaka was thoughtful. "He entered the fort and met the emperor using the ring. If you did not give it to him, there is only one other person from whom he could have got it ..."

"Who are you referring to?" Ambalavan asked coldly.

"Can't you guess who I'm referring to, *anna*? I'm referring to your wife."

The chancellor roared in anger: "Careful, *thambi* ... I'll cut off your tongue!"

Kalaanthaka refused to back down. "Even if you cut off my head, I'll speak my mind now: mesmerized by a beautiful snake, you brought it home. Its poison will destroy us all one day. Send her away ... now."

"I will also speak my mind," the chancellor said. "Listen carefully: you may criticize me. But if you say a word against Nandini, I'll kill you with the very sword I taught you to hold."

Nandini Sulks

IT WAS WELL after midnight when Ambalavan reached his palace. His mind was in a whirl. *Kalaanthaka loves me more than life itself. What he says is because of that love. But he's a coward to blame Nandini for his own foolishness. Anyway, he has apologized ... that's the end of it.* But he could not shake off a sneaking suspicion that his brother's words might be true. *Have I let lust destroy me? As they say, there's no fool like an old fool. I found Nandini on a forest track. I have no idea who she is or where she is from. I was bewitched by her beauty.*

He shook his head. *No, I must not doubt Nandini. She adores me; she serves me dutifully and is ready with sound advice for me. She's beauty personified, yet she married me—an old man.* He frowned. *Why does she often ask for my signet rings? What does she do in that garden pavilion for hours on end? Who is this sorcerer she often meets? I can overlook all this. But why does she refuse to consummate our marriage? She keeps putting me off with vague talk of fasts and penance. But what penance can stop her from sleeping with her lawfully wedded husband? Enough is enough! I'll insist on having my way tonight.*

The chancellor's temper rose when he heard that Nandini was at the pavilion even at this time of night. He strode angrily to the garden. Nandini saw him coming and turned away deliberately. She stood staring into the darkness. Ambalavan's anger died before her beauty. He gently held her shoulder and turned her to him. "My darling, why do you refuse to speak to me?" Nandini burst into tears. "How could you leave me alone for four days?" The chancellor's heart melted with love for his beautiful wife. "And what will you do if I go to war?" he asked tenderly.

"I'll follow you to the battlefield," she declared.

"Sweetheart, I would never let you do that," he whispered. "I can withstand arrows and spears ... but I cannot bear it if you even get pricked by a thorn." He took her hands and led her to her couch. "Every day away from you felt like a year."

Nandini wiped away her tears and smiled up at him. *I'll lay down my life to see her smile,* the infatuated Ambalavan thought.

"Your work kept you away from me for four days. But why didn't you come straight home to me on your return? Your brother means more to you, is it?"

"I had to wait for that fool, Madurandaka, to reach his palace through the underground passage."

"I hate the idea of that man in my palanquin," Nandini grumbled. "Everyone thinks you are dragging me with you everywhere you go."

"But you are the one who gave me this brilliant idea of using the secret tunnel and the palanquin to smuggle Madurandaka to our meetings," the chancellor pointed out.

"It's my duty as your wife to help you in any way I can," Nandini smiled modestly.

"No one could convince Madurandaka to renounce his asceticism and agree to our plans. But you met him just twice—and now, he can't wait to become emperor! What magic did you use? You are an enchantress yourself: why do you need a sorcerer's magic? It makes people talk ..."

"Cut out their tongues!" Nandini spat out. "I need magic to defeat that witch in Pazlayarai, Kundavai. You men bravely fight face to face on the battlefield but you underestimate the power of a woman." Nandini's voice trembled. "You may have forgotten her insults, but I'll remember them until my dying day. Kundavai told me in public, 'I can understand that old buffalo lusting after you, but were your brains addled? Why did you agree to marry that old man?'" Nandini broke into sobs.

The Earth Spins

AMBALAVAN KNEW HE was a laughing stock for marrying a girl young enough to be his daughter. He had heard that Kundavai disapproved of his marriage, but not in these bald terms. Nandini's words kindled a raging fury in him. "The witch! I'll crush her ..."

Nandini twined her soft hand with his. "Darling, leave her to me: we must meet witchcraft with witchcraft. And if you object to the sorcerer, I'll leave this palace."

"Never! You are life itself to me. I give you permission to meet any number of sorcerers. Sweetheart, I'm consumed by a fire only you can put out. We have been married for more than two years ... yet we have not consummated our marriage. Why do you keep putting me off with excuses? Why don't you just poison me and end my agony?"

"Stop! I'll poison myself if you say such cruel things again. On our marriage day, we became one in body and soul: my heart echoes your heartbeat; my mind reflects your thoughts. Why should we bother about our bodies which are only made of dust and will return to dust?"

"No, Nandini, the Creator made your body out of fragrant flowers, divine music, cool moonlight and the elixir of life," Ambalavan crooned into her ears.

"You have many wives," Nandini reminded him mischievously.

The chancellor's voice was sad. "I married them only for sons to continue the Pazluvur line. But they were either barren or gave me daughters. I stopped having a woman in my bed years ago. I devoted my entire life to the Chola empire. I defeated the Pandians and raised the Tiger Flag over their capital, Madurai. And then ..." His eyes were faraway. "As I rode along the banks of the Ponni, I saw you on that deserted forest track. I thought you were an angel who would vanish if

I blinked my eye. You said, 'I'm an orphan, give me refuge.' I couldn't resist the force which pulled me to you. There's only one explanation for this: we have been bound to each other in every previous lifetime ..."

Ambalavan did not see the flash of surprise on Nandini's face. "Dearest," she said, "You are courage and compassion combined. You took me, an orphan with no family or roots, and made me your queen. Please be patient, my penance is almost over. And then, I'll give myself to you completely—all the pleasures you dream of will be yours."

"Let me help you complete your penance quickly. Tell me what it's about."

"Sundara Chola's sons must not become kings and the arrogant Kundavai must be punished."

"Consider that done, Nandini. Except a few chieftains, everyone has accepted Madurandaka as the next emperor."

"But we can relax only after Madurandaka sits on the Tiger Throne," Nandini warned.

"Yes," Ambalavan agreed. "I must remain alert and let nothing interfere with our plan. See what happened today: a young man from Kanchipuram managed to fool my brother."

"Hah! Didn't I tell you your brother's not as smart as you think?"

"Kalaanthaka has been foolish in this matter. But he says the young man has my signet ring ..." Ambalavan looked at Nandini with a raised eyebrow.

She shrugged. "Your brother's looking for an excuse to justify his failure."

"The search is on for that young man. We'll find him soon and the mystery will be solved."

"My dearest, my penance will not end with the crowning of that fool, Madurandaka. When I was a child, an astrologer predicted great suffering for me until the age of eighteen. And then, he predicted I would marry a man who would become emperor and rule a vast empire." She looked up at him with melting eyes. "My beloved, will you make his prediction come true?"

Ambalavan felt the earth spin around him.

The Dark Mansion

VANDHIYA DEVAN CROUCHED in the dark garden, listening to the low murmur of Nandini's conversation with the sorcerer. *Am I mad? Nandini's an enchantress: she's more dangerous than the Pazluvur brothers. And how she hates Princess Kundavai! I'm a fool to trust her.*

He decided it would be safer to find his own way of escape from the fort. As he looked around, his eyes fell on the dark mansion before him. He crept to the huge door, with its strong bolt and padlock. Just as he was about to turn away, the moonlight showed a smaller door set cleverly into the bigger one. Devan pushed this door—to his amazement, it opened at his touch.

He stepped into a hall where the moonlight fell on huge pillars. He closed the door behind him and was immediately engulfed in total darkness. An unreasonable fear gripped his mind. He felt his way forward carefully. His hands reached out to touch a pillar; he made his way around it and put his leg forward ... the ground fell away under him! *It's a staircase. I just missed breaking my neck! Is it the entrance to the notorious dungeon?*

The darkness was impenetrable. Devan decided it was safer to go back to the pavilion and face Nandini than to risk his life in this dark hall. *I must first save my life. Later, I can find a way to deal with Nandini's terms.* He tried to retrace his steps, but lost all sense of direction in the darkness. A sense of panic gripped him. *I'm trapped!*

Suddenly, he heard footsteps and something brushed against his face. Instinctively, he lashed out with his hand and bit his lips to smother his cry of pain—it was a stone pillar. The footsteps echoed in the cavernous hall making it impossible for Devan to pinpoint the direction from which they came. Then, a flare of light and smoke rose from below, outlining the pillars with their carved gargoyles and demons. Devan slipped behind a pillar and waited. Three men emerged from the stairwell. One man, obviously a guard, held a flaming torch in his hand. The second was Madurandaka ... and the third man, armed with a spear, was none other than Kandamaran.

Devan thought excitedly, *This is the secret tunnel which leads outside the fort! Kandamaran has escorted Madurandaka here. This is how the prince secretly enters and leaves the fort.*

The three men reached the ground level and continued up the winding steps to the next level. The torchlight faded. Devan concluded they were going to the commander's palace. Devan made a quick decision and climbed down into the stairwell.

The Underground Vault

DEVAN CLIMBED DOWN dark flights of steps interspersed with landings. The stairwell was so wide that he could not feel the walls. After a while, the steps climbed up. The darkness faded a little and he found himself in a rock-cut underground cave. Devan stared about him in amazement: in the dispersed light were stacks of gold bars, huge bronze urns filled with gold coins and lustrous pearls, and mounds of jewelry and precious gems.

I'm in the Chola treasury. Obviously, it's located near Lord Ambalavan's palace. Mesmerized by the wealth on display, he fingered crowns and necklaces and thrust his hands deep into pools of pearls and gold coins. His eyes fell on a shiny object on the floor. He bent over it … it was a human skeleton. The skeleton stirred. Devan froze in horror … then, he sighed and relaxed as a bandicoot emerged from the bones and skittered away.

Over a heap of gold coins in a corner, Devan watched a spider spin its web to catch an unsuspecting fly. *Lust for women and money and land: these are the three strands with which life spins its web to trap human flies. I faced all three today—Nandini, this treasure and Nandini's offer to restore my kingdom.* He straightened his shoulders. *As my wise ancestors believed, the entire world is my home and every man is my kin. Why do I need land or wealth or women? I'll delight in Nature's beauty; I'll revel in my freedom. Why exchange that for a life of political intrigue and danger?*

Devan heard a door open and close with a soft bang. He melted into the shadows. Footsteps came from two directions. The flame of torches lit up the unfolding scene.

Kandamaran, and the guard who had accompanied him, came from one side; from the other came Ambalavan and Nandini. It was clear that this was an unexpected encounter. Ambalavan questioned Kandamaran who replied softly. Ambalavan pointed to the tunnel: Kandamaran bowed and walked into it. Ambalavan then whispered a command into the guard's ear. The man nodded his head, bowed and followed Kandamaran into the secret tunnel. Ambalavan and Nandini walked into the darkness and disappeared.

Devan quickly followed the light of the soldier's torch. It was obvious that Kandamaran was retracing his steps to the tunnel's exit. The passage wound up and down and made many sharp bends. *I would never have found my way out on my own*, Devan thought. *Thank god for Kandamaran.*

The tunnel ended in a blank wall. The guard twisted a hidden lever and an opening, large enough for one man, appeared in the wall. The guard stood back and beckoned Kandamaran forward. As Kandamaran put one foot across the gap, Devan gasped: the guard slipped a curved dagger from his waistband and stabbed Kandamaran in his back! Devan sprang forward in fury and knocked the guard to the ground.

You Betrayed Me!

THE GUARD BANGED his head on the stone floor and lost consciousness. Vandhiya Devan quickly tied his hands with his waistband and ran to his friend. Kandamaran lay face down with his body half inside the tunnel: the dagger protruded from his back. Devan picked up his friend's spear and dragged him outside the tunnel. There were in a dense thicket of trees at the foot of the fort wall; the ground sloped steeply to the fast-flowing river. *We are on the banks of the Vadavar. The chancellor must have ordered the guard to kill Kandamaran and throw his corpse into the river.*

Devan lifted Kandamaran on his shoulders and staggered down to the water. He used the spear to measure the depth of the river—it was too deep to attempt a crossing with an unconscious man.

Kandamaran groaned in pain. *At least he's still alive.* Staggering under his friend's weight, Devan walked along the riverbank. After a while, he saw a fallen tree floating in the river, forming a makeshift bridge. Holding Kandamaran securely, Devan carefully stepped on to the tree trunk. As the wind howled and the water dashed against the tree, he somehow made it to the end of the trunk. He again measured the river's depth. To his relief, the spear easily touched the river bottom. He waded across the waist-high, icy water to the opposite bank, laid Kandamaran gently on the ground and collapsed shivering beside him. Kandamaran was alive but his breath was shallow and labored. *Chendan Amudhan's house is on the banks of the Vadavar. If I can somehow get Kandamaran there, I may be able to save his life.*

He bent to carry Kandamaran and found his eyes open. "Kandamaran! Do you recognize me?"

"Yes ... Vandhiya Devan ... the friend who stabbed me in the back!" Kandamaran hissed.

Devan was shocked into silence by this accusation.

"You ungrateful wretch! I hurried to Thanjavur only to save you from the Pazluvur brothers ... I promised the commander you would join his guards ... you betrayed me ..." Kandamaran said passionately and sank back into unconsciousness.

Devan eyes filled with tears. *My friend, why did you trust the Pazluvur brothers of all people?*

Carrying Kandamaran once more, Devan walked on. The fragrance of flowers told him that they had reached Amudhan's place. The once-neat garden was a wreck—it was evident that Kalaanthaka's men had been there searching for Devan. Luckily, his horse was still tied to the tree he had chosen that morning. Devan crept to the cottage and found Amudhan asleep on the verandah.

Gently laying Kandamaran on the ground, Devan shook Amudhan awake and whispered, "*Thambi*, this is my friend, Kandamaran, son of Sambuvaraya of Kadambur. He needs help."

Amudhan sat up and exclaimed softly, "Stabbed in the back? Cowards! Thank god you're safe. Soldiers are hunting for you. I'll take care of your friend. Take your horse and escape at once."

Devan hesitated and looked down at his unconscious friend.

"Leave him here," Amudhan urged. "My mother's a skilled healer." Amudhan knocked on the cottage door. His mother opened the door and took in the situation at a glance. The men carried Kandamaran in. She examined the wound carefully and gestured to her son, who held Kandamaran tightly. At a signal from her, Devan pulled out the dagger. Blood gushed from the open wound. Amudhan's mother quickly applied herbal balm over the gash and bandaged it with a clean cloth. The sound of running feet echoed in the still night.

"Hurry! Go!" Amudhan cried.

Devan hesitated. "*Thambi*, I must dash to Pazlayarai. I'm a stranger to these parts: will you come with me as my guide?"

Amudhan and his mother spoke hurriedly in sign language. The two men then raced to the horse and jumped into the saddle. Devan reined the horse to a slow walk, breaking into a gallop once they were past the soldiers. Even as they made their escape, a band of soldiers banged on the cottage door. Pushing Amudhan's mother roughly aside, they stormed inside.

"Here he is," one soldier shouted. "Oh my god! Just look at the blood!"

Amudhan's mother wailed, holding her lamp high above the unconscious man on the bed.

"This is not the man we're looking for," another soldier said.

"Is this the man who came here yesterday?" "Where's your son?" the soldiers shouted.

Impatient with her loud shrieks, their captain said, "Leave the dumb witch alone. This is not the man we are looking for, but he looks suspicious. We'll take him with us ..." He broke off at the sound of galloping hooves. "To your horses!" he shouted. "Catch him!"

The men abandoned Kandamaran and galloped after the horse.

Pazlayarai

PAZLAYARAI, CAPITAL OF the Chola empire, was a glowing city of rivers, mansions and towering temples. The magnificent palace lay at the heart of the city. Pazlayarai's glory dimmed when the emperor moved to Thanjavur, along with the *Velakkara Padai* and his officials. The barracks too were empty as the Chola army was now stationed in Sri Lanka, Kanchipuram and Madurai.

But on this Krishna Jayanthi day, Pazlayarai's streets bustled with citizens, tourists and pilgrims dressed in their festive best to celebrate Lord Krishna's birth. There was a special buzz of activity around the Vishnu temple. The richly dressed ladies of the royal household walked out of the temple and climbed into their waiting chariots. They were led by the Queen Mother, Sembiyan Madevi, Gandara Aditya's widow. She was followed by the beautiful Kalyani, Sundara Chola's mother. Behind her came Kundavai and her companions.

Sembiyan Madevi paused by her chariot; Azlvarkkadian stood at the temple entrance, singing a sweet hymn. The Queen Mother gestured to him. Azlvarkkadian rushed forward and bowed. "Thirumalai," she said. "I haven't seen you in a while …. have you been on a long pilgrimage?"

"Yes, mother," Azlvarkkadian said. "I saw and heard many interesting things on the way."

"Then come and see me this evening," Sembiyan Madevi said and climbed into her chariot.

A burst of laughter drew Azlvarkkadian's attention to Kundavai and her group. Kundavai gave him a meaningful glance; Azlvarkkadian replied with a slight bow.

That Woman is the Cause

SEMBIYAN MADEVI, DRESSED simply in white silk, with a string of *rudraksha* beads around her neck and holy ash smeared on her forehead, sat on a throne in her audience chamber. She was the embodiment of regal devotion and was revered by every Chola emperor. A patron of the arts, she gave generously to all who appealed to her for help. The renovation of temples was especially close to her heart. A group of artisans and temple priests, including Easana Bhattar, stood before her. As she discussed the renovation of a Shiva temple with a sculptor, she sighed. "There are many who criticize my mission to build temples. Even Prince Aditya Karikalan ...."

Azlvarkkadian rushed forward to interrupt. "I too have a complaint, mother. You favor Shiva temples ... you neglect Lord Vishnu ..."

The queen laughed. "Thirumalai, come tell me what I can do for you—the others may go." She lowered her voice, "Thirumalai, you have news for me?"

"Yes, mother. We are surrounded by spies: that's why I interrupted you when you mentioned the crown prince."

The queen sighed. "These are evil times if I can't trust my own family. Karikalan loves me as a mother: would he spy on me? I wish I had entered my husband's funeral pyre, but he died entrusting me with many tasks. Tell me, have I truly lost Karikalan's love and trust?"

Azlvarkkadian replied, "Hiding in a temple, I overheard the prince speaking with Malayaman and Parthibendran. The two men accused your son, Madurandaka, of plotting to become the next emperor with the help of the Pazluvur brothers. They said the conspirators held the emperor hostage at Thanjavur and urged the crown prince to lead an army to the fort. Malayaman insisted you were a part of this conspiracy. The prince said he would make one last attempt to bring the emperor to Kanchipuram without bloodshed. He sent a special messenger to the emperor and to Princess Kundavai. I learnt the young man's identity and tried to get information from him. But he's courageous and resourceful—I could get nothing out of him. Even our Kudanthai astrologer failed with him."

"What happened then?" the queen asked eagerly.

"He met the emperor, delivered his message and evaded the Pazluvur brothers' manhunt."

"A clever young man, indeed!" the queen applauded.

"There's more, mother," Azlvarkkadian said. "I spied on the conspirators at a meeting held in Kadambur Palace. The palanquin of Ambalavan's wife ..."

The queen interrupted angrily: "That woman is the cause of all the conflict in our family. Did you speak to her?"

"I adopted that snake and brought her up as my own sister only because you ordered me to, mother," Azlvarkkadian pointed out. "My blood boils at her ingratitude. She refuses to meet me after marrying the chancellor."

The queen sighed. "That's the way of the world. What happened at Kadambur?"

"Nandini was not in the palanquin ..."

"It was another woman? Is there no end to that old man's lust?"

"It was a man ..."

"A man! Which man would be shameless enough to hide in a woman's palanquin?"

"It was your son, Madurandaka, who attended that meeting in the palanquin."

The queen froze in horror. "My god! Do I deserve such a punishment for my crime?" She bowed her head in sorrow. "My son, I tried to bring you up as a Shiva devotee—will you now be the one to destroy the Chola dynasty?" Sembiyan Madevi sat up erect on her throne. "Thirumalai, I must consult Princess Kundavai. Meet me before you leave Pazlayarai."

"Mother, is it wise to confide in the princess? After all, Aditya Karikalan is her brother."

The queen was firm. "I held Kundavai as a newborn infant and raised her. I have been both mother and father to her. She's dearer to me than my own son. She'll never betray me."

"Tell me, mother," Azlvarkkadian said. "Did the princess tell you about the young man she met at Kudanthai and again on the riverbank?"

"No," said the queen. "What are you trying to say?"

"That young man and Aditya Karikalan's messenger are one and the same. He's a spy."

The queen was unmoved. "If Kundavai chooses not to tell me, she'll have good reason for it."

"Very well, mother," Azlvarkkadian said. "I'll tell the princess you wish to meet her."

An Enemy Spy

IT WAS A pleasant evening and Kundavai and her companions were in the garden behind the palace. The garden, with its tall trees and fragrant flowers, adjoined a large creek which brimmed with fresh water throughout the year and also served as a security barrier for the palace complex. Kundavai and Vanathi sat on a swing suspended by creepers from a banyan tree.

"Vanathi," Kundavai shook her. "Your thoughts are in Sri Lanka … hovering over my brother."

Vanathi blushed. "I worry about him, *akka*," she confessed softly. "How I wish I could be with him on the battlefield to support and comfort him."

Kundavai laughed. "Chola men don't take their women to the battlefield. Our men don't want our help. What if the enemy soldiers are dazzled by our beauty and surrender without a fight?"

"Really, *akka*?" Vanathi smiled.

"Do you remember the young man we met at the astrologer's house and again on the riverbank? When he saw us, he behaved as if he was drunk."

"Not 'us,' *akka*," Vanathi teased. "He had eyes only for you. Why are you bringing up that young man now?"

"What's wrong if I recall seeing him?" the princess was indignant.

They were interrupted by a loud drumbeat. A herald announced, "Attention! An enemy spy infiltrated Thanjavur Fort using a fake signet ring. He escaped with classified information after critically injuring two men. This man, Vandhiya Devan, is dangerous and is an expert in black magic. Anyone sheltering him will be put to death. Anyone with information leading to his capture will be rewarded with a thousand gold coins. These orders are issued in the name of Kalaanthaka Kandar, commander of Thanjavur Fort." As the drumbeats faded, Kundavai shuddered.

A servant rushed up. "Lady, a man calling himself Azlvarkkadian asks to see you urgently."

Kundavai hurried to the palace.

The People Whisper

AZLVARKKADIAN STOPPED TO watch a street play in honor of Krishna Jayanthi. The actors were portraying the duel between Krishna and Kamsa.

"Come and fight me!" the boy playing Krishna challenged.

"I'll kill you, Krishna!" the man playing Kamsa roared. "I'll kill your brother and your father ... I'll also kill that Vaishnava fanatic standing there, smeared with sandal paste."

At this, everyone turned to Azlvarkkadian and burst into laughter. Azlvarkkadian, furious at being made the laughing stock, raised his stick threateningly and advanced towards Kamsa, but the actor's wooden mask with its cruel teeth, huge mustache and terrifying eyes made him pause. Azlvarkkadian shrugged and walked away. *Have I heard that voice before? There's something familiar about it.*

Suddenly, drumbeats were heard and the herald made his announcement about Vandhiya Devan. At once, the festive air vanished and men eyed strangers suspiciously. The citizens gathered in small groups and whispered. Azlvarkkadian's sharp ears picked up their words. "These Pazluvur brothers are tyrants. Pazlayarai has lost its life and wealth because they took the emperor to Thanjavur. Our darling prince, Arulmozli, is in Sri Lanka with our sons and husbands. Our men are fighting the enemy and these wicked Pazluvur brothers are refusing to send them food and supplies. Who would dare to spy on the great Chola empire? These wicked men just need an excuse to throw their enemies into the dungeon ..."

Soon, the streets were empty. Azlvarkkadian reached Kundavai's palace. Kundavai, usually eager to hear his news and listen to his songs, was preoccupied and worried.

"Thirumalai," she said. "Give me news from your travels. What do the people say?"

"They praise the Chola dynasty and your two brothers, especially Arulmozli whom they adore."

Kundavai smiled. "That's only to be expected."

"They ask why the princess remains unmarried. I said a prince worthy of her is yet to be born."

"Oh! If your prince is yet to be born, I'll be old enough to be his grandmother by the time he's ready for marriage," Kundavai laughed.

"People are shocked by Madurandaka's sudden marriage. They praise the Pazluvur brothers …"

Kundavai cut him off angrily: "Enough! How's your dear sister–the to-be saint?" she sniffed.

"As the queen of the chancellor's palace, she enjoys every luxury."

"I hear she's the queen of the entire Chola empire!" Kundavai mocked.

"Let's not talk about her, lady. Let me sing you a song about Krishna …" He broke into a song but the princess seemed distracted.

When he stopped, Kundavai asked, "You heard the public announcement, Thirumalai. Do you know anything about that spy?"

Azlvarkkadian looked around fearfully. "I met the young man in Veeranam. He said he was on his way to Thanjavur. He tried to get information from me."

The princess suppressed her excitement. "What did he look like?"

"He was handsome … courageous … strong … he seemed to come from a noble family."

"And what did he want from you?"

"He asked about the emperor's health and he was interested in Prince Arulmozli and in the line of succession to the throne. I heard he asked the Kudanthai astrologer the same questions."

"Ah!" the princess exclaimed. "So, he visited the astrologer?"

"Lady, he's the one who caused a commotion there during your visit."

"I knew that rude young man would get into trouble. Thirumalai, if you see that man …"

"I'll drag him to the Pazluvur brothers and claim the reward," Azlvarkkadian declared.

"No! No, Thirumalai, you will bring him to me. I have an important task for him."

Azlvarkkadian looked her in the eye. "Lady, he'll come to you soon—on his own accord."

Easana Shiva Bhattar

AZLVARKKADIAN WALKED TO Easana Shiva Bhattar's house, which stood beside the Shiva temple. Easana was his cousin. The outer wall of the temple was a hillock dotted with Jain caves. The only access to the temple was through the single entrance gate. It was dark by the time Azlvarkkadian reached the temple. He walked into the temple, as this was the shortest way to his cousin's house. A crowd stood near the sanctum. *That's the drama troupe I saw earlier today*, Azlvarkkadian thought. Just then, his cousin hurried up, caught him by the shoulder and pushed him outside the temple.

"*Anna*," Azlvarkkadian protested. "What are you doing?"

"Don't step into the temple, Thirumalai. You insulted Lord Shiva before the Queen Mother. I'll kill you if I see you here again!"

Azlvarkkadian stealthily went around the temple: all the cave entrances were blocked. He then took the long route to his cousin's house. Easana's wife welcomed him warmly and served him a delicious meal. The content Azlvarkkadian relaxed on the verandah. He looked back on the events of the previous day.

He had been walking along the bank of the Kudamurutti river when he heard the sound of horses. He quickly hid behind a thick bush and watched. A horse bolted into view, lathered in sweat. A young man was tied to its back. Azlvarkkadian was struck by the determination with which the terrified youth clung to his horse. Five soldiers rode in hot pursuit, armed with spears. They steadily gained on the man. One of them aimed a spear at him, but the captain stopped him. The young man's horse charged into a bamboo thicket and his hair got tangled in a low-lying branch. In a minute, the soldiers surrounded him. They were obviously surprised at the rider's identity.

Azlvarkkadian heard them shout, "Where is he?"

The young man sobbed and pointed to the river. "He was washed away in the floods ..."

Dragging the young man and his horse behind them, the soldiers headed back to Thanjavur.

Azlvarkkadian now saw that this incident was a part of the larger puzzle he was trying to solve. He came back to the actor who had played Kamsa in the street play that morning. *There was something in his voice and manner which reminds me of someone* ... he thought as he drifted into sleep.

The next morning, Easana Bhattar frowned at him and asked, "When are you leaving?"

"When your anger has evaporated, *anna,*" Azlvarkkadian replied.

"Don't call me *anna.* I'll have nothing more to do with you—you wicked heretic!" Azlvarkkadian's sister-in-law tried to pacify her husband but he stormed out of the house. When he returned shortly, he said, "Thirumalai, I'm sorry for my harsh words. Forgive me."

"That's okay, *anna,*" Azlvarkkadian smiled in relief.

"Stay here until I return from my afternoon pooja. I have some important matters to discuss with you. Don't go anywhere," Easana emphasized.

"Okay, *anna,*" Azlvarkkadian agreed. *Ahah!* he thought. *Something's up.*

As soon as Easana left, Azlvarkkadian stealthily left the house and watched the hillock. Soon he was rewarded: Easana emerged from one of the caves, looked carefully around him and beckoned. Another man appeared behind him. *This is the man who played Kamsa. My cousin's anger was only a screen for this secret.* Determined to discover the identity of this mysterious man, Azlvarkkadian followed them as they walked to the broad creek which adjoined the palace complex. He hid in a thicket and watched as they climbed into a waiting boat and left the shore. The stranger turned towards the bank: as Azlvarkkadian had expected, it was Vandhiya Devan.

Where are they headed? Azlvarkkadian thought quickly. *I can guess.* He hurried down the street lined with royal mansions. He stopped at the home of Aniruddha Brahmaraya, the chief minister of the Chola empire. The house was empty at present as Aniruddha was in Madurai, overseeing the transfer of power from the defeated Pandians. The guard stationed at the entrance saluted Azlvarkkadian and opened the gate. Azlvarkkadian hurried to the garden at the back, hid in the bushes and looked across the creek.

The boat stopped at the opposite bank. The two men stepped out and climbed a flight of steps to a marble landing where Kundavai waited.

Whirlpools and Women's Eyes

ONE LOOK AT Kundavai and time stood still for Vandhiya Devan. He stared at her beautiful face. The princess turned away and fixed her eyes on a butterfly which sat on a nearby creeper. They stole glances at each other, only to look away ... and turn back again.

Easana Bhattar cleared his throat noisily and the spell was broken.

With difficulty, Kundavai gathered her wits, assumed her royal posture and said, "Easana Bhattar said you wished to meet me."

Devan, recalled to the present by her regal tone, said, "Lady, this may be a case of mistaken identity. I want to meet the light of the Chola empire—the one and only Princess Kundavai."

Kundavai smiled. "I'm Princess Kundavai. I'm also the woman you met in Kudanthai ... and again on the riverbank."

"Not 'again,' lady," Devan replied. "You were constantly on my mind from the moment I first saw you ... only if you left me could I meet you 'again.'"

Kundavai smiled "You have a way with words ... what do you think of our Chola country?"

"I love your country," Devan declared. "But I tremble before two dangerous things in it..."

Kundavai said proudly, "Yes, the sword and the spear of the Chola soldiers—especially when you are a spy."

Devan said, "I fear no man's sword or spear. I refer to the dangerous whirlpools in your rivers."

Whirlpools?" Kundavai was puzzled.

"When I escaped from Thanjavur Fort and rode towards Pazlayarai with the commander's men in hot pursuit, a young man came with me as a guide," Devan said.

"Who was this?" Kundavai asked.

"A young flower seller, Chendan Amudhan. I spent a night at his house. His mother is dumb."

"Ah!" exclaimed Kundavai. "I was right. Go on."

"When we reached the Kudamurutti river, Kalaanthaka's men were almost on us. I jumped off the horse and told Amudhan to ride on until he was caught. 'Tell them I drowned in the river,' I said. But he refused to lie. I had no other choice but to jump into the river, right into a whirlpool. I fought for my life and somehow managed to escape by grabbing a tree root. While I struggled in the whirlpool, I saw a fish which reminded me of the second dangerous whirlpool in your country—the beautiful eyes of the Chola women." He smiled. "If a man is caught in this whirlpool, he's doomed."

Before Kundavai could reply, the sweet sound of the flute floated to them on the breeze. They fell silent, losing themselves in the beauty of the music.

Kundavai pulled herself together and asked, "Why are you here?"

Devan held out Karikalan's letter. "This letter is from your brother."

Do You Hate Me?

Kundavai smiled as she read the letter. She looked up at Vandhiya Devan. "You have delivered my letter. What next?"

"I plan to go home, lady."

"But your work is just beginning," Kundavai said. "My brother says I can trust you with anything. Will you go back on your promise to him?"

"It's not in my blood to go back on my word," Devan firmly declared.

Kundavai smiled. "Are you reluctant to obey a woman? Do you hate women—and me?"

Hate you? One sidelong glance from you is enough to shake me to the core of my being! Aloud he said, "Lady, I'm surrounded by enemies: the Pazluvur brothers are determined to capture me, dead or alive; my friend, Kandamaran, thinks I have betrayed him; Lady Nandini has sent a sorcerer to kill me. It's not wise to entrust me with any important task … it's only a matter of time before I'm captured or killed."

Devan recalled his journey after he escaped from the whirlpool in the Kudamurutti river. Aware of the manhunt launched for him, Devan stayed concealed in a banana grove that day and set out at nightfall. He trudged on; long past midnight he came to a ruined building. Exhausted, he lay down in a dark corner for a short rest. Just as he was about to doze off, he heard the hoot of an owl. Recognizing the signal made by the sorcerer in Nandini's garden, Devan grew alert and quickly hid behind a tumbled down pillar. He heard muffled footsteps. A shaft of moonlight fell on the man who was stealthily approaching the pillar—it was the sorcerer.

With a bloodcurdling cry, the sorcerer leapt on Devan and caught his neck in a stranglehold. "Give me the signet ring," the man hissed. "Or you will die."

Devan gasped for breath; his eyes started from their sockets; he felt as if his neck would snap. Bracing himself against the pillar, he kicked his assailant with all his might. The sorcerer screamed and collapsed. At the same time, the pillar fell and stones pelted down from the roof. Devan burst from the ruins like a bat out of hell and ran for his life without a backward glance.

Kundavai's sweet voice interrupted his thoughts. "You must tell me all about the adventures and dangers packed into the eight days since you left Kanchipuram."

"It's a long story, lady."

Kundavai turned to Easana Bhattar: "Can the boatman be trusted?"

"He's deaf, lady," Easana replied.

"Excellent!" Kundavai said. "We'll go on a boat ride."

The three of them climbed into the boat which made a round of the creek. Devan, delighting in Kundavai's company, narrated the events of the past week. All too soon, they were back in the garden pavilion. Again, the sound of singing reached them.

Listening to the song on Krishna, Devan smiled. "It was Kamsa who got me here."

"How did that happen?" Kundavai asked.

Devan had reached the outskirts of Pazlayarai. Certain that the commander's men would have reached the city before him and raised the alarm, he hid near the gates and waited. Soon, a troupe of actors arrived, costumed for a street play on Krishna's life. Devan noted that the man playing Kamsa wore a wooden mask which completely concealed his face.

Devan deliberately picked a quarrel with him, boasting, "I'll make a better Kamsa than you!" Grabbing his mask, Devan performed Kamsa's moves with great style. As the drama troupe applauded, the offended actor walked away. "Don't worry," Devan assured the troupe leader. "I'll perform as Kamsa."

Wearing the mask, Devan entered the city. Once the performance was over, he went to the Shiva temple and met Easana Bhattar as instructed by the crown prince.

"The Goddess of Victory has sent you here!" Kundavai exclaimed.

Basking in her admiration, Devan was ready to do anything she asked. Kundavai took a palm leaf from a shelf in the pavilion and wrote, '*Thambi*, please come home. The bearer of this letter will give you all the relevant details.' Below the message, she drew the outline of a fig leaf. She held out the letter to Devan. "Go at once to Sri Lanka and come back with my brother."

As he took the letter from her, Kundavai's fingers grazed his palm. Trembling in ecstasy at her touch, he gazed at her. His eyes said everything his tongue could not.

Easana Bhattar coughed, bringing Devan back to earth.

The Paranthaka Clinic

THE NEXT MORNING, Kundavai, accompanied by Vanathi, went to Pazlayarai's soldiers' quarters. Using her personal revenue, the princess had established a clinic in honor of her great-grandfather, Paranthaka Chola. This clinic served the families of the veterans fighting in Sri Lanka. Kundavai often visited the Paranthaka Clinic and mingled with the soldiers' families.

The women were mounted on the royal elephant. Cheers rose from the spectators: "Long live Princess Kundavai!" A crowd followed the elephant to the clinic. As soon as the two women alighted from the howdah, the princess was surrounded by women.

Kundavai asked, "Do the doctors keep regular hours? Is their treatment effective?"

Several women spoke up: "Yes, lady. The doctor mended my son's broken leg. The naughty boy is now back to climbing trees!"

"My mother was losing her sight but after the doctor's treatment, she can see well."

Kundavai smiled in satisfaction. "How wise our ancestors were!" she exclaimed to Vanathi. "They identified the herbs and their medicinal properties."

The old physician welcomed Kundavai with great respect.

"Doctor, did you meet the young man I sent to you?" Kundavai asked. "You once told me many valuable herbs are found at Kodikkarai: we'll send him there to gather them for you."

"He's inside, lady," the doctor said. "My son, Pinakapani, will accompany him to Kodikkarai and return with the herbs … the young man plans to go on to Sri Lanka."

"To gather herbs there?" Vanathi asked innocently.

"Yes," said the doctor. "Lanka has rare medicinal plants which may be of use to our emperor." He ushered the women to his private room where two young men waited. One of them was Vandhiya Devan. Kundavai smiled at him.

Vanathi whispered, "*Akka*, it's the man we saw at the astrologer's house."

"Yes, it looks like him. The astrologer must have recommended this doctor to him." Kundavai turned to Devan. "Will you go to Sri Lanka for medicinal plants?"

His eyes spoke volumes as he said, "Yes, lady." He paused. "I may run into the prince there. Would you like me to deliver a message to him?"

Kundavai laughed. "Tell my brother Vanathi is pining for him."

Vanathi blushed. "No! Tell him I'm fine …"

Kundavai turned to the doctor. "Have you prepared his papers?"

"Yes, lady," the doctor replied. "I have given him two letters: one ordering all government officials to help him and another addressed to the lighthouse keeper at Kodikkarai."

"It's best that you leave at once," the princess said.

"Yes," agreed Devan.

But Kundavai seemed to find it necessary to give him many directions and Devan, on his part, seemed to have many questions for her. At last, the women climbed on the elephant and the two young men mounted their horses. At a gesture from Kundavai, Devan gave her a last searing glance, spurred his horse into a gallop and disappeared into the distance with Pinakapani struggling to keep pace with him.

As the elephant walked on, Kundavai wondered, *How strange the heart is! I have turned down kings and princes, only to be captivated by this wandering warrior. May he stay safe. May he overcome every danger and return soon ...*

"*Akka*, what are you thinking?" Vanathi asked.

"Nothing. Maybe I shouldn't have trusted that arrogant young man with my messages."

Vanathi smiled. "Yes, he's a thief who plans to rob the Chola empire of its most prized jewel."

"Nonsense!" Kundavai cried. Just then, she saw a group of women standing by the roadside, obviously waiting for her. Kundavai ordered the mahout to stop the elephant. "Come," the princess gestured kindly to the women. "Do you want to speak with me?"

One woman came forward. "Lady, we hear Thanjavur is blocking supplies to Sri Lanka. How can our sons and husbands in the army there fight on empty stomachs?"

Kundavai assured her: "Don't worry. Food is being shipped to Lanka from Mamallapuram. The prince will see your men are well cared for. There's nothing Thanjavur can do to stop this."

The women dispersed, satisfied with her words. Kundavai turned back to her own thoughts.

Mamallapuram

MAMALLAPURAM'S IMPORTANCE AS a sea port ended with the defeat of the Pallavas. Its natural bay grew silted and large ships now anchored at sea, serviced by small boats from the shore. Only the beautiful Shore Temple stood as a reminder of its past glory.

Crown Prince Aditya Karikalan, raced through Mamallapuram in an ornate chariot, drawn by two thoroughbred horses. He was accompanied by Malayaman and Parthibendran. Aditya Karikalan, the emperor's first-born, had proved himself on the battlefield at a young age and had many brilliant victories to his credit. He had defeated the Pandian king, Veerapandian, and beheaded him. The emperor had anointed him crown prince after this great victory.

Once the Pandian kingdom was annexed by the Cholas, Karikalan turned his attention to the north. He forced Kannara Devan's army to retreat to the banks of the Pennai. The prince was eager to press his advantage and annex more territory. He camped in Kanchipuram, recruiting soldiers and consolidating his supply lines. The Pazluvur brothers opposed his northern campaign, insisting the Chola army could not fight simultaneously on two fronts. Karikalan was furious to hear that the Pazluvur brothers were trying to block supplies to Sri Lanka, where his brother, Arulmozli, led the Chola forces.

Parthibendran, a descendent of the Pallavas, was Karikalan's closest friend. He longed to achieve fame and stature in life. Malayaman, veteran of sixty-six battles, was the emperor's father-in-law. His lined face reflected the wisdom of eighty years. His grandson often chafed against his advice to be patient.

Karikalan was furious. "How dare the Pazluvur brothers brand my messenger a spy? How can I be patient? It's time I taught them a lesson with my sword!"

Parthibendran, jealous of the prince's affection for Devan, said, "I knew Vandhiya Devan would get into trouble—he's a reckless fool."

"Stop it, Parthibendran!" the prince exclaimed. "Devan is intelligent and resourceful. The Pazluvur brothers are angry because he outsmarted them and delivered my message to my father."

"I bet he stirred up more trouble after that …."

Karikalan cut off his friend. "*Thatha*, what do you say?"

Malayaman cleared his throat. "Let's stop for a while. I'm too old to talk in a moving vehicle."

The Old Man's Advice

THEY STOPPED THE chariot and walked to the seashore. It was low tide and many rocks stood exposed. Karikalan and Malayaman sat on two adjoining rocks, letting the waves wash their feet.

Parthibendran stood a little away from them. His face darkened as he watched the boats ferrying supplies to the ships anchored at sea. "My blood boils to see supplies meant for the northern invasion being diverted to Lanka," he said.

"Our best soldiers are fighting there," Karikalan reminded him. "They have won many victories: Anuradhapura, under Lankan rule for a thousand years, is now ours. Can we let our men starve?"

"Why can't supplies be sent to them from Nagapattinam or Sethukkarai? Why delay our campaign?" Parthibendran retorted.

"I agree the Pazluvur brothers are plotting something." Karikalan turned to his grandfather. "*Thatha*, say something."

Malayaman said, "Karikalan, how can I talk when the waves and Parthibendran compete to make a noise?"

"Will you keep quiet, Parthibendran?" Karikalan scolded. "Let's hear what *thatha* has to say."

Stung by the criticism, Parthibendran replied, "Okay, I'll be quiet. But your poor old grandfather, although he's the Mountain King, the Ocean King refuses to obey him."

Aware of his sarcasm, Malayaman said, "Young man, there was a time when all the kings of the land trembled at the mention of my name. Now that I'm old and weak, every stray dog is nipping at my heels. I come from a clan whose line goes back a thousand years. These Pazluvur brothers are upstarts ... and they want to finish me off? It will never happen!" The old man sighed and continued. "Karikalan, the Pazluvur brothers are plotting your brother's defeat and humiliation in Sri Lanka; this is to instigate you to fight with your brother."

Karikalan burst out vehemently: "That will never happen, *thatha*! I'm ready to die for Arulmozli. I long to go to Lanka and fight by his side instead of wasting time in luxury here."

"Let's go at once," Parthibendran urged. "We can leave tomorrow with half our troops. We'll crush the Sinhalese and then come back to Thanjavur to finish off the Pazluvur brothers."

Malayaman glared furiously at Parthibendran who fell silent. The old man said, "Karikalan, you are a great warrior. I watched proudly as you cut your way through the enemy at the tender age of sixteen. Parthibendran too is a great warrior. But you are both hot-headed young men. You rush into danger and make mistakes."

"*Thatha*, you have often warned me about this," Karikalan said. "Just tell me what to do now."

"Anuradhapura has been captured. The monsoon is due and no one can attack us in Sri Lanka for the next four months. Let our generals hold the lines. Ask Arulmozli to come back at once. The two of you must stand shoulder to shoulder at this time. The Chola dynasty is in great danger."

"*Thatha*," Karikalan said. "We have nothing to fear as long as I have my sword in hand."

"My dear boy," Malayaman said tenderly. "I'll never doubt your courage. One must be fearless on the battlefield, but one must take precautions against political intrigues and conspiracies."

"What are you referring to, *thatha*?" Karikalan asked.

"A few days back, Ambalavan secretly called some chieftains to a midnight meeting at Sambuvaraya's palace at Kadambur. The conspirators included Mazlavaraya and Vanangamudi."

The prince sniffed in disdain. "What can these old men do, *thatha*?"

"Don't underestimate old men, my boy. Ambalavan recently married a woman young enough to be his daughter. There's no one more dangerous than an old man married to a young woman."

Parthibendran saw a sudden change in Karikalan: the prince's eyes burned with rage, his face darkened and he gnashed his teeth.

Malayaman, absorbed in his own thoughts, did not notice his grandson's reaction. "There were two young men there: Sambuvaraya's son, Kandamaran, and your uncle, Madurandaka."

At this, his two listeners burst into laughter.

"*Thatha*," Karikalan said, "Madurandaka is an old man who has devoted his life to Lord Shiva."

"Not anymore," Malayaman said. "He has taken three wives …"

Karikalan shrugged. "So what? Let him marry as many women as he likes."

"My boy, with each marriage he has cemented a strong political alliance," his grandfather pointed out.

"*Thatha*, stop talking in riddles," the prince said. "What do the Pazluvur brothers want?"

"They want Madurandaka to succeed your father to the throne. They hold your father hostage in Thanjavur to make him agree to this."

Malayaman's Anger

THE TWO YOUNG men froze, shocked at Malayalam's words.

"I have heard these rumors, *thatha*," Karikalan said. "But tell me, is this possible?"

"My boy, Madurandaka's father, Gandara Aditya, ruled before your own grandfather. Seen from that perspective, Madurandaka has a stronger claim to the throne than you," said the old man.

"Never!" Parthibendran burst out. "He's a coward, a weakling! He does not know how to hold a sword ... or even to speak. The crown prince is a brave warrior who beheaded the Pandian king. He has never been defeated on the battlefield. Who then has a greater right to rule the Chola empire?" He turned angrily to Malayaman. "Has old age dulled your mind?"

Karikalan silenced his friend with a gesture. "*Thatha*, I don't covet the empire. I can create any number of new empires with my sword. Tell me, is Madurandaka's claim just? Do you approve of my uncle succeeding my father?"

"Never!" Malayaman roared. "If you agree to this, I'll kill you with my own hands ... then I'll kill your mother–my daughter, and myself. As long as I live, I won't let anyone rob you of your right to the Tiger Throne."

Parthibendran embraced the old man with tears in his eyes.

Karikalan said, "In that case, *thatha*, let's march to Thanjavur. We'll destroy the Pazluvur brothers and their allies, free my father and put Madurandaka behind bars. They don't stand a chance against us."

"This is not a battlefield, Karikalan," the old man said. "We are dealing with conspiracy. When you march on Thanjavur, the plotters will accuse you of wanting to kill the emperor. They may even kill your father and say he died of shame to see his own son marching against him."

"What can we do, *thatha*?" the prince frowned.

"Send a trustworthy messenger to Sri Lanka to persuade Arulmozli to return immediately."

Parthibendran stepped forward. "Let me go, prince."

"This messenger should not be like Vandhiya Devan," the old man said. "He must not get involved in anything other than his mission."

Parthibendran smiled triumphantly. "I told you so," he said to the prince.

"Why, *thatha*," Karikalan said. "Have you some news of Vandhiya Devan?"

"Yes," Malayaman said. "I was suspicious at not being invited to the feast at Kadambur Palace. I waylaid Kunrathur Kizhar on his way back from Kadambur and got all the information I needed from him. I heard Vandhiya Devan was at Kadambur that night as Kandamaran's friend."

"Nothing wrong with that, *thatha*," the prince said. "Vandhiya Devan and Kandamaran became close friends when they were posted together as sentries in our army."

Malayaman continued. "I had my doubts—was Vandhiya Devan a part of the conspiracy? But my suspicions vanished when I heard that Vandhiya Devan escaped from Thanjavur Fort by stabbing Kandamaran in the back."

"Impossible!" Karikalan exclaimed. "Vandhiya Devan would never stab anyone the back."

Malayaman shrugged. "The Pazluvur brothers accuse Vandhiya Devan of stabbing his friend. Obviously, the friends quarreled—that exonerates Vandhiya Devan from the conspiracy."

Karikalan said passionately. "If Vandhiya Devan joins our enemies, the world will end!"

"I agree," Parthibendran said. "Vandhiya Devan would never betray us. His only weakness is his excessive chivalry. He tends to make a fool of himself over beautiful women."

Karikalan laughed. "That's why I ordered him to deliver my father's letter at Thanjavur before going to Kundavai at Pazlayarai. If he sees my sister first, he'll become her slave."

"Once Arulmozli is here, we'll send for Kundavai," Malayaman said. "Then, all we have to do is follow her advice."

Karikalan smiled. "*Thatha,* Kundavai has enslaved you too."

"Yes," the old man agreed happily. "Kundavai ruled us all even as a child. Her word is my command. She's the most intelligent person I have met in my life. Our wise chief minister, Aniruddha Brahmaraya himself, consults her."

Parthibendran's jealousy towards Devan raised its ugly head. He murmured, "And what if Devan met Nandini first and got bewitched?" The prince heard this and glared angrily at his friend.

Malayaman walked slowly towards the chariot. Once he was out of hearing, Parthibendran said, "Prince, some deep sorrow is eating at your heart. It's clear it has something to do with Nandini, Ambalavan's wife. I'm your friend: why don't you confide in me? Maybe I can help you."

Karikalan sighed. "You can't help me. But I'll share my story with you later tonight."

Deadlier Than Poison

KARIKALAN AND PARTHIBENDRAN stood on the palace terrace in Mamallapuram, gazing out at the sea. Malayaman had gone to see a drama troupe perform the story of Aravan.

"Prince," Parthibendran said. "Tell me some of the brave deeds of your youth."

Karikalan smiled. "There's nothing to say. What have I done when compared to the great kings of my dynasty and yours? Look at the sculptures created by your forefathers."

"Sir, my forefathers lost their kingdom because they focused on sculpture instead of war."

"You're wrong, Parthibendran. Dynasties come and go. Emperors who shed blood and ruled vast empires are forgotten or remembered only through epic poems which may be true or false. But these stone sculptures stand as a testimony to the greatness of the Pallavas for all time."

Is this the warrior Aditya Karikalan talking? Parthibendran wondered. He said, "It's clear you are not yourself today, sir. Won't you tell me what's troubling you?"

Karikalan sighed. "Parthibendran, if you tear open my heart, you will not find my father or my mother in it ... or Kundavai and Arulmozli who are dearer to me than life itself ... not even you or Vandhiya Devan, my dearest friends. My heart holds only Nandini, a woman deadlier than poison ..."

"I guessed this from your reaction whenever her name is mentioned. But Ambalavan wedded her with the fire as his witness. He may be your enemy but he has close ties to the Chola dynasty. How can you lust after another man's wife?"

Karikalan said, "I'm tormented by guilt because I know it's wrong. Destiny brought us together and forced us apart many years before her marriage."

"Really?" Parthibendran was surprised.

Karikalan sighed. "It's a long story ..."

Nandini's Lover

"NANDINI CAME INTO my life when I was twelve. I can still picture her beautiful eyes widening in surprise when she saw me playing with Kundavai and Arulmozli. Our grandmother, Sembiyan Madevi, introduced her to us one day: 'This is Nandini. She's from the Pandian kingdom and is here to visit Easana Bhattar. I want you to be friends with her.'

"Kundavai disliked her at once. 'She looks like an owl! Why does grandmother force us to play with her?' she complained." Karikalan smiled. "I think it's a law of nature for one beautiful woman to hate another.

"A few days later, I went with my father to fight the Pandians. We defeated the combined forces of the Pandians and Sri Lankans. Veerapandian, the Pandian king, ran away from the battlefield. We chased the Lankan forces to the coast where the survivors boarded their ships and retreated to Sri Lanka. My father, furious with the Sri Lankans for traditionally allying with the Pandians against us, determined to establish Chola rule over Sri Lanka. It took us two years to recruit a large army and launch it across the strait under the command of Chieftain Paranthaka.

"When I returned to Pazlayarai, Kundavai and Nandini had matured into extraordinarily beautiful women and were now good friends. Nandini was shy and never said a word to me. But my heart was flooded with a strange new emotion which drew me to her side constantly. I saw that Kundavai disliked my attachment to Nandini—she was no longer her friend. My grandmother too scolded me: 'It's not right for you, a prince, to be familiar with the daughter of a priest.' I hated my grandmother for this and deliberately spent time with Nandini.

"Soon, I was told that Nandini had gone back with her parents to their home in the Pandian kingdom. I vented my anger and sorrow on Kundavai." He smiled and went on. "Fortunately, my father gave me the command of our northern forces and I threw myself into defeating our enemies. This is when I met you, Parthibendran. With *thatha's* help, we captured Kanchipuram.

"Remember how furious we were to hear that our Sri Lankan army had been defeated and Paranthaka killed? Veerapandian immediately came out of hiding, mustered a large army and recaptured Madurai. The fish ensign once more flew over the Pandian capital. We rushed to Pazlayarai. My father's health had deteriorated and he had lost the use of his legs. I persuaded him to let me go in his place to fight the Pandians. He agreed and put me under the command of General Velir. We went to Madurai with our army."

He paused and turned to Parthibendran. "My friend, do you remember the Vishnu temple on an island in the River Vaigai near Madurai? One day, I happened to go to the island and came across Nandini in the garden. She was dressed like the saint, Andal. She explained, 'After we parted, I took an oath not to marry. I have dedicated myself to Lord Vishnu.'

"I thought, *Let me win the war ... then I'll win my love.* 'Is there anything I can do for you?' I asked her.

"She replied, 'Please ask your soldiers not to disturb us. Only my aged parents and I live here; my brother has gone on a pilgrimage.'

"That is when I ordered our men not to go anywhere near the island. This was not to protect the temple and its priests, it was to protect Nandini, the woman I loved. I met her secretly a few times. My love for her grew stronger with each day. I told myself, *I'll be patient. I'll throw Veerapandian's head at my father's feet and then ask his permission to marry Nandini.*

"My friend, as you know, you and I were instrumental in the Chola victory over the Pandians. Determined to destroy them once and for all, we chased Veerapandian as he fled from the battlefield. The fish ensign on his chariot was a giveaway and we caught up with him. But his personal bodyguards fought like lions and sacrificed their lives to save him. We killed them all, but Veerapandian once again escaped. Seeing the fish ensign moving in the distance, we gave chase, but we were deceived–the flag had been attached to a riderless elephant.

"We sent our soldiers in every direction, determined to find him and finish him off. As I walked along the dry Vaigai riverbed, I saw the hoofprints of a single horse with a trail of blood behind it. The trail led to the Vishnu temple. I found the horse tied to a tree in that garden. I crept to Nandini's house and looked through the window and that picture remains etched on my memory. Veerapandian lay on a cot; Nandini knelt beside him, eyes brimming with tears; she raised his head tenderly and gave him some water; her face glowed with love for him. I opened the door with a crash and charged into the room. Nandini threw herself at my feet.

"'He's fighting for his life,' she said, 'If you ever loved me, leave him alone.'

"My voice was cold. 'Who is he to you? Why do you beg for his life?'

"'He's my lover ... he's my all ... he's my betrothed,' she sobbed.

"I was consumed by a white-hot rage. I would have forgiven this man if he had captured my empire, but I could not forgive him for having stolen the woman I loved. I pushed Nandini aside, lunged to the bed and beheaded the wounded man with one frenzied thrust of my sword.

"I turned to Nandini who stared at me with unblinking eyes—eyes that burned with rage, with dark evil, with lust, with the desire for revenge.

"Just then, you and our soldiers entered the house and broke into cheers on seeing my bloody sword and Veerapandian lying dead on the cot."

Karikalan sighed. "From that hour, a heavy burden weighs on my soul."

In the Women's Quarters

A CHORUS OF praise for the emperor and the prince carried to them on the breeze. "The performance is over. *Thatha* will be back soon. What stamina he has at his age!"

"Sir, that's because the men of those days did not lose sleep over a common priest's daughter. If a woman attracted them, they simply dragged her by the hair to their harems."

"Nandini's not a priest's daughter," Karikalan said. "There's some mystery about her birth."

"She may be a princess or a penniless orphan. When Ambalavan came across her, what did he do? He dragged her to his harem and kept her with his other wives."

"That's something which puzzles me: why would Nandini, who once loved me and then loved the Pandian king, agree to be that old man's wife?"

"I'm not surprised," Parthibendran declared. "I'm only surprised you listened to that witch begging for Veerapandian's life. If you had agreed, that coward would have run away once more and come out of hiding to make war on us again. You should have cut her head off then and there, or thrown her into prison." He paused. "Ah! I remember we heard a woman crying in some part of that house; you insisted it was a woman from the priest's family and ordered us to leave her alone. Later, you were preoccupied and did not join in our celebrations."

"I was suffering from guilt. I cursed myself for not granting Nandini's wish. I should have spared her lover's life."

"So that we would still be at war with the Pandians?" Parthibendran mocked. "And all for the crocodile tears shed by a witch!"

Karikalan smiled. "My friend, you have yet to fall in love."

"Yes, sir, I'm yet to fall under the spell of a woman's eyes—unlike Vandhiya Devan who forgets everything when he sees a beautiful woman."

"Back to Vandhiya Devan!" the prince exclaimed.

"Did you meet Nandini after that, sir?" Parthibendran asked.

"On the night of our victory, I could not sleep. I longed to see Nandini. I stole out of the camp and rode back to the island. All that remained of the house was a smoldering ruin. I found a terrified old couple crying in the garden. I recognized them as the ones who had brought Nandini to Pazlayarai. They said they had gone to care for their elder daughter who lived in a village on the other bank of the river and was expecting a baby. Nandini had insisted on staying behind. Now, she was nowhere to be found. On their way back that day, they had seen some thugs dragging a gagged and bound woman towards a funeral pyre …

"'Prince, where's our beloved daughter?' they wailed.

"I had always suspected they were not Nandini's real parents and now, I was sure. Would any parent leave a girl alone during a war? I shouted, 'Go jump into the funeral pyre into which your daughter was thrown!' and rode back to the camp."

"Did you see Nandini again before she married Ambalavan, sir?"

"If I had met her, she would never have married that old man! We were not in Pazlayarai for the wedding: remember how repulsive we found the idea of the old man marrying some young girl? My coronation was held a few days later and, with all the festivities, I forgot Nandini. Wearing the ancient Chola crown, I went to the women's quarters to receive blessings. Among all the beautiful faces, one face stood out— Nandini's!

"I thought, *She's alive! But why is she here? It's a miracle!* I was giddy with happiness. She was more beautiful than ever. *Today's my lucky day … I'll make her my queen.*

"Just as my mother kissed my forehead in blessing, my father collapsed with a scream. Leaving the immediate family to attend to the emperor, the other women left the room. I took Kundavai aside and asked, 'What's Nandini doing here?'

"'Don't you know?' she said in surprise. 'She's married to Ambalavan.'

I felt a knife thrust in my heart. That wound has not healed—it never will." Karikalan's hand instinctively covered his heart.

The Enchantress

"THAT'S WHY YOU were so gloomy on the day of your coronation!" Parthibendran said.

"Yes. You all did your best to cheer me with your jokes and talk of my future victories but my heart was filled with sorrow. Soon after that, Nandini sent for me. I hesitated at first. Then I resolved, *I'll go: I must get to the root of the mystery which shrouds her.* Of course, this was just an excuse—I went simply because I couldn't stay away from her. Ambalavan was not in town. As the crown prince, I had no difficulty entering his palace. I suppose everyone thought I was there to receive the women's blessings after my coronation. Nandini met me in a pavilion in the garden.

"She said, 'I'm happy to see you as crown prince.'

"My mind was in a whirl and my tongue seemed to have a will of its own. I said, 'I'm not happy. You threw me over for Veerapandian … and now you have chosen to marry an old man!'

"'You killed my love for you! You killed my lover before my very eyes! Kill me!' She whipped out a dagger from her waist and thrust it at me.

"To my eternal shame, I said, 'It's not too late. Just say the word and I'll give up this kingdom for you. We'll sail to a far-off land and live happily.'

"She laughed hysterically. 'What will we do in this far-off land? Cut firewood? Grow bananas?'

"I mocked her. 'Oh! The priest's daughter has become used to a queen's luxuries!'

"'I aim even higher,' she said, tossing her head. 'Tell me: are you ready to kill the Pazluvur brothers? Are you ready to put your father, the emperor, behind bars? Are you ready to become the emperor of the Cholas and crown me your empress? If yes, I'll be yours.'

"'How can you be so cruel!' I exclaimed in horror.

"'And wasn't it cruel to kill the wounded Pandian king before my eyes?' she retorted.

"I abused and cursed her and turned to leave. Her voice was calm: 'If you change your mind, come to me.' That was the last I saw of her."

Parthibendran was shocked. "What a devil! Thank god, you never saw her again."

"I did not see her, but she fills my thoughts by day and my dreams at night. She never leaves me alone. She laughs like a lunatic; she sobs; she comes at me with a dagger; she rants and raves; she is balm for my soul; she covers me with kisses .... do you know the real reason I avoid Thanjavur? I fear Nandini."

"Sir! I don't believe you fear a woman. Do you think she'll poison you?"

"No, Parthibendran," Karikalan replied. "I fear myself. I fear if she tempts me again, I may give in. I may kill the old man and imprison my father just to make her my wife." He sighed. "My tormented soul will find peace only after my death—or hers."

"Let me put off my trip to Sri Lanka," Parthibendran said. "Just say the word: I'll go to Thanjavur and kill that she-devil."

"No!" Karikalan exclaimed. "If Nandini is to die, it will be by my hands only. I won't allow anyone else to harm even a strand of hair on her head." The prince straightened his shoulders. "Come, my friend, let's forget Nandini. Go to Sri Lanka and come back with Arulmozli. We'll leave this empire to my grandfather and brother and go to Sri Lanka. We'll gather a huge army and sail to Burma and Malaya and Indonesia. We'll plant the Cholas' Tiger Flag on the soil of Arabia and Persia, Egypt and Rome. Let the world marvel at the Tamil warriors' courage." Karikalan smiled. "My friend, in those lands, the rulers are not confined by our laws of morality: they can drag any woman, married or unmarried, to their harems."

They were interrupted by Malayaman. "Why are you still up?" he asked. "Parthibendran, you have to leave early tomorrow for Sri Lanka."

PART 2

THE WHIRLWIND

Poonkuzlali

AS THE SUN set in a blaze of color, Poonkuzlali steered her small boat to the Kodikkarai shore. Singing sweetly, the beautiful young girl dragged the boat on to the white sands of the beach which ended in dense forest. Above the trees rose the tower of the Kuzlagar temple. The lighthouse flamed in the distance. A few houses stood nearby.

Poonkuzlali crossed the sand and walked towards the temple. She skipped behind a herd of deer which raced past her into the forest. As the herd jumped over a patch of quicksand, a little fawn fell short and its hind legs sank into the swamp. The helpless mother stood rooted to the spot. Poonkuzlali ran along the swamp's edge, took the little creature in her arms and tugged it free. The mother nuzzled the trembling fawn and vanished into the forest with it.

"The ungrateful creatures!" Poonkuzlali murmured. "Of course, men are worse."

She reached the isolated temple where the priest welcomed her warmly, giving her a broken coconut and some other food offered to the deity. He said, "Will you wait, my dear? I'll lock up and walk back with you."

Poonkuzlali readily agreed. She perched on the temple's outer wall, eating her coconut. She heard the sound of horses' hooves in the twilight. A vague melancholy filled her heart. *Who can it be?* she wondered. Horsemen often visited Kodikkarai on the emperor's business. Some came to be rowed across to Sri Lanka. Two scoundrels had come the previous day and paid her brother well to take them across the strait. *What can one do with money in this forest? But my brother and his wife are greedy for money ...*

Vandhiya Devan and Pinakapani emerged from the forest.

Embarrassed at being caught scraping a coconut shell with her teeth, Poonkuzlali jumped down from the wall and ran into the forest. When Devan saw the beautiful girl perched on the temple wall, his exhaustion melted away. Instinctively, he jumped off his horse and followed her.

Quicksand

VANDHIYA DEVAN CHASED Poonkuzlali through the forest and across the sand dunes. *This must be Amudhan's Poonkuzlali. She runs like a deer! Why am I chasing her? Am I mad?*

Seeing the lighthouse in the distance, Devan and Pinakapani had entered the forest but soon lost their way. Devan had stopped to ask the girl for directions and she had run away. Gasping for breath, Devan doggedly chased her. Open ground lay before him; beyond that surged the sea. He rushed forward: to his horror, he sank into wet sand—in seconds, the squelching mud reached his thighs. *Quicksand! Is this the end of all my dreams?* "Help! Help!" he screamed at the top of his voice.

Poonkuzlali turned back and immediately grasped the situation. She climbed into a small boat standing on the edge of the swamp and rowed across the wet sand. Jumping out, she planted her feet firmly on dry ground and gave Devan her hands. With one pull, she had him safely on land.

What strength! Devan marveled. Even as his legs trembled, Devan laughed. "Do you think you saved me from the quicksand? It was just a trick to make you stop."

"Very well," Poonkuzlali said. "I'll push you in again."

Backing off, Devan asked, "Why did you run? I only wanted directions to the lighthouse."

"I hate all men."

Devan smiled. "Even Chendan Amudhan of Thanjavur? You are Poonkuzlali, right? Amudhan said he loves you."

She laughed. "If he wasn't safely in Thanjavur, I would push him into the quicksand."

"He said you were his cousin and that celestial nymphs can't match your beauty."

"Oh! He has seen these nymphs, has he? What else?"

"He said you sing like an angel."

This Girl Is Mad!

POONKUZLALI LED DEVAN to the sea, where he washed the mud from his legs. They saw Pinakapani riding to them, with Devan's horse trotting behind him. Poonkuzlali stroked the horse and the animal whinnied softly and muzzled her hand. "All animals love me ... unlike men," she said. "I too hate men, they are deceivers."

"Don't generalize. Amudhan's a good man; so is Pinakapani ... and so am I."

"Why are you here?" she asked.

"To collect herbs for our emperor. If we do not find any here, I'll go to Sri Lanka for them."

"Men are liars. Two men paid my brother to take them to Sri Lanka. They said a sorcerer wanted them to gather tiger nails and elephant hair to make a talisman to cure the emperor."

Devan's mind flew to Ravidasan and their midnight encounter in the forest ruins. *Why do I always get caught in these intrigues? Can I trust this girl?* "I'll be honest with you, I'm on a secret mission to Sri Lanka." Devan paused. "Are you going to marry my friend, Amudhan?"

"Why do you want to know?"

"I like you. If Amudhan's not your lover, I would like to court you," Devan said.

She laughed wildly. "Listen, Amudhan's not my lover and I don't hate you. But I have many lovers ... if you come with me at midnight, I'll show them to you,"

This girl is mad! Devan thought. *I won't trust her with my secrets.*

They came to a cottage near the lighthouse. The lighthouse keeper, Thyaga Vidangar, stood at the door with his wife. "Poonkuzlali," the old man scolded. "How many times have I told you to come home before dark? And who are these strangers?"

"They're here to collect herbs for the emperor, *appa*," she said.

Devan gave the old man a palm leaf. Thyaga Vidangar read the message and smiled. "This is from Princess Kundavai. Poonkuzlali, tell your sister-in-law there are two guests for dinner."

At Midnight

AFTER DINNER, VANDHIYA Devan took Vidangar aside: "I must leave for Sri Lanka urgently."

Vidangar sighed. "All the boats have been commandeered by the army and are in Sethukkarai. I have two boats. My son rowed two men to Sri Lanka in one. I don't know when he'll return."

"Who were these men? Your daughter said they looked suspicious."

"Yes. They were secretive and had Lord Ambalavan's signet ring. I did not want to help them. But my daughter-in-law is greedy. They gave her a bag of gold coins and she forced my son."

"Why does your son obey a woman?" Devan mocked. "Sorry, sir. That's your family matter."

Vidangar sighed. "My boy, a curse runs in my family. My son ..."

"Is a deaf-mute," Devan completed his sentence.

The old man was amazed. "How do you know this?"

"I stayed with Amudhan in Thanjavur," Devan explained.

"You are that man? There's a manhunt on for you! That's why you want to escape to Sri Lanka."

"No, I have an important message for someone there: I can show you the letter."

"Princess Kundavai's word is enough for me. Can you row? You can take my second boat."

"No," Devan said. "To be honest, I'm afraid of water ..."

"Hmm ... Poonkuzlali is skilled at handling a boat, but she's a stubborn girl. We must persuade her to take you. Let's wait until tomorrow and catch her in a good mood."

The old man left for the lighthouse. Devan fell asleep on the porch beside Pinakapani. He was startled awake by the sound of the door opening softly. A figure glided past him. The lighthouse flame showed it was Poonkuzlali. Devan quietly followed her. She crossed the beach and walked along the edge of the forest. Haunted by fear of quicksand, Devan kept her in sight. She turned a corner and Devan hurried behind her. The next instant, she vanished.

Devan looked around. There was flat marshland on three sides: she could not have crossed this unseen. Devan peered at the ground and saw a faint trail in the star light. Heart-in-mouth, Devan followed the track into the forest. Shadows swayed in the wind; mysterious things rustled. Devan imagined wild beasts and venomous snakes on all sides. The trail disappeared. His legs shook. *Why did I follow her? I don't even have my spear! I must find my way back ...*

Just then, he heard a woman sobbing and singing. He followed the sound and climbed the sand dune. Poonkuzlali stood on the summit, silhouetted by the distant flare of the lighthouse; her head raised to the stars, she sang a song of heart-rending grief.

She stopped and asked, "Why did you follow me?"

"You asked me to," he retorted. "Show me your lovers."

"Look behind you," she said.

Poonkuzlali's Lovers

VANDHIYA DEVAN TURNED around—the blood in his veins froze in horror. A hundred spheres glowed in the endless darkness below him. They rose from the earth and hung in the air, as if a black demon was spitting out flaming globes from its countless yawning mouths.

Poonkuzlali laughed like a devil. "These fire-spitting demons are my lovers!"

She's insane! How can I entrust myself to her in the sea? Slowly, Devan's terror dissolved. *I have heard of swamp gas. Sulphur compounds in marshes sometimes cause this phenomenon.* He said, "Come, your lovers will be here tomorrow. Let's go home."

Poonkuzlali burst into sobs.

The exhausted Devan thought, *What now?* He said, "I'm going home."

When he started to climb down, Poonkuzlali stopped weeping and overtook him. "Is the emperor really ill?" she asked.

"I saw him with my own eyes: he's paralyzed. Without the herbs, he may even die."

"Who will succeed him?" was Poonkuzlali's next question.

She's not as simple as she seems. I must be careful. "Aditya Karikalan was anointed crown prince years back," he said.

"And what about Madurandaka? I hear many chieftains support him."

"News travels fast." Devan was noncommittal.

"What happens if the emperor dies suddenly?"

"There will be violence and chaos. Which is why you must help me and take me to Sri Lanka."

"Row yourself there. Aren't you ashamed to ask for a woman's help?" she sneered.

"I don't know to row or to swim," Devan admitted. "I'll get lost or drown in the sea."

Poonkuzlali shrugged. "Why should I care?"

They reached the lighthouse. Devan decided to resume the conversation in the morning. *I must not push her or she may become stubborn. Something in her manner gives me hope.* He fell asleep for the second time that night. He was troubled by dreams. *He is gliding in a small boat with Poonkuzlali; bewitched by her smile, he asks her to sing. 'What will you give me?' she asks. 'I'll give you a kiss,' he says. She waves a dagger: 'Move an inch and I'll feed you to the fish!'*

The Leopard's Den

THE HOT SUN woke Vandhiya Devan the next morning. Poonkuzlali was nowhere to be seen. He walked to the Kuzlagar temple and found Vidangar gathering flowers in the garden.

"My daughter will be chasing deer in the forest or strolling on the beach. Ask her to row you to Sri Lanka. But careful! Any mention of love or marriage and she'll become a Kali," he warned.

Poonkuzlali was not in the forest or on the beach. Exhausted, Devan went to bathe in the sea. *I must get over my fear of the sea to travel by boat and ship. Anyway, the water's shallow here.* He left his waistband and scabbard on the beach and waded into the ocean. He gingerly tested the depth of the water—it was just waist-high. Taking courage, he walked further into the waves. He looked back at the shore. *I have walked too far into the sea. What if the waves rise suddenly?* He saw Poonkuzlali on the beach, gesturing to him and bending over his waistband. Puzzled, he started back to the shore. The girl gathered his belongings and shouted something, but her words got drowned by the sound of the waves. She ran into the forest.

Devan broke into a run, shouting, "Stop! Don't touch that ..." He tripped, swallowed salt water and made it to the shore, sputtering. He chased after the girl. *Is she insane or evil? I must get back my belongings from her.* Devan wandered among the dense scrub and thorns shouting, "Poonkuzlali!" Suddenly, his waistband dropped from a nearby tree. Devan picked it up and found his letters and gold coins intact. He looked up—Poonkuzlali was perched on a branch.

Hot and furious, he asked, "Why did you run? If you need money, you could have asked me."

"Who wants your money? I wanted to stop you from going home. Climb up and look there."

Securing his waistband, Devan climbed the tree and looked towards the lighthouse. A company of horsemen, armed with swords and spears, surrounded Vidangar's house. *They must be Lord Ambalavan's men.* "Why did you save me?"

Poonkuzlali looked confused. Then she said, "I pity fools."

"Thanks for the compliment! How did you know the soldiers had come for me?"

"I knew you were a fugitive as soon as I saw you. Your companion confirmed it."

"What nonsense did he tell you?" Devan asked.

"He asked me to help him search for herbs. Once we were in the forest, he said he loved me. When I said you had already declared your love, he told me you were a fugitive. He warned me not to trust you and to marry him instead. We heard horses and climbed a tree … how your friend's legs shook when we saw soldiers riding towards us!" She burst into laughter.

"Then?" Devan asked impatiently.

"Your companion said, 'They have come to arrest him as I told you.' I said, 'In that case, they'll arrest you too for being with him … you had better hide.' But instead of hiding, he walked up to the soldiers and said, 'I know you are here for Vandhiya Devan. If you promise not to harm me, I'll take you to him.' They agreed, and he has taken them to our house," Poonkuzlali concluded.

"The traitor!" Devan cried.

"I came to warn you. It would have taken too long to explain the situation and convince you to hide. That's why I grabbed your belongings and ran here."

Ashamed, Devan said, "You have saved my life and my honor. Thank you. Will you help me once more? I must go to Sri Lanka on a very important mission. Will you row me across?"

Poonkuzlali was silent. Then, "What will you give me for this?" she asked.

Devan looked at her beautiful face and flushed cheeks. Remembering his dream, he caught himself and said, "I promise to help you whenever you need me."

Poonkuzlali made up her mind. "Come with me. You must hide in the forest until tonight. I'll try to bring you some food. Have you heard the cuckoo's call? That will be my signal for you to come out of hiding. We must set sail at least three hours after midnight."

Poonkuzlali led him to a sand dune in the heart of the forest. She pushed aside the thick branches and creepers which covered its sides and slid down a tree into a pit underneath. Devan found himself on the rim of a ruined pavilion. The stone structure was completely hidden from sight.

"This was a leopard's den. Now, it's my refuge whenever my hatred for men overwhelms me. There's a pot with drinking water. Stay here. Don't peep out whatever happens."

"What about wild animals?" Devan asked. "I don't have my spear."

"Only jackals and boars come here." She picked up something from the ground. "Take this."

Devan examined the strange weapon. It had sharp blades at both ends.

"It's the tailbone of a fish," Poonkuzlali explained. "I killed the leopard with it."

"I'll wait eagerly for the cuckoo's call," Devan said.

Ocean Princess

VANDHIYA DEVAN SLEPT through most of the day. When awake, he thought about Poonkuzlali. *What a strange girl! She's sweet and crazy and wild and brave. How casual she is about killing a leopard! She's a child of Nature. What made her like this? Why has she agreed to help me?*

He heard sounds of a massive hunt for him in the forest. Darkness fell. Devan stood on the summit of the sand dune, looking at the distant lighthouse and the stars twinkling in the sky.

'Cuckoo! Cuckoo!'

Devan eagerly walked towards the cry. Poonkuzlali was waiting for him. She led him silently to a boat on the nearby shore. Refusing his help, she pushed the boat into the water. Some distance from the shore, she climbed in and the frightened Devan somehow managed to clamber on board.

Devan watched Poonkuzlali skillfully steer the craft singlehandedly. "You are an expert!" he said in admiration. "No wonder your father recommended you to me."

"He's my father only on shore. Here, I'm the Ocean Princess."

"When will we reach Sri Lanka?"

"If the winds are favorable, we should be there early tomorrow morning."

Devan tried his hand at the oars but soon gave up as the boat went round in circles. He pointed to two long poles with wooden blocks at their bases. "What are these for?"

"To steady the boat in strong wind. We can cling to the poles if a whirlwind sinks the boat."

Devan, already giddy, panicked. "Can a whirlwind sink the boat? Take me back to the shore!"

"Are you mad?" Poonkuzlali asked.

"If you don't turn back at once, I'll jump into the sea!"

"Go ahead. But give me Prince Arulmozli's letter before you jump."

"How do you know about the letter?" Devan asked suspiciously.

"I read it when I was on the tree. That's why I agreed to help you."

Devan had had enough. Terrified, he jumped into the sea. To his shock, he found himself in deep water. He screamed as the waves lifted him up and then plunged him into the dark ocean depths. He surrendered to god. *Destiny brings me to a watery grave.* Before him flashed his dreams of glory; the evil Nandini; the Pazluvur lords; wicked Poonkuzlali; Kundavai's beautiful face. *I'm sorry, princess, I have failed you.*

Poonkuzlali rowed the boat for a few minutes after Devan jumped into the sea. *Pretender! Let me teach him a lesson.* In the next instant, as Devan came up, she realized her mistake. *Oh my god! He can't swim! He's panicking—he'll drown!* The second time he came up, she steered the boat to him and shouted, "Come on, climb in!"

But Devan was beyond reason. He screamed in despair and went down again. Poonkuzlali took a long rope, tied one end to a pole and the other around her waist. She jumped into the sea. A few powerful strokes took her to the drowning man. *He'll panic and pull me down with him.* She punched him on his forehead. A million sparks exploded in Devan's head before darkness and silence enveloped him.

Boodha Island

VANDHIYA DEVAN REGAINED consciousness to find himself tied to some planks on the boat; he sat up. Poonkuzlali was singing as she rowed. He checked his waistband: the money and scabbard were safe. In a flash, Devan remembered the recent events. *What an extraordinary woman! She rescued me from the sea. I was a fool to suspect her.*

Poonkuzlali hoisted the sails and gave him water from a dried gourd vessel. "You can untie yourself. But don't jump into the sea again."

Devan looked up at the Pole Star on the northern horizon. *The astrologer compared Prince Arulmozli to the constant Pole Star. I'll soon meet him.*

"We'll be on Snake Island by dawn. From there, you can enter Sri Lanka easily. How will you find the prince?"

"God will help me," Devan said. "Didn't he send you to bring me across the ocean?"

"God does not interfere in man's petty affairs. I did not help you for your god or for yourself."

"Why are you helping me then?" Devan asked.

"That's my secret," she replied.

"I'm worried. I heard Sri Lanka is a land of mountains and forests filled with wild animals. How will I find the prince? Even the sun can be hidden by the clouds."

"Not this sun: even the clouds and the ocean glow in Prince Arulmozli's reflected glory."

Her face lights up when she talks about the prince. Like all his subjects, she too worships him.

"Just reach the Chola army," she suggested. "They'll take you to him."

"But the Chola army is stretched from Mathottam to Pulastya, covering almost half the country. The letter I carry is urgent."

She thought for a while: "Very well, we'll stop at Boodha Island ..."

"Ghost Island?!" Devan exclaimed.

"It's Buddha Island–the Island of Enlightenment. It's believed Buddha came there as a spirit. It became corrupted into Boodha Island and is now feared and avoided. Wait on the shore and keep an eye on the boat. I'll find out the prince's location and come back."

The boat skimmed over the waves and the ocean heaved and roared; Devan fell asleep.

This is Lanka

THE SEA WAS molten gold under the rising sun when Vandhiya Devan opened his eyes. He looked around him in wonder: emerald islands rose on every side. "This is paradise," he said.

"This is Lanka," Poonkuzlali announced. "It was paradise until warmongers like you came here."

"That includes Prince Arulmozli, right?"

"Don't drag him into this," she said.

Poonkuzlali steered the boat to Boodha Island. Leaving him to guard the craft, she disappeared into the jungle. She was back in half an hour and they set sail again. "Chief Minister Aniruddha is in Mathottam to meet Prince Arulmozli. The prince is there."

Devan said, "Now, tell me what I can do for you in return."

Poonkuzlali was silent. Then, "When you have given the prince the letter and your messages, tell him it was the Ocean Princess who rowed you across the strait to Lanka."

Ah! Can a little sparrow fly with the eagle? This will end badly. "I'll tell him the Ocean Princess saved me from Ambalavan's men, rescued me from the ocean and rowed me to Lanka, and that I could not have delivered the letter without her."

"Don't tell him I asked you to tell him this," Poonkuzlali said.

"Am I a fool?" Devan retorted.

"If the prince replies, you must let me know every word he says. I'll be either in Kodikkarai or Boodha Island. If you find my boat on the island, do not, on any account, come in search of me. Give me a signal: can you imitate the call of the cuckoo?"

"No, but I can imitate a peacock." Devan screeched like a peacock and Poonkuzlali laughed. The boat reached the shore. Devan said goodbye and set out. Poonkuzlali turned the boat and sailed away without a backward glance.

Aniruddha Brahmaraya

HAVING OVERHEARD THE conversation between Kundavai and Vandhiya Devan, Azlvarkkadian hurried to Madurai to gather some information and then went to Rameswaram. As usual, he got into an argument with the Shaiva priests who lived in this pilgrim town. He was surrounded by a crowd of priests determined to teach him a lesson for his insolence and his insults to Lord Shiva.

"Catch the fat pig!" "Shave off his topknot!" they shouted.

Azlvarkkadian waved his stick and cried, "Just you try! I'll break your heads!"

Just then, a herald announced: "Make way for His Excellency, Aniruddha Brahmaraya, chief minister of Emperor Sundara Chola!"

A boat sailed swiftly to the shore from a fleet of huge ships anchored off the coast. Aniruddha, flanked by men of the secret service, stepped out. He turned towards the commotion on the shore and saw Azlvarkkadian. He gestured to him. Azlvarkkadian hurried forward, his hands folded in respect.

"Thirumalai," Aniruddha said. "What's this ruckus?"

Azlvarkkadian exclaimed: "Gurudeva, can I believe my eyes? You, the staunchest of Vaishnavas, have converted to Saivism—there's holy ash on your body!"

Aniruddha smiled. "Thirumalai, does it matter whether the band of sandal paste on my forehead is vertical or horizontal?" He pointed out to sea. "Meet me in the pavilion on that island."

The priests complained about Azlvarkkadian and insisted he be punished. Aniruddha assured them, "I'll take care of this rogue." He turned to his guards. "Bring this man to my camp."

The Kaikkola Regiment

THE CHIEF MINISTER was surrounded by accountants, scribes and secret service men. A delegation of merchants stood before him.

"How is trade?" Aniruddha asked.

"Trade flourishes in the Pandian kingdom, sir," their leader replied. "The people welcome Chola rule and praise Prince Arulmozli."

"What about overseas trade?" Aniruddha asked.

"We have not lost a single vessel this year. The Chola navy has secured the eastern sea routes by destroying the pirate base on the Minicoy Islands."

"Have you followed my orders to send rice and grains to the Chola army in Sri Lanka?"

"Yes, sir. When is the war expected to end?"

The chief minister laughed. "You must consult your astrologer for that."

"Our astrologer says Prince Arulmozli will plant the Tiger Flag in far off lands."

"More profit for you traders," the chief minister smiled.

He dismissed them with instructions to continue their monthly consignments to Sri Lanka. His next meeting was with the generals of the emperor's renowned Kaikkola Regiment.

The general complained, "We are sitting idle on this island, letting our spears and swords rust, sir. Send us to Sri Lanka to fight under Prince Arulmozli."

"I'll get the emperor's sanction for this when I return to Thanjavur," the chief minister said.

"But what if the war ends before that?"

"There's no chance of that. King Mahinda refuses to fight and hides in the jungle. The war is at a standstill right now. Stay alert for enemies in the Pandian kingdom and be patient."

"Sir," the general said. "We have wiped out our enemies in the Pandian kingdom."

"Some conspirators claim to be heirs to the Pandian throne. The ancient crown and diamond-studded sword of the Pandian kings are hidden in Sri Lanka. Only when we recover these symbols of power can we end the Pandian threat once and for all."

"Let Prince Arulmozli sit on the Madurai throne, wearing the crown and the sword."

"Let's leave politics aside," Aniruddha said diplomatically. "You'll soon have the chance to use your swords and spears: Prince Arulmozli plans to invade Malaya and Indonesia. So, take heart!"

"Sir, we hear whispers of a conspiracy involving the Pazluvur brothers. Our loyalty lies with the emperor alone. We also hear the emperor is ill. If anything happens to the emperor, the Kaikkola Regiment will become Prince Arulmozli's personal bodyguard."

"Ignore rumors. Your only duty is to obey the emperor," Aniruddha was firm. "I'll convey your wishes to him." He dismissed them. *What charisma Prince Arulmozli has! Everyone loves him.*

He ordered, "Fetch that Vaishnava fanatic."

The Guru and His Disciple

AZLVARKKADIAN PROSTRATED HIMSELF at Aniruddha's feet. "Gurudeva, let me become a Shaiva."

Aniruddha smiled indulgently. "What's the matter, Thirumalai? As our Lord Vishnu says in the *Gita*, each man must do his duty: ours is to serve the emperor. Have you forgotten your vow?"

"Gurudeva, I'm confused by the rumors I hear about you: you have received a grant of seventy acres of land from the emperor; for this you have renounced Vaishnavism; you have ignored our Brahmin dharma and crossed the sea ..."

"Thirumalai, ignore the jealous men who want to keep us confined to a narrow sphere. As for the emperor's gift, I served as his chief minister for four years before I received it. My friendship with Sundara Chola goes back to our student days. At that time, there was no chance of him becoming emperor. Who dreamt the previous kings would have such short reigns? Knowing he would face many problems, Sundara Chola insisted he would become emperor only if I agreed to be his chief minister. I have kept my promise to stand by him as a friend and advisor."

"I know all this, gurudeva," Azlvarkkadian said. "But the people gossip about you ..."

"Let them," Aniruddha said. "I sometimes feel guilty for giving up my traditional role as a teacher to get involved in politics. But now I know I made the right decision. Thirumalai, I'm not in Rameswaram to worship at the temple—I have just returned from Mathottam."

"I guessed as much ... did you meet Prince Arulmozli?" Azlvarkkadian asked eagerly.

Aniruddha smiled. "Even you are excited about him. King Mahinda's army had a large number of Pandian and Chera soldiers. They deserted and joined our forces to serve under Prince Arulmozli! Now outnumbered, Mahinda and his army have gone into hiding in the mountains."

"In that case, why doesn't the prince return, gurudeva? What's the point of staying there?"

"The prince knows if he leaves the country, Mahinda will come out of hiding and fight again. The only way to resolve the conflict is to defeat Mahinda decisively or make him our ally. Our soldiers are now busy renovating the Buddhist temples destroyed in the war."

Azlvarkkadian threw up his hands. "Next, the prince will convert to Buddhism!"

"Thirumalai, a good king defends all the religions his subjects choose to follow. I believe Prince Arulmozli is divinely blessed—he will rule the world. A few days back I met a yogi. He predicts that savages from across the Himalayas will fall upon the north and destroy our temples. Our religion will be in danger. Great warriors and kings born in the south will safeguard our temples and scriptures. After my trip to Mathottam, I believe his predictions."

"Gurudeva, once you hear my news, your optimistic dreams will vanish."

"Thirumalai, let's hear your intelligence report."

Azlvarkkadian looked around cautiously. "The news I bring will make even the gods tremble ..."

"Come with me. There's an underground cave where even wind and fire can't enter."

Ponni's Beloved

SUNDARA CHOLA LEFT the women of the royal household, except his queen, in Pazlayarai so that they could enjoy their freedom. In Thanjavur, they would be restricted by Kalaanthaka's rules.

Kundavai avoided Thanjavur also because she hated Nandini. But after Vandhiya Devan listed the dangers threatening the Cholas, Kundavai decided that her place was beside her father. *Both my brothers are far away. I must keep them informed about every development. I must guard my father. The Pazluvur brothers may kill him to make Madurandaka emperor. Madurandaka will be a puppet in their hands and Nandini will have us all at her mercy. Not while I live!*

Kundavai had another reason to go to Thanjavur—she was anxious for news of Devan. She knew that the commander had sent men to Kodikkarai in search of him. *If he's caught, they'll bring him to Thanjavur. I must be there. He's protected by the authority of the crown prince. But the Pazluvur brothers will falsely accuse him of stabbing Kandamaran in the back and punish him. I must ask Kandamaran for his version of the story.*

So, as Devan made his way to Mathottam, Kundavai and Vanathi headed for Thanjavur.

While Kundavai wrestled with many problems, Vanathi had only one thing on her mind: "*Akka*, you have not yet told me why the prince is called 'Ponni's Beloved.'"

"Very well," Kundavai said. "I'll tell you that story."

Years ago, Sundara Chola and the royal household were on a pleasure trip on the River Ponni. Suddenly, the seven-year-old Kundavai screamed, 'Where's my brother?' Arulmozli, then five years old, was missing. After a frantic search of the boat, it was clear that the boy had fallen into the river and been carried away. The women wailed as the boatmen jumped into the flood. Suddenly, they saw a woman in the middle of the raging river, at a little distance from the boat. Only her radiant face and bust could be seen. She held the little prince in her outstretched arms.

Sundara Chola swam towards the woman who gave him the child.

The boat went to them and men reached out for the child and helped the emperor aboard. No one saw what happened to the mysterious woman ... no one came forward to claim the reward offered for saving the prince. And so, it was believed that Arulmozli had been saved by the river goddess. From that day, the prince was called 'Ponni's Beloved.'

Two Full Moons

CROWDS GATHERED AT Thanjavur Fort's gates to welcome their beloved princess, renowned for her beauty, wisdom and compassion. A large delegation, led by the Pazluvur brothers and Nandini, received Kundavai. The two women, each beautiful in her own way, and radiant as the full moon, smiled sweetly at each other and exchanged greetings and compliments.

Some women asked Kundavai to give them free access to the fort for the coming Navaratri festival. Kundavai turned to Nandini, "We must relax security for the festival. Why should we fear these women? After all, the authority of the Pazluvur brothers extends from coast to coast!"

Nandini smiled sweetly. "Soon, their authority will extend even to lands across the sea."

Is there some hidden meaning in the devil's words? Kundavai wondered.

Ambalavan readily granted Kundavai's request. The gates of Thanjavur Fort were left open for the nine days of the festival. The days were filled with celebration and entertainment. Kundavai and Nandini made several public appearances. Under their smiling exteriors rumbled volcanos of fury. They used their words and eyes as arrows and spears and both of them were soon exhausted.

Vanathi was oblivious to everything and lived in a world of her own.

A Wail of Sorrow in the Night

HISTORICAL PLAYS WERE the highlights of the Navaratri celebrations. The final play was based on the life of Emperor Paranthaka, the greatest of the Chola kings. During his forty-six-year reign, he extended the Chola kingdom from the Tungabhadra river to Sri Lanka. The Pazluvur and Kodumbalur chieftains were the emperor's valued commanders. Traditionally, these two clans were the pillars which supported the Chola dynasty. The playwright had taken care to balance the two clans' courage and sacrifice. But the audience was determined to take sides. When the Kodumbalur chieftain appeared on stage, a section of the audience cheered loudly. Another section applauded when the Pazluvur chieftain made his entrance.

Vanathi belonged to the Kodumbalur clan while Nandini was married into the Pazluvur clan. Seated between the two women, Kundavai was fired by the crowd's enthusiasm. When the audience cheered Kodumbalur, Kundavai said, "Vanathi, your supporters are stronger!" When their rivals applauded Pazluvur, Kundavai cried, "Nandini, now your side leads!" Kundavai saw that Nandini was furious with her playful comments. Curious, the princess carefully watched her face.

The play portrayed the Chola victory over the Pandians. The defeated Pandian king went to Sri Lanka; the Lankan king refused to help him; the Pandian king was forced to give up the ancient Pandian crown jewels before fleeing to the Chera kingdom.

Kundavai was surprised at the flood of grief which washed over Nandini's face during this act. Attempting to draw her out, Kundavai said, "Father would have enjoyed this superb play ..."

Nandini spat out, "Now that his beloved daughter is here, he'll recover soon—helped by the medicinal herbs coming from Sri Lanka."

"What herbs?" Kundavai asked.

"Don't play innocent. I hear the person sent to Sri Lanka is your man. Isn't that true?"

Fortunately, the audience erupted into cheers and saved Kundavai the trouble of replying. The crowd dispersed. Kundavai and her mother, Queen Vanamadevi, went to the Durga temple for the late night pooja.

Vanathi could not sleep. She went over the scenes from the play. She thought proudly of her father who had sacrificed his life in Sri Lanka and of Arulmozli now fighting to avenge his death. *I'll wait until the princess returns and discuss the play with her. Till then, I'll stroll on the balcony. At least I can look out on the fort and the temple from there.*

Vanathi stepped into a long corridor lit by oil lamps. Servants slept in some corners but Vanathi was reluctant to wake them to ask for directions. She continued to wander down the passage. Suddenly, she froze in terror at a heart-rending wail of sorrow. "Will no one help me?" Vanathi recognized the emperor's voice. *Is he in pain? Or is it something else?* Knowing that the women of the royal family were at the temple, Vanathi hurried towards the voice. She looked down into a large room and saw Sundara Chola lying on the bed, lamenting.

Vanathi strained to hear his words. "Yes, you wretch, I killed you, but it was a mistake. Twenty-five years have passed and you still haunt me! Will you never let me live in peace? Will no one save me from your torture? Everyone is searching for a cure for my body. Why can't someone find a cure for my mind?" He screamed, "What do you want? Speak … and go!"

Vanathi, trembling like a leaf, searched the room. She saw a woman standing at the foot of the bed. Although she was partially concealed by a pillar and the incense which clouded the room, Vanathi recognized her: *It's Nandini! And that's the chancellor hiding behind the other pillar!* Her mind in a whirl of doubt, Vanathi felt giddy. *I won't faint here.* Gritting her teeth, she retraced her steps. *I can't make it …*

Kundavai returned from the temple to find Vanathi unconscious outside their room.

The Emperor's Madness

THE EMPEROR SENT for his daughter the next morning and dismissed his attendants. He asked Kundavai to sit by his side and lovingly patted her on her back. His eyes filled with tears. "Did your friend who fainted last night tell you what she saw and heard?"

"Yes, *appa*," Kundavai replied. "Vanathi heard someone lament piteously ..."

Sundara Chola's body shook and his glazed eyes stared vacantly into the distance. "This palace is no place for a young girl, my dear. It's haunted. You must go back to Pazlayarai."

"Let's all go to Pazlayarai," Kundavai insisted. "Thanjavur has done nothing for your health."

Sundara Chola sighed. "Nothing can cure me: my disease is not of the body, it's of the mind."

"What troubles you, *appa*?" Kundavai asked tenderly.

"The burden of ruling this empire," he replied.

"Then let your sons shoulder your burden." said Kundavai.

"My sons are matchless warriors and dearer to me than life. But this empire comes with a curse."

"No curse can blight our Chola dynasty which is renowned for its justice, courage and devotion to god!" Kundavai exclaimed. "Some madness grips you in Thanjavur Fort ...."

"Did you see how the Pazluvur and Kodumbalur factions behaved during the play? These two clans have always been the pillars of our dynasty. If I leave Thanjavur, they'll destroy each other and the mighty Chola empire will shatter."

"What if one of those factions conspires against you to deprive your sons of the Tiger Throne?"

Sundara Chola stared at Kundavai in amazement. "And whom do they want as emperor instead?"

"Uncle Madurandaka," Kundavai replied. "And he's only too eager to sit on the throne."

"How I hope this conspiracy succeeds!"

Kundavai was shocked. "*Appa*, will you betray your own sons?"

"I want only what's good for my sons ... let Madurandaka take this accursed empire. Kundavai, you must go to Kanchipuram and convince Karikalan to abdicate his position as crown prince. And you must convince Sembiyan Madevi to let her son ascend the throne: you have always been her favorite. Then, at last, we can be free of the curse and live in peace."

"*Appa*, what's this curse you keep harping on? Won't you tell me?" Kundavai begged tearfully.

"My dear, I'll tell you what I have told no one else. Listen …

"Years ago, a young prince hid in a thicket on the shore of a beautiful island, peering out at a ship. As the vessel hoisted its sails and disappeared into the horizon, he sighed in relief and came out of hiding. This prince belonged to a ruling dynasty, but he was not the heir to the throne. He had commanded a battalion in the overseas army and fought bravely, but their army was defeated. The survivors somehow reached the coast and boarded a ship to return to their motherland. The prince, born in a long line of triumphant warriors, could not face the shame of going home defeated. As his ship crossed a small island, he stealthily jumped out and swam ashore. The island looked uninhabited. The prince leaned against a tree and thought about his future.

"Suddenly, he heard a woman scream in terror. He turned and saw a huge bear chasing a young woman. He charged behind the bear and killed it with his spear. The girl peeped out at him from behind a tree. It was clear that she was a child of the jungle. But her radiant beauty outshone all her shortcomings of dress and manner. The prince went to her, but she ran into the jungle. Exhausted from his duel with the bear, he rested on the beach. Soon, the girl returned with an old fisherman who was obviously her father.

"The old man explained that the bear had actually tried to attack the prince and the girl had screamed to divert the beast's attention. It was she who had saved the prince's life. The prince thanked her warmly but it was the old man who replied. He told the prince that his daughter was a deaf-mute. In the days that followed on that island paradise, the prince's feelings for the beautiful girl blossomed into love. The years passed. He lost track of time.

"And then one day a ship anchored off the island. Men rowed to the shore in boats. They had come in search of him. Due to an unexpected series of events, he was now the heir to the throne. An empire awaited him and war loomed over his country. He was torn between love and duty. No one saw the girl who had hidden herself at the sight of strangers. He promised her he would return once he had done his duty. He hardened his heart and climbed into a boat.

"Kundavai," Sundara Chola said, "I'll never forget that girl standing on the shore with tear-filled eyes. There's another scene, even more tragic, which haunts me and fills me with dread."

Her father's switch of pronouns made it clear to Kundavai that he was telling her the story of his own life. She listened, choked with emotion.

Can the Dead Come Back to Life?

"MY BELOVED CHILD," the emperor continued. "This is not a story a father would choose to tell his daughter. But at least one person in our family must know the truth. I can't confide in your mother or your brothers. I have finally summoned the courage to confide in you. I trust you won't judge me harshly. Aniruddha is the only other person to know a part of the truth.

"My grandfather, Paranthaka Chola, lay on his deathbed, saddened by the Chola army's defeats and the untimely death of his sons. I was his favorite grandchild. He had sent search parties to Sri Lanka to find me. He said, 'My boy, your uncle, Gandara Aditya, will succeed me. After him, the Tiger Throne will be yours. Promise me you'll restore the Chola empire to its past glory.'

"I worshipped my grandfather and I resolved to dedicate my life to fulfilling my promise to him. But what about the girl? Could a fisherwoman be empress? Would I become a laughing stock?

"On my grandfather's death, my uncle became emperor. So that there were no doubts about the line of succession, my uncle anointed me crown prince on the very day of his coronation. I was the darling of the people, as Arulmozli is now. As we stood on the palace terrace, acknowledging the cheers of the crowd gathered below, one sorrowful face stood out among the thousands: it was the deaf-mute from the island. Shocked, I fell unconscious. Everyone thought it was fatigue.

"I confided in Aniruddha and asked him to trace the woman. Her face haunted me day and night. She was not in Thanjavur. Aniruddha then sent his men further afield. A group of them found a deaf-mute at the lighthouse keeper's house in Kodikkarai. The woman was hysterical and refused to come to Thanjavur. Aniruddha and I galloped to Kodikkarai, but the girl had vanished.

"We heard that she was in the habit of climbing to the top of the lighthouse to gaze at the sea. The day after our men met her, it was a moonless night with heavy winds and strong waves. Suddenly, a scream was heard above the roar of the water. A man saw a woman plunging into the sea from the lighthouse. A search was mounted with boats, but the girl was never seen again.

"I was filled with grief … at the same time, to my shame, I was relieved. I returned to Thanjavur, married your mother and was blessed with my three children.

"But I had a recurring nightmare of a woman somersaulting to her death into the stormy ocean. I would wake up screaming. Over the years, the nightmare stopped."

Sundara Chola trembled and his eyes stared at something in the distance. He whispered: "But now the nightmare is back. Kundavai, do you believe the dead can come back to life?"

Kundavai hugged her father and burst into tears. "*Appa*, you have kept all this sorrow buried in your heart. Now you have shared your grief with me, you will regain your health."

He smiled sadly. "Kundavai, you don't believe me. Bring your friend: we'll ask her what she saw and heard last night."

"*Appa*, Vanathi is extremely timid. There's no point in questioning her."

"Very well. Do you remember when Arulmozli fell into the Ponni? You all believed the beautiful woman who saved him was the river goddess. But do you know whom I saw? It was the deaf-mute. It was that shock which made me faint when I climbed back into the boat.

"I saw her again in the women's quarters on the day Karikalan was made crown prince. She looked at him with such hatred! Again, the shock was too much for me and I fainted.

"Now, in Thanjavur, she appears at midnight and says, 'I forgive you for killing me, but don't compound your sin by giving your son the kingdom which rightfully belongs to another.' I have decided: as my father's elder brother's son, Madurandaka is the rightful heir to the throne. I have always felt guilty about becoming emperor. I'm being punished for my crime. Kundavai, help me convince your brothers to renounce their claim to the throne … let us live peacefully in Karikalan's golden palace in Kanchipuram."

"What will grandmother say?" Kundavai wondered.

"I can't understand why your wise grandmother is so against her son becoming emperor. We must bring her to Thanjavur and persuade her to do the right thing."

"She's coming here for the renovation of the Thalikkulathar Temple. Until then, don't worry about anything, *appa*."

Kundavai went to her mother. "*Amma*, on no account must you leave *appa* alone at night. Send someone else to attend the pooja."

Kundavai was now convinced that an evil conspiracy was at work. *I'll save the kingdom and my family from the danger which threatens them.*

The Greatest Betrayal

A HOSPITAL FUNDED by Kundavai from her personal income was inaugurated the next day. A jubilant crowd gathered to watch the ceremony. The emperor's ministers and accountants were present. Ambalavan and Kalaanthaka arrived on magnificent elephants; Madurandaka rode a white Arab horse which he controlled with great difficulty. Kundavai and Nandini sat together under a blue silk canopy.

The ceremony began with the rendition of a hymn composed by Saint Sambandar.

Nandini said, "Sambandar once cured the Pandian king with this song: it has lost its power now."

"Yes," Kundavai replied. "Mantras are powerless in these evil times. There are people who plot against the emperor himself." She watched Nandini's face carefully.

"Really?" Nandini replied calmly. "Who are these traitors?"

"I intend to stay here for a few days and find out," Kundavai declared.

"You can count on my help. There's a guest in my house who may be able to help you—Kandamaran, Sambuvaraya's son. That strapping young man keeps repeating the words 'Traitor,' and 'Spy.' What do you think is worse than betraying the country?"

"Being unfaithful to one's husband, of course," Kundavai replied.

Nandini smiled. "Kandamaran won't agree. He says the greatest betrayal is betraying one's friend. One of his best friends turned out to be a spy who stabbed him in the back."

"Who's this shameless man?" Kundavai asked.

Nandini smiled. "A man called Vandhiya Devan. He's from the clan which once ruled Vallam. He stabbed Kandamaran and escaped. My brother-in-law has launched a manhunt for him."

"I'll pay Kandamaran a visit," Kundavai said.

Once the edicts had been read and inscribed on stone, the ceremony ended with the public raising slogans praising the emperor and his family. Kundavai missed the venomous hatred in Nandini's eyes when the crowd shouted, "Hail Aditya Karikalan who beheaded Veerapandian!" The cheers reduced considerably in volume when the Pazluvur brothers were praised.

The Spy has been Caught!

AMBALAVAN WAS FURIOUS when Nandini told him that Kundavai was coming.

"Why is the demoness coming here? Did you invite her? Have you forgotten her insults?"

"I never forget the good or evil done to me. She invited herself: she wants to see Kandamaran."

"I can't tolerate her presence," Ambalavan announced. "I'm going to Mazlvarpadi."

"Good idea, lord. Leave that venomous cobra to me: I'll pull out her fangs." Nandini gave him a piercing glance. "You plot to make Madurandaka the next emperor ... does that mean our struggle is only to crown that effeminate man?"

The old man took her hands and passionately declared, "My darling, the day will soon come when you sit beside me as empress of the Chola empire." He left the palace.

Kandamaran was filled with excitement at the news of Kundavai's visit. *How I wish I had been wounded on the battlefield and not stabbed by a friend! But I'm conspiring against the princess's family: how can I be a hypocrite and talk with her? I'll be rude and send her away.*

His resolution vanished in the light of Kundavai's radiant beauty and compassion. Kundavai sympathetically asked him about the stabbing.

"Vandhiya Devan stayed with me at Kadambur under false pretenses and used a fake signet ring to meet the emperor in Thanjavur. He said he carried a message for you. The commander suspected he was a spy and ordered his arrest, but the clever fellow managed to escape. I was sure Devan was not a spy; he aroused suspicion only because he's rash. I convinced the commander to pardon him and to let me find Devan and bring him to Thanjavur. Judging he could escape only by climbing the fort walls, I patrolled the riverbank after midnight. Sure enough, I saw him climbing down.

"I said, 'My friend, what's all this about?' He replied by punching me on my chest. We grappled with each other. Within minutes I overpowered him. I urged him to confide in me and assured him of my help.

"He said, 'I'm exhausted. Let's sit and talk.' As I walked ahead of him, that betrayer stabbed me in the back and escaped. When I came to my senses, I was in the house of a deaf-mute woman on the outskirts of Thanjavur."

Nandini silently mocked Kandamaran's lies. As for Kundavai, she didn't know what to believe.

"How did you get to the deaf-mute's house?" the princess asked.

"It's a mystery," Kandamaran replied. "We could get nothing out of the woman. I believe she has a son who went missing at the same time. If he returns, he could throw some light on this. Or we'll have to wait until Lord Ambalavan's men catch my friend."

"Do you think he'll be caught?" Kundavai asked.

"Of course, they'll catch him," Kandamaran declared. "I'm waiting here for that. I hope to get a pardon for him from the Pazluvur lords."

"How large-hearted of you!" Kundavai said. She fervently hoped that Devan would never be caught—whether he was a traitor or not.

Just then a servant ran into the room shouting, "The spy has been caught. They are dragging him down the street and bringing him here."

Nandini suppressed the worried look which flashed across her face but Kundavai was not so quick.

Two Tigresses

NANDINI AND KUNDAVAI rushed to the balcony and Kandamaran struggled out of bed to join them. A group of soldiers, wielding spears, rode down the street. In the middle was a man whose hands were tied behind his back. Two soldiers held the ends of the rope which bound him. There was a tense silence on the balcony. The prisoner's face was not visible. Nandini looked from the street to Kundavai and back again. Kundavai's eyes flashed with eagerness and anxiety.

Kandamaran's voice shattered the silence. "It's not Vandhiya Devan!"

Kundavai's face was radiant. The group reached the gates and the prisoner looked up. The princess recognized him. Hiding her joy, Kundavai said, "What madness! Why are they dragging Pinakapani like this?"

"Oh! My brother-in-law's men are notorious for capturing the wrong men," Nandini mocked.

"My friend can't be captured so easily!" exclaimed Kandamaran.

"Your friend?" asked Nandini.

"Although he betrayed me, he's my friend," replied Kandamaran staunchly.

"Maybe they have killed him," said Nandini. "They followed two spies to Kodikkarai." Nandini saw Kundavai writhe in agony at the word 'killed.' *Hah!* she thought in triumph. *You arrogant woman—now I have the instrument of your torture in my hands. I'll make good use of it.*

Kundavai burst out angrily: "How dare they capture the man I sent to Kodikkarai to gather herbs for my father? Let your brother-in-law explain!"

"Oh, is this your man?" Nandini asked innocently. "Did you send another man with him?"

"Yes, I ordered one of them to go on to Sri Lanka."

"Was the other man a stranger?" Nandini asked.

Kundavai hesitated. "My brother sent him from Kanchipuram with a message for me ..."

Nandini interrupted: "Yes! My husband says he's the spy. That's why he escaped at night after stabbing this poor man."

"I don't believe he stabbed him … why would he then carry him to the deaf-mute's house?" countered Kundavai.

"You seem to have a soft corner for this spy," Nandini mocked. "He has some magic—this man still calls him his friend. But the dead can't come back to life. If he has been killed …"

Kundavai's forehead was bathed in sweat; her heart raced. "I'll go to my father right now," she lashed out in anger. "I'll take up this matter with him."

"Why do you want to disturb your sick father? Take it up with my brother-in-law. Would he dare to contravene your orders?"

Nandini emerged victorious in this duel; Kundavai struggled to hide her wounded heart.

The Dungeon

KUNDAVAI GREW UP in luxury, pampered and indulged by everyone. All at once, grief entered her world: her father was ill; her brothers were far away; the oracles predicted impending danger; important men plotted against her family. She faced all this courageously with a steady heart. But now, a stranger had melted her heart and made her tremble for his safety. *There's no time to examine my feelings. I must act at once.*

Giving notice of her arrival, Kundavai walked to Kalaanthaka's mansion. After being welcomed warmly by the women, she went to the art gallery where he waited. They examined the paintings.

Kundavai said angrily, "The Pazluvur lords have served the Chola dynasty for generations. There's no doubt you have earned the right to rule the Chola empire … but why are you in such a hurry to take over? Surely you can wait until the emperor dies?"

Kalaanthaka broke into a sweat. His voice trembled. "Lady, what's the reason for your fury?"

"Knowing I sent the Pazlayarai doctor's son to Kodikkarai, why did you arrest him?"

"You may not know he's a spy, lady. He admitted his companion is a spy who's carrying letters to Sri Lanka."

"That man's a fool! I'm the one who chose his companion. He's the messenger my brother sent from Kanchipuram. What proof do you have he's a spy?"

"Vandhiya Devan entered stealthily; he visited the Kudanthai astrologer and enquired about the emperor's health; he lied that my brother gave him a signet ring ..."

"Who gave him the ring?" Kundavai interrupted.

"I'll know that only after I capture him. We have ways to make him talk in our dungeon. Fearing this, he escaped after stabbing Kandamaran."

"I don't believe he stabbed Kandamaran."

"It's obvious the lucky spy has earned your good opinion—unlike me," Kalaanthaka said.

"None of your accusations prove he's a spy," the princess protested.

"Why did he hide from my men in Kodikkarai? Why did he leave for Sri Lanka at night?"

"Ah! He escaped! Your men could not catch him. We'll forget about him." Kundavai paused. "But Pinakapani is innocent—release him."

"He's an accomplice, lady. I can't let him go. Danger lurks on all sides; conspirators, including Veerapandian's men, threaten the Chola dynasty."

"Keep your dungeon for the real conspirators. Release him."

"I can't take the responsibility for this," Kalaanthaka stood firm.

"Very well, I'll ask the emperor to order his release," the princess declared.

"It's well known that your wish is the emperor's command. Here's the key to the dungeon. You are responsible for the consequences of your actions."

Controlling her anger, Kundavai took the large key. "I have never shirked my responsibility."

"Two women will bring about the downfall of the Chola empire ..." the commander said.

"I'm one; who's the other?" Kundavai asked.

"Nandini," he replied.

Kundavai smiled for the first time. "Why do you equate me with the most powerful woman in the Chola empire? If your brother hears this, he'll send you into exile."

"I look forward to that, lady." Kalaanthaka's voice was steady.

Chendan Amudhan in Prison

KUNDAVAI HURRIED TO the royal mint with Vanathi. The chief welcomed them and showed them around. They saw a heap of new coins with the tiger on one face and a ship on the other.

"These coins are convenient for those who plot against the emperor," Kundavai said in a low voice. "Gold can turn even the best men into traitors."

"True, lady," the chief said. "We hear strange rumors and have increased our security. The number of people going in and out of the dungeon is increasing."

"Going out?" Kundavai asked. "Do people come out?"

"Even this morning, they took a man down to the dungeon, but he was out within an hour."

Who could this be? the princess wondered.

The women entered a dark, low-ceilinged room at the rear. In the light of the guard's torch, they saw that the room was filled with caged tigers. The beasts paced their cages and roared.

"It's their meal time, lady," the guard explained.

Kundavai tightened her grip on Vanathi. "In that case, let's hurry. Take us to the prison gate."

The guard moved a cage in the corner of the room. Under it was a door which led to the dungeon. As they climbed down in the dim light, they heard piteous cries from the prisoners. To their amazement, rising above the groans, they heard a sweet voice singing a hymn. Kundavai moved from cell to cell, examining the occupants' faces in the light of the torch. Many of them wore manacles and were chained to the walls.

Vanathi said, "What cruelty! Why are they kept like this? Is there no judicial enquiry?"

"This is for traitors, spies and their accomplices," Kundavai explained. "They are released after extracting information from them. Those who have nothing to say are the ones to be pitied."

They reached the cell from which the song came. As the guard raised his torch, Kundavai was impressed by the young man's innocent face.

"Were you singing?" the princess asked. "You have not lost hope even in this place."

"Why should I, lady? God who is everywhere is here with me in this prison too."

"Who are you?" Kundavai asked. "Do you have a family?"

"I make garlands for god. I live with my mother, Vani, near the lotus pond outside the fort."

"I'll meet your mother and tell her you are in good spirits," Kundavai said.

"My mother is a deaf-mute, lady."

"Ah!" exclaimed Kundavai. "You are Chendan Amudhan. Why are you here?"

"Lady, I'm accused of helping a spy."

"Tell us your story," Vanathi urged him.

"I met a stranger at the fort gates some days ago. His name is Vandhiya Devan. I took him home for the night ..." Amudhan narrated the events which ended in his capture.

"Why did you blindly trust this man?" Kundavai asked.

"Lady, sometimes one instinctively likes a person and is willing to lay down one's life for him; sometimes one hates a person on sight. Today, a Pazlayarai doctor's son spent an hour with me in this cell—I hated him! I could have killed him. Luckily, Lady Nandini sent her men to release him."

"And why did you hate him?"

"I have a cousin in Kodikkarai—Poonkuzlali. That rascal spoke ill of her. But he also gave me good news. My friend, Vandhiya Devan, accompanied him to Kodikkarai. This wretch betrayed him to the Pazluvur men, but Devan gave them the slip and Poonkuzlali rowed him to Lanka."

Happiness flooded the women's faces.

"Let me talk to the commander," Kundavai said as they took their leave.

"Lady, don't do that. The man in the next cell has offered to tell me where the Pandian dynasty's crown jewels are hidden in Sri Lanka. All he wants in exchange is to learn a song."

"Do you want to go mad like him?" Kundavai scolded. "Who will look after your mother?"

Within half an hour, Amudhan was released from the prison.

Nandini's Letter

NANDINI SAT IN the garden pavilion, writing a letter:

Prince, I hesitate to write to you. The Chola empire is in danger and your father is seriously ill, but you never come to Thanjavur. I fear I may be the cause for this. I beg you to meet me once and let me clear your doubts. If you wish, we can meet at Kadambur. There is nothing improper in us meeting, as my marriage to Lord Ambalavan makes me your grandmother. You can trust the warrior who brings this letter. Please send your reply through him. The Unfortunate Nandini.

"Fetch Kandamaran at once," she ordered a maid.

Kandamaran came and stood with his face averted, not daring to look at Nandini.

Nandini teased, "After gazing at the beautiful Kundavai, you can't bear to look at me."

One look at her bewitching smile and Kandamaran was lost. "A thousand Kundavais can't equal one Nandini. My blood boils when I think of her supporting Vandhiya Devan."

"Still, your imaginative account of the encounter between you and your friend was too much."

Kandamaran had the grace to be ashamed. "I had to say something …"

"You must have a credible story so that he will be charged and imprisoned when he's caught."

"I want him to be pardoned," Kandamaran insisted.

"Surely you know the truth: do you remember meeting me and Lord Ambalavan that night?"

"How can I ever forget that, lady? Lost in your beauty, I can't remember what I said."

"You said, 'Sir, your daughter is even more beautiful than what I heard!'"

Kandamaran was horrified. "Did I say that? Is that why his face darkened in anger? Even now, it's obvious he hates me ... and I confess I dislike him."

Nandini laughed. "It's enough that I like him. Let's leave that aside: what did you do next?"

"Still dazzled by your beauty, I followed the guard to the wall. He opened the secret gate and stood aside. I started to climb out ... and somebody stabbed me in the back. My mind is blank after that. Vandhiya Devan must have been waiting for me outside."

"No, you are wrong. This is what happened: Vandhiya Devan escaped by entering the treasury. He then followed you. When you stepped through the door, he stabbed you. His conscience pricked him, so he carried you to the deaf-mute."

"Ah! This makes sense. You are a rare combination of beauty and brains, lady."

"Will you do me a favor?" Nandini asked sweetly.

"I'll do anything for you!" Kandamaran declared.

"Will you deliver a letter from me to the crown prince at Kanchipuram? Will you invite him to Kadambur Palace?"

Kandamaran was shocked. "Lady! Are you aware that your husband, my father and many other Chola chieftains are plotting against the ruling family?"

"Yes, and we're all in great danger. That venomous cobra, Kundavai, plans to make Arulmozli emperor. He'll be her puppet and Vandhiya Devan will be the power behind the throne."

"We must warn my father and Lord Ambalavan at once," Kandamaran urged.

"They won't believe us. Leave Kundavai to me. Will you deliver the letter?"

Kandamaran, overcome with desire, took her hands in his. "I'll do anything for you."

Just then, there was a bustle and Ambalavan stormed into the pavilion in a rage. He squeezed the parrot which was tied to a little wooden swing there—the bird fluttered and screeched in terror.

His Anger Melted Like Wax

KANDAMARAN'S BLOOD FROZE in his veins at the sight of Ambalavan. *I must be careful. Did the old man see or hear anything he could misinterpret?*

Nandini turned her radiant face to her husband and gazed adoringly at him. "My dear, you are back! I was afraid you would be delayed."

To Kandamaran's amazement, Ambalavan's anger melted like wax under her smile. He turned to Kandamaran and joked, "What's he doing here? Is he reciting love poems to you?"

Kandamaran turned red in embarrassment. Nandini laughed and said, "He knows nothing about love or poetry—he only knows to get wounded in fights. Luckily, he has recovered and wants to go home."

"How brave today's young men are!" Ambalavan mocked. "I was wounded sixty-four times in battle but never took to my bed. Maybe wounds in the back take longer to heal."

Kandamaran was furious. "Sir, I think of you as my father: that's why I tolerate your insults."

"Or else?" Ambalavan asked, his hand going to his sword.

Nandini intervened quickly. "My dear, he's wounded in body and heart. Don't you remember what happened that night? He was stabbed in the back by his best friend." She gave her husband a meaningful look.

Ambalavan's expression changed. "Let it go, his father's my friend. I have news: our men caught a spy in Mathottam with letters for Prince Arulmozli. From his description, he's obviously this man's handsome friend. Clever fellow—giving us the slip and going to Lanka."

The two men missed the flash of alarm which flitted across Nandini's face.

"Oh! He escaped, is it?" Kandamaran's voice showed his disappointment.

"My dear, haven't I always said your brother is not fit to be the commander of Thanjavur Fort? His men are obviously like him."

"I'm forced to agree," her husband replied. "The spy was carrying a Pazluvur signet ring and refused to say where he got it from."

Nandini exhaled softly.

"And do you know what my brother says? He says you gave the man the signet ring … what a joke!" He roared with laughter.

Nandini laughed along with him.

"He also says you met the spy when you were coming to Thanjavur in your palanquin …"

Nandini's eyes blazed in fury. "The idiot! And did you tolerate my brother-in-law's nonsense?"

Ambalavan wilted under her glare. "Do you think I kept quiet? I gave him such a tongue-lashing, he was reduced to tears!"

For the first time, Kandamaran feared Nandini and pitied her poor worm of a husband. He cleared his throat.

Nandini immediately said, "We have forgotten this man. Can he leave?"

"Yes. His father must be worried about his long absence," her husband replied.

"Can I send a letter through him to the crown prince at Kanchipuram?"

"Why?" asked Ambalavan suspiciously.

"If Kundavai can send a letter to the younger brother, why can't I send one to the elder brother?"

"Was it Kundavai's letter the spy carried? How do you know that?" her husband asked.

"Why do you think I see the sorcerer? He told me this. I don't depend on your men. They told you the spy had a signet ring, but they did not tell you who sent the letter."

"Actually, it was Aniruddha, who is back from Rameswaram, who mentioned the ring."

"And did that Brahmin tell you who sent the letter?" Nandini asked pointedly.

"No."

"Didn't I warn you that we are surrounded by traitors? The doctor's son confirmed the sorcerer's words: the spy carried a letter from Kundavai to Arulmozli," said Nandini.

Ambalavan's thoughts were in a whirl. He looked suspiciously at Kandamaran.

Seeing that he was reluctant to talk in Kandamaran's presence, Nandini turned to the young man. "Take this letter and deliver it to the crown prince. If he gives you a reply, send it here securely. And invite the prince to Kadambur Palace," she instructed.

"Shall I tell my father this is Lord Ambalavan's wish?" Kandamaran asked hesitantly.

"Certainly: my wish is my husband's wish. Isn't that right, my dear?" she smiled at her husband.

"Yes, yes," Ambalavan nodded hurriedly. He felt too giddy to argue with his wife.

When they were alone, Nandini's eyes filled with tears. "My dear, your brother's wicked words have made you suspicious of me. You questioned me before a stranger—I feel so ashamed."

Ambalavan tenderly wiped her tears. "I'll lose confidence in my spear before I lose confidence in you! But my darling, why are you writing to Karikalan: isn't he our arch-enemy?"

"No, Kundavai's our arch-enemy. She plots to make Arulmozli emperor. We must counter her moves. Now you see why I have sent the letter to the crown prince, don't you?"

Without understanding, Ambalavan mumbled, "Yes, yes."

"My dear, the Cholas' rule stands on your courage and the courage of your ancestors. I'll work day and night to see you seated on the Tiger Throne. If you suspect me, kill me," Nandini said.

"My darling," Ambalavan pleaded. "Don't torture me with such words."

Mathottam

AFTER SEVERAL DAYS, Vandhiya Devan reached Mathottam with its famous Ketheeswaram temple. Fruit groves lined the banks and ships unloaded cargo in the port. Armed soldiers were everywhere. Devan reached the fort gates and was refused entrance. As usual, he tried to force his way in and was captured and taken to the fort commander.

Devan declared he had a letter for Prince Arulmozli and must see the Chola general in person. He was frisked and the letter was found, along with the Pazluvur signet ring.

Kodumbalur Velir, the general of the Chola army, was Vanathi's uncle. He was busy with Chief Minister Aniruddha and was going to Rameswaram with him. He ordered Devan to be kept in custody until he returned.

Devan was thrown into a room in a ruined building, with a guard stationed outside his door. Exhausted by his travel, he was only too glad to find a secure place to sleep. On the second day, he was disturbed by shouts from the adjoining room.

"I'll kill you! Don't you dare come near me!"

Some mad soldier is shouting to himself. How can I sleep? Suddenly, something thudded to the ground near him—it was a cat. Devan burst into laughter.

"Oh, you can laugh, is it?" the voice in the next room shouted. "Just don't come back here!"

Devan thought, *The man is mad! Who would quarrel with a cat? But there's something familiar about the voice.* Shrugging his thoughts aside, Devan lay down to sleep. But, ignoring his kicks and shoves, the cat crawled under him, cuddled by his side and stroked his forehead with its tail. Exasperated, Devan got up, caught the cat by the scruff of its neck and threw it through an opening in the wall into the next room. A commotion erupted there; a man's shouts and the cat's howls mingled for a while until the cat's mews faded into the distance and silence reigned. *Peace at last!* Devan prepared to sleep. He dreamed of Kundavai's soft hand stroking his forehead ....

His dream vanished as someone banged on the wall and shouted, "Who threw the cat here?"

Devan was silent and heard someone scaling the wall. He stood alert, his hand on his sword hilt. A pair of hands appeared in the opening, followed by a turbaned head. *It's Azlvarkkadian! What's he doing here?* "Brave Vaishnava, welcome to Lord Shiva's sacred abode at Ketheeswaram," Devan said.

"*Thambi,* it's you!" Azlvarkkadian said and jumped into Devan's room.

A Shaiva Cat

VANDHIYA DEVAN SAID, "You leaped over the wall like Hanuman leapt to Sri Lanka."

"How can you compare me with Hanuman? I couldn't even deal with a cat! Look-" He showed Devan the scratches on his legs.

"It must be a Shaiva cat," Devan teased. "It insisted on cuddling up to me, but it scratched you."

"I came here looking for you. I evaded the sentry and jumped over the back wall. That evil creature decided to place its tail exactly on the spot I landed on."

Devan smiled. "When I was near Thanjavur Fort, your sister's palanquin rammed my horse. I went to demand justice from her and told her I carried an urgent message from you."

"Liar!" Azlvarkkadian exclaimed.

"She was so impressed by me, she gave me a Pazluvur signet ring and asked me to meet her at her palace the next day."

"Did you go?" Azlvarkkadian asked eagerly.

"Of course. Hearing about my achievements, she gave me an important task: she asked me to bring her the Pandian crown jewels which are hidden in the Sri Lankan mountains."

"Isn't Lord Ambalavan's treasury enough for her? What did she promise you in return?"

"She promised to make me commander of Thanjavur Fort. But I'm caught in this place."

"Do you know why you are locked up here?" Azlvarkkadian asked.

"I made a mistake: I carried the Pazluvur ring, thinking it would be of use here too."

"Yes. The general is Kodumbalur Velir. The Pazluvur and Kodumbalur clans have been rivals for generations. Never mind, come with me. We'll escape at once."

"No," cried Devan. "I have not slept for many nights. I want to sleep peacefully here."

"Is this how you honor your promise to Princess Kundavai?" Azlvarkkadian asked and gave Devan the letter he had carried.

Devan took it eagerly, his suspicions about Azlvarkkadian fading. "How did you get this?"

"General Velir gave it to me, along with this ring. You are free to go."

"My heartfelt thanks. Do you happen to know where Prince Arulmozli is?"

"No one knows his whereabouts. He left Anuradhapura for the mountains. The general asked me to go with you—I can be your guide."

Again, Devan was suspicious. "Can I meet the general?"

"Of course," Azlvarkkadian said. "After all, you must give him news of Lady Vanathi."

Is he a magician? Devan wondered.

Jungle Trail

VELIR WAS A seasoned warrior. His younger brother, Vanathi's father, had lost the war, and his life, in Lanka. Velir was determined to avenge his brother's death and defeat. Fortunately for Vandhiya Devan, the general had mentioned him to Aniruddha and the chief minister had sent Azlvarkkadian to Sri Lanka to give the general details of Devan's mission.

Velir sized up Devan and seemed impressed. He smiled. "*Thambi,* I hope you have been treated well."

Devan entertained the general with a humorous account of Azlvarkkadian and the Shaiva cat.

Velir laughed. "Thirumalai, you are lucky to have this brave warrior as your companion. See that he eats before you leave." He turned to Devan. "*Thambi,* there's a severe food shortage here as Mahinda's men have flooded the fields. The people themselves have no food—where do we go? We're not getting sufficient supplies from our country."

Devan replied, "The Pazlayarai women complained to Princess Kundavai that their men in Lanka were short of food. She said Kodumbalur Velir would not let a single Chola soldier starve."

Velir stood tall. "Did she say that? No woman is equal to our princess!"

"There's another princess second only to her," Devan said. "Vanathi of the Kodumbalur clan."

The general smiled. "This young man impresses me. Did you meet Vanathi?"

"Of course. She and Princess Kundavai are as inseparable as a flower and its fragrance."

Velir applauded. "He has a silver tongue! Thirumalai, take him to the treasury and give him the dresses and ornaments he chooses."

"Thank you, sir," Devan said. "I'll accept your gifts when I return."

"Did the princess send me any news about Vanathi?" the general asked.

"Sir, she sent a message—but not to you. She sent news of Lady Vanathi to Prince Arulmozli."

Velir hugged Devan. "What a wise young man! It's time you left on your journey."

"Sir," Devan asked. "Must I take this Vaishnava with me?"

"You can't find the prince without Thirumalai's help," the general said. He also carries an important message for the prince. Don't quarrel and ruin your mission." The general beckoned Devan closer and whispered, "He won't give you any trouble, but be careful. Let me know what message he delivers to the prince."

Devan and Azlvarkkadian set out that same night, accompanied by two soldiers. On the third day, they entered dense jungle. One of the soldiers climbed a tree to survey the land. He clambered down, shouting, "Sir! An elephant in musth is crashing through the trees!" Azlvarkkadian pointed to a hillock and the four men ran for it. But a steep ravine separated them from the hill. Standing with their backs to the edge of the ravine, they faced the charging beast. The elephant trumpeted: unable to bear the sound, the men covered their ears and scattered.

The elephant advanced menacingly towards Azlvarkkadian, who was caught between the ravine and a dense thicket. Devan lifted his spear, only to lower it - no spear could stop that beast. Even at this moment of crises, Azlvarkkadian brought a smile to Devan's face. Waving his two-foot stick at the elephant, Azlvarkkadian shouted, "Stop right there! If you take another step, I'll dig a pit and bury you in it!"

The Highway

THE GUARDS SHOUTED to distract the elephant and Devan raised his spear again. The elephant charged at Azlvarkkadian ... the Vaishnava threw his stick at the animal ... and vanished.

Before the others could grasp what had happened, the huge elephant rushed to the spot where Azlvarkkadian had stood an instant before: unable to stop itself, it toppled into the ravine with a blood-curdling shriek. Dust rose from an avalanche of rocks which rolled down the ravine's side. Azlvarkkadian and the elephant had both died at the same time and in the same way.

Devan was filled with sorrow. Just when his suspicions about Azlvarkkadian had died and he had started to feel a deep affection for the Vaishnava, fate had struck. *How will I succeed in my mission without his help?* Devan walked to the edge of the precipice and peered down.

Suddenly, he heard a voice: "*Thambi*, are you going to stand there doing nothing?"

Devan staggered back in shock. Then he peered down in the direction of the voice: there was Azlvarkkadian, clinging to a tree root on the steep slope of the precipice! Overwhelmed with relief and happiness, Devan called the guards. He made them hold one end of his waistband and passed Azlvarkkadian the other end. The three men heaved the Vaishnava up.

Azlvarkkadian lay prostrate on the ground, panting. Then, sitting up abruptly, he said, "Come, we must reach the highway before dark. The carnivores will soon come to feast on the elephant."

They heard foxes bark, followed by the yowl of leopards; an eagle wheeled overhead. The alarmed men set out at a brisk pace. At sunset they were on the highway.

"Hurry. We must reach Dambulla before dark," Azlvarkkadian said. "I used the jungle trail only to avoid being stopped and questioned."

Pedestrians, carts and elephants plied the road. Devan was surprised to see Lankan civilians calmly going about their business even as Tamil soldiers marched by.

"This highway links Anuradhapura with Singagiri," Azlvarkkadian explained. "The Chola army controls the stretch from Anuradhapura to

Dambulla. From there to Singagiri, King Mahinda rules. Under Prince Arulmozli, civilians are free to go about their business." Azlvarkkadian grimaced. "The Buddhist monks are happy: the prince is rebuilding the monasteries destroyed in the war. When I see the prince, I'll tell him I don't like this."

"Yes, the prince will listen to the brave Vaishnava who faced an elephant with a stick," Devan teased.

Azlvarkkadian said, "There's something about the prince which silences critics when they face him. Only one person has the power to command him ... and that's Princess Kundavai."

"What about your sister, Nandini?" Devan asked.

"If a man was heading to hell, Princess Kundavai would stop him and take him to heaven—that's her magic. Nandini would speed him on his way to hell, convincing him he was going to heaven—that's her magic."

Devan broke into gooseflesh. *How well he knows Nandini. Is he really her brother?*

Engrossed in their own thoughts, the men walked on in silence. Suddenly, four men galloped towards them. Raising a storm of dust, the company crossed them. In that brief instant, Devan recognized one of the riders. It was Parthibendran Pallava. *He has always hated me.*

"Stop!" a voice barked. The riders wheeled around and came back to stop before Devan. Their leader was indeed Parthibendran.

"What are you doing here?" Parthibendran asked. "When you vanished in Thanjavur, I thought the Pazluvur brothers had finished you off."

"I'm not that easy to finish off," Devan said defiantly. "I'm a prince of Vallam ..."

"Yes, you are unmatched when it comes to guarding your own life," Parthibendran mocked.

Devan's unsheathed his sword. "Sir, if I have to die, I'd rather die at the hands of one who descends from the brave Pallavas than be killed by those shameless Pazluvur brothers."

"I have no intention of fighting with you in this alien country," Parthibendran declared. "I'm on an urgent mission. What happened to your assignment?"

"I have accomplished my task and delivered both the letters," Devan said. "I've always wanted to visit Sri Lanka; I've come here with this Vaishnava."

Parthibendran studied Azlvarkkadian. "I've seen you somewhere ..."

"Yes, sir," Azlvarkkadian said. "You were with the crown prince when I met him regarding my sister, Nandini."

"The harm that viper is causing! You should be impaled on a stake for being her brother."

"I have vowed to die by impalement," the irrepressible Azlvarkkadian said.

"It will take a hundred men to lift you onto the stake," Parthibendran retorted. "Have you any news of Prince Arulmozli? Has he returned to Anuradhapura?"

"Sir, we know nothing. We came through the jungle: we were chased by an elephant and ..."

Parthibendran cut him off impatiently. The riders wheeled around and galloped off.

Azlvarkkadian lowered his voice. "*Thambi*, did you recognize the other men?"

"No," Devan said.

"Two of them were at a secret meeting at Thirupurambayam—they swore to destroy the Cholas."

Are these the two men Poonkuzlali's brother rowed from Kodikkarai to Sri Lanka? Devan wondered. *What's their connection to Parthibendran?*

The Mahout

THE ANCIENT MONASTERY town of Dambulla was bustling with monks and pilgrims.

Devan was puzzled. "Isn't Dambulla under Chola control? I don't see a single soldier."

"The prince has ordered our men to stay in their barracks outside the town."

"Why are we looking for the prince here? Parthibendran said he couldn't find him."

"Do you think I would go by what that man said?" Azlvarkkadian countered. He walked up to two Tamil men on the street corner and spoke with them. He came back and said, "Two Chinese travelers are coming here from Singagiri. They saw the cave paintings there and now want to visit the Dambulla monastery. Look ..."

The crowd cheered as a huge elephant strode towards them. Two Chinese men were seated on the howdah on its back. A mahout sat on the elephant's neck, goad in hand.

"*Thambi*," Azlvarkkadian said. "Did you see that?"

"Yes, what a huge elephant! And the Chinese have such flat features and strange clothes ..."

Azlvarkkadian rolled his eyes. "Did you see how the mahout eyes glowed when he saw us?"

"Why should a mahout's eyes glow?" Devan asked.

"I pity Princess Kundavai for having chosen you to be her messenger. Come."

They walked behind the crowd. The mahout whispered into the elephant's ears: it knelt and the Chinese climbed down and entered the monastery. The mahout led the elephant to a group of men near the gates. Entrusting the animal to one of them, he pointed to Azlvarkkadian and whispered to a second man. He then disappeared into an alley with two other men.

The second man came to Azlvarkkadian. "Will you come with me?"

"I've been waiting for this," Azlvarkkadian replied.

"Do you have any identification?" the man asked.

Azlvarkkadian showed him the Kodumbalur signet ring from General Velir.

"Follow me," the man said. He led them to the town's outskirts, down a narrow jungle path and then to some ruins away from the track. He climbed a tree and scanned the four directions.

Devan saw two horses tied to a tree behind the ruins. *Only two horses?* Devan turned to Azlvarkkadian. "Who's this mysterious mahout? Is it Prince Arulmozli?"

"From the sparks flying from his eyes, I think so," Azlvarkkadian replied.

"But won't the people recognize him? And why would he risk entering enemy territory?"

"The people here don't know him. He has gone far into enemy territory with the Chinese."

"Why?"

"To see the sculpture and paintings," Azlvarkkadian said.

"My god!" Devan exclaimed. "Can this foolhardy prince become the mighty emperor the Kudanthai astrologer predicted?"

"I for one don't need any astrologer to tell me that," Azlvarkkadian declared.

They heard the sound of horses' hooves. The man climbed down from the tree. He mounted one horse and gave the other to Azlvarkkadian. "In a few minutes, some horses will pass by. We must follow them," he said.

"What about me?" Devan asked. "I need a horse. I have an urgent message from the princess."

"I've been instructed only to take this man, not you," he was told.

"Give me the letter," Azlvarkkadian said. "I'll give it to the prince."

"No," Devan said emphatically.

"Then you must wait here," Azlvarkkadian said. "There's no other option."

As three riders streaked past them, Devan grabbed one of the guide's legs and gave him a violent push. The man toppled off his horse. Devan jumped on the horse and rode away with Azlvarkkadian's horse following. The guide jumped up with a shout and hurled a dagger at Devan. Devan ducked in the nick of time—the dagger wedged itself into a tree trunk.

"Great going, *thambi!*" Azlvarkkadian applauded.

But Devan frowned in anxiety. *Why did I listen to a woman and end up in this mess?*

The horses streaked along the narrow forest track.

A Duel

THE RIDE SEEMED endless. The dense jungle on both sides was shrouded in darkness. The feeble moonlight silhouetted the three riders who thundered ahead of them.

Has the Vaishnava led me into a trap? Devan wondered. Suddenly, he heard the unexpected sound of soldiers' voices raised in cheer. A circle of light appeared and fires burned under huge cauldrons. *Are we in the enemy camp?*

The three riders stopped suddenly. In the blink of an eye, one man charged back, punched Devan violently and followed up with a push to his knee. Devan fell to the ground. Before he could gather his wits, his attacker bent over him and threw away the dagger in Devan's waistband. The furious Devan jumped up; clenching his hands into fists, he punched his attacker with all his might. The man returned his punches, and the two were soon engaged in a mighty duel.

Azlvarkkadian stood in the circle of men who watched the fight in the flickering moonlight. The spectators increased in number, some holding torches in their hands.

Finally, Devan fell to the ground; sitting astride his chest, his opponent untied his waistband and took the letter. Grabbing a torch from one of the men, he moved to the edge of the crowd and read the message. Two soldiers kept Devan pinned to the ground.

Devan shouted at Azlvarkkadian in fury: "You traitor! Grab that letter from him!"

"That's impossible," Azlvarkkadian replied.

"You coward!" Devan berated him. "I deserve this for trusting you."

Azlvarkkadian bent over Devan's ear. "Fool! The letter has reached the person it was meant for."

The torch lit up the face of the warrior reading the letter and the crowd broke into loud cheers. "Long live Prince Arulmozli!" "Long live Ponni's Beloved!"

Is this the prince? Devan marveled. *He's as handsome as Arjuna and as strong as Bheema. No wonder the entire country sings his praises.* Devan stood before the greatest Tamil warrior of all time–Prince

Arulmozlivarman, who would go down in the annals of history as the renowned Emperor Raja Raja Chola.

The prince's smile was captivating. "My friend, welcome to beautiful Sri Lanka. You have crossed the seas to join the bravest Chola warriors. I gave you a warrior's welcome."

"I have accomplished my mission," Devan replied. "I no longer have to safeguard my life. We can fight again if you want."

"I'll have to answer to my sister if anything happens to you," Arulmozli said. "My friend, this letter is in my sister's handwriting—did she give it to you in person?"

"Yes, sir. I have traveled day and night to bring it to you."

Arulmozli hugged Devan. "How can I repay you for this?"

With that, Devan's aches and pains vanished.

Elele Singan

THE CHOLA ARMY was camped in a large clearing in the jungle. Arulmozli sat majestically on a tree stump, wearing a golden crown and dressed in rich silks and ornaments. With him sat Devan, Azlvarkkadian and the battalion commander.

In the prince's honor, the men performed a play on the life of the Chola warrior, Elele Singan. Centuries ago, Singan led the Chola forces on an expedition to Sri Lanka and decisively defeated the Lankan army. The Lankan prince, Dushtakamanu, was a brave warrior and brilliant strategist. Dushtakamanu challenged Singan to a duel saying, 'Let the winner rule Sri Lanka.' Impressed by the prince's courage, Singan agreed. The soldiers of both armies watched as the two great warriors battled for hours. Dushtakamanu, fighting for his country and his birthright, gave no quarter. Singan, pitying the prince, fought halfheartedly and was killed by the prince. Dushtakamanu built a memorial in honor of the great Chola warrior on the battlefield.

Arulmozli said, "Thirumalai, this story is in the Dambulla paintings: have you seen them?"

"Prince, we can see the paintings any day but we met you only because we happened to be there at the right time. Parthibendran could not find you, we met him on our way."

"Yes, I heard he was here," Arulmozli said. "What do you think he wants?"

"The crown prince wants you to go to Kanchipuram at once," Azlvarkkadian replied.

"And what do you think my sister wants?" the prince asked.

"Princess Kundavai wants you to go to Pazlayarai at once. I hid among the creepers and watched the princess give this warrior her letter."

Devan pinched Azlvarkkadian on his back. Azlvarkkadian slapped himself on the back and exclaimed, "These mosquitoes!"

The prince frowned. "Thirumalai, have you started spying on my sister?"

"Sir, it's only because I knew about the letter that I brought this man safely to you."

"Was that your only reason?" the prince asked.

"No, sir," Azlvarkkadian said. "I too have a letter for you: the chief minister advises you to remain in Sri Lanka for some time."

"If three elders give me three conflicting orders, whom do I obey?!" Arulmozli said ruefully.

Devan said, "Sir, obey your sister, for that's what your heart tells you. I have to obey her. I must take you to Pazlayarai at any cost."

The prince sized up Devan. "I have long prayed for a brave friend like you."

The Magic Elephant

THE SOLDIERS SAT down to a hearty meal of rice and lentils served on lotus leaves. Arulmozli moved among the men, talking and joking. It was clear that the soldiers adored their prince.

Arulmozli then retired to his tent with Devan and Azlvarkkadian. "If only Thanjavur had given us adequate supplies, we could have captured Sri Lanka by now. We have wasted a golden opportunity."

Azlvarkkadian said, "Sir, you should be more worried about Tamil Nadu: the mighty Chola empire, created and nurtured by your forefathers, is in danger of breaking apart."

"You're right, Thirumalai," Arulmozli agreed. "Let me hear the news both of you bring."

Devan narrated all that had happened from the day he left Kanchipuram, leaving out nothing. "Sir," he concluded, "Your father is a hostage and important chieftains are conspiring against the Chola dynasty. The princess is devastated by all this: you must go to Pazlayarai at once."

Azlvarkkadian, in his turn, gave an account of all that he had seen and heard, including the plot being hatched by the Pandians. He concluded, "My gurudeva advises you to remain here. The conspirators will strike soon. You must gather all our forces in Sri Lanka and prepare to crush them. The chief minister asked me to tell you the Kaikkola battalion, along with the Vanniyar and Velaalar battalions, has sworn its loyalty to you."

Arulmozli said passionately: "Thirumalai, does your gurudeva want me to take up arms against my own kin? All authority lies with my father—I won't interfere without his direct orders."

Devan intervened. "Sir, the Pazluvur brothers have made your father a prisoner. And the crown prince swears he will not step into Thanjavur Fort. Under these circumstances, isn't it your duty to safeguard the kingdom? You must come to Pazlayarai."

The prince was lost in thought. "Do you know how many sins have been committed because of the lust for the throne? I'll tell you the history behind Singagiri Fort …

"Five centuries ago, Sri Lanka was ruled by King Dadhusena who had two sons, Kasyapa and Magellan. Kasyapa, lusting for power, conspired with his general, killed his father and usurped the throne. Magellan fled to Tamil Nadu. Fearing his brother's revenge, Kasyapa built Singagiri Fort and hid there for eighteen years. Then, Magellan allied with the Pandians and returned with a huge army. Kasyapa was defeated and killed on the battlefield. What an evil man! To kill one's father and cheat one's own brother! But the paintings in his fort are beautiful."

Azlvarkkadian asked respectfully, "Sir, why do you risk your life going into enemy territory?"

"Thirumalai, is my life worth more than that of a Chola soldier? I wanted to see the paintings and avoid meeting Parthibendran." He smiled. "I also knew the chief minister had sent me a message from Mathottam—and I'm obliged to obey the first letter I receive, right?"

"In that case, you must come to Pazlayarai!" Devan exclaimed happily.

"I recall an old folk song about my ancestor, Killi Valavan. He had a magic elephant which stood with one leg in Kanchipuram, one in Pazlayarai, one in Thanjavur and one in Lanka."

Azlvarkkadian and Devan burst out laughing.

"Since I don't own such a wonderful animal, let's go to Anuradhapura and see Parthibendran," the prince said. "I'll make a decision after hearing what he has to say.

The Statue's Message

ARULMOZLI SET OUT early the next morning, accompanied by Vandhiya Devan and Azlvarkkadian.

As they galloped down the highway, Devan thought, *What a man! He's a brilliant strategist and brave and compassionate too. He treats all men as his equals. He even cares for the civilians in enemy country: look how happily they go about their lives.* Devan could not help comparing Arulmozli with his elder brother. Karikalan's victorious armies always plundered conquered territory, leaving behind a wake of sorrow and cruelty.

They stopped at a huge Buddha statue on the outskirts of Anuradhapura and the prince examined it. "Only the figures of Lord Nataraja and Lord Buddha completely capture the beauty of sculpture. The Lankan kings were large-hearted and devout men: see what huge statues, stupas and monasteries they have built in honor of Buddha. I'm ashamed of our tiny Shiva temples." Arulmozli walked to the statue.

He examined Buddha's feet and the lotus buds scattered on them. He touched the feet reverentially and climbed on his horse again. They rode on.

"What's this?" Devan asked Azlvarkkadian. "Does the prince plan to become a Buddhist?"

Hearing this, Arulmozli said, "There's a reason behind my devotion. There was a secret message for me at Buddha's feet: I must be at the Simhadhara Lake in Anuradhapura at midnight."

Anuradhapura

THE MEN REACHED Anuradhapura at sunset. Vandhiya Devan was dazzled by the city's beauty and magnificence, far greater than that of any city in Tamil Nadu. Excited people and monks crowded the city gates; it was clear that a festival was to be celebrated. Some men pointed to the riders and whispered among themselves.

Arulmozli led the way to a grove of trees a little away from the gates. "The horses are tired. We'll rest and enter the city after dark."

The three men later entered the city along with a group of pilgrims.

Devan saw soldiers renovating monasteries. *Why should the prince rebuild Lankan cities and encourage their festivals? Ahah! He knows there's no chance of him ascending the Tiger Throne —his brother is the crown prince and his uncle, Madurandaka, is another contender. Maybe he plans to found an independent kingdom in Sri Lanka and rule here.*

They dismounted at the gates of a ruined mansion in a deserted side street. There was no sign of life inside. The prince clapped thrice and a door opened at the side of the building.

"The horses know the way," Arulmozli said and pulled Devan into the darkness. After a while, a faint glow appeared which grew into a bright light—they were in the hall of an ancient palace.

"They say Mahasena's ghost haunts this palace," Arulmozli smiled. "He may chase us out."

"Who's Mahasena?" Devan asked.

"King Mahasena ruled Lanka about six hundred years ago. He was very compassionate and the people believe his spirit still wanders the city. They hang clothes on branches for his spirit so that it does not feel cold. And his palace has remained empty since his death."

Attendants waited on the three men. Once they had bathed and dined, they went up to the palace terrace where they remained out of sight but had a clear view of the city.

"Why did the kings build such huge stupas?" Devan wondered.

"The first kings built huge stupas to show the people Buddha's greatness," the prince replied. "Later kings built even bigger stupas to show their own greatness."

A roar rose from below and an endless procession came down the street. A sea of people surged around huge elephants, ornamented in gold plate. Some elephants carried gem-studded gold chests, covered with silk canopies. Musicians and dancers followed the elephants. The dancers wore costumes depicting the legends of Shiva, Vishnu, Muruga and Kannagi.

"This is Sri Lanka's largest festival–the Perahera," Arulmozli said. "The gold chest on the first elephant carries Buddha's tooth. The other chests contain jewels belonging to Hindu gods. The Sri Lankan kings have visited our country and enjoyed good relations with our kings. They have incorporated our festivals into their own."

The procession wended it way through the street and the music and cheers faded away.

"Come," Arulmozli said. "It's time for our appointment."

They walked through deserted streets and came to the bank of a large lake. The water rippled in silver waves under the moonlight and the fragrance of flowers filled the air. They stopped at a small pool formed by water gushing from the mouth of a stone lion carved into the bank.

Devan thought back to the Buddha statue: the twelve lotus buds had signified midnight; a small, water-filled vessel in the shape of a lion's face had indicated this spot. *Who asked the prince to come here? Why are we unarmed? Is romance in the air?* He was transported across the sea to the garden in Pazlayarai with Kundavai and Vanathi. "This looks like a palace garden," he said, hoping to get some information from the prince.

Arulmozli said, "This was Dushtakamanu's palace garden. It has an interesting story. Prince Sali, Dushtakamanu's son, saw a beautiful girl watering the flowers in this garden one day. Her name was Asokamala. The prince fell in love with her. As she was from a low caste, Dushtakamanu forbade Sali from marrying her and threatened to disinherit him. Sali declared, 'I give up the throne—I choose Asokamala.' Would any other prince in the world do such a thing?"

Devan thought, *Is the prince telling us this story with Poonkuzlali in mind?* As he wondered how to bring Poonkuzlali into the conversation, they came to a stone bench in a niche in the wall behind the pool. Devan froze in amazement … a light glowed in one corner of this niche … a hand emerged holding a lamp … finally, a monk's face appeared.

The Lankan Throne

THE MONK SIZED up the three men and addressed Arulmozli: "Welcome Devapriya, beloved of the gods. The Maha Thero waits for you. Who are these men? Can they be trusted?"

"I trust them as I trust my own two hands. But if you wish, I'll leave them here."

"Let them come," the monk said. "The place we are going to is safe, but the way is long and who knows what dangers lurk in the corners."

Vandhiya Devan was deeply touched by the prince's trust. *Something very important is going to happen. What can it be?*

The monk worked a lever in a corner of the niche. A dark passage opened; he picked up a flaming torch and led the way. The door closed behind them and the sound of water faded. The underground passage twisted and turned endlessly. Their footsteps echoed eerily in the silence.

Is this a trap? Devan feared.

The passage widened and they entered a large hall. The flickering torchlight showed pillars of gleaming marble. Buddha statues in all sizes and postures stood everywhere. The way narrowed again. They crossed other halls with copper and gold-plated pillars. Every hall was filled with Buddha statues. Arulmozli looked straight ahead, without glancing at these marvels.

Finally, they came to a hall of plain black granite. Several monks were gathered there, their faces glowing with an inner light. The Maha Thero was seated on a raised dais in the center. Before him stood a gem-studded golden throne on which lay a golden crown, a scepter and a sword. Everything gleamed in the light of the oil lamps burning on all sides.

The monks rose and chorused: "Long live Buddha! Long live Dharma! Long live the Sangha!"

Arulmozli went to the Maha Thero and folded his hands in respect. The guru pointed to a chair beside the throne and the prince sat there.

The Maha Thero spoke in Pali which their guide translated into Tamil: "Prince who is beloved of the gods, the Maha Bodhi Sangha is happy to welcome you. We are indebted to Bharath for giving us Buddhist Dharma. But your past kings waged war on Lanka and destroyed our monasteries. Even our own kings sowed division and hatred among us. Anuradhapura's monasteries lay in ruins and you have renovated them. The Perahera festival had not been celebrated for more than a century and you made it happen this year. The Sangha appreciates your nobility."

Arulmozli bowed in acknowledgement. "Please let me know if there's anything else I can do."

The Maha Thero smiled. "There's a lot more we expect from you. But first, I have something to say: Emperor Sibi was one of Lord Buddha's avatars. The epitome of compassion, he sacrificed his own flesh to save a dove from a predator. The Cholas claim to descend from Emperor Sibi. The Sangha dismissed this claim. But after seeing you today, we support the Chola claim. Look ..."

A monk was carried before them, every part of his body in a state of convulsion.

"The gods speak through this monk," the Maha Thero said. "Listen ..."

The possessed monk broke into a flood of quavering words. When he stopped, the Maha Thero said, "The gods ask you to spread Buddhism throughout the world, starting your work in Anuradhapura. They will give you the glory of Emperor Ashoka. What do you say, prince?" The Maha Thero pointed to the throne. "Every Lankan king has sought the blessing of the Sangha before beginning his rule. Every king, from Dushtakamanu to Mahasena, sat on that throne, wore that crown and carried that scepter. Are you willing to accept this honor?"

The excited Devan was ready to carry the prince and seat him on the throne at once.

But Arulmozli remained calm. "Guru, King Mahinda, to whom this throne belongs, is still alive."

The Maha Thero replied: "Lanka's ruling dynasty, to which Mahinda belongs, has earned the gods' anger for ignoring Buddhist Dharma. The gods decree there be change. Mahinda has no heirs. In such circumstances, the Sangha has the right to choose the new king. We choose you to be the king of Sri Lanka. If you agree, the coronation will be held tonight."

There was silence. Devan's excitement rose to fever pitch. *I'll crown him with my own hands!*

Arulmozli, as calm as ever, rose. "Great saints, I bow to you for your love and trust. But I can't accept your offer. The soil and rivers of the Chola country nurtured me. I'm here at the command of my father, Emperor Sundara Chola. I can't do anything without his agreement …"

"Are you aware your father is a prisoner in all but name?" the Maha Thero asked.

"Yes, he's bedridden. But I'm bound to obey the orders of those who rule the Chola empire under his authority," the prince declared resolutely.

"We can send a delegation to receive your father's blessing," the Maha Thero suggested.

Arulmozli replied, "My conscience is dearer to me than life. Please forgive and bless this unworthy man. I cannot accept your offer."

A deep silence reigned.

"I expected this," the Maha Thero said. "Your decision does you honor. We will not force you. We will summon you again at the end of a year, you may give us your final decision then." He continued seriously. "This sacred monastery has escaped destruction for centuries because it is carved in the bedrock of this ancient city. The path is known only to the abbots assembled here. Even the kings of Sri Lanka come here only once to be crowned. You and your companions must keep your visit secret. If you violate this code, the curse of the gods will be upon you."

"Guru," the prince assured him, "I'll never break my oath of silence."

In half an hour, Arulmozli and his two companions were back on the streets of Anuradhapura.

Devan could not control himself. "What foolishness! The Chola kingdom is nothing compared to Lanka. Why did you turn down the throne?" He added mischievously, "And there I was, standing among the pillars—those foolish monks could have made me the offer."

Arulmozli smiled. "Prince Sali sacrificed the throne for the woman he loved; I have two women standing between me and the throne— Sathya and Dharma. Truth and Virtue made me refuse."

As they walked past an old building on the street corner, they heard someone clap from across the street and saw a figure standing there.

"Follow me," Arulmozli said and crossed the street.

They were halfway across when they heard a huge bang: the building they had just been walking past had collapsed! They had escaped death by seconds.

As Devan followed his companions, the moon lit the mysterious figure standing before them. Devan could not believe his eyes. He stood rooted to the spot. *What madness! How can Nandini, whom I saw in Thanjavur, be on the streets of Anuradhapura?*

The next instant, the figure vanished.

Who's That Woman?

VANDHIYA DEVAN RAN after the woman but Arulmozli stopped him.

"Sir," Devan asked. "Who's that woman?"

"She must be the guardian deity of the Cholas," Azlvarkkadian said. "If we had not moved from there, we would all be dead!"

They looked at the mountain of rubble across the street.

"Prince," Devan asked again. "Who's that woman?"

"Who did you think she was?" Arulmozli countered. "Why did you try to follow her?"

"She reminded me of Lady Nandini, Lord Ambalavan's new wife," Devan replied.

"You're mad!" Azlvarkkadian exclaimed. "How can she be here?"

"He's not mad," the prince said. "I have seen the resemblance myself."

Cautious now, they walked down the middle of the street.

"Sir, what did she tell you?" Devan asked curiously.

"She warned me that two enemies are here looking for the opportunity to kill me."

Azlvarkkadian said, "Sir, I saw two men in the ruins — they were the men with Parthibendran ..."

"Why didn't you say this earlier?" Devan scolded Azlvarkkadian. "I'll go back and check."

Arulmozli stopped him. "Leave it for now. I left my bodyguards behind because you are with me. If you go, who will guard me?"

Deeply moved by these words, Devan vowed, "I won't leave your side even for a second, sir."

Azlvarkkadian smiled. "You guard the prince ... I'll guard you."

They reached the Mahasena Palace and retired to a large hall with three antique beds. As they prepared to sleep, Devan made the prince laugh with his witty comments. He ended with, "Sir, if you didn't want the throne, why didn't you tell them to give it to me?"

Arulmozli laughed again. "My friend, religion and politics don't mix. The monks belong to one Buddhist sect. There are other sects we would have antagonized if we had accepted their offer."

"Does the prince of Vallam now understand Lankan politics?" Azlvarkkadian mocked.

"Yes," Devan retorted. "Like the fools in Tamil Nadu who fight over Shiva and Vishnu, this country has its own share of fools!"

"Now, now," said the prince. "It's late. Let's sleep."

"I can't sleep until I know about the woman who clapped and saved our lives," Devan declared.

"Very well," said Arulmozli. "Come and sit beside me. I'll tell you what I know."

The River Goddess

ARULMOZLI NARRATED A strange story.

"When I was a child, I fell overboard while we were sailing down the Ponni. I remember being carried away by the current. A woman scooped me into her arms and brought me to the surface. She handed me over to someone and disappeared. Everyone decided it was the river goddess who had saved me. Her face remained etched in my memory. Longing to see that face again, I searched the riverbank and the crowds at every festival. The years went by... I gave up.

"A year ago, I came to Sri Lanka. General Velir gave me a battalion of thousand handpicked soldiers and I set out to visit all the areas under our control. One day, we camped in a forest near Anuradhapura. That night, we heard a wail of grief. Whether it was animal or human, it made one's hair stand on end. When I mocked the men for their cowardice, they tracked the sound. They saw a woman run away into the forest; the wails continued.

"The next night, I searched for the woman. When she saw I was alone, she waited. The moonlight fell on her tear-streaked face. It was the goddess who had saved my life in the river!

"'Who are you, mother?' I asked. 'What do you want? Why are you weeping?'

"I could not understand her strange sounds. To my sorrow, I realized she was dumb. She hugged me, kissed me tenderly on my forehead and ran away. I did not try to follow her. I told my men she was a poor woman who had lost her mind due to some great suffering. I gave them strict instructions not to disturb her in any way.

"The next night, I again went to see her. She was expecting me. She led me to a hut. An old man lay inside, delirious with high fever. His eyes were bloodshot and his teeth chattered. This time, I understood her sign language. She warned me to move camp at once, or my men would catch the epidemic which was in the air. I moved camp that very night."

The Drawings Speak

ARULMOZLI STOPPED ABRUPTLY. "Did you hear footsteps?"

"I smell smoke ..." Vandhiya Devan said.

"The room seems hotter ..." Azlvarkkadian added. "Are we safe, sir?"

"Don't worry," Arulmozli said. "Goddess Ponni will warn us if we're in danger."

The prince continued his story. "Although we struck camp that very night, ten of my men caught the fever and suffered badly. If we had not moved, my entire battalion would have been affected. Goddess Durga came in that woman's form and saved us.

"From that day, she has been my guardian angel. She has saved me from wild animals and hidden enemies. She appears from nowhere, speaks to me and vanishes. I have learnt to communicate with her in sign language. I can sense her presence. Even now ..." Arulmozli broke off. "Quick! Lie on your beds and pretend to sleep ..."

Azlvarkkadian and Devan obeyed at once. But their curiosity kept their eyes open. A figure appeared at the moonlit window: it was the woman who had saved them earlier in the day. She gave a soft hiss and Arulmozli went to the window. They spoke in sign language.

The prince and his companions left the palace and silently followed the old woman down a dark path between trees. After a long walk, they came to a moonlit clearing with a huge stupa, supported by hundreds of stone elephants so realistic, Devan was startled. The woman went to an elephant with a broken tusk. She moved a granite slab at its foot: a stairway led underground. They followed her down the steps and into a narrow passage which led to a hall.

Azlvarkkadian and Devan waited by the steps as she took a lighted lamp and showed Arulmozli the beautiful line drawings on the walls. Arulmozli realized that these images depicted her life.

A young woman stands on a beach as her father fishes in the sea; she sees a young prince hiding in a tree; she saves him from a bear; the prince kills the bear; her father explains that she is a deaf-mute; the prince and the woman fall in love and live happily on the island; one day, soldiers arrive on a ship searching for the prince; the prince comforts the woman and leaves with them; moved by her tears, her father rows her across the sea to a lighthouse; a family welcomes them; they travel together to a city with a fort; wearing a crown, the prince stands on a terrace with richly dressed people; filled with sorrow, the girl runs away; she jumps into the sea from the top of the lighthouse; a passing boatman rescues her and leaves her at a temple; thinking she is possessed, the priest tries to exorcise the spirits; the pregnant queen visits the temple and sees the girl; when the queen knows that the girl is also expecting a child, she takes her to the palace; the girl gives birth to twins; thinking about their bleak future, she leaves them with the queen and goes to live in the forest. Sometimes longing to see her children, she hides behind trees on the riverbank and watches the royal family; one day, a child falls into the river and she rescues him.

"I'm that child, you're the rescuer," Arulmozli said in sign language.

The old woman hugged him and kissed his forehead. She then took him to another corner where the images depicted the dangers which surrounded him.

Devan thoughts were in a whirl, seeing the resemblance between the old woman and Nandini. When they climbed the steps again, the old woman vanished. In the distance, they saw a huge fire.

"The Mahasena Palace is burning!" Arulmozli exclaimed. "If we had stayed there, we would have died in the fire. The drawings warned me about this."

"What else did they say, sir?" Devan asked.

"They revealed many secrets about my family and told me to leave Sri Lanka at once."

"Long live art!" exclaimed Devan. "Vaishnava, my side has won."

Arulmozli suggested that they catch some sleep on the top of the stupa and leave at dawn. Devan had nightmares which featured deaf-mutes, fires, bears, monks and crowns of gold.

The next morning, the three men walked to the centuries-old fig tree in the Mahamegha Gardens. The prince joined the monks and pilgrims circumambulating the tree saying, "Emperors and empires come and go, but the righteousness symbolized by this Bodhi tree lives forever."

Arulmozli spoke to some men standing unobtrusively in a corner, with swords and horses. "My men feared we had perished in the fire last night. They are happy to see us," he said.

The three men mounted the horses, mixed with the festival crowd and left the city. After about ten miles, they saw horses galloping towards them. The riders were armed with spears.

"Sir, unsheathe your sword," Devan cried in warning.

The Swordfight

ARULMOZLI JUMPED DOWN from his horse, unsheathed his sword and challenged Vandhiya Devan: "Enough of your arrogance! Let me teach you a lesson!"

The shocked Devan also dismounted. *Is this a game or is the prince serious?* But once the prince advanced on him, whirling his wicked broadsword with both hands, Devan's doubts vanished and his mind steadied. He forgot that his opponent was a great prince; he forgot what the duel was about—all he saw was the sword in his adversary's hands. He threw himself into the fight. Their broadswords whirled and clashed at lightning speed.

Azlvarkkadian, confident that the prince had some motive for his actions, led the horses to the side and watched the approaching battalion. To his relief, he saw the Tiger Flag fluttering above it. Two men rode in the center, mounted on Arab steeds; an elephant followed them.

A herald cried, "Make way for General Velir! Make way for Parthibendran Pallava!"

The cavalry stopped before the duelists. "Move!" the soldiers shouted. Then, a buzz of recognition went through the ranks. The men jumped down from their horses and formed an excited circle around the fighters.

Parthibendran raised his sword. "Didn't I tell you Vandhiya Devan is an impudent rascal? Fighting with the prince himself! I won't let him get away with this."

Velir stopped him. "Wait, it's years since I saw such an engrossing swordfight."

By now, the marching infantry had also joined the spectators.

A woman climbed down from the elephant's saddle. She went to the front of the circle and stood absorbed in the duel, intense emotions flitting across her face: it was Poonkuzlali. At first, Arulmozli faced the girl. As the duelists' position changed, Devan faced her. Recognition flashed in his eyes and in that one instant of distraction, the prince knocked Devan's sword from his hand. Poonkuzlali's excited laughter rang above the spectators' wild cheers.

As Devan lunged to retrieve his sword, Arulmozli hugged him. "You fought like my equal! You did not lose to my sword but to a woman's eyes. That happens to the best of us."

Velir walked up. "Prince, I sent this young man to you. I hope he has not been a nuisance."

"Yes, general. He pestered me to give him a taste of the Lankan war and I obliged him."

Velir patted Devan on the shoulders. "It was a beautiful swordfight! You are a worthy companion to the prince. Every now and then, he gets the itch to fight."

Arulmozli went up to Parthibendran. "I hear you have an important message for me."

Velir said, "We can't talk in the middle of the road. Let's go to that ruined building."

A Council

AS THEY CROSSED the road, Vandhiya Devan asked Azlvarkkadian, "Why did the prince do that?"

Azlvarkkadian replied, "It was a trick to find out who the newcomers were: whoever it was, they would stop to watch the swordfight."

"Thirumalai is right," Arulmozli smiled. "And I always fight with my friends to ward off the jealousy others feel towards them."

"That's okay with me, sir," Devan replied. "Next time, I'll start the fight. Do you know the woman who came on the elephant?"

"No," said Arulmozli. "I'm not in the habit of examining women's faces."

"In all the excitement of collapsing roofs and fighting duels, I forgot her message for you. Do you remember the name, Poonkuzlali ... or Ocean Princess?"

"No," Arulmozli said.

"Her heart will break if you have forgotten her. I could not have reached you without her help. You were waiting at Kodikkarai to board your ship for Lanka. To your surprise, a woman singlehandedly rowed a boat to the shore. 'Who's she?' you asked the lighthouse keeper. 'My daughter,' he replied. You said, 'Your daughter? I thought she was an Ocean Princess.'"

"Ah!" said the prince. "I vaguely remember something now. But what is she doing here?"

Devan saw Poonkuzlali's eyes continuously dart to the prince's face. They entered the roofless building, shaded by trees. While the battalion waited on the perimeter, Velir and Parthibendran sat on a platform with the prince and Poonkuzlali stood behind a nearby pillar.

"I'm eager to hear what my brother and grandfather have to say," the prince said.

Parthibendran said, "Sir, the Chola empire is in great danger. The Pazluvur brothers conspire with important chieftains to deprive your brother of the crown. They plan to make that hypocrite, Madurandaka, emperor. But the army is under our control. With our loyal chieftains, we can nip this conspiracy in the bud. Your grandfather wants you to be with your brother at this time. I'll also tell you what's in your brother's heart: he dreams of conquering foreign lands and planting the Tiger Flag on their soil. When you come to Kanchipuram, he'll attack Thanjavur, destroy the conspirators and crown you king ..."

"Stop!" exclaimed Arulmozli. "I have nothing to do with the Chola throne."

"That's between you and your brother," Parthibendran said. "Once we have killed the Pazluvur brothers and Sambuvaraya, and dispatched Madurandaka to the gods, you can decide."

"Sir, these are matters to be decided by my father, the emperor," Arulmozli said firmly. "Has my brother received a message from him?"

"Sir, I'll be frank: your father is the Pazluvur brothers' prisoner. No one can communicate with him without their permission. If you wish to save his life, come at once."

The prince's distress was evident. He turned to Velir. "General, what do you advise? Aniruddha Brahmaraya, my father's close friend, advises me to remain here; my brother summons me to Kanchipuram; my sister, Kundavai, asks me to hurry to Pazlayarai ..."

Velir said, "Prince, until this morning, I advised you to listen to the chief minister. But this girl brings news which changes everything— you must go to Kanchipuram."

The general signaled to Poonkuzlali who came forward slowly. She looked at every man there except the prince.

"Quick!" Velir said. "Tell us the news."

Poonkuzlali was speechless.

"Ahah!" said Arulmozli. "It looks like the whole world has been struck dumb."

At these words, Poonkuzlali looked up at the prince's face for one split second. Then, her eyes filled with tears and she ran away, vanishing into a dense grove of trees in the distance.

The men were astonished.

Devan spoke up. "Sir, I'm used to her behavior. Let me go and talk to her."

"You do that," Arulmozli agreed. "Meanwhile, general, tell me what the girl said."

Velir said, "The Pazluvur brothers have sent two large ships with soldiers to arrest you and take you back. These ships are anchored in a hidden bend of the Thondaman Channel."

Look!

AT THESE WORDS, Parthibendran jumped up in fury. "How dare the Pazluvur brothers do this? What are you waiting for, general? Let's march at once: we'll kill the men sent to arrest the prince and bury them here in Sri Lankan soil!"

Velir was calm. "Patience, Parthibendran. There's no point in being rash. Think."

"What is there to think?" Parthibendran raged. "We must exterminate the entire Pazluvur clan!"

The prince turned calmly to Velir. "Sir, what do you think?"

Velir asked, "If the arrest order is authorized by the emperor, should we resist?"

Parthibendran laughed. "What a joke! The emperor is a prisoner of the Pazluvur brothers."

Devan spoke up. "True, I saw that the emperor is a prisoner in all but name. No one can meet him without the Pazluvur brothers' permission."

"Let's hear the news first-hand from the girl." The prince turned to Devan. "She seems a little unbalanced: handle her carefully and bring her here."

"Yes, sir," Devan said. "But, as long as I live, the Pazluvur brothers will not lay a finger on you!" He left the hall.

Velir said, "Prince, you must avoid the men sent by the Pazluvur brothers. Go to Kanchipuram at once. I'll meet the emperor in Thanjavur and learn the truth."

"General," Parthibendran cried out. "You'll be putting your head in the lion's mouth—you'll end up in the infamous underground dungeon. You'll never see the emperor."

"Who can stop me?!" Velir roared. "And Aniruddha is there …"

"The chief minister himself can't meet the emperor," Parthibendran retorted. He turned to Azlvarkkadian. "His disciple is here—ask him."

"Speak your mind, Thirumalai," the prince urged.

"We should lock up the prince in the most secure prison in Sri Lanka," Azlvarkkadian declared. "Ask the prince how many attempts have been made on his life …"

"Then the prince must come with me to Kanchipuram," Parthibendran cried.

"Never: we might as well give the prince to the Pazluvur brothers' men," Azlvarkkadian said.

"Vaishnava, what did you say?" Parthibendran unsheathed his sword.

Velir calmed him. "Thirumalai, explain yourself: you know Parthibendran is a good friend to the Cholas."

"Who were the two men who went with him to Dambulla two days ago?" Azlvarkkadian asked.

Parthibendran was shaken. "I met them in Trincomalee and they offered to guide me to the prince. They disappeared when we reached Anuradhapura ..."

"Those two men are part of a group which has sworn to destroy the Chola dynasty. I suspect they were behind the two attempts made on the prince's life yesterday. Look!" he shouted, pointing to where Devan stood talking with Poonkuzlali.

They saw Devan throw a dagger into a thicket ... a shriek of pain came from the bushes.

Poonkuzlali's Dagger

VANDHIYA DEVAN FOUND Poonkuzlali sobbing against a tree. "Why are you angry?" he asked gently.

"I hate all men, especially the prince. He has forgotten me—he didn't even look me in the face."

"He remembers you. When I mentioned you, he asked, 'How is the Ocean Princess?'"

"Why did he ignore me then?"

"He's going through a bad period. The astrologers predict danger for him. He does not want his friends to suffer: you saw how he tried to drive me away by picking a fight with me."

"Then why do you stay with him?"

"For some reason, I loved him from the minute I saw him."

"Me too," Poonkuzlali blurted and then bit her lips in regret at confessing her feelings.

"I know you're fond of the prince. Come tell him your news, or I'll have to drag you to him."

Poonkuzlali pulled out a dagger. "If you come near me, I'll kill you!"

"Very well," said Devan and turned as if to go. He lunged back, grabbed the dagger from her and flung it into the bushes. Devan and Poonkuzlali looked at each other in amazement as a shriek of agony came from the thicket. They stealthily followed the direction of the sound. They parted the bushes and found tracks of fresh blood. There was no sign of beast or man ... there was no sign of Poonkuzlali's dagger too!

"Now, do you believe me?" Devan asked. "I happened to throw your dagger into the bush only to hit someone lurking there to kill the prince. He's surrounded by danger. Do you remember the two suspicious men your brother rowed to Lanka? Mustn't we stand by the prince at this time?"

"What if he tells me to go away?"

"We'll stand by him even if he drives us away," Devan declared firmly.

Poonkuzlali was lost in thought. "Shouldn't we track the man who hid here?"

"No. It's impossible to find him in this dense forest. And the prince won't wait for us. Come." They walked back to the hall. To questions about the dagger and the scream, Devan said, "I thought I saw some wild animal moving in the thicket and threw the dagger ... but we found nothing there."

"Let that be," Velir said. "Let's hear what the girl has to say."

Poonkuzlali stared at Arulmozli, who now met her gaze. *What foolishness! When I have courageously faced raging waves and savage leopards, why does my heart beat so fast and falter? I won't let him think I'm mad. I'll meet his eyes and speak confidently. The world praises his compassion—why would he harm a simple girl like me?*

"Ocean Princess, do you remember me?" Arulmozli asked.

I Am Guilty

WHAT KIND OF a question is that, Ponni's Beloved? We have lived together for eons. We travelled in my little boat on the boundless ocean; we held hands and faced storms; you adorned my hair with stars plucked from the sky ... and you ask if I remember you? Aloud Poonkuzlali said, "Yes."

"Ah!" Arulmozli exclaimed. "How sweet your voice is! Will you tell me about the two ships hiding in the Thondaman river?"

"Yes, sir. I saw them with my own eyes."

"As you told the general, you rowed away from there and hid in the forest, waiting for them to leave. Two soldiers happened to come near and you overheard their conversation. When they left, you hurried to find the general. Will you now tell us what those soldiers said?"

"They said they were here to arrest you on the emperor's orders," she said.

"Did they give a reason for this?" Arulmozli asked her gently.

"Yes; they said you had conspired with the Buddhist monks to make yourself king of Sri Lanka. They said the general should not be told for he would try his best to save you …"

"And that's why you came to the general," the prince concluded for her. "Thank you for your great service, Ocean Princess."

Poonkuzlali moved back and stood with her eyes devouring the prince's handsome face.

Arulmozli turned to Velir. "Your clan has always stood by the Cholas. You are my father's best friend and you love me like a son: I beg you, don't stop me from doing my duty." Before the commander could reply, the prince turned to Parthibendran. "You are my brother's best friend. I beg you too … let me do my duty."

"Prince," Velir said. "I have spent my life on the battlefield. I don't understand political nuances. Tell me clearly what you mean by your duty."

"My only duty is to obey my father," the prince declared. "I'll surrender to his men."

"Over my dead body!" Parthibendran cried.

Velir was calm. "Sir, when you left for Sri Lanka last year, your father ordered me to protect you at all costs. He said, 'Arulmozli is dearer to me than life itself. I'll die if anything happens to him.' How could he order your arrest now?"

"Sir, I am guilty of wanting to be king of Sri Lanka. My sister, Kundavai, always told me, 'You were born to rule. There's no place for you here; go and win the Sri Lankan throne.'"

"General," Devan intervened. "Thirumalai and I bear witness that the prince turned down the Buddhist Sangha's offer of the Lankan throne."

Arulmozli laughed. "My friend, this is the message Thirumalai brought from Aniruddha: 'The Buddhist Sangha will offer you the Lankan throne; turn down their offer before two witnesses.'"

Velir said, "Prince, your father himself has told me that he longs to see you crowned king of Sri Lanka."

"In that case, why should I hesitate to obey my father's orders and go back to Thanjavur? I'll tell him what happened, with these two men as my witnesses. He can then decide what to do next."

Parthibendran stood up angrily. "General, will you tell the prince the truth—or shall I?"

Velir lowered his voice. "Sir, I must bring up an unpleasant subject. Ambalavan's young wife, Nandini, is a witch, expert in black magic. The old man is her slave …"

"This is common knowledge, general," the prince remarked.

"Pardon me for saying this: she has now bewitched your father. The arrest warrant is her work."

"I warn you, general: don't insult my father. As long as he lives, his wish is my command."

Velir said, "Sir, I fear for your father's life. Parthibendran told me some secrets. After we defeated the Pandian army near Madurai, their king, Veerapandian, went into hiding. Crown Prince Karikalan, Parthibendran and I swore to hunt him down. We tracked him to a hut near a temple on an island. Karikalan went into the hut while we stood guard outside. He came out with Veerapandian's severed head and we celebrated the king's death and returned to camp.

"We now know a woman was in the hut. She begged your brother to spare her lover's life but Karikalan pushed her aside and killed Veerapandian. The woman who tried to save Veerapandian was Nandini—the same Nandini who is now married to the seventy-year-old Ambalavan.

"It's clear that she married the old man only to avenge Veerapandian's death. Vandhiya Devan will attest that no man can escape her web of seduction. Thirumalai witnessed the meeting of Pandian conspirators who have sworn to destroy the Cholas: Nandini finances them. Your father seems to have fallen into her web. I hear he wants to make Madurandaka emperor. At this time, you must not take the arrest warrant as coming from your father. Do not go to Thanjavur."

Arulmozli declared majestically: "General, what do I care about my life or the Lankan throne when my father is in danger? I have made up my mind. Please don't stand in my way." He turned to Poonkuzlali. "Ocean Princess, will you help me?"

I long to serve him, she thought and said, "Sir, I wait for your command."

"Take me in your boat to the ships waiting on the Thondaman river," Arulmozli said.

"Tell him you can't," roared the general.

Poonkuzlali's head said, *I won't let him walk into danger.* Her heart said, *Here's your chance to spend two days with him. The wind which touches him will caress you; his voice will fall on your ears. Your foolish dreams will partly come true—who cares what happens after that?*

"Why do you hesitate?" Arulmozli asked. "Shall I find my own way there?"

Poonkuzlali made up her mind. "Sir, I'll be your guide."

Velir cleared his throat loudly. "Very well. But it's my duty to protect you until I hand you over to the men who have come to arrest you."

The prince smiled. "So be it, commander. I won't stand in the way of you doing your duty."

The Elephant Runs

VELIR CONFERRED WITH Parthibendran and then gave some of his men confidential orders.

Parthibendran said, "Prince, I won't be a part of this foolishness. My ship is in Trincomalee. Your brother will be furious that I failed, but these men will bear witness that I did my best." He turned to Vandhiya Devan. "Aren't you coming with me to Kanchipuram?"

Devan hesitated. "No, I'll stay with the prince."

"You'll regret this," Parthibendran said and took his leave, escorted by a few soldiers.

"What does he mean?" Devan asked Azlvarkkadian.

Azlvarkkadian said, "Velir and Parthibendran are plotting something. The Kodumbalur old man is the root cause of this mess. He wants the prince to become the king of Sri Lanka and marry his niece, Vanathi. He arranged for the monks to offer the prince the crown and did not even know how to keep it a secret. The chief minister came to know about it and sent me to the prince with his advice. We must stay alive to testify that the prince turned down the throne."

Velir's men left, leaving only four soldiers as escort. Arulmozli and his companions rode along the highway, followed by Poonkuzlali on the elephant. Somehow, news of the prince's route spread. Crowds stopped them and cheered them on. The horses slowed to a walk. Arulmozli insisted they leave the highway and cut through the jungle. Again, the going was slow because of the thick undergrowth. They came to a large lake and were surprised to find a crowd welcoming them with music and shouts of, "Long live Arulmozli, King of Lanka!"

The prince smiled and asked their leader, "Why do you call me King of Lanka?"

"Prince," the man said respectfully. "Our land has not had stable rule for generations. All the people of Lanka–the Tamils, the Sinhalese and the monks, want you to be their king."

They insisted that Arulmozli join them in a feast. Devan saw the prince frown and sparks fly from his eyes. He was deep in thought.

Azlvarkkadian told Devan, "The prince is unhappy with the general's delaying tactics ..."

Poonkuzlali sat apart from the others, lost in a world of her own. Her dreams of having the prince to herself were dead; he was always surrounded by people. Her mind was in a whirl. *Shall I run away? How long must I bear the pain in my heart? Why can't I die?* She saw her dagger lying on the ground near her and picked it up. *How did my dagger come here? Did someone try to kill me? Or was the dagger meant for the prince? He's surrounded by enemies ... what if I'm lucky enough to block a knife meant for him? He'll take me in his arms ... he'll be drenched in my blood ...* She burst out laughing.

"Are you mad?" It was Devan. "Come, it's already late."

As they continued their journey, an arrow suddenly whizzed past the prince. Arulmozli's superb reflexes made him duck. To Azlvarkkadian's horror, the arrow pierced his turban. The shocked company halted. The general ordered his men to form a cordon around the prince.

Arulmozli took Velir aside. "I must reach Thanjavur alive and prove I'm innocent of the charges made against me. It will be safer if I ride as a mahout on the elephant."

The general hesitated. "The mahout can't ride a horse -"

"In that case, let him walk back," Arulmozli said.

Velir tried again: "The girl may not agree to ride with you ..."

"Then, let her walk," the prince was adamant.

Velir gave up. To Poonkuzlali's delight, the prince exchanged places with the mahout.

Arulmozli asked, "Ocean Princess, will you be afraid if the elephant runs?"

"Sir, when you are with me, I fear nothing."

"Where's your boat?"

"On the other side of Elephant Pass. I walked and swam across the pass at low tide."

"Can you row your boat with two people in it?"

"My hands have held the oars from the age of ten. They are not the petal-soft hands of your princesses. Ask Vandhiya Devan, I rowed him across to Lanka."

"Your boat must take us to the ships," Arulmozli said.

"Sir, why do you make me do this?" she asked sadly.

"My father may be on his deathbed. Can I let him die thinking I tried to usurp his throne? Help me do my duty. Tie yourself to the saddle with the ropes hanging by the sides." Arulmozli gently rubbed the elephant's forehead and whispered into its ears. The animal lifted its trunk, trumpeted and crashed through the forest. The ground shook underneath it.

Poonkuzlali hung on, pale with fright. She closed her eyes.

"The elephant is in musth!" screamed the general.

They reached Elephant Pass–a narrow strait connecting the northern and central parts of Lanka. The animal stepped into the water.

The Prison Ship

ONCE SHE GOT over her fear, Poonkuzlali was ecstatic: *The prince is by my side!*

Arulmozli stopped by a lake filled with lotuses and lilies. He sat on the shore and asked Poonkuzlali to sit beside him. Her flushed face was reflected in the clear water. Looking at her image in the lake, Arulmozli said, "Ocean Princess, I'm very fond of you. All my friends try to make me do what they want—you alone let me do what I want. I'll never forget your help. The general tried to delay me and Parthibendran is rushing from Trincomalee to Thondaman by ship … you helped me foil their plans."

Poonkuzlali was filled with remorse. "They are trying to save you, but I let your sweet words make me betray you." She stood up. "Let me go." Arulmozli held her hand. Helpless at his touch, she sat down again and burst into tears.

"If you cry, I'll go away. I have something to tell you."

She wiped her tears and waited.

"Everyone who loves me wants me to become emperor. But, to me, a palace is a prison and a throne is a sacrificial altar," Arulmozli said.

"But you're a prince," she pointed out.

"Luckily, my elder brother will be emperor; my uncle, Madurandaka, also wants the throne."

"You know that?" she asked in surprise.

"Of course!" He smiled. "I don't want the throne. I dream of sailing on the endless ocean to islands across the seas; I dream of blowing like a gale through forests and rivers; I dream of scaling mountains; I dream of marvels in strange lands …"

Poonkuzlali swallowed every word. "I want the same thing! Will you take me with you?"

"Who knows whether my dreams will ever come true?"

"Then why must you go to Thanjavur now?"

"There's a deaf-mute lady who wanders around Lanka like a mad woman. Do you know her?"

"I lost my mother as a child. That old woman is my aunt, Mandakini. She gave me a mother's love–she's my god."

"Where does she live?"

"She lives in a cave on Boodha Island, off the Lankan coast. I saw your image in the pictures she has drawn on the cave walls there. When I saw you in Kodikkarai, I was astonished."

"Ah!" Arulmozli exclaimed. "Many things are now clear to me. Poonkuzlali, that old woman is my stepmother. By right, she should be seated on the throne of Thanjavur."

"Oh my god!" Poonkuzlali cried.

"Fate interfered. I often suspected my father was tormented by some secret sorrow: I now know the truth. He thinks my stepmother is dead and that he caused her death. Once I tell him she's alive, he'll be at peace. He's also troubled by talk that the comet in the sky is a bad omen. I must hurry to Thanjavur before anything unfortunate happens. Will you help me?"

Poonkuzlali sighed. *Why does god mix grief with happiness?* "Sir, it's my privilege to help you in any way. But why don't you just explain matters to the general and go to Thanjavur?"

"I don't want to tell him my father's secret. There's another favor I need from you. The astrologers who predict I'll be emperor also predict my life will often be in danger. If I die, will you promise to meet my father and tell him the truth? Will you do this for me?"

With tears streaming down her face, Poonkuzlali said, "I will, my prince."

"Come, let's continue our journey." They climbed on the elephant. As they rushed on, Arulmozli said, "Ocean Princess, I have told you the things which are closest to my heart: now, tell me what you like."

"You may think I'm mad, but these are my favorite things: the buffalo-riding God of Death; spending all night on a rock watching fire-spitting demons; riding the waves in a storm ..."

"You're a strange girl, Poonkuzlali ... you don't know the meaning of fear."

They reached the Thondaman estuary.

Poonkuzlali exclaimed, "How can this be? The war ships have vanished! Like the general, you too will think I lured you here with lies."

"Nonsense! Why would you do that?"

"Maybe because I love you," she replied.

"The general may be suspicious, but you and I have no such foolish thoughts in our hearts."

"What about Lady Vanathi in Pazlayarai Palace?" she asked.

"The general and my sister want me to marry her. That poor girl, dreaming of being a queen, may also want it, but I'm not responsible for that. Come, let's go closer."

When they reached the shore, an extraordinary sight met their eyes: a war ship, its mast and sails shattered, lay wrecked in the thick mud. There was no sign of life on it.

The Arab Horse

ARULMOZLI AND POONKUZLALI went to the ship. No one answered their calls. They clambered on board. The ship's hull was broken and the hold was filled with water and sand.

Sad at heart, Arulmozli picked up the Tiger Flag which lay among the sails. "Is this one of the ships you saw, Poonkuzlali?"

"Yes, sir. I think the other has sunk to the bottom." She could not hide her joy.

"You must not rejoice, Ocean Princess; something's wrong. Where are the soldiers? Chola sailors are expert seamen: how could they run the ship aground? Let's look for survivors."

"It will be dark soon," she pointed out. "Where can we search?"

"Let's walk along the riverbank and look for the other ship while there's light," the prince said.

They walked along the bank but there was no sign of the other ship. They went back to the wreck.

"I'll wait here for the general. Goodbye, Poonkuzlali, I'll never forget your help. Go back safely to your boat." Poonkuzlali swayed and clutched at a branch for support. "What's the matter?"

"Sir, I'm exhausted. I have not slept for two days ... let me rest and then leave."

In the moonlight, the prince saw Poonkuzlali's sad, exhausted face and drooping eyelids. "And when did you last eat?"

"More than two days ago. As long as I'm with you, I feel no hunger."

"What a fool I am! We feasted today and I did not ask you if you had eaten. Come, we'll gather the grains scattered on the ship's deck and cook a meal. You can leave after that."

"I'll fall asleep if I eat."

"Good! You can sleep on the deck while the elephant and I stand guard on shore," he said.

They reached the wreck. To their surprise, smoke rose behind it, carrying the aroma of roasted yam. Arulmozli quietly went around the ship. Mandakini was there, kindling a fire. She seemed to be expecting them and served them a kichadi of millet and yam, which was more delicious than anything the prince had eaten at Pazlayarai palace.

"How did she get here so quickly?" Arulmozli wondered.

The old woman pointed: a thoroughbred horse stood near the elephant.

"Can she ride?" the prince was surprised.

"She rides horses and elephants and rows boats. I sometimes think she rides the air!"

"That's an Arab horse. Where did she get it from?" he asked.

Poonkuzlali spoke to Mandakini and said, "She found it wading to the shore near Elephant Pass. She calmed the animal and rode it here." Poonkuzlali wrapped herself in a sail and fell asleep on the deck. She sang softly in her sleep.

Arulmozli looked at Mandakini: *How many joys and sorrows are pent up in her heart.* The old woman sat beside him. She ran her fingers lovingly through his hair and softly stroked his cheeks. Arulmozli bent to touch her feet. She held his hands to her face and wet them with her tears. She signaled to him that she would stand guard while he slept.

The prince lay down to please her, his thoughts in turmoil. Caressed by the breeze, he drifted off to sleep. He dreamt of riding to heaven on an Arab horse. There, Indra, Lord of the Devas, offered him a gem-studded throne. The prince refused it saying, 'Give it to Mother Mandakini.' Indra gave him the divine *amrita*. Arulmozli sipped it and said, 'Our Ponni water is sweeter.' Indra then asked him to choose a wife among the celestial nymphs. The prince replied, 'Poonkuzlali is more beautiful than them all.' Suddenly, Kundavai stood there. 'Arulmozli, have you forgotten Vanathi?' The prince cried, '*Akka,* you make me a slave to your love: set me free.' Kundavai said, 'Yes, love is bondage and you must bow to it.' Arulmozli said, 'True love is not bondage: I'll show you … Poonkuzlali … Poonkuzlali …'

Poonkuzlali was woken by the sound of horse's hooves and saw Mandakini riding away from the wreck. She heard her name and turned to hear the prince calling her in his sleep. Overjoyed, she gently touched his forehead. "Sir, why did you call me?"

"If you can sing in your sleep, can't I talk in my sleep?" he teased. "Where's Mother Mandakini?"

"She rode away early in the morning," she replied.

"You can go now," Arulmozli said. "I'll inspect the ship and wait for my friends."

Poonkuzlali pointed excitedly to the sea: a big ship was in the distance and a small boat was coming ashore with four or five men in it. They hurried to the shore with the elephant lumbering behind them.

Arulmozli was worried. *I should be on that ship which is sailing away. And why is Vandhiya Devan not in the boat? I love him for his courage and loyalty …*

The boat reached the shore. Velir jumped out and embraced the prince. "How could you do this to us, sir? Look how docile the elephant is now! Did you see the ships?"

"I'll tell you my story later," the prince said. "Where's Vandhiya Devan?"

Velir said, "That insolent young man is on that ship. I'm totally confused." He pointed to Azlvarkkadian. "Only Thirumalai understands you and Vandhiya Devan."

Arulmozli said, "Thirumalai, tell me quickly, why is Vandhiya Devan on that ship?"

The Ghostly Voice

AS THE PRINCE and Poonkuzlali dashed away on the elephant, the others thought the animal was in musth and chased it. But the horses could not keep pace with the elephant. They halted at Elephant Pass.

Devan, in the lead as always, galloped into the water. His horse got stuck in the mud and was pulled out with great difficulty. It was useless after that.

Velir slapped his head in frustration. "What do we do? How can we save the prince?"

Azlvarkkadian spoke up: "General, the prince knew you were delaying him. So, he rushed away on the elephant. The animal is not in musth."

Velir was relieved. "Then let's hurry to the Thondaman estuary."

Azlvarkkadian said, "We must find a boat to take us there or wait for Parthibendran's ship."

"Thirumalai," the general said. "You are a scoundrel: did you tell the prince anything?"

"I didn't have a chance to talk to the prince on this journey," Azlvarkkadian protested.

After much searching, they found a fisherman who rowed them across the pass. They decided to go in the same boat to the estuary where ships anchored. The fisherman refused to row any further in the darkness. "The path twists and turns and there are submerged rocks. My boat will shatter if it hits a rock."

The exhausted men slept in a grove near the shore.

Devan was furious with the way things were going. "You're the cause of all this!" he shouted at Azlvarkkadian. "You're always hiding things. If you had told me what the prince was up to, I would have climbed on the elephant with him. What will I tell the princess now?"

"Your duty was done once you delivered the letter," Azlvarkkadian pointed out.

"My duty will be done only when I take the prince before Princess Kundavai," Devan declared. "And you are the biggest obstacle in my way."

"Don't worry," Azlvarkkadian said. "I plan to leave tomorrow."

"Yes, you have done your duty by trapping the prince. My suspicions about you were right."

They quarreled a while and then fell asleep.

The splash of oars woke Azlvarkkadian at dawn. He looked toward the sea and screamed: "General, wake up!"

Velir, Devan and the two soldiers woke with a start. Their boatman was rowing three passengers out to a ship which stood at sea, ready to set sail.

"That looks like a Chola ship!" the general cried. "Maybe it's the ship the Pazluvur brothers sent and the prince is on board. Where's our boat? We must stop the ship." Realizing it was their boat which was being rowed to the ship, he shouted, "Stop! Boatman, stop!"

But the boatman continued to steer his boat towards the ship.

The words, 'The prince is on board,' galvanized Devan into action: he jumped into the sea and went after the boat. He rushed across the shallows and suddenly found himself floundering in deep water. "Help! I'm drowning!" he screamed. He heard voices and laughter. Then the boatman pulled him into the boat and the boat moved on.

Devan examined his co-passengers. One man was obviously an Arab. *What's he doing here?* He turned his attention to the other two men. Their faces were half-concealed by their turbans. *Ah! These are the men who were with Parthibendran: the men Thirumalai says are here to kill the prince. And one of them is Ravidasan–the sorcerer I saw in Nandini's garden. They know the prince in on the ship and are going to kill him. Thank goodness I caught the boat.*

Devan broke the silence. "Where are you going?" he asked.

"Can't you see we're going to the ship?" Ravidasan's muffled voice was ghostly.

"Where's the ship going?" Devan persisted.

"We'll know when we get to the ship," Ravidasan replied. "And where are you going?"

"I'm also going to the ship," Devan replied.

"And where will you go after that?" the sorcerer asked.

"I'll know when I get to the ship," Devan repeated the lesson.

They reached the ship and climbed up a rope ladder. Devan jumped on to the deck. "Where's the prince?" he shouted. What he saw made even his brave heart tremble a little: he was surrounded by large, demonic-looking Arabs who stood glaring at him in silence. *I have made a serious mistake. This is not a Chola ship. These are Arab merchants who have come to sell their horses. The prince can't be on board.*

Devan saw his boat leaving the ship. "Stop!" he shouted and prepared to jump into the sea. An iron hand caught him by the throat and knocked him down. Devan jumped up and punched his attacker on the jaw. The six-foot tall Arab staggered and fell, knocking down the man standing behind him. Devan heard a shriek and turned just in time to block the knife which another Arab was ready to plunge into his back. The knife fell to the deck and rolled overboard. The next instant, Devan was surrounded by Arabs. Their leader barked orders. The struggling Devan was trussed, carried below deck and tossed on a heap of logs. The men tied him to a log for good measure and left.

From the heaving of the ship, Devan realized it had sailed. Logs of wood fell on him. *If only I escape this time, I'll never be rash again. Like Thirumalai, I'll think before I act.* He heard wild laughter and turned his head with great difficulty—Ravidasan stood nearby.

Ravidasan said, "I came hunting for a Chola tiger. The tiger escaped but a Vallam fox fell into my trap ... that's good enough for me!"

The boatman returned to shore but was unable to give the general much information. "Those men woke me up and offered me good money to row them to the ship," he explained. "I agreed as I would be back before you were awake."

Azlvarkkadian told the prince what he knew. "Vandhiya Devan may be in the hands of the Pazluvur brothers. They may throw him into their infamous dungeon."

"Just say the word, prince," Velir roared. "I'll destroy the Pazluvur brothers and throw them into their own dungeon!"

"Sir, don't even dream I'll defy my father!" Arulmozli declared.

They turned at the sound of horse's hooves: to their amazement, a woman came riding bare-back on a horse and stopped a little distance away from them.

The Captain's Death

ARULMOZLI RECOGNIZED MANDAKINI and ran to her, followed by the others.

The old lady spoke to Poonkuzlali in sign language. "Aunt wants us to follow her. She has seen something terrible in the forest."

The company followed Mandakini, marveling at the Arab

thoroughbred she was riding. Where did she find such a horse when there were no army camps nearby? Mandakini led them along the coastline. They came to a forest clearing with a small pool in the middle. Even these battle-hardened veterans were shocked at the ghastly sight which met their eyes: men lay dead by the pool and the stench of corpses and dried blood filled the air. They moved closer—all the dead men were Chola sailors.

"Quick!" the prince cried. "See if there are any survivors."

Mandakini led Arulmozli away from the pool. There, under a tree, lay a man whose body was covered with grievous wounds; blood flowed from the cuts on his head. Seeing Arulmozli, the man struggled to speak even as his mouth filled with blood.

Arulmozli sat beside him and shouted, "Bring water!"

The dying man murmured, "Sir, I'm being punished for betraying you …"

The prince examined his face. "Captain! It's you! What happened? Why would you betray me?"

The captain replied, "I came here to arrest you on the Pazluvur brothers' orders. Here's the warrant." He took a palm leaf from his waist.

"This is not betrayal, captain," Arulmozli said. "You were only obeying the emperor's orders. Tell me what happened … quick!"

The captain stumbled through his story. Unable to defy the emperor's orders, he sailed from Nagapattinam with two ships. The Pazluvur brothers gave him strict instructions: he must anchor at a secret location on the Lankan coast and find out where Arulmozli was; he must meet the prince and serve the warrant without Velir's knowledge; if the prince resisted arrest, he must use force. They sent some of their own secret service men with him. His heart was heavy and his sailors had no idea why they were going to Lanka. He anchored his ships in a hidden bay on the Thondaman estuary and went to Kankesanthurai Port with a few men. There, he heard that Arulmozli was somewhere in the interior jungles. He returned to his ship to find that his men had heard about the purpose of their journey from the Pazluvur men. The sailors protested.

The captain tried to convince them: "We must carry out the emperor's orders."

"These are the Pazluvur brothers' orders," his men cried. "We will not obey. We'll go to Mathottam and join the Chola army under Prince Arulmozli."

"Go then!" the captain shouted. "You will face the consequences of your actions."

Some of the rebels wanted to sail to Mathottam on one of the ships. Finally, the two hundred sailors decided to walk. They left, leaving the captain with ten men, including the Pazluvur brothers' guards. In their hurry, the sailors did not anchor the ship securely and it ran aground.

The captain had heard in the port that an Arab ship had recently sunk near the coast. The survivors were reported to be in this area. As Arabs were notorious for their cruelty, the captain left the wrecked ship and sailed to a secluded cove on the estuary. He decided to go by himself to arrest the prince while the men guarded the ship. Suddenly, they heard a blood-curdling yell. Before they could understand what was happening, the Arabs fell on them. The sailors, unarmed and caught by surprise, put up a brave fight but were massacred by the enemy.

"Prince," the captain said. "I somehow crawled here. I was determined to live to tell the tale of what happened. I'm fortunate you found me. Ponni's Beloved, forgive me."

"There's nothing to forgive," the prince assured him. "You did your duty. You have earned your place in the warriors' paradise." Arulmozli gently stroked his forehead. The dying man took the prince's hand and raised it to his eyes. Arulmozli's own eyes filled with tears. A little later, the captain breathed his last.

The Hunt for the Ship

THE CAPTAIN'S BODY was piled with those of the other dead men and a mass cremation was held.

Seeing Arulmozli's tears, Velir asked, "Why do you shed tears for these traitors?"

"General, I'm weeping for the Cholas. What could be worse than a mutiny on a Chola ship? These are the cracks which will shatter our mighty empire. When the sailors come to you, arrest them and send them to Thanjavur. I'm the cause of all this."

"Prince, justice demands we hear their side of the story, too," Velir pointed out.

"Very well, but I can't delay any longer. I must pursue the Arab ship. Vandhiya Devan is on it, risking his life for me. I will not add betraying a friend to my long list of sins."

"Sir, Vandhiya Devan is a foolhardy thug. You're not responsible for the danger he rushed into. How can he be your friend? There can be friendship only among equals."

Arulmozli said, "I don't have time for this nonsense! Where's the boatman?"

"How can you follow a ship on the ocean in that small boat?" Velir cried.

Arulmozli was firm. "I'll go in the boat; if the boat sinks, I'll cling to a plank. I'll hunt down that ship across the seven seas. If I can't save my friend, I'll die with him."

He found the boatman with Poonkuzlali who was arguing furiously with him, tears in her eyes. The boatman fell at Arulmozli's feet. "Prince, forgive me for betraying you! I was greedy."

The prince turned questioning eyes to Poonkuzlali who said, "Sir, I'm ashamed to say this man is my brother, Murugayyan. He rowed the two assassins to Lanka from Kodikkarai. He waited for them and rowed them to the ship."

"I didn't know they were such wicked men," Murugayyan sobbed. "Kill me, my lord."

"I need you now," Arulmozli said. "Come quickly ..."

Just as the prince was about to climb into the boat, they saw a ship sailing towards them.

"That's Parthibendran's ship coming from Trincomalee," Velir said.

"Excellent!" Arulmozli said. "He may have other ideas, but his timing is perfect. I will now hunt the leopard with a lion. I'll save time by rowing to the ship. None of you need come with me. Thirumalai, you are afraid of water ..."

"Yes, prince," Azlvarkkadian replied. "I was asked to guard you as long as you were in Sri Lanka. I'll go and report to the chief minister in Madurai."

Arulmozli said, "Poonkuzlali, go your way. I'll never forget your help. Now, now, wipe your tears. What will everyone think?!"

Arulmozli bent to touch Mandakini's feet but she stopped him and kissed his forehead.

Arulmozli jumped into the boat; all eyes were on it as it sped towards the ship. The prince too stood looking back at them. But his eyes were fixed on Poonkuzlali's tear-stained face. He broke into gooseflesh as his dream came back to haunt him. Above the roar of the waves, he heard Kundavai's voice: *Thambi, remember Vanathi is waiting here for you.*

King Veerapandian's Bodyguards

PARTHIBENDRAN WAS OVERJOYED to see the boat with the prince in it. *But why is he alone? Does he think this ship is the one sent by the Pazluvur brothers?*

The prince climbed aboard and updated Parthibendran about the recent developments. "We must rescue Vandhiya Devan from the Arabs at any cost," the prince concluded.

"It would have been better if that young man had not been so rash, but we can't sell him out to foreigners. We'll catch that ship," said Parthibendran and gave orders to the ship's captain.

"If the winds remain favorable, we'll catch up with the ship by this evening," the captain assured him. "Once it reaches Kodikkarai, it has to sail along the coast."

But the wind died and by noon, the ship came to a standstill. The sea was absolutely calm; the heat was stifling; the sun was a ball of flame which set the ocean on fire. The silence was unbearable.

"How long will we be forced to stay here?" Arulmozli asked. "Will the other ship escape?"

"This is the calm before the storm, sir," the captain explained. "A cyclone is coming. But the wind and waves are impartial—that ship will also be at a standstill."

"What if it's near the coast?" the prince asked.

"The passengers may have a chance of reaching the shore, but the ship will be wrecked."

Devan lay on the logs, ruing his foolishness. *Whose ship is this? Why's Ravidasan with these Arabs? What will they do with me? As long as I have my life and my wits, I won't lose hope.* He strained to see in the darkness. Slowly, he made out weapons heaped near him. He tested his bonds: his legs and body were tied tightly but the rope around his hands was loose. He could reach out for a knife and cut the ropes. But the door was locked and even if he got out, how could he fight with all those men? And even if he killed them all, he knew nothing about ships. *I won't be rash again. Let me wait. The fact that they have not yet killed me is a good sign.*

As the hours passed, Devan felt stifled; the ship's rolling stopped; his thirst was unbearable. He saw a heap of coconuts in the corner. *Aha! Those will quench my thirst and my hunger.* Just as he reached out for a knife, the door opened and Ravidasan entered with his companion.

"I'm dying of thirst," Devan complained. "Give me some water."

"We are thirsty too," Ravidasan said. "These wretches have not stored water on the ship."

"Kali is even thirstier," his companion added. "She thirsts for blood."

"You're Devaralan …the possessed dancer at Kadambur!" Devan exclaimed.

Devaralan smirked. "Yes. We came to Lanka to sacrifice the prince to Kali but failed. We tried to send the Vaishnava to his Vaikundam but that too didn't happen. At least you came to us voluntarily: Kali will have to be satisfied with the blood of a minor chieftain's son."

Devan challenged: "Go ahead and kill me!"

"We'll sacrifice you when we reach the shore. The priestess, Nandini, must be present."

"If you truly have such plans, give me water," Devan said. "Or I'll die of thirst now itself."

"If you cooperate, you can come up to the deck and drink rain water. We want to kill the Arabs: they want to sail to Kalinga instead of letting us off at Kodikkarai or Nagapattinam."

"There are six of the thugs," Devan pointed out.

"Three are asleep: if we throw them overboard, we can fight the other three man-to-man."

Arulmozli's face appeared before Devan's eyes. *He would never stoop to killing sleeping men.* Devan declared, "I refuse—that's cowardice."

"You fool!"

The men armed themselves and went out, leaving the door open. Devan reached for a knife and freed himself. He broke open a coconut and drank the water. He heard two splashes followed by shouts and the clashing of knives. He grabbed a sword and rushed to the deck to find Ravidasan and Devaralan cornered by four Arabs. Devan screamed and charged. One of the Arabs turned to him. Devan knocked the man's sword into the sea and slashed his face. As the man lunged at him with his fists, Devan dodged. The Arab fell on the deck and a crossbeam from the mast dropped on him and knocked him out. Devan attacked the other Arab and threw him into the sea.

The two Arabs fighting with Ravidasan and Devaralan heard the splash and turned to see who had fallen overboard. Ravidasan and Devaralan quickly pushed the distracted men into the sea. The three exhausted victors sat on the deck to recover.

"My dear fellow, you arrived at the right moment. How did you escape?" Ravidasan asked.

"It must be your magic," Devan said cheekily. "My bonds loosened and a sword appeared in my hand. A coconut hovered over my head, broke into two and poured its water into my mouth."

The two men burst out laughing. "My dear fellow, we deliberately tied your hands loosely and left the weapons and coconuts within your reach. It was a test," Ravidasan said.

Not knowing whether to believe this or not, Devan kept quiet.

Ravidasan said, "Do you want to live? Do you want wealth and power? Join us."

"Who are you?" Devan asked.

Ravidasan looked at Devaralan. "There's no need to hide anything from him. He can join us or be thrown into the sea. We are King Veerapandian's bodyguards, sworn to protect him."

"You failed; Aditya Karikalan killed him," Devan pointed out.

Ravidasan's bloodshot eyes sparked; his face flushed in anger; he gnashed his teeth. "That foolish woman thought she could make the lustful Chola cobra dance to her tune. It danced, but sank its poisonous fangs into our king. They paraded his head through the streets of Thanjavur!"

"The past is past," Devan said. "Can you bring your king back to life?"

"That's beyond my powers," Ravidasan said. "But we'll kill his murderer and wipe out his entire clan; we won't spare even the babies. That will be our revenge. We will then crown the man our queen chooses," Ravidasan declared.

"Who's your queen?"

"Who else but Nandini, pretending to be Lord Ambalavan's wife."

"What about Madurandaka?"

"He's also a Chola snake."

"And Lord Ambalavan?"

"Hah! Why would we make that old man our king? It's only to use his wealth and influence …"

"That your queen lives in his house," Devan completed the sentence.

"You clever young man!" Ravidasan applauded.

"You mentioned a woman's foolishness …" Devan prompted.

"That too was Nandini. We decided to burn her on our king's funeral pyre but spared her when she swore to help us with our revenge. We could never have come this far without her help. Will you join us? You may be lucky enough to rule southern Tamil Nadu."

A few days ago, Devan would have jumped at this offer. But his days with Arulmozli had changed him. He was no longer interested in tricks and lies.

Changing the topic, he asked, "How did you get on this ship and befriend the Arabs?"

"It's all due to my magic," Ravidasan boasted. "We bought two horses from the Arabs at Trincomalee. When the prince crossed Elephant Pass, we used a short cut to get ahead of him. We were surprised to find our Arab friends with a Chola ship. It seems their ship sank and they captured this one. They offered to take us on board as their guides."

"Why do you want to go back to Tamil Nadu?" Devan asked.

"We heard the young Chola snake insist on returning to Thanjavur.

In Lanka there's a mute female ghost who counters my magic and protects Arulmozli. She won't be in Thanjavur." Ravidasan laughed. "You know how ruthless these Arabs are: they don't think twice about killing a man. But they dote on their horses. They think we are cruel because we don't make iron shoes for our horses' hooves. We were ready to set sail when we heard the sound of horse's hooves. Suspecting it was a horse which had made it to shore from their wrecked ship, one of the Arabs insisted on returning to the shore. He took us along. We didn't catch the horse … but we caught you." He grinned. "And you came in handy in killing those Arabs."

"This boy is yet to answer your question," Devaralan reminded Ravidasan.

"I serve the Cholas. I'll never join you," Devan declared.

"You have not sworn an oath to the Cholas. As a warrior, you should join the side which is more profitable," Ravidasan pointed out.

A glance from Princess Kundavai's eyes … her smile … the prince's friendship … what more do I need to serve the Cholas? "Come what may, I won't join your murderous gang," he declared.

"Then prepare to die!" Ravidasan cried.

The Whirlwind

DEVAN QUICKLY STRETCHED his hands to the ocean and intoned, "Om, hreem hraam vashat!" He whirled his sword and roared, "The Sea God demands sacrifices: a sorcerer and a Kali devotee."

Ravidasan burst out laughing. "What game are you playing?"

"It's not a game. When I was in the hold, the Sea God spoke to me in my dream. Only if you two are sacrificed will the ship move." He shouted. "Sea God, give these fools a sign!"

At that moment, the sea became a vast expanse of white foam and a tender breeze caressed the ship. Devan saw a small black cloud on the horizon whose top shone blood-red.

"Looks like we must prepare to be sacrificed," Ravidasan howled. "Young man, just give us a few minutes to pray. We'll be back soon … we'll even leave our weapons here."

The two men dropped their weapons and went out of sight to the other side of the ship. Devan hardened his heart and prepared to kill the evil men. The dark cloud was now huge. It grew under his eyes. The wind picked up speed and waves appeared on the sea's surface. The ship moved. Suddenly, Devan heard a splash, followed by the sound of oars. He ran to the other side of the deck and was shocked to see Ravidasan and Devaralan rowing away from the ship in the boat.

"You wretches! Take me with you!" Devan shouted.

"Shouldn't the Sea God be given at least one sacrifice?" Ravidasan grinned as he rowed away.

I'm alone on the ship. I have no idea how to handle it or to read the directions. Devan considered jumping overboard and swimming to the boat. *I'm a poor swimmer. Those wicked men may hit me with their oars if I try to climb into the boat. I know their secrets but refused to join their gang. Let them go. It's safer to be alone on the ship than with those murderers. I have survived many dangers in the past and god will show me a way out of this too. What if they reach the shore and hatch more evil plots? It's in god's hands. My priority is to find the prince. He should not have tricked me and run away on the elephant. I'll ask him if that's his idea of friendship. Thirumalai would have told him about the danger I'm in …*

The waves rose higher and the sky and the sea darkened as the black cloud covered the sun. The boat vanished from sight. The wind's whisper became an angry roar. The sails fluttered wildly and the planks and timbers groaned. The ship was going around in circles.

A tornado is going to hit the ship! Devan was terrified. He knew the sails must be furled before a storm, but that was impossible to do single-handedly. He resigned himself to his fate. There was no doubt the ship would either sink or be wrecked. *That useless astrologer did not predict my death at sea. If I see him again … Fool! How will I see him again!?*

Suddenly, Devan was pelted by hailstones. His excitement at his first hailstorm revived his spirits. This was followed by heavy rain. Devan admired the sturdy Chola ship which would not sink unless its hull cracked. Feeling more confident, he thought, *If the rain becomes unbearable, I can lock myself in the hold and leave my fate to god.* His thoughts flew to Pazlayarai. *Who will tell the princess I died while on my mission? Why did I meet her? God showed me paradise and then threw me into hell.*

Fearing that he would be washed into the sea, Devan lashed himself to the mast. The wind became a gale; the sea boiled; the sails shrieked like demons; it was pitch dark. Lightning streaked across the sky, followed by a roll of thunder which shook the sky, the sea, the ship. The sky burst and a flood of rain gushed out. It was only a matter of time before the ship sank.

My death will be a wonder! Devan no longer feared death. His heart danced with the waves. He laughed above the roar of the wind, waves and thunder. As the ship whirled, Devan and the mast whirled with it. He closed his eyes and shut his ears with his hands. Soon, Devan's mind was calm and he lost all sense of time and space. There was a lull in the storm. The wind slowed, the rain became a drizzle and the sea a black expanse. Devan opened his eyes.

Have I survived the storm? God has saved me! I'll see the princess. I'll chat with the prince. But how will this ship reach the shore?

A streak of lightning lit up the sky like a hundred suns. The roll of thunder which followed threatened to shatter Devan's eardrums. He closed his eyes and ears. After a while, he heard the crackling of flames and slowly opened his eyes—the sails above him were burning! The mast had been struck by lightning. The ship had withstood the wind and the water but was now being destroyed by fire.

Vandhiya Devan realized this was the end of the ship—and him. He laughed in the face of death and untied himself from the mast. *I'd rather die in the cool water than by fire.*

He looked around at the beautiful ocean, lit up by the fire. *They say the spirit of a person who dies a premature death lingers on in that place. Will my spirit float on the wind and the waves? Maybe the princess will sail this way. They'll say, 'This is where Vandhiya Devan went down with the ship.' If she cries, will I be able to wipe her tears?*

As his ship stood poised on the crest of a huge wave, Devan saw a ship in the distance, flying the Tiger Flag. *Thank god! The prince has come to rescue me!*

The Boat Shatters

PARTHIBENDRAN'S SHIP WAS manned by seasoned sailors: the sail was furled and stowed away and the ship was steered so that it did not bear the full brunt of the storm. Even when the whirlwind spun it like a top, the ship righted itself under the expert hands of the Tamil seamen.

"I have weathered fiercer storms," the captain said. "There's no need to worry. I fear only one thing: visibility is zero. The other ship will also be floundering in the dark. If the two ships collide, both will shatter and that will be the end of everyone on board."

Arulmozli stood in a corner of the deck, scanning the sea. *My sister's messenger is in the clutches of Arab thugs and a murderous sorcerer. Will I be able to rescue him? What if the ships collide? Who'll give my father the crucial news about his first wife? I have never failed in anything I set out to do. I won't fail now.* The prince closed his eyes in reflex as lightning streaked across the sky, followed by an earsplitting roll of thunder. When he opened his eyes, he saw a ship dancing like a ghost upon the waves. The sails were on fire. In the light of the fire, he saw a man standing by the mast. *Oh god! It's a miracle! It's the brave Vandhiya Devan. Why is he alone?*

"There! Look!" others on board had spotted the ship.

Arulmozli ran to the lifeboats. "Who will come with me?" he shouted.

Although the sailors were horrified at what the prince planned to do, many of them volunteered. Parthibendran and the captain ran to stop the prince.

"Sir," Parthibendran said. "It's impossible to rescue anyone from that burning ship. But there are many of us here who are ready to try. You must stay here."

The prince roared, "I'll never forgive anyone who tries to stop me! I need only two men."

The boat was lowered into the sea and the prince and two sailors jumped in. The boat swirled in the sea. The men slowly brought it under control and rowed to the burning ship.

"Jump! Jump into the sea!" the prince shouted.

But Devan was in shock: he stood staring helplessly at the ship and the approaching boat. In minutes, the fire would reach the deck and the ship would sink.

Arulmozli grabbed the heavy rope tied to the lifeboat, fastened it around his waist and jumped into the sea. Fighting the waves, he swam to the burning ship. A huge wave threw him on the ship's deck. The prince held Devan by the neck and shouted, "Hold on to me—don't let go!"

The next instant, they were in the water. The sailors stopped rowing and pulled in the rope. The prince, and Devan who clung to him like a leech, somehow reached the boat.

"Grab your oars!" Arulmozli shouted. "Row quickly!"

As the burning ship sank, huge waves battered the small boat. Somehow, the boat managed to ride the waves. But without the fire, they were in total darkness. If they collided with their ship, the boat would be smashed; if they missed the ship, they would be lost in the sea. The whirlwind vanished as quickly as it had appeared, but the sea continued to seethe and heave. The small boat was tossed by ferocious waves. The men stopped rowing: it was pointless to row without knowing where their ship was.

Unknown to them, an unexpected danger was coming near. As the burning ship sank, one of its huge sails detached itself and came straight at the boat. In the pitch dark, no one saw it until it was too late.

"Row for your lives!" Arulmozli shouted just as the sail rammed the boat and the boat shattered. "Courage, my friend," the prince shouted to Devan. "Grab the sail, it's safer than the boat."

Let Me Die!

THE COMPANY ON the shore of the Thondaman estuary watched the boatman row the prince to Parthibendran's ship which immediately set sail.

Velir was pleased. "God is on our side. Parthibendran will take the prince safely to Kanchipuram. I'll gather my army and leave for

Thanjavur." He noticed Azlvarkkadian nearby. "Thirumalai! You heard my plans? Never mind—there's nothing Aniruddha's spy does not know. Are you coming to Mathottam with me?"

"No, sir," Azlvarkkadian replied. "I still have some work … my master said if I ever came across a mute woman in Lanka, I must somehow persuade her to come with me to Thanjavur."

Velir smiled. "She's very fond of the prince. What do you know about her?"

"I know she's a deaf-mute by birth. I also know it will be easier to cage a tempest than to take her with me. But I'll give it a try," Azlvarkkadian replied.

"The boat girl and the mute woman are good friends," Velir remarked. "Look at them talking together in sign language. Send the boat girl here, Thirumalai. I have a warning for her."

Azlvarkkadian went to the women and gave Poonkuzlali Velir's message. She came and stood before the general.

Velir said, "Look here, you're a clever girl. You have done the Cholas great service by bringing your news at the right time. I'll reward you for that."

"Thank you, sir," Poonkuzlali replied. "But I don't want any reward."

Velir laughed. "Let things calm down. I'll find a brave Chola warrior to be your husband. He must be an extraordinary man—otherwise he won't be able to keep you in check." He paused. "But just because you helped the prince, don't think you have any claims over him. Catch your fish in the sea, but don't try to catch the prince. If you come near him, beware!"

Poonkuzlali kept her eyes lowered to hide her anger. Velir's harsh words poured like molten lead into her ears. She wanted to give the old man a piece of her mind but her voice choked. Eyes brimming with hot tears, she walked away. *I hate the sound of cruel human voices. All men should be born dumb. I must hurry to my boat and row into the sea where no human voice can be heard … only there will I find balm to heal my heart. That wicked man! What a dirty mind he has. As if I'm trying to catch the prince.*

Her anger lent her wings and by noon she had reached her hidden boat. Her boat was her friend and her refuge from the world of sorrow and betrayal. *Let the old man guard the prince and saddle him with his* niece. *Who cares? I have my boat ... my oars ... my strong hands ... and the sea. The Ocean King won't let me down.*

Poonkuzlali knew the signs of a coming cyclone–the dark ring around the moon the previous night, the stillness and humidity, the dark clouds in the southeast. She would row to Boodha Island and watch the magnificent storm. Once the cyclone was spent, she would go across to Kodikkarai. *The prince must have reached Kodikkarai or Mamallapuram. What do I care? As long as he's not caught in the storm.*

Poonkuzlali reached Boodha Island just before the storm and climbed to the top of a stupa. She swayed in the wind, drenched by the rain, her hair streaming behind her. She watched as the coconut palms on the island waved in frenzy, waves rose like mountains and dissolved into froth, lightning streaked across the sky and the roar of wind and waves joined the rolls of thunder. The storm reflected the tempest raging in her soul. *The prince must be safe in Kodikkarai by now. Even if he's at sea, his ship will withstand the storm. Will he think of me? Never! He'll think of Vandhiya Devan or Vanathi. Why would he remember this poor girl of the fisher folk?*

Poonkuzlali went to sleep in the cave, troubled by dreams: she was in a boat, casting her net ... the prince was caught in her net ... she and the prince were fish swimming together in the sea ... She awoke. *'What madness is this?'* she thought before falling asleep again.

Poonkuzlali rose at dawn and walked to the shore. The storm had died but the sea still heaved. Suddenly, she saw a raft floating to the shore with a man tied to it. She rushed to untie him—he was half dead. When he revived, he told her that he was a fisherman from a village on the Lankan coast. He was caught in the storm and, while his companion died, he made it to the shore.

He said, "When we were stranded in the sea, lightning lit up the darkness and we saw two ships. One was burning and there were men running on its deck. It sank and we lost sight of the other ship."

Poonkuzlali was worried. *Was it the prince's ship? Impossible! Ships come and go in the sea: can I worry about each one of them? But some men may have jumped into the sea from the burning ship; they may be clinging to some floating object and fighting for their lives. If I don't try to save them, what's the purpose of my life?*

Poonkuzlali jumped into her boat and rowed against the waves which dashed on the shore. Then she was in the sea and the boat sped across the water. As she rowed, Poonkuzlali instinctively broke into song. Her sweet voice rose above the roar of the waves.

Arulmozli and Vandhiya Devan clung to the spar of the sail as they were tossed about by the turbulent waves.

Devan soon lost all hope of ever reaching land again. Every time the waves lifted them and threw them down, he thought, *I'll die now.* Filled with remorse, he lamented, "My rashness has put you in danger, sir!"

Arulmozli comforted him. "Men have survived three or four days in the sea. We have not been in the water for even one night."

"Lies! Many days have passed. I'm dying of thirst."

"Patience," Arulmozli said. "Once the sun rises, we'll be washed ashore somewhere."

"Sir, I can't bear this torture. Please untie me from the plank … let me die!"

Refusing to listen to Arulmozli's words of comfort, Devan struggled to untie his own bonds. Arulmozli gave him a blow on his head. Devan lost consciousness.

When Devan came to himself, it was morning. The sea was calm.

The prince said, "My friend, we are near land. I saw the top of a coconut tree a while back."

"Sir," Devan pleaded. "Let me die. Save yourself somehow."

"I'll never abandon you. Don't lose hope." Arulmozli paused. "I hear someone singing …"

Devan cried, "It's Poonkuzlali—we are saved!"

Poonkuzlali's sweet song breathed fresh life and spirit into them. Soon, the boat came to them. Poonkuzlali was speechless in wonder: *Is this a dream?*

The prince untied Devan's rope, jumped into the boat and then pulled Devan in. Poonkuzlali stood frozen like a statue.

PART 3

THE KILLER
SWORD

In Kodikkarai

MALAYSIA WAS AN important trading partner of the Cholas and many Malaysian nationals lived in Nagapattinam, the Chola empire's main port. The Malayan king, Maran Vijayathunga, built the Choodamani Monastery in Nagapattinam in honor of his father. The Chola emperors, renowned for their devotion to Lord Shiva, were also known for their religious tolerance. They supported the monasteries in their kingdom with grants and subsidies.

Ambalavan arrived at Nagapattinam a few days before the storm. The chancellor inspected the busy port and checked the tax-collectors who levied duty on the ships' cargo.

Earlier, two Buddhist monks from the Choodamani Monastery had visited the emperor in Thanjavur and praised Arulmozli for renovating the Buddhist monasteries in Sri Lanka: 'The Sangha offered the prince the Lankan throne—what a testimony to his greatness!'

This gave Ambalavan an idea. "Your Majesty, your authority extends from coast to coast but your sons refuse to obey you. Aditya Karikalan, advised by Malayaman, refuses to come to Thanjavur. As for Arulmozli, Velir blocks my messages to Sri Lanka with your orders to return. Let's issue an arrest warrant for the prince, accusing him of conspiring to become the Lankan king. The general cannot ignore it and the prince will be forced to return to Thanjavur."

Sundara Chola thought, *It might work. I long to see Arulmozli before I die. He'll agree to let Madurandaka become the next emperor and will convince Karikalan too.*

And so, the warrant was sent to Lanka.

Ambalavan decided to hurry to Nagapattinam, meet the prince and escort him to Thanjavur. He knew that Kundavai and Sembiyan

Madevi disliked him. Knowing their influence over Arulmozli, he did not want them to meet the prince first and upset his own plans. As the arrest warrant included Vandhiya Devan, he could also find out what that young man knew and take necessary precautions. He was worried about the mysterious man who had attacked his guard in the Thanjavur vault. *Was it Vandhiya Devan? In that case, he knows too many dangerous secrets. What message has Kundavai sent Arulmozli? Has that female snake heard of our conspiracy?*

Nandini was also eager to go to Nagapattinam. She wanted to know Kundavai's reply to the message Devan carried; she also wanted to know whether Ravidasan's plans had succeeded. Ambalavan happily agreed to take her with him. The old man dreamt of sailing along the coast with his beautiful wife and finally getting a chance to satisfy the lust which was consuming his body and soul. But the cyclone hit Nagapattinam and shattered his dreams of pleasure cruises.

Some fishermen reported seeing two ships floundering in mid sea between Sri Lanka and Kodikkarai: one of the ships had sunk after being struck by lightning.

Ambalavan worried: *What if the ships are the ones I sent? How will I answer to the people and the emperor if anything happens to the prince? Arulmozli is the people's favorite.* He decided to go to Kodikkarai as any survivors would wash up there.

Nandini agreed readily to this. "I have never seen Kodikkarai. I hear it's beautiful."

They went by road with a large retinue. Nandini was relieved. If they took the coastal channel, she would have to deal with her husband's passionate demands in the privacy of their boat.

Nandini refused Vidangar's offer of his modest house, and chose to pitch tents on the beach. As the men pitched the tents, they sighted a ship with tattered masts. An excited buzz ran through the crowd: could it be the prince? Ambalavan immediately sent a boat to the ship. Two men climbed into the boat—one was Parthibendran.

On the night of the cyclone, Parthibendran was filled with grief when Arulmozli did not return from the burning ship. The next morning, he searched the sea and picked up one of the sailors who had accompanied the prince. The man told them how the prince had rescued Devan from the burning ship and how their boat had been shattered by the mast pole. Hoping the prince had survived and been washed up at Kodikkarai, Parthibendran had hurried there.

His hopes dashed, Parthibendran was irritated to find the chancellor and Nandini in Kodikkarai. But he was curious to see the woman whose beauty had bewitched Aditya Karikalan. Seeing Ambalavan standing majestically at the tent entrance, he thought, *This is no 'old man!' He's a lion: he's braver and stronger than most young warriors...*

Nandini came out of the tent and stood in front of Ambalavan. One look at her radiant beauty and Parthibendran was lost.

"My dear," Nandini crooned. "Who's this brave warrior?"

Parthibendran froze, drunk on the sweetness of her voice.

Web of Seduction

AMBALAVAN WAS UNHAPPY with Nandini for standing in front of him, but he could not scold her. "The world is filled with strangers, my dear," he said jealously. "That's nothing to you."

"Sir, the loss is mine. Let me introduce myself, I'm Parthibendran."

"Ah! I have heard of you," Nandini said.

Ambalavan sneered. "My dear, this is Parthibendran Pallava who beheaded Veerapandian."

For a split second, Nandini's face darkened like a stormy sky and lightning flashed in her eyes. "Is there no end to the number of men who claim to have beheaded Veerapandian?" she laughed.

"Lady, the chancellor is wrong–only Aditya Karikalan can claim credit for that."

Ambalavan laughed loudly. "Don't you want to share the credit for beating a dead snake?"

Parthibendran's eyes were glued to Nandini's face. "My lord, that snake, Veerapandian, was very much alive when Karikalan raised his sword. A beautiful woman begged Karikalan to spare his life. If I was the prince, I would have thrown away my sword and spared Veerapandian."

Nandini quickly said, "My dear, why waste time on old stories? Why is this man here?"

Ambalavan turned to Parthibendran. "Why did you leave Kanchipuram? Why are you here?"

The dazed Parthibendran shook himself. "Sir, I bring sad news. Prince Arulmozli, who came with me from Sri Lanka, jumped into the sea and is missing. I came to Kodikkarai hoping he may have been washed ashore here."

The chancellor wailed and collapsed. Parthibendran lunged forward but Nandini stopped him with a gesture. She sat down, took her husband's head in her lap and shouted for water. She signaled everyone to keep their distance. She sprinkled water on Ambalavan's face and softly crooned, "My dear, my dear."

The chancellor stirred and sat up. He beat his head with his hands and lamented, "Arulmozli is lost at sea! I carried him on my shoulders when he was a child—and I sealed his arrest warrant. What will the Chola empire think of me?"

No one had ever seen the old man in such a state.

Nandini said, "My dear, let's hear the rest of the story; then we can decide what to do next."

Eyes flashing, Ambalavan turned to Parthibendran and roared, "Don't play games with me! Did you say Arulmozli died at sea?"

"Forgive me, sir. I did not say he's dead. I said he jumped into the sea and is now missing."

The chancellor gnashed his teeth in rage. "Tell me the truth: why did he jump into the sea during a storm? Why did you let him do that? What was he doing on your ship?"

"I always speak the truth. News reached Kanchipuram that you, along with Sambuvaraya and some other chieftains, were conspiring against the Cholas ..."

"Lies!" shouted Ambalavan.

"I hope so. Anyway, Karikalan and Malayaman sent me to Lanka to bring back Arulmozli ..." Parthibendran related the sequence of events with ended with the shipwreck.

Ambalavan wailed, "I'm responsible for this disaster: it was I who ordered the prince's arrest."

"Lord, fate is responsible, not you," Nandini said. She whispered something to him.

The chancellor's face cleared. "Parthibendran, I'm going to search your ship. Stay here. If you try to escape, my guards will kill you."

Nandini intervened. "Don't worry, lord. Go to the ship and question the sailors. If this man tries to escape, I'll plunge my dagger into his chest." She drew a knife from her waist.

Ambalavan said, "Go to your tent or to Vidangar's house. My men will guard him."

She lowered her voice. "This man may have come to spy on us. We must not let him spread the news about the prince."

Ambalavan left for the ship. Nandini's eyes followed his boat but she knew that Parthibendran was staring at her. She waved her dagger at him. "Don't try to escape."

"How can I escape? You have bewitched me."

Nandini smiled, asking him to sit beside her on the ground. "How chivalrous the Pallavas are!"

"I have heard of women with power over the earth and the sky: today, I have met one."

"I deliberately sent the chancellor away. There's something I want to ask you. Do you know the name of the foolish girl who tried to save Veerapandian from Karikalan?"

"Nandini," Parthibendran replied at once.

"If I'm as powerful as you say, why was I not able to save Veerapandian's life?"

"Karikalan was carried away by blood lust. He has been tormented by regret for three years."

"How do you know that?"

"He confided in me before I left for Lanka. Since then, I have wanted to meet you."

"You may be pretending to be captivated by me ... you may be trying to learn my secrets."

Parthibendran cried, "If I'm a spy, may lightning strike me!"

"Don't say that. Vandhiya Devan tried to learn my secrets and lightning did strike him."

"Unfortunately, he was not struck by lightning: lightning struck his ship's mast and the mast caught fire. And the prince was caught in that catastrophe."

"Poor Princess Kundavai! I pity her—the two men she loved are dead."

"Two?" Parthibendran asked.

"Prince Arulmozli and Vandhiya Devan of course."

"What!" Parthibendran was disgusted. "The princess and that arrogant, insolent young man?"

"Yes, the princess loves him. She sent hm to Sri Lanka to avoid punishment. My poor husband blames himself for the prince's death when actually it's the princess who's responsible."

"True: if she had not sent that message, none of this would have happened."

"I'll be grateful if you tell my husband this when he returns from the ship," Nandini said.

"Is there nothing else I can do to earn your gratitude?"

"Will you do anything for me?" she asked.

Parthibendran's hair stood on end and his voice quavered. "I'll sacrifice my life and soul for you. I'll throw my dearest friend's head at your feet if you ask for it …"

"Stop, sir! I'm going to ask you only for something which will make us both happy."

This is human nature: a sinner can become a saint and a virtuous man can slip and fall into hell.

The Owl Hoots

NANDINI SIGHED AND looked after the boat in which Ambalavan sat. Her sigh was a tempest in Parthibendran's heart. *The Devil! How dare he marry a girl young enough to be his granddaughter?*

Nandini watched Ambalavan climb into the ship. "Thank goodness, he has made it safely on board. However brave he may be, he's still an old man."

Parthibendran thought, *Why does she care? If he falls into the sea, she'll be free.*

Nandini said, "Only now do I realize how attached the old man is to the Cholas. How he wailed when he heard the prince is missing! Could the prince have survived the cyclone?"

"It would be a miracle," Parthibendran said. "One's fate can't be changed."

"Kundavai is to blame for this, not fate. She believed her beloved younger brother would rule the world. How I would love to comfort her when she hears he's dead!" Nandini's voice overflowed with happiness. Parthibendran decided his hearing was at fault. "If that beauty sheds a tear, a thousand men will weep," Nandini said.

"Her beauty is nothing compared to yours. Tell me what you want from me."

"Kundavai wanted to make Arulmozli the next emperor and this made the chieftains angry. Now, they can come to an agreement. The emperor wants to make Madurandaka his successor -"

"Really?!" Parthibendran exclaimed.

"Why else did he issue the arrest warrant?" Nandini pointed out. "But it would be better to divide the empire along the Vellar river: Karikalan gets the north and Madurandaka gets the south."

Parthibendran said, "Let's not talk about the Chola empire. I want to live for myself. Shall I bring you corals and pearls from the sea? Shall I bring you the full moon to be your mirror?"

"Stop, sir! Kundavai already says I'm mad. Don't make me truly insane with your words."

Parthibendran was embarrassed. "I'm the one who's going mad. What do you want me to do?"

"I'm accused of instigating the chieftains and Madurandaka and bringing bad luck to the Cholas. I need your help to clear my name." She paused. "Do you believe in palmistry?"

"Show me your palm," he said and looked at her extended hand. "What amazing lines! You'll meet a young man on a beach who loves you and will be ready to die for you." Parthibendran grabbed her outstretched palms and lifted them to his eyes.

Nandini shook free her hands. "Chi! What are you doing? If the chancellor sees this, he'll have you impaled on his spear."

"I'm ready to die for you! What do you want me to do?"

"Bring Aditya Karikalan to Kadambur Palace. There will be peace if he marries Sambuvaraya's daughter, Manimekalai. The Chola empire will be divided between Karikalan and Madurandaka and my name will be cleared."

"And after that?" he asked.

"I'll be mistress of my own destiny. I'll throw myself into the sea ..."

"I'll rescue you ... I'll establish a new kingdom across the sea and make you queen."

"Stop! I come from a line of chaste Tamil women: I'm married to the chancellor."

"Tell me the truth: did the old man force you to marry him?"

Nandini sighed and rolled her eyes. "You must not blame him. I chose to marry him."

"I don't believe it!" Parthibendran exclaimed.

"When I was a child, a girl mocked me for being a poor orphan and said I had no right to play with royal children. I made the mistake of marrying the old man because of that."

"Was Princess Kundavai the girl who insulted you? I'll make her pay for this."

"God has punished her: she has lost her brother and her lover at the same time. And if you help me, she will no longer be the darling of the Chola empire."

"What will you give me for my help?"

"Anything you want which does not detract from a Tamil woman's chastity."

"There are Arabian countries where a woman can leave her husband and marry again. Come with me to one of those lands," Parthibendran pleaded passionately.

"Quiet!" Nandini said urgently. "My husband is back. Come to Thanjavur. We must talk again."

The old man was in a towering rage to find the two of them sitting together for so long.

"My dear," Nandini crooned. "Did you question the sailors? Is this man's story true?"

Pacified by her sweet tone, Ambalavan said, "Yes, the prince is gone." He turned to Parthibendran and roared, "And all because of this murderous devil!"

"Sir, don't blame me. It's the demoness who controls the Chola kingdom who's responsible for the prince's death."

"You wretch!" roared Ambalavan. He snatched up a spear and aimed it at Parthibendran. "How dare you insult my wife!"

Nandini stopped him. "My dear, he's not talking about me."

"I'm referring to Princess Kundavai," Parthibendran explained. "She sent Devan with the letter and the prince jumped into the sea to rescue Devan—so, the princess is responsible."

A little embarrassed by his hasty reaction, Ambalavan shouted, "You are also to blame! Why did you let the prince jump into the sea in a cyclone? Get lost! Don't let me see you again."

Nandini intervened. "My dear, let him come to Thanjavur and tell the emperor his story. There are people ready to accuse us of pushing the prince into the sea."

Ambalavan roared, "I'll cut their tongues! But this man had better come with us." He turned to Parthibendran. "What are you staring at? Are you planning to escape?" The chancellor ordered his guards to tie up Parthibendran.

Four men approached Parthibendran, who sent them flying in four directions. "Sir, I'll let the brave Lord Ambalavan with his sixty-four battle scars tie me but no one else!"

Ambalavan stood tall. "Very well, give me your word that you will come with us to Thanjavur."

"Yes. I want to tell the emperor what happened. No one should be wrongly blamed."

Suddenly, the hoot of an owl was heard from the forest a little distance from them. Nandini turned towards the sound. The men did not notice the change that came over her face.

"Strange," remarked Parthibendran. "The Kodikkarai owls hoot in broad daylight."

Nandini said, "Why don't we stay for a day? The prince may drift ashore on a plank …"

Ambalavan smiled. "Parthibendran, see how clever my wife is! We did not think of this. We'll stay one day. I'll send men to stand watch all along the coast."

Parthibendran said, "If you had been in the cyclone, you would not be so optimistic."

Ambalavan ignored him, stationed his men along the shore and paced restlessly on the beach.

The Screw-Pine Thicket

POONKUZLALI ROWED SLOWLY. The little boat rocked like a cradle in the calm sea. It was hard to believe that mountainous waves had surged on the same sea a day ago.

Devan insisted, "We must go to the princess at Pazlayarai. I gave her my word."

The prince was firm. "I will not disobey my father's orders. We will go to Thanjavur."

"Those are the Pazluvur brothers' orders," Devan declared. "If you go to Thanjavur as their prisoner, the people will revolt. Do you want your beloved country to become a battlefield?"

Arulmozli thought this over. "In any case, how can I avoid being arrested by Lord Ambalavan's men? They'll be waiting for us at Kodikkarai."

"This boat girl will help us," Devan said. "Poonkuzlali, can you hide us in the forest?"

Poonkuzlali was delighted. She had saved the prince and now, she had the chance to spend more time with him. "A little west of Kodikkarai, there's a canal which runs inwards from the sea. I can take the boat there. Both banks are covered by swamps: no one can approach easily. There are many places where I can hide the boat."

Arulmozli smiled. "I'm stealing like a thief into my own country! My friend, all your plans are useless. I'm not going to Pazlayarai or Thanjavur; god is taking me to heaven. I have the fever which was spreading in Sri Lanka: almost everyone who catches it dies."

Arulmozli was shivering. Soon, he became delirious. Devan was filled with dread. Poonkuzlali's oars fell from her hands and she stood still as a statue. Suddenly, Arulmozli jumped up and staggered in the boat. "Take me to my sister at once!" he cried. "I'm coming, *akka*!" With that, the prince tried to jump into the sea.

Devan caught him but the fever gave Arulmozli abnormal strength and he fought against Devan. Unable to hold the prince, Devan shouted, "Poonkuzlali, come quickly!"

Poonkuzlali snapped out of her daze, ran and caught one of Arulmozli's hands.

Suddenly, the prince's strength ebbed and he sobbed like a child. "*Akka*, I'll lie down, don't be angry with me. What would I do without you?" Arulmozli lay at the bottom of the boat, his eyes staring vacantly at a point and mumbling.

Devan realized it was up to him to save the prince. And he had the resourceful Poonkuzlali with him ... she shared his concern for Arulmozli. "Poonkuzlali, speed up. Shall we risk going to Kodikkarai? Can we depend on your family?"

"Sir, it's best to trust no one. My sister-in-law is greedy for money and my father is on the Pazluvur brothers' pay roll. Their men may be waiting there." She pointed to the shore: "Look!"

A large ship was anchored off shore.

"It may be Parthibendran's ship!" Devan exclaimed. "We can take the prince to Kanchipuram."

Poonkuzlali pointed to the lighthouse. "Look up: I see men standing there looking out to sea."

"Can they see our boat?" Devan asked anxiously.

"Not yet."

Devan made up his mind. "Let's go to the canal you mentioned earlier."

"We'll be there by sunset. I'll hide the boat. You and the prince must hide in the forest pavilion: it's nearby. I'll gather information and come back."

"Does the canal end there?"

"No, it continues all the way to Nagapattinam."

Arulmozli's murmur was louder and clearer. "*Akka*, as you predicted, the Buddhist Sangha offered me the Lankan throne ... I refused ... I'll do whatever you ask ... except that ... I don't want to rule a kingdom ... I'll be happier sailing the seas ... there's a boat girl in Kodikkarai ..."

Poonkuzlali's delight at these words contrasted with Devan's outrage. Both of them waited with bated breath for the prince to continue. But

Arulmozli lost consciousness once more. When he came to again, he looked around and asked weakly, "Have we reached Kodikkarai?"

"We are in sight of the shore," Devan replied.

The prince sank back into unconsciousness. Embarrassed by the prince's words, Poonkuzlali averted her face and rowed steadily. As darkness fell, they entered the canal. The dense jungle reached the high banks on both sides. Poonkuzlali stopped the boat, softly asking Devan to keep an eye on it. She jumped out and climbed a tall tree. She scanned the four directions and quickly came down.

"There are men posted all along the coast and a crowd is standing near the lighthouse."

"Did you recognize anyone?" Devan asked eagerly.

"No, but they must be Pazluvur men. I'll go home after nightfall and find out everything." Poonkuzlali rowed soundlessly up the canal. The trees' shadows made the water black. The stars twinkled above. After an endless hour, she stopped the boat on the shore and walked into the forest, but her heart hovered over the boat. Ignoring the thorns, shadows and wild creatures, she hurried to the Kuzlagar temple and reached there just as the priest was locking the sanctum door. She looked around to make sure there was no one else there and then went to the priest.

The startled priest cried, "Poonkuzlali, it's you! Where have you been?"

"I was away from home, *swami*. What's all the excitement about?"

"Don't you know anything?" the priest cried. "Haven't you been home?"

"You know I hate strangers. I saw people gathered there and came straight to the temple. Who are all these men?"

"Lord Ambalavan and his wife are here, along with their men. A man called Parthibendran Pallava came with terrible news: Prince Arulmozli was on that wretch's ship when the cyclone hit; the prince jumped overboard to save someone and is now missing! The Pazluvur men are combing the shore in case he washes up here. And the rumors about Lord Ambalavan's wife are false: she's a good woman. She was here a while back and grieved over the prince's fate."

"Really? I'm glad to hear she's a good woman. But what was she doing here, *swami*?"

"She came to offer prayers for the prince's safe return." The priest looked accusingly at Poonkuzlali. "Not everyone is as hard-hearted as you: you don't care about the prince."

"*Swami*, haven't you always told me that it's all up to fate? With important people around, I don't want to go home. Give me the food you offered the deity. I'll eat and sleep here tonight."

"You're a strange creature, Poonkuzlali," the priest said affectionately. He gave her a few coconuts and bananas.

"This won't satisfy my hunger," she complained. "What's in that kettle? Drinking water?"

"That's the milk poured over the deity. I'm taking it home for my child."

"I'll be your child today," Poonkuzlali said.

The priest smiled. "Here you are, don't lose the kettle. Bolt the entrance door before you sleep." He went on his way.

An owl hooted in the distance. Poonkuzlali froze—the call was repeated. Taking the food and milk, she followed the direction of the hoot. She came to a small canal bordered by screw-pine and followed the canal, ignoring the thorns. She walked silently, her ears alert. She heard a man and a woman talking softly ahead of her. Poonkuzlali hid in a thicket and listened carefully.

The woman said, "Sorcerer, like you, everyone believes the prince has drowned. My husband is heart-broken. But I don't believe the prince is dead."

Rakamma

NANDINI STOOD ALONE on the shore, lost in thought as she gazed at the waves.

"Lady," a voice called.

She turned to see a woman standing beside her. "Who are you?"

"I'm Rakamma, the lighthouse keeper's daughter-in-law ..." the woman broke off and stared at Nandini's face in amazement.

"What are you gaping at, you fool?" Nandini barked.

The women came to with a start. "Sorry, lady, there can be no connection between you and the deaf-mute woman."

"Which woman are you talking about?" Nandini asked.

"My husband's cousin, lady. She lives in Sri Lanka and sometimes comes here. There must be something wrong with my eyes: your face is just like hers!"

"Is she here now?" Nandini asked.

"No, lady, she comes here very rarely."

"When she comes next, bring her to me. I want to see this face which is a copy of mine."

"You are from Pandian country, so am I. The deaf-mute is a Chola woman: it's not possible."

"Never mind. I have heard of her from others too. Bring her to me and I'll reward you richly. What do you want?"

"A few days back, two men came here and said they had to go to Sri Lanka urgently on a mission for you. I sent my husband to row them across. My husband has not returned. I'm worried about him."

"Don't worry—if anything happens to him, I'll take care of you. What about the two men?"

"They are back: didn't you hear the owl hoot some time back?" Rakamma asked.

"What about that?" Nandini said casually.

"Didn't you recognize the sorcerer's call?" Rakamma asked.

"Are you one of his gang?" Nandini asked in surprise.

In reply, Rakamma drew a symbol on her palm. "The sorcerer is waiting to see you."

"Why can't he come here?" Nandini asked.

"He does not want to meet your husband or Parthibendran, whom he met in Sri Lanka. He asked me to bring you to the stream near the Kuzlagar temple. Shall we go?"

"Just like that?!" Nandini exclaimed.

"We can say we're going to the temple. If you want, Chendan Amudhan can escort us."

"Who is he?"

"The Thanjavur deaf-mute's son," Rakamma replied.

"God help us!" Nandini cried. "How many deaf-mutes are there?"

"It's a curse which runs in this family, lady. Some are born mute, some are dumb, even if they can talk. My husband can talk but I have intentionally made him dumb."

"Does the Sri Lankan deaf-mute have children?" Nandini asked.

"I believe she had twins, but no one knows what became of them," Rakamma said.

"And why's the Thanjavur boy here?"

"He came to see my sister-in-law, Poonkuzlali. As she's not here, he's waiting for her to return."

"Where did she go?"

"The day after my husband left with the sorcerer, two men came here, chased by Pazluvur soldiers. Poonkuzlali rowed one of them secretly to Sri Lanka that night. They say someone has drowned, but I don't believe it. We'll know the truth when she comes back."

"Maybe she has drowned," Nandini said.

"Never! The sea is her cradle. I saw a boat from the top of the lighthouse before it moved away. I think Poonkuzlali saw the crowd and took the boat into the canal in the marsh."

"Let the Thanjavur boy search for his cousin—we'll go to the temple," Nandini decided.

Like Poonkuzlali, Rakamma was familiar with the forest and guided Nandini safely through the swamp to the temple.

The astonished priest stammered, "Lady, why didn't you send word? I would have received you with every honor."

"Where was the time for that? I rushed here to pray that Kuzlagar saves the prince from the sea."

"Don't worry, lady. The prince's horoscope says he'll rule the world. God will save him." The priest offered the ritual aarti. "Lady, I'm glad to see you in this high position," he said.

"Have we met earlier?" Nandini asked.

"I have seen you in Pazlayarai and in the temple near Madurai. How's your brother, Thirumalai? He regrets that you have not met him after your marriage."

"Yes, I have not seen him in years. What can I do? I'm married into a family of Shiva devotees. My brother wanders from place to place

singing the songs of Vaishnava saints and picking up quarrels with
Shaivas. I have to be careful not to hurt my family."

"Absolutely right, lady. Let Thirumalai go his way—your first duty is
to your husband. I'll take you safely back to the beach."

"Please don't worry about us: this woman knows the way. And
Kodikkarai is crawling with our men. I'll go back safely," Nandini said.

As soon as they were out of sight of the priest, Rakamma took
Nandini to the canal behind the temple. They walked along the bank
in the starlight.

The Footsteps

POONKUZLALI, HIDING BEHIND the screw-pine, held her breath
and listened carefully.

"Why don't you believe me when I tell you the prince is dead?"
Ravidasan asked.

Nandini said slowly, "His horoscope says otherwise. You didn't see
Vandhiya Devan die or the prince rescuing him from the burning ship.
Whatever you say, my instinct tells me they are both alive. Do you know
Poonkuzlali?"

"I saw her in Lanka: she was a nuisance," Ravidasan said. "She may
have died in the cyclone."

"No. Rakamma saw her boat from the lighthouse earlier with two
or three people in it."

"Take your husband and leave at once: I'll deal with it. If the old man
is here, he'll welcome the prince with open arms and all our plans will
be ruined," Ravidasan said.

"Sorcerer, tell me: must they die?" Nandini asked. "If everyone
agrees to let Madurandaka become emperor ..."

"Foolish woman! Vandhiya Devan knows our secrets and he must
have told the prince. Leave Kodikkarai before dawn." He turned to
Rakamma. "Where would Poonkuzlali hide the men?"

"There's a pavilion in the forest which is her favorite hiding place,"
Rakamma replied. "I found out later that she hid the spy there for an
entire day before rowing him to Lanka."

"I know that place. I'll go and wait there." He turned back to Nandini. "How is our emperor?"

"Which emperor?" she asked.

Ravidasan snarled, "That diseased Sundara Pandian is no emperor of mine! I'm asking about our emperor."

"I heard he's in good health," Nandini replied. "How long it is since I last saw him!"

"Okay, okay, leave quickly," Ravidasan urged. "What about that fool, Parthibendran?"

"We are taking him with us to Thanjavur," Nandini smiled. "Don't worry about him. He'll do anything I ask him to."

"Still, be careful. Vandhiya Devan fooled you, didn't he?" Ravidasan pointed out.

"Yes," Nandini agreed. "That's why I want to meet him again."

They moved away from Poonkuzlali who trembled as she considered the dangers which threatened Arulmozli: the prince had caught a toxic fever; Ambalavan waited to arrest him; the sorcerer was ready to kill him; an enchantress in human form helped them; she had cast her spell on Parthibendran; the plotters even knew the secret hiding place.

I'm responsible for the prince's safety. I must hurry back to the boat. The weight of her burden crushed her mind and, for the first time, she lost her bearing in the forest. *Am I going round in circles? No, here's the canal.* She ran to the spot where she had left the boat. Her heart stopped—the boat had vanished! *Have they been arrested by the Pazluvur men? Or has Vandhiya Devan taken the prince to the hidden pavilion? Is the sorcerer waiting for them there?*

She ran towards the pavilion; again, she was troubled by doubts as to the way. Suddenly, Poonkuzlali stopped as she heard footsteps behind her. *Who can it be? Is it the sorcerer?* She took her dagger from her waist. *Whoever it is, I'll face him.* She thought again, *No, I must not risk my life. The prince's life is in my hands. I must live.*

Poonkuzlali ran deeper into the dense forest. The wild animals screeched and scattered but the footsteps continued behind her. She heard the thud of legs and panting breath. *Enough!* she decided in a rage. *Whoever it is, I'll show him who I am!*

A Song in the Forest

AS POONKUZLALI TURNED and faced the darkness, she heard a sweet voice singing. Recognizing the voice, she burst out laughing. "Cousin, is that you?" she asked.

"Yes, Poonkuzlali." Chendan Amudhan stood before her.

"Why did you frighten me like this?"

"I came all the way from Thanjavur and then I had to wait here for days. When I saw you at last, I had to catch you. Sing for me."

"Fine place and time for singing!"

"If you don't sing, I will, and all the wild animals will run for their lives." Amudhan bent to her ear and said, "Poonkuzlali, a man is chasing you—my song was a warning. I saw him whispering with your sister earlier. Do you know him?" He raised his voice: "Will you sing or shall I?"

Poonkuzlali sang a few lines and then quietly asked, "Amudhan, how did you find me?"

She continued to sing aloud while Amudhan explained softly, "I saw your boat from the lighthouse and came looking for you. Some Pazluvur men were nearby. I found the boat with the prince and Vandhiya Devan. I warned my friend. We submerged the boat in the canal and carried the prince to your hiding place."

"We have made a serious mistake, Amudhan," Poonkuzlali said quietly. Then, loudly, "Amudhan, I have forgotten the song in praise of Lord Kuzlagar. You sing it."

When Amudhan finished his song, he whispered, "There's no sound of footsteps: the man must be hiding nearby."

Poonkuzlali raised her voice. "These days, even men hoot like owls in this forest. Let me show you ..." She hooted like an owl.

"Where did you learn that?" Amudhan laughed.

"I learnt it from a sorcerer. You must hoot for your magic to work."

"You know magic?!"

"A little," Poonkuzlali said. "Let me demonstrate: my magic tells me someone is hiding nearby, listening to us ... look for him."

The bushes rustled and Ravidasan appeared, roaring with laughter.

"It's you, you wretch!" cried Poonkuzlali. "You tried to kill the prince in Sri Lanka. When you failed, you called up a storm and killed him and his friend at sea."

"Did you see them die?" Ravidasan asked.

"Their bodies washed ashore at Boodha Island and I buried them there," she declared.

"Don't try to fool me, girl!" Ravidasan shouted. "I know you countered my magic and revived them. I was only testing you. Tell me where you have hidden them, or else I'll burn you both into ashes!" His eyes flashed fire.

Poonkuzlali whispered to Amudhan, "I'm going to run; try to delay him." In a trembling voice, she told Ravidasan, "Please don't harm us: I'll show you where they are."

She ran from the pavilion. As the sorcerer followed her, Amudhan grabbed him from behind. Ravidasan gave Amudhan a blow, knocking him flat on the forest floor. Poonkuzlali sprinted through the forest with the sorcerer chasing her. Amudhan struggled behind them. Whenever the sorcerer seemed about to give up the chase, Poonkuzlali stopped as if to catch her breath. She ran up a sand dune and stopped at its summit, waiting for him. When the angry man puffed and panted his way there, she pointed: "Look at my lovers."

Ravidasan saw the floating globes of light which Devan had earlier seen. The sorcerer knew what they were, yet the eerie sight made his hair stand on end. "Are you trying to cheat me? I asked you to take me to the prince—why did you drag me here?"

"You refuse to believe they are dead. What can I do?" she retorted.

"Do you swear they are dead?"

She pointed to the comet in the night sky. "Isn't that proof enough? Don't you know a comet means a death in the royal family?"

Poonkuzlali broke into a run again. The furious sorcerer lost his cool and charged behind her, paying no attention to the terrain. After leading him straight on, Poonkuzlali suddenly swerved to the side. Ravidasan, hurtling after her, could not stop—he ran straight into the quicksand. To his horror, the wet clay slowly rose higher. He struggled in vain to free his legs.

Poonkuzlali laughed from the edge of the swamp. "Why don't you use your magic to escape?"

Controlling his anger, Ravidasan pleaded, "Give me a hand and pull me out. I won't harm you." The quicksand had reached his thighs. He grabbed a clump of grass on the shore and tried to pull himself up, but he only sank deeper into the swamp. "Girl! Have mercy!" he shrieked.

Amudhan arrived and took in the situation in a glance. His eyes filled with compassion.

"Let's go," Poonkuzlali said.

"And leave him like this? I'll have nightmares for the rest of my life!" Amudhan exclaimed.

"He wanted to kill me," Poonkuzlali pointed out.

"God will punish him for his sins. We must save him."

"Very well, give me your upper garment." Poonkuzlali tied one end of the cloth to the stem of a large bush near the swamp and threw the other end to Ravidasan. "Hold this end. Don't pull it or try to get out on your own: you'll uproot the bush. Someone will come in the morning and rescue you."

"I can't bear this for an entire night!" Ravidasan howled. "Kill me!"

Poonkuzlali ignored him and dragged Amudhan away. The sorcerer's cries followed them for a long distance before fading away.

"Cousin," Poonkuzlali said. "You arrived just in time. Why did you come to Kodikkarai?"

"After the dungeon, I was tired of Thanjavur ... and I also wanted to hear you sing. I went to Pazlayarai and met Princess Kundavai. She sent me here with a message for Vandhiya Devan: he is to take the prince to the Choodamani Monastery in Nagapattinam. Poonkuzlali, the Buddhist monks there are skilled healers. They'll cure the prince."

"How do we go to Nagapattinam?" she asked.

"By boat through the canal. We just have to pull up the boat and empty the water."

"But the boat will not hold us all ..."

"We have decided Vandhiya Devan will go straight to Pazlayarai from here while we take the prince to Nagapattinam."

Poonkuzlali was overjoyed at the thought of spending a few more days with the prince.

They reached the pavilion and Amudhan clapped his hands.

"Who's there?" Devan shouted.

"Me, Amudhan—and my cousin."

Devan stepped out. "Speak softly, the prince is sleeping. Sometime back, I heard someone and came out, thinking it was you. The man looked like Ravidasan. Before he could see me, you started singing—perfect timing, my friend! He turned away: did you meet him?"

"Yes, and this girl has left him standing waist-high in quicksand," Amudhan said.

"We heard her singing too," Devan said. "Her song brought the prince out of his delirium. He asked, 'Who's singing?' I said, 'It's the boat girl.' He listened for a while and then fell asleep."

Poonkuzlali's heart thrilled to hear this. Amudhan heard the distant barking of foxes, mingled with the screech of an owl. He shuddered as he pictured the sorcerer hooting to chase away the foxes that circled him.

"If we wait until sunrise, we'll be trapped. We must leave at once," Poonkuzlali said.

The two men carried the sleeping prince and followed her to the boat. Laying him gently down on the bank, they waded into the canal, carefully lifted out the boat and carried it to the shore.

The prince stirred and weakly cried, "Water." Poonkuzlali gave him milk from the kettle. Arulmozli drank some milk and looked up. "Poonkuzlali, is that you? I thought it was an angel feeding me nectar."

Aiyo! Ghost!

ECSTATIC AT THESE words, Poonkuzlali said, "Prince, I'm only a simple boat girl."

"No, you are the Ocean Princess. How many times you have saved my life! What can I do for you in return?"

"Stay with me for another day and let me take you to Nagapattinam as the princess wants."

"Who's the boy in the boat with Vandhiya Devan?" Arulmozli asked.

"My cousin, Amudhan. He brought the princess's message asking you to go to the Choodamani Monastery."

Arulmozli smiled. "My sister has finally given up her plans to make me king. How lucky I am! I'll become a monk and go on pilgrimages to Java … China … come, let's go!"

He's still delirious, Poonkuzlali thought.

Suddenly, they heard a shriek of agony in the distance. The startled prince jumped up. "What's that?"

"It's an owl hooting," Poonkuzlali said.

"No! It's the sound of a man in pain—we must save him." Saying this, the prince lunged forward, only to fall. Poonkuzlali held him as the two men came running. They carried the unconscious prince to the boat and gently laid him down.

"I'll leave you here," Devan said. His eyes brimmed with tears in the moonlight and his voice shook. "It's up to you to take the prince to safety. There's nothing more for me to say."

"Why don't you come with us to the edge of the forest?" Amudhan suggested. "I left my horse there and you can ride on from there."

"No," Devan replied. "I'll sleep in the Kuzlagar temple for a few hours and leave at sunrise. I need to rest if I'm to face the dangers tomorrow's journey may bring."

"Take this." Poonkuzlali gave him the parcel of food she had carried carefully all this while. "We can get food from the villages, but you have to stay hidden all the way to Pazlayarai."

"Remember that the prince is in the boat," Devan warned.

"No one will give this old boat a second look," Poonkuzlali assured him. "No one will believe this man's a prince. Don't worry."

Again, the pitiful shriek was heard. The prince stirred and murmured, "What's that?" before sinking back into a faint.

Poonkuzlali stood. "The prince will never forgive me if I leave the sorcerer in the swamp—it's nearby. Wait here; I'll pull him out and come back." She ran into the forest.

Devan stopped Amudhan from following her. "Stay here and guard the prince. I'll go with her. I have some unfinished business with that sorcerer."

Poonkuzlali imagined Ravidasan being devoured by foxes and the prince accusing her of murder. This lent her wings and she was at the swamp in minutes. To her horror, the swamp was empty.

"Maybe it was a different patch of quicksand," Devan suggested.

Speechless, Poonkuzlali pointed to Amudhan's garment which was still knotted to the shrub.

Devan comforted her. "That man has a hundred lives. He must have escaped." In his heart, he rejoiced that the wicked man had met his end in the swamp.

Taking Amudhan's garment, they walked back to the canal. Suddenly, ahead of them, they saw two figures hiding behind a large tree and peering at the canal.

"It's the sorcerer and my sister-in-law," Poonkuzlali said. "She's the one who rescued him from the quicksand. They have spotted the boat in the canal."

Just then, one of the figures turned in their direction. The next instant, both figures vanished.

"Sir, they have seen us," Poonkuzlali said. "They are hiding."

"Don't worry," Devan said. "I have an idea. Just go along with anything I say." He led her to a place on the canal bank within earshot of the hidden pair and sat down with her. "Look here, Poonkuzlali," Devan said loudly. "The sorcerer is dead—good riddance to him!"

"But what a dreadful way to die!" she replied.

"You're the one who pushed him into the swamp," Devan pointed out. "You're a murderess."

"Me, a murderess!?" she cried.

"I'm no better than you. I pushed the prince into the sea and you pushed the sorcerer into the swamp. If you promise to keep quiet about the prince, I promise to keep quiet about the sorcerer."

"You killed the prince? Some time back, you said you had not seen him."

"I lied, but now there's no need to hide anything from you. Do you agree to my terms? If you don't, I'll tell Lady Nandini you killed the sorcerer. She'll see you buried up to your neck in sand and trampled by an elephant. Remember, no one saw me kill the prince, but I saw you kill the sorcerer."

"What do you want me to do?" she asked.

Devan said harshly, "Get into the boat with your cousin and go to Sri Lanka: you can grieve for your prince there. If I let you stay here, you may tell the Pazluvur brothers about me. All said and done, they have a soft corner for the prince and will punish me. I don't want to die."

"You wretch! At least tell me why you killed the prince."

"Listen, the prince and his sister were plotting to grab the throne from my master, Aditya Karikalan. My master's enemies are my enemies, and so I killed the prince."

"You'll be punished for your sins. I'll go to Lanka—what choice do I have?"

"Get into the boat and head out to sea. If I see you turn towards Kodikkarai, that will be the end of you. Now, go!"

Poonkuzlali hurried to the boat and climbed in. Devan remained seated and watched as the boat set off down the canal and disappeared from view. Suddenly, he heard wild laughter behind him. Devan jumped up as if startled and turned around—Ravidasan stood in the middle of the dense bushes, laughing hysterically.

"Aiyo! Ghost!" Devan shouted and sprinted into the forest.

Three in the Boat

A BEAUTIFUL NEW day dawned as the boat glided up the canal. The song of birds and the paddle of oars woke Poonkuzlali. Her heart leaped at the sight of the prince's radiant face before her.

"Where's the boat headed?" the prince suddenly asked.

"To the Choodamani Monastery," Poonkuzlali said.

The prince murmured, "So, it was not a dream. Amudhan, does my sister want me to become a monk? Where's my friend, Vandhiya Devan?" and sank back into sleep.

They heard a horse; Poonkuzlali and Amudhan looked at each other anxiously. The next minute, Vandhiya Devan rode up. The boat stopped and he jumped off his horse. "I just stopped to see if everything was okay," Devan said. "There's no immediate danger. The sorcerer believed my story: he does not suspect the prince is in this boat."

"Did you see him?" Poonkuzlali asked.

Devan smiled. "Yes. I screamed as if I had seen a ghost and ran."

"I've never seen a liar like you!" she exclaimed.

"Not lies—call it imagination," Devan laughed. "How's the prince?"

Poonkuzlali was worried. "He wakes up now and then and says a few words. He goes back to sleep again. How long will he be like this?"

"It can last for months. But the Buddhist monks will cure him. Poonkuzlali, you are responsible for the prince. Knowing Amudhan, if he sees a temple, he'll forget the prince and go to worship the gods with his songs."

"Not after becoming your friend," Amudhan countered. "My devotion has decreased."

"Is that because of me or the girl?" Devan teased.

Amudhan ignored this and asked, "Did you find the horse?"

"The horse found me! It's the horse I left with you in Thanjavur, right? It recognized me in the dark and neighed. I don't know whether I'll see you again. When the prince awakes, tell him I'm going to Pazlayarai and will send news from there at the earliest: he'll be worried." Devan turned his horse and rode away.

The boat glided down the canal, lined with flowering trees. The blossoms filled the air with fragrance and carpeted the surface of the water. *This is the road to paradise,* Poonkuzlali thought. When the prince was awake, she turned aside. But when he was asleep, she feasted her eyes on his face. When Amudhan went to buy food and milk from the villages, she stroked Arulmozli's forehead and ran her fingers through his hair.

They took turns to row. At sunrise the next day, they reached Nagapattinam. They took the branch canal which led straight to the monastery and stopped the boat behind the building. They heard the roar of a crowd and saw monks hurrying about. Leaving the others there, Amudhan went to see what was happening.

Choodamani Monastery

AMUDHAN FOUND THE monastery's back courtyard deserted and made his way to the front. He pushed his way through the crowd gathered there and reached the steps. He soon understood the situation.

Parthibendran's ship had reached Nagapattinam the previous day and the town was abuzz with rumors. The abbot had summoned one of the sailors that morning, questioned him and found that the news of the prince's disappearance at sea was true.

The crowd wailed in grief and tears streamed down the abbot's face. He turned away and climbed up the steps with the other monks. Amudhan mingled with them and entered the monastery.

The monks listened in tears to the abbot. "Is this Buddha's mercy? When I went to Thanjavur, Princess Kundavai took me aside and told me she would fund a hospital at our monastery. She said these are dangerous times and asked me whether I could keep Prince Arulmozli as a guest here if necessary. I assured her I would guard him with my life. But all is lost! The prince is dead. The hopes of all the good people in the Chola empire are dashed."

When the abbot finished speaking, Amudhan moved towards him. He was stopped by several monks who shouted, "Who's this man?" "How did he come in?"

Amudhan spoke up. "I'm Chendan Amudhan from Thanjavur. I must speak to the abbot."

The abbot said, "Speak, there are no secrets here."

Amudhan said, "Sir, I came here by boat with a man who is ill ... he has the chills. Please -"

The abbot exclaimed, "That's contagious! Why did you bring him here? And now of all times?"

"I saw one of Emperor Ashoka's pillars near Kanchipuram," Amudhan said. "It said caring for the sick is the most important part of Buddhist Dharma, but you are chasing us away ..."

The abbot turned to the monks. "Stay here. I'll go with this man." When he saw Poonkuzlali in the courtyard, he was horrified. "Don't you know women are not allowed here?" He froze in joyful surprise when he recognized the prince. "Isn't this Prince Arulmozli?"

"No," the prince replied. "I'm a boatman. These two are trying to fool me. I asked this girl to marry me and sail with me to distant lands. She says I'm born to rule the world. She won't marry me as she's from the fishing community. She says all she wants is for me to recover and she'll rejoice in my future victories ..."

Realizing that the prince was delirious, the abbot told the monks, "This young man is suffering from the chills. I'll keep him in my room and care for him myself. If we send him away, the fever will spread: thousands died in Sri Lanka. Ignore anything he says in his delirium."

The abbot, supported by Amudhan, took the prince up the steps. Saying a few words to Amudhan, the abbot went into the monastery, followed by the other monks. The door closed. Poonkuzlali stood looking after them—it was as if the door to her heart had banged shut.

The Smithy

VANDHIYA DEVAN RODE towards Pazlayarai. He did not need to ask for directions as he remembered the route which he had taken earlier on his way to Kodikkarai. The horse struggled along the rough forest path. Devan was exhausted and badly in need of sleep.

Once I reach Pazlayarai and meet Princess Kundavai, I'll sleep for days. He imagined her beautiful face radiant with happiness that he had fulfilled his task. He felt a tinge of regret: *How many lies I have said since I left Kanchipuram! I thought cunning and deceit were the only ways to deal with danger. Prince Arulmozli's integrity has changed me.* Devan was worried that his lies to the sorcerer might reach the princess and lead to disaster. *No, she won't believe them. In future, I'll leave spying and intrigue to Thirumalai and Ravidasan. I'll stick to the truth and face the consequences. My sword will be my strength. No more lies …*

Lost in thought, Devan did not notice his horse limping. He nodded off for a few minutes. Only when the horse stumbled did he startle awake and jump down. He found a small, sharp stone wedged in the horse's front hoof. He picked out the stone, comforted the horse and rode on. He remembered Ravidasan talking about Arabs fixing iron shoes to their horses' hooves. *I'll enquire about this at the first smithy I come to.* Devan left the forest track and took the highway. *No one here knows me. The Pazluvur brothers' men and Ravidasan are behind me. On the highway, I can find a smithy and shoe my horse.*

Devan came to a village where the streets and houses were decorated with welcome arches. *Are they expecting the Pazluvur brothers? I must hurry away from here.* He noticed groups of villagers in sorrowful discussion. Some men came to stop him, but Devan spurred his horse on. He did not want to get involved in any trouble. He came to a smithy on the outskirts of the village. He stopped the horse and went inside. The smith was at work while a small boy stoked the furnace. Devan saw a man leaving by the back entrance just as he entered by the front door. But all his attention was caught by the beautiful sword in the smith's hand: one side shone like polished silver while the other glowed a golden-red. *What a marvelous piece of work!* Devan thought.

Throw Him into the Fire!

VANDHIYA DEVAN CLEARED his throat noisily to catch the smith's attention.

The smith said, "A few years ago, there was a demand for weapons. Now, people come to sell their old weapons to me. Do you want to sell your sword?"

"No," Devan replied. "Once I complete my mission, I'll go on a pilgrimage. I'll bring my weapons to you then. What about the sword in your hand?"

"This has come to be polished," the smith said. "What can I do for you?"

"Do you know how to shoe a horse?" Devan asked.

"Yes, that's now picking up in Tamil Nadu. But you must wait until I finish with this sword."

Devan agreed to wait. *I need some rest, and so does the horse.* He stared at the sword in the smith's hand. "That's a marvelous sword. Who does it belong to?"

"Ask me no questions and I'll tell you no lies." The smith smiled and continued to work.

Devan examined the sword: a fish was engraved on its hilt. *Does it mean something? Or is it just ornamentation?* The smith plunged the hilt into the furnace and hammered it, as if he was trying to erase the fish symbol. *Why would he do that?* As he stared at the sword, drowsiness overtook Devan. He lay down by the furnace and slept.

He was troubled by horrible dreams. A man came to claim the sword and the smith said, 'There's no charge: it's my gift to Lady Nandini.' 'No one must know of this,' the man threatened. 'If that young man sleeping there suspects anything, throw him into the furnace.' They dragged Devan to the fire. The images changed: Devan stood before Yama, the God of Death. 'He's a liar,' accused Chitragupta. 'No,' shouted Devan. 'I lied only to serve the Cholas!' 'A lie is a lie!' shouted Yama. 'Throw him into the fire!' A million voices howled as the Pazluvur brothers dragged him to hell. Princess Kundavai said, 'He lied for me: punish me instead.' Nandini said, 'Throw them both into the fire' …

"No!" shouted Devan and sat up. Even as he rejoiced that it was only a dream, his body shook. *I'll never again lie,* he resolved. "Have I been asleep for long?" he asked.

"Six hours in broad daylight!" the smith mocked him.

"Have you shod my horse?"

"Not yet. A sleepyhead like you will probably lose the horse and yourself too."

Devan ran out—his horse was gone! He faced the smith with his hand on his sword. "Where's my horse?"

"Don't worry," the smith smiled. "Your horse is safe. Look in the yard."

Devan found his horse stabled in the yard. The small boy from the forge was feeding it grass. The boy said, "My father asked me to bring the horse here as Lord Ambalavan and his retinue were passing by. If the Pazluvur men saw the horse, they would have taken it."

Devan was ashamed of his suspicions. As the smith worked on the horse shoes, he said, "Thank you for safeguarding my horse. How long is it since the Pazluvur men went by?"

"About an hour," the smith replied. "You slept through all that commotion."

"Why didn't you start work on my horse after they left? You've wasted all this time."

"How could anyone have the heart to work after hearing the news those men brought? Where are you coming from, *thambi*?"

"Sri Lanka," Devan answered.

The smith lowered his voice. "Did you see the prince there?"

"Yes," said Devan, sticking to his resolution to speak only the truth.

"When did you last see the prince?"

"This morning," Devan replied.

"Really?" the smith sneered. "And where's he now?"

"At the Choodamani Monastery in Nagapattinam."

"I have never met a bigger liar than you!" the smith exclaimed.

Devan smiled. *Everyone believes my lies, but no one believes me when I speak the truth.*

"You have not heard the news, *thambi*," the smith said. "The prince is missing at sea."

"What!" Devan pretended surprise.

"We heard rumors yesterday. Lord Ambalavan confirmed it as he passed through. May that wretch be struck by lightning! It's all because of a plot hatched by him. The people cancelled the reception arranged for him."

"Do the people love the prince so much?" Devan asked.

"The Chola empire is drowning in sorrow. People curse the Pazluvur brothers. The emperor is ill: what will the effect of this news be on him? The comet rightly predicted disaster. If god is merciful would the prince have died? Would the evil Pazluvur brothers prosper?"

Thank goodness the smith did not believe me. I need not lie about the prince, but I need not say the truth either. "The Pazluvur brothers are powerful—be careful what you say," Devan warned.

"You're the one who should be careful. I speak when I'm awake, you blabber in your sleep."

"Aiyo! What did I say?" Devan asked anxiously.

"You said the Pazluvur brothers are devils and Lady Nandini's a monster: it's true, but imagine your fate if anyone overheard you! The Pazluvur men were passing by just then. I quickly hid your horse, shut the smithy door and stood outside."

"Did I say anything more?" Devan asked.

"Much more. You begged some prince to come to Pazlayarai; he insisted on being arrested by the Pazluvur brothers. You also spoke a lot about Princess Kundavai ... be careful, *thambi!*"

Devan bowed his head in shame. *I hope I didn't say anything to embarrass her. From today, I must sleep alone in a room with the door locked - or in a mountain cave or a desert!*

"You spoke about surviving a cyclone—maybe the prince will also be saved by god."

"Sir, I need to go to Pazlayarai urgently without being seen by the Pazluvur men …"

"The Pazluvur company is on the highway. Take the path along the Mullai river to Pazlayarai."

The smith hammered the shoes. With each blow, he shouted: "That's for Lord Ambalavan! That's for Lord Kalaanthaka! That's for Sambuvaraya!" The smith refused payment for his work. "Why are you going to Pazlayarai?"

Devan said, "Ask me no questions and I'll tell you no lies."

The smith laughed. "Young man, you learn quickly. Be as careful in your sleep."

Dusk was falling as Devan rode along the banks of the Mullai. Under the starlit sky, Devan was suddenly filled with joy: the prince was alive; he had outwitted the sorcerer; he had completed his mission—above all, he was going to see Kundavai. He burst into a love song. As he finished the last note, he heard foxes barking. Above the barks came a man's loud laughter. Devan looked around fearfully as his hand went to his sword hilt.

A man walked out from behind a tree—it was Devaralan. "Young man, your song was wonderful, and so was the barking of the foxes."

Poisoned Arrow

VANDHIYA DEVAN'S HEART quailed at meeting Devaralan at this time and place. He recalled the man's frenzied dance at Kadambur and the conversation on the ship. *Shall I make a run for it?* He looked around and saw the light of a funeral pyre in the distance. *Prince or pauper, we all must die one day.* His fear vanished as swiftly as it came. *Why should I run from this villain? Let me hear what he has to say. Maybe he was the man who slipped away from the smithy when I entered; maybe that sword is his. He may know the meaning of the fish symbol.* Devan slowed his horse and asked, "How did you suddenly turn up here?"

Devaralan sneered. "How did you escape from the ship?"

Devan laughed. "Do you think you're the only one who knows magic? What do you want? You told me your secrets on the ship, but I won't reveal them to anyone. I'll forget everything."

"I'm not worried about that: if you reveal our secrets, your tongue will rot and fall out."

How can I get rid of this man? Devan wondered. *No use pushing him into the river–the water is shallow. I'll use my trusty sword ...*

"Don't even try it!" Devaralan said, as if he had read Devan's mind.

Needing time to think, Devan changed the topic: "Where's your friend, Ravidasan?"

Devaralan laughed wildly. "You tell me, where's Ravidasan? And where's that boat girl?"

Devan felt he had stepped on a snake's tail. "Let me go. I have urgent work."

"Let me tell you why I waited here for you. This river fulfils all wishes. The person for whom you sang your love song is waiting for you. Look ..." he pointed.

A little way ahead, Devan saw the vague outline of a palanquin. *Where have I seen it before? Ah! It's Nandini's palanquin.* Devan suddenly longed to see Nandini. He stopped his horse at the palanquin and dismounted. Devaralan gave a cry—seven or eight men rushed out of hiding behind the trees and pounced on Devan. They bound his hands and legs, blindfolded him, grabbed his sword and threw him into the palanquin. Some men carried the palanquin and hurried behind Devaralan; others walked ahead and behind it; one man followed, leading the horse.

All this happened in the blink of an eye, taking Devan completely by surprise. When his confusion cleared, he shook off the loose blindfold. He moved the screen with his tied hands and peered out: they had left the riverbank and were headed somewhere else. He could easily free his hands and legs, jump out of the palanquin, deal with those men, climb on his horse and gallop away. But something held him back. A strange fragrance filled the palanquin. His instincts told him he was on his way to meet Nandini. He was obsessed by his desire to see her. *Let me see her just this once and hear what she has to say; I may never get a chance again. I'll meet cunning with cunning. I must find out the connection between her and the mute old woman in Sri Lanka who looks like her.* Suddenly, Devan felt giddy and sleepy. *Something's wrong! The perfume in the palanquin ...*

Even as he struggled to free himself, his eyes closed and he slipped into unconsciousness. When he woke, he was in a spacious room, brightly lit with lamps. The invigorating scent of incense filled the room. He sat up in bed and looked expectantly at the open door—Nandini walked in. Devan was mesmerized by her beauty, by this unexpected meeting and by her striking resemblance to the mute woman.

Her sweet voice said, "You're a good man. Do good men leave without saying goodbye?"

Devan bowed his head in embarrassed silence.

"I gave you my ring and helped you enter Thanjavur Fort: surely you could have returned it before you left? Where's it? You no longer need it; give it to me."

"Forgive me, lady. General Velir took it forcibly from me in Sri Lanka."

"He's my arch-enemy. I don't believe a brave warrior like you can be forced into anything."

"Your men brought me here by force," Devan pointed out.

"Be honest, sir. You had the opportunity to escape from the palanquin."

"I came willingly," Devan admitted. "I had to know why you wanted to meet me."

"To get my ring. When you were in the underground treasury..." She paused at Devan's shock. "My goodness! How could you have escaped that night if I hadn't known you were there? My husband and I both knew you were hiding there. He ordered the guard to kill you; I changed his orders and saved you, or your skeleton would be piled beside that heap of pearls by now."

Devan was amazed. *How could she know I was there? I had better thank her just in case ...*

Nandini said, "Don't say what you don't believe. I don't want your thanks. I brought this up only to warn you not to return to the treasury—the guard has been strengthened."

"I have no intention of going back there," Devan said.

"You don't care about those who help you. Your friend was wounded. I took him home, healed him and sent him away. Are you glad, or are you a born betrayer of friendship and trust?"

Nandini's words pierced Devan's heart like poisoned arrows. He suffered in silence.

"What about the doctor's son you left to be caught in your place? Do you care about him?"

"I planned to ask you about him," Devan said.

"I'll tell you about him, if you tell me about Prince Arulmozli,"

She brought me here for news of the prince. I must not let her get the better of me. "Lady, please don't ask me about that," he said.

"I know I won't get a word out of you about that. Can I ask about your lover? How is she?"

Devan's eyes flashed fire. "Who are you referring to? Careful!"

"I am careful. I'm not referring to the Maharani of Pazlayarai: you are less to her than the dust under her feet! I'm talking about the boat girl who rowed you to Sri Lanka—Poonkuzlali."

"She's not my sweetheart. She showed me the marsh lights and said they are her lovers."

"She's lucky: her lovers are figures of light. My lovers are shrouded in darkness. Have you ever spent a night in a ruined jungle pavilion with the wings of formless bats and owls fluttering in the darkness? Such figures haunt my soul; their fluttering wings beat against my heart and caress my cheeks. Where do these dark figures come from? Why do they haunt me? Do you know?" Nandini's mad eyes darted here and there.

Devan's hard heart melted with pity and fear. "Lady, calm yourself," he urged.

"Who are you to advise me?"

"I'm Vandhiya Devan of Vallam. Who are you, lady?"

"Who am I? I don't know ... am I a woman or a demon?"

"You may be an angel who lost her way and fell to earth because of a divine curse ..."

Nandini cut him off. "Yes, a divine curse is on me: what it is, I don't know. I don't know who I am or why I was born. This is the only token god has given me ... look!" Nandini raised the sword which lay near her. The newly polished, sharp sword glowed blindingly in the light.

Devan recognized the sword as the one he had seen in the smithy. His warrior heart, accustomed to swords and spears from childhood, was fearless before this wonderful weapon. "Lady, I see an exquisitely crafted sword worthy of royalty. Why is it in your delicate hand? What does it mean?"

A Flying Horse

NANDINI HUGGED THE shining blade and kissed it. Her face took on the awesome beauty of Kali thirsting for blood. Then, she put the sword down and became her usual charming self. "I have yet to find the sword's meaning. I keep it sharpened and polished and guard it like a tigress guards its cubs. Maybe I'll plunge its blade into a wicked man's chest; maybe I'll plunge it into my own chest and let my blood stain my rich silks and ornaments. I'm prepared for whatever may happen. My poor husband thinks I dress like this daily as a tribute to him and his position—little does he know the fire which burns in my heart!"

Devan came to his senses. "Lady, where's your husband?"

"Why?" she asked. "Are you afraid of him?"

"My dear lady," he replied. "I'm not even afraid of you."

"Ah! That's why I like you. My husband, the man with sixty-four battle scars, fears me; my brother-in-law, the fearless Kalaanthaka, trembles before me; Madurandaka, who dreams of being king, stands in awe before me; Sundara Chola, the emperor with one foot in the grave, faints at the sight of me. And now, the fearless Parthibendran, Karikalan's closest friend, follows me, ready to do anything for me; yet, he trembles to come near me. When I was a little child, I was fascinated by fire. I longed to touch it but whenever my hands neared the flame, I would draw back in fear. Aditya Karikalan is the same. Even when we were children, he loved me but also feared me. How my life has changed because of that! Sir, when you see your master, give him a message from me: tell him I have forgotten the past. My marriage to Lord Ambalavan makes me his grandmother—he no longer needs to fear me ..."

"Lady, I don't know if I'll reach him alive. And I have many important messages for him. I can't promise to give him yours. Forgive me."

"Yes, you're the bravest man I know: you're not afraid to speak your mind."

"It's no use hiding anything from you: you penetrate a man's heart and find his secrets."

"But I can't read your heart. Anyway, leave it. You asked about my husband. Parthibendran and he have gone to a village to see the *Velanattam*. The fools hope the Devaralan will make predictions about Prince Arulmozli. Instead of catching and questioning the right person, they are listening to astrologers! They will be away for hours, that's why I brought you here. Sir, I ask you once again, will you tell me the truth about the prince?"

"No, lady, I will not. I have resolved to speak only the truth from today, but I forgot my resolution and lied to you earlier. Forgive me." He took the signet ring from his pouch and extended it to her. "The general gave it back to me."

"I'm not in the habit of taking back what I give. I was testing you. You have passed the test. I need not ask my men to search you. Keep the ring in memory of me."

"My dear lady, are you sure? If the need arises, I may use it again."

"You can do whatever you want with it. Now, my men will take you back to the river."

"Where are we, lady?" Devan asked.

"Long ago, when the Chola country was under Pallava rule, the Pallava kings built this palace and fort. Later, the Pandian kings captured this territory and used this palace. A great battle took place here, leaving the fort in ruins. We are now in a small portion which is undamaged. This fort is called Pallava Fort by some and Pandian Fort by others. Do you want my men to escort you? It's difficult for anyone who does not know the way to find the path."

"Lady, I'm in a hurry: please ask your men to guide me. Before I leave, is there anything I can do for you?"

"Can you get me a flying horse?"

"Do you mean a fast Arab horse?" Devan asked.

"No. I have heard of horses which spread their wings and fly in the sky ..."

"To fly to heaven?" Devan smiled.

"Do I look like the kind of woman who goes to heaven?" she asked. "I'm a sinner."

"Many of those in heaven are sinners who atoned for their sins on earth and returned to heaven."

"I have no desire to go to heaven. There's an outcrop of bare rock in a desert in the Pandian country. There are caves there which the Jain monks once used. Now only snakes and jackals go there. That place is dearer to me than heaven."

"You have strange wishes, lady."

"If I had a flying horse, I would go to those caves. Then I would fly to see all the wonders I have heard of: mountains whose summits are always covered with snow and ice that shine like silver in the sun; vast deserts whose white sands burn like fire in the afternoon heat; lands so cold that the seas are frozen and men and animals walk over the ice ..."

Devan smiled. "I can't get you a flying horse, lady, but if you sail on a ship ..."

"Sir, I'm terrified of ships: I can't even get into a boat without trembling! You may go."

Devan asked, "Were you in Lanka recently? Were you on a street in Anuradhapura one night?"

"I have not set foot outside the Pazluvur mansion. Why do you ask?"

"Lady, I saw you in Lanka: in a simple sari, hair uncombed, wearing no ornaments ..."

"It was not me. Did this woman speak?"

"No, she used sign language. If it was not you, she's a copy of you."

Nandini's eyes looked into the distance. She sighed. "If you really want to do something for me, bring that mute woman to me, or take me to her."

Within an hour, Devan was back on the riverbank. His escort vanished into the night. Devan rode on in the darkness. He looked at the comet and wondered whether it was truly a bad omen. He thought of Nandini. Her words were etched in his memory. The revulsion he had felt when he first met her at Thanjavur gave place to pity. She was a woman scarred by deep sorrow. Her past and her plans remained a mystery to him. Her incomparable beauty and bewitching charm were dangerous. He decided that it would be best to have nothing more to do with her. *Shall I throw her ring into the river? No, it may be useful later. I'll keep it till I report to Princess Kundavai. And I won't get involved in such dangerous missions again.*

Venus rose in the east. Devan tied his horse to a tree and slept awhile.

The Kalamukhas

THE RAYS OF the rising sun fell on Vandhiya Devan's face. He reluctantly opened his eyes and saw two men walking towards him. Their matted locks and the tridents and fire pots they carried showed that they were Kalamukhas. Many believed that Kalamukhas did penance in the cremation grounds and could predict the future. People feared their curses and tried to please them. Many chieftains gave them charity through temples and rest houses, but the Chola kings were not their patrons.

Pity Thirumalai is not here to pick a quarrel with them. Devan decided to pretend to be asleep until they passed. He sensed them stopping beside him. Devan kept his eyes closed as one man cleared his throat.

"*Shivoham!* It would be good if this young man joined our cause."

"*Shivoham!* Don't be fooled by his good looks," the other replied. "He'll be useless to us. Very soon, he'll face great danger."

Devan was becoming breathless. *If I open my eyes now, they'll know I was pretending. I'll keep my eyes closed. They may say more about the danger which threatens me.*

But the first man said, "*Shivoham!* That's his fate. Come," and the two men moved on.

Devan waited for them to go a little ahead and got up. *Let them babble. After all I've been through, what more dangers can come my way?* But he was rather eager to hear what his future held. He saw the ascetics standing by a ruined pavilion. Behind it was a former Jain cave which the Kalamukhas now used. Leaving his horse tied to the tree, Devan walked to the pavilion, planning to speak to the men. As he neared the ruins, he heard them talking on the other side.

"That boy was really asleep; I have not yet met a man who can ignore a prediction of coming danger," one man said.

"I still say that strong young man would help our cause," the other insisted.

"Why do we need him? Soon, Madurandaka, the next Chola emperor, will be joining our sect."

"How's that possible?" the second man said. "What about the other two princes?"

"One is missing at sea and the other's life is coming to an end," the first said.

Devan lost all interest in talking to the Kalamukhas. He decided to deliver his message to Kundavai at Pazlayarai and hurry back to Karikalan in Kanchipuram. *My first duty is to Aditya Karikalan. Even Parthibendran has fallen under Nandini's spell. The prince is rash and rushes into danger. I must stand by him.* Devan turned back, mounted his horse and rode away. As he crossed the pavilion, the Kalamukhas stared at him. One of their faces seemed familiar; he ignored that and galloped away.

He passed villages where people went peacefully about their tasks. It was clear that news of Arulmozli's death had not yet reached them. *Good. I must get to Pazlayarai before the news reaches the city. Princess Kundavai may not believe it but that Kodumbalur girl might kill herself.*

But his horse, not yet comfortable with its new shoes, refused to gallop. Devan reached Pazlayarai only by late afternoon. Slowing the horse to a walk, he wondered how to get through the gates. Just then, a procession came from another direction. Men with spears and banners marched before a gilded, lotus-shaped chariot. In the chariot was Madurandaka. In a flash, Devan hit upon an idea to gain entry into the fort: *Didn't the Kalamukha say no one can ignore a warning of coming danger?*

Devan spurred his horse forward. Taken by surprise, the guards failed to stop him in time and he reached the chariot. Devan stood up in his stirrups and shouted, "Danger!" Even as the guards unsheathed their swords and aimed their spears, he jumped off his horse and rolled on the ground. Seeing Devan on the ground, the escort relaxed and laughed. Madurandaka joined them. Ignoring his fall, Devan jumped up and stared at the prince.

"Bring him here," Madurandaka said. Two guards took Devan to the prince. "Who are you?"

Devan stared at the prince's face. "Great emperor! Don't you know me?"

The prince waved away the guards. "Who do you think I am?" he asked Devan.

"Forgive me, prince, I made a mistake. You are not yet … not yet …" Devan stammered.

"Have you seen me anywhere before today?" Madurandaka asked.

"I'm not sure," said Devan. "Nowadays, one person looks like another: the one in a screened palanquin one day is in an open chariot the next day …"

Madurandaka was startled. "What do you mean?"

"I have seen you, or someone like you, twice before. I had my doubts and so I stood up on my horse to check. I'm still not sure whether the person I saw was you or not."

The prince grew angry. "You rascal -"

Devan interrupted: "Don't be angry, sir. Let me tell you where I saw you, or somebody like you. I saw a big fort … a gathering of warriors … the dim light of a lamp … a palanquin … the leader walked to the palanquin and lifted the screen … a handsome man stepped out … the men cheered him: 'Long live the crown prince!' 'Long live the emperor!' Sir, the man who stepped out of the palanquin looked like you. If it was someone else, please forgive me."

Madurandaka's face paled in fear; perspiration stood on his forehead. "Were you in the gathering?"

"No, sir," Devan said. "I swear I was not."

"Then how do you know this?"

"I don't know whether it was real or a dream. Listen to the second picture. There's a dark underground vault … a passage winds up and down … three men come through the passage … the first holds a lighted torch … the third is a guard … the second man is a handsome young prince … his face resembled yours. You're the one who must say whether this is true or not."

"Stop! Enough!" Madurandaka's voice trembled in fear. "Are you a soothsayer?"

"No, sir, that's not my profession. But I can read the past and the future."

The prince thought for a while. "What did you shout when you were on your horse?"

"I said you were in danger. At the same time, great honor awaits you. I must speak with you at leisure. Your men have confiscated my sword. If you take me with you into the fort …"

"Very well, come with me." He gave the captain instructions which the man obeyed reluctantly. The fort gates opened and Devan entered the fort as a part of Madurandaka's escort.

Prince Madurandaka

MADURANDAKA'S PARENTS, GANDARA Aditya and Sembiyan Madevi, were ardent devotees of Lord Shiva. They dedicated their lives to the renovation and upkeep of Shiva temples in the Chola kingdom. Gandara Aditya was passionate about compiling the *Thevaram* hymns of the Shaiva saints and hated war. Due to his pacifist policies, the Chola empire shrunk during his reign. Gandara Aditya married late and his son, Madurandaka, was born when he had not much longer to live. His younger brother, Arinjaya Chola, was wounded on the battlefield and lay on his deathbed. The Chola empire was surrounded by enemies. Arinjaya's son, the young Sundara Chola, was already a great warrior and battle veteran. Determined to avoid conflict in the family, Gandara Aditya made his nephew crown prince and also announced that Sundara Chola's sons would succeed their father to the throne.

Gandara Aditya asked his wife to bring up their son to be a Shiva devotee, detached from worldly life. Until the age of twenty, Madurandaka obeyed his mother. He did not interfere in the workings of the empire and was not interested in being king. He then married Kalaanthaka's daughter. The desire for power raised its ugly head in his heart. Under Nandini's influence, it became an all-consuming passion. Led by the Pazluvur brothers, some chieftains conspired to make Madurandaka the next emperor. However, Madurandaka was impatient to ascend the throne at once. *After all, the emperor is on his death bed*, he thought

The Pazluvur brothers tried to control Madurandaka's impatience, in case it ruined their well-laid plans. Sundara Chola's two sons were great warriors who had captured the peoples' hearts. They were supported by the powerful chieftains, Velir and Malayaman. The majority of the armed forces were loyal to the two princes. The Pazluvur brothers judged it wiser to wait until Sundara Chola's death before making their move. There were also signs that the emperor himself would make Madurandaka his heir, saving them the trouble.

Only Kundavai and Sembiyan Madevi would raise objections to this. Kundavai's moves could be countered by the Pazluvur brothers, but the people revered the Queen Mother as a saint. It was common knowledge that the queen had no wish to make her son emperor. If Madurandaka was seen to be a son disobeying his saintly mother, the people would not accept him as their ruler. The Pazluvur brothers urged Madurandaka to convince his mother to agree to their plans. But the prince was reluctant to discuss this matter with his mother.

Now, Sembiyan Madevi had asked Madurandaka to meet her at Pazlayarai to discuss her plans to fulfil his father's wishes. Kalaanthaka urged Madurandaka to use this opportunity to persuade his mother to support his claim to the throne.

Naraiyur Nambi

MADURANDAKA AND HIS escort went to the royal palace. The streets were largely deserted; a few onlookers casually glanced at the procession. It was clear that Madurandaka was not popular in Pazlayarai. This suited Vandhiya Devan who did not want to be recognized by anyone.

They crossed a large procession led by musicians with cymbals and drums. Behind them came a palanquin carrying a young Shaiva ascetic. Shouts of, 'Hara Hara Mahadeva!' and, 'Long live Naraiyur Nambi!' filled the street.

Madurandaka stared at the procession with jealous eyes and complained, "The people ignore us, but look at the fuss they're making over Naraiyur Nambi."

Devan recognized the man walking beside the palanquin: it was the Shaiva who had shared their boat when they crossed the Kollidam river. Azlvarkkadian had picked a fight with this man.

Sembiyan Madevi was waiting on the palace steps. She kissed Madurandaka on his forehead. "Son, you have come at the right time. Naraiyur Nambi is on his way here. Refresh yourself and come quickly to the durbar hall."

Madurandaka's face fell. He had assumed that his mother was waiting to receive him. Seeing himself as the next emperor, he could not accept that her welcome was meant for the Shaiva ascetic. The prince took his time to get ready, ignoring his mother's messages asking him to hurry. Finally, he made his way to the durbar hall, taking Devan and a few other men with him.

The young Naraiyur Nambi was seated on a throne. With holy ash on his forehead and rudraksha beads around his neck, his handsome face glowed. Bundles of palm-leaf manuscripts lay before him. The Shaiva who had used the Kollidam ferry stood beside him. Sembiyan Madevi, Kundavai and other women of the royal family sat on one side of the hall.

Devan's eyes took in all the people in the durbar hall but came back time and again to feast on Kundavai's beautiful face. Kundavai's eyes widened in surprise at seeing him, but she did not look in his direction after that. *Has she forgotten me?* Devan wondered with a pang of pain.

Sembiyan Madevi told Madurandaka, "My son, this young boy, Naraiyur Nambi, is blessed by god. He has found some rare *Thevaram* manuscripts of Saint Sambandar' songs."

"Let's hear the songs, mother," Madurandaka said dutifully, without enthusiasm. He was disgusted: *Seating that young nobody on a gem-studded throne!*

Naraiyur Nambi began to sing the hymns. While tears flowed down the Queen Mother's cheeks as she lost herself in devotion, Madurandaka dreamt of wearing the crown. *I have the Pazluvur brothers' support. I'll soon be emperor.*

Devan did not hear a single word of the songs. His eyes and heart were fixed on Kundavai. *Is she pretending not to recognize me? Is she angry with me? How can I meet her?*

When Naraiyur Nambi finished singing, Sembiyan Madevi spoke to the man by the boy's side. "Sir, please take this boy throughout Tamil Nadu to collect *Thevaram* manuscripts. It was my husband's dearest wish to have these hymns recited daily in our Shiva temples. I'll arrange for your travel and other expenses and ask my son to get the emperor's permission for this."

The Soothsayer

Sembiyan Madevi turned to Madurandaka. "Son, come and see me after these men leave. I have something important to discuss with you."

Madurandaka burned with rage. *A royal reception for a wandering beggar! The Pazluvur brothers are right: if someone comes to her with holy ash and rudraksha beads or a forgotten hymn, she'll empty the treasury for him. And whatever remains will be spent by Kundavai on hospitals. If these women go on like this, how can I become emperor and conquer the world? What does she want to discuss? Meditation? The meaning of the crescent moon on Shiva's head? She has made me a madman in the public eye. I won't listen to any more nonsense from her.*

Madurandaka saw Devan hesitating in the durbar hall. *How did that soothsayer know about those two incidents? He has some wonderful power. I must ask him to predict my future.* The prince gestured to Devan to follow him and left the hall.

Devan tried to catch Kundavai's eye, but she left without giving him a glance. He decided that she did not recognize him as she would not have expected to see him with Madurandaka. *She meets hundreds of men daily. Why would she remember a man she has met only twice? I'm a fool. Through all those dangerous days and nights I remembered her face. She looks worried. I must find a way of meeting her.*

"Soothsayer, what about my fortune?" Madurandaka's voice startled Devan from his reverie and brought him back to the prince's room.

Stalling for time, Devan said, "You must sit behind a lighted lamp in a room filled with incense smoke. Only then will images of the future come to me."

The excited prince arranged for the lamp and incense. Devan closed his eyes in meditation. He mumbled an incantation and shook like one possessed. Then he opened his eyes wide and stared into the flame: "Your fortune is extraordinary. I'm stunned by what I see …"

"Tell me what you see," said Madurandaka excitedly.

"I'm at a loss for words. Kings, ministers and officials stand in line; beyond them is a sea of soldiers, their armor shining in the sun; crowds of people on terraces and fortress walls roar …"

"Tell me: tell me what the crowds roar!"

"They shout, 'Long live the Chola heir!' 'Long live the emperor!' The Tiger Flag flutters above the crowd. A gem-studded golden throne stands in a hall, with a white canopy above it. Golden pots with holy water are arranged in a row. Everything is ready for the coronation."

"Whose coronation? Tell me that, my man!"

"The door opens; an old man walks in with his brother; behind them comes a handsome prince - Sir, it's you! The men lead you to the throne; you reach the throne. Like a bad omen, a woman with untied hair stands in your way and cries, 'No!' You push her away. I see no more …"

"Look, my man! Look!" cried Madurandaka. "Do you recognize the woman?"

"Prince, the visions are gone: someone in this palace with magic power has blocked my sight." He covered his face with his hands. When he opened his eyes, he saw Madurandaka's eyes blaze. *Have I stirred up his greed too much?* Devan worried.

"Look again!" the prince ordered.

"That image is gone, sir. I see a different image now: a messenger comes with news that someone from the royal family is lost at sea … the people are mad with grief and anger … they are beating the poor messenger. Prince, if this happens, please don't go among the crowd."

"Who is the person who drowned?" Madurandaka asked eagerly.

"I can't hear the name," Devan held his head in his hands and cried, "Forgive me, sir. I can see no more."

Just then, a messenger came with summons from Sembiyan Madevi.

Devan said, "Sir, my head is splitting. Let me breathe the fresh city air for a while."

Madurandaka nodded his permission and went to vent his anger on his mother.

The Timely Rescue

PINAKAPANI, CONTENT TO be his doctor-father's apprentice, changed after his trip to Kodikkarai. Vandhiya Devan opened his eyes to a larger world. As any newly-in-love person does, Devan prattled on about falling in love and told Pinakapani that he was in love with a woman. Pinakapani was eaten up with jealousy and resentment when Devan refused to tell him who that woman was. By the time they reached Kodikkarai, Pinakapani saw Devan as his enemy. Pinakapani was furious when Poonkuzlali refused his love and showed her preference for Devan. He betrayed Devan to the Pazluvur men. And when the soldiers arrested Pinakapani and locked him in the Thanjavur dungeon, he blamed Devan for his misfortune.

Before Kundavai could arrange his release, Pinakapani was freed by Nandini. Nandini was furious that Devan had escaped from Thanjavur Fort, reached Pazlayarai and gone to Sri Lanka with Kundavai's message. Guessing that Devan would return to Pazlayarai at some point, she decided that the doctor's son would be a suitable spy.

Nandini said, "The man who betrayed you will return to Pazlayarai. Keep your eyes open for him and send me reports of where he goes, what he does and whom he meets. I'll reward you richly."

Kalaanthaka, thinking along the same lines, told Pinakapani, "If you catch Devan on his return to Pazlayarai, I'll give you a high position in the secret service."

Pinakapani lost all interest in healing. Building castles in the air, he wandered the streets of Pazlayarai peering at passersby and muttering, "No, it's not him!" The people decided that the doctor's son was mad, but Pinakapani did not give up.

Pinakapani paid no pay attention to Madurandaka's escort as he did not expect to find Devan with them. But he examined every face in the crowd around Naraiyur Nambi. He happened to look back casually at the man riding with the prince. Suddenly suspicious, he ran towards him but the group went into the palace. Unable to enter the durbar hall, Pinakapani waited at the door, staring at Devan. Another man quietly watched him—it was none other than Azlvarkkadian.

When Devan came out of the palace, Pinakapani walked up to him and asked, "Who are you?"

Recognizing Pinakapani, Devan hid his alarm and said, "Who am I? Are you referring to my body or my soul or my supreme spirit …?" Devan then galloped away on his horse.

But Pinakapani's suspicions were confirmed. He rushed to the city guard captain who sent two men with him. They searched the streets and finally found Devan in the marketplace. "He's the spy who escaped from Thanjavur Fort. Arrest him!" Pinakapani shouted.

A crowd gathered around them.

"You're mad!" exclaimed Devan.

"Who's mad? 'My body or my soul or my supreme spirit?'" mocked the doctor's son.

"See—he's babbling … he's mad," accused Devan.

"I'm not mad!" Pinakapani cried. "He's the man the Pazluvur brothers are looking for."

At this, a rumble went through the crowd. Their sympathies were immediately with Devan.

Devan warned the guards, "Careful! I'm Prince Madurandaka's personal soothsayer."

Azlvarkkadian quietly made his way through the crowd and shouted, "Where's Prince Madurandaka's soothsayer? The prince has sent me to fetch him."

"Here I am," Devan said.

"Don't let the spy escape!" Pinakapani screamed.

Azlvarkkadian gave Devan a meaningful look and said, "Let him prove he's a soothsayer. Two riders are galloping here and it's clear they bring important news: tell us what the news is."

Devan stared at the riders and said, "A member of the royal family is lost at sea."

The riders stopped at the edge of the crowd and one of them said, "Sad news: Prince Arulmozli's ship was caught in a cyclone. The prince jumped into the sea to rescue someone and drowned."

The people wailed and beat their chests in grief. The crowd grew larger by the minute and a whisper ran through it: the Pazluvur brothers had tried to arrest the prince; they had pushed him into the sea and killed him. The people sobbed and cursed the Pazluvur brothers. The messengers could not ride on as they were blocked by the crowd asking them questions.

Azlvarkkadian urged the guards, "Make way for the messengers and escort them to the palace." The guards escorted the messengers and the crowd followed them, growing even bigger.

Pinakapani, engulfed by the crowd, shouted: "It's a trick! Don't let the spy get away!" Ignoring him, the crowd carried him along with it.

Azlvarkkadian pulled Devan. "Leave the horse and come with me."

"My dear fellow, you came at the right time!" Devan exclaimed.

"You make it a habit to get into trouble and have someone rescue you," Azlvarkkadian teased. He took Devan to Aniruddha's locked house and through the courtyard to the garden at the back. They went to the river where a boat was moored. Devan's heart thrilled at the sight of the woman who waited in that boat.

Mother and Son

Madurandaka once loved his mother above all else, but his love had changed into a deep anger. *Why am I cursed with a mother who favors my cousins over her own son?* The sight of her serene face calmed him. He touched her feet and she blessed him.

"How's the emperor?" she asked.

"He grows weaker by the day. His mental suffering is greater than his physical pain. Of course, those who steal what rightfully belongs to someone else must suffer."

"What do you mean? What wrong has the emperor done?"

"He's sitting on the throne which rightfully belongs to me: isn't that wrong?"

The queen's eyes showed her pity. "My child, who has poisoned your pure heart?"

"Do you think I'm such a fool that I can't think for myself? Tell me why you sent for me."

"You were at the reception today ..."

"Yes, I saw you treat a wandering boy like royalty; it must have gone to his head by now."

Sembiyan Madevi sighed. "I never dreamt that two years with the Pazluvur brothers would change you so much. Let it go. I must do my duty towards your father. Before I give you my reason for calling you here, let me tell how I met your father–"

Madurandaka settled down comfortably in his chair.

"My father descends from the powerful Mazlapadi chieftains. When they allied with the Pandians, the Cholas defeated them and annexed Mazlapadi. My family lost much of its influence. As a young girl, I was devoted to Lord Shiva. I made garlands for Shiva in the Mazlapadi temple, sang hymns and meditated for hours before the sanctum. I wanted to marry Shiva and no one else. People called me mad, but I didn't care. One day, I opened my eyes and saw a man standing before me. My heart leaped in joy: I thought my beloved Lord Shiva had come to marry me! I bowed to him, with tears coursing down my cheeks.

"'Who's this girl?' the man asked.

"'She's my daughter,' my father replied. 'She's completely devoted to Lord Shiva.'

"Realizing that the man was not Lord Shiva, I ran home in embarrassment. But that man asked for my hand in marriage—he was none other than your father." Sembiyan Madevi wiped her eyes and continued. "I learnt that your father had become king a few years back. He was forty and was in the habit of visiting the Shiva temples in the kingdom. His wife had passed away years ago and he had resolved to remained single. But on seeing me, he longed to make me his wife. He asked for my consent and I gave it wholeheartedly. We were married and your father restored the Mazlapadi chieftainship to my father. My son, your father and I decided to dedicate our lives to Lord Shiva's service and not have children. There was an important reason for this. I never dreamt I would have to tell you this, but circumstances force me. Listen carefully ..."

You Are a Demon!

SEMBIYAN MADEVI SIGHED. "Your grandfather, Emperor Paranthaka, was a great warrior whose kingdom stretched from Sri Lanka to the River Krishna. During the last years of his life, the Rashtrakutas invaded the Chola country. Your uncle, Crown Prince Raja Aditya, defeated the enemy in a great battle at Thakkolam. But he was killed in the battle and Arinjaya Chola, his younger brother, was badly wounded and missing. Arinjaya's young son, Sundara Chola, had gone to Sri Lanka with the army and was also missing. Only your father was with the emperor.

"Your father had stayed away from affairs of state. He hated war; he did not carry a sword or learn warfare. He spent his time on pilgrimages and avoided political intrigues. He believed that a king who conquered another king's territory was a thief. Paranthaka Chola, on his deathbed, asked your father to become king. Your father could not refuse.

"Your father's first wife was dead and he had not yet met me. Emperor Paranthaka was worried the Chola dynasty would end with your father. Luckily, Prince Sundara Chola was found on an island in Sri Lanka. The emperor was overjoyed: he doted on the prince and believed he would take the Cholas to great heights. He decreed that Sundara Chola would succeed your father and that Sundara Chola's sons would succeed their father to the throne.

"Your father was not interested in being emperor. He delegated state affairs to his younger brother, Arinjaya Chola, and his son, Sundara Chola, and dedicated himself to Lord Shiva. He married me because my devotion to Shiva matched his. Your father was a saint. I'm fortunate to have been his wife. My son, we have a duty to fulfill his wishes."

Madurandaka was furious. "My father told me nothing. I have no duty towards him."

"My son, you were a baby when your father died: how could he tell you anything? We had resolved not to have children, but I was a foolish woman. I loved your father more than I loved Lord Shiva. I longed to have a child to love and hold in my lap. God granted my wish. I was afraid your father would be angry with me, but he understood my feelings. He made me promise to see you became a Shiva devotee, detached from worldly pleasures. I believed I had kept my promise. But now, my beloved son, I hear troubling rumors about you."

Madurandaka said angrily, "Mother, just tell me what you want."

"Very well, I'll say it. I hear you want to become king; I hear our enemies are leading you down the path of evil. Tell me this is not true."

Madurandaka forgot Kalaanthaka's advice to gently persuade his mother to support him. He shouted: "Those who are ready to die to see me crowned are not my enemies. You are my greatest enemy. Aren't you ashamed to call yourself a mother? Why are you determined to give someone else the throne which rightfully belongs to me? You're a demon! I don't believe your words about my father. Come what may, I won't give up my right to the throne." Madurandaka pulled the rudraksha beads around his neck. "I wore this out of respect for you but they made me a laughing stock. I throw them back in your face—take them!" He tugged at the beads like a mad man but was unable to remove them. His beautiful face darkened with rage.

Sembiyan Madevi closed her eyes in pain. When his fury was spent, she said quietly, "I may be a demon, but listen to what I have to say."

Madurandaka calmed down a little. "I'm listening."

"Like any mother, I'm trying to protect you. If you try to grab the throne, your life will be in danger. The emperor's two sons are great warriors; the generals and soldiers support them; they have allies in neighboring kingdoms. Who do you have? The comet is a sign of a death in the royal family. I fear for your life."

The prince was touched. "Why didn't you tell me this earlier? You need not fear for my life. The most powerful chieftains of the Chola empire, including the Pazluvur brothers, Sambuvaraya and your brother, Mazlavaraya, support me. They can raise an army in no time."

"What about the people? You know the people adore the two princes. Did you see how they ignored you today? That's because of your closeness to the Pazluvur brothers."

"I don't care about being popular—all I expect from the people is obedience."

"My son, a king who does not have the support of his subjects, will not rule for long ..." She stopped on hearing raised voices, wails, curses and shouts of anger. "Stay here. Some great catastrophe has fallen on the Cholas. I'll go and see what's wrong."

The Roar of the Mob

VANDHIYA DEVAN LOOKED at Azlvarkkadian and hesitated.

Azlvarkkadian smiled. "My dear fellow, the princess has been waiting for some time. First give her the good news that the prince is safe. You can boast about your brave deeds after that. We have unleashed the mob; I must go back and try to control it." He hurried away.

How does he know everything? I'm an accidental spy who keeps falling into trouble while he's a professional who goes coolly about his work. Who does he work for? Did he tell me the truth about himself? One look at Kundavai and he forgot Azlvarkkadian, himself, his mission and the world. Here was the face which had filled his mind day and night, in storm and rain, on the mountains and in the sea. His heart beat fast. He waded into the water and climbed into the boat.

Kundavai gestured to the deaf-mute boatman who paddled away into the middle of the river. "Soothsayer," Kundavai teased. "If you stare at my face, how can I let you read my fortune?"

Devan smiled. "I'm not reading your fortune. I'm trying to remember where I last saw this face."

"Let me remind you. About a month back, you saw me at the Kudanthai astrologer's house ..."

"I don't believe you. I have seen your face in a thousand past lives. I was the hunter who caught colorful birds for you; you laughed and set them free. I was the fisherman who dived into the sea and gathered pearls for you; you filled the little hands of street children with them ..."

"Aiyo!" Kundavai cried. "This soothsayer is mad! We must go back to the shore."

"Lady, I was sane when I came to the boat. How else did I enter Pazlayarai, fool Prince Madurandaka and escape from Pinakapani? But when I see your face, I become a drunken fool."

"In that case, look at the river or the sky. But tell me whether your mission was successful."

"Would I look you in the eyes if I had failed? I crossed a hundred hurdles and brought Prince Arulmozli back. When I left him, he was suffering from a fever but he's in safe hands. Poonkuzlali and Chendan Amudhan will lay down their lives to guard the prince."

They heard the angry roar of a mob and turned fearfully in the direction of the sound.

The Underwater Wedding

THE BEAUTY OF dusk brings peace laced with melancholy. Vanathi's beauty was like dusk–joy tinged with sorrow. She would not smile for days and then her laughter would light up the room. Her fainting spells happened when she swung between extremes of grief and joy; it was nature's way of healing her mind. This was because of her past. When her mother was expecting Vanathi, her father was away at war. News of victory and defeat would reach Kodumbalur, making her mother alternate between joy and sorrow. Her mother died early; her father lavished his affection on Vanathi until he died in the Sri Lankan war. Vanathi grew up in luxury, but was scarred by her parents' deaths.

Someone comforted her saying, "Don't worry, your father will be reborn as your brave son." Little Vanathi took these words to heart. She consoled herself with dreams of her brave son. She imagined him seated on a golden throne, sailing to far off lands and dedicating his victories to her. As she matured, she realized that she must marry to have a son. But she did not give much thought to her husband.

Once she came to Pazlayarai, Kundavai's style of dress and speech opened her eyes to a new world. The princess's affection was a comfort and joy to her. Vanathi's sweet nature endeared her to everyone in the palace. The other girls' jealousy gave her spirit: *There must be something special in me which they don't have.*

When she fell in love with Arulmozli, Vanathi's dreams of a son were shattered. The prince would never marry her and it would be wrong for her to marry another man when she loved Arulmozli. She was sad. Kundavai, reading Vanathi's mind, encouraged her to hope and the Kudanthai astrologer's words revived her dreams.

Vanathi became aware of the enmity between her family and the Pazluvur clan. She saw how powerful they were: Nandini, that beautiful cobra, was even more powerful. *Will they allow my dreams to come true? Nandini hates Princess Kundavai—won't she hate me too? Was it Nandini in the emperor's room that night in Thanjavur? Why does the princess refuse to talk about it? It's clear the princess is worried: she's quiet and likes to be by herself.*

Just then, Varini came running and cried, "The prince has drowned at sea!"

The girls burst into tears and all their eyes turned towards Vanathi as if in accusation: 'You wretch! It's because of your bad luck that the prince is dead!'

Unable to stand their looks, Vanathi ran to the lake. She remembered that during the last few days, she had seen the prince's face in the water— it had disappeared when she touched it. *The prince was calling out to me when he drowned. But I stood here like a fool. There's only one thing to do. The lake flows into the river which flows into the sea. The prince is waiting for me at the bottom of the sea. I'll meet him there …*

Vanathi became calm. She stood on the marble steps leading to the water. She saw a boat in the distance with Kundavai and Devan in it. *He must have brought the news about the prince. If they come here, they'll stop me. How can I leave the princess without a word of thanks for all her love? No, I won't wait. I see the prince in the water, he's calling me. I feel giddy …* Vanathi fainted and fell into the lake. She sank to the bottom. Her body was cool; palaces of gem-studded gold shimmered in the water; a crowd of radiant figures walked to her; they took her to a pavilion were the prince welcomed her with a smile; to the sound of auspicious music, they exchanged garlands and were married; unable to bear the happiness, she fainted.

Hands lifted her. She thought it was the prince who held her close and revived her on his lap. The she heard the sound of bangles and Kundavai's voice: "Vanathi! What have you done?!"

Vanathi struggled to open her eyes; Kundavai was bending over her. "*Akka*," Vanathi mumbled. "Did you come for my wedding? I didn't see you there …"

Vanathi Recovers

VANATHI SLOWLY CAME to her senses. She realized that her marriage to the prince was just a dream and that he was dead. *Why did the princess save me? Why couldn't she let me die?* She couldn't open her eyes but heard the princess talking with someone.

"She's rambling," Kundavai said. "Thank goodness our boat was near the shore and we were able to save her. I tremble to think what would have happened otherwise!"

"It may have been better if we had not saved her; she would have died happily."

Ah, it's that young warrior the princess sent to Sri Lanka. Let me hear what he says.

"Have you no heart?" Kundavai exclaimed.

"She was talking about marrying the prince and she's going to be disappointed."

"Yes, she loves my brother. And she's from the Kodumbalur clan—who could be a more suitable match for him?"

"You'll be disappointed," Devan said.

"Why? Didn't you tell me the prince is safe in the Choodamani Monastery?"

The prince is alive and safe! What sweet news! Thank goodness I didn't die in the lake.

"The prince is safe, but I doubt he'll marry this girl."

"If there's one man who will obey my every command, it's my brother."

"I'm another," Devan declared. "The prince's love for you knows no bounds. Although he doesn't want to rule, he'll agree to become king if you insist. But he won't marry this girl … what if his heart is set on another girl?"

Devan's words were like molten lead being poured into Vanathi's ears.

"I told you about Poonkuzlali, the boat girl. She rowed me to Sri Lanka, saved the prince and me from the sea and rowed the prince to the monastery. She will lay down her life for him."

"Never!" Kundavai exclaimed. "I won't let my brother fall into this boat girl's net."

"Is clan that important? Is a boat girl worthless? Isn't her blood red and doesn't her heart beat like that of a princess? A princess's love may be tinged with the desire to be queen, but Poonkuzlali's love is pure … sacred! The prince too feels that way. Why should others stand in their way?" Devan paused. "Take my case: if I could show you what's in my heart …"

"No! It's best to let what's in your heart stay there safely. Love is not for kings. If kings follow their hearts, there will be endless trouble and grief. My father is an example of this. He once saw a girl in the jungle … why am I telling you this? This girl is recovering; her eyelids are fluttering. Tell me about the dangers you faced in Sri Lanka."

"One night in Anuradhapura, we would have been buried alive under a building. We escaped only because a woman warned us … that woman was known to the prince. She was old enough to be his mother and she was a deaf-mute."

"What?" Kundavai exclaimed. "Tell me more about her: where was she born?"

"She was born on an island off the Lankan coast."

The princess could not hide her excitement. "Who does she look like?"

"She's older, and wears a simple sari, but she's a copy of someone here: can you guess who?"

"Nandini?"

"Yes, Nandini," Devan said.

"My god! My suspicions are correct—the woman I hate like a poisonous snake is my sister. Fate is cruel. This shows why a prince should never fall in love with a woman of no lineage."

"My ancestors ruled Vallam for more than three hundred years: I know the value of lineage. But now, though I don't have a kingdom, I have my sword ... strong shoulders ... a brave heart ..."

"Sir, let's discuss your greatness later. There are things to be done at once. Will you help me?"

"I'll lay down my life for you," Devan declared.

"You and the boat girl must be brother and sister. Shh! This girl is opening her eyes ..."

Vanathi had recovered. *I'll prove to the prince that my love is greater than the boat girl's.* She also began to understand the meaning of what she had seen that night in the emperor's room.

"My darling, how are you feeling?" Kundavai asked.

"I'm fine, *akka*," Vanathi replied. "I'm so sorry for giving you all this trouble."

Azlvarkkadian came up. "Lady, I'm also here to trouble you. An angry mob has gathered at the palace. You must come and calm them or there will be disaster."

The Chief Minister Arrives

WAVES OF PEOPLE surged towards the palace. They were of all ages and faiths. Some sobbed; others cursed the Pazluvur brothers; young men banged thick sticks in anger. The crowd shouted, 'Break your sticks on the Pazluvur brothers' heads!' The soldiers at the entrance let in the two messengers and guards and barred the palace gates. But the crowd shouted, 'Go in! Go in!' and became a tidal wave which pushed aside the soldiers, broke open the gates and burst into the courtyard.

Sembiyan Madevi came out to stand on the balcony. At the sight of her calm face and folded hands the crowd was silent for a few seconds.

"Mother!" a voice shouted. "Where's Ponni's Beloved? Tell us!"

The crowd again wailed and shouted angrily. Sembiyan Madevi froze in horror: what misfortune had fallen on Arulmozli? The messengers pushed their way through the crowd and stood before the balcony. "Mother, we bring sad news. As Prince Arulmozli was returning to

Kodikkarai on the emperor's orders, the ships were caught in a cyclone. One ship sank and the prince jumped into the water to rescue the men. He is now missing at sea. The emperor is heart-broken and asks you to come at once to Thanjavur along with Prince Madurandaka and Princess Kundavai."

Tears coursed down Sembiyan Madevi's face. The crowd wailed louder. Shouts came from the courtyard: "Mother, don't go to Thanjavur, let the emperor come here!" "The Pazluvur brothers have murdered the prince!" "We want Princess Kundavai!"

Azlvarkkadian, standing on the edge of the crowd, rushed to fetch Kundavai. Leaving Vanathi to the maids, Kundavai hurried to the balcony. One look at the Queen Mother's tears and Kundavai broke into sobs herself. This inflamed the crowd more. "Princess, the Pazluvur brothers must be punished!" "Princess, the Pazluvur brothers have imprisoned the emperor: just say the word and we'll march to Thanjavur and free him!"

I must keep my brother's rescue a secret, but I must also calm the people and send them home. Kundavai signaled to Azlvarkkadian who immediately joined her on the balcony. She whispered to him and he shouted to the crowd: "The princess believes that just as the Ponni saved Prince Arulmozli then, the Ocean King will save him now. This is what the soothsayer also predicts. The princess has taken steps to search for the prince and bring him here. She asks you all to stay calm and go home."

The crowd heaved a collective sigh of relief. Some men shouted, "Where's the soothsayer? Let's hear him." Seizing the opportunity, Devan went to the balcony and stood beside Azlvarkkadian. "It's true the prince was in danger, but his life is not at risk. I have studied the planetary positions and read his horoscope: he will soon return home safely."

"Lies!" Pinakapani shouted from the crowd. "You are a spy for the Pazluvur brothers!"

With a roar, Devan leaped down the twelve feet from the balcony and attacked Pinakapani. As they fought, the excited crowd moved to give them space and formed a circle around them.

Conches and horns blared and a herald announced: "Make way for Chief Minister Aniruddha Brahmaraya!"

Aniruddha's Plea

AS ANIRUDDHA'S PALANQUIN cut through the crowd, the people greeted him and called out their grief. Aniruddha, his face sober, nodded to them in sympathy and blessed them. He stepped out of the palanquin and bowed to the ladies on the balcony. Azlvarkkadian whispered to him.

Aniruddha ordered the guards, "Arrest the two ruffians fighting in the palace courtyard." The guards separated Pinakapani and Vandhiya Devan and bound their hands. Azlvarkkadian looked pointedly at Devan who allowed himself to be arrested.

Aniruddha went up to the balcony and addressed the crowd. "I understand your pain and anger. But the royal family is grieving and you must not do anything to make things worse for them. I have organized the search for the prince. I ask you all to go home peacefully."

There were shouts: "We want the emperor!" "What about our men in Sri Lanka?"

"The emperor is guarded day and night by the *Velakkara Padai*. I will personally escort him to Pazlayarai soon. As for Sri Lanka, the war has been won. Our men will be back soon."

The satisfied crowd cheered and dispersed.

Aniruddha turned to Sembiyan Madevi. "Lady, there are important matters I must discuss with you. Shall we go inside?" He paused to tell Kundavai, "Princess, I'll see you later."

Kundavai walked back to her palace in confusion. If there was anyone she feared in the Chola kingdom, it was Aniruddha. His eagle eyes could read the secrets in one's heart. *How much does he know? How much shall I tell him?* Kundavai was furious with Aniruddha for having arrested Devan along with Pinakapani. She could not protest in public and had to hide her anger. *You'll see me later, is it? I'll deal with you then!*

Sembiyan Madevi waited for Aniruddha to sit before taking her seat. "Sir, blow after blow is falling on my head. Is the news about Arulmozli true? I can't believe it!"

"No one can know for sure, but the news of his death has spread throughout the land."

"If it's true, what misfortune will it bring? I have never seen a mob in the palace courtyard!"

"There was rioting in Thanjavur too. The *Velakkara Padai* refused to leave the fort. An angry mob surrounded the Pazluvur brothers' houses and had to be chased away by elephants in musth. It's fortunate that Prince Madurandaka was not there: he may have been attacked too."

"Sir, Madurandaka has changed; you must help me with him."

"Prince Madurandaka believes he's the emperor's rightful heir. He wants to be king. It would be best if he's allowed to have his way."

"Sir, what are you saying? Are you too ready to betray the emperor?"

"My queen, I would not dream of betraying the emperor. The emperor himself wants to crown Prince Madurandaka and retire from all affairs of state. He sent me to get your consent to this."

Sembiyan Madevi cried, "I'll never give my consent! I'll never betray my husband! How can you ask me to do this? Have you forgotten the secrets we share?"

"I have forgotten nothing: in fact, there are some secrets you don't know. That's why I'm here on the emperor's behalf. I'm here to beg you to save the Cholas from great danger."

"What great danger can we avert by making Madurandaka king?"

"My queen, the riots will spread from Kanchipuram to Rameswaram. General Velir has sailed from Lanka with his army and intends to march on Thanjavur. When Aditya Karikalan hears this, he'll join him with the northern army. The Pazluvur brothers and their allies are also raising armies. You'll watch your near and dear ones kill each other in a civil war …"

"My country is dear to me but my Lord Shiva's world is larger. If there's no place for me in the Chola country, I'll go on a pilgrimage to my Lord's abode in the Himalayas."

"Mother, Lord Shiva's world itself is under threat. Turks, Mughals and Arabs are ready to invade this land; their faith encourages them to destroy our temples. The kings in the north can't stop them. I dream our Chola kings will defeat these invaders and save our faith. Please make my dream come true. I beg you to stop the civil war which looms over us."

Sembiyan Madevi pondered on this. "Sir, if Bharath is threatened, my Lord Shiva will protect it, not I. I'll never forget my husband's dying wish: I'll never betray him."

"In that case, I have no other choice but to tell you a truth which has remained secret …"

Madurandaka bustled in and asked, "Mother, is it true Arulmozli is missing at sea?"

"My queen, I'll leave you to console the prince. I'll tell you what I have to say some other time."

Madurandaka said loudly, "That man's my arch-enemy. Has he been poisoning your ears?"

Aniruddha heard the prince's words as he crossed the threshold.

Kundavai's Predicament

ANIRUDDHA WALKED TO Kundavai's palace. The princess stood and bowed to him. He blessed her: "May you live long, may you be blessed with a brave and wise husband."

"Sir, is this the time for such a blessing? The whole kingdom is worried about my father's health and my beloved brother's fate …"

"But I see no signs of worry on your face," Aniruddha pointed out.

"I come from a courageous lineage: do you want me to break down like some ordinary woman?"

"Never. But women should confine themselves to song and dance and not get involved in political affairs. See how much trouble you have caused."

"Aiyo! What have I done?"

"I asked the prince to remain in Lanka, but you sent a messenger asking him to return at once. Of course, he obeyed you and not this old man. Now, he's lost at sea. Did you see the mob today? Who's to blame for all this but you?"

"It was the Pazluvur brothers who sent two ships to arrest Arulmozli," Kundavai countered.

"I know, my dear. But their ships sank in the storm. If they deny sending an arrest warrant and accuse you of being the one who asked the prince to return, how can we refute their claim?"

"How did you and the Pazluvur brothers know about my message?"

"Your messenger got arrested when he reached Sri Lanka, so everyone there knows about it. The doctor's son went with him to Kodikkarai, so everyone here knows about it. See how your secret became public knowledge. That's why women should not interfere in politics."

Kundavai was speechless. She had to admit that there was some truth in Aniruddha's words. Her anger turned to Devan. *Yes, he's brave, but he has ruined everything. I must give him a piece of my mind when I see him.* Kundavai remembered that Devan had been arrested. *How much of trouble he gets into! Why couldn't he have just ignored the nonsense said by the doctor's son?*

"Sir, I have a request ..."

"Just say the word, lady. Is there anyone in this kingdom who can refuse you?"

"You arrested two men who were fighting in the courtyard ..."

"That was a serious crime, to fight before the queen in the middle of an angry mob. If the spectators had taken sides and joined in, the riot would have got out of hand."

"I agree, sir. Yet, I ask you to release one of the men: he's the messenger I sent to Lanka."

"Excellent!" exclaimed Aniruddha. "He's the very man I wanted to arrest. He's accused of being the one who pushed Prince Arulmozli into the sea."

Kundavai was shocked. "Who makes this serious accusation?"

"Parthibendran. The Pazluvur brothers are non-committal ... I too have my doubts."

"Acharya! Are you accusing me of sending a man to push my brother into the sea? Karikalan sent him to me and said he was trustworthy."

"My dear, Aditya Karikalan and you trusted him, but he could be a spy for the enemy camp. I heard someone shout, 'spy,' as I arrived. What was that about?"

"The doctor's son accused Vandhiya Devan of Vallam of being the Pazluvur brothers' spy. What nonsense! He escaped from the Pazluvur brothers and they are hunting for him ..."

"My dear, how come he carries the Pazluvur signet ring?"

"That demon, that poisonous snake–forgive me, Nandini gave it to him."

"I'm glad you know that. Vandhiya Devan may not be the Pazluvur brothers' spy, but he could be Nandini's spy. He met Nandini outside Thanjavur Fort and got the ring from her; he met her in her house; Nandini hid him in the treasury and helped him escape; she knew he had a message for you; when he returned from Lanka, he met Nandini again at midnight in the ruined Pandian fort; he still has her the signet ring. Do you still trust your messenger?"

Kundavai said, "If you continue talking to me, I won't trust even myself!"

A Spy to Spy on a Spy

"IT'S DIFFICULT TO know who to trust in these troubled times. Our enemies conspire and plot."

"But you seem to know of every plot—how is that?" Kundavai asked.

"I have a thousand eyes and ears. My men watch the Pazluvur brothers and Nandini. Others, like Thirumalai, travel and gather news. But who knows? Some people may get the better of me."

Does this clever man know Arulmozli is in the Choodamani Monastery? Kundavai controlled her urge to blurt it out to him.

Aniruddha continued: "Think, my dear. Madurandaka fell into Nandini's coils and changed from a Shiva devotee to a power-hungry man; Kandamaran became her messenger to Karikalan; Parthibendran, sworn enemy of the Pazluvur brothers, is now her slave–he proposes to divide the Chola empire between Madurandaka and Karikalan ..."

"Blasphemy! To talk of dividing the empire which our ancestors built with such difficulty! What powers of bewitchment does this Nandini have?"

"I was going to ask you the same question. Let that be. Why are you so confident Vandhiya Devan alone would not have fallen for her charms?"

"I can give you no reasons. I instinctively know he's not a traitor."

"Very well, let's test his loyalty. Nandini is worse than a poisonous snake and plans to annihilate the Cholas. She's instigating Sambuvaraya to invite Aditya Karikalan to Kadambur. She proposes to let Karikalan marry Sambuvaraya's daughter and one of the Pazluvur girls. She plans to divide the kingdom. All this is known. But no one knows her true motives, not even I." He paused. "We must stop Karikalan from going to Kadambur. We must send urgent messages to him through Vandhiya Devan. If he does not obey us, Devan must go with him to Kadambur, stick to him like his shadow and guard him. He must not let him meet Nandini alone."

Kundavai knew how crucial this mission was. *Does he know everything, or is he only looking at it from the political angle?* "Sir, why do you think it's so important to prevent their meeting?"

"My dear, some of Veerapandian's bodyguards have sworn to destroy the Cholas and they are using newly minted coins from the Chola treasury: need I say more?"

"No," she murmured. "Sir, we are truly fortunate to have you as the chief minister in these troubled times. What arrangements have you made in Arulmozli's case?"

"I have asked all temples to organize prayers for his safe return. The monks at the Choodamani Monastery will hold special prayers for the next forty days. What else do you want me to do?"

Kundavai watched him carefully: there was no change in his expression. *Arulmozli's life may be at risk in the monastery.* "The Pazluvur brothers are angry with the monks because the Buddhist Sangha offered Arulmozli the Lankan throne. You must protect the Choodamani Monastery."

"I'll send a small army to guard the monastery. What about sending Devan to Kanchipuram? We need a fearless warrior for our mission and I have heard of his courage. I saw at firsthand how he fought the doctor's son. If I had not intervened, the doctor's son would have died."

Kundavai rejoiced at this but hesitated. "He's brave, but he's rash. See how he jumped into a fight."

"If you want, I'll send Thirumalai with him—he's known for his cool reasoning."

Kundavai thought, *Only god knows what's in the chief minister's mind. He's sending a spy to spy on a spy!*

Vanathi's Transformation

AS KUNDAVAI PREPARED to secure Vandhiya Devan's release from prison, Vanathi came to her.

"Darling, I have some work; I'll be back soon. Wait in the garden, and don't go near the lake."

"*Akka*, I won't trouble you anymore. Please let me go back to Kodumbalur."

"What! Are you angry with me? Why this sudden fondness for your family?"

"I would never be angry with you and I have no family. My mother died before she could hold a special pooja at the Kali temple. My fainting fits are because of this. I want to fulfill her oath."

"There's no need to go all that way, Vanathi: I'll see your mother's oath is fulfilled."

"That's not the only reason, *akka*. My uncle is coming from Sri Lanka. I want to be at Kodumbalur to meet him and hear his news. My father sacrificed his life there, *akka*. But my uncle is hurrying back with the war only half won."

"Now I understand. You want the general to tell you about Arulmozli's brave feats on the battlefield. I think you are unhinged by the news of my brother's death. Vanathi, don't worry."

"When you are not worried, why should I be?"

"Tell me the truth: did you faint or did you jump into the river?"

"Why would I jump into the river, *akka*? I'm grateful to you and that warrior for saving me."

"You don't seem very grateful. Listen, Vanathi. I don't believe Arulmozli's life is in danger. My intuition tells me you will soon hear good news."

"I don't believe in intuition. I'm haunted by a strange dream. I see your brother's face in the water and he calls to me …you'll think I'm mad. When I fell into the lake, I saw a wedding …"

"Whose wedding?"

"I don't want to talk about it, *akka*. From today, I'll only believe my own eyes and ears."

"Vanathi, sometimes our eyes and ears may be wrong. Trust your instincts and your heart …"

Vanathi interrupted her. "*Akka*, let's talk about this later. Please let me leave. And give me permission to consult the Kudanthai astrologer on my way."

"I too want to see him, but you're in such a hurry."

"*Akka*, I want to meet him on my own."

Where did her sudden courage and stubbornness come from? Kundavai wondered. "Vanathi, wait for a few days. These are troubled times. I must send you back safely."

"Why should I be afraid? I'll go back with the palanquin bearers and four soldiers who brought me here from Kodumbalur."

"Very well, Vanathi. I'll release that Vallam warrior from prison and come to see you off."

Two Prisons

KUNDAVAI HURRIED TO the prison. Leaving the guards behind, she went to the separate cell in which Vandhiya Devan was kept. She found him singing at the top of his voice.

On seeing her, Devan said, "I have disgraced my ancient lineage by becoming a woman's slave. And when I tried to vent my anger by killing the doctor's son, I was stopped …"

"Sir, why were you so angry with Pinakapani?" Kundavai asked.

"He betrayed me at Kodikkarai; he tried to get me arrested by the Pazluvur brothers' men; and he called me 'Lady Nandini's spy,' in front of hundreds of people!"

"Is that true?" she asked.

"I have sworn to never tell the truth. Now let me go my way …"

"In that case, you'll have to remain in this prison."

Devan laughed. "Lady, do you think I can't escape from this prison without your help?"

"For the clever man who escaped from the Thanjavur treasury, this is nothing. But there's one prison you can never escape from."

"Which prison is that?"

"The prison of my heart ..."

"Lady, I have no home to call my own; the greatness of my clan lives on only in the imagination of poets. You are the emperor's beloved daughter; everyone bows to your authority ..."

"Haven't you heard the saying, 'Can anything stop love?'"

"Doesn't that apply to Poonkuzlali and the prince too?"

"Yes, it does. I believed my brother was born to be king. So, I tried to thwart their love."

"And I dreamt of standing by the prince to earn glory as he conquered the world, but he prefers a peaceful life to the burden of a throne. He would rather build temples than go to war."

"And Madurandaka longs to be king: the lion wants to be a lamb and the lamb a lion."

"And, because of you, I became a fox—hiding, lying and playing tricks to evade my enemies. I can no longer do this. Let me go."

"Aiyo! My dearest friend, Vanathi, is leaving. Will you also abandon me?"

"How can I abandon you? I'm just a servant on an errand. Kings line up for your hand ..."

Kundavai gave him her hand.

Am I dreaming? Devan wondered. He took her hand in both his and raised it to his eyes. His heart and soul thrilled to her touch.

"Warrior of Vallam," Kundavai declared. "I come from an ancient line which treasures the chastity of its women: our women have even entered their husbands' funeral pyres. After holding your hand in mine, I'll never touch another man's hand!" Kundavai paused and her eyes filled with tears as she continued. "Sir, if you risk your life because of your rashness, what will happen to me?"

"Can the man you love be a coward?"

"Cowardice is different from caution. Even the chief minister is confident of your courage ... but he fears you may be Nandini's spy."

"Set me free. I'll give him the same reply I gave Pinakapani."

"Sir, he's my father's dearest friend. If you insult him, you insult my father and me."

"In that case, how can I earn his trust?"

"Aniruddha wants someone trustworthy to go to Kanchipuram. I have said you'll go."

"Lady, don't send me there. A voice tells me, 'Don't go to Kanchipuram!'"

"Is it Nandini's voice?"

"Do you think I would listen to that venomous snake instead of you?"

"Sir, please don't talk about Nandini like that. After hearing the news you brought from Lanka, my feelings for her have changed."

"Does this mean I must obey her if she gives me the sword she worships and orders me to bring her a particular man's head?"

Kundavai trembled and her voice quavered. "You can respect her without obeying her. Maybe she doesn't know what she has got herself into."

"Yes. She said she doesn't know why she's worshipping that sword."

Kundavai's voice shook even more. "Only god can save the Cholas!"

"May god use me as his instrument," Devan said.

"I'm confident he will."

"Don't send me to Kanchipuram. If my master questions me, I'll have to tell him everything. He'll immediately march on Thanjavur. Maybe he's already on the way ..."

"If my brother's on the march, join him wherever he is. Lord Ambalavan and Nandini are on their way to Kadambur. They have invited Aditya Karikalan to join them there, supposedly for marriage alliances. I hear the division of the Chola empire is to take place there."

"Aditya Karikalan will never agree to that."

"I'm not worried about that. A dreadful fear grips my heart and haunts my dreams ..."

"I won't leave you: I'll guard you with my life!"

"Sir, I fear for my brother and Nandini, not for myself. I'm terrified of what may happen if they meet. Somehow, you must prevent them from meeting alone."

"Lady, can anyone stop them from doing what they want?"

"You must be my brother's armor. If the need arises, tell him who Nandini is."

"And if I fail?"

"Whether you fail or succeed, I'll keep you a prisoner in my heart forever," Kundavai said.

Green Silk

THE NEXT MORNING, Vandhiya Devan was riding along the banks of the Arasalar with Aniruddha's message. Nature seemed to be dressed in beautiful green silk. Devan rode slowly, taking in the different shades of green in paddy sprouts and leaves and grass and water. So many of his dreams had come true in the two months since he last rode along this river: he had met the emperor, befriended Arulmozli, seen Thanjavur, Pazlayarai, Anuradhapura and Mathottam. Above all, he had earned Kundavai's love. But a strange melancholy filled his heart.

Do I deserve such good fortune? Will there be more obstacles in my way? He shrugged. *I have faced sorcerers like Ravidasan, enchantresses like Nandini, plotters like the Pazluvur brothers, betrayers of friendship like Kandamaran and Parthibendran, lovesick girls like Poonkuzlali and Vanathi, Vaishnava spies, Kalamukhas, quicksand and marsh lights: I somehow survived them all!* He frowned. *Now the chief minister has thrown me into greater danger—on one side is the short-tempered Aditya Karikalan, on the other is the enchantress Nandini who has made even Lord Ambalavan her puppet. Can I stand between them and win? Maybe Aniruddha is doing this only to separate me from the princess. And there's no sign of Thirumalai; he's a good man to have beside me. How long must I ride slowly, waiting for him to catch up with me?*

Devan came to the spot where he had thrown his spear at the dummy crocodile. Old memories flooded his mind and he stopped. Climbing down from his horse, he looked into the river—Kundavai's beautiful face shimmered in the water. He heard a voice singing and looked up to see Azlvarkkadian seated on a branch above him, singing a hymn to Lord Vishnu.

"Hah! It's you! Be careful, there were some Kalamukhas in the crowd yesterday. I heard them say they plan to sacrifice Vaishnava fanatics to Kali, pile up their skulls and dance around them."

Azlvarkkadian touched his head. "My skull is thick enough to withstand their dance. Look!"

A palanquin passed along the bank. It was obviously a lady from the royal household. A servant walked along with the palanquin bearers.

"Do you know who's in the palanquin?" Devan asked.

"*Thambi*, don't bother about what doesn't concern you. Spur your horse on."

"And what about the man who once asked me to deliver a message to a lady in a palanquin?"

"Let's not bring up old stories. Ride to the Kollidam river. I'll meet you there tomorrow morning," Azlvarkkadian said.

Devan jumped on his horse and galloped away. *I bet he's on some other secret mission today. The Kudanthai astrologer's house is on my way. I'll pay him a visit. Who'll become emperor? Will Prince Arulmozli achieve greatness? Will my dreams come true? Will I recover my lost fiefdom? Will I succeed with Nandini and Aditya Karikalan?* Devan's heart thrilled at the thought of Nandini. *She has treated me with love and respect but I just can't read her mind. Does she plan to use me for something? What could it be?*

Devan rode past the palanquin. The screen parted a little and he glimpsed Vanathi. He hesitated but then rode on. He saw two Kalamukhas staring at the palanquin: they were the same men he had seen earlier on his way to Pazlayarai. *Why is Vanathi traveling without security in these troubled times?* Devan did not care for Vanathi, seeing her as the woman who stood between Poonkuzlali and the prince. But he knew that if Vanathi met with any disaster, Kundavai would be heart-broken. Devan rode on, recalling Azlvarkkadian's advice to mind his own business. However, the image of the Kalamukhas staring at Vanathi's palanquin haunted him. He reached the astrologer's house. *Ah! Vanathi too is headed here,* he guessed.

Skulls

VANDHIYA DEVAN'S HEART rejoiced as he walked into the astrologer's house. His mind was filled with images of Kundavai's beautiful face as it had been when he saw her here for the first time.

The astrologer was getting ready for his pooja. "Come in, come in! It's Vandhiya Devan, right?"

"Yes, your memory is accurate even if your predictions are not," Devan replied.

The astrologer smiled. "A good memory is essential in my profession. Planets, stars, directions, fortunes, hours—all need to be remembered. Now, didn't my predictions for you come true?"

"Why can't you predict the answer to your question?" Devan asked.

"You have a sense of humor," the astrologer said.

"And a temper: I would have left my temper at the door with your disciple but he's missing."

"It's a new moon today. My disciple is a Kalamukha; he has gone to participate in the gathering of Kalamukhas on the banks of the Kollidam."

"The repulsive sight of the human skulls these Kalamukhas carry is enough to make me want to become a Vaishnava," Devan said.

"Is a warrior like you afraid of skulls?"

"Killing the enemy in battle is different from wearing their skulls as a garland around my neck."

"You and I smear holy ash on our foreheads to remember that this body is temporary and we will all become ash. The Kalamukhas carry skulls to remind themselves that life is fleeting."

"What about your predictions of glory for Ponni's Beloved? The Pole Star seems to have fallen into the sea!"

"The Pole Star remains constant. But sometimes it's hidden by clouds."

"Is that what you think? Do you know something about the prince that I don't?"

"Aren't you the one who saw him last? You are the one who will know."

Devan quickly changed the topic. "What about the comet?"

"The disaster it heralds will come soon. What will happen in the royal family, and to whom?"

Devan's mind darted here and there—the paralyzed emperor in Thanjavur; Arulmozli sick in Nagapattinam; Aditya Karikalan going to Kadambur; Madurandaka longing for the throne; Nandini fondling the sword ...

"Let's leave all that aside. Tell me, will I succeed in my present mission?"

"Like last time, you will face many dangers but you will get help from unexpected quarters."

Both men turned to the door at the sound of footsteps and Vanathi walked in with her maid. Devan stood and said respectfully, "Forgive me, lady. I didn't know you were expected."

Vanathi's Request

"WHAT HAVE I done to make you want to avoid me?" Vanathi asked pathetically.

Devan said, "Forgive me, lady, I meant I'll wait outside for you. I'm not in a hurry." *Why should I vent my anger on this girl because of Poonkuzlali?*

"I'm glad you're not in a hurry. I came here to meet you, not the astrologer. I don't believe in his predictions," Vanathi said.

"Lady, my predictions will come true one day and you will praise me then," said the astrologer.

"We'll see," Vanathi said sharply. She turned to Devan. "Sir, I saw you ride past and expected you to stop. But why should you care about this orphan?"

Devan's heart melted. "Velir's niece ... Princess Kundavai's dearest friend ... an orphan?! I did not stop as it might be seen as disrespect, that's all. If there's anything I can do for you ..."

"Yes, there's something I need from you. Will you promise to help me?"

Devan hesitated. "It would be better if you tell me what you want."

"You feel I must not cheat you into making a promise. I'll tell you—I plan to become a Buddhist nun." Vanathi ignored the men's cries of objection and surprise. "I have made up my mind; many women have taken this path in our history. I tried to end my life but failed. Since god seems to want me to live longer, I'll spend my years serving my fellow men. Will you help me?"

A small suspicion crept into Devan's startled mind. "Lady, you should consult your uncle ..."

"I have made up my mind. I need no one's advice. I plan to join the Choodamani Monastery in Nagapattinam. Will you escort me there?"

This lady is no fool. She heard Princess Kundavai and me talking yesterday and plans to meet the prince at the monastery. I won't be her accomplice. "Forgive me, lady. I can't help you."

"Why not? This is nothing compared to the feats you accomplished in Lanka."

"The chief minister and the princess have ordered me to go to Kanchipuram. I'm carrying an urgent message for them. At some other time -"

Vanathi cut him off. "Very well. I planned to travel on my own. I was a little alarmed at the sight of some Kalamukhas. I'll place my trust in god who protects every life, great and small. What harm can anyone do to a woman who has renounced everything? Goodbye, astrologer."

Vanathi walked out.

The astrologer hurried after her. "Lady, night is falling and there are rain clouds in the sky. Spend the night in my humble house and leave in the morning."

"Forgive me, astrologer. I'll spend the night in Thiruvarur. As this man refuses to escort me, I'll find someone else there. I do not fear for my useless life."

The two men watched the palanquin until it disappeared from sight.

"This lady was so timid, her companions frightened her with fake crocodiles. What has made her courageous enough to travel on her own? And how did Princess Kundavai agree to this?"

"Yes," the astrologer agreed. "I can't believe this fearless, determined woman is the same woman who fainted the last time she was here.

Maybe it's the shock of the prince's death. It is said she was to marry the prince."

I wonder what shocked her: the prince dying at sea or the prince being safe in Nagapattinam or my news about Poonkuzlali. "Why should a woman from a devout Shaiva family want to join the Buddhists–and that too particularly the Choodamani Monastery? Can your astrology give us the answer?"

"That's not part of astrology texts. It will be in the texts on espionage," the astrologer smiled.

Turning down the astrologer's invitation to spend the night with him, Devan rode on. He came to the cross roads. One road led to the Kollidam river and the other led to Thiruvarur. Devan glimpsed Vanathi's palanquin in the distance on the Thiruvarur road. He hesitated for a moment. *I'll never forgive myself if anything happens to her. But my mission is urgent. I have got into enough trouble by jumping into things that don't concern me; Thirumalai also warned me. No, I can't even dream of escorting her to Nagapattinam.*

Devan turned his horse towards the Kollidam. Just then, he heard a woman's faint cry of terror. He turned back—the palanquin was gone! *It must have turned a corner, but I had better check: it won't take much time.* Devan galloped back in an instant. His heart stopped at the sight which met his eyes: Vanathi's servant was gagged and tied to a tree. He jumped off his horse and ran to her. He untied her loosely tied bonds and removed the gag from her mouth. "Woman, quick! What happened?"

The servant said that when the palanquin turned the corner, about eight men jumped out of hiding from behind the trees. They carried skulls and tridents. One of them banged her on the head, pushed her to the ground and gagged her. The others threatened the palanquin bearers and made them carry the palanquin along a side road. She pointed out the narrow path.

"Run to the astrologer's house," Devan shouted and galloped down the dark path.

The Torch Goes Out

IT WAS THE night of the new moon and darkness shrouded the forest. The stars were hidden by storm clouds. Vandhiya Devan rode by the dim light of the glow worms which hovered over the thick bushes. Even after an hour, there was no sign of the palanquin. Devan stopped his horse. *This is foolishness!* Just then, he heard the sound of horse's hooves ahead of him. *I must be careful.* He rode slowly, stopping often to listen to the faint sounds ahead. He saw a horse standing on the high canal bank. He climbed off his horse and peered around. There was a ruined building nearby. He hid his horse behind a wall and walked to the rise.

Devan jumped as a familiar voice suddenly shouted, "Who's there?" Another voice answered. "It's me, Your Majesty—your slave."

A man came out of hiding from behind a tree, holding a lighted torch. As he walked to the horse, the dim light fell on the rider's face—it was Madurandaka. The horse panicked at the sight of the torch: it reared back on its hind legs, whirled, broke into a wild gallop and plunged into the floodwaters of the canal. Shouting, "Your Majesty! Your Majesty!" the torchbearer ran after the horse, tripped and fell into the canal. The torch went out. A heavy drizzle began. Devan heard the men's shouts faintly above the sound of the rain, the wind in the trees and the buzz of insects.

Madurandaka is not a brave man. His horse may bolt and throw him into the canal. Shall I continue searching for Vanathi or help Madurandaka? There's no sign of Vanathi, but Madurandaka is in danger before my eyes. I'll help him and then continue my search for Vanathi. There goes my resolution not to get involved in matters which don't concern me!

Devan fetched his horse and rode in heavy rain and pitch darkness to the spot where the prince's horse had bolted. He climbed down into the canal and peered around. There was no sign of anyone. In the distance, he heard faint shouts of alarm. He rode across the canal and climbed to the other bank. Paddy fields stretched into the distance. He slowly rode along the narrow, slippery canal bank, overgrown with thick thorn bushes.

Why's Madurandaka alone? Who's the man who met him? What's happened to Vanathi? Are the two incidents connected? Shall I just find the highway and go to Kanchipuram? Maybe all this is related to my mission, but if my horse falls and breaks a leg my mission will fail. Just as he decided to return to the ruins and shelter from the rain, lightning flashed and he saw a horse standing in a farmyard in the distance. *I have come this far. Let me check … if I rescue Prince Madurandaka it may serve me well in the future.*

He rode down into the fields towards the farmyard. A flash of lightning showed a riderless horse standing there. Lightning flashed again, followed by a roll of thunder—the horse bolted. Thinking the prince may be lying somewhere close by, Devan shouted, "Anyone there?" His voice echoed above the sound of the rain which poured down, soaking him and his horse. A cold wind blew, making him shiver. *It's pointless staying here. Why did I get into this? From today, I'll mind my own business.* His horse instinctively found its way back to the ruined building. Devan was drenched. He decided to shelter there with the horse, dry his clothes and leave in the morning.

Suddenly, a cry came from a dark corner of the building: "*Amma! Amma!*"

Devan jumped out of his skin in fright. *Is it a ghost? No, it's a child crying for its mother.* Devan walked closer and asked, "Who are you? What are you doing in the dark? Come out."

"Are you a tiger? My mother said if I come out a tiger will pounce on me."

"No, I'm a horse. I won't pounce on you. Don't be afraid, come out."

"Why should I be afraid?" and a little child walked out of the ruins.

The rain had stopped and the sky was clear. In the starlight, Devan saw a beautiful four-year-old boy, dressed in silk and wearing a necklace of precious gems. *This child belongs to a noble family. What's he doing here? Where's his mother?*

"Oh, you have brought me a horse! But they said a palanquin would come …"

Devan's thoughts were in a whirl. *Who's this child? How fearless he is!* "Why did your mother leave you?"

"She did not leave me: I left her. A horse went running past. I wanted to catch it but *amma* said 'no.' So I ran away to catch it. Is that the horse?"

"No, this is another horse. What happened then?"

"I couldn't find the horse and I couldn't find *amma*. It started to rain. I came here for shelter."

"Aren't you afraid to be alone in the dark?"

"Why should I be afraid? I live like this every day."

"Aren't you afraid of tigers?"

"I'm not. It's my mother who's afraid of tigers. I'm a big fish–a whale. I can swallow tigers and elephants!"

"Oh my! Can a fish swallow a tiger?" *Who has taught this child to talk like this?*

"Look," the child pointed.

Devan saw a crowd with torches coming towards them with a palanquin. The men were running in excitement, along with a woman. Shouts of "Here!" "Over here!" reached them. One man pointed to the ruins and the crowd converged on it.

The child said, "I don't like palanquins. Will you take me on your horse?"

Charmed by the child, Devan wanted to pick him up and embrace him. But something held him back. "I have some urgent work in Kanchipuram …"

"Kanchipuram!" the child cried. "My greatest enemy is in Kanchipuram."

Devan was shocked. *It's wrong to even stand beside this child.* But it was too late to run. The crowd was almost there. Devan hid in a dark corner and watched.

The woman came running ahead of the others. Gasping for breath, she hugged the child and cried, "Pandya, how could you do this?!"

The next person to come forward was Ravidasan. "My king, what a fright you gave us!"

The boy laughed. "This is how I frighten you. I wanted a horse, but you brought a palanquin."

Soman Sambavan, Idumbankari, Devaralan and other men surrounded the child.

"We'll get you a thousand horses, just ride the palanquin this once," urged Sambavan.

"I'll ride that horse," the child pointed to the dark corner. All eyes turned to the horse and Devan.

Ravidasan's face blazed with shock and rage. "You wretch, how did you come here?"

"You ghost, how did you come here from Kodikkarai?" Devan countered.

Ravidasan roared with laughter. "Did you really think I was a ghost?"

The child said, "Don't fight with him: I like him. Let's take him with us."

Ravidasan said, "I'll bring him, Your Majesty. Please ride the palanquin for this one day." The boy walked to the palanquin and Ravidasan turned to Devan. "Come with us; you know our secrets and we can't let you go. There are twenty of us: don't try to escape."

"Where are you going?" Devan asked.

"To Lady Nandini of course. She's waiting at Thirupurambayam. Are you coming?"

"I'm headed in that direction. I'll be happy to have someone show me the way," Devan said.

The palanquin with the boy moved forward. Ravidasan and his group surrounded it, holding torches and cheering. Devan followed the company, his thoughts in a whirl. *What's happened to Vanathi? What's happened to Madurandaka? What will happen to me? This conspiracy is more dangerous than the Kadambur meeting. These people will kill me if I don't join them. Maybe Nandini will let me go once more. Her name was enough to make me agree to go with them ... what magic does she have? But I had no choice. I'll gather information about this murderous group and watch out for a chance to escape ...*

The child's words, "My greatest enemy is in Kanchipuram," echoed in his ears. *God! How will all this end? And when?* A voice in his mind whispered, 'Very soon.'

The strange procession hurried past fields, canals, and forests. Finally, it crossed the floodwaters of the River Manni and reached the Thirupurambayam memorial in the thick jungle.

The Time Has Come

RAVIDASAN LED VANDHIYA Devan and his horse to a corner of the outer wall. "Stay here until I call you. Don't try to escape: you can't find your way out of the forest. You'll die."

"Even if I find a way, you'll kill me with your magic, right?" Devan mocked. As Ravidasan laughed, a fox barked somewhere in the distance. As if in reply, an owl hooted. Devan shivered. The rain had stopped. He removed his waistcloth and spread it on a rock to dry. He sat on the same rock, leaned against the wall and waited. One man stood guard over him while the others walked to a nearby clearing. They extinguished their torches except for two. A man brought an old throne from the ruins. Seating the little boy on the throne, the men sat in a circle around him.

"Why is the queen not yet here?" a man asked.

"She'll be here soon," Sambavan replied. "Why don't we sing of the glory of the Pandians?"

Devaralan sang, accompanied by Idumbankari on a small drum. Devan listened to the sad song of the Pandians' heroic exploits at the Battle of Thirupurambayam. He drifted into sleep.

Devan woke with a start. Devaralan was singing about the Pandians killing their enemies and his audience was roaring in appreciation. The song stopped abruptly as the light of a torch was seen, followed by a palanquin. The bearers set it down and Nandini stepped out. Devan shuddered: she stood like Kali before the men, without her usual silks and ornaments, her hair loose. She walked to the little boy on the throne and the child stared at her. The woman whom the boy had earlier called, 'Amma,' stood behind the throne.

Nandini held out her hands to the child who looked from her to the woman standing behind him. "You're my mother, not she–right?" he asked Nandini.

"Yes, my darling," Nandini said.

"Then why does she call herself my mother?"

"Because she's the mother who brought you up," Nandini explained.

"Why does she keep me hidden in a mountain cave? Why don't you keep me with you?"

"My darling, this is to fulfill your father's wishes and avenge his death."

The boy went to Nandini who hugged him and kissed his forehead. The child clung to her as if he would never let her go. Nandini gently unclasped his arms and seated him on the throne. She went to the palanquin and took out the sword she had shown Devan. She gestured to the bearers who carried the palanquin some distance away and sat out of sight of the company. She placed the sword across the throne.

The boy eyed the sword eagerly: "Can I hold it?"

"Wait, darling." She examined every man. "Is there anyone here who has not taken the oath?"

"No, my lady," Sambavan assured her.

Nandini said, "The Cholas are powerful. We are few and our emperor is a child. We have waited for years and are now on the threshold of success only because we have been patient. Do any of you have anything to say?"

The men remained silent. All eyes were on Nandini. "Many of you were in a hurry—you even accused me of forgetting my oath. I have more reason than any of you to remember it. I have worked day and night over the past three years, looking for opportunities for revenge. Everything I did was directed towards our mission. The time has come: the Chola chieftains are divided. One group, led by Ambalavan, has decided to make Madurandaka the next king; the other, led by Velir and Malayaman, is against it. I hear Velir is marching on Thanjavur with his army and will be joined by Malayaman's forces. Civil war will break out at any moment."

"But you are trying to prevent the war with peace talks at Kadambur," Ravidasan accused her.

"Let me tell you why. If civil war breaks out now, Sundara Chola and Aniruddha will somehow stop it. Again, if either side wins, our vengeance will fail. We must complete our mission before war breaks out. Only then will the two warring factions fight until both are destroyed. Understand?"

Amazed at Nandini's cleverness, the men broke into excited murmurs. Ravidasan applauded in admiration. "Brilliant thinking! But tell us the details of your plan."

"Under the cover of peace talks, I have seen that our arch-enemy is invited to Kadambu: he'll definitely be there. We'll take revenge on him there. Veerapandian's Men, today is Saturday—by next Saturday, our oath will be fulfilled."

Devan could see Nandini announcing some important news but he could not hear her words. The excited men jumped up and cheered; someone beat a tattoo on the drum; the sleeping owls hooted and flew to other branches; the bats fluttered on their perches; Devan's horse trembled.

Ravidasan signaled for silence. "Lady, who's the lucky man who'll do the job?"

"We all want to do it. To avoid hard feelings, I asked you to bring King Veerapandian's son, our emperor, here. Whoever this little child hands Veerapandian's sword to will be the chosen one. The others must help him. If the chosen one fails, the others must complete the task. I'll be in Kadambur Palace and Idumbankari will be posted as a guard there. We'll see that the chosen one gains entry to the palace. Do you all agree?"

The men looked at each other in agreement and Ravidasan spoke up. "We agree to your plan. But, until the emperor's time comes, we must all agree to obey the chosen person in all things."

The men hesitated. It was clear that some of them were not happy with this. "It's not fair to include Lady Nandini in this stipulation ..." Sambavan objected.

Nandini said, "I live only to avenge King Veerapandian's cruel murder. I'll be a slave to whoever fulfills our oath." She turned to the child who sat without understanding what was being said. "My darling, this is your father's sword. Take it and give it to the person you like best."

Ravidasan came close to the boy. "Your Majesty, look at us all carefully. Give the sword to the one you think is the bravest and most courageous of us all."

The child looked around him. Twenty men stared at him in wild eagerness. Every eye seemed to say, 'Give it to me! Give it to me!' The little boy looked at each man in turn. He touched the sword ... he struggled to lift it ... the excitement reached fever pitch ...

The boy turned abruptly to Nandini. "Mother, you are the one I love most. You are the one who must rule the kingdom until I become a man." He handed the sword to her.

A Shape in the Dark

NANDINI TOOK THE sword and embraced it. Tears streamed down her face. She picked up the boy and held him to her chest along with the sword. The men were speechless in shock.

Ravidasan recovered first. "Lady, the emperor did not understand. Let me explain ..."

Nandini stopped him. "No, he gave me the sword understanding what it meant. Don't let my tears confuse you—these are tears of joy at being chosen to avenge King Veerapandian's death."

Sambavan said, "Lady, consider: when there are so many of Veerapandian's guards here ..."

"There's nothing to consider. The responsibility is mine. You'll all have your own duties. Half of you take the emperor safely to the Pancha Pandava Mountains. The others go to Kadambur. Those of you who can gain entry to the palace, go in. The others wait outside with horses. Once our work is done, we must all make a quick getaway."

Ravidasan spoke up. "Lady, I have some news for you."

"Tell me quickly. Lord Ambalavan has gone to take part in the gathering of Kalamukhas on the banks of the Kollidam. I must be back at the palace before he returns."

"You can't be sure Aditya Karikalan will come to Kadambur. Kundavai and Aniruddha have sent messages to Kanchipuram warning him not to go to Kadambur at any cost."

"You don't know Aditya Karikalan—if anyone tries to stop him from doing something, he'll be determined to do it. He can't be guided like Arulmozhi and he's not a coward like Madurandaka. He'll come to Kadambur because he's forbidden to do so."

"Lady, he may not get their message," Ravidasan said.

"What do you mean?" Nandini was alarmed.

"Lady, we caught the messenger. He was in the ruins where the emperor sheltered from the rain. He knows all our secrets. We risk our lives if we let him go. Idumbankari, bring that spy here." Idumbankari, along with two men, went to the ruined memorial.

Nandini's face, which had flashed with anger, again assumed its charming smile. The men pounced on Devan who was pretending to be half-asleep. Eager to find out what they were up to, he gave up the idea of fighting with them. They tied him with a thick rope and dragged him to Nandini.

Devan smiled at Nandini, who looked calmly back at him. "Sir, you again!" she said.

"Yes, I'm back, but I didn't come voluntarily." Devan looked pointedly at the men.

"Mother, this man saved me from the monsters in the dark. Why is he tied?" the little boy asked.

Devan said, "Child, don't interrupt your elders—a tiger will swallow you."

"I'll swallow the tiger!" the child declared.

"Can a fish swallow a tiger?" Devan asked. His skin prickled at the men's growls.

"Lady, did you hear that!" Ravidasan exclaimed. "This time he must be killed!"

Nandini calmy asked, "How and when did he come here?"

"This spy tried to kidnap the emperor. We stopped him in the nick of time," Ravidasan said.

"Sir, is this true?" Nandini asked.

"Lady, you are the one who knows whether your men are in the habit of telling the truth."

Nandini's smile came and went in a flash. She turned to Ravidasan. "All of you, please move back. There are some things I must discuss confidentially with this man."

The men moved away with the boy.

Nandini turned to Devan. "Sir, there seems to be a strong bond between us."

"Yes, lady: it's so strong, it has bound my hands tightly to my body!"

"Stop joking for some time. Tell me, did you come here by choice or by accident?"

"Your men dragged me here by force or I would be on the banks of the Kollidam by now."

"It's clear you are sorry to see me and eager to leave me."

"No, I'll be sorry to leave you. You are caught between the Pazluvur brothers and this terrible gang of sorcerers. Just say the word and I'll take you away from them all. I'll take you to your mother who is wandering like an orphan on Sri Lanka's islands."

Nandini sighed in disappointment. "Do you want me too to wander like an orphan? If the time comes for that, I'll come to you. But before that, I must carry out my plan. Will you help me?"

"Lady, I can tell you that only after you tell me what you want."

"If you truly care for me, you would agree to do anything I want."

"If I truly care for you, I'll warn you and guard you from danger. Lady, these villains have hatched a plot and are pushing you into danger. They are using you for their own purposes. They are fooling you with a little child from some forest."

"You're wrong: I'm the one using them for my purpose. Do you know what the child is for?"

"Yes, to crown him king and seat him on the Pandian throne."

"Wrong again: it's to crown him Chola emperor."

"Oh my! And how will you do this? Will you defeat the Chola empire with its army of twenty lakh warriors with these twenty foxes who hide in their dens by day and come out at night?"

"I put my faith in this sword!" Nandini declared.

"Lady, you'll never use that sword: you don't have the heart or the strength for it."

"I can prove you wrong right now!"

"In that case, I'm indeed fortunate to die at your hands." Devan bowed his head as if in readiness to be beheaded by her sword.

"Wouldn't you rather be crowned by me?"

"Many people have complimented me on my curly hair. I don't want to hide it under a crown."

"You and your jokes! Very well. How did Kundavai react when she heard the news about Arulmozli? Was she very upset? And is it true the Kodumbalur girl tried to drown herself in the lake? Who rescued her?"

Devan was taken aback. He did not reply.

Nandini's voice hardened. "I know you won't discuss all that with me. Tell me, are you going to convince Aditya Karikalan not to go to Kadambur?"

"I'll try, but once the prince makes up his mind to do something, it's difficult to stop him."

"You know him well," Nandini said.

"Not at well as you know him, lady."

"However much I ask, you won't join me; you'll always be on my enemy's side."

"Lady, who's your enemy?"

"Who else but that Pazlayarai princess?"

"That's your imagination. Let me tell you an important truth …"

"Keep your truth to yourself!" Nandini said angrily. "I know your truth will be a lie." She clapped: Ravidasan and his men surrounded him, growling like a pack of wolves at its prey.

Devan thought, *I have not made good use of my opportunity. This demon will order her men to kill me. What a death! Why could I not die a heroic death on the battlefield?*

Ravidasan said, "Queen, this man will never join us. Let's sacrifice him on this holy ground …"

"Sorcerer, beware!" Nandini cried. "If any man touches him, I'll kill that man with my sword. I need him for many more things. Let him go his way. Let's all leave now."

Ravidasan protested. "Lady, he has a horse—it will not do to let him go first."

"Tie him to a pillar: by the time he frees himself, you would have crossed the forest."

The men tied Devan to a pillar and his horse to another. Nandini left in her palanquin; two men carried away the throne; Ravidasan and his group went with the little boy. The light of their torches faded into the distance and Devan was engulfed in darkness. Giant bats fluttered their wings; owls hooted; foxes howled in the distance. Devan thought the howling of the foxes was coming closer and remembered his nightmare at Kadambur Palace. He struggled to free himself from the rope, but it was not easy, especially in the pitch dark.

What's that? It sounds like footsteps. Devan's horse neighed softly.

Devan again tried to free himself, but it was useless. *How tightly those monsters have knotted the rope! I'll teach Ravidasan a lesson the next time I see him.*

A dark shape came towards him. Devan gathered his courage and his strength and gave it a powerful kick. "Aaaah!" the figure shrieked and banged against the wall. Devan felt eyes staring at him. The figure went into the memorial and Devan heard the sound of flint stones being scraped. The figure came out holding a lighted lamp: it was a Kalamukha with matted hair, a wild beard and a garland of skulls. The Kalamukha raised his lamp and peered intently into Devan's face.

Identity Revealed

DEVAN FELT A pang of fear on seeing that dreadful figure. Then his courage reasserted itself. *Where have I seen this man before? Ah! He was one of the two men who examined me as I slept under the tree. But I have seen those sharp eyes somewhere else …*

The Kalamukha burst out laughing. "It's you! To think I took all this trouble to follow you!"

It seemed as if the Kalamukha was trying to disguise his voice. *Where have I heard this voice before?* Devan asked, "Why, whom did you think you were following?"

"The prince. Because of a spy like you, our grand conference fizzled out. We waited but the prince did not come to swear that once he was king, he would make our guru the Royal Guru."

"Untie my ropes. I'll tell you why Prince Madurandaka did not attend your meeting."

"When I came searching for the prince, I saw some men leaving the forest. I know them: they tied you up because they think you're a spy. What I can't understand is why they let you live."

"I'll tell you why–untie the rope."

"If I free you, will you mind your own business in future and do hundred-and-eight squats?"

All this while, Devan had been busy with his hands. He freed himself, knocked down the Kalamukha, sat on his chest and tugged at his beard. It came away in his hands. The Kalamukha pushed Devan off his chest and jumped to his feet. Devan held up the flickering lamp and looked into Azlvarkkadian's face. The two men burst out laughing.

"My boy," said Azlvarkkadian. "If I had not come here now …"

"Was it you who untied the rope?" Devan countered.

"You'll never find your way out of this forest without my help. Was anyone with those men?"

"Yes, a little fish which wanted to swallow tigers."

"Ah! Tell me the details—who was there? What happened?"

"Why are you disguised? Where did you go? If you tell me, I'll tell you what happened here."

"I assumed this disguise to attend the Kalamukhas' conference. Lord Ambalavan was there; so was the Kalamukhas' chief guru. But the important guest who was expected did not turn up."

"Prince Madurandaka. If he ascends the throne, what a great government we'll have! He can't even control a spirited horse—how will he control chieftains like the Pazluvur brothers, rebellious Kalamukhas and fanatic Vaishnavas?"

Azlvarkkadian laughed. "Did you see Prince Madurandaka? What happened to him?"

Devan described how he had followed Madurandaka, the man who came with the torch, how the horse had bolted and stood riderless in a farmyard. "The poor prince must be lying hurt somewhere. Shall we go look for him?"

"That's nothing to do with us. We must be at the Kollidam ferry by sunrise."

"What if the prince is lying dead in a canal or field?" Devan asked.

"The chief minister will handle it: nothing happens in the kingdom without his knowledge."

"Oh! Does he know about the meeting of conspirators at Kadambur Palace?"

"I asked you to give a message to the person in the palanquin and you thought I wanted you to deliver a love letter. It was a message from the chief minister to Prince Madurandaka saying, 'Do not trust the conspirators and ruin your life.' The man whose torch made the horse bolt was probably one of the chief minister's men. By now, someone would have rescued the prince and he'll be on his way to Thanjavur. I hear Karikalan has left Kanchipuram: we must fly!"

"I can't come with you. You must carry my message to the prince." Devan told Azlvarkkadian how Vanathi had been abducted. "I must find out what happened to her."

"Why do you care about that girl?"

"She's the general's niece, Princess Kundavai's companion and is to marry Prince Arulmozli ..."

"So, you think the prince is alive?"

"Don't try to pull secrets out of my mouth! The Kalamukhas may sacrifice that young girl ..."

"If the Kalamukhas have kidnapped Vanathi, you needn't worry: the Kodumbalur chieftains are Kalamukhas. Her kidnappers will treat her like royalty. Many powerful men in the kingdom and in the army are Kalamukhas. That's why Lord Ambalavan arranged for Prince Madurandaka to gain their support. A horse ruined his plans. Now, are you coming or shall I go?"

Devan reluctantly followed Azlvarkkadian through the dense jungle. The comet's tail covered the sky. A cold breeze made him shiver. Somewhere in the distance, a village dog howled.

What Happened to Vanathi

NIGHT FELL AS Vanathi left the Kudanthai astrologer's house. She longed to go to the Choodamani Monastery and care for Arulmozli. She had resolved to travel alone to Nagapattinam. Now she was discouraged and filled with doubt. She tried to stiffen her resolve. *Nothing can be achieved without a struggle. When that boat girl braved the storm to save the prince, how can I be scared to travel to Nagapattinam? Even if I can't enter the monastery, I can stay somewhere close by and get news of the prince. Maybe the boat girl will take me to him. It's enough to just see him once and show my love for him ...*

Vanathi parted the screens to ask the palanquin bearers when they would reach Nagapattinam. She saw some Kalamukhas hiding behind the roadside tees. Vanathi was not alarmed as she was used to seeing these frightening men at the Kodumbalur palace. Her uncle was their patron and she was confident they would not harm her. *But why are they hiding behind the trees?*

Suddenly, the men charged forward, surrounded the palanquin, dragged her shrieking maid to a tree and tied her to it. One man waved his trident at the maid and said, "Quiet! If you scream, I'll kill you!"

Vanathi picked up courage and declared, "I'm General Velir's niece: watch out!"

The Kalamukha said, "We know whom you are and we were waiting for you. Be quiet!"

Vanathi heard the crack of whips and her palanquin bearers screamed in pain. Indignant, she tried to step out of the palanquin but the bearers lifted it and took off at a run. The Kalamukhas ran with the palanquin, shrieking loudly. Vanathi realized that there was no use in her shouting for help. *If I jump out, they'll be on me in a second. Let's see where they are taking me.*

After about half an hour, the men stopped at an ancient Durga temple hidden among the trees. One man went in and returned with a lighted torch which he shone on Vanathi's face. He said, "Woman, if you give us the information we want, we won't harm you; we'll take you wherever you want. Tell me, who's the man you are going to meet in secret?"

Vanathi, the timid mouse, became a fearless lion. "That's none of your business!"

The Kalamukha laughed. "You are going to meet Prince Arulmozli: just tell me where he is hiding and we'll let you go."

Vanathi said defiantly, "I'll never tell you. Do what you want."

He lifted the torch. "First, I'll burn your beautiful hands; then I'll burn your black hair ..."

These men are part of the group which is plotting against the Cholas. I'm lucky to get this chance to protect the prince. Vanathi's courage grew. "You can kill me inch by inch; you can cut me into pieces—I won't say a word!"

"Very well, let me begin my work," the Kalamukha said. "Give me that torch ..."

Vanathi saw a long procession of horses, elephants, soldiers and palanquins coming towards them. *God has saved me,* she thought in relief. "Careful! That's the chief minister's company. If I shout, they'll hear me—run for your lives!"

"Yes, woman, that's Aniruddha's company. We brought you here on his orders."

Vanathi covered her mouth to stifle the terrified scream which rose from her throat.

The Elephant

VANATHI STEPPED OUT of her palanquin and looked at the procession. The Kalamukhas stood silently beside her. She had no thought of escape. *Even if I run from the Kalamukhas, I can't run from the chief minister. He's known for his intelligence, cunning and political skills. He's the emperor's closest friend and Princess Kundavai respects him. Are these Kalamukhas lying? Maybe it's the Pazluvur brothers or Prince Madurandaka who's coming here. Whoever it is, even if I die, I won't say a word. I'll show them who I am—I belong to the brave Kodumbalur clan!*

A palanquin detached itself from the procession and came to her. Aniruddha stepped out. His bearers and the Kalamukhas moved away, leaving him alone with Vanathi. "Can this be true? Is it the brave Kodumbalur chieftain's daughter who stands before me?!"

"Yes, and is this the Chola empire's most respected Chief Minister Aniruddha Brahmaraya who stands before me?"

"As you know who I am, my task becomes easier. Just answer a few questions and ..."

"Before that, let me ask you a few questions," Vanathi said.

"I think of you as my own daughter; your uncle and I have been close friends for more than forty years," Aniruddha replied. "Ask me whatever you want. Be quick, it's going to rain."

"You are the arbiter of justice in this kingdom. I thought the roads were safe under Emperor Sundara Chola's reign. Isn't it wrong to kidnap a woman traveling on the road and torture her?"

Aniruddha said, "I heard a woman was going to Nagapattinam with an important state secret. I ordered my men to stop her. Maybe they made a mistake and stopped you instead. Were you on the way to meet a traitor in Nagapattinam? Were you on your way to meet Prince Arulmozli?"

Vanathi controlled her fury. "Sir, I'll never give you information about the prince. Even when your men threatened to burn my hand, I did not say a word."

"I applaud your courage, but I have already gathered information from you. The entire kingdom is mourning the prince's death. But you did not say, 'How can I meet him when he's dead?' This shows you know he's alive. Just tell me where the prince is hiding in Nagapattinam and how you came to know about this. Once you tell me this, you can leave at once."

Vanathi was devastated that she had unknowingly betrayed the prince to this clever man. "Sir, as my father, do one thing for me. Ask your men to sacrifice me on this temple's altar."

"My child, when it comes to matters of state, there are no friends or family. Look at the emperor —he ordered his own son to be arrested when he came to know he was a traitor."

"How can you call the prince a traitor?"

"The prince tried to use the Chola army's victory to make himself king of Sri Lanka; he defied the emperor's arrest warrant and jumped into the sea to spread the false news of his death; he's now in hiding. My dear, it's a serious crime to protect such a traitor."

Vanathi could no longer control her anger. "Lies! The prince turned down the Buddhist monks' offer to crown him. He honored the emperor's arrest warrant and sailed back voluntarily. He jumped into the sea to save his friend … and you call him a traitor!"

Aniruddha chuckled. "Anyone hearing you would think you're in love with the prince."

"I love him with all my heart. There's no need to hide the truth from you. But there's no chance of the prince returning my love. I'll never tell you where the prince is."

"Then I'm forced to punish you as a traitor to the country. Look at that elephant -"

Vanathi saw an elephant with curved white tusks standing like a black mountain in the darkness.

Aniruddha laughed. "My girl, this elephant has sent many men to their deaths …"

Vanathi's hair stood on end. *He's a demon!* "Sir, shall I go to the elephant, or will you ask it to come here?" she asked defiantly.

Aniruddha signaled and said something in a strange language. The earth shook; the elephant walked to Vanathi, encircled her fragile body in its trunk and lifted her off the ground.

Vanathi thought, *Princess Kundavai called me a coward: how surprised she'll be when she hears this. Someday the prince will know how courageously I faced death. Will he admit I'm braver than that boat girl?* The elephant lifted her higher. Vanathi closed her eyes … the elephant whirled its trunk … by god's grace, Vanathi fainted.

Anaimangalam

VANATHI FELT HERSELF swaying from side to side; she heard the patter of rain; her body shivered in a cool wind; she was surrounded by darkness; flashes of lightning came and went. *I'm flying to heaven. Why am I swinging like this? My head is on something soft … it feels like Princess Kundavai's lap … she loves me like a mother … has she heard the news of my death?*

"Vanathi! Vanathi!"

"*Akka!* Is that you? Are you coming with me to heaven?"

"Nonsense! We are going to Anaimangalam. We're riding an elephant there."

"Aiyo! An elephant!!"

"Mad girl! Why are you shivering? Are you so afraid of elephants? You fell asleep; you were mumbling something about Kalamukhas and sacrifices … you called the chief minister a wicked man: serves him right!"

"I had a horrible nightmare. The Kalamukhas kidnapped me and the chief minister threatened to let an elephant kill me if I did not tell him where the prince was. You would have been proud to see how brave I was. I can't believe it was only a dream!"

"Sometimes our dreams seem very real. I see Arulmozli clearly when I close my eyes at night. You also blabbered something about becoming a Buddhist nun—are you that tired of life?"

"I'm not as brave as you, *akka*. Now that the prince is dead -"

"Don't say that. Let the Pazluvur brothers and Nandini and that crazy Madurandaka say it and rejoice, but we don't have to say it."

Vanathi was silent for a while. Then, "Where's Anaimangalam, *akka*?"

Kundavai chuckled. "It's on the coast near Nagapattinam. In fact, it's near the Choodamani Monastery you were talking about in your sleep. It's conveniently located if you want to become a Buddhist nun. But wait until we get confirmed news about Arulmozli before you decide."

"How can you laugh, *akka*? Are you so confident the prince is alive?"

"I believe the conch and chakra sign on my brother's hand foretells a great future for him. The astrologers predicted he will face danger when he is young—that's happening now."

"Why are we traveling at night, *akka*?"

"If we travel by day, the people will crowd around us, cursing the Pazluvur brothers and Nandini and even the emperor. The Pazluvur brothers will accuse me of instigating the people. It's better to travel by night. We must sleep seated on this swaying mountain."

Vanathi kept quiet. But she was sure that the events of the night were not part of her dreams. *I'm not mad. What happened after the elephant picked me up? Did Princess Kundavai rescue me from the chief minister? Is this the elephant which picked me up and put me in this howdah? Did the princess and the chief minister plan this? Was it to stop me from traveling alone? Was it to test my courage as the princess did with the dummy crocodile? How comforting it is to have the princess by my side. She makes me confident the prince is alive somewhere. Who knows? Maybe I'll see him at the end of this journey.* She looked up at the stars. *The astrologers say the prince's star matches mine. And they say my son will rule the world—will this happen?*

Vanathi drifted off to sleep. When she awoke, it was morning and they had reached the Chola mansion at Anaimangalam. They went to the terrace overlooking the canal which ran to the sea.

Kundavai said, "Look: Chendan Amudhan and Poonkuzlali are coming here by boat … maybe they bring us news of Arulmozli."

Vanathi saw the small wooden boat. "*Akka*, I don't want to see that girl. I'll go inside."

"Why are you afraid of her? Don't worry, I'll take care of you. Stay here."

Madurandaka's Gratitude

VANATHI'S SUSPICIONS ABOUT Kundavai and Aniruddha were correct. The elephant lifted Vanathi gently to the howdah, where the princess was ready to hold her.

Aniruddha climbed into his palanquin. "Lady, may you have a happy journey and may you find happiness at its end."

"Sir, thank you for your help."

"You said Vanathi was timid, but I have never met a more courageous woman in my life."

"She was a coward until a few days ago," Kundavai said.

Aniruddha smiled. "It must be your training. That girl probably thinks I'm a demon. Never mind: many people say such things about me! Goodbye."

Aniruddha set off in his palanquin with four guards. Suddenly, the palanquin halted.

"Master," one of the advance guards said. "Someone is lying under that tree."

Aniruddha peered out: a sudden flash of lightning showed a man on the ground. As the chief minister walked towards the tree, he heard a groan of pain. "Who's there?"

A weak voice said, "It sounds like the chief minister … it's me, Madurandaka."

"Prince! Why are you here?" Aniruddha asked. He lifted the prince and tried to make him stand.

Madurandaka screamed. "Aaah! I'm dying! Don't touch me—my legs are broken!

The worried chief minister asked, "How did this happen? How dare your attendants abandon you? They'll be severely punished."

"Chief minister, no one is to blame. I rode from the palace by myself last evening. It started to rain when I was riding along the banks of the river. My horse, afraid of the thunder and lightning, bolted. I got tangled in the branches of this tree and fell down. I don't know where the horse is. My legs are either broken or I have cramps. Thank goodness you came here!"

"I came this way by your saintly father's grace. Let me take you to my house in Nathankovil." Aniruddha called the palanquin bearers and carefully lifted the prince into the palanquin. Ordering the men to be gentle, the chief minister walked behind the palanquin to his house near the Perumal temple. They carried Madurandaka inside and laid him on a bed. The prince's legs were examined: he was only suffering from cramps. Madurandaka's fear subsided.

After they had shared the food offerings from the temple, Aniruddha said, "Prince, sleep peacefully. I'm going to Thanjavur in the morning. If you want, I can escort you safely there."

"Sir, you have wronged me in many ways. But you have made up for that today. I'm grateful to you for your help. If I become the next king, I'll make you my chief minister."

Aniruddha exclaimed in surprise: "Prince! It's my duty to advise and help all the Cholas— there's no need to thank me. But I have never deliberately wronged you."

"Sir, you are a renowned genius and political strategist but don't try your tricks with me. I know you have wronged me. But I forgive you. Tell me if there's anything I can do for you."

Aniruddha laughed. "Yes, prince, please don't ride a horse. A screened palanquin would be safer. The best thing would be to ride in Lady Nandini's palanquin."

Madurandaka was shocked and alarmed. He tried to bluff his way out. "Sir, are you trying to insult me? Are you suggesting I travel in a woman's palanquin?"

"Prince, since when have you considered it an insult to travel in

Lady Nandini's palanquin? Aren't you used to it? The last time you used it was to travel to Kadambur Palace ..."

Madurandaka was now in a panic. "I ... I ... Kadambur Palace ..." he stammered.

"Prince, you went to Kadambur Palace on the eighteenth of *Aadi* with the chancellor, Lord Ambalavan. You traveled there and back in Lady Nandini's palanquin. A palanquin is for old men like me. You should ride an elephant or a horse: I'll arrange riding lessons for you."

"Just because of today's accident, don't think I don't know how to ride. And just because I once used Lady Nandini's palanquin, don't think I always travel in it. I'm being patient with you."

"Prince, as the saying goes, the patient will rule the world. If I have offended you in any way, you who wish to rule the world must be patient with me."

"Do you accuse me of wanting to rule the Chola empire?" Madurandaka's fear changed to rage.

Aniruddha stayed calm. "How can I accuse you? You have every right to the throne: you belong to the Chola dynasty and you are Gandara Aditya's son. Your parents had other plans for you but you have now changed. No one has the right to criticize you for that. Make your wish known openly: talk to the emperor. There's no need for you to steal out alone at night to seek the Kalamukhas' support—or to join men who meet like thieves at night in Kadambur."

Madurandaka was amazed and angry. "Sir, who betrayed me to you?"

"No one," Aniruddha replied. "I have eyes and ears all over the kingdom."

"Does the emperor know this?"

"The emperor is my dearest friend. But he's suffering from a cruel disease and has many heartaches. I don't want to hurt him further by telling him about this conspiracy among the chieftains. I assure you I won't tell him about you."

"Why this sudden love for me?" the prince mocked.

"Prince, I love you just as I love all Emperor Sundara Chola's sons."

"If I had fallen off my horse a few days back, you would have strangled me under that tree."

"What are you saying, prince?!"

"Sir, you were my enemy even when I was in my mother's womb. You arranged to kill me as soon as I was born. There! The surprise on your face is proof of what I say. Do you think you're the only one who knows this country's dreadful secrets?"

Aniruddha was shocked: a range of emotions flitted across his face. He smiled sadly. "My pride has taken a beating. But, if I arranged to kill you as an infant, how is it you are alive?"

"Are you trying to see how much I know? Very well! My mother delivered a baby girl. You decided to let it live and gave it to a temple priest. I was born half an hour later. As you did not expect twins, I escaped with my life. Once your plan failed, you decided to stop me from becoming emperor. You tried to make me a Shiva devotee—a madman. You failed in that too. Why are you shocked? Why don't you deny it all?"

Aniruddha was at a loss for words. "Prince, what's the point of me denying anything?"

"Exactly! And I know the reason for your sudden affection: you dislike Aditya Karikalan and planned to make Arulmozli emperor; now that Arulmozli is dead, you are leaning towards me. But I'll forgive your past sins and be grateful to you for today's help. If you agree to be on my side from now, I wish to make you my chief minister."

"Prince, your words give me great happiness." Aniruddha replied.

Am I in Heaven?

ARULMOZLI LAY IN a room adjoining the abbot's cell. He had high fever for three days and was mostly unconscious. The monks cared for him day and night. When he was conscious, the prince tried to understand where he was. A large painting on the wall showed a host of celestial beings with musical instruments, parasols and trays of flowers. *Am I in heaven*? *How did I come here*? He remembered a canal, the fragrance of screw-pine and a small boat with two angels. The boy sang sweet *Thevaram* hymns; the girl was quiet but gazed at him lovingly. Where were they?

On the fourth day, the prince was very weak but his mind was alert. He realized that the walls were covered with paintings depicting

Buddha. *I'm in a Buddhist monastery, but where?* Slowly, all the events of his days in Sri Lanka came back to him. He remembered floating on the mast pole in the sea with Vandhiya Devan, but everything was a jumble of confusion after that.

A monk came in with a cup of milk mixed with some medicine. Arulmozli asked, "*Swami*, where am I? How many days have I been here?" The monk turned away without replying.

The prince heard him in the next room. "Acharya, his fever is gone and he's fully conscious."

The old abbot entered the room and examined the prince carefully. "Prince, you are in the Choodamani Monastery. You had high fever for three days. We took care of you."

"Sir, you have taken great trouble to heal me. But I won't thank you … you brought me back from the threshold of heaven to this grief-filled life on earth."

"You must not thank me. Buddhist dharma sees healing as the highest form of service. And we are obliged to your father, Emperor Sundara Chola, and your sister, Princess Kundavai, for being our generous sponsors. As for going to heaven, you still have much to do on earth."

Arulmozli sat up suddenly. "Acharya, you are right: there are things I must do. The stupas in Sri Lanka make me ashamed of our own temples and monasteries. I'll rebuild the Choodamani Monastery to match the grandeur of Abhayagiri Vihara in Anuradhapura. I'll build a Shiva temple in Thanjavur whose tower reaches the sky. Generations to come will marvel at it!" Arulmozli fell back on his bed, exhausted.

The abbot said, "All this in good time—but first you must regain your strength. Rest."

The Nandi Pavilion

The following afternoon, the abbot came again. "How are you feeling?"

"Acharya, I want to ride a horse and swim in the river. I have such an appetite! I can't believe I was at death's door a few days ago—your medicines have worked a miracle."

"The after-effects of the fever make you feel like this. But if you are careless, the fever will return and threaten your life. In every city and village, the people are crying their hearts out …"

"Why should they worry? Surely they know your medicines will cure me?"

"Sir, the people don't know you have fever or that you are here …"

The prince sat up in bed. "Acharya! How did this happen?"

"One morning, we heard that the ship in which you were sailing from Sri Lanka to Kodikkarai sank in the cyclone. The news that you had died at sea spread like wildfire through the land. We were mourning your death when a boat came to the monastery with you in a high fever."

"Who brought me here?"

"A young man and a girl. The man is Chendan Amudhan, a Shiva devotee. I don't know the girl's name, but she's strong and courageous."

"She must be Poonkuzlali, the boat girl. Did they tell you why they brought me here?"

"No—and they asked me not to tell anyone you were here."

"Something suspicious is happening. I left Sri Lanka submitting to the emperor's arrest warrant. Now, someone plotting to accuse me of disobeying the emperor has spread rumors of my death. Acharya, keeping me here makes you a traitor. Send me to Thanjavur at once."

"Sir, even if this monastery is razed to the ground for keeping you, I will not regret it. It's our duty to care for the sick and Princess Kundavai told me you would be coming to spend a few days here. Amudhan also said the princess had instructed him to bring you here."

"Can I meet the two who brought me here? I have some urgent questions for them."

The abbot smiled. "I won't keep you here against your wishes. The two people who brought you here are waiting for you in a boat in the canal."

Arulmozli hesitated. "Did they tell you where they are taking me?"

"Yes, two women are waiting for you at the Nandi Pavilion about an hour's journey from here."

Amudhan and Poonkuzlali grinned happily as Arulmozli walked majestically to the boat.

The abbot sent off the prince saying, "Please come back here for a week to regain your strength."

Arulmozli said, "Acharya, I'll be back."

As the boat moved down the canal, the prince looked from Amudhan to Poonkuzlali. "Tell me everything that happened to me from the time I lost consciousness in the sea–but first tell me who's waiting for me in the Nandi Pavilion."

Amudhan said, "Sir, Princess Kundavai and Lady Vanathi are waiting for you at the pavilion."

"Ah! The lady who faints for no reason at all! Why has my sister brought her here?"

Amudhan smiled. "Sir, all the women of Tamil Nadu want to become Buddhist nuns."

"Who are these women?" the prince asked.

"Lady Vanathi and this woman here." He smiled at Poonkuzlali.

"Only two of them, Amudhan—the Shaiva faith can bear the loss. I know many Buddhist monasteries in Sri Lanka; I can take these two women there if they want."

Amudhan and Arulmozli laughed together. Amudhan then told the prince what he knew about events from the time Arulmozli and Vandhiya Devan had fallen into the sea. The prince listened eagerly, trying to match Amudhan's account with his own memory of events.

"There's the Nandi Pavilion," Poonkuzlali pointed.

The two men turned in that direction.

The Nandi Grows

STEPS LED UP to a pavilion in a corner of the steep canal bank. On each end of the pavilion was a finely sculpted Nandi statue. People flocked here during the spring festival to pray and picnic in the moonlight. On other days, due to its distance from the city, the pavilion was usually deserted. By the time the boat reached the pavilion, Kundavai stood on the lowest step while Vanathi stayed half-hidden behind a pillar.

Amudhan and Kundavai helped the prince climb out of the boat. Amudhan then rowed the boat a little distance away and waited with Poonkuzlali.

Arulmozli touched Kundavai's feet in respect. She laid her hand on his head in blessing and kissed him on his forehead. "*Thambi,* how thin you are!" Kundavai's eyes filled with tears.

"*Akka,* leave that aside. Something has happened to cause you grief. Or you would never have sent me an urgent message asking me to return from Sri Lanka."

"Sit here. The abbot said you had recovered from the fever but it's clear you're still weak. I should not have asked you to come so soon. But once I came to Anaimangalam, I couldn't wait."

"*Akka,* if you hadn't sent for me, I would be on my way to Pazlayarai by now. Your message was always on my mind. I have never met a braver man than Vandhiya Devan. I was amazed at his cunning and scheming. I thought he would be here with you, but you have brought the lady who faints for no reason."

"You don't know how brave she is now! Yesterday, the chief minister's elephant lifted her ..."

"Enough about your friend—tell me about my friend."

"What is there to say? He has gone back to Aditya Karikalan."

"Then he has broken his word. He assured me he would stay in Chola country."

"What would he do here? If you're so fond of him, ask father to restore Vallam to him—then he will stay here."

"What would a great warrior like him do with a chieftainship?"

"What every chieftain does! Do you think he would refuse it like you refused the Lankan throne?"

The prince smiled sadly. "I refused the Lankan throne in the presence of witnesses. In spite of that, father has accused me of being a traitor and issued an arrest warrant for me ..."

"Father knows you refused the Lankan throne. He issued the arrest warrant just to make you come back. He would have been happy if you had become king of Sri Lanka. He would have divided the Chola empire between Karikalan and Madurandaka and been at peace. There are plans to divide the empire into two kingdoms, one south and the other north of the Kollidam."

"I'll never be a part of such a disaster. Better to give the entire empire to Madurandaka."

"The chief minister feels the same."

"Yes, he discussed this with me when he came to Sri Lanka. *Akka*, shall I tell you the real reason why I refused the Lankan throne? I imagined Sri Lanka to be a great land. But I saw how small it was: one can ride by horse or elephant from coast to coast in one day."

"The Chola kingdom is no bigger, *thambi*: you can ride from one end to the other in a day."

"If anyone offered me the Chola throne, I would refuse. Sadly, Tamil Nadu is divided among the Cholas, the Pandians and the Cheras. We have no great emperors like Chandragupta and Harshavardhana who ruled vast empires. If I become emperor, I'll rule an empire which stretches from Sri Lanka in the south to the Ganga in the north. I'll plant the Tiger Flag in distant lands like Java and the Maldives … you must think I'm mad."

"If you're mad, I'm madder! Arulmozli, I rejoice to see you dream big like me. I'll see the Chola empire you dream about come true before I die. I thought Aditya Karikalan would make my dream come true, but I have lost faith in him. He's a brave warrior, but he can't control his passions: he won't achieve greatness. I hope you'll build this great empire, but I won't lose hope if you don't. I believe your son will build it. I'll raise your son from the day he's born. I'll make him a warrior the likes of whom the world has never seen."

"*Akka*, you're definitely madder than I am! You are talking about my son when I have no intention of getting married. If any of the companions you dote on dream of marrying me and sitting on the throne, you had better tell them it will never happen." Arulmozli's eyes rested for an instant on Vanathi's face before moving on to the Nandi. "*Akka*, even though Sri Lanka is small, its kings had large hearts: they built stupas which reach to the sky, monasteries with thousands of rooms, Buddhas as tall as that coconut tree there. Look how small this Nandi is! He who is Lord Shiva's vehicle, he who guards Mount Kailash." Arulmozli's eyes seemed to gaze into the future. "I see this Nandi grow to touch the sky …. I see a temple whose tower is so high it's called 'Mount Meru of the South.' I don't care who sits on the throne—I'll be happy to be in charge of temple renovation!"

"*Thambi*, the Chola kingdom is surrounded by danger from internal and external enemies and from friends turned foes. I'm haunted by a terrible dream: a wicked sword hangs over us. Will it fall on a member of our family? Will it cut this empire into two? You and I must somehow stop this sword."

"I suppose you know who's the greatest threat to the Cholas?"

"Nandini, right?"

"Yes. Do you know who she is?"

"Yes, that's why I hurried here to meet you."

Vanathi in Danger

"*AKKA*, IN SRI Lanka, I met the goddess who saved me from drowning in the Ponni ..."

"I'm not surprised, just eager to hear everything about her."

"There is too much to tell. I'll just give you the important details. She saved my life many times and lavishes her love on me ... in fact her love for me is even greater than yours."

"You're right. For me, the Chola kingdom comes first. If you stand in the way of my country, my love for you will become hatred. But that mute woman shows her love for our father by loving you—her love is priceless."

"*Akka!*" Arulmozli exclaimed. "How do you know this?"

"From what father and Vandhiya Devan told me. Does she treat you as her own son or as her stepson? Our mother is seated on the throne which rightfully belongs to her."

"My age is proof I cannot be her son. She tried to tell me what she could through her paintings. My heart melts at how much she loved father. Tell me, *akka*, do I look like father did when he was my age?"

"No. At your age, father was as beautiful as Manmatha, the God of Love. Our family is not renowned for its good looks—we prize courage above beauty. But our grandmother, Kalyani, was beautiful and father inherited her beauty. We get our looks from our mother's side."

"I don't know whether there's any connection between courage and love, but I do know that love has nothing to do with beauty. Otherwise ..."

"Otherwise, why would Vanathi stare at you? Why would Amudhan stare at Poonkuzlali?"

Arulmozli laughed. "*Akka*, I'm talking about our stepmother's love for me while you are talking about something else. Let that be. Is it possible for one person to be a copy of another?"

"Why not? Twins can be a copy of each other; a daughter may be a copy of her mother at the same age; and rarely, strangers may resemble each other exactly."

"I have not looked closely at Nandini in recent years. I remember her only as a child. Vandhiya Devan insists our stepmother is a copy of Nandini. What do you think?"

"I have not seen our stepmother. But, from what father said, I believe Vandhiya Devan."

"What did father tell you? When?" Arulmozli asked excitedly.

"I was in Thanjavur recently. Father told me the story of his youth. He stayed behind on a small island near Lanka ... he met a beautiful young girl there and fell in love with her ... his grandfather's men brought him back here to be made crown prince ... from the palace balcony, he saw the girl in the crowd ... she disappeared ... the chief minister told father the girl had jumped into the sea from the top of the Kodikkarai lighthouse. For the past twenty-four years, father has been plagued by guilt that he drove her to her death. *Thambi*, let our dreams for the country wait: we must first do our duty to father. You must somehow bring our stepmother here. Only if he knows she's alive will father find peace."

"Even when I lay at death's door, my only regret was I had not brought her to father. *Akka*, my heart aches when I think of her: she cannot tell anyone her sorrows or hear anyone's words of comfort. Anger, curiosity, sorrow, love, longing ... she must keep everything bottled up inside her. No wonder she wanders like a madwoman. But do you think father will want to see her?"

"Whether he does or not, it's our duty to bring them together. Father cries at night thinking the dead woman is haunting him—that's why he does not recover."

"Did father tell you this?"

"Father and Vanathi."

"Vanathi? How does she come into this? Did you tell her anything?"

"No, no! I'll ask her to tell you what she saw one night at Thanjavur. Where are your manners? You have not greeted Vanathi: is this how you respect the Kodumbalur chieftains?"

"*Akka,* when you take care of Vanathi, why should I bother?"

"Will you shut up?!" Kundavai scolded. "Vanathi, come here. The prince wants to see you."

Vanathi came up to them. Ignoring the prince, she said, "*Akka,* your brother does not want to see me. All his attention is on the boat waiting in the canal. It looks like he must leave in a hurry."

Arulmozli laughed. "Your friend can talk! I feared she was dumb like many members of our family."

"*Akka,* when I see him, I become speechless," said Vanathi.

"Vanathi used to talk non-stop. But since you left for Sri Lanka, she prefers to sit by herself, lost in dreams. Leave that aside. Vanathi, tell the prince what you saw at the palace that night."

"Let her sit, *akka.* If the general sees his niece standing, his heart will break! He keeps asking about her when he sees me—as you do not send me news of her, I'm at a loss for words."

"Didn't Vandhiya Devan give you my news about her?" Kundavai asked.

"He must have," Vanathi said. "But the prince must have had other things on his mind."

"True," Arulmozli agreed. "Once I read your message, nothing else got my attention."

Vanathi narrated all that she had seen and heard that night in the emperor's room at Thanjavur Palace. Each time she happened to look up at the prince, she stopped talking and had to be prodded by Kundavai to continue. When Vanathi finished her story, Arulmozli smiled and said, "*Akka,* I think your friend has left out one thing: after seeing all this, didn't she faint?"

Kundavai burst into laughter while Vanathi bowed her head in embarrassment.

The princess said affectionately, "Vanathi, why don't you take a walk along the embankment? Arulmozli will be here for a few days and you can see him again later."

Vanathi skipped away, her heart filled with joy. The prince's eyes followed her with a smile and then turned to Kundavai. "*Akka,* what did father and Vanathi see that night? Was it imagination?"

"No, it was a midnight drama and the main character was played by Nandini. I suspected as much and now, you and Vandhiya Devan have confirmed my suspicions."

"But what's the reason behind this?"

"Nandini is suspicious about her parentage. Father saw her once before and fainted. She stayed away from him after that. She hoped to gather information from father with her midnight act."

"Did she learn anything, *akka?*"

"I have no idea—no one can read her mind. I pity Lord Ambalavan for the way she tortures him. Nandini is the epitome of beauty and the rest of us are nothing compared to her. Any man who sees her becomes her slave: Lord Ambalavan, Madurandaka, Thirumalai, Kandamaran and now, Parthibendran. The chief minister avoids her; Karikalan refuses to come to Thanjavur because of her. The only man who has not been bewitched by her is Vandhiya Devan. That's why I have sent him to Kanchipuram. Nandini has asked Aditya Karikalan to meet her in Kadambur. I have asked Vandhiya Devan to stop this. And if he can't stop it, I have asked him to guard Karikalan. Karikalan does not know Nandini is his sister. I have no idea if Nandini knows this."

"Is it certain she is our sister?"

"What doubt can there be? When we were children, I hated and insulted her. I was jealous of her beauty. I would scheme to stop you and Karikalan from talking to her. I hated and envied her even after she left for the Pandian kingdom. Even after she became that old man's wife, I heaped insults on her … but the next time I see her, I'll fall at her feet and beg forgiveness."

"Never! I won't let you do that–you are not to blame. It's Nandini who's jealous of you."

"Just as your heart bleeds for our stepmother, my heart bleeds for Nandini. Instead of growing up in luxury, she suffered. For no fault of her own, she ended up marrying an old man."

"*Akka*, how did all this happen? How did Nandini grow up as an orphan?"

"I have thought about this day and night but can't discover the truth. There are two people who know the answers—grandmother Sembiyan Madevi and the chief minister. But both of them will not share their secrets with us. Thirumalai probably knows a part of it, but he's worse than his master: he won't open his mouth. *Thambi*, our priority now is to stop Nandini from bringing disgrace and danger on our family. Vandhiya Devan told me, 'Lady Nandini worships a sword with the fish symbol etched on it.' From that moment, my heart shudders. I worry that Nandini, not knowing that she belongs to the Chola dynasty, may do something dreadful."

"Why don't we tell Nandini everything?"

"It may only make her angrier with us. But we must do our duty."

"Sending Vandhiya Devan to Kanchipuram is important, but we must also hurry to Thanjavur to tell father that our stepmother is alive. Why must he suffer unnecessarily?"

"No! I'll go to Thanjavur in a couple of days, but you must stay in the monastery."

"Are you asking me to hide and disobey father's orders?"

"If you come to Thanjavur now, there'll be unrest in the country. The people are angry with Madurandaka and the Pazluvur brothers. They are even angry with father for ordering your arrest. If they see you now, they may get carried away by their passion and insist on you being crowned emperor at once; they may lay siege to the palace and fort. I asked you to come here because the kingdom was in danger. Now I think it's better you return to Lanka."

"*Akka*, I'll come to Thanjavur secretly if you want, but I won't go back without seeing father and telling him that our stepmother is alive."

"I can tell him all this at the right time. Must you come?"

"He'll believe me as I have seen her with my own eyes. I will also be able to ask his permission to bring her here."

"I won't stand in your way. Stay in the monastery for a week. I'll tell father you're alive and send for you." She paused. "Men must take risks; I'm proud of your courage and fearlessness. But before you risk your life again, grant me a boon. I won't disturb you after that."

"Why this preamble, *akka*? Have I ever disobeyed you?"

"Aditya Karikalan is not married and I doubt he will ever marry. Our Chola dynasty can live on only through you. Will you follow my wishes in this matter?"

"If I agree to get married, will you agree to let me marry the woman I love?"

"Why are you asking me this? Have we ever differed in our thoughts in these twenty years?"

"I have a reason—the woman I marry must be one who will help me achieve my dreams."

"*Thambi*, do you want to depend on a woman to achieve your dreams?"

Just then they heard a cry of terror. "Aiyo! *Akka!*" It was Vanathi.

Vanathi Laughed

POONKUZLALI AND AMUDHAN waited in the boat while the others were at the pavilion.

"Amudhan," Poonkuzlali said. "I'll ask you something—will you answer truthfully?"

"I speak only the truth, Poonkuzlali. That's why I have not talked to anyone for four days."

"Some people are habitual liars, like Vandhiya Devan."

"But he's a good man and his lies never harm anyone."

"He told me something about you and I want to know if it's true."

"What did he say?"

"He said you love me and want to marry me."

"I must thank him for being my messenger. I would never be brave enough to tell you myself."

"So, it's true?"

"It's true, Poonkuzlali."

"Why do you love me, Amudhan?"

"No one has yet found a reason for love, Poonkuzlali."

"Don't people fall in love with each other's beauty?"

"It's true that people are attracted by beauty and lust after it. But that's not true love. It will not last. Vandhiya Devan became my friend from the minute he met me and I'll give my life for him. Tell me: did he become my friend because of my looks?"

"But he described my beauty at great length ..."

"Yes, he did, but he does not love you. He praised Nandini's beauty even more, but he does not love her either."

"I know the reason: he loves Princess Kundavai."

"Doesn't that prove there's no connection between love and beauty?"

"Do you mean to say I'm more beautiful than the princess?"

"There's no doubt about that, Poonkuzlali. Princess Kundavai or Lady Vanathi or even the enchanting Lady Nandini—none of them can match your beauty. And that beauty is my greatest enemy. It's your beauty which stops me from telling you about the love which overflows my heart. Your beauty is worthy of gods and kings and puts you beyond my reach."

Poonkuzlali thought a while. "Amudhan, what would you do if I said I don't love you?"

"I'll wait for you to change your mind. Sometimes our minds are confused. Once the confusion clears, our minds will see the truth ..."

"Okay, you'll wait ... but if I don't change my mind?"

"I'll try to erase my love for you."

"Is that possible?"

"It's possible if one tries; it's possible if one disciplines one's mind by devoting oneself to god."

"Amudhan, I don't think your love is true ...if you truly loved me, and I turned you down, you would kill me. And if I loved some other man, you would kill him too."

"No, Poonkuzlali, vengeance is for demons, not men. If you truly love someone, that person's happiness will make you happy. Yes, you will suffer for a while, but if you are patient and do good in return, your happiness will be multiplied."

"You're wrong. The doctor's son who came with Vandhiya Devan desired me. When I rejected him, he blamed Vandhiya Devan and betrayed him to the Pazluvur men. He would have tried to kill me."

"Then he's not a man–he's a demon."

"Look at Lady Vanathi: she loves the prince. If she finds he doesn't love her, she'll poison him. And if he loves another woman, she'll kill her too."

"Never! Lady Vanathi is a model of virtue."

"If it was me, that's what I would do."

"I'll pray for you, Poonkuzlali."

"Amudhan, you have inherited our aunt Mandakini's virtuous character."

"Are you talking about my mother's elder sister? Your father's sister?"

"Yes. She's not dead as our family says. She roams like a madwoman in Sri Lanka. She lived on a Lankan island when she was young. A Chola prince pretended to love her and she trusted him. He then abandoned her and went away to become king."

"What!! How do you know this?"

"My aunt told me this in sign language. My blood boiled at the injustice done to her. Soon after, some men from the Pandian kingdom asked me to help them take revenge on the Chola dynasty which had betrayed my aunt. I decided to join them. Then I came to know my aunt not only forgave the man who betrayed her, but also saved the life of the son born to him and the other woman he married. Yes, my aunt's love is divine, but mine is not. If any prince betrays me, I'll kill him. If he loves another woman, I'll kill her too. Then, I'll kill myself."

"My god! What kind of talk is this?"

"Amudhan, you don't know how my mind has been seething for the past two years. Is Lady Vanathi superior to me in any way?"

"She's no better than you in any way. You grew up among the ocean waves and she grew up in a palace. You kill wild animals with your bare hands; you row your boat in whirlwinds; you rescue men fighting for their lives at sea. Vanathi fears the sea; she shrieks in terror at a domestic cat; she faints if she hears any bad news ..."

"In that case, why does Princess Kundavai treat me like dirt? Why does she love and cherish Vanathi?"

"Poonkuzlali, you're being unfair to the princess. Vanathi is her long-time friend while she has just met you. Didn't she thank you for saving the prince?"

"She can keep her thanks to herself! Amudhan, if we have to take the prince back to the monastery, you had better row the boat by yourself—I might upset it on purpose."

"You would never do that! What harm has the prince done to you?"

"I'm mad, Amudhan. I'm not in my right mind! When I think how his father betrayed my aunt, I might overturn the boat. You take him."

"Very well, and what will you do?"

"I'll follow Vanathi and break her head with a stone!" Just as Poonkuzlali picked up a large stone from the shore, a majestic bull came out from a dense coconut grove. Poonkuzlali vented her anger on the animal and threw the stone at it. The stone hit the bull's head. The animal shuddered and turned towards the boat.

"Aiyo! Poonkuzlali, why are you punishing this poor animal for what someone did to our aunt?"

"This animal has sharp horns to protect itself. My aunt was defenseless."

"You will throw stones on the bull, especially when you are safely out of the bull's reach."

"If the bull can't gore me, let it gore someone else."

Whether the bull understood her or not, that's what it decided to do. It turned and dashed into the grove just as Vanathi walked towards it from the opposite side. When Vanathi saw the bull charging towards her with lowered head, cruel horns and raised tail, she was terrified. She had no option but to turn and run back. She was near the pavilion but could go no further as there was a steep drop from the embankment to the canal. *I'll run along the embankment*, she thought and turned around— the bull was almost on her. "Aiyo! *Akka!*" Vanathi cried.

Kundavai and Arulmozli turned in the direction of her call. They saw Vanathi standing on the high embankment with her back to the canal; they heard an angry roar: the next second a huge bull came into view. Vanathi turned and jumped headfirst into the canal! Arulmozli took in the situation at a glance: he leaped into the canal, ran like lightning and caught Vanathi.

Kundavai's terror turned to joy when she saw Arulmozli catch Vanathi and carry her back to the pavilion.

"*Akka*, hold your friend. I can't believe she belongs to the brave Kodumbalur clan."

"*Thambi*, what have you done! How could you touch an unmarried girl?"

"My god! Would you rather I let her fall headfirst into the water? Luckily, she won't know I carried her, she's unconscious. Here, hold her."

Vanathi burst into laughter and jumped out of his hands.

"You naughty girl!" exclaimed Kundavai. "You were alert!"

"Ask her why she pretended to faint," Arulmozli said.

"I did not pretend, *akka*. When he touched me, I felt shy and closed my eyes."

"How was I to know that?" Arulmozli countered. "After all, she's in the habit of fainting."

"I won't faint again, at least not in front of him," Vanathi declared. "Let him never forget the favor I have done him today."

"What!! How has she helped me today?" the prince cried.

"*Akka*, when he was a child, he fell into the river and was rescued by a woman. Recently, he fell into the sea and was rescued by a boat girl. He's in the habit of being rescued by women. Now, I have helped him remove this stain on his honor. I have given him the glory of being the man who rescued a woman from falling into a canal—he should be grateful to me."

Vanathi laughed; Kundavai joined her; Arulmozli roared with laughter.

"Amudhan, can you hear those three mad people laugh?" Poonkuzlali asked and burst into laughter herself. Amudhan laughed with her.

Nature laughed with them.

PART 4

THE CROWN

On the Bank of the Kedilam

TRAVELERS STOPPED AT the busy junction where the highway crossed the River Kedilam to watch the procession of elephants, horses and palanquins making its way to the ford.

A herald announced: "Hail Crown Prince Aditya Karikalan, son of Emperor Sundara Chola, Commander of the northern forces, the valiant warrior who beheaded Veerapandian!"

Three young warriors rode behind the herald.

"The one in the middle is Aditya Karikalan. How his crown sparkles in the sun!"

"The Chola kingdom is a mess after Prince Arulmozli's death. Civil war may break out between the Pazluvur brothers and Velir. Sambuvaraya is holding peace talks at Kadambur: Aditya Karikalan is on his way there."

"Keep your voices down. How sad Aditya Karikalan looks!"

"He loved his brother and his father's paralyzed."

"No, he's furious with the Pazluvur brothers for not financing his northern campaign."

"No! Karikalan loved a woman from the Pandian kingdom. When he was away fighting in the north, Lord Ambalavan married the girl— she's the Lady Nandini who now controls the kingdom. The prince is broken hearted and hates the Pazluvur brothers."

"Quiet! They're here. The man on the prince's right is Parthibendran Pallava."

"And the one on his left is Kandamaran, Sambuvaraya's son."

The three riders stopped at the river. The chariot behind them halted a little distance away and eighty-year-old Malayaman climbed down from it.

Grandfather and Grandson

AT A GESTURE from his grandfather, Aditya Karikalan turned his horse and rode to the chariot.

Parthibendran said, "Thank goodness! I was afraid the old man would come with us."

"I would have drowned him in the Vellar," replied Kandamaran. The two young men laughed.

Malayaman looked affectionately at his grandson. "Aditya, there are some important things I want to tell you before I leave. Let's sit on that platform under the peepal tree ...my child, you were born on this day, twenty-four years ago. I emptied my treasury to host a three-day feast for thirty thousand chieftains and warriors. Your great-grandfather, Paranthaka Chola, and your father, Sundara Chola, were overjoyed at the birth of a male heir to continue the Chola line."

Malayaman paused and pointed: "Look, Aditya. Can you see the Navalur temple tower? That's where your grandfather's eldest brother, Raja Aditya, camped twenty-five years ago. He was the greatest warrior I've ever known. He recruited and trained a huge army to fight Kannara Devan, king of the Twin Provinces. People came from miles to see the mock battles between his elephant brigades, cavalry and infantry. Just when Raja Aditya was ready to attack the Twin Provinces, war broke out in Sri Lanka. Emperor Paranthaka refused to fight a war on two fronts. He ordered his son to put off his attack until the Sri Lankan war was won. But the enemy attacked and the allied forces of Kannara Devan and Buthugan, the king of Kanga, swept like a tidal wave towards us. Raja Aditya led an army of three lakh foot soldiers, fifty thousand horsemen, sixteen thousand war elephants, two thousand chariots, three-hundred and twenty chieftains and thirty-two petty chieftains. The two armies met at Thakkolam, near Kanchipuram. Aditya, the Battle of Thakkolam was the Mother of all Battles! It raged for ten days with countless casualties on both sides. We were outnumbered one is to two, but with Raja Aditya leading us, the enemy began to give way. Their commanders realized that wherever Raja Aditya went with the Tiger Flag fluttering proudly on his war elephant, our men fought with renewed courage and spirit.

"Buthugan hatched a wicked plot. He planted a white flag on his elephant and cried, 'Surrender!' The evil man came close, hands folded in entreaty and tears in his eyes. Raja Aditya's heart melted. He waved away his bodyguards and gestured to Buthugan who said, 'Kannara Devan refuses my advice to surrender. I have deserted him and come to join the Cholas.' Raja Aditya was disgusted and said, 'There's no room in my army for traitors.' In the blink of an eye, Buthugan took his hidden bow, shot a poisoned arrow at Raja Aditya's chest and dashed away on his elephant. The news of Raja Aditya's death spread like wildfire through the battlefield. Taking advantage of our confusion, the enemy pressed its attack and soon, we were fighting for our lives and retreating. We made a stand at the Kedilam river and pushed back the enemy. But they held Kanchipuram and harassed us from there for years. It was only after you captured Kanchipuram that this ended ..."

"*Thatha*, I never tire of hearing about Raja Aditya and the Battle of Thakkolam. But why are you talking about it now?"

"My child, Raja Aditya dreamt of extending the Chola empire from Sri Lanka to the Ganga. He died before he could do it. The people believe that you, my grandson, will make his dream come true. You must not be destroyed by cunning men like he was."

"*Thatha*, he was killed on the battlefield by a cunning enemy. I'm not going to war."

"Aditya, the *Thirukkural* says you need not fear the enemy with his sword, but you must fear the enemy who pretends to be your friend. You insist on meeting enemies who pretend to be your friends. I hear they want you to marry Sambuvaraya's daughter and divide the kingdom between you and Madurandaka, but we don't know what they really want. I'll go to Thirukoyilur, gather my forces and camp on the banks of the Vellar. If there's any trouble at Kadambur Palace, send word to me at once."

But Aditya Karikalan's attention was elsewhere: in great agitation, he cried, "*Thatha*, look!" He pointed to an old stone pavilion. It had intricate sculpture on its pillars, worn away by time and weather.

The Falcon and the Dove

"ADITYA," SAID THE old man. "That pavilion is empty."

"*Thatha*, your eyes have dimmed with age. Can't you see that huge falcon? It's holding a little dove in its claws and tearing it apart. Can't you see the blood dripping? Look, *thatha*, another dove is circling the falcon. The dove in the falcon's claws must be her lover. She's fighting with the falcon to save her lover. What courage! You wretched falcon! I'll kill you!" Karikalan threw a stone at the pillar and roared with laughter. "Take that, you demon!"

Malayaman often worried about his grandson's sanity. He went to the pillar and saw a sculpture of a falcon tearing apart a dove with its talons; another dove hovered above it. He walked back to Karikalan and said, "Yes, it's a very realistic sculpture."

Karikalan said, "What a cruel piece of art! I feel like burning the pavilion to the ground."

"Now, Aditya, why are you so disturbed by this? An emperor must kill his enemies. It's the falcon's nature to kill its prey, or it would not be a falcon."

"*Thatha*, if your enemy's wife begged you to spare his life, what would you do?"

"I would kick her aside and kill my enemy. Aditya, a woman's tears are dangerous; a man who lets himself be moved by a woman's tears will never become great."

"*Thatha*, if you criticize women, aren't you belittling my mother?"

"My child, I love your mother above everything in this world. I did not grieve when my five sons died on the battlefield. But my heart ached when your mother married and left me. I hid my pain. I told her, 'Daughter, don't be proud of marrying a king, be prepared to suffer. If you don't give him sons, he'll marry another woman: don't grieve over that. If you have sons, raise them to be brave warriors; don't shed a single tear if they die on the battlefield. If your husband rejoices, rejoice with him; if he grieves, try to cheer him; if he's ill, nurse him; if he dies, jump into his funeral pyre. This is the code of honor of the women of the Malayaman clan.'" The old man stood tall. "Your mother has followed my advice. She has raised her sons to be brave warriors and she nurses your father day and night. I'm proud of my daughter."

"But tell me, if an enemy comes to kill my father, won't my mother plead for my father's life: especially if that enemy is known to her?"

"My child, your mother would never disgrace her father's or husband's clan by crying or begging the enemy. She would die with your father or live only to avenge his death." He paused. "I don't believe Arulmozli is dead."

"Nor do I," Karikalan said.

"He'll be back. But the news of his death has caused an upheaval in the kingdom. You should be with your parents at this time to comfort them. But I don't want you to go to Thanjavur as the Pazluvur brothers' enemy. That's why I'm letting you go to Kadambur. I would have come with you but Sambuvaraya has deliberately not invited me."

"*Thatha!* Do you think I'm that helpless?"

"I would confidently send you to face thousand armed men ... but I'm afraid to let you meet a woman whose tears may melt your heart."

"I doubt Sambuvaraya's daughter will try such tricks on me. Kandamaran told me his sister is a timid girl. I won't marry her in a hurry without consulting my parents and I know you have two granddaughters of marriageable age ..."

"My child, I don't want that. As it is, the other chieftains are jealous of me. I'm old and weak: you need new friends to stand by you. I'll be glad if you make an alliance with Sambuvaraya. But my heart is filled with dread. I fear this is the last time I'll see my beloved grandson ... Aditya, I overheard your two friends say you are going to Kadambur only because the witch who married the old Pazluvur man sent you a message. Is this true?"

"Yes, *thatha.*"

"Listen Aditya, you belong to an ancient lineage of kings. Some were great emperors, others were petty chieftains; some had one wife, others had many; some were Shaivas, others were Vaishnavas. But every one of them was a righteous man. My child, marry as many virgins as you want: your great grandfather had seven wives. But don't even look at another man's wife."

"*Thatha*, I would never shame my ancestors by doing such a thing.

I'm going to ask her to forgive me for a great wrong I once did to her."

"Ask forgiveness of a woman? I can't bear to hear this!"

Karikalan bowed his head. He told his grandfather how he had killed Veerapandian, ignoring Nandini's pleading, and how he was tormented by guilt. "Only if I see her once and ask her forgiveness will I find peace. She seems ready to forget the past and is keen to settle the matter of the royal succession. I'll finish my task and hurry back. I'll then go and find my brother."

Malayaman sighed. "Many things are now clear to me. No one can defy the dictates of destiny."

The Ayyanar Temple

AS KARIKALAN AND Malayaman said farewell on the banks of the Kedilam, Vandhiya Devan and Azlvarkkadian stood on the banks of the Kollidam which was in flood. Leaving behind their horses, they took an overcrowded ferry which sank near the shore. As Devan swam to the shore, his waistband was lost in the river, along with his money, the signet ring and Kundavai's message. They reached the other bank which was bustling with people celebrating a temple festival and hit upon an idea to get money to buy horses.

Azlvarkkadian planted a jamun tree branch in front of him and shouted, "I'm here to prove Vaishnavism is the greatest religion. I challenge any Shaiva or Buddhist or Jain to a debate. If you win, I'll carry you on my shoulders all around the town; if you lose you must give me everything on you, except your waistcloth." Soon, he had won a heap of *rudraksha* beads, ear studs, silk garments, gold coins and water pots.

Devan stood nearby, leaning on a tree. When a group of angry Shaivas prepared to attack Azlvarkkadian, Devan twirled his dagger and warned, "No violence!"

When no new debaters came forward, Azlvarkkadian proclaimed the victory of Vaishnavism. A group of Vaishnavas cheered him and invited him for lunch. Azlvarkkadian and Devan gladly filled their stomachs with good food. Azlvarkkadian then asked the Vaishnavas to buy his winnings, saying that he was on a pilgrimage and needed money. The men paid him generously and the two friends set off for Kadambur in the mid-afternoon.

They now had money but there were no horses for sale. They finally decided to walk to Kadambur to see if they could get any news of Aditya Karikalan's plans. They would have to stay hidden, especially from Kandamaran and the Pazluvur brothers.

The friends reached the town at sunset. The place was bustling with activity. Banners and welcome arches lined the streets and security had been strengthened. After all, the crown prince was expected, along with Lord Ambalavan. They heard that none of the guests had arrived yet and that Kandamaran had gone to Kanchipuram to bring the crown prince. People talked about Arulmozli in hushed voices and murmured at all this celebration going on at a sad time like this. Agreeing that it was too risky to stay in Kadambur, the friends crossed the town and walked along the road looking for some ruined building or pavilion; both of them needed a good night's rest.

Devan pointed to an Ayyanar temple standing in a dense bamboo thicket. "Vaishnava, I can't walk another step. Let's spend the night at this temple. It's a good place in which to hide."

They walked around the bamboo thicket until they found a narrow track to the temple. Struggling through the thorns, they reached the clearing. A sacrificial altar stood facing a small temple. Clay elephants and horses brought by devotees stood in rows before the altar.

Devan teased: "Ayyanar is powerful—let's ask him for two horses."

"If your Ayyanar gives life to these clay horses, all the better. We'll save money …"

Just then, to Devan's shock, a horse and an elephant moved. Before Devan could say a word, Azlvarkkadian put his fingers on his lips and pulled him deeper into the bamboo. A man's head appeared in the gap between the elephant and the horse. As the head turned and looked around, Devan's hair stood on end. But Azlvarkkadian's steady grip on his hand gave him courage. The head was followed by a body and finally a man emerged from a dark hole which seemed to be the gateway to hell. They exchanged surprised looks: it was Idumbankari. Leaving the hole open, Idumbankari again looked around carefully and then went into the temple and lit a lamp.

"Idumbankari is in Ravidasan's gang," Azlvarkkadian said. "The lamp is a signal ..."

"I'll see where the opening leads; it may be useful to us later. You stay here ..." They heard voices in the distance. "There's no time to lose! I must go. Will you wait here for me?"

"I'll wait for you as long as I'm alive," Azlvarkkadian said. "But how do I know whether you'll come back?"

"I'll come back if I'm alive," Devan replied. He ran to the opening and entered it. He disappeared as if the ground had swallowed him.

Idumbankari came out of the temple and looked around. He walked to the altar and turned a trident planted before it: the horse and the elephant once again moved close together and the opening disappeared. At the same time, Ravidasan and Soman Sambavan arrived. Ravidasan sat on the temple steps and the others sat on the ground before him.

"Comrades," Ravidasan said. "Our wait is over: within a few days we will fulfill our oath. Aditya Karikalan is on his way here from Kanchipuram. Malayaman could not stop him."

"What if the message from his sister reaches him?"

"How can it? We left her messenger tied up in the forest."

"Hah! I saw him this morning on the bank of the Kollidam. He was with another one of our enemies—that false Vaishnava."

"We must be extra careful," Ravidasan said. "We must stop them from meeting the prince."

"We should have killed him when we had the chance. I wonder why the queen let him go ..."

"Comrades, I too had my doubts. But I now realize that the queen is even more cunning than I thought. She plans to use him for something very important. Forget about Vandhiya Devan, but if you see the Vaishnava, kill him at once."

The Hunters' Hall

VANDHIYA DEVAN CLIMBED down some steps and reached level ground. The light was very dim. He heard wheels turning and darkness engulfed him. *Why do I let my rashness get me into trouble? Where does this lead? What dangers lie ahead?* Devan decided to go back. But when he retraced his steps, he could not find the opening. He heard voices in the distance and broke into cold sweat. *Someone has closed the gap. Idumbankari's comrades have arrived. They are talking near the temple. They'll probably be there for some time. If I find the opening and go out, they'll catch me. Let Thirumalai listen to their evil plans. I might as well see where this passage leads.*

Devan walked down the tunnel. The ground was uneven; the tunnel had been carved out of rock. Devan guessed that it led to Sambuvaraya's palace. Such tunnels were commonly found in palaces as a way of escape when danger threatened. Devan thought this tunnel would probably end in the treasury or in the women's quarters: to carry away the treasure or to lead the women to safety. *Idumbankari came through this tunnel, so it must lead to the treasury. I wonder what their plan is. Do they plan to rob the treasury?* Devan remembered Nandini's sword and shuddered. *They may have something more dreadful in mind than robbery. Let me see where this tunnel leads. I may be able to foil their plans.*

It was only a few minutes since Devan had entered the tunnel, but it felt like ages. He sweated and panted in the airless passage. The thought of the long distance he and Azlvarkkadian had traveled from the palace to the Ayyanar temple frightened him. Then he realized that the tunnel would take a straight underground route from the temple and could not be more than an arrow's flight from the palace. He felt a gust of cool air from above. He looked up and saw a faint light and heard distant voices. *I must be under one of the guard posts on the fort walls.* Air entered the tunnel at this point but no one could enter or leave the tunnel. Sensing that he was now under the palace, Devan walked on with fresh energy. *I'll soon be in the treasury.* His feet stumbled against steps leading up. *If it's the women's quarters, I must be careful. Kandamaran's sister, that dusky beauty, may be there.* Devan smiled at the thought that he had once considered marrying her. *What if I barge into the women's quarters when they are in a state of undress?* He burst out laughing.

He reached the topmost step and looked around him. The next instant, his eyes almost fell out and the blood froze in his veins: hundreds of eyes glowered at him. They were the eyes of wild animals! Devan turned back in panic, but there was nowhere for him to go. He had heard a sound earlier: it must have been the sound of the tunnel entrance closing. He was trapped with the wild beasts. Tigers, lions, leopards, bears, bison, wolves, foxes - even a hippopotamus! *Aiyo! Two huge elephants ... look at the size of that vulture ... that bat can swallow a man ... a giant owl ... a crocodile with its jaws gaping open ... but crocodiles can't live on land ...*

Devan laughed in relief. He remembered Kandamaran telling him that his ancestors were great hunters. They stuffed the wild animals they killed and mounted them on the walls of the Hunters' Hall in their palace. *I'm in the Hunters' Hall.* He kicked the animals to prove they were dead, but it took some time for him to stop trembling. The way back to the temple was closed. Should he find a way to open it or should he see where this room led to? He walked along the walls but could not find any exit. He grew increasingly angry. He came to an elephant in a corner of the wall. "You wretched elephant! It's because you moved that I'm caught in this situation." Devan grabbed the elephant's tusks and gave an angry twist. To his shock, the elephant's ear folded back on itself, revealing a large opening in the wall.

Devan peeped through the opening. He saw a dusky young beauty with large eyes. To his shock, Devan saw his own face near hers, so close that he could kiss her. The girl's eyes widened in surprise and she shrieked. The startled Devan let go of the elephant's tusk: at once the opening closed. The girl vanished and her scream faded. Devan's heartbeat slowed; he considered what he had seen.

Manimekalai

SAMBUVARAYA'S BELOVED DAUGHTER, Manimekalai, was a spirited young woman. She had been pampered all her life by her parents and her elder brother, Kandamaran. Until recently her happy days were filled with song, dance and celebration. All this changed about five months ago. For the first time in her life, her family was determined to make her do something against her wishes —and she was equally determined not to obey them.

For the last three years, whenever he came home from the army, Kandamaran told Manimekalai about his friend, Vandhiya Devan. He praised his courage, resourcefulness and intelligence. "He'll be a good husband for you: he'll tame you and keep you in your place."

"Oh! Why don't you bring him here? Then I can deal with his resourcefulness." Manimekalai day-dreamed about Devan, building an imaginary world in which she laughed and talked and played and quarreled with him. She confided her dreams to her closest friends.

Then, four months ago, Kandamaran changed his tune. "Vandhiya Devan's an orphan with no home, no position, no status: forget him!" He told her that she was to marry Madurandaka and hinted that Madurandaka would be the next emperor. If she married Madurandaka, she would be an empress and her sons would rule the world. Her parents supported Kandamaran in this matter.

Manimekalai, dreaming of Devan, hated the idea of marrying Madurandaka who was a coward and had never set foot on a battlefield. Until recently, he wore *rudraksha* beads and holy ash and was to become an ascetic: to cap it all, he was already married to Kalaanthaka's daughter. And the women in the Thanjavur palace were snobs who looked down their dainty noses at women from other places. Manimekalai was determined not to marry Madurandaka. She also heard that when Ambalavan and the chieftains visited Kadambur, Madurandaka came there in Nandini's palanquin, disguised as a woman. *Chi! What a coward! I'll never marry him.*

On the same day, Kandamaran brought Devan to the women's quarters. Suddenly feeling shy, Manimekalai hid behind her mother, but

Devan's handsome, smiling face etched itself on her heart. Manimekalai made it clear to her brother that she would never marry Madurandaka and hinted that she loved Devan.

Kandamaran was furious. "Vandhiya Devan is my arch-enemy. He stabbed me in the back. If you want to marry him, I'll kill both of you!" He showed her the scar on his back, telling her it was Nandini who had saved his life. "If you love me, forget Vandhiya Devan."

Manimekalai, who dearly loved her brother, decided to forget Devan. But this was easier said than done; his smiling face continued to haunt her dreams and her heart. Manimekalai lost her high spirits and became tired and sad. Her friends tried to distract her but it was no use.

Manimekalai was now happier: her parents and brother had decided against her marrying Madurandaka. They hinted that she should marry the crown prince, Aditya Karikalan. Karikalan was known for his courage. It was also known that, for some reason, he had refused to marry. It was every woman's dream to become his wife. Manimekalai's spirits recovered somewhat.

She was excited that Karikalan and Ambalavan were to be guests at the palace, along with Nandini. Kandamaran raved about Nandini's beauty, virtue and intelligence and instructed her to take good care of Nandini. He told her that it was Nandini who had suggested Manimekalai's marriage to Karikalan. Manimekalai decided to be friends with Nandini. She was also keen on picking up beauty tips from Nandini to beat the Thanjavur women at their fashion games. Manimekalai enthusiastically supervised all the arrangements for the guests. She went through the rooms allotted to the prince and his friends. *A friend called Parthibendran is coming with him. Vandhiya Devan was also the prince's friend. If he had not turned traitor, he would also be coming ...* she had not forgotten Devan.

Nandini was expected that night. Manimekalai checked her rooms one last time. A mirror stood against the wall in a corner. She looked at her face in the mirror. *I'm beautiful too,* she thought in satisfaction. Just as she was about to turn away, another face appeared in the mirror, cheek to cheek with her. It was the face which still haunted her dreams: it was Devan! Instinctively, she screamed and Devan's face disappeared.

The Tail-less Monkey

WAS IT MY imagination? Or a dream? Manimekalai pinched herself: she was definitely awake. She examined the wall opposite the mirror. She knew that there was a hidden entrance to the secret passage at this spot—the door could be opened from either side. She placed her ear against the wooden door and heard a faint sound. Manimekalai quietly opened the secret door and peeped into the Hunters' Hall. The room was dark except for a lamp burning in a corner. Suddenly, the lamp flickered as if someone had flitted past it. She clapped her hands and called softly, "Who's there?" She heard someone clear his throat and a bat fluttered from its perch on the ceiling ... again, a faint cough. Manimekalai shouted to her maid: "Chandramathi! Bring a lamp. I want to check the Hunters' Hall: I heard a sound."

The servant came with a lamp and said, "It's probably a bat, lady. What else could it be?"

"I was looking at my face in this mirror and I saw another face reflected beside mine."

"Lady," Chandramathi teased. "Maybe the man you see in your dreams appeared in the mirror. Once you see the crown prince, you'll forget the old face completely."

"We'll see. Now let's check the Hunters' Hall."

"Lady, that's a waste of time and it's dusty. You'll ruin your sari and catch a cold. You'll be sneezing tomorrow when the guests are here ..."

"Never mind," Manimekalai said. "Hold the lamp steady." The two women entered the Hunters' Hall. Manimekalai noticed footprints on the dusty floor.

"Lady!" Chandramathi cried. "That tail-less monkey moved!"

Manimekalai smiled. "Maybe it's happy to see you."

"It's directly opposite the mirror: maybe the reflection was the monkey's face. It moved again!!"

"Nonsense! That's just your lamp flickering. There's no one here. Let's go. Maybe it really was the handsome face I see in my dreams which appeared in the mirror ..."

The women went back the way they had come.

Devan emerged from hiding behind the monkey. He sneezed a couple of times and said, "Long may you live, monkey! Even if that servant compared my face to yours, you saved me from being caught by those women." Devan guessed who they were from their conversation. *What was that about the face in her dreams and the face in the mirror being the same? Kandamaran said he often spoke to his sister about me: is that foolish girl dreaming of me by any chance?*

There was no time for such thoughts. He had to find a way out. It was clear that there were different ways to open the doors from either side but he had to find the entrance. He examined the walls but could find no sign of a door. He remembered seeing a stuffed crocodile near the opening through which he had entered the hall. He went to the crocodile and searched the wall near it but could find nothing unusual. Time passed. *What if I'm trapped here? What if the door to the women's quarters is the only way to get out? It's too dangerous.* Maybe Manimekalai would pity him, but what reason could he give her for being there? Could he say that he was there to see her? Would she believe such a cruel lie? And what if her companions were with her? *If Sambuvaraya catches me, he'll kill me …*

Devan saw the crocodile at his foot. "Why are you staring at me with your jaws wide open?" He kicked it in a fit of anger: the crocodile moved and Devan saw an opening on the floor. "You stupid crocodile! Why couldn't you tell me you were blocking the way?" When Devan moved the crocodile, the opening widened and a flight of steps was seen.

Hands in the Darkness

VANDHIYA DEVAN MARVELED at the ingenious ways in which the secret passages and doors of Kadambur Palace had been designed. Afraid that the door would close while he was halfway down the first step and trap him against the wall, Devan made sure that the crocodile stood still. He then put his foot on the first step. He stopped at the sound of footsteps in the tunnel. *It's Idumbankari and his gang.* In a flash, he hid behind the monkey once more.

A head emerged from the opening—it was Idumbankari. He stood with one leg in the room and the other on the step to keep the door from closing. Just then, the elephant moved and Manimekalai entered the hall with a lighted torch. Idumbankari jumped into the hall and the opening in the floor closed. He unwound his turban and started dusting the tiger near him.

Manimekalai lifted her torch and looked around her. When she saw Idumbankari, her eyes widened in surprise. The equally surprised Idumbankari stopped dusting and looked at her. "Lady, what are you doing her at this hour?" he asked.

"Idumbankari, is that you? What are you doing here?" Manimekalai countered.

"Lady, guests may visit this hall tomorrow. Master Kandamaran asked me to clean the room."

"I was checking Lady Nandini's room when I heard a sound here. I thought it must be you: who else knows the secret passages so well? How long have you been here?"

"More than an hour, lady. I have another hour's work. Why are you alone? Where's that chatterbox, Chandramathi?"

"I sent her to fetch my father when I heard noises here." Manimekalai lifted her torch and saw Idumbankari's expression change at her words. She also saw the monkey move again. "I'll go and stop her."

"Yes, lady. The master is busy; tell Chandramathi not to disturb him and then go and sleep peacefully. I'll see to all the work."

Manimekalai went out and the secret door closed behind her. Idumbankari stood for a minute with his ear to the door. When there was no sound from behind it, he moved the crocodile and stood on the step with half his body above the opening. An owl's hoot came from the tunnel and Idumbankari hooted in reply.

A bat fluttered past ... as Idumbankari turned towards it, the tail-less monkey fell on him from behind. The startled Idumbankari lost his footing and stumbled down two steps ... he thrashed about, waving his hands in panic. Once he realized that it was a stuffed animal which had fallen on him, Idumbankari recovered and tried to make it stand upright again. Just then, what felt like a man's hands pushed him further down the steps. Unable to believe this, Idumbankari froze in horror.

Slowly, he looked around him. The stuffed monkey's head and upper body were in the tunnel while its lower half was above ground: the opening was closing on it. Idumbankari decided that he had imagined the pair of human hands.

Ravidasan called from the tunnel: "What's up? Why were you gibbering and waving your hands? Is there danger? Shall we go back?"

"No," Idumbankari replied. "There's no danger. A stuffed monkey demon fell on my head and startled me. Now it's half in and half out of the tunnel, blocking the way. Let me move it ..."

Devan, with Lady Luck on his side, had turned the situation to his advantage. As Idumbankari looked at the bat, Devan pushed the monkey on him; hiding his face and body, he pushed Idumbankari further down the steps with his hands; he pushed the stuffed monkey upside down on Idumbankari; finally, he moved the crocodile. Devan then ran to the elephant and tugged at its tusks with all his might. A narrow opening appeared in the wall. There was no time to find out how to widen it as Ravidasan's murderous gang was almost in the hall. If they caught him, it would be the end of him. Devan tried crawling into the opening. He got his head, hands and chest through it and then he was stuck. He could find no hold to pull himself out. At the same time, the lamp in the room went out leaving him in darkness.

Devan cried in alarm, "Chandramathi, save me!" A woman laughed. Devan recognized Manimekalai's voice but pretended, "Chandramathi, I'm here only because you asked me to come. There are men chasing me: pull me in quickly or I'll be in trouble!"

Manimekalai laughed again. "I'll teach both you and Chandramathi a lesson."

"It's Lady Manimekalai! Lady, forgive me and help me. I'll never do such things again." In the darkness, two soft hands took Devan by the shoulders and gently pulled him into the room. The opening closed behind him. "Lady, thank you a million times."

"You can thank me later. I have not yet decided what to do with you."

"You saved me from those murderers: that's enough for me."

"My goodness! What a hero you are! Let me light a lamp and see your face."

"Lady, do you want to see my face again? The monkey face you saw in the mirror was mine."

Devan heard a woman's laughter, accompanied by the tinkling of bangles. Manimekalai held up the lamp which now blazed with light. She looked at Devan's smiling face and lost herself.

The sound of footsteps came from the Hunters' Hall.

The Dog Barked

AS MANIMEKALAI GAZED at him, Vandhiya Devan wondered how to escape from her.

A voice shouted from the distance, "Lady, did you call me?"

Manimekalai recovered herself. "No, get back to your work." She closed the opening through which Devan had entered. Signaling him to follow, she walked away from the wall. She stopped abruptly and said, "Tell me the truth: did Chandramathi really ask you to come?"

"Yes. When you came to the hall, I was hiding behind the monkey. When you turned to go, Chandramathi looked at me and said, 'Will you come and stay in my room? I'll use you to frighten away unwanted visitors.' It looks like you did not hear her."

"Your face is far from being like a monkey's. But you're as naughty as a monkey and stare like an owl. You were the one I saw in the mirror, right? Why did you go and close the door?"

"I was afraid my face would frighten the divine woman looking into the mirror. I let go of the elephant's tusks and the opening closed."

"Did you know who the woman was?"

"Not then, but I soon guessed she was Manimekalai, Sambuvaraya's precious daughter and my dearest friend, Kandamaran's beloved sister."

Manimekalai frowned and laughed sarcastically. "Really? Are you my brother's friend?"

"Yes. Don't you remember him bringing me to the women's quarters?"

"How could I forget so soon? Are you Vandhiya Devan Vallavaraya?"

"Yes, lady. I'm a poor man who has no kingdom or home but carries an ancient clan name. When your brother and I were at the army camp, he often talked of you. My head was filled with dreams but I have now forgotten them all."

A happy thought came to Manimekalai: *Did he stab my brother because Kandamaran refused to let him marry me?* "Let's not talk about the past. Tell me why you sneaked into the palace. Or I'll ask my friend to call my father."

"Lady, a murderous gang was chasing me; I saw an opening in the ground and jumped into it; it led to a tunnel which brought me here."

"What a great warrior you are! Running from the enemy!"

Devan was surprised. *I thought Manimekalai was an innocent girl: and here she's taking a dig at me.* "Lady, they are eight: I'm one; they are armed: I'm not. I lost my precious sword in the Kollidam floodwater."

"I'm glad the river washed away the wicked sword which stabbed my brother in the back."

"My god!" Devan exclaimed in horror. "I would cut off my hand before harming Kandamaran. Lady, who accuses me falsely?"

"My brother. I would not have believed anyone else."

"Kandamaran told you this? Someone stabbed him and left him by Thanjavur Fort's wall. I carried him to Chendan Amudhan and saved his life. Did he tell you why I tried to kill him?"

"He said that you criticized my looks and said that the Thanjavur women were more beautiful. He slapped you. Instead of fighting him face to face, you stabbed him in the back like a coward."

"Lies! I would cut out my tongue before calling you ugly. It was Kandamaran who begged me to forget you as kings are waiting to marry you."

"And did you forget me?"

"Not completely, but I began to think of you as my sister. Let me meet Kandamaran. I must find out why he lied about me or, if he believes this, I must convince him he's wrong."

"Why did you come by the secret tunnel?"

"Listen carefully: can't you hear the footsteps and voices of the men who want to kill me?"

"Why do they want to kill you?"

"Some of them are sorcerers; maybe they want me to be a sacrificial offering."

"It looks like they have chosen a handsome prince," Manimekalai laughed.

"I too wonder why they chose someone who's a cross between a monkey and an owl. After talking to you, I suspect Kandamaran has arranged for them to kill me. Lady, take me to him at once. I'll either convince him I'm innocent or ask him to kill me with his own hands."

"Kandamaran's not here; he's gone to Kanchipuram to escort the prince. They'll all be back tomorrow night. Lady Nandini will soon be here. If Lord Ambalavan finds you here, he'll cut you into pieces. How the old man loves his wife!" She laughed. "The last time they were here, the old man wouldn't let her out of his sight. This time, they'll be here for a few days. I wonder whether the old man will allow us to see her."

"What shall I do now?" Devan asked.

"My brother has a private armory. I'll take you there. Stay there until Kandamaran returns tomorrow evening. Then you can prove your innocence."

"Lady, that's too dangerous. Kandamaran will ask how I came here ..."

"Tell him the truth."

"Will he believe me? You don't believe me even when you can hear my pursuers in the next room."

"I'm going to the hall right now to question those men –"

"Aiyo!! They're wicked villains. If they catch you ..."

She showed him a folded knife hidden at her waist. "No one can harm me in my palace. And you–the great hero, are here to protect me."

"Lady, I'm unarmed."

She laughed. "Even a woman can fight if she's armed: why does a man need a weapon? Don't worry, the man who was dusting the animals is a palace servant. He must have brought the others here. I may know them too. I'll question them. Stay away from the door. Go stand by that store room and stay out of sight." Manimekalai opened the door to the Hunters' Hall and went in.

Devan hid himself by the store. Amazed at Manimekalai's courage, Devan consoled himself by saying that no harm would befall her. He looked into the store room whose doors happened to be open: it was a repository for musical instruments. There were steps in the room on which veenas, drums and cymbals were arranged. These steps reached up to the ceiling.

Just then, another door into the room opened and Chandramathi walked in calling, "Lady!"

The startled Devan dashed into the store room.

"Lady," Chandramathi said. "The Thanjavur party is at the palace gates. The queen sent me to call you …" She looked around and walked to the open door to the Hunters' Hall. From there, if she turned around, she would be able to see Devan in the store room.

Devan quickly climbed a few steps. His knee banged against a veena which gave a musical note. Alarmed, he climbed higher until his head bumped against the roof. To his surprise, the plank on which he hit his head lifted a little. He pushed the plank with his hands. It lifted and Devan saw the starlit sky through the opening. Devan shifted the plank and climbed out. He found himself on the terrace where he had slept on his last visit to Kadambur. Devan replaced the plank and walked forward stealthily: there was no one on this upper terrace. Devan quickened his steps. In the light of hundreds of torches, he saw that most of the palace was deserted. The commotion and sound of music showed that the people had all gathered at the gates to welcome the Pazluvur contingent. This was the perfect time to escape.

He looked down into the courtyard: it was deserted. He looked at the opposite wall—there was a head among the branches! *It looks like Thirumalai. No, it can't be. I saw his head there because my mind recalls seeing it in the same place during the conspirators' midnight meeting.* Deciding it was the right place to climb the wall, Devan looked for some way to reach the courtyard. He saw a tall bamboo pole, probably used as scaffolding. He jumped on the pole and slithered down to the ground. He looked around: the place was still deserted. He heard the sound of anklets from the terrace where he had stood minutes ago. *It must be Manimekalai looking for me. If she catches me this time, that will be the end of me.*

Devan ran to the base of the fort wall and looked back. He saw a woman standing on the terrace. He could not make out whether it was

Manimekalai or Chandramathi. Whoever it was would definitely have seen him run across the yard. *Thank goodness she did not shout and raise the alarm! God bless her.* Devan ran along the fort wall. When he reached the spot where he had seen Azlvarkkadian's head, he stopped and wondered how to climb the wall. His eyes fell on some bamboo poles lying on the ground. He immediately grabbed a pole and leaned it against the wall. Hoping the pole would hold steady, Devan started to climb up the pole.

When he was halfway up, the pole began to shake. *That's it! I'm going to fall and break my bones.* Suddenly, the pole steadied as if a hand was supporting it from above. *I'm imagining things.* When he was on the top of the wall, the bamboo pole fell with a crash as loud as thunder. Luckily, the sound was drowned by the roar of the crowd at the gates. But the woman on the terrace would certainly have heard. Devan looked back: the figure still stood there. Devan could not resist waving goodbye to her before climbing down the wall on the other side. This was quite easy, as this outside wall was not smooth and he could find footholds. He clambered down with the help of the tree branches which touched the wall.

Devan laughed at the thought that he had fooled Manimekalai and escaped …he heard a laugh echoing his own. His blood froze in horror. His hands shook and he prepared to jump to the ground. One look down and he changed his mind: a dog waited below him, barking wildly. *Is someone hiding nearby after setting the dog on me? If I jump down, the dog is sure to get a mouthful of my flesh. Shall I go back up the wall or jump down?* Devan wavered, swinging his legs from side to side to avoid getting bitten by the dog which kept leaping up at him.

The Ghosts

VANDHIYA DEVAN GLIMPSED white cloth among the trees and remembered the laugh he had heard earlier: someone was hiding among the trees. *There may be many men lying in wait for me. I can't escape both the dog's teeth and the men's hands. Maybe Thirumalai got*

*tired of waiting at the Ayyanar temple. Maybe he's hiding here, laughing
after setting the dog on me ....*

"Vaishnava!" Devan shouted. "What kind of a joke is this?" Again, he
heard the laugh: it was not Azlvarkkadian. Devan decided to climb back
into the fort. In the bustle of the reception for Ambalavan's company,
he could find an opportunity to escape. He could throw himself on
Manimekalai's mercy or even plead with Nandini. He started to climb
up the wall. The dog jumped higher, barking wildly. He heard the laugh
again and a man came out of hiding in the forest: it was Devaralan.

Devaralan held a spear in his hand. "You won't escape this time!"
Devaralan raised his spear.

Devan was clinging half-way up the fort wall. "Devaralan, remember
your queen's command not to harm me."

Devaralan laughed wildly. "I obey no one except Goddess Durga."

"My clan worships Durga: the goddess will be angry if you harm
me."

"Prove you are Durga's devotee. If you help me find the Vaishnava,
I'll let you go. I have sworn to sacrifice him to the goddess."

The small plant on the wall to which Devan was clinging began
to give way. Devan calculated how to avoid the spear and jump on
Devaralan's neck. "The Vaishnava is my dear friend. I won't betray him.
Sacrifice me instead."

"Very well, prepare to die!" Devaralan aimed his spear.

Devan jumped from the wall, caught the handle of the spear and slid
down to fall flat on the ground. Devaralan recovered from his shock and
lifted the spear. Just then, Azlvarkkadian charged out of the forest and
bashed Devaralan on his head with a stout stick. Devaralan collapsed
on Devan. The dog rushed at Azlvarkkadian who was ready for it: he
covered its head with his upper cloth, blinding it. He then tied the dog
to a tree with a vine which he had in hand. The two friends gathered
more vines and tied the unconscious Devaralan's hands and feet. Devan
picked up the spear, Azlvarkkadian his stick and they hurried along the
fort wall.

Azlvarkkadian said, "You're a fool! Why didn't you agree to help
Devaralan find me?"

"It's Prince Arulmozli's influence: I hate saying lies."

"Even to save your life?!"

"I had an ulterior motive. I knew you were hiding nearby. What if I told Devaralan I would help him catch you and you believed it? You would not come to my aid …"

"You're a genius! I was eagerly waiting to hear what you would say."

"See, I was right. I do not betray my friends by word or deed. But why are you here? What if I had returned to the Ayyanar temple and you were not there?"

"Minutes after you entered the tunnel, Ravidasan and his gang were behind you. I knew you were too clever to come back that way. I guessed you would climb the fort wall here. I didn't know that Ravidasan had left Devaralan behind as a lookout. I went to the altar to see if I could find the lever to operate the tunnel opening in case you were in danger and needed my help. I turned around at the sound of footsteps and found Devaralan standing there with his spear. I charged into the forest with him behind me. After a while, I thought he had given up the chase. I saw a lamp flickering in a small hut ahead of me and walked towards it to ask for directions to the highway. Luckily for me, I spotted Devaralan talking to a woman in front of the hut. There was a dog with them. Devaralan took the dog and continued looking for me. I ran into the forest. The dog's barking marked their position and I was able to avoid them.

"I knew it was impossible to spend the entire night like that; just then I came to the fort wall. I decided it would be easier to climb into the fort and escape from there. When I reached the top, I saw you running from the palace terrace and I jumped down again. I was confident the two of us together could handle Devaralan and his dog. I heard them come closer and hid in a nearby tree. Devaralan came to the tree: just then, he saw you climbing down the wall … you know the rest."

"Do you believe in fate?" Devan asked. "My fate saved me today."

"No, it was your brain which saved you," Azlvarkkadian countered.

Debating on this issue, the friends came out of the forest. From where they stood, they could see the fort's entrance which was a hive of activity. Ambalavan's contingent of elephants and cavalry had reached the gate where Sambuvaraya and his company waited to receive him. Trumpets, cymbals and conches blared a welcome and thousands of torches turned the night into day.

Azlvarkkadian pulled Devan. "Let's go! Someone may recognize us."

"No one can see us from there. And if they do, my fate will protect me. Let's watch Ambalavan get off his elephant and see whether Lady Nandini's on the elephant or in her palanquin."

"*Thambi*, don't trust fate blindly: an enchantress may pull the rug from under your feet."

"I'm not the man to fall under anyone's spell that easily, Vaishnava."

Ambalavan got off the elephant, followed by Nandini.

"He's brought her openly with him," Devan remarked. "Let's go."

But now, Azlvarkkadian did not move. His eyes were fixed on Nandini. Whether by chance, or because of the magnetism of his glance, Nandini turned towards them. She saw Azlvarkkadian's face peering at her from the trees and paled in fear. Ambalavan noticed her expression and turned: he saw two figures disappear into the shadows of the thick trees. Ambalavan whispered to Sambuvaraya who immediately gave orders to his soldiers. While the rest of the company entered the fort, two soldiers went into the forest. Riding their horses with difficultly among the dense trees, the two men searched the forest and finally came to a small clearing.

"Brother," one man said. "There's no one in the forest: it was the old man's imagination."

Just then, a dog came howling towards them.

"Do you know that a dog howls when there are ghosts nearby?" the second man asked.

"Maybe it thinks you're a ghost," the first man teased.

The men heard wild laughter above their heads. They looked up fearfully: two ghosts were perched on the branch above them! Before the startled soldiers could recover, the ghosts jumped on them and pushed them off their horses. The ghosts then galloped towards the highway.

Friend or Traitor?

ADITYA KARIKALAN, PARTHIBENDRAN and Kandamaran laughed and joked as they continued on their way to Kadambur.

"Why does god make us old?' Parthibendran complained.

"Why blame god?" Karikalan asked. "Growing old or dying young is in our hands."

"How is that?" Kandamaran asked.

"Think of Raja Aditya: he died young and remained young all his life. I wonder how many of us will be that lucky." The other two found this talk unpleasant and kept silent. "Why are you so quiet? Why fear death? This body dies and we get a brand-new body. If Vandhiya Devan was here, he would agree. He would laugh even if he was at death's door."

They saw two horses galloping towards them. The riders halted abruptly a little distance away from the company: Devan and Azlvarkkadian jumped off their horses. Karikalan could not control his happiness on seeing Devan. He dismounted and rushed to embrace him.

"May you live to be a hundred, *thambi!*" Karikalan said. "I was just praising you."

Parthibendran and Kandamaran rode a little ahead and looked on jealously. Another group of riders galloped up. Kandamaran recognized them as Kadambur men and went to question them. Kandamaran then went to Karikalan. "Prince, Vandhiya Devan is your friend. He was also my friend but he stabbed me in the back, wounding me seriously. He's a traitor: I must warn you."

The Spear Breaks

ADITYA KARIKALAN ROARED with laughter at Kandamaran's accusation. "Vandhiya Devan stabbed you in the back? Why did you turn your back on him?"

Kandamaran's dark face flushed with anger. "Sir, this is no laughing matter."

"It's so long since I had a good laugh," Karikalan said. "Laughter is god's gift to man."

"Sir, I have no objection to you laughing. But I did not turn my back on this great warrior: he hid and stabbed me. I survived only because of Goddess Durga's grace and Lady Nandini's care. Hold an enquiry and give me justice. Or let me punish him myself."

"My friend, I belong to a dynasty whose emperors sacrificed their own flesh and the life of their sons in the cause of justice. I'll see that you receive justice. Be patient." Karikalan turned to Devan. "Vallavaraya, before you tell me about your voyage, tell me this: did you stab Kandamaran in the back? If yes, what was the reason for this cowardly act?"

"Sir, I never stabbed him. I found him lying in a pool of blood, stabbed in the back. I carried him to Chendan Amudhan and saved his life. I now regret not having stabbed him in the chest. I let my loyalty to my friend override my loyalty to my king. Sir, he accuses me of betraying a friend, but he has betrayed his master. Ask him whom he took to the Pazluvur bothers' palace through the secret tunnel; ask him whom he saw in Lord Ambalavan's treasury that day; ask him what meeting was held at Kadambur Palace in the month of *Aadi*; ask him who came there in a screened palanquin ..."

Kandamaran shook with rage. "You low-born fool! I'll kill you!" He raised his spear.

Shocked at this outburst, Karikalan grabbed Kandamaran's spear and snapped it into two with his strong hands. Flinging the pieces away, he said, "Careful! I won't tolerate my friends fighting before me. Parthibendran, if either of them picks up a spear or a sword, arrest him."

Devan immediately handed his sword to Parthibendran who took it with revulsion.

"Kandamaran," Karikalan said. "Vandhiya Devan has replied to your accusation: I'll see if it's true later. Now, do you want to answer his questions?"

Kandamaran was speechless. Then, "Sir, I have sworn an oath not to talk about these matters."

Parthibendran intervened. "Sir, I suspect some woman is involved in this. I think it would better to question them individually."

Karikalan laughed. "Exactly! All three of you met Lady Nandini separately and got caught in her web of lust. That's why you are trying to eat each other."

Parthibendran's face darkened. "Sir, I too have my suspicions about Vandhiya Devan. Prince Arulmozli jumped into the sea in the middle of a raging storm to save him. The prince has not been seen after that, but this man springs up here unharmed. Ask him what happened to your brother. This wretch is the cause of his death."

Karikalan turned to Vandhiya Devan. "What do you have to say to this?"

"Sir, before I answer his question, I have a question for him: The chief minister and General Velir advised Prince Arulmozli to stay in Sri Lanka. But the prince, determined to obey your summons, boarded Parthibendran's ship. Why didn't Parthibendran stop the prince from jumping into the sea? Prince Arulmozli jumped into the sea to save a poor orphan like me: why didn't the brave Parthibendran and his men jump into the sea to save the prince? Did they entertain themselves watching him drown?"

Parthibendran shook with rage. "Sir, this fool accuses me of causing the prince's death. I won't stand for it!"

"Parthibendran, the three of you are fighting with each other because of Lady Nandini. Ride ahead with Kandamaran. I'll follow with Vandhiya Devan. I must hear the news of his voyage. I must also question him about your accusation. But remember, I insist you three be friends: I'll be very unhappy otherwise."

Parthibendran and Kandamaran were forced to ride ahead.

Azlvarkkadian said softly to Devan, "My dear boy, you have learned to save yourself without telling lies or telling the truth either."

Karikalan's eyes fell on Azlvarkkadian. "Who's this? I've seen you somewhere before ..."

"Sir, you saw and heard me three years ago at a crucial moment ..."

A dark cloud crossed Karikalan's face. "Three years ... a crucial moment ... can it be? Is this the voice I heard when I was searching for my enemy on the island in the Vaigai river?"

"It's the same voice, sir. I hid among the trees and told you where your enemy was."

"What a terrible day that was! I shudder even now to think of the blood lust which coursed through my veins. Vaishnava, why did you hide like a ghost?"

"Sir, didn't you just mention the frenzy which possessed you? You were ready to kill anyone who came in your way: I wished to live a little longer."

"Why didn't you come out of hiding even when I shouted for you to show me the way?"

"I did not want to earn the undying hatred of my foster sister, Lady Nandini."

"You wretch! What about me earning her undying hatred?" Karikalan drew his sword.

Devan, frightened for Azlvarkkadian's life, quickly intervened. "Sir, he comes from the chief minister. Let's hear what he has to say before you punish him."

Karikalan sighed and replaced his sword in its scabbard. "What's the point of punishing him? What's the point of punishing anyone?"

Azlvarkkadian was not daunted by the prince's anger. He smiled. "Sir, knowing you would be angry with me, I avoided meeting you all these years. My sister is still angry with me: she refuses to meet me. But it seems her anger towards you is gone; it's because of her loving message that you are going to Kadambur Palace as a guest."

"You wicked Vaishnava! How do you know this?" Karikalan asked.

"Nothing happens in this kingdom without my master Aniruddha Brahmaraya's knowledge."

"Wait and see! One day, I'll banish both you and your master from this kingdom. Now, you two: ride on either side of me. We'll talk as we go."

Manimekalai's Secret

NANDINI LAY ON a soft bed in her room in the women's quarters of Kadambur Palace. She was richly dressed and more beautiful than ever. Her half-closed eyes flashed like lightning. She stared at the bowl of incense and sighed. "My dreams vanish like incense smoke. At least the incense leaves behind a sweet fragrance: my dreams leave behind only sorrow and pain."

Manimekalai's soft voice called, "Lady, may I come in?"

"Come in, my dear. Why do you need my permission to enter your own house?" Nandini sat up.

"Lady, my brother told me about southern courtesy: one must not barge into another's room without permission."

"To hell with southern courtesy. And don't call me lady: call me 'Akka.'"

"Akka! I have never seen anyone as beautiful as you, not even in paintings."

"My girl, don't you start! As it is, I'm accused of being an enchantress who casts spells on every man who sees me."

"If I hear anyone say that, I'll cut out their tongues!" Manimekalai cried.

"I married an old man: that's why they talk. Let them. Tell me about yourself."

"There's nothing to tell, akka."

Nandini pinched Manimekalai's pretty cheeks. "Fraud! Didn't you tell me you had something to confide in me? I have longed for an affectionate friend like you, Manimekalai. All the chieftains' daughters run to that Pazlayarai monster. At least you are here for me."

"I'd love to stay with you always, akka. If only women could marry women, or stay unmarried."

"Impossible! You must marry a man: only then will your parents and brother be satisfied. Your brother invited me here specially to arrange your marriage. Tell me who you want to marry: Madurandaka the Shiva devotee or Aditya Karikalan the brave warrior?"

Manimekalai burst out laughing. "*Akka*, Prince Madurandaka came here in your screened palanquin. We women did not know that and wondered why Lady Nandini did not visit the women's quarters. If I marry Prince Madurandaka, it would be like marrying a woman."

"As I expected. I told your brother you would not like to marry Madurandaka. He's married to my brother-in-law's daughter: she's an arrogant woman whom you would not be able to live with even for a day. So that means you love the crown prince."

"No, *akka*. I have not seen him. How could I love him?"

"Come now, surely you have heard of his exploits?"

"Yes, *akka*. I know he's a great warrior. I heard he cut off Veerapandian's head with one swing of his sword—is it true?"

Manimekalai missed the dreadful expression which flitted across Nandini's face. Smiling again, Nandini said, "Is that a sign of courage? Think of someone you love dearly, like your brother or your future husband. What if he was lying wounded and helpless and his enemy came and cut off his head? Would that enemy be a hero or a demon?"

Manimekalai thought a while. "A strange question, *akka*. I'll tell you one thing: if such a thing happened to me, I would grab the enemy's sword and kill him with it."

Nandini hugged her and said, "My darling, what an answer! I must find you a husband worthy of you. I doubt even Aditya Karikalan is good enough for you."

"After hearing about Karikalan, I'm afraid of him. *Akka*, can I tell you what's in my heart?"

Will My Dream Come True?

NANDINI LIFTED MANIMEKALAI'S chin and looked into her eyes. "Keep your secrets: you have known me for just a day."

"*Akka*, I feel I have known you for years. I long to confide in you."

"Very well, tell me, sweetheart."

"Can we feel the presence of someone who's not really present?"

"Yes, it can happen. If you have extreme love or extreme hatred for someone, that person will appear before you. Who's this man whom you love?"

"*Akka*, I saw him for the first time about four months back. My brother often spoke to me about him before that. I began to dream of him day and night ...

"You saw him yesterday, right?"

"*Akka!* How did you know? Are you a magician?"

"You must have heard people say I'm a witch. You can test me ..." Nandini closed her eyes. "The man you love is Vandhiya Devan."

"*Akka*, you really do know magic!"

"My girl, if you love him so much, why don't you tell your brother? Why unnecessarily bring Madurandaka into it? Why invite Aditya Karikalan here?"

"My brother hates him now. He says that he stabbed my brother in the back and that you saved my brother's life."

"He exaggerates my role. But what will you do now?"

"But he says it's not true ..."

"Who says?"

"The name you said earlier ..."

"When did he tell you this?"

"Yesterday."

"Did you actually see Vandhiya Devan yesterday or did you feel his presence?"

"I'm confused. *Akka*, when a person dies, can their ghost talk to us?" Her voice trembled in fear.

Nandini too shuddered. She gazed into the distance: "Yes, the ghost of a person whose life was cut short will haunt the living. If it's someone who was beheaded, the ghost will appear as a severed head, or a headless body, and ask, 'Have you taken revenge?'" She recovered. "Why are you bothered about this? Are you afraid something has happened to Vandhiya Devan?"

"There's a man possessed by spirits in the palace. I sent for him; it seems someone beat him up yesterday. His wife came instead and she's the one who told me this. I don't believe it. After all, one can't touch a ghost."

"Now, tell me everything that happened yesterday," Nandini said eagerly.

"At about this time yesterday, I came here to see if everything was ready for you. I looked in this mirror and saw his face coming towards mine from behind as if to give me a kiss. I turned back: there was no one. The mirror was in front of the secret entrance to the Hunters' Hall which I showed you earlier. I decided to see if anyone was inside. A servant, Idumbankari, was cleaning the room. He insisted no one had come there, but I sensed someone else hiding there. I came back here and waited; soon, I heard bangs and thumps in the hall. The small door within the secret door opened and he tried to get in, shouting, 'Help!' I pulled him into this room. He told me a murderous gang was chasing him and denied stabbing my brother in the back …"

"Did you believe him?"

"I did, but I had doubts later. As I was talking to him, I heard voices in the hall. Asking him to stay here, I went into the hall. I saw five or six men in the dim light. Just as I was about to challenge them, I heard Chandramathi call me; afraid that she would find him in the room, I decided to deal with those men later and came back here: he was nowhere to be seen. I went back to the hall: the men had disappeared too! Idumbankari swore he had seen no one. Chandramathi said you had arrived. I took a short cut across the terrace to get to the entrance quickly …. from the terrace I saw him cross the open courtyard and scale the fort wall with a bamboo pole. I don't know whether I really saw all this or whether it was a hallucination."

Nandini remembered the two figures at the edge of the forest last evening. *Had they been caught? Would they be brought here?* Aloud she said, "Is there any other exit from this room?"

"Not that I know of, *akka*."

"Didn't you tell your father all this?"

"I felt rather shy and afraid to tell him. I'm wondering whether to tell my brother …"

"Better not to involve the men: and Kandamaran is now determined to marry you to Karikalan."

"*Akka*, help me! Kandamaran has great regard for you: he'll listen if you tell him."

"You're asking me to work against the very purpose for which I am here. But even if we drop the idea of you marrying Karikalan, how do you know whether the other man loves you?"

"I don't care! Whether he loves me or not ..."

"It seems women are fated to love men at any cost. Very well, let's see how lucky you are. And don't forget to tell me if anything else happens."

"Who else can I tell, *akka*? I had a dream last night: someone was coming to stab him with a knife; he was unarmed; I pounced on a knife gleaming on the ground; I ran to stab the other man in the back; when I went closer, I saw the other man was Kandamaran ... I screamed and woke up. It was so real, *akka:* do you think it will come true?"

"My dear girl, you are totally confused. What's real seems to be a dream and a dream seems real. A fine pair we are: I'm mad and you're madder!"

Chandramathi came to say the company was expected soon.

Royal Welcome

THOUSANDS CROWDED KADAMBUR Palace's entrance at the news of the crown prince's arrival. The crowd surged like an ocean towards the fort's entrance. The guards had a difficult time holding it back. People had traveled miles to see Aditya Karikalan: the brave warrior who had gone to battle at the age of twelve; who had defeated the Pandian forces at the Battle of Sevur and forced King Veerapandian to hide in a desert cave; who had destroyed the Pandian king's bodyguards and beheaded Veerapandian at the age of nineteen. Rumors about Karikalan buzzed through the crowd: the crown prince and his father were not on good terms; the emperor did not want Karikalan to succeed him to the throne; Karikalan wanted to establish an independent kingdom in Kanchipuram; Karikalan was angry with his father because of the emperor's partiality towards Arulmozli; Karikalan and Arulmozli were inseparable; the emperor was angry with Karikalan because he wanted to marry a temple priest's daughter; sorcerers from the Pandian kingdom had cast spells on Karikalan and made him mad ...

Suddenly, someone perched on a tree shouted, "Here they are!"

A rider galloped through the crowd: it was Kandamaran. He reached the entrance, jumped off his horse and hurried to where his father and Ambalavan waited. "The crown prince is coming. I came ahead to warn you he's in a bad temper. We must give him a warm reception and if he says anything inappropriate, it's best to keep quiet." Kandamaran looked up at the balcony above the entrance and saw the women gathered there. He climbed the steps leading up to it and went straight to Nandini. "Lady, I have done what you wanted: the prince is here. But he's like an elephant in musth! I don't know how we're going to manage him."

"Don't worry," Nandini replied. "Your sister's eyes will be the goad which tames him."

"*Akka*, what kind of talk is this?" Manimekalai cried.

"Manimekalai," Kandamaran said. "You'll be lucky if you get a husband like the prince."

Nandini intervened. "Who else has come with the prince?"

"Parthibendran and Vandhiya Devan."

"Which Vandhiya Devan? Your friend?" Nandini asked, with a meaningful look at Manimekalai.

"Yes, the good friend who stabbed me in the back. He came out of nowhere and joined us at the Vellar river. If it wasn't for the prince, I would have killed him there itself!"

Manimekalai's face fell. "*Anna*, if he stabbed you in the back, why do you let him come here?"

"Darling," Nandini said. "Stay out of this: it's men's business. Today they'll fight, tomorrow they'll be dearest friends."

Kandamaran smiled. "Nothing like that: I have to consider the prince. Oh! You have baskets of flowers … your showers of blossoms may cool his temper. They're here; I must go welcome them." He ran down the steps.

Aditya Karikalan, Parthibendran and Vandhiya Devan reached the fort entrance. The prince's cavalcade was far behind, blocked by the crowd. Musical instruments blared a welcome.

A herald announced: "Here comes Aditya Karikalan, first born of

Emperor Sundara Chola; Crown Prince; Commander of the northern army; Killer of Veerapandian!"

A second herald cried, "Sambuvaraya, Eternal Friend of the Chola Emperor, Commander of five thousand soldiers, welcomes the prince to his humble palace. May his arrival bring prosperity to the Chola kingdom!"

Flowers rained down on the men. Devan and the prince looked up. Among the beautiful faces there, Devan had eyes only for Manimekalai's smiling face: he returned her smile for an instant before catching himself and turning away. As the three men walked into the fort, the gates closed with a clang behind them.

Karikalan's face darkened. "Why are they closing the gates in such a hurry? Are they planning to imprison me here as they have imprisoned my father in Thanjavur? Where's my escort?"

The two old chieftains were taken aback. Ambalavan recovered first and said, "Lord, your father and you are locked in the people's hearts—there's no need for any other prison."

Sambuvaraya added, "Prince, this crowd cannot be allowed into my small house. Once they disperse, your escort can come in. Until then, my servants will see to your needs."

"How does one go up to the balcony?" Karikalan asked Kandamaran who pointed. The prince ran up the steps followed by his three friends.

Sambuvaraya turned to Ambalavan. "It looks like we have invited trouble: his brain is addled!"

Ambalavan shrugged. "If our plan works, well and good. If not, no harm done."

"I'm not referring to our plans. I'm afraid some disaster may happen while he's in my house. He is like an elephant in musth—see the anger on his face and the poison in his words."

"We must put up with him for a few days. Parthibendran will help us to control him. It's the other one I am afraid of: I suspect he's a spy. He was here on the day of our meeting and I saw him hiding among the trees last evening."

"He's my son's friend, we don't need to worry about him. Now why is he rushing to see the women? Maybe we should go up too?"

Parthibendran heard the chieftain's last words and turned back from the bottom of the steps. "Sir, there's one thing you don't need to worry about: the prince has no interest in women."

Ambalavan smiled. "Then what's the point of bringing him here?"

"Leave that aside," Sambuvaraya said. "Why's he in such a bad temper? I'll be satisfied if you just take him from here peacefully."

"He was okay until Vandhiya Devan and the Vaishnava joined us. I suspect they have said something to him. Leave Vandhiya Devan to me—I'll pick a quarrel with him at right time."

Just as Karikalan and his friends started up the stairs, the women came down. Saying, "We must not make the women wait," Karikalan gave way to them and greeted them in turn with folded hands as Kandamaran introduced them. When he came to Nandini, Karikalan said, "Oh, it's the grandmother from Pazluvur! I'm glad she has come." Nandini gave him pointed look and walked past silently. Karikalan trembled, recovered himself and turned to Manimekalai who came behind her. "This must be your sister, Manimekalai. She's as pretty as a picture! We must find a good husband for her." Manimekalai bowed in embarrassment, gave Devan a sidelong glance and hurried down the stairs.

Karikalan went up and stood on the balcony. The crowd which was just beginning to disperse, gathered again. The prince beckoned to the herald and gave him orders.

The herald beat his drum and announced: "The crown prince will be staying at Kadambur Palace for a week. He will visit the surrounding villages and hear the people's grievances!" A roar of approval rose from the crowd; the people cheered, clapped and praised the prince.

Karikalan came down and went to Parthibendran. "Parthibendran, why did you stay back? Are you planning to join these old men in their conspiracies?"

The old men looked in alarm at the prince who smiled back at them.

Sambuvaraya recovered first. "Lord, you mentioned imprisonment and now conspiracies. I promise as long as you're a guest in my humble house, no harm will come to you. I'll give my life to keep you safe!"

"Sir, I was fearless when surrounded by thousands of enemy soldiers: why would I be afraid among friends? But please don't call your palace a 'humble house.' Look at the thickness and height of these walls: they beat Thanjavur Fort! Which enemy are these walls meant for?"

"The Cholas' enemies are my enemies; the Cholas' friends are my friends!" Sambuvaraya declared staunchly.

"I'm happy to hear that: you must make it clear to your son, Kandamaran. He considers my friend, Vandhiya Devan, his enemy—that's a big mistake, right?"

Kandamaran bowed his head.

Malayaman's Worry

KANDAMARAN LED THE prince across the open courtyard and the others followed.

Karikalan paused before the stage. "Ah! What's this for?"

"Sir, we have made arrangements to stage plays if you want," Sambuvaraya replied.

"Excellent! Make arrangements to stage plays and songs. We'll hunt during the day and pass the night in song and dance. My grandfather, Malayaman, warned me not to sleep while in Kadambur Palace. I told him I have not slept for the past three years: which enemy would dare to attack me while I'm awake?" The prince laughed heartily.

Sambuvaraya's voice shook with anger. "Prince, whether you are asleep or awake, no one will dare to harm you in this palace."

"Yes, my grandfather is old and worries unnecessarily. Some old men become timid. But look at my Pazluvur grandfather's majestic walk: will anyone think he's sixty?"

Ambalavan cleared his throat—it sounded like a lion's roar.

"How true is the saying that when Lord Ambalavan clears his throat, the earth trembles! My friends, will you be as strong as him when you are old? You'll never marry a new wife at his age." He turned to Ambalavan. "*Thatha,* you brought Lady Nandini with you. How did she travel: by palanquin, chariot or elephant?"

"She was seated in the elephant's howdah for all the world to see," Ambalavan declared proudly.

"Excellent! Never let her travel in a screened palanquin. They say my uncle, Madurandaka, sometimes travels in Lady Nandini's palanquin. Have you heard anything so ridiculous?" Karikalan roared with laughter.

No one else laughed. Devan was alarmed. *He's out of his mind! I made a big mistake in telling him everything—he's going to disclose it all to these men.*

Ambalavan fumed like a volcano and cleared his throat before erupting. Without giving him a chance, Parthibendran stepped forward to say, "Prince, Lady Nandini's chastity is beyond reproach. If any man speaks ill of her, I swear I'll cut him down with my sword!"

Kandamaran declared, "If anyone insults Lady Nandini, I'll break his neck with my bare hands!"

Not to be outdone, Devan said, "If anyone abuses Lady Nandini, I'll burn him to ashes with a look!"

Karikalan said, "Wait a minute, friends. It seems like you're ready to fight with me! No one is insulting Lady Nandini: if anyone did, I would kill him myself. It's her palanquin people are talking about. If that coward, Madurandaka, travels in her palanquin, there will be talk about it."

"Why would he do that?" the confused Parthibendran asked.

"For a ridiculous reason," the prince replied. "He goes secretly from place to place, gathering support to become the next Chola king. Four months back, he traveled here in the palanquin to attend a meeting of conspirators. Parthibendran, didn't my grandfather say Madurandaka was so eager to become king, he might even murder my father?"

"I remember, prince, but I don't believe it ..."

"Nor do I," Karikalan said. "Otherwise, would I have come to Kadambur as a guest?"

Sambuvaraya cleared his throat. "Prince, there's a long history of enmity between Malayaman's clan and mine; even if we forget it, Malayaman holds on to it."

"Didn't I say the old man's brain is addled by age? I'm worried he may land up here with a big army, thinking my life is in danger."

"Sir," Sambuvaraya stammered. "If you have any such doubts ..."

Karikalan laughed like a mad man. "Why should I have doubts? Malayaman's association with the Cholas goes back two generations while the Pazluvur association with the Cholas dates back to six generations. Lord Ambalavan is here: am I mad to think he would betray me?"

Ambalavan said majestically, "Sir, I swear I'll never betray the Cholas! I doubly swear I'll never go against the dictates of righteousness!"

"You and I must discuss the dictates of righteousness when we can spare the time." Karikalan turned to Sambuvaraya. "Where are my friends and I to stay in your palace?"

"Sir, I have reserved all the guest rooms at the back for you and Lord Ambalavan. The other chieftains and my family will use the front rooms."

"Ah! Are we expecting more chieftains?"

"Yes, prince. The chieftains from the surrounding area are eager to meet you."

"Good! We can hold discussions and come to a decision. Leave Madurandaka's conspiracy aside: I have a conspiracy of my own. This palace will be the best place for it."

Poonkuzlali's Wish

POONKUZLALI AND CHENDAN Amudhan rowed down the canal from Nagapattinam to Kodikkarai. The fragrance of screw-pine was in the air. Poonkuzlali watched a parrot perch on a flower. "How I would love to be a parrot! It's free to roam the skies—what more could one want?"

"People catch parrots and cage them," Amudhan pointed out.

"Yes, princesses cage parrots and play with them: the cruel demons! If I worked in a palace, I would poison the princesses along with the parrots."

"Why do you hate princesses? They are to be pitied. Like parrots in cages, princesses are caged in palaces. They can't row a boat in the sea or leap around like the deer in the forest."

"Who's asking them not to?"

"You grew up by the sea and so you have the freedom to roam where you want. A woman born in a palace does not have that freedom. And another thing: a parrot which has been caged and fed for some time will not fly away even if it's set free. I have seen this in palaces."

"If I was a caged parrot, I would bite the hand of the princess who fed me."

"You don't want to be a caged parrot in a palace; you don't want to be a princess in a palace; you don't want to marry a prince who lives in a palace."

Poonkuzlali's eyes flashed like angry lightning. "Who said I wanted to marry a prince?"

"No one. If you have no such wish, all the better."

They were silent for a while. The only sounds were the splash of the oars, the croaking of frogs, the call of sea birds, the crash of the waves and the distant sound of thunder. Amudhan cleared his throat and gathered his courage. "Poonkuzlali, there's the Kodikkarai lighthouse in the distance. I won't get a chance to see you alone after this. I have to return to Thanjavur tomorrow; my mother needs me. Vandhiya Devan told you I love you …"

"Don't you have a tongue? Can't you speak for yourself?"

"Very well. Will you marry me?"

"Why do you want to marry me?"

"Because I love you dearly."

"Does love have to end in marriage?"

"That's the way of the world."

"Can you give me the palaces, jewels, dresses, elephants, servants and palanquins I want?"

"No, but I'll give you something better: a life of peace. My mother and I live in a hut in a beautiful garden. My mother will love and cherish you. We'll wake up at dawn, gather flowers and weave beautiful garlands; while I go to the temple with the garlands, you can bathe in the pond and help my mother in the house; in the evening we'll water the plants; when the sun sets, I'll teach you sweet hymns; if you want, we'll sing them together at temples to delight devotees. Where else in the world would you find a better life?"

Poonkuzlali burst out laughing. "Amudhan, do you know the life I want? I want to marry Indra, King of the Gods; I want to ride the skies on his elephant, Airavat; I want to grab his vajra and beat the storm clouds with it; I want to see those dark clouds split the sky with streaks of lightning; I want to shatter all the royal palaces with thunderbolts …"

"Stop, Poonkuzlali, some bitterness in your heart makes you say this. I'm sorry for talking about marriage now. I'll pray day and night for god to give you peace."

Suddenly, Poonkuzlali jumped up and stared at a tree on the bank. For an instant, Amudhan thought that the woman standing among the branches was his mother; then he realized that it must his aunt from Boodha Island. Poonkuzlali leaped from the boat and ran up the canal bank.

The Arrow Whizzes

POONKUZLALI SAW MANDAKINI disappear into the nearby forest.

Amudhan joined her on the bank. "Was that our aunt? I saw her resemblance to my mother. Why did she run away?"

"She ran away from you. She hates strangers; she doesn't know you're her nephew. I'll look for her in the forest."

Amudhan was curious about Mandakini. He also hoped that she would help him win Poonkuzlali. "Let me come with you. I want to meet her."

Poonkuzlali hesitated. "Okay, but having you with me will make it more difficult to find her."

They concealed the boat in a screw-pine thicket, tied it and walked into the forest.

"Poonkuzlali, does our aunt come here often?"

"No, she comes here very rarely–only if I have not visited her for a long time. I think she has come here now for news of her foster son. She's worried about him."

"Prince Arulmozli is her foster son? Then who's her real son?"

"I don't know, but I intend to find out. Amudhan, you saw a resemblance to your mother: did you see a resemblance to anyone else?"

Amudhan thought a while. "Yes, Lady Nandini looks like her. How is that possible?"

"I have many things to discuss with our aunt today."

"How our grandparents must have suffered when both their daughters were born deaf-mute!"

"I believe the two sisters quarreled non-stop when they were young. That's why grandfather took our aunt to live with him on Boodha Island. He doted on her. An astrologer predicted she would be a queen and grandfather was heart-broken when she was born dumb."

They searched the forest but could find no trace of Mandakini.

"We can't find her. She's staying away because of you, Amudhan." A strange sound, half human and half animal, came from the forest. A herd of deer ran towards the sound. "Amudhan, follow me without making a noise."

They walked softy in the direction of the sound and a wonderful sight met their eyes. Mandakini sat on the forest floor, her hands filled with tender leaves. A herd of deer crowded around her, eating from her hands. Amudhan and Poonkuzlali stood frozen in amazement. The deer sensed their presence and bounded away into the forest. Poonkuzlali signaled to her aunt and walked up to her. Mandakini hugged her and kissed her on her forehead. They spoke in sign language and Poonkuzlali then called to Amudhan. Mandakini placed her hand on his head in blessing and they walked to the canal bank together.

"Amudhan, let's go. Aunt refuses to come home. I'll bring her food here."

As they walked towards the lighthouse, Amudhan asked, "Poonkuzlali, what's your answer?"

"I planned to go with you to Thanjavur, but that's not possible now. Aunt wants to see her beloved foster son and I'm taking her to Nagapattinam. If you come with us, she may run away again–and I want to ask her many questions."

"In that case, I'll say goodbye here," Amudhan said.

"No, you must come home, see father and have lunch; otherwise he'll scold me."

In the distance, they saw Rakamma and a man concealed in the thick bushes. *Who's my sister-in-law talking to? Is it the Pandian spy or someone else?* Poonkuzlali wondered.

Rakamma emerged from the bush and was startled to see Poonkuzlali.

Recovering herself, she said, "Where have you been all these days? Your father and brother are worried."

"Why? This is not the first time I've been away from home."

"But this time, you went with your cousin. What if you decided to marry him secretly?"

"Please don't talk like this to me ..."

"Okay, okay. What do I care whether you marry your cousin or a prince? Your aunt from Sri Lanka was here looking for you. Did you see her?"

"No," replied Poonkuzlali. She took Amudhan aside when she got the chance and warned him, "My sister-in-law has joined the Pandian conspirators. Don't tell her anything."

"I'll pretend to be dumb for the short time I'm here," Amudhan smiled.

Late that afternoon, Poonkuzlali rowed her boat back to Nagapattinam, taking Mandakini with her. The two women were kindred spirits and Poonkuzlali always felt a deep peace when she was with her aunt. But today, she was troubled. Her heart ached to think that she had saved Arulmozli and taken him to Nagapattinam only to let that princess get him. She also pitied Amudhan for having rejected him. Her father's warning echoed in her ear: 'My child, it would be best if you stayed at home for a while. Strangers come and go and I don't know what they want. Don't get caught in any plots. Always remember that our family's loyalty is to the Cholas.'

Thinking of Rakamma, Poonkuzlali worried that these strangers were after her, hoping that she would lead them to the prince. Her anxiety increased as she heard a rustling along the canal bank and saw Mandakini look up with worried eyes. Poonkuzlali saw a herd of deer among the bushes. *Deer are the most beautiful of all living creatures but some human wretches hunt and kill them.* Lost in the deer's beauty, Poonkuzlali stopped rowing and the boat came to a standstill.

Suddenly, Mandakini gave a cry of warning and the startled deer turned and ran. An arrow whizzed out of a bush and hit a deer. As the animal bleated in pain, Mandakini jumped out of the boat and ran to the wounded deer. The bushes rustled; eight men rushed out of hiding and surrounded her, many of them armed with spears. Knowing there was no chance of escape, Mandakini stood quietly while the men tied her hands. Rakamma looked on from a distance. All this happened in seconds.

Poonkuzlali jumped out of the boat and charged towards the men, screaming in rage and waving an oar. Five men ran to her, dragged her to the boat and threw her into it after tying her up tightly. They disappeared, taking Mandakini with them.

Fire and Laughter

POONKUZLALI STRUGGLED TO untie the rope, but the men had knotted it well and she could not free even the fingers of one hand. Her knife lay on the floor of the boat. With great difficulty, she bent and gripped the knife handle with her teeth. Painstakingly, she sawed at the rope. At long last, it loosened slightly. She managed to free one hand and then cut the rope which bound her arms. This took her more than an hour. Just when she freed her hands, she heard footsteps. Thinking that one of the men had come back to check on her, Poonkuzlali gripped her knife and prepared to throw it at him as soon as he showed himself on the bank.

"Poonkuzlali! Poonkuzlali!" It was Chendan Amudhan. His terrified face peered down from the canal bank. "You're alive!"

"What took you so long?" Poonkuzlali scolded. "Do you know how long it took me to free myself?" She tried to stand but tripped, as her feet were bound.

Amudhan jumped into the boat and caught her. "The villains tied you up and left you here. Look how your feet and hands are swollen!"

"All this concern now! Why didn't you come earlier?"

"How was I to know you were in danger? You're the one who said, 'Go, go!' And so, I went ..."

"Then why did you come back? To perform my last rites?"

"Lord Shiva has poison in his throat and you have poison on your tongue. Serves me right for running here when your sister-in-law said you might be in danger."

"Where's that witch? I'll kill her with this knife before doing anything else! She's the one who betrayed our aunt."

"You're wrong. The men who took our aunt away also tied your sister-in-law to a tree after hitting her on the head."

"I don't believe such nonsense! Tell me everything that happened," Poonkuzlali said excitedly.

Amudhan told her his story. He was walking along the road to Thanjavur with a heavy heart. Suddenly, he heard a woman scream and men running. He hid behind a tree on the roadside and saw a group of soldiers armed with spears emerge from the forest track and take the highway. He saw a woman with them who looked like Mandakini but thought it was just his imagination. Again, he heard a woman scream in the forest. *Why get into unnecessary trouble? Better to go my way.* But he did not have the heart to ignore that cry. He found Rakamma tied to a tree. Her face was covered with blood from a wound to her head. Amudhan untied her, asking, "*Akka*, who did this to you? Was it those men who took the highway now? Who was the woman with them?"

Rakamma said, "Your aunt and Poonkuzlali were going in the boat when those men stopped them and dragged out your aunt. When I tried to stop them, they hit me and tied me to this tree. God alone knows what happened to Poonkuzlali! Go and see." As Amudhan turned to go, Rakamma stopped him. "One second, *thambi*. Do you know where Poonkuzlali and that dumb devil were going?"

Put off by her calling his aunt a 'dumb devil,' Amudhan said, "I'll tell you later," and ran to the canal. Terrified that the men may have killed Poonkuzlali, he was relieved to find her alive. "What shall we do now?" he asked. "Do you agree your sister-in-law is innocent?"

"It looks like it from what you say. Bet let's go to her first."

"Do you think she'll still be there?"

"She'll be there or somewhere nearby. Or she'll come to us. Amudhan, don't tell my sister-in-law anything. We don't know for sure that she has nothing to do with these men. And why was she following the boat? Don't trust her."

"Poonkuzlali, your brother pretends to be dumb before your sister-in-law: I'll do the same." As she burst into laughter, he said, "Your laugh is nectar to my ear."

"Don't let my laughter fool you—a fire is raging in my heart!"

"The flood of god's compassion is the only thing which will put out that fire."

Pinakapani Again

THEY WALKED INTO the forest.

"Amudhan, there must be some bond connecting us from our past lives. At noon, I thought I wouldn't see you again: yet, here we are together two hours later."

"Don't worry, once we reach the Thanjavur Road, I'll go my way and you can go yours."

"You won't get rid of me so easily, Amudhan. After meeting my sister-in-law, I'm coming with you to Thanjavur. I'll meet the emperor and get justice for my aunt."

"Do you think it's that easy to see the emperor? People like us can't enter Thanjavur Fort."

"I'll break the gates; I'll scale the walls; I'll scream so loudly the guards are forced to take me to the emperor! If I can't meet the emperor, I'll meet the Pazluvur brothers; if they ignore me, I'll go to the chief minister; I'll go to the queens in Pazlayarai. I won't rest until my aunt gets justice. Amudhan, will you come with me?"

"Of course, I will. But first, we must find our aunt and rescue her from those men."

"Amudhan, my aunt has divine power—no one can harm her. I'm not worried about her. People believe a young girl can move about safely in the Chola kingdom. But an old deaf-mute woman has been abducted by villains in broad daylight."

"Yes, it's dangerous for unmarried girls to move about in this kingdom. It would be best if these girls married soon."

Poonkuzlali burst out laughing. "If a girl married you, will you be able to protect her?"

"I learnt to make garlands and sing hymns, not to fight. But, didn't you teach me to row a boat? In the same way, I'll learn to use a sword.

If Prince Madurandaka can dream of becoming king, why can't I learn to fight?"

There was no sign of Rakamma near the tree where Amudhan had found her. He pointed to the drops of blood on the ground.

"It looks like my sister-in-law is not working with the men who kidnapped my aunt. But we must find out who else she's working with."

"Poonkuzlali, there are plots within plots and secrets within secrets. And it's clear they concern the royal family. Why do we want to get involved? Why are we asking for trouble?"

"How can I turn away when it concerns my aunt? Don't you care about her?"

"Poonkuzlali, it looked like she was going with those men voluntarily ..."

"She must have gone with them to find out where they were taking her. I'm not worried about what happened to her today. I want justice for the wrong done to her twenty-five years ago."

Amudhan sighed. "What an impossible task you have set yourself!" They heard voices in the distance and saw Rakamma and Pinakapani at the highway junction. Poonkuzlali's face darkened at the sight of the doctor's son.

"Here you are, Poonkuzlali," Rakamma said. "I was afraid those men had killed you. See the wound I got trying to save your aunt. I was asking the doctor's son for medicine."

"If Poonkuzlali has a wound, I can apply medicine to it," leered Pinakapani.

Poonkuzlali ignored him and told her sister-in-law, "Please tell father that Amudhan and I are going in search of our aunt." She turned to go.

"Poonkuzlali," Pinakapani said. "Those men had horses—you can't catch up with them. I'll ride after them like the wind and come back to tell you where they went. In return, just tell me this: where were you and your aunt going by boat?"

"We don't need his help," Poonkuzlali told Rakamma. "Just give father my message."

Pinakapani persisted. "How angry the lighthouse keeper's daughter is! Am I the one who stopped you from marrying the prince? You cheated me and took Vandhiya Devan in your boat. He pushed your beloved prince into the sea and killed him." He roared with laughter.

Poonkuzlali looked daggers at him and pulled Amudhan along the road with her. "Amudhan, once you learn to fight with a knife, first kill that wicked doctor's son!"

Poonkuzlali and Amudhan traveled night and day. They made enquiries about a woman with a party of horsemen. People first reported seeing this group on the highway but after that, there was no news. They decided to go to Thanjavur anyway. Amudhan was in high spirits. He enjoyed Poonkuzlali's company. He bought a sword at a smithy near Kodikkarai. As they walked along, he whirled it about and cut and slashed with it; Poonkuzlali gave him some pointers. When Thanjavur Fort appeared in the distance, they worried how they could gain entry into it.

Amudhan thought of Devan and his resourcefulness. *How would he have reacted in this situation?* Just then, a screened palanquin with the Pazluvur palm tree symbol came along the road. *It's Lady Nandini's palanquin. What if I get a signet ring from her like Vandhiya Devan did?* Amudhan told Poonkuzlali his idea and the two of them waited for a chance to talk to Nandini.

A Palanquin Ride

THE SUN BEAT down on them; by afternoon, they were sweating even under the shade of the trees. Shortly after the Pazluvur palanquin passed them, the north-east horizon darkened. Soon, the wind roared and rain poured down. Trees shook and huge branches crashed down on the highway. Travelers ran for shelter as lightning flashed and rolls of thunder split their ears. As night fell, Amudhan and Poonkuzlali gave up their idea of entering the fort that day and decided to go to Amudhan's hut for the night. They carefully made their way towards Thanjavur.

"Poonkuzlali, you row your boat fearlessly in storms; how come you are afraid now?"

"There are no trees to fall on my head in the ocean."

They heard a tremendous crash just ahead of them and stopped.

"Let's shelter in a pavilion until the rain lets up a little," Amudhan decided. As lightning flashed, they saw a pavilion nearby and ran for it. Once there, they wrung out their drenched clothes. "I hope you don't catch a cold, Poonkuzlali," Amudhan worried.

"I'm the Ocean Princess–the rain won't harm me." Poonkuzlali's thoughts went to Arulmozli in the Choodamani Monastery.

Another streak of lightning showed them the uprooted banyan tree lying on the road just opposite the pavilion. Two horses and four or five men were trapped under its huge branches and prop roots. Other men were struggling to lift the branches and rescue them. They heard muffled cries of 'Aiyo!' 'Here!' 'Quick!' The palanquin was on the ground a little way from the tree. Only two guards stood by it. The others had gone to lend a hand with the rescue.

"Amudhan, do you see the palanquin? Shall we go and talk to Lady Nandini?"

"At this time and place? The men will think we're robbers in the darkness."

"If I use my sister-in-law's name, or say the sorcerer Ravidasan sent me, she'll help us."

"Look!" Amudhan exclaimed as lightning flashed again.

They saw two men pick up the palanquin and bring it to the pavilion's entrance.

"Looks like Lady Nandini's coming to us," said Poonkuzlali, standing her ground as Amudhan tried to pull her to the back of the pavilion.

"Who's there?" shouted one of the bearers.

"We're travelers like you, brother," Poonkuzlali said. "We're sheltering from the rain."

"Okay, but don't come near the palanquin," the bearer warned. "How many are you?"

"We are only two," Amudhan replied.

Unknown to Amudhan, a third man stood hidden behind a pillar at the back of the pavilion. Lightning flashed; Poonkuzlali's and Amudhan's eyes were fixed on the palanquin. They saw a woman part the screens and smile at them in recognition. Darkness descended on them again.

"Amudhan," Poonkuzlali whispered. "Did you see who's in the palanquin?"

"Isn't it Lady Nandini? She looked a little different …"

"It's our aunt."

"What!" Amudhan exclaimed.

"Shh! Come, let's take her and go."

"Will she agree to come with us? Don't we want to know where she's being taken, why and on whose orders?"

"And what if she's taken to the dungeon? What can we do then?"

"I'll find a way. I have some influence in the palace. Keep quiet now."

Poonkuzlali decided that she had no choice but to be patient. The palanquin's screen parted. In the darkness of the pavilion, the two guards saw nothing. Mandakini stepped out and stole like a cat towards the cousins. She took them by the hand to the back of the pavilion. She hugged Poonkuzlali and kissed her on the forehead. The two women spoke in sign language.

Poonkuzlali told Amudhan, "My aunt wants me to take her place in the palanquin. She'll go home with you. This is a good opportunity to find out who sent these men to catch her."

"Think, Poonkuzlali: it may be dangerous!"

"Don't worry, Amudhan. If I do as my aunt says, I won't be in danger. And remember, I have my knife." Poonkuzlali hugged her aunt again, crept into the palanquin and closed the screen.

Aniruddha's Disappointment

ANIRUDDHA'S THANJAVUR MANSION was a hive of activity: officials, chieftains, army commanders, merchants and foreign ambassadors bustled in and out. Kalaanthaka was unhappy with the increased traffic of people into the fort, especially as the chief minister's home adjoined the emperor's palace. But he did not have the courage to confront Aniruddha when Ambalavan was away in Kadambur. Kalaanthaka also resented Aniruddha giving him orders disguised as requests. Two days back, Aniruddha asked for some soldiers to go to Kodikkarai; Kalaanthaka had obliged. Aniruddha had then asked to borrow Nandini's palanquin and bearers to escort a noble woman from nearby Thiruvaiyaru. Kalaanthaka had again agreed, but he was suspicious. *Who's this woman who must travel in a screened palanquin? What's Aniruddha up to? I wish my brother was here.*

Azlvarkkadian was as eager as Kalaanthaka to know the identity of the person in the palanquin. He was at the chief minister's palace bright and early on the day after the storm.

"Thirumalai, was your mission successful?"

"Gurudeva, forgive me, I failed. I told the crown prince everything you asked me to but could not stop him from going to Kadambur."

"As I expected. Who's with him now?"

"Parthibendran and Vandhiya Devan, along with Lord Ambalavan and Lady Nandini. I heard more chieftains are to join them. Lord Malayaman left the prince at the Kedilam river."

"That brave old man will not stay quiet. He'll probably raise an army and march to Kadambur. I hear Velir is marching here with his army. God alone can save the kingdom! And what are the people saying?"

"They mourn Prince Arulmozli; they curse the Pazluvur brothers; some of them criticize you."

"They are justified, Thirumalai. I plan to resign my chief ministership soon."

"Then I'll be free to wander the land singing the *Azlvars*' hymns. When do you plan to resign?"

"I'm making one last attempt to save the kingdom; I'll resign after that. I have already taken the first step, Thirumalai. And I have succeeded in doing what you failed to do: last night, the deaf-mute woman from Sri Lanka arrived at my palace."

"Amazing! How did you do this, sir?"

"I suspected she would go to Kodikkarai for news of Prince Arulmozli. I sent some men there. Luckily, she came willingly with them. And how's this? I had her brought here from Thiruvaiyaru in Lady Nandini's screened palanquin!"

"But there was a big storm last night."

"Yes, I was worried. I heaved a sigh of relief when the palanquin reached here at midnight."

"So late? Did you receive her?"

"I left that to the women in my family. I was worried she would make a fuss. Luckily, she had her dinner and went to sleep. Thirumalai, I'm a little afraid to meet her. You came at the right time. She knows you as Prince Arulmozli's friend … she'll be comfortable in your presence."

The two men walked to the women's quarters and Aniruddha ordered the servants to bring the woman who had arrived the previous night. The servants brought the woman: Aniruddha gaped at her in amazement. Azlvarkkadian could not hide his smile.

Can the Dumb Speak?

THE CHIEF MINISTER dismissed the servants and turned to Azlvarkkadian. "Thirumalai, something is wrong. This girl is about twenty years old … the woman we want must be at least forty. You saw Lady Mandakini in Sri Lanka: is this her?"

"No, gurudeva, this is definitely not Lady Mandakini."

"Then who is she?"

"Why don't you ask her?"

"What's the point of asking a dumb woman?"

"Whom did you send to Kodikkarai to bring her?"

"The Pazlayarai doctor's son. He seemed capable and said he had been to Kodikkarai once before. He even sent me a message from Thiruvaiyaru saying his mission was a success …"

"Sir, where's that clever spy who succeeded where I failed? Let's question him."

"We can't do that, Thirumalai. A huge banyan tree crashed down on the highway. Luckily, it missed the palanquin, but it fell on the men riding behind it; the doctor's son was one of them."

"Why did just the tree fall on that devil's head? Why wasn't he struck by a thunderbolt?"

Aniruddha stared at Poonkuzlali in amazement. "You are neither deaf nor dumb!"

"There are times when I wish I was deaf, but I'm delighted to hear the tree fell on that devil. I hope he's dead!"

"By the smile on your face, I suspect you know more than you let on, Thirumalai." Aniruddha turned to the girl. "Why did you pretend to be dumb?"

"Sir, the grand welcome I received in your palace made me speechless! The women here spoke to me in sign language; I thought they were deaf-mutes and replied in the same way."

Aniruddha said, "I wonder how Pinakapani managed to catch you."

"If he had tried to catch me, he would be dead by now." Poonkuzlali took the knife from her waist.

"Girl, for heaven's sake, put that knife away. Why are you so angry with him?"

"His men tied me to my boat; they tied my sister-in-law to a tree …"

"At least he was clever enough to follow my instructions …" Aniruddha said.

"Sir, are you the one who ordered him to catch my poor voiceless aunt?"

"Your aunt? The fisherman's daughter, Mandakini, is your aunt? In that case, what's your relationship to the lighthouse keeper, Thyaga Vidangar?"

"I'm his daughter."

"Girl, just tell me this: where's your aunt? How did you exchange places with her?"

"Sir, why did you send men to capture my aunt?"

"Daughter, that's a state secret. I can't answer your question."

"Father, then I too can't answer your question."

"Why are you here?"

"I wanted to see Thanjavur's palaces. I heard the emperor is ill. Is he better? Can I meet him? I must tell him women are being kidnapped under his righteous rule."

"Girl, I can't waste time arguing with you. Did anyone force you into the palanquin?"

"Certainly not. It was raining and so I climbed into the empty palanquin."

"I begin to understand," Aniruddha said to Azlvarkkadian. "The bearers put down the palanquin during the storm and this girl exchanged places with her aunt. This happened somewhere near the fort. Is my guess correct?"

"That's exactly what happened, gurudeva. I saw it with my own eyes," Azlvarkkadian said.

"What! Why did you keep your mouth shut all this while? Tell me quickly."

"Last evening, as I neared the fort, the storm worsened. I took shelter in a pavilion. This girl and her cousin came there. The boy was wearing rudraksha beads. I thought I would pass the time arguing with him about Lord Vishnu's superiority over Lord Shiva. Just then, two bearers brought a palanquin with the palm tree emblem to the pavilion. A woman got out stealthily, went to these two and conversed in the dark. A flash of lighting showed that the woman getting back into the palanquin was not the same one who had climbed out. The bearers did not notice anything; when the rain stopped, they picked up the palanquin and went on their way."

"Ahah! And what happened next?"

"The other two left together and I too left the pavilion."

"Thirumalai, why didn't you stop them at once? Are you a part of this plot?"

"Gurudeva, what a thing to say! How was I to know this was your plan? I assumed it was Lord Kalaanthaka's business as it was the Pazluvur palanquin. Even otherwise, Lady Mandakini knows me and would have disappeared if she saw my face. Blocking a whirlwind would be easier than catching her!"

"Looking at it like that, Pinakapani was clever enough to catch her."

"Gurudeva, you are wrong. Lady Mandakini let herself be caught. Something made her change her mind when she neared Thanjavur."

"Could be. But she could not have gone far in the storm. She'll be somewhere nearby. We must find her." He turned to Poonkuzlali. "What's your name, daughter?"

"Poonkuzlali, sir."

"What a beautiful name! Tell me where your aunt is: no harm will come to her."

"Sir, I know where she is. If you'll tell me why you want her, I'll tell you where to find her."

"There's no point in talking to this girl, Thirumalai ..."

"Okay, sir, I'll bring her to you on one condition: you must crown her queen," Poonkuzlali declared.

"Thirumalai, is she mad?!"

"Gurudeva, has it taken you so long to realize that? Don't worry, I know where Lady Mandakini is: she's at Chendan Amudhan's house. Send two men with me; I'll bring her here."

"If you do that, I'll raise a hue and cry outside the emperor's palace! I'll proclaim your secrets to the public." Poonkuzlali cried.

"We have no choice but to send her to the dungeon," Aniruddha said.

"I'll kill anyone who comes near me!" Poonkuzlali raised her knife.

"Sir, I have a better idea: let's send her to Princess Kundavai. The princess will cure her madness —she may also need the girl."

"Why would the princess need this girl?"

"Gurudeva, haven't you heard? Last night's storm has left a trail of devastation along the coast. Messengers from all parts of the country are waiting to see you."

"Yes, yes! This girl has taken up too much of my time; it would be better if she was dumb!"

"So, you would have no one to question you, is it?" mumbled Poonkuzlali.

"I hear Nagapattinam is in great danger," Azlvarkkadian said. "The sea has flooded the city." Both Aniruddha and Poonkuzlali looked at him in alarm. "Princess Kundavai will probably come to see you about that ..." Azlvarkkadian stopped as Kundavai and Vanathi came in. When Kundavai saw Poonkuzlali, her worried face bloomed with surprise and happiness.

She's a Wicked Girl

Aniruddha said, "If you had sent word, I would have come to you, lady. Is the emperor alright?"

"My father didn't sleep all night. He's very anxious about the effect of the storm on the poor. He insists that those affected must receive aid at once. That's the main reason I'm here."

"Lady, what can I do? Lord Ambalavan is away at Kadambur and the key to the treasury is with him. You must have seen the crowd at my door. I'm ashamed to meet them: even Lord Kalaanthaka can't open the vaults without the chancellor's permission."

"I'll donate all my personal wealth and so will my mother," Kundavai said. "You may take what you want from the palace. My father asks you to organize emergency relief at once."

"Your donation will be just a drop in the ocean, lady. Last night's storm has wreaked havoc all along the coast. Thirumalai heard that the sea has flooded all the coastal areas from Kodikkarai to Nagapattinam." Aniruddha saw the fear in the women's faces. "It's probably a rumor. We'll know the truth when messengers reach here this afternoon. Meanwhile, I'll see what we can do."

Kundavai controlled herself. "Sir, if it's true, what will the monks in the Choodamani Monastery do?" She turned to Poonkuzlali. "Isn't this Vidangar's daughter? What is she doing here?"

"She's a wicked girl who pokes her nose into matters that don't concern her," Aniruddha said.

Kundavai was suspicious. *Has the chief minister brought her here to get information about Arulmozli? I had better support her.* "Poonkuzlali is a good girl. Come here, dear. The chief minister is angry with you: have you done something to bother him?"

"Lady," Poonkuzlali said. "It's the chief minister who's bothering me!"

"Oh, you too are angry! Come sit beside me," Kundavai said. "Sir, why did you bring her here?"

"I did not even know of this wicked girl's existence," Aniruddha said. "She came here searching for her aunt."

"Chendan Amudhan's mother?" Kundavai asked. "Why, she lives in the garden outside the city."

"No, she has another aunt: the deaf-mute who lives in Sri Lanka. You must have heard of her. I wanted to bring her here on an urgent matter. I succeeded ..."

Kundavai stood up in excitement. "Is she here? I must see her at once!"

"Forgive me, lady. This girl ruined everything at the last moment." Aniruddha gave Kundavai a brief account of events regarding Mandakini. "She's now in Chendan Amudhan's hut."

"Come," Kundavai said. "Everything else can wait; let's go and bring her here."

Azlvarkkadian stopped her. "Lady, if she sees a crowd, she'll run away and we'll never be able to find her again. Let this girl go and bring her here. There are only two people who can control her: Poonkuzlali is one of them."

"Who's the other?" Aniruddha asked.

Azlvarkkadian hesitated. "The prince who is rumored to be missing at sea."

Kundavai ignored this and said, "Poonkuzlali, bring your aunt here. I promise you no harm will come to her. I must see her at once over an important matter. Will you help me?"

"I will. But the chief minister should not have done this …"

"Yes, I agree that doing things in secret leads to unfortunate situations. Bring your aunt quickly; I have another important job for you," Kundavai urged.

"Thirumalai, go with her," Aniruddha said. "If you find it difficult to bring them through the main entrance, use the secret passage to the palace."

Poonkuzlali and Azlvarkkadian left.

Kundavai said, "Sir, please see to those waiting. I have an important matter to discuss with you."

"I'll be back soon, lady."

Vanathi spoke for the first time. "*Akka*, are you sending Poonkuzlali to Nagapattinam again?"

"Yes," Kundavai said. "Don't worry, Arulmozli will be safe."

"*Akka*, that boat girl hates me: she did not even look at me once. She's angry."

"All the unmarried girls in the country are angry with you—no point worrying about that."

Aniruddha's Sin

ANIRUDDHA CAME BACK. "Lady, I have done what I can to start relief efforts. I have also sent word to Lord Kalaanthaka that he and I must jointly open the treasury."

"Is it true there's a vault full of treasure under Lord Ambalavan's palace?"

"I have heard of it but have never seen it, lady. Those who enter it once, never come back."

"Leave that aside. Do you think they'll bring my mute mother here? I'm so worried …"

"Lady, how did you come to know of her?"

"A few months ago, my father told me …"

"What! That she's alive??"

"No. He believes she's dead: that's the reason for his mental distress. You were the one who told him she had died in the sea. How did you find out she's alive?"

"How did you find out, lady?"

"Vandhiya Devan told me about her when he returned from Sri Lanka. Later, Arulmozli told me that …" Kundavai realized her mistake and covered her mouth with her hand.

"Lady, if you don't want to talk about Prince Arulmozli, I'll erase all mention of his name from my mind."

"No, I came here to tell you everything. I realize that hiding things only leads to disaster. Sir, Arulmozli did not die at sea—he's at the Choodamani Monastery. I went to Nagapattinam to see him. I suspect you know all this."

"Lady, I know. But I never interfere in your affairs and I have instructed my men to leave you alone. Lord Malayaman, General Velir and I often say that if only you were born a man, you would plant the Chola flag over the entire world."

"I dreamt of achieving this through my brothers. But now, I have decided women should not interfere in affairs of state. I hid Arulmozli at the monastery—see what's happened!"

"Nothing will happen. The ocean which spared the prince won't harm him when he's on shore."

"Come and tell my father this: he'll be comforted."

"Ah! Does the emperor know the prince is alive?"

"I was forced to tell him last night."

"I wish you had waited a little longer. It was a good idea to keep him hidden in Nagapattinam. The people are agitated; they curse the Pazluvur brothers and Prince Madurandaka. Some believe that the Pazluvur brothers used the arrest warrant to kill Arulmozli at sea. If Prince Arulmozli comes now, the people may rebel and insist that he be crowned king at once. The Pazluvur brothers are spoiling for a fight and General Velir is marching here with a huge army. I fear the Chola kingdom is headed towards a bloody civil war. I pray this will not happen."

"I pray for the same thing. I wanted my brothers to succeed my father. But now, I have no objection to Madurandaka becoming king."

"But the people object to that. If, god forbid, something happens to your father, there will be anarchy."

"I fear for my father's life. Last night, he was so bad, I had to tell him Arulmozli's alive. He believes the fisherman's daughter's ghost is out to take revenge on him through his sons."

"Oh my god! What a tragedy! Tell me everything."

"I'm here to confide in you and ask for your advice. The last time I was in Thanjavur, my father told me what took place twenty-five years ago. All these years, he has been tormented by guilt. He says that recently, the fisherman's daughter appears before him as a ghost and tortures him."

"Lady, do you believe this?"

"I was confused. I thought it was hallucination. Later, other doubts crept in. Vanathi heard my father scream one night and saw a figure resembling Lady Nandini in his room. I suspect there's some connection between her and the fisherman's daughter; Vandhiya Devan and Arulmozli have reinforced my doubts. Sir, could Lady Nandini be her daughter?"

"Like you, I can only guess. There are only three people who know the truth."

"Who are they, sir?"

"The first is Sembiyan Madevi: she hides a painful secret which she confided to her husband, Gandara Aditya, on his deathbed. He died before he could tell me. The other two are the deaf-mute sisters. We'll get nothing out of Amudhan's mother: she's totally devoted to Sembiyan Madevi. As long as the Queen Mother's alive, she'll guard the secret. That's why I have worked so hard to bring her sister, Mandakini, here from Sri Lanka."

"Oh! Is her name Mandakini? When did you know she's alive?"

"Lady, I have known this for more than twenty-five years."

"What! How could you not tell my father? Don't you know how much he has suffered?"

Aniruddha sighed. His face showed the conflict in his heart. Then, making up his mind, he said, "Lady, I did something wrong twenty-five years ago: you are the first person I'm confessing this to. Your father sent me to find the fisherman's daughter. I galloped to Kodikkarai. There, I heard from eye witnesses that she had jumped into the sea from the top of the lighthouse. This is what I told your father." He paused. "The fisherman's daughter jumped into the sea, but she did not die. A boatman saved her and came ashore miles away from Kodikkarai. On my way back to Thanjavur, I happened to see that boat. I paid the boatman handsomely to take the woman back to Sri Lanka and keep her there. I then told your father that she was dead. I did this in your father's interest. Little did I know it would come back to cause so much trouble."

"Sir, even if you did wrong, it was for my father's good. What happened after that?"

"After becoming crown prince, Sundara Chola went to fight the Pandians. I left for Kashi to study the Vedas and returned to Pazlayarai after several years. One day, I was shocked to see Esana Bhattar's father talking secretly to the fisherman's daughter. He told me she had stayed in Sembiyan Madevi's palace garden for some time and given birth to twins. Leaving the babies behind, she had run away. Now and then, she would return to see her children. He refused to give me further details about the children, saying it was Sembiyan Madevi's secret. I thought it best not to stir things up and left it at that. Lady, when Prince Arulmozli fell into the Ponni as a child, I think it was the fisherman's daughter who saved him."

"You're right; Arulmozli recognized her when he saw her in Sri Lanka. But strangely, my father believes it's her ghost which has come to take revenge on his children. Last night, he insisted it was her ghost which pushed Arulmozli into the sea and killed him. He's sure the ghost will take revenge on Karikalan too. 'Why can't I die while at least one my sons is alive?' he cried. I was forced to tell him Arulmozli is alive."

"Was he comforted by your words?"

"No, he became even more agitated. At first, he didn't believe me. When I said I had seen Arulmozli with my own eyes, he asked why I did not bring him here. I said Arulmozli was still recovering from the fever and could not travel. I hinted that seeing him might push the people into rebellion. He said, 'This kingdom will be the death of my sons; without it, they'll be alive and well.' When a loud roll of thunder split the air, he jumped up in bed crying, 'I'll never see Arulmozli again! The storm will flood the coast. Nagapattinam will sink into the sea like Poompuhar. The Choodamani Monastery is between the sea and the canal: there's no chance of it escaping the flood. That vengeful ghost could not kill Arulmozli at sea—now she'll kill him on land. I must save my son!' He tried to walk but fell back on his bed; his sobs would have melted even the hardest hearts." Tears flowed down Kundavai's face.

Trouble in the Street

VANATHI BURST INTO tears on seeing Kundavai weep; even Aniruddha's hardened heart melted. I'm responsible for the emperor's suffering. How can I make amends for it?" he grieved.

"Sir, the only way to give my father peace is to tell him that the fisherman's daughter is alive."

"Yes, but he won't believe me unless Lady Mandakini stands before him."

"Sir, we must not take her to my father suddenly: he can't bear the shock."

"I planned to meet him this morning and prepare him to see Lady Mandakini. But Vidangar's daughter ruined my plans. I'll see that she's punished."

"Aiyo! Please don't do that. Whether she's good or bad, she saved Arulmozli's life. I'm planning to send Poonkuzlali to Nagapattinam, but if you think it's better Arulmozli comes openly to Thanjavur ..."

"No! Until the matter of the succession is resolved, he must stay away. I intend to ask the emperor what his final decision is today. If Prince Madurandaka is to succeed your father, then it would be best if your brother goes back to Sri Lanka. As long as Arulmozli is here, the people will never accept Madurandaka as king. They will revolt—blood will flow in our rivers!"

"I'll send Poonkuzlali and Chendan Amudhan to Nagapattinam again."

"Yes. If your father wants, Prince Arulmozli can visit him secretly once. Is the emperor worried about Prince Aditya Karikalan?"

"No. My father is confident no one can harm him."

"I don't share your father's confidence. The prince is undefeatable on the battlefield but it's easy to cheat him. The Pazluvur brothers are his enemies and Lady Nandini is plotting secretly against him. Thirumalai could not stop him from going to Kadambur."

"Sir, I asked Vandhiya Devan to tell him Lady Nandini may be our sister and also asked him to protect my brother."

"I'll send Thirumalai to Nagapattinam behind Poonkuzlali and Amudhan ..."

"Why have they not come yet? When I see my stepmother, half my worries will be over. I must tell my mother everything."

"Ah, your mother will be heartbroken! And I wonder how your grandfather will react. If his grandsons don't succeed to the throne, Malayaman may decide to destroy the entire kingdom."

"Leave my grandfather to me: it's General Velir I'm worried about. He dreams of Vanathi becoming queen and Vanathi shares his dream—"

Vanathi intervened angrily. "*Akka* ..."

Just then, Poonkuzlali hurried in. Their faces fell on seeing that she was alone. "Sir, my pride is humbled. I could not bring my aunt here."

"What happened? Has she run away? Did she refuse to come?"

Poonkuzlali told them what had happened. The storm knocked a big tree down on Amudhan's house, shattering it. Amudhan himself had caught a cold and fever in the rain. So, Mandakini remained with her sister to help her. She was glad to see Poonkuzlali, who assured her that Azlvarkkadian was her friend. As they had decided earlier, Poonkuzlali and Azlvarkkadian told Mandakini that the emperor was on his deathbed and longed to see her one last time. Poonkuzlali told her that the emperor had not forgotten her all these years: maybe seeing her would give him new strength. Poonkuzlali explained that the chief minister had sent men to bring her to Thanjavur for this. She also told her that Kundavai waited at Aniruddha's palace to take her to her father. Mandakini agreed to come with them. They reached the fort gates just as the *Velakkara Padai* was marching in. Mandakini was fascinated by the king's bodyguards. The crowd pushed through the guards and surged into the fort behind the *Velakkara Padai*. Azlvarkkadian suggested that they use the secret passage to Aniruddha's palace, but Mandakini ignored him and joined the crowd. Once they were inside the fort, Azlvarkkadian tried to take another way, but Mandakini insisted on following the crowd. Poonkuzlali was amazed to see her crowd-fearing aunt behave like this.

As they passed Kalaanthaka's palace, people began to notice Mandakini. "Doesn't this woman look like Lady Nandini?" someone said. The worried Azlvarkkadian tried to stop Mandakini. A bystander shouted, "Is this Vaishnava troubling you, lady?" On hearing this, some of the king's bodyguards turned back and came to Mandakini.

"Lady," one guard said. "Tell me who's troubling you: I'll hang him before your eyes." Mandakini remained silent.

Another man said, "Doesn't she look like Lady Nandini? That's why she's so arrogant. All Pazluvur people are arrogant."

One of Kalaanthaka's soldiers shouted, "Who insulted Pazluvur? Come forward if you dare!"

One of the king's bodyguards stepped forward. "I'm the one who said that—what will you do?"

As the two soldiers attacked each other, the crowd broke into boos and cheers. Poonkuzlali and Azlvarkkadian were pushed aside. When Kalaanthaka arrived there on horseback, the crowd scattered and the king's bodyguards marched on. Azlvarkkadian and Poonkuzlali looked for Mandakini, but there was no sign of her.

Azlvarkkadian sent Poonkuzlali to update Aniruddha and ask for help, while he continued the search. "Don't worry," he said. "Your aunt's not in danger. I saw her staring at a particular spot in the crowd: she saw someone familiar to her. She's following that person. We'll find her." Poonkuzlali had hurried back to the chief minister.

"How will we find her?" cried Kundavai.

"Don't worry," Aniruddha said. "She's inside the fort: there's no way she can go out without my knowledge. Lady Mandakini will not leave without meeting the emperor."

In the Treasury Vault

AS THE CROWD surged into the fort behind the king's bodyguards, Mandakini spotted Ravidasan. Instinctively knowing that he was up to no good, Mandakini followed him: after all, he was the man who had tried to kill Arulmozli in Sri Lanka. When the crowd scattered at Kalaanthaka's arrival, Ravidasan and another man hurried into an alley. Mandakini followed them. She had lost sight of Poonkuzlali and Azlvarkkadian in the crowd. She now looked back to see if they were behind her, but there was no sign of them. Deciding that it was more important to find out what Ravidasan was up to, Mandakini continued to follow him.

Ravidasan and his companion, Soman Sambavan, hurried on without looking back to see whether they were being followed—even if they had, they would not have seen Mandakini. They came to the wall behind Ambalavan's palace and climbed it with the help of an uprooted tree which leaned against it. They jumped into the garden. Mandakini waited a few minutes and then jumped into the garden after them. Ravidasan and Sambavan waited some distance away from Ambalavan's palace. With Ambalavan and Nandini away, the place was deserted but they could hear voices. After some time, two maids came to the garden and remarked on the damage caused by the storm. As they turned back towards the palace, Ravidasan hooted like an owl.

"An owl hooting in broad daylight!" one maid said. "The owls have gone mad after the storm."

The other woman remained silent. Shortly after that, she came back and went to the pavilion which stood between the palace and the vault. She peered into the garden. Ravidasan hooted again and she walked in the direction of the sound. Ravidasan stepped out from behind a tree.

"Sorcerer, it's you! Why have you come? Lady Nandini's not here."

"Lady Nandini sent me."

"Lord Kalaanthaka is suspicious. He called me and warned me to tell him immediately if the sorcerer returned."

"To hell with him: his days are numbered! Here's Lady Nandini's signet ring: bring me the keys to the vault."

"No! How do I know whether you stole it?"

"How dare you! Even Lady Nandini trembles when she sees me. I'll summon nine ghosts to carry you alive to the graveyard ..."

"No, keep your ghosts to yourself! Show me the ring: I'll bring you the keys. But be patient; the women come this side often to see the damaged garden. Wait until they are at lunch."

"I have not eaten for two days: bring me plenty of food."

Ravidasan and Sambavan sat on a fallen tree trunk, talking. Mandakini understood that something was going to happen. After a long time, the servant came back with a bunch of keys and a parcel of food. Ravidasan went to meet her and walked to the vault with her. They tried the keys: the third key opened the door. Peering into the darkness of the vault, Ravidasan said, "Fetch me a torch or a lamp."

"What if someone sees me with a lamp or a torch in broad daylight?"

"You'll find a way or else, I'll send twelve ghosts at midnight –"

"Aiyo! I'll do it somehow." She left.

Ravidasan walked back to Sambavan and gave him the food parcel. "Keep this. You may have to wait in the vault for a few days for the right opportunity. Take your spear and come with me. You must be in the vault before the maid comes back with the torch."

The men hurried towards the vault and Mandakini followed them.

The Underground Passage

RAVIDASAN LOOKED AROUND and then opened the door to the vault. "Go in quickly," he told Sambavan. "Don't stand near the door: wait some distance away from it."

The darkness swallowed Sambavan. Ravidasan went to the pavilion and watched the palace, waiting for the servant. As Ravidasan stood with his back to the vault, Mandakini crept forward and slipped quietly through the door. Accustomed to the dark forest, she had excellent night vision. She saw Sambavan bump into a pillar some distance away. She walked in the opposite direction and came to a staircase leading down. She went down two steps and waited.

Sambavan heard a slight noise. "Who's there?" he shouted.

Ravidasan heard the muffled shout through the open vault door. At the same time, he saw the servant enter the garden with a torch. He hurried into the vault and scolded Sambavan: "Why did you call? What if anyone heard you? As if I would leave you and run away!"

Sambavan came to Ravidasan. "I just wanted to ask you something …" Just then, a light appeared at the door.

"The maid is here!" cried Ravidasan. "Go hide behind a pillar, quick!"

"Sorcerer! Where are you?" the servant called.

Ravidasan took the torch from her. "Lock the door from the outside. Come back with the key after an hour. Make sure there's no one around and knock on the door. After you hear me answer, open the door."

"Very well, but I warn you: Lord Kalaanthaka is suspicious. If he catches you, don't pull me into this. Why do you need me again? Isn't there another way out of the vault?"

"The river is in flood: that way is blocked. Go and come back after an hour."

The servant locked the door and Ravidasan bolted it on the other side. Carrying the torch, he hurried to Sambavan. "What did you want to ask me?"

"Did you come here before this?"

"I have come here many times. Where do you think that the treasure we have comes from?"

"No, did you come back just after leaving me here? After you left, a figure blocked the light from the door for a second. I also heard footsteps."

"This vault plays tricks: you'll see sudden flashes of light and hear strange sounds. Men who enter this vault have died of fright—their skeletons still lie on the floor."

"Can anyone enter the vault?"

"No one enters this vault and leaves alive. As far as I know, I'm the only one who has entered and lived to tell the tale, but there may be two others: Vandhiya Devan and Kandamaran."

"Why are they still alive?"

"How many time must I tell you? Lady Nandini needs Vandhiya Devan for something. He'll die along with the Cholas. Come, I'll show you the underground passage. Remember one thing: don't let the heaps of gems blind you and make you forget your mission."

"Ravidasan! Like you, I have sworn an oath on King Veerapandian's headless corpse."

"I myself have been tempted by those gems. Come, I'll show you the tunnel to Sundara Chola's palace. You can explore the rest of the vault on your own. It may come in useful later."

In the dim torchlight, the pillars loomed like monsters; bats fluttered above them; giant spiders watched from their webs; strange creatures slithered on the ground. They heard queer noises and the distant sound of the storm and the rain.

Sambavan stopped suddenly. "Did you hear footsteps?"

"I hear our footsteps. Sambavan, stop this! If you're so scared with me here, how will you stay here by yourself for three days?"

"I'm not scared of ghosts or snakes, Ravidasan. But I'm a little hesitant about staying here for three days. If I get an earlier opportunity …"

"Don't ruin everything by being in a hurry. Today is Tuesday: you must wait until Friday. Sundara Chola's wife sticks to him like a leech, but on Friday night, she'll go to the temple, leaving him alone. That's when you must strike. On Friday, we'll wipe out the Chola dynasty."

The men hurried across the vault. Mandakini followed them soundlessly, hiding behind the pillars. They came to a wall. Ravidasan used the rough stones as footholds and climbed to a small latticed window at the top. He peered through it and slithered down the wall again.

"Do I have to jump out through the window?" Sambavan asked.

"Only a rat can get through that window," Ravidasan replied. "But you can see Sundara Chola's bedroom from it and check people's movements. Now, watch carefully …" Ravidasan bent and examined the floor; he pressed his foot on a circular stone; at the same time, he pushed a square stone with his two hands—a passage appeared.

"God!" exclaimed Sambavan. "An underground passage in a vault!"

"After Lord Ambalavan, Lady Nandini and me, you are the only one who knows about it."

They disappeared down the passage and the light of the torch faded. Mandakini placed one foot on the steps and hesitated. She stepped back and scrambled up the wall to perch on the latticed window's narrow ledge. She saw an adjoining garden and palace. Her instincts told her that her loved ones were in that palace and that the two men meant to harm them. She prayed for the strength to defeat their wicked plans. As she was about to get down, she was shocked to see Ravidasan and Sambavan hiding behind a pillar on the upper floor of the palace. The men peered into the palace in the broad daylight. Mandakini's heart stopped as Ravidasan took Sambavan's spear, aimed it at the palace interior and made as if to throw it. He then gave the spear back to Sambavan and the two men disappeared from view. Mandakini slid down the wall and hid behind a pillar. Soon, the men were back in the vault.

"Are you sure you know how to open the entrance to the passage?" Ravidasan asked.

"Don't worry, I'll kill Sundara Chola on Friday. Make sure the rest of you do your parts."

"The queen will see to Aditya Karikalan. The tiger cub is in Nagapattinam: he won't escape this time. The two witches who saved him last time are in Thanjavur—I saw them both in the crowd today, along with the Vaishnava traitor. I'm sending an assassin to Nagapattinam. Sundara Chola's dynasty will be wiped out on Friday."

"What about Madurandaka?"

"Let him be. If an idiot like him rules the Chola kingdom, it's good for us: remember our king has to come of age."

They retraced their steps to the vault door.

How he has Changed!

ONCE THE MEN were out of sight, Mandakini went to the place where the secret passage began. She tried to open it but failed. She had been too far away to see Ravidasan's demonstration clearly. Certain that the men would return, she waited. Sure enough, Sambavan came back to that spot after Ravidasan left the vault. His torch was now dim. In spite of his brave talk, he looked around fearfully before sitting there. Soon, the torch flickered and died. Sambavan looked up at the sunlit window. When the light dimmed and the sun set, he opened the passage entrance. Mandakini stood near him. Just as Sambavan was about to enter the passage, he heard a frightful screech nearby. He froze and waited until its echo faded. The second time he heard that dreadful screech, his hair stood on end. At the third screech, which was even closer to him, his courage failed: he panicked and ran blindly around the vault.

As soon as he disappeared, Mandakini entered the passage. After a few steps, the ground was level and she rushed down the tunnel which was like an endless, dark passage to hell. Finally, the tunnel ended in a high wall with a slight gap at the top. Mandakini's hands felt some steps. She climbed until she bumped her head on a ceiling. Between the steps and the ceiling, there were narrow openings. Mandakini went through one of the openings and found herself in a hall filled with huge statues. Accustomed to Sri Lanka's gigantic statues, Mandakini was not afraid. She carefully noted the spot where the tunnel ended and opened into the Art Gallery.

A ten-headed Ravana held up an uprooted Kailash Mountain with his twenty hands: and in between two of Ravana's hands was the gap through which Mandakini had entered the hall. Although the light was dim, Mandakini's sharp eyes took in the details of the other statues in the hall. She came to a section depicting the birth of the Ponni from Sage Agastya's *kamandalam*. The Ponni flowed down rocks and through groves and ended against a wall. Instinctively, Mandakini pushed the wall with her hands: a small door opened, leading to the palace garden. Just across the way were the palace balconies. Among all the broken branches and trees, no one saw Mandakini come out of the Art Gallery and hide by its door.

Soon, oil lamps were lit and the palace became a blaze of light. Mandakini thought, *I must be careful not to be seen.* She noticed that the part of the palace closest to the Art Gallery was darker than the other parts. This was the part that Ravidasan and his companion had visited. *Why are very few lamps lit there?* When night fell, Mandakini ran across the dark garden to the palace. The rear of the palace had many yards filled with large cooking vessels, old palanquins and other discarded articles. Steps led to the top floor of the palace. Mandakini summoned up her courage, climbed a flight of stairs and wandered around the deserted balconies, hesitating to go near the inner wall of the palace. Finally, she went to a window through which the dim light of a lamp could be seen. Mandakini was transfixed by what she saw.

A man lay on a carved bed in the middle of a large room; four women and two men stood respectfully around the bed while two maids waited at a distance. A lamp glowed dimly from a niche near the bed. Mandakini recognized her beloved Poonkuzlali and the others were familiar to her by sight. Slowly, she turned her eyes to the man on the bed—her heart stopped. Yes, it was him! The man who had stolen her heart all those years ago and made Boodha Island a paradise.

Ah, how he has changed! Mandakini had seen him many times over the years without his knowledge: hiding in the bushes along the bank as he sailed down the river; standing in the crowd as he rode by in his golden chariot. She had not seen him for the past three years and those years had brought these changes. His unshaven face, gaunt cheeks and wrinkled forehead tore at her heart. He looked like the fever-struck men in Lanka who lay at death's door. *Can a man change so much? Where's the fire which once sparked in his eyes? Is he dying?* She suddenly remembered that Ravidasan had stood at this spot when he mimicked aiming and throwing the spear. *Are they planning to throw the spear at him?* Mandakini's head whirled; she held tightly to a pillar to stop herself from fainting.

The Accusation

SUNDARA CHOLA'S HEALTH had deteriorated considerably over the past few days and Kalaanthaka's afternoon visit aggravated his suffering. The commander complained that Aniruddha's visitors ignored his rules for entry into the fort and compromised the emperor's security. The emperor smiled at this but was troubled by his other accusations. Kalaanthaka said that he had narrowly prevented a riot that morning when the King's bodyguards clashed with the crowd. He said this was due to Aniruddha's security lapses. The chief minister was renowned for his virtue but a few days ago, he had kidnapped a woman from Kodikkarai and brought her to Thanjavur. He had borrowed the Pazluvur palanquin for this—any disgrace would now reflect on the Pazluvur clan. Suspecting a sorcerer who often visited Ambalavan's palace, Kalaanthaka had stationed a spy there. When the spy reported that a man had scaled the back wall and was lurking in the chancellor's garden, Kalaanthaka had sent men to catch the intruder. To his shock, it was none other than Azlvarkkadian, Aniruddha's man. Azlvarkkadian said that he was there on the chief minister's orders.

"Your Majesty, if Aniruddha Brahmaraya behaves like this, how can I keep the fort secure?"

"Very well, I'm expecting Aniruddha; I'll question him about this woman he abducted."

"Ask him about Azlvarkkadian too, Your Majesty," Kalaanthaka said before hurrying away. He did not want to run into the chief minister who was in the habit of asking him uncomfortable questions. More importantly, he did not want Aniruddha to get permission from the emperor to open the treasury to fund the storm relief. How could he face his brother if that happened?

Sundara Chola had expected the chief minister that morning but

Aniruddha came to him only after sunset. The fearless Aniruddha was shaken; all his well-laid plans were ruined. Confident that he would soon find Mandakini, he had put off his visit to the emperor, but Azlvarkkadian had failed. Azlvarkkadian had followed the alley which he guessed Mandakini had used. He had glimpsed a woman climbing the back wall of Ambalavan's palace. He had also climbed the wall and was searching the garden when Kalaanthaka's men caught him.

"I couldn't give them my reason for being there, gurudeva. I was forced to use your name."

"Of all the palaces in Thanjavur, she had to choose the chancellor's!" Aniruddha said. "We can't search it openly. Luckily, Lord Ambalavan is away. I'll post guards around his palace and alert my spy who's inside." He frowned. "And all because of that boat girl!"

"Gurudeva, I suspect she would have run away even without the boat girl."

"Hmmm ... I have a feeling she won't leave the fort without seeing the emperor. Anyway, I can no longer delay meeting him. Bring the boat girl and come with me, Thirumalai. If he hears about Prince Arulmozli directly from the boat girl, he'll be reassured."

They met Kundavai and Vanathi at the entrance to Sundara Chola's palace and went in together. Kundavai was upset to hear that Mandakini had been seen in the chancellor's garden. "Sir, I heard there's a secret tunnel from that palace: what if she gets out that way?"

"Lady, not everyone is as lucky as Vandhiya Devan—the tunnel is not easy to find. But I'll post my men outside the fort walls."

Aniruddha went in first. He greeted the emperor and his queen and explained that he was late because he had been studying reports of the cyclone damage and plans for relief work.

"I'm glad you are here in the chancellor's absence," the emperor said. "But what's this I hear about you kidnapping a woman from Kodikkarai? And Kundavai tells me Arulmozli is alive at the Choodamani Monastery. Why was I not told? I'm ignorant of things taking place under my rule. I would rather die than ..." The emperor choked and his eyes filled with tears.

Aniruddha intervened. "Lord, our friendship goes back forty years. In all this time, I have never done anything against your interest. Not wanting to trouble you, I may have kept a few things to myself. If that's wrong, forgive me. I'll answer all your questions. Please stay calm."

"How can I stay calm? My own children and my dearest friend are plotting against me!"

"Lord, you'll soon know who the plotters are: I'm not one of them. I'm ready to give up the chief ministership. As I told you earlier, you are welcome to give it to Lord Ambalavan ..."

"Yes," the emperor interrupted him. "You are ready to abandon me. The only person who'll stay with me until my last breath is Malayaman's daughter. I'm blessed to have her as my wife." At this, Vanamadevi, seated on the bed beside the emperor, sobbed and ran from the room.

"Your Majesty, like their mother, your children too are devoted to you."

"Yet they disobey me. Why didn't you tell me Arulmozli's in Nagapattinam?"

"I received confirmation only yesterday, Your Majesty. His horoscope can't be wrong."

"I'm thinking of banning all astrologers in my kingdom. Because of Arulmozli's horoscope, some people want to crown him king while I'm still alive. Are you one of them?"

"My lord, I advised the prince to remain in Sri Lanka. But, with your approval, the Pazluvur brothers sent men to arrest him and bring him here. The people blame the Pazluvur brothers for his death and accuse them of deliberately throwing him into the sea."

"Lies! Parthibendran told me Arulmozli was on his ship; refusing to listen to Parthibendran, he jumped into the sea on the pretext of rescuing someone."

"Your Majesty, the prince jumped into the sea to save his friend. The boat girl who rescued them both is waiting in the next room to see you."

The emperor said eagerly, "Send her in at once! Is she the woman you kidnapped?"

"The woman who came here in the Pazluvur palanquin is in the next room." Aniruddha clapped: Poonkuzlali and Azlvarkkadian came in.

Evening Dreams

THE EMPEROR LOOKED at Poonkuzlali and said, "This girl's face is familiar—who is she?"

"This is the Kodikkarai lighthouse keeper's daughter, Poonkuzlali, Your Majesty."

"That explains it," Sundara Chola muttered to himself. "She resembles her aunt."

Poonkuzlali had heard of the emperor's great beauty. She was shocked to see this man worn out by physical and mental illness. She was ashamed to think that she had planned to fight with him for abandoning her aunt. Awed and shy, she was tongue-tied.

"Girl, how's your father?" Sundara Chola enquired.

Coming to herself, Poonkuzlali prostrated herself before the bed and stood with folded hands.

"Is she dumb like her aunt?" The emperor's face showed his agony.

"She talks enough for nine women, lord. She's awed by your presence: that's why she's silent."

"Yes, when anyone sees me, they fall silent. No one tells me anything." Sundara Chola turned to Poonkuzlali. "Is it true that you rescued Prince Arulmozli from the sea? Tell me one thing first: how did you know that it was the prince?"

"I have seen the prince many times when he went to Sri Lanka with his army. He once called me Ocean Princess."

"Ah, she can talk!" the emperor said.

Prompted by Aniruddha, Poonkuzlali narrated all the events from the time she had rowed Vandhiya Devan to Lanka up to her taking the prince to Nagapattinam. Warned by the chief minister, she avoided all mention of Mandakini.

"Girl, the Cholas are indebted to you. But why didn't you bring the prince here?" Sundara Chola asked.

"The prince was unconscious and burning with fever. He could only travel by boat. We took him to Nagapattinam as the Buddhist monks are skilled healers."

"Why didn't you take him to Lord Ambalavan in Kodikkarai?"

Poonkuzlali hesitated. "Lord, knowing the Pazluvur brothers are the prince's enemies, how could I do that?"

"Chief minister, the storm would have been severe in Nagapattinam. My heart trembles with anxiety about Arulmozli ... I want to see my sons at least once before I die."

"Sir, please don't talk like that. I'll send men to Nagapattinam at once to escort the prince safely here. I'll send my disciple, Thirumalai, with them."

The emperor noticed Azlvarkkadian for the first time. "Oh! Has he been standing here all this while? Is this the man who jumped over Lord Ambalavan's wall?"

"There was good reason for that, lord. I'll talk with you again tomorrow. You are tired now."

At that moment, the queen returned with Kundavai and Vanathi and said, "Chief minister, that's enough: the doctor says he must not be tired." She turned to Poonkuzlali. "I hear she sings beautifully ... the emperor loves songs."

"Yes, lady," Aniruddha said. "Thirumalai also sings."

Poonkuzlali sang a *Thevaram* hymn which Azlvarkkadian followed up with a hymn by the *Azlvars*. Sundara Chola closed his eyes; his face grew calm and his breath even. Soon, he was asleep. A maid placed a lighted lamp in the niche. Everyone walked out quietly.

The only sound in the room was the emperor's breathing. Although he was worn out by his sleepless night and soothed by the songs, the emperor's mind was troubled. His memories of the past and the events of the present mingled in his dreams.

Sundara Chola was sailing on the calm blue sea with Poonkuzlali, who sang sweetly. Suddenly, the sky darkened, a gale blew and mountainous waves tossed the boat. But the boat glided on under Poonkuzlali's skilled hands. The storm vanished and the sun rose over a shining blue sea. He saw the coconut-grove-filled islands of Sri Lanka. He said, 'Poonkuzlali, you have brought me back to paradise.' She did not reply; he turned to find Mandakini in her place. Shocked, he said, 'Mandakini, is that you?' Reading his lips, she smiled. 'Mandakini, even if anyone offers to make me emperor of the three worlds, I won't leave you. Let's not go to Lanka: they'll find me there. Let's cross the seven seas to an island far, far away.' Mandakini smiled again.

Sundara Chola was sailing with his wife and children in a swan-shaped boat on the Ponni. Suddenly, voices cried, 'Arulmozli is missing!' He looked around and saw a woman in the river: she was pushing his son under the water, trying to drown him. Furious, he was about to jump into the river when he saw the woman's face—it was Mandakini. He fainted and fell on the deck.

Sundara Chola woke up with a start, bathed in sweat. *Thank goodness, it was only a dream!* He looked around: the room was deserted. *Everyone must be in the next room. I'll call them after I recover from my dream.* A slight noise made him turn ... he saw a figure sliding down a pillar from the terrace above.

Why Do You Torture Me?

SUNDARA CHOLA WAS shocked. *Is this part of my dream?* He closed his eyes for a minute and slowly opened them—there was no one there. *It's my imagination.* He thought back to the events of the evening. He regretted criticizing Kundavai: in her wisdom and foresight, she had sent Arulmozli to Nagapattinam to avoid trouble. *I'm the one who has lost my mind. I must bring Arulmozli here. I hope he has not been harmed by the storm. I must ask Kundavai ...*

He was about to clap his hands for the maids when he heard a catlike tread and felt someone standing behind him. "Who's there?" Sundara Chola called softly. When there was no reply, he called a little louder, "Come stand before me!" *Is it the fisherman's daughter? But her ghost comes only at midnight, decked in silks and jewels. It's only late evening now, or have I slept till midnight? Why did they leave me alone? That devil will torment me until I go mad ...*

"You wretch! Why are you hiding behind me? Come and kill me with the knife you keep at your waist, but leave my children alone. What harm have they done to you? Did I ask you to jump into the sea from the lighthouse? Why do you torment me for what you did?" Sundara

Chola felt someone very close to his head. His eyes bulged and he trembled. *It's her. She's come for revenge. She'll plunge her knife into my heart or strangle me with her bare hands! Let her kill me … let her spare my children.* He felt the presence close to him; he even felt her shadow fall on his face, but he could not summon the courage to tilt his head back and look at her. He closed his eyes and waited. Nothing happened. After a while, he felt the presence move away from his head. *Has she let me off so easily today? Let me call for help.*

Shouting, "Who's there? Where have you all gone?" he opened his eyes. The ghost stood at the foot of his bed. It was her: her hair was loose and blood flowed down her forehead. Sundara Chola screamed: "Why do you torture me like this? Why are you standing there crying? Tell me what you want. You witch! You tried to kill Arulmozli; he escaped by god's grace. You devil! Go!"

Sundara Chola grabbed the brass lamp near the bed and flung it at the figure. The lamp missed her and fell on the floor with a clang. Her cry froze the very marrow in his bones. By the dim light of another lamp in the room, he saw the agony on her face. She gave him a last look of longing and turned to go. He felt a stirring of doubt. *Is this Mandakini's ghost … or her twin … or … or … maybe … could it be her? Is she still alive?* Sundara Chola shouted, "Woman, are you the fisherman's daughter, Mandakini … or her ghost … or her sister … tell me the truth!"

The queen, Kundavai, Vanathi, Aniruddha, Poonkuzlali and Azlvarkkadian rushed into the room. They stood frozen in shock at the emperor's frenzy and at the sight of Mandakini.

Sundara Chola cried, "Stop her! We must find out who she is."

Recovering first, Aniruddha asked Poonkuzlali, "Is this your aunt?" At her nod, he turned to Azlvarkkadian. "Thirumalai! Why are you standing there like a statue? Stop Lady Mandakini!"

For the first time in his life, Azlvarkkadian defied his master. "Gurudeva, command me to catch a whirlwind instead."

Poonkuzlali leaped to her aunt and held her by her shoulders. Mandakini shrugged her off and ran. But Azlvarkkadian bolted the entrance door and stood before it with his arms extended. Mandakini trembled like a deer surrounded by hunters. Poonkuzlali again went to her aunt; this time she spoke to her in sign language. Mandakini replied by pointing to the lamp on the floor.

Kundavai saw this and asked, "*Appa*, did you throw the lamp at her?"

"Yes, my dear," Sundara Chola said. "I couldn't bear the look the ghost gave me."

"She's not a ghost, *appa*! She's a woman: ask the chief minister; he'll tell you everything." Saying this, Kundavai went to Poonkuzlali and Mandakini who were arguing.

Sundara Chola tried to get up. "Kundavai! Don't go near her, that demon will hurt you!"

Vanamadevi held her husband gently by his shoulders and made him lean back. "My lord, be calm: Kundavai's not in danger."

Kundavai surprised everyone by falling at Mandakini's feet. Mandakini's eyes filled with tears as she lifted Kundavai and hugged her.

Goddess of the Chola Clan

VANAMADEVI SAW MANDAKINI'S forehead and cried accusingly, "My lord, you hurt her!"

Sundara Chola quickly denied it. "She was bleeding when she came here. But the wretch will probably blame me and you will all believe her. It's clear that everyone's on her side. Are you too pitying her? Do you know whom she is?"

"She's our clan's guardian deity: she saved Arulmozli's life."

"Ahah! Is that what you believe? Did Kundavai tell you this?"

"No, Kundavai was only a child then. I saw it with my own eyes. She is also the one who saved you from the bear on Boodha Island."

"My god! You know that too! And did you also know she's alive?"

"Only recently. I immediately asked the chief minister to bring her here from Sri Lanka."

"Aniruddha, is this really the fisherman's daughter? Don't drive me completely mad!"

"Lord, she's the fisherman's daughter and she's alive. I committed a great sin ..."

Sundara Chola interrupted. "So, this is the woman you brought from Kodikkarai. You call me 'Emperor,' but there can be no greater fool than I! Why didn't you tell me earlier? Lord Ambalavan is right: you too are part of the conspiracy against me."

"We may have conspired, lord, but not against you. When the queen told me how you suffered and blamed yourself for Lady Mandakini's death, we decided to somehow bring her to you; it was not easy. Lady Mandakini was almost here last night, but this girl exchanged places with her in the palanquin. Today, we searched for her everywhere. Thirumalai saw her enter the Pazluvur palace garden but before he could find her, Lord Kalaanthaka's men caught him. My lord, I beg you to forgive Thirumalai for this ..."

"Is this the only thing for which you need my forgiveness?!" Sundara Chola rolled his eyes.

"We could not find her. We were wondering how to break the news of her being alive to you; luckily, she came here on her own," Aniruddha concluded.

Sundara Chola turned to where Kundavai and Poonkuzlali were wiping Mandakini's forehead with a wet cloth. "Vidangar's daughter, ask her how she was wounded."

"I asked her, sir," Poonkuzlali replied. "But I can't understand: she says she hurt her head when she bumped into the mountain ..."

To everyone's surprise, Sundara Chola burst into genuine laughter for the first time in years. Seeing everyone staring at him, he said, "Aniruddha, I'm not mad. We all know there's no granite in the Chola kingdom. Ask her which mountain she bumped into."

Vanathi's face lit up suddenly: "Lord, something occurs to me ..."

Sundara Chola smiled. "Velir's niece, I did not notice you. How come you have not fainted in all this excitement? Tell us what you think."

"Sir, there's an Art Gallery in the palace garden with a statue of Ravana holding up Mount Kailash. Maybe she banged her head on it."

Poonkuzlali spoke to her aunt and said, "Yes, it's the statue in the Art Gallery." She added, "And I too would have known that if I had been to that gallery."

Sundara Chola looked pointedly at Mandakini. "She must have lost her way, banged her head there and ended up here by mistake."

"She was looking for you. I was sure she would not leave Thanjavur without seeing you," Aniruddha said.

Sundara Chola said, "If that's the case, why has she waited twenty-five years? Why has she haunted me? She has been roaming Lanka like a ghost while I lived in a palace. Do you know the agony of a guilty conscience? Who knows: maybe she has been visiting me secretly and I imagined it to be her ghost. Twenty-five years! Twenty-five ages!" He turned to Aniruddha with a frown. "Your guilt is written on your face. You fooled me with your report of her death and held fast to your lie for twenty-five years. Your crime is indeed unforgivable."

"I'm not the only one who's guilty, lord. Lady Mandakini is equally guilty—she made me promise not to tell you she did not drown in the sea. She threatened to kill herself if I refused to go along with her lie. You can ask her, if you like."

"There's no need for that. But it's true you have all conspired against me," the emperor said.

Aniruddha said, "You can't forgive me but at last, this burden has been lifted from my soul. Please let me spend the rest of my days worshipping Lord Ranganatha at Srirangam."

"No way!" Sundara Chola said. "You are responsible for this mess. How can you go to worship Lord Ranganatha without clearing it up?"

Ravana in Danger

SUNDARA CHOLA TURNED to his daughter. "Kundavai, I have something to discuss with Aniruddha and your mother. Go—and take that thing with you." Kundavai's face fell at hearing her father disgustedly refer to Mandakini as 'that thing.' Reading her face, Sundara Chola continued, "Take her to the mountain and find out what happened there. I can't stand the sight of her!"

The disappointed Kundavai took Mandakini by the hand. As she passed her mother, Vanamadevi whispered, "Why blame your father?

She does look disgusting. Let your cosmetics work their magic on her." Kundavai smiled and left with the other women.

Sundara Chola looked at his wife and chief minister in turn. "I don't know why the two of you did this. You are mistaken if you think it makes me happy. Aniruddha, tell me why you brought this savage here. Don't hide anything."

Aniruddha was indignant. "I'll never again make the mistake of keeping anything secret from you. It was to reveal the truth that I went to all this trouble. You felt guilty a woman died because of you; I thought you had got over your pain; recently, the queen told me you were still tormented by guilt and had nightmares; we decided to bring the woman to you and show you she's alive. If I'm at fault, forgive me."

Sundara Chola said passionately, "Yes, you are at fault! All these days, she haunted me like a ghost. Now, you have brought a mad woman to me. If you had bothered to ask me, I would have forbidden it. Never mind; how are you going to get rid of her?"

Hearing this, Aniruddha was speechless.

The queen said, "*Swami*, I have no intention of sending her away. I'll keep her with me and care for her as my elder sister."

Sundara Chola said, "My dear, there's no need for you to bring me a madwoman from the forest to prove your love for me. For twenty-five years, you have been my devoted wife; you neglected your children to care for me after I fell ill; you have fasted and done penance for my recovery. Listen, both of you: years ago, I met this mad woman on a deserted island. Yes, I loved her, but if you think I have longed for her all these years, you are fools. My love for her has changed to hatred. I can't bear the very thought of her living in this palace. Get rid of her at once!"

Aniruddha and Vanamadevi were shocked at Sundara Chola's fury. Aniruddha had expected the emperor to scold him only for his past silence; Vanamadevi had expected her husband to praise her large-heartedness. Both of them were disappointed and a little angry and disgusted.

Sundara Chola said, "Why didn't this madwoman drown in the sea? Which fool saved her life?"

This was too much for the queen. "*Swami!* Enough! Being ungrateful is a sin. Forget about her saving your life: how can you forget she saved Arulmozli's life?"

"That story again!!" The emperor rolled his eyes.

Vanamadevi was indignant. "It's not a story: it's the truth. Arulmozli himself told me that when he saw her in Sri Lanka, he recognized her as the woman who had rescued him from the Ponni. She saved his life many times in Lanka. Luckily, Arulmozli has recovered from his fever; send for him and question him yourself."

"Yes, Arulmozli's in Nagapattinam. But how do we know he's safe after yesterday's storm? Aniruddha, my heart is troubled: I sense some unknown danger looming over my family. The madwoman coming at this time is a bad omen."

"*Swami*, her coming is a good omen. She will protect our family: she's Goddess Durga's answer to my prayers. Let her stay here at least until Arulmozli returns."

"Chief minister, my innocent wife never asks for anything and I don't have the heart to refuse her this. But every moment that madwoman is here will be hell for me. Make immediate arrangements for the prince to come."

"Yes, sir. Shall I arrange an escort of elephants and cavalry brigades or ..."

"Or bring him here in secret ... you fear there may be riots if he comes here openly, right?"

"I'm sure about that, lord. The people are simmering: if something triggers their anger, I don't know what will happen to the Pazluvur brothers and Prince Madurandaka."

"What kind of talk is this, Aniruddha? If the people revolt, what's the Chola army doing?"

"Your Majesty, the people will shout and disperse. But the army will march on Thanjavur, smash the fort walls, put the Pazluvur brothers and Prince Madurandaka in the dungeon and crown Prince Arulmozli emperor."

"And you will be glad if that happens. The people are confused by some stupid astrologers' stories. Let me be clear: my uncle Gandara Aditya's son, Madurandaka, is the rightful heir to the Tiger Throne.

I won't let the people or the gods or my sons stop me from crowning him."

The queen protested. "Your sons have never disobeyed you. Arulmozli refused the Lankan throne: he does not want to be king. As for Aditya Karikalan, he agreed to be crown prince only because you wanted it. Karikalan is a great warrior: if he wants, he can establish new kingdoms with his mighty sword. All you have to do is tell him what you want …"

"Then why has he not obeyed me and come to Thanjavur?"

Aniruddha said, "They say that if he crosses the Kedilam, the Pazluvur brothers will arrest him."

"Someone's poisoning his mind: Malayaman, Velir… maybe you have joined them."

"Lord, I don't talk behind people's backs. Your premonition of danger to your family is correct. The danger is coming from two fronts: the Pazluvur brothers and Sambuvaraya."

"Stop! The Pazluvur clan has served the Cholas for more than a hundred years. Lord Ambalavan is a veteran of twenty-four battles and wears sixty-four battle scars as badges of honor. The sun will become dark before such a man betrays the Cholas."

"Your Majesty, the sun darkens during an eclipse. I did not accuse Lord Ambalavan of betraying the Cholas: he's plotting to make Prince Madurandaka king."

"Madurandaka is the rightful heir to the throne—I'm grateful to Lord Ambalavan."

"But the Pazluvur brothers are also making plans to divide the kingdom so that Prince Karikalan rules the part north of the Ponni and Prince Madurandaka rules the south."

"Chief minister, I'll never agree to split the kingdom. Maybe Lord Ambalavan wants to please me by giving my son half the kingdom. Once I tell him my wishes, he'll drop the plan. I'll crown Madurandaka king of the undivided Chola empire. No one can stop me."

"Majesty, Sembiyan Madevi, whom we all revere, will refuse to let her son become king."

"Someone must have misled her into thinking I want to crown my son king. Chief minister, make immediate arrangements for her to come here. I will change her mind."

"That won't be easy. She promised King Gandara Aditya that Prince Madurandaka will not become king. I was with the king during his last moments. He said, 'There's an important reason why Madurandaka must not be king; my wife knows this reason.'"

"Do you know what it could be?"

"No, lord. You will have to ask Sembiyan Madevi."

Sundara Chola smiled. "Let's send Kundavai to her." He turned to his wife. "My dear, bring Kundavai here."

Vanamadevi had listened to Sundara Chola and Aniruddha with half an ear: her mind was on Mandakini. She was only too glad to hurry to the women's quarters. She found Kundavai, Vanathi and Poonkuzlali in great agitation—Mandakini was missing!

Kundavai said, "*Amma*, it wasn't easy, but we managed to bathe Lady Mandakini. We dressed her in new clothes and Vanathi combed and braided her hair. While we were sorting ornaments and Poonkuzlali was preparing flowers for her hair, she disappeared."

Vanamadevi smiled. "Did she see herself in a mirror by any chance? She may have felt shy about her makeover; she's probably hiding in the garden."

The women searched the garden, but there was no sign of Mandakini. Just as they decided to tell the men that she had run away, they heard the sound of a hammer on stone from the Art Gallery. Asking a servant to bring a lamp, the women hurried there. Mandakini stood before the Ravana statue, pounding its hands with a long-handled chisel. Under her strong blows, the stone statue was dangerously close to breaking: if even two of the hands cracked, Mount Kailash would fall on Ravana's head, shattering it. Seeing them, Mandakini dropped the chisel and came to them with a smile. Except for Poonkuzlali, the other women thought, *She's a madwoman ... no wonder the emperor finds her disgusting ...*

Vanamadevi warned, "Girls, no one is to mention this to the emperor."

The King's Fury

AS SOON AS Vanamadevi left, Aniruddha said, "Your Majesty, there are some issues I did not want to raise before the queen. Veerapandian's bodyguards still lurk in our kingdom waiting for an opportunity to fulfill their terrible oath."

"That's nothing new. That's why the Pazluvur brothers keep me here under strong security."

"The bodyguards are financed by the Chola Treasury."

"What!!"

"There's more to come: Thirumalai saw newly minted gold coins from Lord Ambalavan's treasury heaped before the bodyguards. If you permit, Thirumalai will tell you the details."

"There's no need for that. Even if Harishchandra tells me the Pazluvur brothers are giving my would-be assassins gold from my treasury, I won't believe him."

"Anything's possible when an old man marries a young girl. The traitor is Lord Ambalavan's wife."

"I find it revolting to blame an unfortunate, helpless girl."

"Let me tell you some facts about Lady Nandini. Please bear with me."

Sundara Chola reluctantly nodded his head.

"Some sorcerers come to Pazluvur palace to see Lady Nandini. Lord Kalaanthaka is suspicious but he does not have the courage to confront his elder brother with it."

"These things are common among brothers."

"But loyalty to a brother should not harm the kingdom. Sir, I suspect these men are not sorcerers: the gold from our treasury reaches the enemy through them."

"What proof do you have?"

"If you order a search of Lord Ambalavan's palace and treasury today, we'll find proof."

"Aniruddha, you are my friend but Lord Ambalavan is a friend to three generations of Chola kings. He has been their armor and spear. How can I search his palace? That too in his absence?"

"His palace serves as the enemy's headquarters without his knowledge. Lust blinds him to what's happening right under his nose. I suspect Lady Nandini of being one of the conspirators."

"What else are you going to accuse that poor girl of?"

"A few days ago, the conspirators met at the war memorial in Thirupurambayam. They crowned a five-year-old boy king of the Pandians and swore an oath to destroy the Cholas."

"Are you trying to frighten me with such tales?"

"I'm not interested in that farce. I want you to know Lady Nandini was there."

"And who's the genius who saw all this and reported it to you? That man there, I suppose."

"Thirumalai got there after the meeting was over. It was Vandhiya Devan who witnessed it."

"That young man who came here once and escaped? That spy?"

"He's not a spy, lord. He's Prince Aditya Karikalan's dearest friend."

"My son has many such friends. Anyway, even if this is true, there's nothing we can do about it now. When Lord Ambalavan returns, I'll question him. I'm now curious about Lady Nandini. As I disapproved of his marriage, I told Lord Ambalavan not to bring his bride to me. Maybe she resents this. I'll invite her and her husband to the palace and pacify her."

"Your Majesty, I too want to make peace with Lady Nandini: there are other reasons for this. Until she returns, please let Lady Mandakini stay here."

"Why? What's the connection between the two women?"

"That's what we have to discover, lord. If the two women meet, we may find out their relationship and Lady Nandini may no longer be the Cholas' enemy."

"Aniruddha, I'm amazed you give so much importance to a woman's enmity."

Aniruddha hesitated. "Lord, what I have to say is complicated: you will not be pleased to hear it. Please be patient ... everyone who has seen both Lady Mandakini and Lady Nandini is amazed by their strong resemblance to each other."

"What's so surprising about this? One madwoman resembles another madwoman."

"Nandini disguises herself and pretends to be Mandakini's ghost to torture you."

Sundara Chola sat up in fury. "If that's true, I'll strangle that devil with my bare hands ..."

The agitated Aniruddha interrupted quickly: "Your Majesty, I have tested your patience. Punish me if you want, but don't talk about punishing Lady Nandini. She's not just Lord Ambalavan's wife ... she's also your daughter."

Sundara Chola was shocked for an instant, then he burst out laughing. "Aniruddha, I thought there is a madwoman in my palace today, but you are a bigger madman!"

Late at Night

JUST THEN, THE queen came in, followed by Kundavai and Vanathi who pulled Mandakini along with them; Poonkuzlali and a maid followed. Kundavai, an expert cosmetician, had transformed the wild-looking madwoman into a matchless beauty. She had instinctively combed Mandakini's hair in the style adopted by Nandini and they were stunned at the resemblance between the two women. Even the twenty-five-year difference in their ages did not show because of Mandakini's healthy forest lifestyle. Poonkuzlali was pleased to see the women's respect and affection for Mandakini.

In those times of frequent war, princes often risked their lives on the battlefield. To ensure that their clans were not wiped out, kings had several wives. The senior queen was expected to rise above petty jealousy and welcome the other wives. Vanamadevi was proud to have fulfilled her duty to her husband with regard to Mandakini.

The women smiled at the sound of Sundara Chola's laughter. Mandakini looked at him before bowing her head again. Sundara Chola's laughter stopped abruptly: he could not believe the transformation in

Mandakini. He noticed the slight differences between Mandakini and the figure which had haunted his nights. He began to take Aniruddha's words seriously.

Deciding to get to the truth of the matter, he hid his revulsion towards Mandakini and turned to Aniruddha. "Chief minister, these women seem to be enjoying each other's company; let them stay together in the palace. Sembiyan Madevi respects you. Go to Pazlayarai and bring her here. Send Thirumalai to Nagapattinam. I'll ask Lord Kalaanthaka to arrange for Lord Ambalavan and his wife to return immediately to Thanjavur."

"My lord, it will take several days for everyone to gather here. The rivers are in flood."

"After waiting all these years, a few more days won't matter. If Karikalan also comes, everything can be resolved. If he refuses this time, I'll have to go to him. We'll discuss that later. Don't let these family matters distract you from your storm relief work."

"Your Majesty," the chief minister said. "Relief work has begun." He bowed and left the room.

Seeing Mandakini alive lifted a great burden from Sundara Chola's mind. He was relieved that Arulmozli was in Nagapattinam and was confident that the monastery could withstand the storm. He was also amused at Aniruddha's suggestion that Nandini was his daughter. He chatted lightheartedly with the queen and Kundavai and questioned Poonkuzlali further about Arulmozli.

Poonkuzlali said, "Sir, may I go back to Kodikkarai? I need not worry about my aunt anymore."

Sundara Chola said, "Aren't you worried about your cousin who's ill? Stay here for a few days." For the first time in years, Sundara Chola slept peacefully that night. The women too slept peacefully in the adjoining room.

Only Mandakini, worrying about the vault and the secret passage, stayed awake. She had not finished breaking the Ravana statue's hands to seal the entrance to the tunnel. She looked around in the dim light of the night lamp, especially at the windows opening on to the upper terrace. Long after midnight, Mandakini saw a dreadful face peering through the window. Recognizing the face, she jumped up in horror and stared at the window: the face disappeared. She crept to the emperor's room. Sundara Chola slept peacefully. She examined the upper windows: no one was there. Mandakini went back to the next room, shook Poonkuzlali awake and signaled her to follow her. Poonkuzlali, devoted to her aunt, obeyed her without questions. Mandakini picked up a night lamp and headed to the Art Gallery.

Poonkuzlali worried, *Is she going to break the Ravana statue? If she does that, everyone will decide she's mad. I must stop her.* Poonkuzlali stopped short: she saw a man's head between Ravana's head and Mount Kailash. The next instant, it disappeared. *It's my imagination. It must be the play of lamplight on the shadows.*

Mandakini went to the Ravana statue and held the lamp so that its light fell on the gap between Ravana's head and the mountain. Poonkuzlali saw an opening. *Ah! This is a hidden entrance to some secret passage. That's why she was trying to break the statue's hands.* Mandakini gestured to Poonkuzlali to follow her and wriggled into the opening, taking the lamp with her. Poonkuzlali squirmed her way into the gap and disappeared behind her aunt. The Art Gallery was dark again.

In the morning, the women were shocked to find Mandakini and Poonkuzlali missing. After searching the palace, the garden and the Art Gallery, they told the king.

Sundara Chola said, "Good riddance to bad rubbish!" But in his heart, the king was worried.

I'll Plant the Tiger Flag on the Himalayas

EVERYONE IN KADAMBUR Palace was on tenterhooks since Aditya Karikalan's arrival. Karikalan often made them nervous by hinting at their plot to make Madurandaka king. Ambalavan could no longer put up with this and suggested that they bring up the matter openly before the prince.

Sambuvaraya put him off. "Patience, he's our guest, and a ruffian. What if things get out of hand? Let's wait for the right chance."

Karikalan solved the problem by bringing up the matter himself one day. "I came here to ask *Thatha* Ambalavan and Sambuvaraya for their advice on a particular matter. Three years ago, my father made me crown prince with your approval. Now I hear he wants to make Madurandaka his heir and calls me to Thanjavur to tell me this. I refuse to go there as I don't want to defy him to his face. Tell me, is it fair on my father's part to deny me the throne after all these years?"

Everyone was shocked at this direct question. Ambalavan cleared his throat and tried to buy time. "Prince, what does your grandfather, Malayaman, say?"

"You know the old man: he'll kill my mother and me before he lets anyone deprive me of the throne. He's gathering an army to ensure I become the next king. But I won't listen to my grandfather. I'll agree to what you say," the prince replied meekly.

Forced to reply, Ambalavan said, "It's our duty to point out that, in the interests of the kingdom and the dictates of justice, we must come to a compromise. Prince Madurandaka has a right to the throne. The Chola kingdom is vast: we recommend we split it into two—Prince Madurandaka gets the part south of the Kollidam and you get the north. If you agree to this, I myself will meet the emperor and get his consent."

Karikalan roared with laughter. "Sharing the kingdom is like sharing one's lawfully wedded wife. Old men like you may agree to this, but I'll never agree."

Ambalavan's eyes blazed with fury. He jumped up and prepared to draw his sword.

"*Thatha*," said Karikalan majestically. "Hear me out. Our ancestors gave their lives to build this kingdom—they'll curse us if we divide it. I'll never consent to this. I'm ready to give up my claim to the Tiger Throne. Madurandaka too has a just claim. He can rule the entire kingdom, but on one condition. I want an army of three lakh soldiers, equipped and armed to invade the north; I want provisions for one year and a fleet of three hundred warships. I'll march overland with the army while Parthibendran sails along the coast with the fleet. We'll meet at the mouth of the Ganga and go further north. Like my ancestor, Karikal Valavan, I'll plant the Tiger Flag on the Himalayas. I'll become emperor of all the land I conquer north of the Krishna river, or I'll die a hero's death and reach the warrior's paradise. Sambuvaraya! *Thatha!* What do you say? Do you accept my condition?"

The two old men were stumped at his direct question. Ambalavan stammered, "Prince ... who are we ... what right do we have ... it's the emperor who must ..."

Karikalan jumped up angrily. "Who do you think you are fooling? I know my father is a prisoner in Thanjavur Fort–he's a puppet in your hands. Can anyone meet my father without your permission? Didn't you force my father to issue an arrest warrant for my brother? The people accuse you of murdering Arulmozli and throwing him into the sea ..."

Ambalavan shouted, "Who makes these false accusations? I'll cut them into pieces ..."

"Will you cut ten lakh people into pieces and make the Chola kingdom one large crematorium? The people are fools who believe and spread rumors. You have supported the Cholas for generations and I don't believe you would commit such an evil crime. However great a warrior you may be, I doubt you can command the waves and the storm. Maybe it was the work of the Pandian sorcerers; maybe it was Arulmozli's fate to prove the astrologers wrong. I don't hold you responsible for my brother's death. But don't expect me to believe you need the emperor's or chief minister's approval: they can't defy you. Of course, if you tell me that you must get Grandmother Nandini's approval ..."

Kandamaran intervened and stammered, "Lord, they are guests in my house ..."

Eyes blazing with fury, Karikalan walked up to him. "Of course, I must be careful in your house and in your presence! Why are you shivering? Have you caught the Lankan fever without even going there?"

Vandhiya Devan said, "Prince, Kandamaran does not have the fever— he's trembling with rage because you called Lady Nandini a grandmother."

Kandamaran gave Devan a look of hatred and touched his sword. Parthibendran held him back and whispered to him. Kandamaran calmed down but shook in anger for a while. Karikalan laughed at him and turned back to Ambalavan. "Young bulls often strain at their leashes: ignore him. If you're my grandfather, Lady Nandini's my grandmother. When you and your wife don't mind, I wonder why this young boy is angry. Let's get back to the point. Don't use my father as an excuse: you're the one who controls the Chola treasury. Men will rush to join my army and the ships are not a problem. Only you and Prince Madurandaka need to agree. What do you say?"

Ambalavan cleared his throat. "Prince Madurandaka must agree to your proposal and you must see your father before you start on your victorious northern campaign. Let's go to Thanjavur ..."

"That's out of the question. If I go to Thanjavur, I may not be able to defy my father or go against the wishes of my mother and sister. No, this issue must be resolved in Kadambur. Bring Madurandaka here. We'll decide and then inform my father. When my army is ready, I'll go to Thanjavur and take leave of my parents. Or, my father can crown Madurandaka now and come to Kanchipuram to stay in the golden palace I have built for him."

Ambalavan looked at Sambuvaraya whose eyes were fixed on a spot on the ceiling. Realizing that he could expect no help from that quarter, Ambalavan cleared his throat and said, "Prince, what can I say against your orders? Very well."

"My thanks, *thatha*," Karikalan said. "Go at once and bring Madurandaka here: this time, bring him openly by elephant or chariot—not in a screened palanquin." Karikalan turned to Kandamaran. "Kandamaran, let Lord Ambalavan go to Thanjavur–we'll go hunting. I must polish my archery skills; I haven't touched my bow for years. Shall we hunt in the Kolli Hills?"

Sambuvaraya spoke up. "Sir, the forests near Veeranam Lake are rich in wildlife. The trophies in our Hunters' Hall are from there. It's also at a convenient distance. We can leave in the morning and be back here for dinner."

"Very well, as long as I'm your guest, your wish is my command. Shall we take your daughter, Manimekalai, with us? She adds life to any gathering."

"I have no objection," Sambuvaraya replied. "Let's leave it to Manimekalai."

Kandamaran protested. "Why take women with us? We can't concentrate on the hunt if we have to worry about their safety. Moreover, Lady Nandini needs company here."

"Kandamaran is always concerned about Lady Nandini. Let the women stay here; we men will hunt. See that the huntsmen are ready early in the morning. Let tonight's entertainment be short so that we sleep soon." Karikalan took Devan's hand and said, "Come, let's go to our room."

Parthibendran and Kandamaran followed them with jealous eyes; Sambuvaraya went to give the huntsmen orders; Ambalavan went to the women's quarters in search of Nandini.

You Must Kill Him!

AMBALAVAN WAS ENTHUSIASTIC over the results of the meeting. When he came to Kadambur, he thought that it would be simple for him and Sambuvaraya to control the young Aditya Karikalan with promises and threats. He knew the danger of crowning Madurandaka king of the entire country: Malayaman and Velir would be up in arms, and if Karikalan joined them, civil war was unavoidable. Who knew what the outcome would be? The people would support Sundara Chola's sons and Sembiyan Madevi would oppose her own son. There could be mutiny in the Pandian and Chera kingdoms. It was better to let Madurandaka rule the southern part of the kingdom, with Thanjavur as his capital, and then slowly work from there. Velir's influence could be reduced; Malayaman could be taught a lesson; Karikalan was a thug who would meet an early death. And then, all the problems would be solved. For now, division of the kingdom was the wisest course. Ambalavan had reached this conclusion with Nandini's advice.

But nothing had gone as planned. The insolent Karikalan did not respect the old men. Ambalavan could not bear his mockery and double meanings. Karikalan calling him 'Thatha,' was like a poisoned barb to him. To cap it all, Ambalavan was unhappy with Sambuvaraya's attitude: instead of helping him deal with Karikalan's insolence, Sambuvaraya kept quiet. Maybe he did not want anything unfortunate to happen under his roof.

Ambalavan had no idea whether Karikalan was sincere or just mocking him. *What if he wants Madurandaka here for some evil purpose? What if he plans to take over Kadambur Palace with Malayaman's help?* He decided that going to Thanjavur was the best option. Kalaanthaka was a wise man and Ambalavan could ask his younger brother for advice. If necessary, he could ask him to raise an army and come to the Kollidam shore. Come what may, he must take Nandini to the safety of Thanjavur.

Ambalavan's spirits rose once he made up his mind. But his good mood evaporated at the laughter coming from Nandini's room. *She never laughs like this in Thanjavur. Who's with her?*

At Ambalavan's entrance, Manimekalai, who was with Nandini, covered her mouth and stifled her laughter as she ran from the room. Nandini stopped laughing and became her dignified self. "Lord, you are here: are the discussions over?"

"Nandini, why was that girl laughing so much?"

"Must I tell you? Manimekalai could hear some of your discussion from the adjoining room. She was laughing at the prince's mocking reference to grandfathers and grandmothers."

"The wicked girl! And why were you laughing along with her?"

"I laughed with her, knowing I could weep once I was alone. You came here before that." Nandini wiped away the tears that flowed down her cheeks.

"I was wrong to bring you here among these fools. Be patient for one night: we leave for Thanjavur at dawn." Ambalavan told Nandini what had happened at the meeting.

"*Swami,* I won't leave Kadambur until I teach Aditya Karikalan a lesson for insulting you. That arrogant prince must apologize to you or you must kill him."

"Nandini, our clan and the Cholas have been friends for six generations. Can I kill Sundara Chola's son just because that foolish young boy blabbers nonsense?" Ambalavan was agitated because he himself had often found his hand on his sword hilt at Karikalan's barbed speech. Nandini's words only openly reinforced his own desire.

Nandini frowned and her face darkened. "Lord, you hesitate to pick up your sword because you are bound to the Cholas by ties of duty and friendship. But I have no such obligations. If Aditya Karikalan refuses to apologize to you, I'll kill him with my own hands!"

His Days Are Numbered

THE ROOM SHOOK with Ambalavan's laughter. He swelled with pride at the thought that Nandini cared so much about his dignity that she was ready to kill anyone who insulted him.

"Lord, why are you laughing? Don't you believe me?"

"I'm laughing at the thought of you holding a knife when I have my two strong arms."

"Lord, I know the strength of your arms which crown and protect the Chola kings and killed countless enemies on the battlefield. But others have forgotten; foolish boys mock you and call you an old man. If I have to defend my chastity or your dignity, my soft hands will find the strength to hold a sword. They became strong when you held them as we walked around the sacred marriage fire. Look …" Nandini opened a box, parted the clothes in it and took out a shining sword which she lifted effortlessly and held above her head.

Ambalavan was shocked. "I thought you had your dresses and ornaments in that box!"

"This sword is my greatest ornament: it guards my virtue and my husband's reputation."

"There's no need for that as long as I'm alive. I'll always be with you."

"You are busy and can't always be with me. I must be ready to defend myself. This once, you must go to Thanjavur without me."

Ambalavan frowned. "Why so stubborn? Why must I leave you here?"

"First, if you take me with you, these fools will mock us: 'The old man does not trust his wife.' Second, Karikalan loves Manimekalai; I hear he even suggested she goes hunting with the men. Your friend Sambuvaraya now dreams of his daughter being the next empress. He has forgotten all the old plans."

"Just two months ago, we took an oath to make Madurandaka king and now Sambuvaraya is ready to go back on his word. What kind of a man is he?"

"That's why I want to stay back. I'll find out if these men hatch any new plots in your absence and foil their plans: that's why a wife is called a man's 'life companion.'"

"Whatever be your reason, I don't want to leave you here with these fools and villains."

"I have Manimekalai—she'll do anything for me. If I ask her to kill Aditya Karikalan with this sword, she won't hesitate to do it. If you want, I can prove it now …"

Ambalavan shuddered. "I know your power. Karikalan's a foolish young man—ignore his rambling. If he wants to marry Manimekalai, let him."

Nandini's eyes were far away. "I'm fond of Manimekalai and think of her as my own younger sister. How can I encourage her to marry someone who's fated to die young?"

Ambalavan became even more nervous. "Nandini, I was once captain of the king's bodyguards. I have sworn an oath to protect the king and his family. If you harm Karikalan, it will be said, 'The wicked old man did this just because he couldn't ignore a young boy's thoughtless words.' My family's reputation, earned over six generations, will be ruined."

Nandini smiled mysteriously. "You know Goddess Durga has given me extraordinary powers. I proved it when I showed you that Sundara Chola was responsible for a woman's death when he was young. Now, I see Karikalan's days are numbered. There's danger ahead of him. He won't die by my hands or yours. A friend's arrow may strike him down; a wild animal may attack him; a woman's dagger may kill him while he sleeps. I promise you I won't kill him with my hands. You married me when I was a nobody: I'll see that nothing damages your reputation." Nandini looked up at him with melting black eyes. "But you must leave at once. There's nothing you can do to prevent his death. If you're here when he dies, they'll accuse you of killing him. If you take me with you, they'll suspect you knew what was going to happen. Do you trust me?"

The poor old man surrendered to her beautiful eyes.

Water Sports

BECAUSE OF THE ancient enmity between the Malayaman and Sambuvaraya clans, Sambuvaraya was against Malayaman's grandson, Karikalan, ascending the Tiger Throne. Karikalan's arrogance and disrespect towards the chieftains aggravated Sambuvaraya's dislike. Sambuvaraya joined Ambalavan's conspiracy to make Madurandaka the next king.

But after Karikalan's arrival at Kadambur Palace, Sambuvaraya's attitude changed. Karikalan spent a lot of time with the women and often praised the lively Manimekalai, who was in high spirits these days. Sambuvaraya decided that Manimekalai loved Karikalan. He began to dream of his daughter becoming the next empress; his grandsons would be heirs to the Chola throne. *Why should I stand in the way of my daughter's advancement?* He no longer wanted Manimekalai to marry Madurandaka who already had two wives. The elder, Kalaanthaka's daughter, had a son. If Madurandaka became king, Kalaanthaka's grandson would be the heir to the throne. Manimekalai would be little more than a servant in Thanjavur Palace. And making Madurandaka king was not easy: Sembiyan Madevi was against it; the people disliked him; Malayaman and Velir must be defeated. *Why get involved in all this trouble?* On the other hand, Karikalan was already the crown prince. Only the obstinate Pazluvur brothers stood in the way of his becoming king. *The old man is his wife's slave. God alone knows how long he'll live. Why should I trust him and risk everything?*

Sambuvaraya was aware of his oath to support Madurandaka. But he was confident that he could find a way around this: Madurandaka was a simpleton who could be convinced to renounce his claim to the throne or Sembiyan Madevi's consent could be made compulsory. Sambuvaraya enthusiastically made arrangements for Ambalavan's trip to Thanjavur. In his absence, he could sound out Karikalan and make good use of any opportunity which came his way.

Ambalavan left for Thanjavur and Karikalan and his friends went hunting. Kandamaran, suspecting that Karikalan's interest in Manimekalai was only for Nandini's benefit, refused to let his sister accompany the men. His hatred for the prince grew.

The palace seemed empty after the men left.

Nandini said, "Men are a nuisance, but we miss them when they are away."

Manimekalai said, "I love to watch the hunt and often accompany my father and brother. I wonder why Kandamaran didn't let me go with them—maybe it's because you hate hunting."

"I hate the sight of blood. But that's not why Kandamaran refused to take you along. He wants to keep you away from one of the men in the hunting party."

Manimekalai's cheeks dimpled. "To hell with the men, *akka!* Let's have nothing to do with them. Let's go to the pavilion on the shore of the lake. We can swim there."

Nandini agreed and Manimekalai got Sambuvaraya's permission. Dense forest stood on the western end of Veeranam Lake; the water was shallow near the shore and dotted with small islands with thick vegetation. One of these islands had a pavilion with steps leading to the water. This was a favorite picnic and bathing spot for the Kadambur women. To reach the pavilion one had to walk around the lake for ten miles and so the women always had the place to themselves.

Nandini and Manimekalai went to the island by boat with two servants rowing them. Once there, they sat and chatted on the pavilion steps while the servants prepared their meal. Manimekalai entertained Nandini with her mischievous mimicry of Ambalavan, Karikalan, Kandamaran, Parthibendran and Devan. Nandini laughed but it was clear that her mind was somewhere else.

Suddenly, Manimekalai jumped up and pulled out the knife at her waist. "*Akka*, we missed the hunt but the hunt has come to us!"

The alarmed Nandini looked in the direction Manimekalai faced: a leopard crouched on the low branch of a tree, ready to pounce. At the same time, they heard horses splashing through the water.

Karikalan's Murderous Frenzy

NO ONE WHO saw Aditya Karikalan hunt that day would believe that he had not touched his bow for years. His arrows felled hares, bears, deer and leopards; he shot eagles and falcons. His murderous frenzy increased as the hours went by. The others in the party only served to bring the animals out of hiding.

When Kandamaran shot his arrow at a bear which threatened Karikalan, the prince turned on him and asked, "Kandamaran, were you trying to kill the bear … or me?"

Kandamaran's face darkened. He joined Parthibendran at the rear and complained, "Isn't this enough? Does he want to kill every animal in the forest? Tell him it's time to go home."

Parthibendran calmed Kandamaran. "Giving up the right to a kingdom is not easy. Be happy he's venting his anger on the animals and not on us. Let him tire; it's better not to interfere."

By the time the sun was directly overhead, everyone was exhausted and eager to rest before heading back to the palace. But Karikalan spurred his tired horse deeper into the forest, with Vandhiya Devan riding beside him. Devan, who was not an expert archer, was armed only with his spear. Suddenly a loud growl shook the forest.

Kandamaran was terrified. "Aiyo! It's a wild boar! Tell the prince to stop."

"Why are you so scared of a wild pig?" Parthibendran asked

"The wild boar in this forest attack bears and elephants. Arrows and spears can't pierce their thick hides. Lord, stop! Stop!" Kandamaran shouted. The bushes shook as if in a whirlwind and two wild boars, as large and black as small elephants, charged out. As Kandamaran shouted, "Careful, lord!" the huntsmen beat their drums and shrieked as if their lives depended on it. The two wild pigs scattered in different directions. Kandamaran said, "Prince, let them go. It's difficult to hunt wild boar without a pack of hunting dogs."

Karikalan ignored him and shot an arrow at one of the pigs. "Ahah!" he shouted in triumph as the arrow found its mark. The boar shook itself—the arrow splintered and the pig charged into the forest. Kandamaran's laugh was tinged with mockery.

Karikalan turned to him. "Kandamaran, a challenge: Vandhiya Devan and I will hunt one boar while you and Parthibendran chase the other. We won't return to the palace without killing both the pigs."

The prince spurred his horse after the boar, with Devan behind him.

For a little distance, the crushed bushes were a pointer to the boar. But they soon came to a jungle stream and lost track of the animal. As they wondered whether to cross the stream or ride along its bank, they saw a boat on the lake. They could make out that the occupants were women, but the boat was too far away for them to identify them. The boat disappeared towards an island near the shore.

"Could that be the women from Kadambur Palace?" Karikalan asked.

"Maybe, but why would they come this far?"

"You're right." Karikalan paused. "Are you sure Lord Ambalavan left this morning?"

"Absolutely. I saw him ride out of the palace gate on his elephant."

"Was he alone?"

"Yes, the old man was alone. Lady Nandini did not go with him."

Karikalan said, "I conspired to send Lord Ambalavan away so that Nandini is alone. But when I think of meeting her, I'm terrified."

"Lord, that's only natural. All these years, you had a certain regard for Nandini; now you know she's your sister. To complicate matters, she's involved in the Pandian plot to wipe out your family. Explaining all this to her will not be easy. I had an opportunity but could not tell her ..."

"My friend, it's hard to believe what you told me but when I think back, it all makes sense. When Sembiyan Madevi forbid me from having anything to do with Nandini, she did not tell me the entire truth ... if she had, we could have avoided so much trouble."

"Maybe Sembiyan Madevi thinks Nandini is just some deaf-mute woman's child; she may not know Nandini is Sundara Chola's daughter."

She's Not a Woman

KARIKALAN SIGHED. "LET'S not talk about the past. We have lost the challenge: the boar has disappeared. I brought you here alone to discuss what can be done. I'm terrified to tell Nandini about our new relationship. I can't meet her eyes and if by chance I look at her, I see her begging me to spare Veerapandian's life. My heart breaks to think my own sister begged me to spare her lover. Do you think Nandini doesn't know the truth?"

"Prince, if she knew the truth, she would never join the Pandians against your family; she would not try to make a little boy the Chola emperor; she would not swear an oath on a sword."

"I'm amazed she let you live after seeing all that."

"Maybe it was a woman's instinctive compassion."

"A woman's heart can be filled with treachery. I don't know why she let you live, but I know why she asked me to come here: she plans to kill me to avenge Veerapandian's death."

"Lord, Princess Kundavai and the chief minister sent me to you because of this but you insisted on coming to Kadambur."

"No one can defy destiny. Do you think Kandamaran aimed his arrow at me or at the bear?"

"I didn't see him, lord. But I'm sure he would never stoop to shooting you from behind, especially when you are his guest and the crown prince. He's not a traitor."

"My friend, the seductive power of a beautiful woman can make a traitor of even the best man."

"Lord, I know the power of a beautiful woman but I'll never let it make me a traitor."

"Ahah! Manimekalai's a good girl. She'll never push you into betrayal."

"After seeing the radiant full moon, how can I find a glow worm attractive?"

"Who's this full moon?"

"Prince, don't be angry … I'm referring to Princess Kundavai."

"You rascal! Kings are waiting to marry my sister; you should not even think about her. What's the point of being angry with you? I'm the one who sent you to Kundavai. But don't let Parthibendran hear this: he dreams of marrying Kundavai and becoming king of Thondainadu."

"Both Parthibendran and Kandamaran are now Nandini's slaves."

"I noticed: that's why I'm cautious with them."

"I think it would be best to tell Lady Nandini the truth at the earliest."

"My friend, I don't have the courage. Will you speak to her on my behalf?"

"Lord, Lady Nandini won't believe me: I have fooled her once before."

"But how can I meet Nandini alone—she's in the women's quarters."

"Manimekalai will help me arrange for you to meet Lady Nandini."

"You have Manimekalai eating out of your hands. Whatever happens, I'll make you happy by marrying you to her."

"Lord, I see Manimekalai as my sister. I suspect you love her. Except for Princess Kundavai, no woman is as intelligent and good as Manimekalai. If you marry her, all our problems will be solved: Sambuvaraya and Kandamaran will support us; the Pazluvur brothers will be isolated; Lady Nandini's power will decrease; Prince Madurandaka will forget his claim to the throne. We can destroy the chieftains' conspiracy and the Pandian plot at one go and ..."

"*Thambi,* I did not come to Kadambur to get married. A great danger lies ahead: when Lord Ambalavan comes back with Madurandaka, he'll bring a large army with him."

"In that case, why don't we send word to Lord Malayaman to raise an army and march here?"

"I want to burn Kadambur Palace and hang the conspirators at the entrance. I'm controlling my temper because my father is in their hands. If you had brought my parents to Kanchipuram ..."

"Prince, delivering your message itself was difficult."

"I wonder whether I'll ever welcome them to my golden palace; I wonder whether I'll leave Kadambur alive." He paused. "Will you go to Malayaman?"

"Forgive me, lord. I have promised your sister to stay by your side and guard you. Why don't you send Parthibendran? He's bored and idle here."

"Yes, he pines for Nandini all the time. I never thought Parthibendran would fall under a woman's spell. I'll send him to Malayaman. I fear no man who attacks me face-to-face or from behind, like Kandamaran: the only thing I fear is the treachery buried in a woman's heart. Every mysterious look from Nandini is a spear piercing my heart. I tremble in fear ..."

"Lord, Lady Nandini must be feared: I know the hatred in her heart. I'm afraid she let me go only because she plans to use me for some evil purpose. But once she knows you're her brother, there'll be no need to fear her."

"You're clever, but you don't understand a woman's heart. When Nandini knows she's Sundara Chola's daughter, her anger will multiply a hundred times."

"In that case, let me talk to Nandini. I'll try to pacify her."

"That's impossible, my friend. There's only one way to save the Chola dynasty: either Nandini or I must die ... or both of us."

"Prince, what dreadful talk!"

"It's okay to sacrifice one person to save a dynasty, even if that person is a woman or my sister. She's not a woman–she's an enchantress. If I don't kill her, the Chola kingdom will shatter ... what's that?!"

The bushes shook near them. They rode closer and saw a wild boar and a leopard fighting.

"Ahah, here's the boar we were searching for!" Karikalan said.

"It looks like the leopard will finish our job for us," Devan replied.

The two men watched the fight. The leopard used its teeth and claws but the boar's thick hide was impenetrable. The boar charged the leopard, knocked it down, dashed it against the tree roots and tore its skin with its tusks: the leopard collapsed.

"*Thambi*, the leopard is dead!" cried Karikalan. "The boar will attack us next. Be ready!" Karikalan's arrow struck the boar's neck: it shook itself and charged his horse. Before the prince could nock another arrow to his bow, his horse's rear leg caught in a tree's roots and the horse stumbled and fell. Karikalan was trapped under his horse. The boar moved back and charged again.

Where's the Leopard?

IN THE BLINK of an eye, Vandhiya Devan charged forward on his horse and plunged his spear into the wild boar's back. The spear grazed the animal's hide and fell to the ground. The boar shook itself and charged towards Devan. Devan leapt from his horse to the low branch of a nearby tree. The boar butted his horse which stumbled and ran away. Karikalan struggled to come out from under his horse; Devan clung to the tree; the wild boar stood between them ...

The prince may be badly hurt. He's not armed; he needs time to get out from under his horse ... I must distract the boar. Devan shook the branch on which he was and shrieked at the top of his voice. His ploy worked: the boar turned to him and charged. *Let it charge and bang against the tree.* But just then, there was a crack and the branch on which he sat gave way. Devan immediately jumped to another branch but he could catch it only with one hand. The branch was thin and bent under his weight. Devan hung from the branch with one hand, his legs swinging in the air ... his hold began to slip. *This is the end; at least I saved the prince. Princess Kundavai will be pleased ... she'll shed a few tears for me.* Devan closed his eyes and fell from the tree, immediately losing consciousness.

He recovered to find Karikalan splashing water on his face. He cried, "Lord, you're alive!"

"Yes, thanks to you and your spear. Look ..." Karikalan pointed to the dead boar.

"Kandamaran was right about boars. How much trouble the animal caused! How did you kill it?"

"While you distracted it, I came out from under my horse and picked up your spear. I threw it on the poor animal with all my pent-up anger. Its squeal was enough to rupture my ear drums. But it did not die only because of the spear: you fell right on top of it ... it died of shock."

Karikalan and Devan roared with laughter at this.

The boar broke my fall; that's why I'm alive, Devan thought.

Abruptly, Karikalan asked, "*Thambi,* did you throw your spear at me or at the pig?"

Devan was indignant. "If you believed that, you would not have killed the boar and saved me."

"And if you had not distracted it, the boar would have killed me. But nowadays, I'm suspicious about everyone and everything. I can't shake off the thought my death is near ..."

"Come, lord. We have won the challenge: let's drag the boar back to the palace."

"Let's not go into the forest to join those fools. Let's cross the lake and get back to Kadambur. We saw a boat some time back ... let's look for it."

"What about the horses? We can't abandon them to the wild animals ..." Devan stopped and started in alarm. "Where's the leopard?!"

They looked around. "There!" pointed Karikalan.

The stream narrowed as it went to meet the lake. At that point, a fallen tree formed a bridge from one side to the other. The leopard was slowly making its way across the tree.

The men shouted together, "The women in the boat!"

"They must be on the island adjoining the stream," Devan pointed out.

"A wounded leopard is very dangerous," Karikalan said. "We must kill it."

"The water is shallow; the horses can wade across the stream."

The men climbed on their horses and forded the stream. The water level was low, but the horses had a tough time stumbling through the mud and slush. They reached the shore of the island. The two men looked around as they advanced. Karikalan held his bow and Devan had his spear. Their hair stood on end as a scream split the air: "Lady, a leopard!" One of the servants cooking in the pavilion had spotted the animal at the same time as Manimekalai.

The men spurred their horses in the direction of the scream and were shocked at the sight which met their eyes. Nandini and Manimekalai were in the water and the leopard crouched on a low branch spreading towards them from the shore. Devan was reluctant to use his spear in case it hit the women, but the prince did not hesitate: he aimed his arrow and let go. The arrow pierced the leopard's belly and the animal roared and jumped on the women in the water. The next second was a jumble of images ... the leopard and the two women disappeared under the water only to resurface at three different places ... the water reddened with blood.

Love and Revenge

THE MEN JUMPED off their horses and ran along the shore. It was clear from the way the leopard floated on the current that it was dead.

The men rushed into the water to check on the women. Devan waded towards Manimekalai—something kept him away from Nandini. Manimekalai was unhurt; she was just a little breathless from being underwater. Thrilled to see Devan coming towards her, she closed her eyes tightly and waited. She did not see Karikalan stop Devan and send him to Nandini instead. Two hands lifted her from the water and gently laid her on the ground; when Karikalan tested her breath with a finger under her nose, she slowly opened her eyes. When she saw the prince, she jumped up and moved to sit a little away from him.

Karikalan laughed at the disappointment in her eyes. "Manimekalai, do I disgust you so much?"

"Lord, any woman would be shy at a stranger's touch," she replied.

"Am I a stranger?" Karikalan asked. "Our marriage is being considered seriously."

"Until that happens, you are a stranger to me."

"Very well, tell me if you would like to marry me."

"Lord, this is something you should discuss with my father; it makes me uncomfortable."

Karikalan laughed. "Manimekalai, you clever girl! Don't try to fool me. You closed your eyes thinking it was Vandhiya Devan who carried you. Poor girl … now, you are disappointed."

Manimekalai picked up courage and said, "Lord, you know my heart—why do you test me?"

"I know Vandhiya Devan's heart too; he's not worthy of you. Look at him … look at the happiness on Nandini's face."

Manimekalai looked where Karikalan pointed and felt a prick of jealousy. Nandini did not close her eyes as Devan carried her to the shore, nor was she in a hurry to leave his arms. But Devan hurriedly laid her on the ground as if she was scorching fire. The leopard had clawed Nandini's shoulder and blood dripped from the wound. A strange fear gripped Devan and he shuddered.

Nandini smiled. "Sir, why are you so afraid? Do you think I'm the leopard, or do you regret saving me?"

"I shuddered at the danger you were in."

"Maybe it's because you have a guilty conscience. I gave you my signet ring to help you enter Thanjavur Fort and I protected you when you sneaked into my rooms. And what did you do in return? You left the fort secretly. I asked you to come back to me after delivering Princess Kundavai's message but you didn't keep your word…"

"It's wrong but I had my reasons. I'm bound to obey Aditya Karikalan."

"Yes, you need his permission to rescue a woman from a leopard and from the water. I saw how eager the prince was to rescue Manimekalai. He would be happy to see me dead."

"Lady, don't say such things. The prince is in Kadambur only because you asked him to come."

"And you could not stop him from coming: you will always fail if you interfere with my plans." Nandini's words increased Devan's confusion. He tried to read her face but it was as pleasant as always. She continued. "You were caught in the forest at midnight. Again, I saved you from my men. You are the most ungrateful man on earth!"

"Lady, I swear I'll always be grateful to you."

"How can I believe that? You did not try to meet me after coming to Kadambur …"

"How can I meet you alone? You are the wife of Lord Ambalavan, the chancellor."

"Don't call me his wife. If a woman is forced to stay with a man, does that make her his wife?"

"But …"

"You wonder why I let myself be forced into this marriage. You have not helped me with my love—will you at least help me take revenge on my enemy?"

"Lady! What do I have to do with your love or your revenge?"

"I can't tell you now … meet me in my room at midnight tomorrow. You escaped from those rooms once before so you can find your way there again."

Devan was shocked, but Nandini smiled as usual.

You Are My Sister

KARIKALAN AND MANIMEKALAI joined them. The prince saw the claw marks on Nandini's cheek and shoulder. "Aiyo! That wretched animal has hurt you!"

"Yes, lord. But it has hurt only my body, not my heart."

These words pierced Karikalan's heart. Before he could say anything, Manimekalai hurried to Nandini and cried, "*Akka*, these are deep scratches! Thank goodness I have medicine with me."

Nandini said, "This is nothing. Do you have medicine to heal the wounds in my heart?"

"Oh yes. There's medicine for that too," Manimekalai said as she led Nandini to the pavilion.

Karikalan and Devan followed them and sat on a stone platform near the pavilion. Devan said, "Sir, let's go. If we stay here with the women, Kandamaran and his father may take offense."

"I don't care. I want to make sure the women have not taken offense. We'll leave after that."

The women came back wearing dry clothes. Nandini's wounds were covered by an ointment.

"We waited to say goodbye," Karikalan said.

"Nonsense! You must stay and have lunch with us or Manimekalai will never forgive me."

"We'll stay on one condition," Karikalan replied. "Manimekalai must show us the medicine that heals wounds of the heart."

"Why don't you guess what it is?" Nandini suggested.

"Maybe she's referring to time which heals all wounds," Karikalan said.

"No, there are wounds which time cannot heal," Nandini said.

Devan said, "There's a good medicine for women's wounds: tears!"

"Vandhiya Devan never misses an opportunity to insult women," Nandini said. "Some wounds make one so emotionally drained, one can't even shed tears."

"If we're both wrong, why don't you tell us the answer?" Devan said.

"Manimekalai, aren't you talking about the power of music to heal all wounds?" Nandini asked.

"Yes, *akka*. How did you guess?"

"Didn't I tell you I'm a magician? Do you men agree music can heal all wounds?"

"Yes," said Karikalan. "I remember Kandamaran saying Manimekalai is an expert *yazl* player."

"Yes, and she has brought her *yazl*. You saved us from the leopard. You must let us thank you by sharing our lunch and listening to Manimekalai's music," Nandini insisted.

Ignoring Devan's signal to refuse, Karikalan said, "Your wish is our command."

"Manimekalai, your wish has come true," Nandini said. "Go and see to the lunch."

Manimekalai went to supervise the servants.

Devan looked around. "The leopard is alive!" he exclaimed. "Look!"

"What!" cried Karikalan. "We saw its corpse floating on the water."

The women's boat was tied to a branch within calling distance from where they stood: they saw the leopard clinging to the boat with its fore paws, trying to climb in.

"Sir, let's go and finish it off —a wounded leopard is dangerous," Devan said.

"Two men to deal with a wounded leopard?" Nandini mocked. "Let's send Manimekalai. She'll finish it off with her little dagger."

"My friend, Lady Nandini questions our courage. Why don't you go alone?" Karikalan said.

"I should cut the wounded leopard's head and throw it at Lady Nandini's feet as an offering. Maybe that will prove our courage to her satisfaction," Devan replied before stalking off.

Karikalan laughed. "Did you hear what the rascal said? Does it need courage to chop off a wounded leopard's head?" He stopped abruptly at the look on Nandini's face. In a choked voice, he said, "Nandini, I'm here only because you sent word that you have forgotten the past."

"How can I forget the past? Have you forgotten?"

"You wept and asked for a boon … mad with blood lust, I turned you down. I'll never forget that. Why did you ask me to come?"

"You refused to come to Thanjavur for three years. You have not visited your father who's ill."

"He's not only my father, Nandini."

"He's also father to Princess Kundavai and Prince Arulmozli. But it's you he wants to see. He heard that you stay away from Thanjavur because of me ... do you want to add to my troubles?"

"But it's true. I stay away from Thanjavur because of you."

"In that case, I'll leave Thanjavur. Come see your father and take your place as king."

"Nandini, I have no wish to be king. Madurandaka can be king; you and the Pazluvur brothers can advise him. I don't want to chase you from Pazluvur palace."

"Sir, isn't Thanjavur big enough for both of us? We don't have to see each other."

"Yes, but we can't stop thinking of each other. Didn't you say we can't forget the past?"

"We can't forget but can't we forgive?"

"When I left Kanchipuram, I planned to ask your forgiveness. But I heard something on the way: now I know I don't deserve your forgiveness."

"You have always been kind to me. Even when we were children, you fought with Princess Kundavai on my behalf, although she's your sister."

"Nandini, you too are my sister—I'm your brother."

"Your chivalry makes you call me your sister because I'm another man's wife. How can I consider the crown prince my brother?"

"Nandini, you don't understand ... you are really my sister. You are a princess."

Nandini laughed. "I don't know which one of us is mad! Are you mocking me?"

"Look at me, Nandini. Do I look as if I'm mocking you?"

"Look at me, lord. Do I look like a princess?"

"Nandini, I have been amazed by your beauty from the time you were a five-year-old girl. Only recently, I discovered the reason for it. My grandmother, Kalyani, is renowned for her beauty; even now, at the age of seventy, her beauty dazzles the eye. You have inherited her beauty through my father, Sundara Chola."

"Am I mad? Or is there something wrong with my ears?"

"Neither. You are my father's daughter: you are my sister. Before he married my mother, my father loved a woman living on an island in Sri Lanka. You are her daughter."

Nandini stared at Karikalan in shock. "Did Vandhiya Devan tell you this?"

"Yes, but it was Kundavai who sent word about this through him."

"Ahah, she has always tried to separate us! It looks like she'll never give up."

"You are wrong. I did not understand why Sembiyan Madevi tried to keep us apart when we were children: now I understand. She should have told us the truth. They have been unfair to you and hurt me. Anyway, let bygones be bygones. If we can't forget the past, let's forgive …"

"Lord, is this the only story Vandhiya Devan told you?"

"Why do you call it a story? Don't you believe it?"

"Is it easy to believe? But tell me, what else did Vandhiya Devan say?"

Karikalan hesitated. "He also said you were part of a Pandian plot to destroy the Cholas; he said you have sworn an oath on a sword with a fish symbol on its hilt; he said you crowned a little boy king at a ceremony in a forest. Forget all that, Nandini. I'll make amends for all the injustice done to you."

"Lord, if you believe all this, why didn't you tell me earlier?"

"I was confused. I needed time to get used to our new relationship and had to find the opportunity to talk to you alone. Luckily, the wild boar and leopard gave me the opportunity today." He paused. "My sister, can you forgive me for hurting you in the past?"

"Prince, I'll forgive you for all your past betrayals and mistakes but I'll never forgive you for what you did today."

"Aiyo! I have done nothing today."

"Do you see that villain?"

"Do you mean Vandhiya Devan?"

"Yes, the man who's returning empty-handed now. He met me once in Thanjavur. He said he was ready to fall at my feet and worship me; he ran away when I called my guards. Because I would not give in to his lust, he made up these stories about me. He told me he would bring me your head if I asked him to. Now, he's afraid I'll tell you everything.

That's why he tried to stop you from coming to Kadambur; that's why he stays by your side all the time." Her eyes blazed with fury. "That wicked man … that man I would not touch even with my feet … you made that man carry me and touch my body …"

The prince's head whirled. "My sister! Nandini! I don't know what to believe. Can Vandhiya Devan be so wicked? I was thinking of getting him married to that foolish Manimekalai …"

"Lord, you don't have to take my word for this. Don't be rash as usual … be patient for two days and observe him. Everything will be clear to you."

The Boat Drifts Away

KARIKALAN SAW VANDHIYA Devan hurrying towards them on one side and Manimekalai calling out, "Lunch is ready," as she approached them on the other. "Nandini, Vandhiya Devan is not the only one who tried to stop me from coming to Kadambur. Thirumalai brought me the same message from the chief minister—he's my father's dearest friend and I'm devoted to him."

"Aniruddha's the man who wants to kill your father and deprive you of the crown. He thinks you are violent and not devoted to god. He planned to make your younger brother king and persuade him to become a Vaishnava. All his plans were upset when your brother drowned."

"But why would he want me to stay away from Kadambur?"

"He's afraid I'll reveal all his secrets to you. Don't forget Azlvarkkadian is my brother."

"Are you really his sister? Do you expect me to believe that?"

"I don't believe it either, but I grew up in his father's house. He planned to marry me and have many children who would propagate Vaishnavism."

"Chi! Did that monkey-faced Thirumalai really think of marrying you?"

"Sir, that's my misfortune—every man who comes near me has evil thoughts in his head."

"Why talk about other men when old Lord Ambalavan leads the pack?"

"Prince, please don't insult Lord Ambalavan to my face. He desired me: he made me his lawfully wedded wife and gave this orphan an honored place in his palace. I'm eternally grateful to him, but I don't live with him as man and wife. There's only one man I love. That will never change."

"Nandini, who's that lucky man? No, don't tell me that. Just tell me who you really are … without knowing that, I'll go mad!"

"Your friend and mine are almost here. I'll tell you when we get another opportunity." Nandini called to Devan, "Sir, where's the leopard's head?"

"Lady, the wounded leopard died. I could not bring myself to cut off a dead animal's head."

"How is that? I saw the leopard stumble into the boat," said Karikalan.

"It climbed into the boat and died. Maybe it died out of regret for wounding Lady Nandini."

Karikalan's anger cooled and he smiled. "Why climb into the boat to die?"

"Maybe it's afraid of water … like me," Devan said.

"But you jumped into the water to save us women," Nandini pointed out.

"I'm more afraid of women than water. I jumped in only because the prince forced me. Now it's clear there was no need for it."

"Yes, you are afraid of falling into the water and drowning but you are not in the least afraid of pushing other people into the water and letting them drown," Nandini said sarcastically.

Manimekalai was unhappy with this conversation. "*Akka*, the food is going cold. Let's eat."

The four of them walked to the pavilion. Manimekalai stole a glance at Devan; she knew instinctively that Nandini and Karikalan were troubling him. *Whoever is against you, don't worry. I'm on your side.* Manimekalai tried to tell Devan this with her eyes, but Devan did not even glance at her. He looked like a man drowning in a sea of worries.

Character is inherited from one's parents at birth. It is changed by environment and experience. The deaf-mute Mandakini spent most of her life in the forest where she had to stay alert for wild animals and sometimes kill them to save herself. Then love gushed like a spring in her innocent heart only to dry up soon—the shock unbalanced her mind. But time healed her wounds and love again enriched her heart as a wife's love for Sundara Chola became a mother's love for Arulmozli.

Nandini inherited many of her mother's traits but suffered more: her mother abandoned her; she grew up in others' houses; men were cruel to her. The insults she faced from the royal family as a child took root in her heart and turned to hatred. She never experienced the magic of love. Those she loved either rejected her or died; those who insulted her flourished. Disappointment killed all love and pity in her hardened heart, leaving room only for revenge. Nandini's wicked accusation and betrayal of Devan was nothing surprising, considering the circumstances of her birth and life.

Nandini, Karikalan and Devan were absorbed in their own thoughts during lunch. Manimekalai was happy when Karikalan and Devan arrived there unexpectedly. Her pure heart had recovered from its little pang of jealousy on seeing Devan holding Nandini. But now she was disappointed: the other three had long faces and spoke in double meanings which she did not understand or like. So, immediately after lunch, Manimekalai said, "*Akka*, shall I ask the servants to bring the boat? Are the men coming with us or riding back?"

Karikalan came back to earth and said, "No, we can't go without hearing Manimekalai sing."

Nandini said, "You men don't look like you are in the mood for music. Anyway, Manimekalai, fetch your *yazl*."

"*Akka*, why should I play before people who are not interested?"

"The prince wants to hear you. As for his friend, if he's not interested, he can close his ears."

"My goodness! When I heard the boat girl, Poonkuzlali, sing, I had goosebumps," Devan said.

"Some people like only particular songs. What if you don't like my song?" Manimekalai asked.

"I'll see he enjoys your music," Karikalan assured her. "Now, bring your *yazl*."

Manimekalai fetched her eight-stringed *yazl*, sat on the topmost step of the pavilion and began to play. Karikalan and Devan soon lost themselves in her music and forgot their troubles. After a while, Manimekalai began to sing to the *yazl's* accompaniment. After she sang several hymns from the *Thevaram*, Karikalan said, "Manimekalai, I'm not as devout as Madurandaka. Sing a love song for us."

Manimekalai beautiful cheeks dimpled in embarrassment and she hesitated.

"Girl, don't hesitate. Vandhiya Devan and I won't think you are singing the love song for either of us," Karikalan assured her.

"And if anyone thinks that, Manimekalai doesn't care," Nandini added.

"*Akka*, how can you tease me before two men!"

"Those who can't even bring us a dead leopard's head are not men. In the past, brave men tore open a live leopard's jaws, pulled out its teeth and gave them to their women as ornaments. Those days are gone. Never mind. Sing the song you sang for me the other day."

Manimekalai began a love song. Somehow her voice sounded even sweeter now and her listeners drowned in her music. Nandini's hard heart melted and her eyes brimmed with tears; Karikalan was lost in a world of his own. Devan's startled eyes fell on Manimekalai—her eyes were fixed on his face alone. *Aiyo! What harm have I done to this girl?*

Immersed in the music and their thoughts, they did not notice the wind growing stronger and the waves rising. Only when the storm uprooted a tree did they snap out of their trance and look around them.

Nandini shouted, "Where's the boat?" They saw the boat being tossed about by the waves at a distance. "What shall we do now?" Nandini cried.

"If you can ride, take the horses," Devan said. "The prince and I will manage."

"What? Do you want to kill us? What if a tree falls and crushes us?" Nandini asked.

"Let's stay here until the storm ends. We have food and Manimekalai's music. I have not been so happy in a long time," Karikalan said.

Devan objected. "What will Sambuvaraya and Kandamaran think?"

"He untied the boat when he went in search of the leopard," Nandini accused Devan.

"*Akka*, why are you making false accusations? The boat was on the shore when he came back. Don't worry, my father would have sent boats for us."

Sure enough, two huge boats soon came to the island; Sambuvaraya himself was in one. He was relieved to see that they were all safe. They boarded the boats and crossed the lake which was now heaving like an ocean. Their four hearts also seethed like the stormy sea.

PART 5

RENUNCIATION

Three Voices

ARULMOZLI CONTROLLED HIS impatience and waited at the Choodamani Monastery. He enjoyed his discussions with the well-travelled and learned abbot about the Srivijaya empire which included Cambodia, the Philippines, Indonesia and Malaysia. He learnt that Srivijaya was the Chola kingdom's equal in agriculture and natural resources and had ancient connections with Tamil Nadu. Pallava sculptors had built exquisite temples there; Tamil arts flourished; people worshipped Buddha, Shiva, Vishnu and other Tamil gods. Arulmozli questioned the abbot about the land and sea routes and filed away this information in his mind.

"Prince, why did you refuse the Buddhist Sangha's offer of the Sri Lankan throne? If you were the king of Lanka, you could commandeer a fleet and sail to Srivijaya."

"Acharya, the *Maha Vamsam* lists the atrocities of the Lankan royal family: sons imprisoning fathers … fathers killing sons … was it wrong to turn down a throne stained by such evil?"

The abbot was indignant. "That holy text also shows people the path of righteousness and tells them how these crimes were punished. The Buddhist Sangha wants to create a new royal dynasty with you. If you embrace Buddhism, you'll become as great as Emperor Ashoka."

"The Hindu gods are enshrined in my heart. Forgive me."

"Prince, don't forget the Cholas have a connection with Buddhism: your ancestor, Sibi Chakravarthi, who sacrificed his flesh to save a dove, is an incarnation of Buddha."

"How can I forget? My ancestors live in my flesh and bone and blood. On one side, the just Sibi Chakravarthi tells me, 'Serve the people!' On the other side, the great warrior Karikal Valavan thunders, 'Pick up your sword and conquer the world!' On yet another side, the Shiva devotee Kochenkan says, 'Build temples whose towers touch the sky!' I'm torn apart by these conflicting voices—I sometimes feel like becoming a Buddhist monk." Arulmozli thoughtfully studied a painting on the wall which depicted Buddha's life. "Acharya, Siddhartha did not gain enlightenment under the Bodhi tree. He became enlightened on the very day he sacrificed his kingdom, his wife and his child to find a way to ease his people's suffering." He paused. "I want to follow Siddhartha's path: will you take me as your disciple?"

"Sir, a rumor has spread in Nagapattinam that you are here and that we are trying to make you a Buddhist monk. The people are furious. Think what would happen if you really became a monk. We live here peacefully under your father's protection. I'm not brave enough to risk that ..." The abbot stopped at the roar of a crowd at the monastery entrance. "The people are here! How do I deal with this? Lord Buddha must show me the way."

Murugayyan Comes

"ACHARYA, I'M SORRY for causing trouble. I hate this secrecy. I have recovered completely from the fever; let me tell the people you gave me refuge and cured me."

"Your enemies are spreading these rumors to flush you out. You must stay hidden."

"Who are these enemies? I can let the people know I'm alive and make it clear to my enemies I'm not interested in becoming king. What harm can that do?"

"Princess Kundavai asked us to keep you in hiding until we hear from her. She is wise and must have an important reason for this. We know that some chieftains are conspiring against you and that there's a Pandian plot to wipe out your family ..."

The abbot was interrupted by a young monk who rushed in and cried, "Acharya! The crowd is shouting, 'We want to see the prince!' We told them he's not here. They refuse to believe us and insist on coming in and checking for themselves. They'll soon become violent."

"Acharya, your disciples have told the crowd I'm not here: I must not be seen."

"Yes, the crowd will go mad if they realize we have lied to them."

"The Chola palace at Anaimangalam is about four miles from here. I'll go there by canal."

"Good idea!" cried the abbot. "But how will you get to the canal without being seen?"

The young monk spoke up: "Why don't we let one man come in to search the monastery? We can delay him until it's dark and the prince can steal away. And there are signs of a storm–the waves are high and the sea is seething."

"If it's just one man, maybe I can convince him to help us," Arulmozli said.

The abbot said, "A couple from Kodikkarai came here two days ago, insisting you were inside. The woman made a big commotion. They are now in the crowd. The man said he was Murugayyan, the lighthouse keeper's son."

"I know him well; Murugayyan will obey me blindly. I'll ask him to row me Anaimangalam after dark."

The abbot said, "Prince, in these times, it's better not to trust anyone. This boatman and his wife are the ones who have been spreading the rumors about you."

"We have to allow one man inside anyway. Murugayyan is a little henpecked but he won't betray me even for his wife. See if you can bring him to me."

The young monk hurried away. The abbot followed him saying, "I'm uneasy. Let me go and judge the situation. I must ensure that no harm comes to this ancient monastery or to you."

The Storm

THOUSANDS OF ANGRY people surrounded the monastery, armed with swords, spears, sticks and axes. During the frequent wars between the Chola kingdom and Buddhist Sri Lanka, the people sometimes vented their anger against the enemy by attacking the monastery. It was clear that they were now a hair's breadth away from violence.

The crowd roared, "Give us Prince Arulmozli!" "We'll break down the monastery!"

The abbot heard the angry sea above the shouts. *May Lord Buddha save us! A storm is coming. We must escape the fury of the crowd and the storm.*

The young monk raised his hands for silence. "Please calm down. Obviously, all of you can't enter the monastery. We'll let one man search the place and you must all be bound by what he says. I suggest you choose a man who has seen Prince Arulmozli recently. That will make it easy for him to identify the prince if he's in the monastery."

Rakamma, standing in the front row of the crowd, cried, "We have seen the prince recently."

Murugayyan said, "Lord, she's a liar; she has not seen the prince. I saw him last month in Sri Lanka. His smile is engraved on my heart. I'll recognize him at once."

The young monk said, "Your wife knows women are not allowed into the monastery." He took Murugayyan by the hand and led him up the steps. "Murugayyan, a boatman, has seen the prince recently. He will search the monastery and report to you. Do you agree?"

Some voices shouted, "We agree!" Others mumbled, "Are they trying to cheat us?"

The young monk shouted, "I'll take the boatman inside. The abbot will answer any questions."

The old abbot's dignified posture and calm face discouraged the crowd from asking any questions. The abbot said, "It's clear that you are here because of your love for Prince Arulmozli. I wept with you at the news of his death. Every day we pray he's alive. We have more reason than you to love the prince."

A man shouted, "That's exactly why we're afraid you'll shave his head and make him a monk!" The men around him laughed mockingly.

The abbot declared, "I swear on Lord Buddha's lotus feet that I'll never let Prince Arulmozli become a monk, come what may!" His impassioned words subdued the crowd. The abbot continued, "Now it's time to think about your own families. A storm, the likes of which we have never seen, is going to strike Nagapattinam. Look!!"

A fearsome sight met their eyes: the sea rose behind them in a huge wall of black waves which moved steadily towards them. On the other side, the sea had flooded the port and the town. Boats and small ships hung on the crest of huge waves with their sails ripped apart by the wind.

"May Lord Buddha save Nagapattinam!" the abbot shouted. "Go, take your families to safety."

The crowd scattered in all directions. Soon, the place was empty. But Rakamma stood her ground. "How can I go without my husband? Let me into the monastery."

The abbot replied, "You know that women are not allowed to enter the monastery. No harm will come to your husband; take care of yourself."

A man who had stayed behind when the crowd dispersed came to Rakamma and whispered to her. He took her hand and pulled her away; Rakamma reluctantly went with him.

Who's this man? What's his connection with this woman? wondered the abbot. He went back to Arulmozli's room and said, "Prince, there's no need to wait for nightfall. The crowd has dispersed."

"In that case, there's no need for me to leave," argued Arulmozli.

"They may be back," the abbot pointed out.

Arulmozli sent Murugayyan to fetch his boat.

In fact, the abbot feared that the storm would engulf the monastery. The Anaimangalam palace was large and was some distance from the sea; the prince would be safe there. The abbot addressed his monks: "We are followers of Buddha, the Compassionate. Go and help those in need. I'm old —I'll stay here and pray."

The monks quickly left to carry out his orders. Murugayyan came with his boat and Arulmozli climbed into it. The abbot stood by the canal, staring at the boat until it disappeared from view. A radiant halo glowed around the abbot's face.

The Nandi is Submerged

AS THE BOAT went down the canal, Arulmozli noticed the water level rising steadily. Trees groaned and crashed down on the canal banks. As they passed the Nandi Pavilion, Arulmozli saw that the Nandi was submerged. "Murugayyan, stop the boat," Arulmozli said.

Murugayyan obeyed and the boat bobbed wildly in the current. Arulmozli jumped to the pavilion and clambered up a fallen tree to its roof. He saw that the lower part of the canal was flooded completely and that the water had risen to the top steps of the monastery. Arulmozli shuddered and said, "Murugayyan, back to the monastery!"

The devoted Murugayyan obeyed unquestioningly. They moved fast, but every second seemed an age to Arulmozli. Water now surrounded the monastery and was rising rapidly. Soon, the modest building would be completely submerged. Arulmozli jumped on the roof of a pavilion and ran from room to room in the monastery's upper floor, wading through chest-high water. At last, he came to a room with a statue of Lord Buddha—water covered the statue up to its chest. The prince looked carefully into the water. "Ahah!" he shouted in relief. The abbot was seated on the ground, underwater, with his arms around Lord Buddha's feet. Arulmozli bent and forced the abbot's hands from the statue. Staggering under the weight of the abbot, he struggled to the boat and jumped in.

The Motherless Calf

THE SMALL VESSEL wobbled wildly but Murugayyan somehow prevented it from overturning. "Murugayyan, to the Anaimangalam palace!" shouted Arulmozli.

Unable to hear the prince above the roar of the storm, Murugayyan guessed his command and bent to the oars. With his experience on the high seas, he skillfully steered the boat between the statues on the submerged monastery towers. As they crossed a half-submerged Buddha statue, the abbot tried to jump out of the boat but could not escape Arulmozli's iron grip. The abbot wept as the statue disappeared under the rising flood.

"What were you trying to do?" Arulmozli asked.

The abbot said sadly, "This five-hundred-year-old monastery is built of brick: it won't survive the flood. Why should I live after seeing it sink before my eyes?"

"If the monastery is destroyed, I can build it again. If you die, can I bring you back to life?"

Their argument was drowned by the roar of the storm. Soon, they were speechless in shock at the piteous sights around them. Boats and ships crashed into houses and trees and shattered; the wind threw thatched roofs into the flood; men clung to roofs and uprooted trees, crying for help; cows and goats floated in the flood. Their hearts ached as they looked on helplessly. Murugayyan rowed carefully, not letting himself be distracted by anything.

They crossed the Nandi Pavilion where the water had now reached the base of its roof. A little calf stood shivering and bleating on the highest point of the roof. *Poor creature! What will happen to it without its mother?* Arulmozli thought. Just then, a coconut tree crashed on the roof, missing the calf by inches. The force of the tree's fall created a huge wave which washed the little calf into the flood. The next instant, the abbot jumped into the water. Murugayyan dropped his oars and grabbed the prince, refusing to obey when Arulmozli shouted angrily, "Let me go!"

The calf instinctively held its head above the water as the abbot swam to it and pulled it to the boat by its front legs. The prince helped to drag it into the boat where it collapsed. Arulmozli then pulled the abbot into the boat. The abbot stroked the calf and said, "My heart is at peace after saving this calf. I won't grieve even if the monastery is destroyed in the flood."

"Acharya, what about the thousands of men, women, children and old people who are struggling in the flood? Countless cows, horses, goats and birds will die. What can we do?" Arulmozli asked.

"All we can do is help any living creature suffering before our eyes."

"But why does the all-powerful god allow such calamities and human suffering?"

"Sir, there's no answer to that question. Lord Buddha does not refer to god at all. He says relieving the suffering of others will give you true happiness and lead to enlightenment."

Arulmozli compared the abbot's words with the religion of his own ancestors. While they believed that the very purpose of birth was to help others, they also emphasized devotion to god. They praised god both as Rudra, the destroyer, and as Vishnu, the protector; they depicted god both as Uma, the embodiment of love, and as the violent Kali. *Why not? The mother who caresses her child is also the mother who beats him. Sometimes the child does not understand why it's being punished ... does that mean the mother does not love her child?*

They boat reached the Anaimangalam jetty as darkness fell. They saw that the palace was untouched by the flood. They climbed out of the boat with the calf. People crowded the palace gates, arguing with the guard.

The guard saw the boat and raised his torch: one look at Arulmozli's face and he ran to them, forgetting everything else. His torch fell into the canal, flared for an instant and went out. "Prince, I was worried about the Choodamani Monastery—thank goodness you are safe!"

"How did you know I was at the monastery?" Arulmozli asked.

"I came to know when Princess Kundavai was here; she asked me to keep it a secret."

"You must continue to keep it a secret. Luckily, the torch went out. Who are those at the gate?"

"They are from the flooded coastal villages. They want shelter; I'll chase them away ..."

"No, no! Give them place to sleep and let them cook and eat as long as the provisions last. But don't tell them about me. Take us to the palace's top floor by another route."

Murugayyan Weeps

THIS WAS THE storm which uprooted the tree which blocked Mandakini's palanquin outside Thanjavur and freed the boat

Manimekalai had arranged for the picnic. The storm battered Nagapattinam all night; the abbot and Arulmozli worried about the damage it caused.

Arulmozli questioned the palace caretaker who said, "Lord, the granary is full; the treasury has twelve copper pots of gold coins which Sembiyan Madevi sent for renovating a nearby temple."

"Acharya, distribute the grain to the hungry and donate the gold coins to those who have lost their homes. I'll satisfy my grandmother later by building hundreds of Shiva temples with towers so high, no flood can reach them. I'll rebuild the Choodamani Monastery in stone so that it can withstand any storm," Arulmozli declared.

The abbot said, "You must organize the flood relief. I can't accept such a huge responsibility ..."

They stopped at the sound of Murugayyan sobbing loudly. Arulmozli asked gently, "What's wrong, Murugayyan?"

Murugayyan stammered his way through his explanation. "Lord, my wife insisted you were at the Choodamani Monastery and forced me to come here. I suspected her of wanting to harm you but now I see how wrong I was."

Arulmozli was alarmed. "My dear fellow, how did she know where I was?"

"My aunt Mandakini, the deaf-mute who saved your life in Sri Lanka, and my sister, Poonkuzlali, left for Nagapattinam by boat. My wife guessed you were here."

"Ahah! Where are they now? You said they left for Nagapattinam."

Murugayyan sobbed and told them that Mandakini had been kidnapped by thugs and that Rakamma had been beaten and tied to a tree when she tried to stop them. Arulmozli forgot his suspicions about Rakamma and his respect for her increased.

The furious prince declared, "If the Pazluvur brothers have harmed Lady Mandakini, I'll wipe out their clan! I won't forgive even my own parents if they have wronged her. I'll leave for Thanjavur tomorrow, disguised as a merchant, taking Murugayyan with me. Acharya, organize the relief work in the name of the 'Sri Lankan Queen's Trust.' Who knows? Maybe Lady Mandakini's a Buddhist. She spends most of her time in a deserted monastery on Boodha Island."

The next morning, the storm weakened and the sea receded. Arulmozli, disguised as a merchant, walked down the streets inspecting the damage. Murugayyan, carrying a sack, followed him.

Rakamma hid in a ruined house and waited. When they were almost at the house, she ran out, fell at the prince's feet and shouted at the top of her voice: "Prince, you're alive! I'm blessed to see you!"

Murugayyan tried to hush her but it was useless. The attention of all the passersby in the street turned to Arulmozli.

The People Celebrate

THE SHOCKED MURUGAYYAN signaled to his wife and said, "Woman, are you mad?"

"I'm not mad," Rakamma said. "Don't you recognize the prince? Where are you going?"

Arulmozli interrupted, "Woman, I'm a merchant from Sri Lanka. I have asked him to be my guide. Take him and go; stop making a scene."

People began to gather and stare at the prince. Rakamma said loudly, "Is the prince mad? Have those wretched monks bewitched him into thinking he's someone else? Prince, you are Emperor Sundara Chola's son. Examine your palm: you'll see the lines of the conch and chakra."

Arulmozli immediately closed his fists and said, "Woman, won't you shut your mouth?"

Murugayyan whispered to Rakamma: "I beg you, keep quiet. The prince wants to go to Thanjavur secretly, disguised as a merchant."

Rakamma shouted, "Why didn't you tell me this earlier?" She turned to Arulmozli. "Lord, I have unknowingly exposed you to danger. But don't worry, there are millions like my husband and me who are ready to defend you from those wretched Pazluvur brothers who want to arrest you." She shouted at the crowd, "If any one of you is a Pazluvur man, step forward. You must kill me before you touch the prince!"

The wonderstruck crowd broke into cheers: "Long Live Prince Arulmozli!"

Realizing that it was useless to hide his identity, Arulmozli said, "I'm deeply moved by your affection. I'm on my way to Thanjavur on urgent business: that's why I'm in disguise. Please let me go."

A voice in the crowd shouted, "The prince must stay with us at least for a day!"

A town councilor pushed through the crowd and said, "Sir, you must let the people show their hospitality and love for you. Yesterday, they were ready to tear down the monastery …"

"The monks cured my fever and saved my life. I'm sorry the monastery is destroyed."

"My apologies, sir, we thought you were being held captive. We'll rebuild the monastery with the town funds. It will take you weeks to reach Thanjavur on foot; the roads are damaged and the rivers are in flood. We'll give you an elephant and follow you to Thanjavur."

Arulmozli said, "Thank you for your affection. I'll stay with you today and leave in the evening." *The boatman's wife has ruined my plans. Was it foolishness on her part … or a deliberate, sinister plan? Anyway, I can't hurt the people by refusing their hospitality.* Murugayyan was with him, but Rakamma had disappeared before he could question her.

The prince was escorted to the palace in a grand procession. Arulmozli moved among the subdued people, comforted them and promised to send relief supplies from Thanjavur. There was widespread bad feeling against the Pazluvur brothers, concern for Sundara Chola's health and anxiety about who would be the next emperor. A grand feast was organized for thousands.

Arulmozli stood on the palace terrace, hands folded in thanks. He looked down at the decorated elephant waiting for him, followed by an endless procession of bulls and horses, flag bearers and musicians and hundreds of people. Even as he smiled at the public, the prince was troubled. *The Pazluvur brothers have spread rumors that I want to seize my father's throne. People will believe this if I enter Thanjavur at the head of this procession.*

The council chairman declared, "Prince, we are worried about the emperor's health. Prince Madurandaka, who has never set foot on a battlefield, will be a Pazluvur puppet. Prince Aditya Karikalan has not been seen in the Chola kingdom for three years and is not interested in becoming king. Only you can succeed the emperor." He turned to the crowd. "Do you agree?

The crowd erupted into cheers and a mighty roar of approval.

Arulmozli held out his hands for silence. "I'm honored by your regard for me. But it's wrong to talk about the next emperor while my father is alive. Let's pray he has a long life."

The chairman was prepared for this. "Sir, by tradition, the emperor names his successor while he is alive. We doubt whether your father has the freedom to choose his heir, we doubt if he's even alive. We'll come with you to Thanjavur, meet the emperor and petition him to name you his successor. We will then be bound by his decision."

Arulmozli's heart was filled with dread. *My father's life may be in danger and I'm too far away to save him. Lady Mandakini is in the hands of some villains. I must hurry to Thanjavur; I can't waste time arguing with these men. I'll find a way to leave them behind later.* Saying, "Sir, I bow to your wishes," the prince mounted the elephant.

The thousand-strong procession set out for Thanjavur. More people joined it along the way.

Ambalavan in the Boat

AMBALAVAN SET OUT for Thanjavur with a small company of ten horsemen. Not wanting to call attention to himself, he avoided the villages. When they reached the ford, they found the Kollidam in flood. Leaving their horses on the northern bank for their return journey, Ambalavan and his ten warriors crossed the river by boat. As the storm worsened, the boatmen struggled to steer the whirling boat in the strong current.

Ambalavan's mind was also a whirl of confusion. When he was with Nandini, everything she said seemed correct and he couldn't stop himself from nodding, 'Yes.' He had agreed to go to Thanjavur and return with Madurandaka. Now, he was haunted by doubts. He had confidence in Nandini, but he hated to think of her alone with three young men whom he disliked.

Kandamaran had referred to Nandini as Ambalavan's daughter in the treasury; furious, Ambalavan had secretly ordered the guard to kill Kandamaran. He had regretted this later and luckily, Kandamaran was alive. But how the guard had died instead of Kandamaran was a mystery to Ambalavan; he also resented Nandini keeping Kandamaran in their palace and caring for him.

Ambalavan had disliked Vandhiya Devan from the time he had met that insolent young man. His dislike increased after Devan tried to warn the emperor and escaped from Thanjavur Fort. Kalaanthaka had suspected Nandini of helping Devan to escape: but now that Devan was known to be Kundavai's and Arulmozli's secret messenger, there could be nothing between Nandini and Devan. Yet, Ambalavan burned with jealousy when he thought of Nandini and Devan together.

As for Karikalan, Ambalavan had heard rumors that Karikalan loved a temple priest's daughter and wanted to marry her: some insisted that this woman was Nandini. Karikalan was from the Chola dynasty and would never covet another man's wife. But what about Nandini? How could he believe blindly in her virtue when he had no idea about her ancestry? Kalaanthaka often warned him about her. *Can my brother be right? Will Nandini betray me?*

Ambalavan's lust for Nandini grew along with his anger. He controlled his urge to beat his head with his hands. He sighed and cleared his throat. Holding tightly to the rim of the boat, he gnashed his teeth and vowed, *I'll find out the truth in two days …*

The River Breaches its Banks

AMBALAVAN HAD A reputation for bravery. When his men saw his agitation, they thought he was afraid of the storm; immediately, they became anxious and began to consider ways to save their own lives if the boat sank. Finally, the boat reached the shore about four miles away from the jetty. Just at the men sighed in relief, a huge tree fell into the river and crashed into the boat. The boat capsized, dumping its passengers into the water. The alert men swam the short distance to the southern bank; some clambered on to trees or clung to any floating object they could find.

But Ambalavan, deep in thought, was caught unawares: he sank and the strong current dragged him a long distance. He swallowed water and thrashed and finally fought his way to the surface—there was no sign of the boat or his men. Ambalavan's old fighting spirit revived. He grabbed a floating branch and swam towards the shore. When his arms tired, he floated. He tried to climb on to the shore only to slip on the wet mud and fall back into the river. Finally, an hour after sunset, he pulled himself up the bank with the help of a clump of reeds on the riverbed.

He was surrounded by thick forest; there was no sign of habitation. *I must be about ten miles east of Kudanthai. Can I make it to Kudanthai by night?* The storm was at its peak. The wind howled; thunder split the skies; the rain poured down; trees crashed all around him. *I had better find shelter for the night in some ruined temple or pavilion and move on in the morning.* Ambalavan steadied his trembling feet and walked along the riverbank. It was pitch dark. The flood waters touched the riverbank which was wet in the heavy rain. The brave old man did not pay attention when water flowed across his path, but he hesitated when the water suddenly rose to his thighs. Before he could react, he fell head over heels into the water: the flood had breached the bank. As the land near the bank was low, he was pulled into deeper water and tumbled helplessly with the flood. He could not see or hear; he was drowning. *My feet can't find the ground. I can't breathe. Goddess Durga, is this the end? Nandini! I have left you with three villains. I was captivated by your beauty and married you. I lost my peace of mind. You gave me no happiness. I'm going to die in a flash flood. If I had died in battle a memorial would stand as a testimony to my courage … now I won't even get a proper funeral. My body will be lost in the river or rot on the bank and become food for jackals … what a shameful death …*

Ambalavan lost consciousness. He came to when he banged his head against something hard: he was gripping a stone surface. With a gigantic effort, he pulled himself up on to a stone floor. He opened his eyes to a bright glare—he was looking into Durga's beautiful face! *Compassionate mother, you have taken me to your abode.* No, he was not dead: he was in a Durga temple. The bright light was an oil lamp which burned in the sanctum in spite of the wind and rain outside. *The lamp is a sign of Durga's love for me. I'll triumph over the dangers which surround me ...* The old man stood up, shivering. He removed his wet clothes, dried himself with the screen in the temple and wrapped the screen around his waist. He decided to spend the night in the temple. *The temple may sink in the flood, but I can't move another inch.* Ambalavan found fruits, broken coconuts and other offerings in the sanctum. He ate the food gratefully, keeping some aside for the next day. He lay down at the goddess' feet as if in worship and fell fast asleep.

Are You Dead?

AMBALAVAN WAS EXHAUSTED and slept like a log. Later, he was troubled by dreams. Durga stepped out of her statue and stared at him with blazing eyes. 'Ambalavan, you and the Pazluvur clan are close to my heart. Hear my warning: the Nandini you keep in your palace is a demon waiting to wipe out the Cholas. Banish her from your heart and your palace at once or the Pazluvur clan will be disgraced forever.' Durga merged with her statue once again. Ambalavan started awake, trembling. *Was it only a dream? It was so real.*

It was morning; the storm had weakened and the rain had stopped. But he heard the sound of rushing water. From the temple's outer corridor, Ambalavan saw that the river had breached a vast stretch of its bank and more than half the flood water flowed through the breach. The temple was surrounded by the flood to the east and south. To the west, the water flowed near the temple but short trees and thickets went on to become a dense forest beyond the water.

Ambalavan guessed that he was in the forest near Thirupurambayam village and that this was the ancient temple near the Prithvipathi memorial. He thought of the war fought here a hundred years ago and the heroic deeds of his ancestors as they stood shoulder to shoulder with the Chola kings. *Did Durga state the truth? Will Nandini bring shame on my ancient clan? I must discover Nandini's secret ... but first I must somehow go to Thirupurambayam and get help.*

Ambalavan looked around. The flood water vented all its force on the temple foundation—the temple was in danger of collapsing. He saw a huge neem tree in front of the temple and guessed that the tree would fall before the temple collapsed and that the water would push the tree to the shore somewhere. If the temple collapsed, he must quickly leap on to the tree. And if the temple survived through Durga's grace, he must wait for the water to drain. That would take days. *Thank goodness I have food for another day. There's nothing to do but wait. I have much to accomplish in this world. Durga must have saved me for a purpose.*

That day and night and the next day passed; the storm abated and the skies cleared. The river ebbed but the water around the temple seemed to rise. There was no way to judge its depth and swimming across was out of the question. Finally, at sunset, what Ambalavan expected happened —the neem tree fell. Luckily, it fell across the water to the west and formed a bridge to the forest. Ambalavan hesitated at the thought of finding his way in the forest at night but finally decided to leave at once. He went into the sanctum to give thanks to Goddess Durga.

The next moment, he shuddered at a call from nearby: "Sorcerer! Ravidasan!" The voice sounded familiar. Ambalavan went to the outer corridor and hid behind a pillar. He saw a figure standing on the forest side of the fallen neem tree. Recalling his brother's words about Ravidasan, the sorcerer who visited Nandini, he stayed motionless. *By Durga's grace, I'll learn the truth today.* He saw the figure coming to the temple, using the tree as a bridge. Ambalavan lay down and pretended to be asleep. *Who's this man looking for Ravidasan in this deserted place? If I get my hands on that sorcerer, I'll make him talk.*

The man came nearer and shouted, "Ravidasan, where are you?"

Ambalavan recognized the voice: it was Devaralan, the man who had performed at Kadambur Palace. *Shall I force him to tell me everything? No, I must let him lead me to Ravidasan.*

"Sorcerer, are you asleep even before sunset? Or are you dead by any chance?" Devaralan turned the sleeping man's face, shrieked in terror and ran for his life. Even before Ambalavan could sit up, Devaralan had dashed across the make-shift tree bridge and disappeared into the forest. Ambalavan followed him. The old man could not leap across the tree like Devaralan; he steadied himself by holding the branches. He reached the other side and followed the footprints in the wet mud of the narrow track. There was no moon in the cloudy sky and soon the forest was engulfed in darkness. He heard strange cries and wild creatures rustled through the thick bushes. The track ended abruptly, but Ambalavan continued deeper into the forest, determined to find Devaralan. After wandering around for more than an hour, he saw a light moving in the distance. He went towards the light and saw a flaming torch disappear into a ruined building which he guessed must be the Prithvipathi memorial. He hid behind one of the walls and heard two men talking.

"Sorcerer, I've been looking for you for hours. I thought you were not coming. I even thought you were dead!" It was Devaralan.

Ravidasan laughed. "It's Sundara Chola and his two sons who will be dead by tomorrow."

The Memorial Collapses

A FLASH OF lightning streaked across the sky, showing Ambalavan the two men's faces. He had seen Ravidasan once or twice in his palace. Nandini had called him an accomplished sorcerer and Kalaanthaka had warned him about this man. The other man had acted as Devaralan at Kadambur Palace. But Ambalavan had seen him earlier. *Ah! He's Parameswaran, a man I dismissed from government service twenty years ago. Let me hear what they are up to.*

"Ravidasan, I'm tired of hearing you say this. Sundara Chola, bedridden for three years, is still alive. And so are his sons—how many times we tried to kill Arulmozli in Sri Lanka!"

"All three of them will die tomorrow. But why are you shivering? Have you brought the boat?"

"Yes, it was difficult to keep it safe in the storm. I'm trembling because I saw Death itself!"

"Parameswaran, stop blabbering nonsense!"

Ambalavan longed to pounce on Parameswaran and wring his neck.

I must be patient and hear what they have to say. Ravidasan predicts that Sundara Chola and his sons will die tomorrow ... is he an accomplished sorcerer as Nandini says? If this happens, my problems will be solved and we need not divide the kingdom. But what about Parameswaran? He's the man who swore twenty years ago that he would wipe out the Cholas ...

"I came here this morning, but you were not here. I wandered around looking for you. There's a small temple at the spot where the Kollidam has breached its bank. I saw a man sleeping there and thought it was you. Whom do you think it was? None other than Lord Ambalavan."

Ravidasan roared with laughter. "Was it Ambalavan you saw or his ghost?"

"I saw the same face, moustache and battle scars. Can there be two men like him?"

"There's no doubt you saw Ambalavan. Last evening, his boat capsized when he was crossing the Kollidam. His men were searching for him along the shore up to the breached bank. They fear he has drowned. Maybe you saw Ambalavan's corpse."

"No, he was alive: I saw his eyes. I wish I had thrown him into the flood."

"It's good that he's alive. When Sundara Chola and his sons die, the chieftains will form two factions, led by Ambalavan and Malayaman. We can raise a Pandian army during their civil war."

"How are you so confident about Sundara Chola and his sons dying tomorrow? I heard that Arulmozli is alive in Nagapattinam and that the people are insisting he becomes emperor."

Ravidasan laughed again. "Who do you think flushed him out of the monastery? None other than Rakamma, our Kiramavithan's daughter; she's now married to the boatman, Murugayyan."

"How does this help us? He's now surrounded by thousands of people."

"Arulmozli is riding an elephant to Thanjavur. On the way, his mahout will meet with an accident and Kiramavithan will take his place. Then see what happens ...'

"Ravidasan, you're a genius! But what plans do you have for Sundara Chola?"

"I left Soman Sambavan in Ambalavan's underground vault. He's armed with a spear. There's a secret passage from the vault to the palace. I showed Sambavan Sundara Chola's bedroom: even a blind man could not miss if he threw his spear at the emperor from that spot. I told Sambavan to be patient for two days."

"But why? Wouldn't it be better for him to finish the job at the first opportunity he gets?'

"Fool! If Sundara Chola dies first, his sons will become alert. What's the use of only that sick old man dying? What news from Kadambur? It's the most important part of our plan."

"There's great confusion there with romances and talk of marriages. Somehow I'm not happy about you trusting Lady Nandini of Pazluvur."

"Call her Pandimadevi, the Pandian queen! Remember that King Veerapandian married her two days before he died. Remember that she has taken an oath to destroy the Cholas. Didn't she receive the sword of the Pandian dynasty from the Pandian prince in this very spot a week ago?"

"You should have seen your Pandimadevi return from her pleasure cruise last evening."

"Nandini is the mistress of deceit, or she could not have lived in Ambalavan's palace for three years and helped us. You can read her mind from the fact that she sent Ambalavan away."

"She may have sent the old man away to have a romance. Remember she let Vandhiya Devan escape …"

Ravidasan laughed. "You'll soon know why she let him escape. Princess Kundavai especially will be shocked to hear that the man she loves has killed her brother."

"What?! Vandhiya Devan is going to kill Karikalan?! Has he finally joined our group?"

"Why do you care who kills Karikalan? He'll be killed by the sword which carries the Pandian fish emblem and Vandhiya Devan will be blamed. Come what may, Karikalan will die tomorrow. Our clever queen will do her duty—and we must do ours."

"What must we do?"

"Tomorrow night, we must wait in the secret passage which leads from Kadambur Palace. Once Nandini comes, we must go to the Kolli Hills. If we can, we must carry away all the gold from Ambalavan's vault through the secret tunnel. We'll raise an army to fight the Cholas with money stolen from the Cholas themselves!" Ravidasan laughed again.

"Don't build too many castles in the air. First let's get back to Kadambur. Shall we start?"

"We'll leave at dawn. The wind will die down and the flood will ebb by then."

A fox barked and the sorcerer shivered. "Ravidasan, shame on you," Parameswaran said. "Trembling at a fox's bark!"

"My dear fellow, if you were buried up to your neck in quicksand in Kodikkarai, surrounded by a hundred foxes waiting to eat you, you too would shiver. Come, let's spend the night in some temple or pavilion near a village, or even go to the temple you mentioned. If Ambalavan is still there, we'll throw him into the flood and save him from the grief he must suffer tomorrow."

Every word Ambalavan heard was like molten lead poured into his ear. He could hardly bear the shame and the pain of knowing that his wife had fooled him for three years and that she had vowed to avenge Veerapandian's death. Ambalavan thought of the six-generation-old bond between the Pazluvur clan and the Cholas. Sundara Chola's grandmother was from the Pazluvur clan. Only recently had Ambalavan developed his dislike for the princes. *How could I think of betraying the Cholas just because of Karikalan's childish behavior and my dislike of Malayaman? I let the Chola's arch-enemies, the Pandians, use my palace. I let the enemy use treasure from my vaults to finance their schemes. As long as there's breath in my body, I'll stop these assassins! I'll kill them with my bare hands now ...* Ambalavan hesitated. *I must not get into a fight now. My first priority is to save Sundara Chola and his sons. And saving Karikalan is most important. If that demon in woman's form kills Karikalan, the Pazluvur clan will be blamed. I'll never get over the disgrace. Can such poison hide inside such a beautiful body?*

But Ambalavan was glad that although Nandini had cheated him, she did not love Karikalan or Vandhiya Devan or Kandamaran. She was using those young men for her own wicked purpose. *Maybe Nandini is being manipulated by those villains. Maybe I can show her she's wrong. I'll kill those men and save her ...* In his excitement, Ambalavan cleared his throat.

"Who's there?" Parameswaran shouted.

Ambalavan showed himself. The shocked men saw his tall figure silhouetted against the night and turned to run for their lives. Ambalavan reached out with his long arms and caught them. *I'm stronger than either of them. But I'm no match for two young men together.* He quickly knocked Parameswaran down and pinned him down with one foot. He caught Ravidasan by the neck and squeezed. Parameswaran, fighting for his life, pulled out his dagger and tried to stab the leg which pressed on him; Ambalavan used his free leg to kick the hand holding the dagger. Parameswaran's hand went numb, but he somehow managed to wriggle out from under Ambalavan's foot. He rained blows on the old man: it was like hitting a stone wall. Meanwhile, Ambalavan continued to strangle Ravidasan whose eyes were now bulging. With his last breath, the sorcerer gurgled, "Parameswaran, bring down the roof. Quick!"

Parameswaran immediately jumped on the dilapidated roof of the memorial which was on the verge of collapse. Using all his might, Parameswaran knocked it down, along with a tree growing from it. Seeing the roof fall, Ambalavan shielded himself with his hands and Ravidasan was free. The roof fell on Ambalavan and he lost consciousness.

The Comet Disappears

HALF-CONSCIOUS, AMBALAVAN FOUND himself on a battlefield. War drums beat a tattoo and swords clashed. Thousands of voices shouted, "Long live the Pandian king! Death to his enemies!" On the other side, thousands cried, "The Pallava king has fallen! Run for your lives!"

The battlefield fell silent. Ambalavan saw a mighty warrior carrying Vijayalaya Chola on his shoulders. The legless old king held two curved broadswords in his hands and roared, "Chola warriors, stop! Pallavas, don't run! Follow me: we'll cut the enemy to pieces!" At these words, the Chola and Pallava soldiers took heart and the retreating army advanced once more.

To Ambalavan's amazement, the warrior who carried the legless king looked exactly like Ambalavan. The Pazluvur man held the old king on his shoulders with one hand; in his other hand, he held a long sword which he whirled as he pushed his way through the battlefield. Wherever the pair went, the heads of Pandian soldiers fell to the ground. The tide of the battle turned. The Pandians fled and the war drums celebrated the victory of the Cholas and Pallavas.

Vijayalaya Chola sat beside the Pallava king who said, "Great warrior, you have snatched victory from the jaws of defeat. From today, the Chola country will be an independent kingdom. You and your sons may rule as kings in your own right."

Vijayalaya turned to the Pazluvur man standing at his side. "Cousin, we won today because of you. I appoint you General and Chancellor of the Chola kingdom. Your descendants too will hold these posts." The Pazluvur man beamed with pride. Suddenly, his expression changed and he stared furiously at Ambalavan. "You wretch! How could you betray your clan and your king? The Chola dynasty is ending because of you. You are cursed forever!" Tears streamed down Ambalavan's face.

Generations of Malayamans and Velirs appeared. "You call yourself a man? You boasted that your clan is the pillar of the Chola dynasty: what do you say now?"

As the people of the Chola kingdom threw stones and mud at Ambalavan, Sundara Chola stumbled through the crowd on his wasted legs. "How dare you throw stones at Ambalavan, the greatest of warriors? If he betrays me, it's between us. Come, chancellor, let's go to my palace."

Ambalavan's brother, Kalaanthaka, stood before him. "*Anna*, how can you betray the emperor who trusts us? How can you keep that demon in our palace?"

Vandhiya Devan and Kandamaran mocked Ambalavan: "Old man, your moustache has aged, but not your lust. Are your sixty-four battle scars badges of courage or rewards for treachery?" Ambalavan reached for his sword, but it was not in its usual place at his side. Princess Kundavai silenced the young men. "*Thatha*, ignore them. Just chase that poisonous snake from your house and everything will be okay."

Ambalavan was surrounded by six generations of Pazluvur women who wept, "We sent our men to fight for the Cholas. They shed their blood and gave their lives for the glory of our clan but you destroyed it in a second!" Ambalavan tried to stand, but some weight was pressing on him; he could not move. He shouted, "Women, shut your mouths and go to your quarters!" But the women's laments became louder. Unable to bear it, Ambalavan tried to cover his ears, but he could not move his hands. With a great effort, he shook free his hands and opened his eyes. He realized that he had been dreaming and that the sound he heard was not the lament of women but the barking of foxes. He vaguely recalled two voices near him when he was half conscious.

"The old man's dead; even if he's alive, the foxes will finish him off by morning."

"You pulled down the roof just in time: otherwise, the old man would have killed me. Let's see … the roof's not budging even an inch. We have used the stones of one enemy's memorial to build a gravestone for another enemy."

"Let's go before the boat gets washed away. How will we cross the Kollidam then?"

Ambalavan's mind cleared. He was pinned down by part of the memorial's roof. How was he able to breathe? The tree which had fallen down with the roof had broken the roof's fall and supported its weight. If the roof had fallen directly on him, it would have shattered his head and chest. His extraordinary strength had saved him. *I must live. I must save the royal family, or I'll be blamed by the people and cursed by my ancestors. Aiyo! How long have I been unconscious? What if the assassinations have already taken place?*

Meanwhile the howl of foxes came nearer; soon he could hear heavy breathing near his head. *Even the foxes are not afraid of me. I'll show them!* With all the strength he could gather, Ambalavan pushed against the tree. The tree lifted a little and the roof above it also shifted. His grunts and cries chased away the foxes. After what seemed an age to him, the tree and the roof shifted, giving Ambalavan room to move and breathe freely. Exhausted after this stupendous effort, he lay still, taking deep breaths.

He looked up and saw hundreds of twinkling stars. The comet which had appeared in the sky some days ago was now shrunken and its tail was short. *I wonder what that means.* He looked around and saw a pack of about fifty foxes nearby, their eyes blazing like coals in the dark. *They are waiting for this old man to die.* Suddenly, a dazzling light covered the earth and the sky. A shining ball of fire flared across the sky; it grew smaller and smaller and finally disappeared. Darkness engulfed the forest once more. The comet was no longer in the sky. *Ahah! The comet has fallen. People believe that when a comet falls, it means a death in the royal family. We'll know if this is true tomorrow ... no, today.*

Ambalavan saw dawn breaking in the east. *By tonight three assassination attempts will be made at three different places and I'm the only one who can stop them. If I succeed, I'll celebrate my victory over the comet; if I fail ...* Ambalavan could not even consider the possibility of failure. *I'll save Sundara Chola and his two sons at any cost. I must go to Kudanthai and send urgent messages to Thanjavur and Nagapattinam; then I must cross the Kollidam and hurry back to Kadambur. That's all I can do. I must leave the rest in destiny's hands.*

Ambalavan tried to stand; the pain was almost unbearable; his chest hurt and he guessed that he had fractured a leg. He ignored the pain, gritted his teeth and stood up. The ground was water-logged and fallen trees and branches slowed him, but he walked steadily towards Kudanthai. It was almost two hours after dawn when he finally reached Kudanthai. He avoided the town and searched the outskirts for someone whom he could send to Thanjavur and Nagapattinam. He must also find a horse to take him to Kadambur.

Ambalavan remembered the astrologer who lived near the Durga temple on Kudanthai's outskirts. *The astrologer's reliable, but he's also close to the chief minister and the royal family. That doesn't matter: and this is my chance to see whether astrology is an accurate science.*

Ambalavan went to the astrologer's house. The huge tree before the temple had fallen. A chariot stood there, drawn by two horses. The body of the chariot was a boat; these vehicles were specially designed for floods—in case the water rose suddenly, the boat could be detached and rowed across the river while the horses swam across. *This chariot either belongs to the chief minister or the royal family. I can borrow the chariot to go to Kadambur.* Ambalavan heard women's voices when he went to the door of the house and sighed in relief. *It's Princess Kundavai. I can warn her about the danger to her father and brothers and leave the matter in her capable hands. Then I can rush to Kadambur where my main duty lies.*

The astrologer's disciple, unable to recognize Ambalavan in this state, blocked his way. Ambalavan caught the poor man by the neck, roared angrily, threw him on the road and charged into the house like an elephant in musth.

Grant Me a Boon

KUNDAVAI WAS TROUBLED by Poonkuzlali's and Mandakini's disappearance. She became more anxious when Aniruddha told her that the storm had forced Arulmozli out into the open and that he was on his way to Thanjavur at the head of a huge procession of excited people. If Arulmozli tried to enter the fort with this crowd, the Pazluvur soldiers would stop him. Velir and his army had reached Kodumbalur. If the two armies clashed, the Chola kingdom would explode into civil war. Her father would be devastated and his life would be at risk.

Determined to prevent all this, Kundavai decided to intercept Arulmozli and take him to Pazlayarai until things calmed down. She would ask Ambalavan to come there from Kadambur and tell him that Arulmozli was not interested in the throne; she would then take Arulmozli to Thanjavur with the chancellor's consent. Kundavai confided her plans to her mother and Aniruddha and set out from Thanjavur with Vanathi. On her way, she stopped at the Kudanthai astrologer's house to see if his predictions gave her any comfort.

Kundavai had just started to tell the astrologer her worries when they heard a commotion at the door. She recognized Ambalavan's angry roar and her hair stood on end. *Why's he here? He must have come to consult the astrologer. This is a good chance to find out what's in his mind.* Kundavai quickly signaled her intention to the astrologer, pulled Vanathi behind her and hurried into the next room. No sooner had she shut the door than Ambalavan barged into the house.

Ambalavan stared at the agitated astrologer and then looked around, disappointed. He recovered and said, "Yes, it's me, Lord Ambalavan, the chancellor. Why are you gawking at me? Have I changed so much? I need a favor from you, but first bring me food ... I'm starving!"

The astrologer stammered, "Forgive me, lord. I was so shocked to see you, I failed to welcome you. What can I do for you? Whatever simple food I have is yours. I can't even offer you a comfortable chair ... please sit on this bench." The astrologer pointed to the low bench on which Kundavai and Vanathi had been seated.

Ambalavan noticed the flowers strewn on the bench. "Just wrap the food in a leaf and give it to me: I'll eat it on my way. I must send an urgent message to my brother, Kalaanthaka. I don't have time to write, I'll give you an oral message and my signet ring. Go to Thanjavur at once or send your disciple; he looks quite strong ..."

"Lord, I beg you to take a few minutes to eat in my poor house ..."

"Astrologer, how can you be poor? I hear kings and princesses consult you."

"Lord, I'm shocked to see you like this. I hear the Kollidam has breached its bank. Did you get caught in the flood? Is Lady Nandini safe?"

Ambalavan laughed wildly. "The demon I married in my old age is safe in Kadambur. But I'm not sure she'll be alive tomorrow! Can you predict how long Nandini will live?"

The shaken astrologer said, "Lord, I don't understand, is this some kind of a test? I assure you I don't have Lady Nandini's horoscope but I can cast it in a few minutes."

"I'll write her horoscope myself: I'll end her lifeline with my own hands. Leave horoscopes aside. The comet fell early this morning - is it a sign that the emperor and his sons are in danger?"

"Lord, by tradition, we astrologers don't make political predictions. Some people believe a comet means good luck for the royal family. I heard this morning that the emperor is fine."

"We are blessed! If nothing happens to the emperor until tomorrow, we don't need to worry about him. What about Prince Arulmozli?"

"I heard he reached Thiruvarur last night. He's surrounded by thousands of people who are forcing him to go to Thanjavur."

"Even thousands of people may not be able to prevent his death. Let me tell you my predictions. The emperor and his two sons are in great danger today. Death lies in wait for the emperor in Pazluvur palace's underground vault. Death waits for Prince Arulmozli in the mahout's goad. Now it's up to you to save the emperor and the prince. Send your disciple to Thanjavur at once with my signet ring while you hurry to Thiruvarur and warn the prince. Will you do this?"

The astrologer was shocked. *Is he mad? No, he's excited, but he's telling the truth. I wonder what Princess Kundavai thinks.* Aloud, he said, "With Durga's blessings, I'll carry out your orders."

The two men heard the sound of anklets from the adjoining room. Ambalavan smiled. "Durga has given us her consent. I can now leave for Kadambur. I saw a chariot outside. I'll ride it up to the Kollidam and send it back. I'll cross the river in its boat."

The astrologer stammered, "My Lord ... the chariot ... I beg you ... don't take it ..."

"Don't worry, astrologer. I'm taking the chariot to save Prince Karikalan's life. Goddess Durga won't object to this. Now listen: she'll sound her anklets to give me her permission."

They heard the sound of anklets; Kundavai opened the door and walked in. Not in the least surprised, Ambalavan said, "Lady, I guessed you were in the next room. I hope you heard everything: I was almost shouting for your benefit."

"Forgive me for hiding from you."

"I'm the one who should apologize. But I'll earn your forgiveness only if I reach Kadambur before nightfall and save the crown prince's life. Lady, for three long years, this old man has been blinded by lust. You and Kalaanthaka tried to warn me, but I did not have the sense to listen to you. By Durga's grace, I overheard two Pandian conspirators talking last night. And now I know the complete truth. I kept that she-devil in my house: she made me betray the Cholas and gave the enemy gold from my vault. Only if I kill her will the anger in my heart be satisfied."

To Ambalavan's shock, Kundavai fell at his feet. "My father is devoted to you; you are my grandfather. I beg you to grant me a boon. Promise me you'll give me whatever I ask for."

"Princess, I betrayed your family: I can never compensate you for that. My first priority now is to save the lives of your father and brothers. But whatever you want is yours. Quick!"

"Promise me you won't harm Lady Nandini: that's the boon I want from you."

"Are you joking? My old age has addled my brain, but I'm not mad. I'll let her know I'm aware she cheated me. Then I'll kill her with my sword. Only then will justice be served; only then can I punish her accomplices. Go, my dear girl, go and save your father and brother."

"I will, *thatha*. But I must also save my sister: Lady Nandini is my own sister."

The shocked Ambalavan murmured, "Am I still dreaming?"

"Nandini's mother was my father's first love. It was she who saved Arulmozli when he fell into the Ponni. My father believed she was dead. He fainted when he saw Nandini in the women's quarters because he thought he was seeing her mother ... the shock of seeing her look-alike was too much for him."

Ambalavan remembered that Nandini had insisted that he take her to the emperor's room at midnight. Sundara Chola had shrieked with terror on seeing her. Nandini had used him for her own plans. "You have convinced me. Does the emperor know this?"

"He came to know only recently. We had a hard time convincing him she wasn't a ghost."

"Does Karikalan know Nandini's his sister?"

"He must know by now: I sent a message to him through the same messenger he sent me."

"Ah! You're talking about Vandhiya Devan. I don't think he told Karikalan. And even if he did, I doubt Karikalan would have believed him. I myself couldn't believe you. And it makes no difference whether Nandini knows this or not. The conspirators will somehow find a way to assassinate Karikalan tonight. You have made my task even more urgent. I must stop Nandini from committing the unforgivable crime of killing her own brother. I'll take your chariot and go to Kadambur. It's up to you to save your father and brother."

"I'll arrange a vehicle from Pazlayarai and rush to Thanjavur. As for Arulmozli, I'm confident his stars will protect him."

"My girl, don't trust astrologers and their predictions. They'll make a prediction with a double meaning and later say, 'I told you so!'" Ambalavan hurried away.

Seconds later, Azlvarkkadian came in saying, "I agree: never trust astrologers."

Vanathi's Oath

"Thirumalai, how did you turn up here? What do you want?" Kundavai asked.

"Lady, this morning, the astrologer told me my mission would be a success. But I couldn't go even a short distance from his house. I came back to ask him if he had deliberately fooled me. I was suspicious on hearing Lord Ambalavan's voice. But I didn't expect to find you here."

"Why are you here? What's this mission? Is it a secret?"

"Are there any secrets you don't know? The chief minister asked me to go to Nagapattinam and bring Prince Arulmozli to Thanjavur. He also asked me to stop at Pazlayarai and give Sembiyan Madevi a message. When did you leave Thanjavur, lady?"

"Shortly after dawn. Why do you ask, Thirumalai?"

"The chief minister received two pieces of news last night. One, Prince Arulmozli is on his way here with a huge crowd of supporters …" He paused and looked at Vanathi.

"Thirumalai, you know how close Vanathi is to me. You can say anything to me before her."

"This concerns her. The chief minister heard that General Velir and his army were near Thanjavur last night. The general sent him a message accusing the Pazluvur brothers of imprisoning the emperor in Thanjavur Fort and Prince Arulmozli in some secret prison. He demands the Pazluvur brothers immediately surrender the posts of Chancellor and Commander of the Fort and bring Prince Arulmozli here. Or, by this evening, he'll lay siege to Thanjavur Fort. The Kodumbalur army is camped along the fort's southern and western walls."

"What! The chief minister didn't say a word to me!"

"Maybe he wanted Lady Vanathi to leave the fort. Lord Kalaanthaka may use her as a hostage."

"Really? Would he dare to do that?"

"Yes, lady. The general's message also demands that Prince Arulmozli and Lady Vanathi be married immediately. He says that since Prince Karikalan is not interested in the throne, Prince Arulmozli must immediately be anointed crown prince. The general insists that if all his conditions are not met within three days, he'll raze the fort to the ground. He says the people support him."

Vanathi said angrily, "*Akka,* has my uncle gone mad?"

"Your uncle has only openly said what has been in many people's mind for years."

"Lady, Malayaman is probably near Kadambur with his army; the situation is spiraling out of control—it looks like a Mahabharata is inevitable."

"Well said, Thirumalai! This civil war will be a war between blood relatives. The Pazluvur, Kodumbalur and Malayaman clans have all mingled their blood with the Chola dynasty: yet now they are raring to fight with each other. The Chola kingdom will be destroyed in this war."

"Let them fight and die! But why's my uncle dragging me into this? I want to go and ask him."

"Vanathi, old men like your uncle pay no attention to girls. Only Arulmozli can stop this war. Thirumalai, why did you come back? Where's Arulmozli now?"

"I heard that he planned to leave Thiruvarur last night but was stopped by the flood. I too could not go to Pazlayarai; the Kudamurutti has breached its banks and become an ocean."

"The flood waters will drain and Arulmozli must come this way. There's nothing to do but wait. I'm afraid disaster will strike Thanjavur before that. Thirumalai, go back to Thanjavur and give the general a message from me: he must not lay siege to Thanjavur Fort till Arulmozli arrives."

"*Akka,* let me go with him to Thanjavur; I'll ask my uncle not to drag me into this."

"Why? Don't you want to marry Arulmozli?"

"Whether I want to or not, I hate him linking my wedding with the prince's coronation. It gives the impression my uncle is starting this war only to make me queen," Vanathi said angrily.

"It looks as if Lady Vanathi hates the idea of being queen ..." It was Poonkuzlali.

Kundavai was amazed. "My girl, what are you doing here? Where's Lady Mandakini?"

"Lady, forgive me. My aunt dragged me through the secret passage under Pazluvur palace and forced me to leave Thanjavur Fort. I hate palace life. If Lady Vanathi herself hates the thought of being queen, how can someone like me enjoy living in a palace?"

"*Akka*, she's mocking me. She's hinting I want to marry your brother only because I want to sit on the throne," Vanathi said.

"Stop it! This is not the time to quarrel. Poonkuzlali, where's your aunt?" Kundavai asked.

"She's in the Pazluvur vault," Poonkuzlali replied.

"Why?" exclaimed Kundavai.

"Because an assassin is waiting there with a spear." Poonkuzlali laughed. "You should have seen the time we gave him … he thought we were ghosts and ran around like he was possessed!"

Is she mad? Kundavai wondered. "Who's he? Why's he hiding there?"

"That's all I know, lady. My aunt has extraordinary powers to compensate for being a deaf-mute. She senses that he's waiting to assassinate someone in the palace. Lady, my aunt's not mad as you think. The entrance to the secret underground passage to Pazluvur palace is between Ravana's arms: that's why she was breaking the statue."

"We now know how Lady Mandakini entered the palace," said Azlvarkkadian.

"We did not know about this all these years," Kundavai said. "But, Poonkuzlali, why didn't you let us know at once? Why did you leave your aunt alone with that assassin?"

"My aunt is stubborn. She insisted she would take care of that man and made me leave. Her instincts tell her Prince Arulmozli's in danger. She asked me to go to him."

"So, you were going in search of Arulmozli! Why did you stop here then?"

"Lady, I'll be frank. I decided not to get involved in palace affairs any more. I was on my way to Kodikkarai. I met this Vaishnava and he brought me here."

"My girl, why do you dislike us? What have we done to you?" Kundavai asked.

"No one has done anything to me. Just as some people dislike the throne, I dislike palace life." Poonkuzlali gave Vanathi a sidelong mocking glance.

Vanathi stepped forward angrily. "*Akka,* she's teasing me again. I swear on your blessed feet, with the sky and the earth as my witness: If Prince Arulmozli survives today, if he marries me, if I'm fortunate enough to be his wife, I'll never sit on the throne of Thanjavur. This is my oath!"

The Thatched Roof Floats

THERE WAS SHOCKED silence.

Kundavai's voice showed her anger and pity. "What foolishness! What have you done?"

"*Akka,* I have thought about this for days: I have now made it public."

Poonkuzlali burst out laughing. Then, the boat girl covered her face with her hands and sobbed as though her heart would break. Finally, she began to sing.

Kundavai turned to Azlvarkkadian. "These two girls will drive me mad! Thirumalai, why did you come back here with this girl?"

"Lady, this girl and I were stopped by the flood. She offered to row me to Thiruvarur if I got her a boat. I came back here to ask the astrologer for help. I was glad to see your chariot and hoped to take the boat but Lord Ambalavan has taken both."

"You heard everything Lord Ambalavan said. What do you suggest now?"

"Lady, we're wasting time here. The emperor's life is in danger. Even the chief minister is not aware of this. Hurry to Thanjavur Fort with Lady Vanathi. You have the best chance of getting through General Velir's army and Lady Vanathi will come in useful. I'll console the boat girl and go to Prince Arulmozli. I have already sent the astrologer's disciple for a boat."

Vanathi jumped up. "Never! I'll go to Prince Arulmozli: if I die, I'll die at his feet!"

At this, Poonkuzlali shrieked, "I have to go back to my fire-spitting lovers in Kodikkarai!"

The astrologer shouted, "Ladies, quiet!"

In the silence, they heard a loud roar which made their hair stand on end.

"Lady, the Arasalar has breached its bank, sending its water into the Ponni. My house is near the Ponni—it will be washed away in the flood!" The terrified astrologer ran out, followed by the others. They saw a green wall of water, half the height of a coconut palm, roaring towards them. "Come! Our only hope is to climb on the temple's roof. Run!"

The flood reached the temple and the water rose to their ankles. Poonkuzlali was the first to jump on the temple's roof. The astrologer and Azlvarkkadian somehow clambered up after her. Poonkuzlali caught Kundavai's hand and pulled her up. Then, Kundavai and Poonkuzlali each took one of Vanathi's hands and pulled. When Vanathi realized that Poonkuzlali was holding her, she shook her hand free. The force of Vanathi's action made Kundavai lose her grip … Vanathi fell into the water which was now up to her neck and the flood carried her away. All this happened in a second.

Those on the temple's roof shouted desperately as the flood carried Vanathi to the thatched roof of the astrologer's house; she somehow climbed on to it. *Thank goodness, I'm out of danger.*

The others shared her relief. *When the disciple comes with the boat, we can rescue her.* "Hold on to the thatch! Don't let go!" they encouraged her.

The house's roof shook, the walls fell and the thatch floated on the water. Clinging to the thatch, Vanathi turned back to the temple and shouted, "*Akka*, Mother Ponni is taking me to him!" Vanathi was sure that they heard her: especially Poonkuzlali. Vanathi was carried away by the flood.

Poonkuzlali Leaps into the Flood

KUNDAVAI WATCHED VANATHI cling to the thatched roof. *She's brave and confident. My efforts to make her worthy of Arulmozli have paid off. The boat will be here soon ...*

She was startled by Azlvarkkadian's shout. "Lady, the thatch is floating! Astrologer, how long will it take for your disciple to bring a boat?"

"We can't wait for the boat. Thirumalai, save Vanathi, or I'll jump into the water. If anything happens to her, I'll die!" Kundavai said.

"Lady, let me think ... I'm ready to sacrifice my life for Lady Vanathi, but what good will that do? I can swim to the thatch and cling to it with her. But will it bear both our weights?"

Poonkuzlali mocked: "By the time the Vaishnava finishes thinking, Lady Vanathi will be dead." Her face darkened in anger as Azlvarkkadian said, "If that happens, the boat girl will be happy. Lord Vishnu will protect Lady Vanathi ... look! The boat is here!"

They saw the boat fighting against the current; by the time the boat reached the temple's roof and they all climbed in, Vanathi might drift out of sight. They shouted and gestured to the disciple to row the boat to Vanathi first but, thinking they were urging him to come quickly, he only tried rowing faster to them.

Poonkuzlali said, "Lady, let me swim to the boat, pick up Lady Vanathi and come back here. She fell into the water because of me; it's my duty to rescue her. Trust me."

Kundavai hesitated. "My girl, I trust you: it's Vanathi I don't trust."

"Aha, you're afraid she won't get into the boat with me! In that case, I'll climb out and let her have the boat." With that, Poonkuzlali leaped into the water and swam steadily to the boat.

The Elephant Throws the Mahout

ARULMOZLI STARTED HIS journey on elephant from Nagapattinam, accompanied by a huge crowd shouting, 'To Thanjavur!' That night, the procession reached Thiruvarur where the people gave the prince a grand reception. Arulmozhi heard that the Kollidam and the Ponni had breached their banks; it would take days for the water to drain. *I must leave the crowd behind. If I travel alone by elephant, I'll soon be in Thanjavur.* He ordered a servant to bring his mahout to him. The man came back to say that the elephant was tethered by the gate, but there was no sign of the mahout. "Send someone to look for him and bring him to me as soon as he returns."

The servant said, "Lord, there's a man who wants to see you urgently: his name is Murugayyan."

Feeling rather guilty for having forgotten the boatman, the prince asked the servant to send him in immediately. Murugayyan fell at the prince's feet and sobbed as he told his story.

Separated from his wife in Nagapattinam, Murugayyan had searched for her in the crowd in Thiruvarur. After more than an hour, he saw her walk into a side street with the elephant's mahout. The suspicious Murugayyan followed them. Another man joined them and the three of them left the town, crossed canals and fields and came to a crematorium on the outskirts. The terrified Murugayyan hid behind a tree and watched them.

The man who had joined Rakamma and the mahout smeared ash over his body and uttered some dreadful incantations. He then told the mahout, 'Beware! Your life is in danger!'

The agitated mahout cried, 'What danger? From where will it come?'

'Tomorrow morning, the elephant will be in musth; it will push you aside and run wild; the people will blame you—they'll beat you with your goad and kill you.'

'Aiyo! How can I save my life?' the mahout asked.

'Don't go near the elephant tomorrow,' said the sorcerer.

'How can I do that?' the mahout cried. 'I'll be punished by the king.'

'Come to my house. I'll give you a magic charm. Wear it and leave your goad behind.'

Unable to stand there any longer, Murugayyan had rushed back to warn the prince. Now, he began to sob again. "Lord, my suspicions are back: what has Rakamma got to do with all this?"

"Don't worry, I'll deal with her. Now go and find the mahout and bring him here."

Arulmozli recalled Kundavai's warning about the Pazluvur brothers and the Pandian conspirators. *This could be connected to one of those groups, or it could be nothing.* In either case, he made his plans and fell asleep.

Arulmozli was at the palace gate before dawn. The elephant sniffed him affectionately. There was no sign that it was in musth. "Where's the mahout?" Arulmozli shouted.

Seeing Murugayyan in the crowd, Arulmozli called him forward. The boat man said that he could not find the mahout. Rakamma had denied going to the crematorium and said that Murugayyan was mad.

"Don't worry, Murugayyan, just untie the chain around the elephant's foot," Arulmozli said.

Just then, the crowd shouted, 'Here's the mahout.' Arulmozli was shocked at the overnight change in the mahout: he looked like a man possessed by demons.

Holding a goad in one hand, the mahout touched the elephant's trunk with his other hand. The elephant suddenly curled its trunk around him, lifted him above its head and threw him. The man crashed to the ground far away and his goad fell even further. People shouted, 'The elephant's mad!' and scattered in all directions.

The Elephant's Mad!

ARULMOZLI DECIDED, *I must grab this opportunity. That man was not the mahout; the elephant sensed his evil intentions and attacked him. There's no time to make enquiries now.* Arulmozli whispered into Murugayyan's ears, climbed on to his shoulders and leaped from there on to the elephant's back. He knocked down the howdah and spoke quietly to the elephant: the elephant trumpeted and ran.

Murugayyan shouted, "Run! Run! The elephant's mad!" The panicked crowd charged into side streets and houses. After all, no one wanted to face an elephant in musth.

Once Thiruvarur was behind him, Arulmozli left the Thanjavur Road and went across the fields towards Pazlayarai. He decided to meet

Kundavai there before going to Thanjavur. The elephant set a good pace, easily crossing rivers, fields and canals.

Murugayyan shouted, "The elephant's mad!" and ran to where the false mahout had fallen. He saw a man splashing his way out of a lotus pond: it was the man who had accompanied the real mahout and Rakamma to the crematorium the previous night. It was also the man who had pretended to be the mahout. Murugayyan went to him and said, "Mahout, luckily you escaped with your life. Where's your goad?"

Kiramavithan looked Murugayyan up and down. "Who are you? I just had a bath in the pond."

"In that case, where's the mahout? Where's my wife, Rakamma?"

The shocked Kiramavithan said, "How would I know? Mahout? Rakamma? Are you alright?"

"Sorcerer, you can't fool me. You took the mahout to the crematorium last night and warned him that the elephant would be mad in the morning," Murugayyan said fiercely.

Kiramavithan looked around to see if anyone was watching them. He smiled. "You are a greater sorcerer than I: you seem to know everything. I'll take you to your wife and the mahout. I came to warn the prince and see what I got as a reward! Anyway, I hope the prince is not hurt."

"The prince is fine; he's the one who sent me to find you and the mahout."

"You should ask him to reward me for saving his life." Kiramavithan stopped and pointed to some bushes. "Look … it's my goad." Kiramavithan ran to the bushes but Murugayyan was faster. He reached the bush, picked up the goad and turned around—Kiramavithan had disappeared.

Murugayyan went in search of the sorcerer's house. The alley was deserted and it was difficult to identify the house which he had seen the previous night. As he went slowly down the narrow street, he heard a moan from a locked house. Murugayyan climbed up to the terrace of a ruined house next door and jumped into the backyard of the locked house. He found the mahout tied to a pillar, frantically trying to bite the ropes which bound his legs and hands.

Relieved to see Murugayyan, whom he knew from Nagapattinam, the mahout cried, "Cut these ropes, Murugayyan. Is the prince safe?"

He told Murugayyan that Rakamma and the sorcerer had brought him there saying that they would give him a magic charm. They had burned some incense which made him faint. When he regained consciousness, he had found himself tied to the pillar.

The two men hurried to the palace where a worried crowd was gathered. The prince was missing. Some people insisted that they had seen him on top of the elephant while others refused to believe that. When they heard the mahout's story, the crowd's anxiety and anger grew. *The false mahout was sent by the prince's enemies ... maybe he was sent by the Pazluvur brothers! The prince is an excellent mahout ... he'll be safe.* The crowd took the highway to Thanjavur while a few people cut across the country and followed the path taken by the elephant.

Thirunallam

VANATHI CLUNG TO the thatch. Sometimes she drifted; sometimes the flood swept her along rapidly; sometimes she was whirled around by the current. She did not try to save herself when she had the chance to climb onto pavilion roofs. She believed that the Ponni was taking her to Arulmozli and that she was the one who would save him from the danger Ambalavan had referred to. *How arrogant Poonkuzlali is! How dare she be familiar with the prince? He would have survived even without her help: after all, the astrologer says it's his destiny to rule the world ...*

She noticed a boat some distance behind her with a man and a woman in it; the woman was at the oars. *Is it Poonkuzlali? Has the princess sent her to rescue me? The prince is indebted to Poonkuzlali for saving his life. Will I too end up being grateful to her? No, I must not be rescued by her!* The boat was sometimes near her; at other times, it faded into the distance as the rapid current carried the thatch faster.

Vanathi crossed a vast expanse of water and finally reached the other shore. She realized that the Ponni had breached its bank, flooded all the land in between, and finally emptied into the Arasalar whose high southern bank now contained the flood water. That southern shore, with its dense trees, was familiar to her. She recognized Thirunallam; she had accompanied Kundavai and Sembiyan Madevi there a few times. They had stayed at the Chola mansion on the riverbank.

The Fledglings

VANATHI LOVED THE garden pond in the Chola mansion in Thirunallam. One day, she sat there, waiting for Kundavai. A mahua tree blanketed the ground with flowers whose fragrance spread throughout the garden. Vanathi sat on a huge root, leaned back against the tree and listened to the birds. *How happy life is!* Vanathi saw the river between the trees. A young man was swimming in the river. She was captivated by the sight of his golden body partly submerged in the dark water. *Chi! How can I be so shameless as to admire a young man's body?* But in spite of her inherent modesty, she couldn't help looking towards the river once or twice.

Vanathi looked up at the sound of birds and saw a nest in a forked branch above her. She heard the little fledglings in it cheeping piteously in fear as a wild cat slowly went towards the nest.

Vanathi shouted, "Aiyo! Aiyo!"

"What is it?" She turned to see the young man who was bathing in the river running towards her.

Two adult woodpeckers circled the nest, trying to chase away the cat. Vanathi, orphaned when she was a child, was moved to tears to see the small birds trying to protect their babies. The cat touched the nest; Vanathi screamed and pointed out the nest to the young man now standing beside her. His smile melted her heart and she even forgot the birds for a second. He stood behind the nest and shooed the cat which stared into his eyes and growled. He picked up a stone and threw it at the cat. The stone struck the branch and the frightened cat leapt to another tree and disappeared. But the cat had dislodged the nest with its paw and the young man's stone had moved the nest further. The nest was now hanging precariously from the tree: if it fell, the fledglings would die. The parent birds circled the nest, crying.

The young man said, "Girl, spread the edge of your sari under the nest and catch it if it falls. I'll be back in a minute." He was back on an elephant. Vanathi went down the steps leading to the pond and sat there watching him. He stopped the elephant under the tree, stood on its back and gently replaced the nest securely. "Girl, where are you?" he shouted. Suddenly shy, Vanathi was quiet. He climbed down from the elephant and looked around. Suddenly, Vanathi laughed and he came towards her. "What's the joke?" he asked.

Vanathi was filled with happiness at the sound of his voice. She looked everywhere but at him as she said, "You brought an elephant to chase away a cat!"

He laughed. "Was it a cat? From your screams, I thought it was a tiger."

Vanathi asked, "Why should anyone fear a tiger—we have a tiger on our Chola flag."

He gave a radiant smile and said, "You chatterbox! I too belong to the Chola country. I have ridden an elephant on many battlefields. Who are you? Where are you from?"

"Mahout, don't be cheeky! Why do you want to know who I am? Will you take me for a ride?"

"What wages will you pay?"

"I'll ask my uncle to make you the head of Kodumbalur's elephant brigade."

His smile disappeared and he frowned. "Oh! You are the lady from Kodumbalur. There are hundreds of elephants and mahouts there. You don't need me." He walked away from her without turning back even once. He climbed on to his elephant and disappeared.

The handsome mahout, his smile and his voice were etched in her heart. She often thought of the incident and laughed in pleasure, to her embarrassment and guilt.

The mansion was abuzz with talk of Arulmozli coming to Thirunallam to see Kundavai. All the girls longed to see the prince, but he did not visit the women's quarters. On the day he left Thirunallam, Vanathi stood on the terrace and saw Arulmozli for the first time. As he rode by on an elephant, she realized that he was the mahout who had saved the fledglings. *My god! I offered to make him the commander*

of the elephant brigade in Kodumbalur, a small fiefdom in his mighty
kingdom. He must have thought I was an arrogant country bumpkin.
She felt like jumping into the pond and killing herself. She considered
telling Kundavai about it but could not bring herself to speak. To
Vanathi's relief, Kundavai also did not bring up the matter: obviously
the prince had kept it to himself.

Vanathi considered apologizing to Arulmozli in Pazlayarai but
felt she would rather die. She hid herself if he was anywhere nearby.
Kundavai and the other girls thought she was timid. Vanathi guessed
that the prince disliked her because it was widely known that her
uncle planned to arrange her marriage to Arulmozli, expecting him to
become the next emperor. Velir himself often dropped hints about this.
Vanathi was hurt when the other girls mocked her: 'You clever thing!
That's why you hide from the prince!'

When Arulmozli was leaving for Sri Lanka, Vanathi planned to
apologize with her eyes. But she had dropped her oil lamp and fainted
when he came near her. The prince had been very concerned and had
shown his regard for her on that day.

As she floated on the thatch, Vanathi thought, *I know he has a soft*
corner for me, but something stops him from loving me. She decided that
Arulmozli disliked being manipulated by her uncle into marrying her
just because Velir wanted his niece to become the next queen. *Once the*
prince knows I have sworn an oath never to sit on the Tiger Throne, he'll
understand the only thing I want is his love. But how will I tell him this? I
become speechless before him. The next time I see him, I'll tell him I want
him as a humble mahout and just want to ride with him on his elephant.
But will there be a next time? What if I die in this flood? No, I can see the
riverbank; I can see the dome of the Thirunallam mansion.

Vanathi saw a huge elephant wading through the flood with its
mahout sitting majestically on its back … it was Arulmozli. *No, it's*
my imagination. How can it be the prince? "Help, Mahout!" Vanathi
shouted. But the man did not turn. He rode on and disappeared around
the corner. Before she could get over her disappointment, the thatch
swirled in the current and entered deep flood waters which pushed
it towards the huge trees and roots on the bank. If the thatch crashed
on them, it would shatter. *If the thatch breaks, can I make it to the*
shore? Then, she saw a huge crocodile with yawning mouth near the

roots towards which the thatch was headed. She closed her eyes and surrendered herself to Durga: "Mother Durga, give me peace at your holy feet."

Crocodile!

VANATHI FELT THE shock of the thatch crashing into a tree's roots and shattering. But luckily, half her body caught in a curving branch of the tree and saved her. She clung to the branch as the flood waters dragged at her feet and pulled her sari. In a rush of courage, Vanathi gritted her teeth and climbed up to sit on a fork between two strong branches. As she squeezed the water from her sari, she heard a splash and looked down: the crocodile, covered by broken pieces of thatch, threshed the water with its tail and came to the surface. It looked up with its jaws open, as if inviting her to fall into its mouth.

In high spirits after her narrow escape, Vanathi spoke to the crocodile: "It's no use baring your teeth at me. Go find someone else to eat!" The crocodile stared unblinkingly up at her. Vanathi looked around. She was still in a dangerous position. The tree's branches were low and tilted steeply towards the water on one side; on the landward side, the branches were high; if she climbed down the trunk, she would directly face the crocodile. *I must jump to the ground from the higher branches; that's the only way out.* She tried to stand but her legs shook so badly, she was forced to sit down again. *Let's see who's more patient: the crocodile or I.*

She heard an elephant trumpet and saw the elephant which had gone past her earlier coming back towards her. At the same time, she saw the boat with Poonkuzlali and the astrologer's disciple approaching her along the shore. *Finally, it has to be Poonkuzlali who saves me.*

The boat came to the tree and Poonkuzlali saw Vanathi clinging to the branch. The boat girl laughed and said, "Lady, jump in quickly. Do you know who's on that elephant? It's the prince."

Vanathi looked at the man on the elephant as he came closer. *I don't want him to see me like this. As Poonkuzlali said, I had better jump into the boat at once.* Just then, the flood pushed the boat away from the tree. Not wanting to go with the boat, Poonkuzlali jumped into the water. *She has not seen the crocodile!* The horrified Vanathi shrieked a jumbled warning.

Poonkuzlali heard the word "Crocodile!" and turned to see the reptile close behind her with its open jaws. The crocodile threshed the water with its tail. Even Poonkuzlali's brave heart quailed at seeing the huge crocodile ten feet away from her. She had split seconds to make up her mind: she decided to swim for the boat. The astrologer's disciple, unaware of the danger, had rowed the boat a little distance away. As Poonkuzlali swam towards it, the whirling flood waters of the Ponni pulled her down, the crocodile chased her and her sari caught on a branch of the tree.

Vanathi saw all this from her perch on the tree. *The Chola kingdom and I are indebted to her for saving the prince's life. He'll be heartbroken if the crocodile kills her before he reaches here. What will he think of me? And she's in this situation only because she came to rescue me ...*

Vanathi climbed quickly to a lower branch, lay on it, reached a hand into the water and caught Poonkuzlali by her hair. Poonkuzlali looked up and stretched out a hand. Vanathi took it and pulled her up. With her other hand, Poonkuzlali caught a branch and pushed herself out of the flood. She climbed onto the branch on which Vanathi lay. Not strong enough to bear both their weights, the branch bent. Poonkuzlali tried to climb to a higher branch and stumbled: the next second, she hung between the tree and the water, held only by Vanathi's grip. The crocodile came out from under the tree roots and opened its mouth right under Poonkuzlali's swinging figure. Vanathi's delicate arm felt like it was being pulled out of its socket; her heart raced with fear that Poonkuzlali would fall into the crocodile's jaws. *I can never look the prince in the face if she slips. If she falls, I'll jump in after her.*

The elephant walked along the shore, stopped under the tree and trumpeted. The crocodile retreated to its place under the tree roots. It was impossible for Vanathi to bear Poonkuzlali's weight any longer. *Poonkuzlali means flower, but her body is made of steel. I can't take it ...* Vanathi heard Poonkuzlali scream and closed her eyes in terror; she could not bear to see the girl fall into the crocodile's mouth. She felt somebody pulling Poonkuzlali and tightened her own grip.

Then she heard Arulmozli's sweet voice: "Vanathi, let her go."

Vanathi let Poonkuzlali go and felt her shoulder relax; she opened her eyes. The elephant was gently placing Poonkuzlali on the riverbank. Poonkuzlali's eyes were closed. *She must have screamed when the elephant lifted her in its trunk. I remember how I fainted when an elephant lifted me. Princess Kundavai would be proud if she saw me now.* The elephant's trunk came towards her. Vanathi closed her eyes and felt herself being lifted and placed on the ground. When she opened her eyes, she was standing beside Poonkuzlali on the shore. Vanathi's heart brimmed with love for the boat girl and she hugged Poonkuzlali tightly.

Poonkuzlali was in tears. "Lady, I came to rescue you from the floods, but you saved my life. I'll never forget what you have done."

"Poonkuzlali, it's the mahout who saved us both: it's him you should thank." Vanathi gave the mahout a mischievous smile. "Mahout, will you take us for a ride on your elephant?"

My Father and Brother are in Danger!

THE PRINCE LAUGHED and climbed down from his elephant. "Managing an elephant is as difficult as managing a royal throne: climbing on to it is difficult, sitting on it is difficult and getting off it is even more difficult."

"But some people do it for the silliest reasons—like saving fledglings on trees."

"You remember that? You never mentioned it and I assumed you had forgotten. But I have to go to Thanjavur urgently. What happened? How did this girl get caught in such danger?"

"I'm glad you remember I'm here," Poonkuzlali said. "If you let me talk to you in confidence for a minute, I'll be on my way."

Arulmozli laughed. "Ocean Princess, you were in such a hurry, you refused to stop your boat when I called out to you. I never expected to see you later swinging on a branch over a crocodile's open mouth! And

I'll never forget how Vanathi struggled to hold you. But, how and why did the two of you come here? One of you tell me quickly!"

"Princess Kundavai and I were on our way to stop you from going to Thanjavur. She fears it will precipitate a civil war. She wanted to meet you first ..."

"Where's she now?"

"In Kudanthai. We stopped at the astrologer's house which got carried away in the flood. The princess and the others climbed to safety on the temple's roof, but because of my foolishness, I was carried away on the house's thatched roof ..."

"And I suppose Poonkuzlali came in the boat to rescue you. Finally, my elephant had to save you both. He lifted you as tenderly as he would a garland of flowers. And just this morning, the same elephant threw the mahout ..."

"I wanted to ask whether you were harmed by the mahout's goad!" Vanathi exclaimed.

"I managed to escape. But how did you know? Did the astrologer tell you?"

"Lord Ambalavan told us your life was in danger from a poisoned goad."

"Has he now become an astrologer—or, as many suspect, is he the reason behind this?"

"He overheard a Pandian conspiracy to kill your father, your brother and you on the same day."

"My god! Since his warning was true in my case, my father and brother are in danger." He turned to Poonkuzlali. "Ocean Princess, what message do you bring?"

"My aunt wants me to take you to Thanjavur at once."

"Is it true someone kidnapped her and took her to Thanjavur?"

"The chief minister did it only because he wanted her to meet the emperor." Poonkuzlali hesitated. "My aunt believes she's going to die soon: she wants to see you before that ..."

"My god! Vanathi, ask Kundavai to forgive me, I must go!"

Look! An Army!

THANJAVUR WAS IN a tumult. After the storm came the news that Arulmozli was alive and was marching to Thanjavur at the head of a huge crowd which was determined to crown him emperor. The people of Thanjavur lined the roads, prepared to give Arulmozli a grand welcome.

Inside the fort, there was an air of tense expectation. The fort gates had opened as usual that morning. But once the king's bodyguards marched in, the gates closed with a clang, heavy iron bolts slid into place, padlocks clicked and the drawbridge was raised.

Rumors spread like wildfire among the people. *The Pazluvur brothers want to stop Prince Arulmozli from entering the fort! If they dare to stop the prince, we'll break down the walls of the fort! Sundara Chola is dead! Will there be civil war?*

Suddenly a shout was heard: 'Look! An army!!' People rushed to climb trees and terraces and saw armed soldiers marching along all the three roads leading to the capital. It was the army of the southern command led by the Kodumbalur chieftain, Velir. It was known that Velir wanted his niece, Vanathi, to marry Arulmozli and make Arulmozli the next emperor.

What perfect timing! Prince Arulmozli is on his way here from the east and the general has arrived from the south with his army. Anything could happen!

The crowds cheered Velir who was here to support Arulmozli, the people's favorite. By sunset, Velir had sealed three of the fort's entrances. He ignored the fourth entrance as the Vadavar flowed along that wall of the fort and the river was in spate; no one could enter that way. Velir pitched his tent before the main northern entrance and summoned a meeting of the powerful Merchants Guild, the City Council and other city officials.

The Council

AFTER A FEW introductory remarks, the general said, "From the time of Vijayalaya Chola, we have given our lives to found and protect the vast Chola empire. Our enemies may accuse us of assembling here without the emperor's permission, but we are unable to meet the emperor and do not know what his wishes are. Using his illness as an excuse, the Pazluvur brothers have imprisoned him in the fort."

Voices shouted, "Yes!" "It's true!" "The emperor's a prisoner!"

"Can we believe that Sundara Chola, who belongs to the brave Chola dynasty, refuses to come out of his palace because of his illness? His enemies have clouded his mind with their black magic. Otherwise, would he choose the cowardly Madurandaka to be his successor, instead of his own two sons who are brave warriors?"

"How do we know the emperor wants to make Madurandaka king?" several voices asked.

"We don't know, but we are here to find out the truth. In spite of the rumors, I'm confident the emperor is alive. We'll meet him and let him directly tell us what he wants." He paused. "If by chance the emperor wants to make Madurandaka his successor, will you agree?"

There was a loud chorus of "No! No!"

"I too will not agree. Sundara Chola is not in his senses if he chooses Madurandaka as his heir. The question of the succession was settled clearly by Emperor Paranthaka on his deathbed: Sundara Chola and his heirs were to succeed Gandara Aditya. And the revered Sembiyan Madevi is against her son becoming king—she must have a good reason for this. In such circumstances, why would Sundara Chola want to make Madurandaka his successor? Prince Arulmozli and I destroyed the Lankan army, captured Anuradhapura and forced King Mahinda into hiding in the forest. It was Prince Arulmozli's inspiring leadership which gave our men the courage to defeat the Lankan army. If the emperor is mentally fit, would he issue an arrest warrant for the prince?"

"General, how do you know the arrest warrant was issued by the emperor?"

"We are here to find out the truth of that too. A rumor was spread that the prince is dead, but I did not believe this. Many of you here agreed with me that the prince, aware of the conspiracy against him, was in hiding, waiting for the right time to show himself. We are vindicated: the prince is on his way here from Nagapattinam with a huge crowd and we are here to support him. But the conspirators have made their next move ..."

"What? What?"

"Just a few minutes ago, I heard that when the prince was leaving Thiruvarur, his elephant went mad, threw its mahout and ran away. In that confusion, the prince is missing."

"Aiyo!" "What new disaster is this?" "Even god is on the side of the conspirators!"

Velir waved his hands for silence. "Prince Arulmozli is not only a matchless warrior, he is also wise. He will not fall into the enemy's traps. I expect to hear good news about him soon. In the meanwhile, we must decide our next course of action. What are your opinions?"

It was decided that their representatives would ask for a meeting with the emperor the next day. They would tell the emperor clearly that they were against Madurandaka succeeding him. Some insisted that the emperor should either remove the Pazluvur brothers from their commands or move out of their control and go to Pazlayarai. A few said that if they were not allowed to meet the emperor, they must enter the fort by force. Some advised patience until they heard from Arulmozli and suggested that Aditya Karikalan be asked to come to Thanjavur. As the men declared their opinions, a sentry came and whispered to Velir.

"Just a minute," the general said and rushed out of his tent.

Make Way for Lady Vanathi

VELIR JUMPED ON his horse and galloped to the fort's northern gate. He saw an elephant there, with a mahout and two women on its back.

The mahout blew a horn and announced, "Make way for Lady Vanathi, General Velir's niece and Princess Kundavai's companion!

Lady Vanathi brings a message for the emperor from Princess Kundavai. She also brings an important message for Lord Kalaanthaka from his brother, Lord Ambalavan. Open the gate for Lady Vanathi and her companion, Madam Poonkuzlali!"

The mahout's voice sounds familiar … that doesn't matter. But if it's really Vanathi on the elephant, I must not let her enter the fort. Better to keep the child with me until all this trouble is over. The general stopped his horse near the elephant and his guard raised a flaming torch high. The amazed general saw that it was indeed Vanathi and Poonkuzlali on the elephant.

"Vanathi, my child!" Velir said. "Couldn't Princess Kundavai find another messenger?"

"Uncle, we heard you have laid siege to Thanjavur Fort. The princess judged I had the best chance of getting through your men and into the fort. She sent Poonkuzlali with me."

"But what message is so important that you have brought it at night?"

"I bring the emperor urgent news of Prince Arulmozli."

"Is the prince okay? Do you know where he is?"

"The prince is fine, uncle. I have promised I won't tell anyone where he is now."

The general was furious. "Girl, Princess Kundavai has made you stubborn! Get down from the elephant. The first thing I must do is send you back to Kodumbalur!"

"Uncle, don't come too close to this elephant. Just this morning, it threw its mahout. Let me deliver my message. After that I'll come to you and you can send me to Kodumbalur."

The general stepped back quickly and thought it over. "Okay, child, I won't stop you. But, what will you do if they don't open the gate?"

"Uncle, if they refuse to open the gate, you can break it down with your army."

The general straightened his shoulders proudly. "Spoken like a true Kodumbalur woman! Lord Kalaanthaka will not dare to stop you from giving the emperor a message from Princess Kundavai. Give Kalaanthaka a message from me: tell him that if he harms a hair on your head, I'll annihilate his entire clan; tell him that if I don't meet the emperor in person by tomorrow evening, I'll attack Thanjavur Fort."

"Very well, uncle," Vanathi agreed.

The mahout shouted again, "Make way for Lady Vanathi! Open the gate for Lady Vanathi!"

Where Have They Gone?

KALAANTHAKA WAS WORRIED. He was brave, but he was not used to acting independently of his brother. Right from dawn, bad news flowed steadily into the fort. It was two days since Ambalavan had left Kadambur for Thanjavur. A man who had traveled with him said that their boat had capsized in the Kollidam and that he himself had made it to the shore with great difficulty. Kalaanthaka feared that Ambalavan had drowned in the Kollidam. Another spy came with news that Arulmozli had come out of hiding in Nagapattinam and was coming to Thanjavur with a huge crowd of supporters. Next, Sambuvaraya sent word that Malayaman was marching to Kadambur with an army and Aditya Karikalan was acting like a madman. Sambuvaraya asked Ambalavan to return to Kadambur at the earliest. The next piece of news fell on Kalaanthaka's head like a thunderbolt: Velir was marching on Thanjavur with his army. Kalaanthaka ordered the gates to be closed. No one was to be allowed into or out of the fort. He stationed the king's bodyguards around the emperor's palace and used his own men to guard the fort.

Kalaanthaka decided to inform the emperor of all these developments after consulting the chief minister. Kalaanthaka did not trust Aniruddha, but he was glad to have him in the fort today as he could keep an eye on him. He could also pretend to ask for his advice, so that if things went wrong, he need not shoulder the entire blame. Kalaanthaka believed that Arulmozli and Velir were conspiring together to capture Thanjavur Fort. The emperor might find this hard to believe, but Aniruddha could convince him.

Aniruddha was not happy about Kundavai leaving in the morning. The disappearance of Mandakini and Poonkuzlali also bothered him. *Where have they gone? How?* He was alarmed at the news that Velir was marching on Thanjavur with a huge army.

But Aniruddha insisted that there was no need to trouble the emperor. "The queen sent word confidentially that the emperor's mental distress is very bad. If we tell him about the general now, we risk him rupturing a blood vessel. The city is abuzz with rumors of the emperor's death ... think what would happen if he really died now! Your enemies will accuse you of killing him. Let's find out what the general wants and wait until we get reliable news of Prince Arulmozli and Lord Ambalavan."

Kalaanthaka was relieved. "I'll leave it to you to inform the emperor at the right time. I'll focus on the fort's defense." Kalaanthaka walked along the fort's perimeter and reviewed his defenses. He also needed to know what was happening outside the fort. There were only two secret passages out of the fort. The tunnel from Ambalavan's treasure vault could not be used now as the Vadavar was in spate and the vault would be flooded if the exit gate was opened. The second passage was in Aniruddha's house. No one could use it without Kalaanthaka's knowledge as he had set up a sentry post at the point where it crossed the fort wall. Kalaanthaka decided to send his men through it to Kadambur and Pazlayarai to gather information about Ambalavan and Arulmozli.

A soldier ran up to him with news about the elephant at the northern gate. *How dare Vanathi ask to come in when her uncle is outside with his army?* His first instinct was to refuse to let her in but by the time he reached the gate, he changed his mind. *Why should I fear a young girl?* He was also curious to hear her news. He climbed to the terrace above the gate and saw the mahout and the two girls. He recognized Vanathi and overheard a part of her conversation with Velir. His suspicions vanished when he realized that she was stubbornly insisting on coming into the fort against her uncle's advice. *It's strange that my brother's sending me a message through this girl. It may be a trick ... we'll see ...*

A horn from the terrace above the fort's entrance blared in reply to the mahout's horn. A torch flared and showed glinting spears and bows ready to spring into action. A loud voice announced, "The fort's gates will be opened for Lady Vanathi. Only the elephant and the people it carries will be allowed inside. If anyone else tries to follow, he will be killed!" At this, Velir and his escort moved back. The gates opened and the drawbridge was lowered. The elephant crossed the moat and entered the fort. The gates closed again and the drawbridge was raised.

Kalaanthaka waited for them on his elephant. He declared majestically, "Lady, welcome. I'm glad you disobeyed your uncle to be our guest. I assure you no harm will come to you here."

Vanathi said, "Once I have delivered my messages, you can throw me into your dungeon for all I care!"

Stop Right There!

"GIRL, I'M BUSY: quickly give me my brother's message."

"He asked me to tell you Veerapandian's bodyguards are targeting the royal family today. He warned you to guard the emperor."

Kalaanthaka mocked her: "If my brother takes care of the Kodumbalur army outside the fort, I can take care of the emperor inside. None of you need worry about that!"

"Lord, knowing you might not trust me, Lord Ambalavan gave me another message about a sorcerer who often visited Lady Nandini. Lord Ambalavan says, 'Thambi, I made a serious mistake: that sorcerer is Ravidasan, the leader of the Pandian conspirators who have sworn to destroy the Cholas. One of his men will try to assassinate the emperor today. Be very careful.'"

Kalaanthaka was shocked; no one but his brother could have sent this message. "Girl, if this is true, why didn't he come here at once? Why did he send you? Where did you meet him?"

"We met him at the Kudanthai astrologer's house. Lord Ambalavan's boat capsized in the flood; he escaped and was sleeping in a memorial when he overheard the conspirators' plans. Prince Aditya Karikalan's life too is and danger and Lord Ambalavan has returned to Kadambur."

"Girl, even if what you say is true, no one can enter the fort."

"What if they are already inside the fort? Anyway, that's your responsibility. Now, I must deliver Princess Kundavai's message to the emperor."

"You can give me the message."

"Princess Kundavai commanded me to meet the emperor in person: here's her signet ring."

"Everybody seems to carry a signet ring these days! The emperor's health is not good today."

"The news I bring about Prince Arulmozli will be the best medicine for him."

"Come, come! Let's not delay: tell the emperor what you have to say."

Kalaanthaka rode ahead on his elephant. He had never seen Arulmozli as a rival to his son-in-law, Madurandaka. He knew that the emperor had no idea of crowning Arulmozli and that the prince would never disobey his father. He was only worried that Kundavai would cause trouble. *Is Kundavai hatching some plot? If this girl gives the emperor news of Arulmozli, the emperor will let me know. Once I know Arulmozli's intentions, I can make plans accordingly.*

Both elephants reached the palace entrance and everyone dismounted. At Kalaanthaka's command, a guard opened the palace door. Kalaanthaka gestured to his men and gave them orders. He commanded the captain of the king's bodyguards to ensure that the palace was guarded securely at night. He was troubled by Vanathi's message and particularly worried that Veerapandian's bodyguards had penetrated Thanjavur Fort. *But what can the sorcerer or any of his men do? Not even a fly can enter the emperor's palace without my permission. I'll strengthen the security around the palace. Thank goodness I locked the gates today. I'll order the detention of any suspicious-looking people in the fort …*

Kalaanthaka turned to see the two women cross the open courtyard and reach the palace door. The mahout was behind them. Kalaanthaka was furious. *Why is the mahout following them? Can the mahout be the assassin? Is he one of the general's men? Has he fooled the girls—and me?* Kalaanthaka ran to the mahout and caught his hand. "You rogue! Stop right there! Why are you entering the palace?" he roared.

The women turned, alarmed and curious. Vanathi smiled and stammered, "He is … he is …"

Kalaanthaka ignored her. He tightened his iron grip on the mahout's arm. "Who are you? The truth, now!" With his other hand, Kalaanthaka turned the mahout's face to the light of the torch mounted on the wall.

The mahout said, "Commander, I'm a mahout too. I'm here to surrender to my father in obedience to the arrest warrant issued by him."

Kalaanthaka saw his face and froze. Slowly, his hand loosened its grip on Prince Arulmozli.

Why the Disguise?

ARULMOZLI STOOD THERE with a mischievous glint on his handsome face.

The shocked Kalaanthaka broke into a sweat and his voice trembled. "Sir, what's the meaning of this? Forgive me …"

Arulmozli stopped him. "There's nothing to forgive. You were only doing your duty."

"Why the disguise? Did you think I would stop you from meeting your father? I would have given you a hero's welcome with every royal courtesy …"

"The general is outside with his army and would not have let me enter the fort. This disguise is for him—thank goodness he did not look closely at me. Your eyes are sharper." He paused. "You too are a father to me. I don't want to defy you and see my father."

"Prince, do you want me to stand guard here or come in with you? Your wish is my command."

"Commander, it looks like you will have to stand here. Look!"

Kalaanthaka turned to see his men coming towards them, along with the king's bodyguards. The awed soldiers stared at the prince whose face was lit by the torch. Under Kalaanthaka's stern eyes, subdued cheers of "Long live Prince Arulmozli!" rang through the courtyard.

"Now, do you see the need for my disguise, commander?" Arulmozli smiled.

"Yes, lord. I'll manage these men. Hurry inside."

My Death is Near

KALAANTHAKA ADDRESSED THE soldiers sternly. "What's the meaning of this? Don't you know the emperor is lying ill inside and our enemies are waiting outside?"

The captain spoke up: "How can Velir's men be our enemies? We hear they have laid siege to Thanjavur Fort to make Prince Arulmozli the next emperor." He turned to his men. "And what do you say to that?"

"We agree!" "Long live Ponni's Beloved!" the men shouted.

Kalaanthaka's face darkened and his moustache twitched. "Is it up to the general to choose the next emperor? Is it up to you? Do you have no respect for the emperor's wishes?"

The captain said, "Commander, we are worried that we have not met the emperor today."

"The emperor is not well and refused to hold court today. Now that the prince is back …"

"We want to see the prince!" "Long live Prince Arulmozli!" the men shouted.

"Let the prince meet his father. Then he'll see you."

"Really? Or will he be sent to the dungeon?" the captain asked.

Kalaanthaka controlled his urge to draw his sword and cut down the captain. His eyes blazed and he roared with laughter. "Whether the prince sits on the throne or goes to the dungeon depends on the emperor. And if he goes to the dungeon, he has to come this way—you can see him then."

Ignoring their shouts, Kalaanthaka climbed the palace steps and saw Poonkuzlali standing there. "Girl, what are you doing here? Did anyone stop you from going in?"

"No. I did not want to intrude on father and son when they are meeting after months. It was my idea which ensured that the prince could meet his father while the emperor is still alive."

"Are you mad? Is this about stupid rumors and predictions? Or is there something you know?"

"If anything happens to the emperor, everyone will blame you," Poonkuzlali pointed out.

"I won't wait to be blamed by anyone: I'll take my own life. When the king's bodyguards swore their oath before Goddess Durga, I was the one who took the first oath."

"What's the use of that? The Chola kingdom will lose its emperor and also a brave warrior. Doesn't it make more sense to prevent the assassination?"

"Girl, even the chief minister cannot enter the palace without my knowledge."

"But what if the danger lies inside the palace? Isn't there a secret passage to the palace?"

The commander was shocked. "Girl, how do you know about this? Only a handful of people know the secret. No one who goes in comes out alive …"

"My aunt took me there this morning. A Pandian conspirator is hiding there with a sharp spear."

"Your aunt?"

"The lady who came from Kodikkarai in the Pazluvur palanquin. We are wasting time … pick up a torch and come with me. I'll tell you the rest on our way."

Kalaanthaka dispatched a company to Ambalavan's palace. He took a torch from a guard and said, "Girl, lead the way. Let's see if you're speaking the truth." *Maybe this girl is trying to cheat me. Maybe she wants me to show her the passage so that she can lead the Kodumbalur men inside. I'll let her go ahead and see if she knows the way. And if an assassin is really hiding there, I'll trap him like a fox in its hole and kill him.* Kalaanthaka hurried to keep pace with Poonkuzlali who rushed ahead of him.

Before dawn that day, Mandakini and Poonkuzlali had groped their way down the tunnel, climbed a few steps and reached a large, dark hall with pillars. Soon, faint sunlight came in from a high window on one wall; it was morning. They were in an underground treasury. Poonkuzlali thought: *How can we find the man we saw? There are a hundred places for him to hide in. He could creep up on us from behind and kill us …*

Mandakini suddenly hollered in that strange voice between that of man and beast—a man rushed out from the shadows with a cry of terror.

Poonkuzlali smiled. *That thug thinks that aunt's a ghost and he's running for his life.* Mandakini howled again: the man dashed madly about the hall until he crashed into a wooden door. He banged desperately on it until it opened. A woman stood on the other side. The woman hesitated as the man argued and threatened her. Finally, she nodded and went away, while the man stood at the open door, looking fearfully around him. The woman came back with a lighted lamp and they entered the hall together. Mandakini quickly pulled Poonkuzlali into hiding behind a large pillar. The couple passed them and went into the treasury.

"Stop blabbering about witches and ghosts!" the woman exclaimed. "It's obvious you're frightened out of your wits. Why did you accept this assignment?"

Mandakini dragged Poonkuzlali through the open door and into a large garden. In a secluded corner, she signaled, "My death is near. I must see Arulmozli before I die—bring him here."

Poonkuzlali was reluctant to leave her beloved aunt, but she could not refuse. Glad to have an excuse to meet Arulmozli, she jumped over the garden wall and went to the fort entrance. She happened to meet Azlvarkkadian who told her that he was on his way to meet the prince. She traveled with him. When they met Kundavai at the astrologer's house and heard Ambalavan's news about the Pandian conspirators, Poonkuzlali guessed that the man hiding in the vault was one of the gang. After Arulmozli rescued her and Vanathi, Poonkuzlali recalled how he had disguised himself as a mahout in Sri Lanka. She suggested that they ride together to Thanjavur on his elephant, with him acting as their mahout. She was delighted when he agreed: "Ocean Princess, excellent idea! You are worthy of being the chief minister of a great kingdom."

But now, her aunt was missing. Poonkuzlali's heart ached when she thought of her aunt's words: 'My death is near.' *What's the use of my bringing the prince here? I can't find my aunt. Maybe she's in the vault … maybe that assassin has killed her. I must get into the vault.*

But people hurried about in excitement at Arulmozli's arrival. If she was seen going to the Art Gallery, they would be suspicious. And if the assassin was there, it was better not to be caught alone. Poonkuzlali cleverly manipulated the commander to come with her and rushed to the vault. Her instincts screamed that some great doom was around the corner. *I don't care what happens to me. Let my aunt be safe.* When they reached the entrance to the Art Gallery, Poonkuzlali thought she saw a dark shadow on the palace's upper terrace and a figure walking along the wall. She paused ...

Kalaanthaka sneered, "Why have you stopped? Are you afraid your lies will be exposed?" Poonkuzlali showed him the opening to the tunnel. "You go first," Kalaanthaka said.

Just then, Poonkuzlali heard her aunt shriek and rushed past Kalaanthaka to the emperor's room. She heard her aunt shriek again. The emperor leaned on his bed, holding Arulmozli's hand. Vanamadevi and Vanathi stood on his other side while Mandakini stood before the bed, screaming like a madwoman. No one saw the spear whizzing towards the emperor from the terrace window. Poonkuzlali raced towards her aunt ...

Guardian Deity

BEFORE POONKUZLALI REACHED her aunt, the spear pierced Mandakini's chest and she fell to the ground with a last scream. Pitiful cries filled the room as everyone turned to Mandakini. At the same time, clay vessels rained down into the room through the terrace window; one knocked down the oil lamp by the emperor's bed and the room was plunged into darkness. There was chaos.

Above the sound of running footsteps, Kalaanthaka roared, "A lamp! Get a lamp!"

"Aiyo!" a woman's voice wailed. It sounded like the queen and everyone trembled in fear.

In all this confusion, Poonkuzlali reached her aunt. But someone else was there before her and held her aunt in his lap. She heard heart-breaking sobs near her and heard Kalaanthaka shout, "Who's that running there? Stop!" Poonkuzlali guessed who the runner was.

Two servants came in with torches which illuminated the strange scene in the room. The emperor, who had lost the use of his legs and had stayed bedridden for three years, was now seated at Mandakini's side with Arulmozli beside him. Blood dripped from the spear which had pierced Mandakini's chest and protruded from her side. Arulmozli gently lifted Mandakini's head and placed it on the emperor's lap. Tears flowed down the prince's cheeks and the emperor sobbed. Vanamadevi stood by the emperor's bed: a sharp dagger was embedded in the pillow where the emperor's head had rested. Vanamadevi stared in horror at the pillow and then turned her amazed eyes to where her husband sat on the floor.

Poonkuzlali knelt beside the emperor and wailed, "Aunt! Aunt! Why did I leave you alone?" But Mandakini did not turn to Poonkuzlali or to the prince who held her hand and sobbed. Her eyes were fixed intently on the emperor's face.

Arulmozli controlled his grief and rose. "Ocean Princess, remember where you are."

Poonkuzlali stifled her sobs and stood. "Sir, my aunt is my only refuge in this world."

Arulmozli wiped away his own tears. "Poonkuzlali, she's your aunt and she's a mother to me. But she did not even look at us. My mother and father who were separated for thirty years have found each other again; who are we to stand between them?" He paused. "Your aunt sacrificed her life to save the emperor. When your aunt was pierced by the spear thrown from the terrace, my father recovered the use of his legs and rushed to her. When his spear missed its mark, the assassin knocked out the light and jumped into the room to stab my father. My mother, who instinctively threw herself on my father to protect him, screamed when she realized that his bed was empty. If my father had remained in his bed, I would have lost either him or my mother to the assassin's knife. Your aunt saved the emperor's life twice."

Arulmozli stared at Kalaanthaka and continued, "Poonkuzlali, if the assassin had succeeded, the Pazluvur brothers would have been blamed and the general would have used this as an excuse to wipe out the Pazluvur clan. Why, if you had not brought me here today, I too would have suspected the commander. Lord Kalaanthaka is more indebted to you than anyone else. Ask him what you want as your reward—he will even give you half his wealth."

Kalaanthaka's pained expression showed that he was aware of the prince's implicit accusation that he had failed in his duty as Fort Commander. Kalaanthaka's customary arrogance and bravado disappeared and he bowed his head in shame.

Poonkuzlali, moved by Arulmozli's praise, became her usual self at his mention of a reward. "Sir, I don't need anyone's gratitude or reward. There's nothing more for me to do here. The Ocean King will shelter me and my boat waits for me in the canal." She paused. "If you and Lady Vanathi happen to come to Kodikkarai one day ..." She saw Vanathi staring at her and the prince. "Chi! What kind of a wish is that? Goodbye." She hurried to the door.

Vanathi, frozen in shock all this time, recovered herself. She went to Poonkuzlali and said, "My dearest friend, where are you going? I too am an orphan like you ..."

Poonkuzlali interrupted her. "Lady, I'm not your dearest friend and you're not an orphan like me. Princess Kundavai will be here soon."

Only then did Vanathi remember Kundavai. "Aiyo! We must send word to *akka*."

Poonkuzlali gently moved Vanathi aside and walked to the door. Kalaanthaka blocked her way. "Girl, the prince is right. The Pazluvur clan is indebted to you: name your reward."

Poonkuzlali smiled sadly. "Commander, everyone is glad the emperor is alive, that he can walk and that the Pazluvur clan has not been disgraced. No one mourns my aunt's death. Mustn't I at least grieve for her? I must hunt down her murderer and kill him. Let me go."

"Girl, you shame me! I'm standing here doing nothing to catch the assassin. He pushed me aside and ran .... he must be in the secret passage. Come with me." Kalaanthaka took Poonkuzlali's hand in his iron grip and led her to the Art Gallery.

In obedience to Arulmozli's wishes, the others in the room stood frozen in their places. But all eyes were on the emperor as he sat with Mandakini's head on his lap.

Mandakini and Sundara Chola were in a world of their own, living thirty years in minutes. Mandakini spoke with her eyes to Sundara Chola who had not forgotten the language of love they had used in those happy days on Boodha Island. Mandakini's face was calm and showed no sign of sorrow or pain. *I don't blame you for anything. I avoided you all these years. It was enough for me to see you once in a while from a distance. I never dreamt I would be blessed to die in your lap ... what more could I want, dearest?*

Sundara Chola whispered to her and Mandakini understood every word: she nodded in agreement, shook her head furiously in objection, smiled happily and comforted him in turn.

"My beloved, you have sacrificed your life for me. I deserted you. I came to Kodikkarai in search of you, but those villains told me you had jumped into the sea and killed yourself. Even Aniruddha, my best friend, hid the truth from me. If I had known you were alive, I would never have given you up, even for this vast empire. You saved my son from drowning in the Ponni but in my madness, I thought your ghost was trying to kill him. I saw you in my room at midnight once and thought your ghost had come to torture me and curse my children. My hatred made me throw the lamp at you when you really came to me two days ago. Forgive me, my love. You came here as our clan's Guardian Deity to protect me and my children. How I have wronged you! You are dying without giving me a chance to show my love for you. You asked me not to let my sons succeed me ... why are you shaking your head? You said that for my good and the good of my family. Is it true you had a child? Tell me if you had a son: I'll do what I can for him and make amends for my sins."

Mandakini stared at him and then looked around. Her eyes rested on Arulmozli who stood by the door. The prince came and sat beside her. Mandakini touched the prince and looked into Sundara Chola's eyes: *This is my son.* Mandakini looked from Arulmozli to Sundara Chola and back again. She closed her eyes and her head sank back deeply into the emperor's lap ... she was dead. Sundara Chola sobbed as though his heart would break.

Arulmozli was unmoved. "Father, don't grieve for my mother. She's not dead; she will live forever as the patron goddess of the Chola dynasty." Arulmozli stood by his words of comfort. When he ascended the throne as Raja Raja Chola, he built a temple in Mandakini's honor in Thanjavur: the Sinhala Nachiar Temple.

Your Time Has Come

NANDINI PACED HER room in Kadambur Palace, her ears alert for footsteps. Her eyelids twitched nervously and she shuddered. She lifted the bed curtain: the sword on her bed glowed red-hot. Nandini raised the sword and admired its brilliance under the light of the lamp. She held it against her breast and kissed it. "Divine sword, your time has come. You won't let me down—it is my hands I can't trust!" She looked at her trembling hands. "I must find other hands to do the job."

A mad light shone in her eyes as she looked up at the ceiling. "Ah, you are here! Come, my love, my king! Come, Veerapandian's head! Why are you hiding in a corner of the ceiling, staring at me? Speak! You said that if you survived you would seat me on the Pandian throne. I don't want a throne. They brought some child to me and said he is your son—he has been crowned. Once I avenge your death, leave me alone and let me sleep at night. Go to the warriors' paradise. What? You refuse? We'll talk about this later. I hear footsteps. Hide! I must hide the sword ..."

Just as Nandini was hiding the sword, Manimekalai came in. At once, the ranting madwoman disappeared. With a calm face, Nandini said, "Is it you, Manimekalai? Come, come."

"*Akka*, why do you always have this sword with you?"

"What else can I do when men are so wicked? It's my only protection."

"I'll always be there for you, *akka*. But I hurried here to give you some bad news ..."

The startled Nandini asked, "What?"

"*Akka*, the chancellor has not reached Thanjavur. On the way ..."

"What? Is he coming back here?" Nandini's alarm was obvious.

"When the chancellor was crossing the Kollidam, the boat capsized near the shore ... those who reached the shore could not find your husband. One of the Pazluvur men who was with him came back here with the news." Manimekalai broke into sobs.

Nandini hugged her and said, "My darling, how much you love me! Don't worry."

Manimekalai looked up at her calm face in surprise: *Her heart is like stone!*

Guessing her thoughts, Nandini said, "My heart tells me my husband's life is not in danger. Maybe your brother and Parthibendran plan to harm my husband and they are making up this story as a safeguard."

"I don't understand, *akka*. Why would they want to harm your husband?"

"You innocent girl! Didn't I tell you your brother and Parthibendran lust after me?"

"I no longer consider Kandamaran my brother. But why would they harm Lord Ambalavan?"

"If he dies, they think I'll be happy to be rid of the old man and surrender to their lust."

"*Akka*, I'll stay by your side always. If either one of them comes here, I'll kill him!"

"Don't worry, I can deal with those young men myself. I'm only afraid of that thug, the prince. Luckily, you have taken care of him for me."

"Me? How?"

"Don't you know he loves you? Wasn't it obvious when he pushed Vandhiya Devan aside and carried you to land himself? Can't you see it?"

"I can, but I'm afraid of the prince. My body shudders when he comes near me. And my devil of a brother keeps pestering me to marry the prince." Manimekalai burst into tears.

Nandini wiped her tears. "Darling, is it true you love Vandhiya Devan?"

"Yes, but I don't know what he thinks."

"What does it matter what he thinks? What matters is he must stay alive. Manimekalai, you and Vandhiya Devan are in danger. No one can harm my husband; Sundara Chola will even defy his own children and chief minister for him. And I can take care of myself. My darling, it's you I'm worried about."

"*Akka*, what do you mean? How am I in danger?"

"Foolish girl! The greatest danger a woman faces is to be forced into an unwanted marriage. Your brother is determined that you marry the prince and your father agrees with him."

"That will never happen! I'll tell the prince to his face that I don't want to marry him. I'll tell him that I love his friend, Vandhiya Devan."

"Foolish girl! He already knows this. They won't force you or ask for your consent: they'll just remove the man who stands in their way. Didn't I tell you the man you love is in danger? Your brother hates Vandhiya Devan and accuses him of stabbing him in the back. He's also furious with him for telling the prince about the conspirators' meeting at Kadambur. Parthibendran has his own reasons for hating Vandhiya Devan."

"Are you saying they'll kill him?"

"They'll cut him into pieces and feed him to the dogs! How will you bear it?"

"My body and soul scream in agony at the very thought! Can they really do this? He's a brave warrior and the prince's close friend …"

"Your brother and Parthibendran have poisoned the prince's ears."

"The wretches! But how do you …"

"How do I know all this? Parthibendran told me today when he came to say goodbye. He's off to meet Malayaman who's marching here with his army. The prince declared, 'If Manimekalai does not marry me, I'll raze Kadambur Palace to the ground!' Kandamaran replied, 'It's Vandhiya Devan who stands in the way.' The prince asked, 'Can't you get him out of the way?' Your brother said, 'If you give the order, it can be done.' Your beloved is in danger. If you don't act at once, you'll lose your husband even before you are married."

Manimekalai stammered in panic, "I must warn him!"

"Yes, and your 'brave warrior' will stubbornly refuse to run from danger."

"My head is spinning! What do you suggest, *akka?*"

"The only way to save his life is to send him away from here. I have an idea. I'll beg Vandhiya Devan to go and see what's happened to my husband. You must support me; he won't be able to refuse two helpless women. After he leaves, you can tell your brother and father how you feel. I will also tell them, 'Forcing a girl into marriage is against the Cholas' code of honor.'"

"If they refuse to listen to you … I have my knife."

"Okay, okay. First, we must send your beloved from here. You know where he is: send Chandramathi or Idumbankari to him with a message asking him to come here."

"Even if he agrees to go, how will he leave the fort? My brother will stop him."

"He can leave by the secret passage in this room. Quick! Your brother's assassins may strike at any minute!"

"I won't come back without him," Manimekalai declared as she hurried out.

Hardly had she crossed the door when there was a knock on the secret door leading to the Hunters' Hall. Nandini opened the inner door and saw a ghastly face in the dim light.

"Sorcerer, you have come."

"Yes, my queen: and the time has come."

It Had Sharp Teeth and Claws!

NANDINI CLOSED AND bolted the room's main door, picked up a torch and entered the Hunters' Hall. Ravidasan's savage appearance was aggravated by the cuts and wounds on his head and face. "What's this?" Nandini asked. "These are fresh wounds!"

"My queen, do you think we are lounging in luxury like you? Parameswaran and I narrowly escaped with our lives today. It was King Veerapandian's spirit which saved us."

"No, Ravidasan, his spirit is always with me. Just before you came, he asked, 'Will you fulfill your oath?' I replied, 'I'll fulfill my oath, or die trying!'"

"You must succeed in your mission and live. Much remains to be done. You must hold Veerapandian's son's coronation in Madurai for all the world to see; you must help us shift all the treasure in Ambalavan's vault to our mountain hideout …"

"Let's not talk about him. Tell me how you got these wounds."

"Last night, a tiger attacked us in the forest. Even though it was old, it had sharp teeth and claws. We escaped by pulling down the war memorial's dilapidated roof on its head."

"Aiyo! The poor thing! Couldn't you fight an old tiger face to face?"

"When an old tiger was so difficult to deal with, think how fierce the young tiger, Aditya Karikalan, will be. My lady, if he escapes tonight, we'll never catch him."

"Sorcerer, have you any news about Sundara Chola and Arulmozli?"

"By now, they'll be dead—no doubt about it."

"That's what you and Parameswaran said when you went to Sri Lanka ..."

"That dumb madwoman stuck to our heels and foiled our plans."

"You said Vandhiya Devan died at sea, but he also escaped."

"We had him in our clutches at the war memorial and you let him go," Ravidasan pointed out. "Now he stands by Karikalan like his shield."

"Don't worry about him."

"We must worry; this is our last chance. Lady, what do you want us to do? We are here to take you away safely after our task is accomplished. We are prepared to come to your aid if any unexpected obstacle comes up."

"There will be no obstacles and I don't want to stay alive after I fulfill my oath."

"No! You must come with us. Saying that it needed repairs, Idumbankari has taken the Pazluvur palanquin to the forest Ayyanar temple where the secret tunnel ends. Once we have killed the man who beheaded Veerapandian, we'll carry you to the Kolli Hills."

"How many of you are here?"

"There are four of us." Ravidasan clapped softly and three faces peeped out from behind the stuffed animals.

"Where's Parameswaran?" Nandini asked.

"I left him at the Ayyanar temple. A Kalamukha was doing penance there and we had a hard time convincing him to move. Parameswaran is there to see that he does not come back."

"Why should we care about a Kalamukha? Have you heard the news about Lord Ambalavan?"

The startled Ravidasan asked, "What news?"

"His boat capsized on the way to Thanjavur. Sambuvaraya heard that he did not reach the shore and is feared to have drowned. What if he swims back across the river and comes here tonight?"

"Don't worry. Last night, I saw a giant of a man on the road to Thanjavur. I did not recognize him in the dark, but now, I'm sure it was Lord Ambalavan. You can be confident he won't come back here tonight. Now, what are your orders?"

"Sorcerer, wait here patiently. Don't come into my room for any reason or you'll ruin my plans. Come only when I call you."

"How will you call us?"

"If you hear me laugh heartily, it will be my signal that our mission is accomplished. If you hear me weep, come in at once: that will be my signal that my plan has met with an obstacle."

"Very well, my queen: I look forward to hearing you laugh."

Aiyo! Ghost!

VANDHIYA DEVAN WAS wandering dejectedly in the garden. The night air was filled with the fragrance of flowers. *If only I was in the Pazlayarai garden. If only I could hear the music of Princess Kundavai's anklets. Instead, I'm trapped here with a mad prince.*

Karikalan had been furious with him that evening, screaming, 'Don't ever look me in the face again!' *He has never before attacked me like this. But I can only pity him when I see how confused his mind is.* That entire day, Karikalan's mood had swung between happiness and sorrow, friendship and enmity. Those around him lived in fear, not knowing what to expect from him from one minute to the next. The news which streamed in only increased his frenzy. Sambuvaraya said that Malayaman was marching on Kadambur with his army and condemned the old man.

Karikalan said, "Sambuvaraya, it is I who asked my grandfather to come here with an army. I'm trapped here alone. What if something happens to me?"

"Lord, the Tiger Flag flies on the fort's ramparts. With your permission, I'll leave the palace with my family. You can then receive Malayaman and feel safe."

"Are you accusing me of being a coward?"

"Lord, at the age of eighteen, you hunted down Veerapandian and beheaded him ..."

Karikalan laughed wildly. "The Pazluvur witch has made the whole world mock me for being the tiger who beheaded a dead man!"

Sambuvaraya gave up. "Lord, you are determined to misunderstand whatever I say. I'll leave you to do what you want..."

"I won't leave this palace until I find out the entire truth about the conspirators' meeting here four months back. And I won't let you leave."

Sambuvaraya's lips twitched and his eyes brimmed with tears.

Parthibendran intervened. "Sir, you are being unfair to Sambuvaraya. This conspirators' meeting has already been discussed and resolved. It was only because you stayed away from Thanjavur that the chieftains considered making Madurandaka the heir."

"Yes, it's impossible to make someone else the king while I'm alive and so, they are planning to kill me!" he laughed hysterically. "Parthibendran, I know you too are part of the conspiracy. I saw you and Kandamaran plan and aim the spear at me when we went hunting. I'm alive only because my good friend, Vandhiya Devan, was with me that day."

Parthibendran gave Devan a killing look. "Lord, this wretch has poisoned your ears against me. Let him prove that I have betrayed you even in my mind ..."

"My dear fellow, how can anyone prove what's in your mind? Can you deny that you and Kandamaran brought me here only because you fell under Lady Nandini's spell?"

"I don't deny that, lord. Lady Nandini arranged this with the best intentions: she wants you to marry Manimekalai and avoid civil war." He glared at Devan. "I'll tolerate criticism, but if anyone says a word against Lady Nandini, I'll kill him!" Parthibendran drew his sword.

"My brave friend, put your sword back in its scabbard. Vandhiya Devan too has been bewitched by Lady Nandini and swears she's my own sister. But he accuses you of pushing my brother into the sea and killing him. What do you have to say to that?"

Just then, Kandamaran rushed in excitedly. "Lord, I have good news! Prince Arulmozli did not die at sea. He stayed in Nagapattinam's

Choodamani Monastery until he was forced out of hiding by the storm. He's now on his way to Thanjavur, surrounded by a huge crowd of supporters."

Karikalan did not rejoice at this news. Instead, he turned angrily on Devan. "You said Arulmozli would stay in Nagapattinam until I made my intentions clear: why's he going to Thanjavur?"

"Lord, that's what Princess Kundavai told me. I don't know what happened to make him change his plans. If you want, I can go and ..."

"You too want to go! You are all my enemies! Arulmozli is going to Thanjavur because of Velir who wants my brother to marry his niece and sit on the Tiger Throne. I heard that Velir's marching to Thanjavur with his army. Kundavai is a part of this conspiracy ..."

Devan interrupted. "Lord, I swear that Prince Arulmozli and Princess Kundavai have no such plans. If you want, I'll go and find out the details ..."

"You want to go and join the plotters. Kandamaran, put him in your dungeon!" Kandamaran eagerly went to Devan, but Karikalan stopped him. "No, Cholas are just. I won't punish him until he's proved guilty. Vandhiya Devan, don't let me see you for the rest of the day! Tomorrow, I'll decide whether to send you to Thanjavur or to the dungeon. Go! At once!"

Devan stared at Karikalan: he thought the prince gave him a sidelong glance telling him he was just pretending. But he decided to stay away from the frenzied prince to be on the safe side. "Your wish is my command, lord," Devan said and left the room.

Later, he heard that the prince had sent Sambuvaraya and Parthibendran to meet Malayaman and bring him to Kadambur. He also heard that Karikalan had had a confidential talk with Kandamaran. Devan was depressed by all these developments. *Will the prince send me to Thanjavur and Pazlayarai? How dull Kadambur is! Everyone here is steeped in sorrow. After sunset, this palace becomes a haunted mansion. When, and how, do I get away?*

Suddenly, he heard a woman's terrified shout, "Aiyo! Ghost!"

I Too Have a Dagger

VANDHIYA DEVAN RAN towards the cry. *It sounds like Manimekalai. What's she doing here at this time? It can't be a ghost, but the fear in her voice is real. Will I get into trouble if I go to her? Her brother is ready to tear me apart. The prince is mad and god alone knows what Nandini's up to.* Devan tripped on a tree root and crashed to the ground. His shoulder cloth caught in a bush and it took him time to extricate it carefully from the branches. He smiled to himself. *Is this a bad omen? Or has this root saved me from trouble?*

He heard Chandramathi's voice, "Lady, where are you?"

"I'm near the lily pond; come quickly!" came Manimekalai's reply.

He heard footsteps and the sweet tinkle of anklets. The lily pond was a small marble lake near an artificial hillock in the center of the garden. Devan realized that he was near it. *Thank goodness the women didn't see me fall. If it had been daylight, they would have laughed and embarrassed me. Now that Chandramathi is with Manimekalai, I can steal away ...*

As he turned to leave, he heard them talk.

"Lady, why did you scream?"

"I saw a head on the fort wall. It had plaited hair and a beard and moustache. And around its neck ... I'm scared to even say it ... it had a garland of skulls! It vanished when I screamed."

"Nonsense, lady, it was your imagination. How can anyone climb such a high wall? You came to the lily pond at sunset and waited with the fragrance of jasmine floating in the breeze. But Vandhiya Devan didn't come ... a ghost came instead."

"Enough of your jokes; I did see that dreadful figure on the wall. What happened to your errand?"

"There's no sign of Vandhiya Devan. Idumbankari told me the prince was angry with Vandhiya Devan; he shouted at him and told him to stay away from him till tomorrow."

"The prince is mad! He's angry with everyone."

"Maybe it was Vandhiya Devan who disguised himself as a ghost and frightened you."

"There are many here who are playing parts, but he's not a pretender. Go and look for him again. Ask Idumbankari to search for him too."

"Lady, I'm scared of Idumbankari: he leers at me."

"Very well, it may be better not to tell him anything. You go and search; I'll wait here."

Devan heard the music of Chandramathi's anklets fade into the distance.

Could the figure on the wall be Azlvarkkadian? Has he come here disguised as a Kalamukha to give me important news from Thanjavur? Why's Manimekalai so eager to see me? I suspect she loves me: that's why I have been staying away from her. I don't want to further provoke Kandamaran. But it must be something very important which makes her wait alone by the lily pond. Is she in trouble? Or has Nandini sent me a message through her? Manimekalai is right: this palace is filled with traitors and this helpless girl is caught in the middle. I don't know what treachery Nandini plans to use this poor girl for. Manimekalai must have sensed some danger ... that's why she wants my help ...

Devan recalled how Manimekalai had helped him earlier. If she now needed his help, he was obliged to her. *This is a good opportunity to find out the truth ... she's alone. Who knows? Maybe I'll need her help again to get out of this palace. Let me talk to her ...*

Manimekalai was seated on a marble bench near the lily pond in which the flowers glowed like stars among the dark leaves. Startled by his footsteps, Manimekalai jumped up and almost stumbled into the pond.

Devan caught her saying, "Lady, it's me."

Manimekalai shivered. Her instinctive modesty made her push him away but that only made her stumble backwards again. Devan held her tightly and pulled her forward. She struggled from his grasp and said angrily, "Let go! Don't touch me!" Her voice steadied. "You were not concerned when I was struggling in the lake, but now you are eager to save me from falling into knee-high water. When you startled me by entering my room from the Hunters' Hall, I should have raised the alarm and let my father catch you."

"I'm sorry for startling you now, lady. And I'm indebted to you for your help that day."

"You are the most ungrateful man I have met in my life. You told me a story about being chased by murderers and ran away like a thief before I came back from the Hunters' Hall."

"Chandramathi came in suddenly. I ran to the music room to hide from her."

"And then you disappeared by magic."

"No, I climbed the stairs, crossed the terraces and climbed the fort walls. I did not get an opportunity to tell you why I ran away."

"Empty words! You have not even looked in my direction all these days."

"My sister ..."

"I'm not your sister!"

"You are my friend Kandamaran's sister: that makes you my sister."

"Kandamaran's not my brother and he's not your friend: he's our enemy."

"Lady, Kandamaran hates me; Parthibendran's waiting for a chance to harm me; the prince's mood swings from one extreme to another. I don't know what danger lies around the next bend. How could I meet you in such a situation? As long as I live, I'll never forget you or your help."

"You'll be grateful to me as long as you live and so, you must stay alive—for me, if not for yourself. Tell me the truth: did you hear me asking Chandramathi to bring you here?"

"Yes, lady, forgive me. That's why I came to you."

"Otherwise, you would have stayed away. But however hard-hearted you are, I can't bear it if your life is in danger. Sir, you must leave the palace."

"Are you asking me to run away?"

"Lady Nandini was right."

"Ahah! What did Lady Nandini tell you?"

"She said you would refuse to go away to save your life. She said we would have to find another way. We heard Lord Ambalavan's boat capsized when he was crossing the Kollidam. Lady Nandini wants you to go and find out what exactly happened there."

Devan considered her words. "Didn't she warn you not to tell me about all this now?"

"Yes."

"Then why did you tell me?"

"Because my mind is troubled. I was never in the habit of being suspicious. But now, I suspect everyone and everything. When Lady Nandini asked me to bring you to her, it seemed right. But when I think back on it, I suspect she wants to harm you."

"Why? How can she harm me?"

"I don't know. There's something suspicious about her. She mutters over a sword ..."

"I do not fear a sword in a woman's hand; I would rather..."

"Fear the daggers in her eyes," Manimekalai completed his sentence. "That's what every man says. I'm not asking you to fear Lady Nandini's sword ... do you remember the Hunters' Hall?"

"Very well."

"You told me you were being chased by murderers, but I did not believe you. I went to the hall and realized that some men were hiding behind the animals. I didn't know whether they were your enemies or your accomplices. I kept quiet as I did not want to tell anyone about you."

"I realize only now how much you have done for me."

"That's not why I'm mentioning this now. Some time back, Lady Nandini sent me to bring you to her. I went back to her room to ask her something, but she had bolted her door. I could hear faint voices from the Hunters' Hall. I suspect some men are hiding there and there's a connection between them and Lady Nandini."

Devan had instinctively sensed impending danger. Manimekalai's words confirmed his fears. "Lady, you must help me. There's a secret passage leading from outside to the Hunter's Hall. One entrance to the hall is through Lady Nandini's room ... is there another entrance?"

"Yes, there's another way for the servants. My father also uses that way to bring in new guests."

"Lady, take me to the Hunters' Hall by that way. I must find out who's hiding there and why."

"I'm trying to save you from danger and you're asking me to put you in danger."

"I carry a dagger at my waist. It's easier to face a known danger than an unknown one. It's even better to meet danger head-on."

"I'll take you to the Hunters' Hall on one condition: I'll come with you. I too have a dagger."

Devan agreed to this.

"Follow me quickly. We must go before Chandramathi comes looking for me."

Manimekalai led Devan across the garden and along the shadows of the palace walls. She entered the palace and took him through deserted corridors to a closed door. She took an oil lamp and opened the door. They went down a flight of steps and along a passage. Suddenly, she stopped. "Wait!" she whispered. "Do you hear footsteps?"

The Road to Hell

VANDHIYA DEVAN HEARD footsteps: they stopped abruptly ... started again ...and faded into the distance.

"Sir, let's go back."

"I never retreat ..." Devan tried to overtake Manimekalai and she blocked him. They banged into each other and the lamp in her hand fell to the ground with a clang. The passage was engulfed in darkness. "Lady, what have you done?"

"Why did you try to go ahead?"

"Because I'm not in the habit of hiding behind women. If you're scared of the dark, you go."

"Why would I be scared with a brave warrior like you beside me?"

"Let's go then. Follow me." Devan tried to go ahead and stumbled.

Manimekalai held him and broke his fall. "Sir, this path is uneven; I'm familiar with every step and bend. Hold my hand and follow me. Otherwise, you'll fall and break a leg."

Devan smiled. "Thank you, Your Majesty. I will obey your command!"

Manimekalai held Devan's hand; it was cold. *He does not fear enemies or traitors: why's he afraid to hold my hand?* They walked on in silence. Devan stumbled often in the darkness and Manimekalai had to grip his hand tightly to stop him from falling.

"The road to hell must be dark like this," Devan said.

"Who knows? If I follow a brave man like you, hell may be my passage to heaven," she said.

"If I hold the hand of a lady like you, hell may become heaven." Devan immediately bit his lips in regret. *Now, why did I say that? This girl may misunderstand …*

"Judging by your cold hand, one would think you are going to your execution: not to heaven."

"Who knows? Maybe I'll be executed at the end of this journey."

"You're the one who stubbornly refuses to go back. God alone knows how many murderers are lurking in the Hunters' Hall!"

"I'm not afraid of murderers. I'm trembling at the thought of Kandamaran seeing us walking in the dark, holding hands."

"Sir, as long as I'm alive, my brother won't harm you."

The sound of a door closing startled them into stopping.

Manimekalai whispered, "We are near the Hunters' Hall."

A light flared ahead of them and grew brighter as it came towards them. Manimekalai dropped Devan's hand and stepped a little away from him. The next instant, Idumbankari stood before them with a lighted lamp in one hand and an ornate dagger in the other. When he saw them, he pretended to be shocked. "Lady! Sir! Where are you going in the dark? If you had sent for me, I would have come with you and lighted the way."

"Idumbankari, Malayaman is marching here with his army. We are checking to see if all the entrances to the fort and its secret passages are locked," Manimekalai replied.

"What a surprise! That's exactly what I'm doing," the man said.

"I thought so. Our lamp fell and went out; I saw a light and walked on, knowing it must be you."

"All the entrances to the passage are locked. We can go back, my lady."

"Give me your lamp and go. This warrior wants to choose a spear from the Hunters' Hall: he lost his spear in the Kollidam. We must be prepared for war."

"Yes, my dear lady. But, at such times, it's better not to take strangers into the Hunters' Hall."

"You're right. But this man is not a stranger: he's my brother's dearest friend. And he may soon become a part of our family. Give me your lamp and go."

Idumbankari reluctantly gave her the lamp and left. Devan and Manimekalai reached the Hunters' Hall. They heard an owl hoot somewhere.

"What's that?" exclaimed Manimekalai. "How did an owl get into the palace?"

"Maybe the stuffed owl in the Hunters' Hall has come back to life," Devan said.

The door to the hall was locked. Manimekalai opened it with a key and they walked in. At first, all they could see were the stuffed animals. But when they raised the lamp, they saw some men half hidden behind the animals. The door banged shut; Devan turned towards the sound. In that instant, someone pushed him violently and Devan banged into the monkey he had once hidden behind. Two hands caught him in a vice-like grip. He tried to reach his dagger but could not move; another pair of hands removed the dagger from his waist. Manimekalai, rushing towards him, shrieked and stopped as Devan's dagger pointed at her.

"Don't scream. If you are both obedient and keep quiet for a while, your lives will not be in danger. Otherwise, you'll die—and this insolent young man will die first." Devan recognized Ravidasan's voice.

"Lady," Devan said. "Be quiet for a while. Let's hear what they have to say."

Pandimadevi

THE MEN TIED Vandhiya Devan to the monkey and Manimekalai to a deer's antlers.

"Sorcerer, it is I who am your enemy. Untie the lady; let her go," Devan said.

"Wait my boy, wait. You have crossed our path many times and each time we have let you go. But you insist on following us."

Devan laughed. "You accuse me of following you, but I can say the same about you. The lady and I are on an important mission and you have come in my way."

"This is the last time our paths cross. If you survive tonight, you'll never see us again."

"In that case, I must try to survive. Sorcerer, teach me a spell to save my life."

"I'll teach you an excellent one: whatever happens in this hall and in the next room, stay quiet and do nothing rash. You'll save your life."

"Why are you being so merciful? Why don't you kill me?"

"Lady Nandini, Emperor Veerapandian's brave wife, insists on letting you live. The task for which Pandimadevi voluntarily imprisoned herself in Pazluvur Palace will be completed today."

"What task is that?"

"Wait and see." Ravidasan turned towards the opposite wall.

"Sorcerer, you let me go because your queen ordered you to. And now, it's your queen who ordered this lady to bring me to her. That's why we came here together."

"There are other entrances to the queen's room. Why did you choose to come this way?"

"I don't have to tell you. I'll tell the queen if she asks me."

"Then wait until you see the queen."

"Sorcerer, release me and the lady at once, or I'll bring down the roof with my shrieks!"

"Careful! If you shriek, three spears will tear you apart simultaneously."

Devan looked around him: three conspirators were ready with their spears.

"You are a clever young man. At one point, I was eager to make you a part of our gang. But that enchantress in Pazlayarai has bewitched you. Now, be wise: if you scream, you'll die." Ravidasan walked to the elephant mounted on the opposite wall. He put his ear against the wall and listened intently. Then he gripped the elephant's long tusks and twisted them. A small opening appeared in the wall; the light of lamps shone through that circular hole into the hall.

Devan saw that Manimekalai had used her dagger to cut the ropes which bound her hands. The small lamp she had taken from Idumbankari sputtered in a corner without throwing its light on her. The men had focused on Devan and ignored her. Devan hooted like an owl. The conspirators were taken aback and the startled Ravidasan, who was peering into the room, turned back in alarm.

"Ahah, this is your work!" he exclaimed and hurried towards Devan. As soon as he took his hands from the elephant's tusks, the opening closed and the hall was dark again.

The three conspirators rushed at Devan with their spears. A stag with large, twisted antlers attacked one man; another man was knocked down by a huge bear; a crocodile with yawning jaws pounced on the third man; a giant bat crashed on Ravidasan's head. In that one second when the stunned conspirators stood frozen to the spot, Manimekalai cut Devan's ropes. Devan threw the monkey at the conspirators. The four men pushed aside the stuffed animals and got up carefully. Devan picked up a spear and prepared to defend himself.

At that moment, the door to Nandini's room opened and light flooded the Hunters' Hall. "Sorcerer! What foolishness is this? Why are you making all this noise?" Nandini walked into the hall.

The Sword Falls

NANDINI WAS STUNNED to see Vandhiya Devan and Manimekalai in the Hunters' Hall. "Goodness! How did you come here?"

"Lady, your friend said you asked her to bring me here: because of her, I got caught by these murderers."

"Sir, if I had not come here now, it looks like you're the one who would have murdered these men," Nandini said.

Manimekalai said, "*Akka*, these men are murderers. These are the men I saw hiding here the day before you arrived."

"Why did you come this way, Manimekalai?"

"*Akka*, just a short while ago, Kandamaran said he was going to meet you. I brought him this way so that my brother would not see him."

Nandini turned to Ravidasan. "Sorcerer, if you harm either of these two people, you will be harming me. From now, you will respect them under all circumstances."

"Forgive me, lady," Ravidasan said. "This man knows our secret signal: it was he who hooted like an owl some time ago."

"Sorcerer, doesn't that prove this man is one of us? Not a sound from you until you hear from me. Careful!"

Nandini, Manimekalai and Devan went to Nandini's room through the gap behind the elephant and the secret door closed behind them.

"My dear, you are clever indeed!" Nandini said. "Your brother just left: he said he'll bring Aditya Karikalan to me. Before they come, I must say goodbye to you two and send you away."

"*Akka*, what's this about saying goodbye? You said you wanted him to go and find out the truth about your husband ..."

"I changed my mind after talking to your brother. Whether Lord Ambalavan is alive or dead, I can't stay here." Nandini turned to Devan. "Sir, you are in danger. If you wish to live, please go at once—at least for my sake!"

"*Akka*, ask him to take me with him. I can't stay here like a caged bird after both of you leave."

"Lady Nandini means that after I leave, you'll marry Aditya Karikalan and become the queen of Thanjavur," Devan said.

"I'll never let Manimekalai, who is dearer to me than life, have the misfortune of marrying Aditya Karikalan. If you go now, you can live to marry Manimekalai later. Manimekalai, if you truly love him, tell him to go at once."

Devan said, "There's something I beg from you: if you give it to me, I'll go at once."

"Sir, what do I have that you want? Tell me."

"You have a sword on which the fish symbol is etched. Give it to me and I'll go. You know I lost my sword in the Kollidam river."

"Sir, there are any number of swords and spears in the Hunters' Hall. Take your pick and go. Why do you want the sword I keep for my protection?"

"Lady, tell me the truth: do you keep that sword only for your own protection ... or to avenge Veerapandian's death?"

"I did not expect you to bring this up before Manimekalai. There's no longer any need for me to hide the truth." Nandini picked up the sword from her bed. "Manimekalai, I did not come to Kadambur to prevent civil war, to divide the kingdom between Karikalan and Madurandaka or to arrange your marriage. I came here to take revenge on the wicked man who beheaded Veerapandian. This is the sword of the Pandian dynasty. I have sworn an oath on it and tonight, I'll fulfill my oath or take my own life!"

"Are you trying to send me away because you think I'm an obstacle to your plans? Are you trying to frighten me by telling me my life is in danger?" Devan asked.

"You think you can stand in my way? Why don't you go and tell your friend what I just said and stop him from coming here?"

"Lady, I know I can't stop him: that's why I came to you. I'll even fall at your feet and beg you – don't commit this sin!" Devan pleaded.

Nandini turned to Manimekalai. "You love a man; when that man is wounded and helpless, his enemy comes to kill him; you fall at the enemy's feet and beg him not to kill your lover; in spite of that, he kills your lover. Is it a sin to take revenge on such an evil man?"

"No," said Manimekalai. "But I would not have fallen at his feet. I would have killed him with my knife!"

Devan looked at Manimekalai. "Lady, what if the enemy was your own brother?"

Nandini said, "I'm not going to kill my brother. I took pity on you and saved you from danger many times because you are my brother, Thirumalai's, friend. Sir, if I die today without fulfilling my oath, ask Thirumalai to forgive me."

"My dear lady, why continue this pretense? Thirumalai's not your brother … Aditya Karikalan is your brother. I beg you, give me the Pandian sword."

Nandini smiled mockingly. "And what did the prince have to say when you told him this imaginary story? Did he believe you?"

"He seemed to believe me, but I don't know what's in his mind …"

"I know what's in his mind: he's amazed at the Pazlayarai enchantress' imagination."

"My dear lady, I saw a mute woman in Sri Lanka who saved Prince Arulmozli, Thirumalai and me from great danger …

"What's that got to do with me?"

"When I saw her at a distance in the moonlight, I thought, 'What's Lady Nandini doing here?' Lady, if you removed your ornaments and parted your hair, you will be her replica!"

"Why should I believe you? I know your power of imagination."

"Lady, you do believe me: you are using this truth for your own purposes. When I met you in the Pazluvur palace garden, the sorcerer suddenly came there. I hid in the treasury vault which happened to be open. I saw Kandamaran and Prince Madurandaka go through the secret passage. A little later, I saw you and Lord Ambalavan in the vault. At that time, I did not know where you were going; later I realized you were acting like your mother's ghost to torment the emperor ..."

Nandini's shoulders sagged and she sank into a chair. "Sir, what else do you know?"

"While you and Lord Ambalavan were crossing the vault, Kandamaran, who was on his way back, said something to Lord Ambalavan. Lord Ambalavan signaled to the guard who had accompanied Kandamaran with a torch ..."

"What signal was that?"

"You know what it was: Lord Ambalavan ordered the guard to kill Kandamaran. I stopped him and saved Kandamaran's life ... and was blamed for it."

Nandini glanced at Manimekalai. "Sir, why are you rambling and confusing this girl?"

"Lady, I have told no one this. If you give me your sword, I promise I'll never mention it again."

Nandini's eyes filled. "I won't give you the sword! Tell anyone whatever you want. Don't bother me. Go to Aditya Karikalan and stop him from coming here. Go!"

"If I try to stop the prince, it will only make him more stubborn: that's why I'm asking you."

"What right do you have to ask me anything? What if the woman you saw in Sri Lanka is my mother? The emperor has wronged her: it only strengthens my cause for revenge."

"Lady, the emperor's children are dearer than life to your mother. If you kill one of them, she will hate you for it. As long as she lives, her accusing eyes will haunt you and make you suffer."

Nandini covered her eyes with her hands and sobbed. "*Amma!* Isn't it enough that Veerapandian torments me? Do you want to haunt me too?" Eyes brimming with tears, Nandini walked to Devan and held out the sword to him. "Sir, you have succeeded where everyone else has failed. Here's the sword: take it!"

But as Devan reached out for it, Nandini backtracked. "Before you take the sword, tell me whether you'll help me. If I try to leave this place without fulfilling my task, the men in the Hunters' Hall will burn me alive. I don't fear death, but I want to see my mother once before I die. I believe every word you said about the woman who wanders in the forests of Sri Lanka with uncombed hair. I myself have seen her ..."

"Where?" Devan asked eagerly.

"When I was a child, I would sometimes be startled out of my sleep and see a woman staring down at me. She would disappear as soon as I opened my eyes. I was amazed to see the resemblance between my face and the face which looked down so intently at me in my sleep. I wondered whether it was my spirit hovering over me or whether I was going mad. Once I grew up, I realized that the figure was a real woman. This was confirmed by Sundara Chola's reaction on seeing me. Thirumalai also let slip a few things which proved that I had a mother who resembled me. I long to see her once, to lie in her lap and sob my heart out. Sir, if you are willing to take me to my mother, I'll give up my quest for revenge. I'll give you the sword right now."

Manimekalai urged, "Sir, promise you'll do this."

With great reluctance, Devan said, "I'll see if I can do this." *Is this some new scheme?*

"We must leave before Kandamaran and Aditya Karikalan come," Nandini said. "How do we go from here? It's too risky to use the entrance: we may bang into them on the way."

Devan said, "I'll take you through the secret passage in the Hunters' Hall."

"*Akka*, take me with you," said Manimekalai.

Nandini ignored her. "I don't want to go to the hall: Ravidasan and his men will kill us."

"My dear lady, just give me your sword. I can handle those four men," Devan declared.

"No, it will cause trouble. Manimekalai, is there any other way out?"

Manimekalai frowned. "*Akka*, I don't know any other way; but he vanished from here last time ... ask him."

Nandini looked at Devan who said, "Yes, there's another way. I stumbled upon it by accident. But it's hard: you have to leap from terrace to terrace and climb the fort wall. I don't think you can do it. The easiest way is for me to deal with Ravidasan and his men ..."

The startled Manimekalai said, "Aiyo! It looks like they are here ..."

They listened intently and heard footsteps coming towards the room.

"Sir, go to the Hunters' Hall. Quick!" cried Nandini.

"I have a better hiding place," Devan said. "Lady, give me the sword."

Nandini held out the sword to him but her hand slipped and the sword fell to the floor with a clang.

It's a Tigress!

NANDINI LAUGHED SADLY. "Sir, it looks like destiny has other plans. Leave the sword: go and hide."

Devan ignored her and bent to pick up the sword. He held the sharp tip just as Nandini stamped on the hilt with her foot. "No. The prince would have heard the sword fall—he'll be suspicious if he doesn't see the sword here. And he's already suspicious about you. Go!" As Devan straightened up, Nandini saw the blood on his palm where the sword tip had cut him. "I'll keep my word. I won't kill my brother with my hands. Go! If he sees you here ..."

"Go! Go at once!" Manimekalai pleaded.

The footsteps were closer. Devan reluctantly went to the music room and closed the door.

Nandini said, "Manimekalai, hide behind the curtains and steal away quietly later."

Just as Manimekalai hid behind the curtains, Kandamaran and Karikalan entered. Karikalan looked around the room: he saw the bed curtains move but gave no sign of it. He saw the shining sword at Nandini's feet and stared at her. Unable to meet his eyes, she bent to pick up the sword. Karikalan beat her to it. He picked up the sword and examined it, noting the fresh blood on its tip.

Karikalan said, "Lady, the clang we heard must have been the sound of this sword falling from your hands. It looks like you were ready to welcome us with a sword."

"Isn't that the right way to welcome brave tigers and young lions?" Nandini asked.

"Tigers and lions need sharp teeth and claws, but not the spotted deer," Karikalan replied.

"There are times when the deer thanks god for its antlers. Give me that sword. I need it to guard the dignity of the man who took me to his palace from the rubbish heap where he found me."

"Or do you need it to fulfill your oath to take revenge on the wretch who ignored you when you fell at his feet and wounded your heart?"

Nandini bowed her head and sighed. "Sir, I admit that I once worshipped this sword and longed for the day of vengeance. But now, there's no strength in my hand or determination in my heart. This sword will only guard my chastity and my husband's dignity. Please give it to me."

"Lady, leave it to me to punish the wretch who wants to harm you or your husband."

"Can you punish your closest friends?"

"I did not believe you when you accused Vandhiya Devan at the lake. But after listening to Kandamaran, I believe every word. Even if you forgive that wretch, I won't. Tell me where he is … I'm not blind!" Karikalan roared angrily and walked to the bed.

Nandini knelt at his feet, folded her hands and pleaded, "Lord, no!" She saw Kandamaran standing like a statue by the door. "Aiyo! Stop him!" she screamed. Kandamaran sneered and stayed rooted in place.

Holding the sword in one hand, Karikalan swept aside the curtain with the other. Manimekalai, standing there with her dagger in her hand, shrieked. The stunned Karikalan froze for an instant; he then slashed the curtain with the sword and burst out laughing. "It's a tigress! She has sharp claws!" He turned to Kandamaran. "My friend, take this tigress to your mother."

Manimekalai calmed down and readily left the room with her brother.

"Lady, I acted a part and sent them away. Now, can we talk frankly?" Karikalan asked.

The amazed Nandini exclaimed, "What a performance! I too was fooled."

"Nandini, there's no better actor than you in this world. Why didn't you stop me when I walked to Manimekalai with the sword? Did you want me to commit the sin of killing a woman?"

"She's the only one in the world I truly love: would I let her die? I knew you would see her when you parted the curtain."

Karikalan laughed. "Or did you think that if I killed Manimekalai, Kandamaran would kill me? Or that Manimekalai would kill me with her dagger?"

"Aiyo! What imagination!"

"Your intentions are darker than my wildest imagination. Tell me the truth: why did you ask me to come here? Why did you send Lord Ambalavan away to Thanjavur? Don't expect me to believe you are here to partition the kingdom or arrange my marriage to Manimekalai."

"Then why did you come, lord?"

Karikalan said in a pitiful voice, "I wish to leave this country: and this world. I came to see you one last time and say goodbye. Once, you fell at my feet and begged for a boon—I refused you. I have regretted it every minute of my life. Tell me if I can make amends for it in any way."

"Sir, you cannot make amends. The dead are dead: they can't be resurrected."

"But one can give one's life in atonement for taking another's life. Nandini, from the time we were children, I could read your mind. You begged for Veerapandian's life only to push me into violence; you married Ambalavan only to torment me; you called me here because you couldn't bear the thought of me living peacefully in Kanchipuram. Here, take your sword: kill me and avenge Veerapandian's death." Karikalan held out the sword.

Nandini took the sword and shuddered; her hand trembled; her eyes brimmed with tears; she sobbed as if her heart would break …

"Nandini! How can you lose heart? You grew up in a temple priest's house, but you were born into a clan of warriors. A lion cub does not lose its ferocity even if it grows up in a sheep's pen. Don't use Parthibendran or Kandamaran or Vandhiya Devan for your revenge: use your own hands. Hurry before someone comes … you'll never get such a good opportunity again. You'll be helping me by killing me."

Nandini stifled her sobs. "What you said is true. But when the opportunity came, my heart and hands failed me. At the sound of your footsteps, I dropped the sword. See how my hands shake!"

"Yes, I see that, but I don't understand why your heart, harder than stone, has now melted."

"Your friend Vandhiya Devan's news melted my heart."

"Is this about him saying we are brother and sister? You said you didn't believe him."

"I did my best not to believe him, but the news he gave me today changed my heart."

"What new fantasy did he come up with?"

"He told me he saw my mother in Sri Lanka. Sir, I asked you for a boon once and you refused me; you say you regret this. Now, I ask for another boon: will you grant me this?"

"Tell me what you want. I'll tell you whether I can grant it."

"Prince, I took an oath to kill you, or to kill myself if I failed. I don't have the strength or the heart to kill you, nor do I have the strength to kill myself: I'm afraid I'll make a mess of it. Sir, help me to fulfill my oath … kill me with your own hands. I'll be grateful to you for all eternity."

Karikalan took the sword which Nandini held out to him; the room echoed with his wild laughter.

I Love Only You

KARIKALAN'S LAUGHTER REACHED Vandhiya Devan in the music room and made his hair stand on end. He sensed the coming of some great calamity. Death stalked that room waiting its chance. *Will Nandini kill Karikalan? Will Karikalan kill Nandini? Will they kill each*

other? Princess Kundavai sent me here to prevent their deaths; I have
done all I can. I have told them they are brother and sister; I have tried
to melt their hearts. Can anyone stop this wild, mad pair from rushing
to their doom? If I interrupt now, I may risk my life; I may make matters
worse. Let me be patient … Devan gritted his teeth and decided to wait.

"Prince, let me die by your sword: can death be any sweeter than
this? Sir, time passes …what are you waiting for?"

"We have waited for years; a few more minutes will make no
difference. Nandini, marry me. If anyone stands in our way, I'll kill
him!"

"It's destiny which stands in our way. We can't change the
circumstances of our birth."

"Are you talking about you being a priest's daughter? We both don't
believe that."

"I'm talking about the news that we are sister and brother. Have you
already forgotten that?"

"Nandini, you told me at the lake that this was just a trick to separate
us from each other …"

"I have no doubts about that. We are not blood relations. But I'm
married to Lord Ambalavan who's your grandfather: that makes me
your grandmother …"

"Nandini, don't try to cheat me again with that story. You may act
like Lady Nandini of Pazluvur before the world but you told me once
in Thanjavur that you were not really Ambalavan's wife; you said you
stayed in his palace for a reason of your own. You said you would marry
me only if I killed Ambalavan, imprisoned my father and sister and
made you empress. I called you a demon and left for Kanchipuram. But
you haunted my dreams and tortured me …"

Nandini's voice became cruel and angry. "Do you think I didn't
suffer? Do you think I was wallowing happily in luxury in Pazluvur
Palace?"

Devan shuddered as Karikalan too raised his voice. "In that case,
why are we wasting time talking? I'm ready to sacrifice this kingdom for
you. I'll leave my country, my family, my friends. Come with me: we'll
cross the seas and live on a beautiful island."

The sparks flew as Nandini mocked him. "You would rather give up your kingdom than let a low-born girl like me sit on the Tiger Throne!"

"Girl! Does the Chola throne mean more to you than I do? Did you only pretend to love me so that you could be queen one day?"

"Yes, I only wanted the throne! That's why I married Lord Ambalavan … that's why I begged for Veerapandian's life …"

Karikalan roared, "You wicked woman! Now I know your plan: I'll go mad when I hear Veerapandian's name … I'll come to kill you … one of your young admirers will kill me. Where have you hidden your new lover, Vandhiya Devan? You plan to elope with him; that's why you refuse to come with me; that's why you sent Ambalavan away. Where's that wicked Vandhiya Devan?" He whirled the sword and ran around the room in a fury.

Karikalan came to the music room. Nandini immediately ran and threw herself at his feet. "Sir, Vandhiya Devan is innocent. If you harm him, my dear friend, Manimekalai, will die. Cut my heart with your sword: you'll find only your image in it. I swear that's the truth!"

Karikalan calmed down. "Why do you refuse to come with me? Why are you goading me into killing you? Tell me the truth."

"I love only you. But I can't marry you. I came here to tell you this truth, ask you to forgive me and beg you to forget me and marry someone worthy of your status. But I'm scared I'll make you angry. Promise me you'll stay calm …"

"Nandini, tell me: why can't we marry and make the dreams of our youth come true? Tell me the truth, however bitter it may be. The truth will give me peace. It's doubt which makes me angry, frightened and confused. No more lies …"

"Prince, I no longer need to weave a web of lies to get through life. I hid some truths from you because I didn't want to hurt you or make you hate me. How I suffered with my heart torn between my duty and my love for you! I pray the truth truly gives you peace. But it will prove I can't marry you. Death is my only redemption. Vandhiya Devan brought me true news of my mother: she's the madwoman who wanders in the Lankan forests. A few days ago, I discovered why my mother went mad. I have no idea whether anyone else knows this secret. You are the first one to hear who my father is. Sir, remember your promise—please stay calm." Nandini went to Karikalan, whispered, "My father is …." and began to sob.

Karikalan jerked as if stung by a thousand scorpions and shouted, "Impossible! Lies! Lies!" Then, his anger died; his voice was grief-stricken. "It must be true. Everything is clear now: your confusion, your hesitation, your dreadful request … how much you have suffered! There's no forgiveness for my sin and there's no way to break the wall between us. There's only one way to atone for your life and mine … Here, Nandini: here's my atonement!"

Devan did not catch the name which Nandini whispered into Karikalan's ear, but he instinctively guessed who it must be: he had never been so shocked in all his life. Karikalan's calm speech frightened Devan more than all his roars and shouts. *What's he going to do?* Devan peeped out from the Music Room. Karikalan and Nandini were out of his sight, but the mirror was directly in front of him. He saw Ravidasan's savage face peering into the room from the secret door into the Hunters' Hall. Then, the door opened slowly and a tiger crept through it.

Galvanized into action, Devan charged out of hiding. But someone from behind caught his neck with an iron hand. He looked up to see the massive figure of a Kalamukha. *Who's this? How did he come here? My neck's breaking! I can't breathe!* With a mighty push, Devan leaped out of that iron grip and crashed to the ground. He felt as if a huge rock had fallen on his head; a million suns exploded before his eyes; everything went dark …

The huge Kalamukha stepped on Devan's body which lay still at the Music Room entrance and walked into Nandini's room. Nandini turned at hearing the crash and saw the Kalamukha coming towards her with a knife in his hand. Nandini's eyes bulged in shock … she stared at the Kalamukha… she rubbed her eyes and turned back … Karikalan lay on the ground, pierced by Veerapandian's sword. She burst into hysterical sobs and laughter.

The Kalamukha shouted, "You wretch! You evil woman! You have fulfilled your vow."

Just then, Ravidasan came out from under the tiger skin. Seeing the Kalamukha, he flung the tiger skin at the lamp and the room was plunged into darkness. In the second before the lamp died, its light fell on Manimekalai's terrified face before she shrieked and ran from the room. The sound of running footsteps, racking sobs, wild laughter and the moans of a dying man mingled in the darkness of the room.

I Killed Him with This Sword

VANDHIYA DEVAN STIRRED, gasped for breath and slowly opened his eyes to pitch darkness. He was dazed and had no idea where he was. His head throbbed and his neck screamed in pain. *Why is my head aching? Why can't I breathe?*

Devan's confusion cleared. *The Kalamukha ... why did he strangle me? To stop me from shouting out? To stop me from running into the room? What happened to Nandini and Karikalan? What did Ravidasan do? What did the Kalamukha do? Where am I now? In a dungeon? In the secret passage?* Devan rubbed his eyes but could see nothing. *My god! How dark it is!* He remembered being at the door between Nandini's room and the Music Room. *Am I still lying there? Or have they carried me somewhere else?*

Devan groped about with his hands and felt an object: it was a knife. *It has a twisted blade ... if it strikes anyone, it means death. Where have I seen this knife before? Idumbankari had it when we bumped into him in the passage. How did this knife come here? There's blood on its edge! Is it my blood?* Devan gingerly touched his neck and the back of his head: there was pain but no blood and there were no knife cuts on any other part of his body. *Why's the knife lying by my side? Did Idumbankari stab someone with it? Was he disguised as the Kalamukha? Impossible! Idumbankari is not so huge ...*

Devan heard the sound of footsteps. *Someone's coming. Shall I shout or keep quiet? If they bring a lamp, I can at least see where I am. What if they step on me in the dark?*

Devan sat up abruptly, held the dagger in defense and shouted, "Who's there?" His voice came out as a soft squeak. He shouted again,

"Who's there?" Again, his voice was just a whisper. He heard the sound of hurrying footsteps which died away.

Someone must have thought I'm a ghost and run away. He laughed at this but, again, only a squeak came from his throat. *No point sitting here like this. Let me find out where I am ...* Devan stood and stumbled; he steadied himself and groped his way forward. Something glinted in the distance—it was a mirror. Devan remembered seeing the tiger-skin-clad Ravidasan reflected in that mirror. *I'm in Nandini's room. But why's it so dark and silent? Where's everyone?* Devan stumbled forward, hoping to reach the room's entrance. *I can find some light there, or find someone to tell me what happened here ...*

He tripped over something and crashed to the floor again. But this time, something cushioned his fall. It was the tiger skin which Ravidasan had thrown. The knife had slipped out of his grasp when he fell; Devan groped around for it and touched something soft. Devan's hair stood on end; he shuddered; his heart raced. *Could it be... could it be...* he groped with his hands again—it was a body. He felt a man's palm. He flung the tiger skin aside and stared at the body. The dim light reflecting off the mirror fell on it: it was Aditya Karikalan's body.

Devan's heart was in his mouth; his eyes brimmed with tears. He touched the body with trembling hands: there was no life in it. Devan's hands were covered with the blood which had seeped from Karikalan's side and pooled on the ground. *How will I look Princess Kundavai in the face? I have failed! I did my best but destiny defeated me.* Devan lifted Karikalan's corpse on his lap. His mind was numb; he couldn't even cry. He had no idea how long he sat like that. He came back to himself only when he saw men enter the room with lighted torches. He gently laid Karikalan's corpse on the ground and stood.

Led by Kandamaran and Sambuvaraya, a dozen men entered the room with torches and spears. Their faces showed their fear; they looked like men possessed.

The excited Kandamaran shouted angrily: "Traitor! Murderer! Haven't you run away yet?" He turned to Sambuvaraya. "Father, here's the murderer! His guilt is written on his face ..."

Sambuvaraya went to Karikalan's body. He sat by the head for a while and stared at it. He beat his head with his hands and cried, "Aiyo! Fate! Why did this have to happen in my house? I'll be accused of inviting the prince to my house and killing him."

"Father," Kandamaran went on. "No one will accuse you. We have caught the murderer red-handed. There's the blood-stained knife he used. When I came here earlier, there was no sign of him or the knife. He must have come back when he realized he could not escape. Maybe he came to make sure the prince was dead: the wicked traitor!"

Devan was speechless at Kandamaran's words. He realized how suspicious his position seemed to others. *It's all that witch Nandini's work; this is why she saved me; she has taken revenge on Princess Kundavai through this. Where's that beautiful monster? She must have escaped with Ravidasan and his gang through the secret passage. Who killed Karikalan? Was it Nandini ... or Ravidasan ... or the Kalamukha ... or Idumbankari with his knife ... or Manimekalai whom I glimpsed for a moment? Did Kandamaran, besotted with Nandini, kill Karikalan? Did Karikalan, shattered by Nandini's news, kill himself?*

Devan came back to the present when Kandamaran shouted, "Guards, tie up this murderer!"

Devan looked at Kandamaran with sorrowful eyes and cleared his throat with great difficulty. "Do you really believe I would do such a cruel thing? What do I get out of this? My friend ..."

"Chi!" Kandamaran spat at him. "I'll cut out your tongue if you call me friend! What's in it for you? Nandini's love, of course! Where's that Pazluvur enchantress?"

"I have no idea. I was unconscious until just before you came. Maybe Nandini left by the secret passage; four of Nandini's men–Veerapandian's bodyguards, were hiding in the Hunters' Hall."

"Don't pretend you know nothing. Nandini bewitched you and you were ready to do anything for her. Nandini told Aditya Karikalan the truth about you, and he told me. You murdered the prince because she pushed you into it or because you thought it would please her."

"Kandamaran, I swear I did not kill the prince. Princess Kundavai sent me to guard him."

"That's what you said to fool the prince. How did you come to this room? Why did you come?"

"I couldn't save the prince's life. But it's not my fault. Ask Manimekalai …"

"Chi! Don't mention my sister. I'll strangle you with my bare hands right now." Kandamaran pounced on Devan and tied him. He turned to Sambuvaraya. "Father, what shall I do with this murderer? Just say the word and I'll cut him into pieces!"

The dazed Sambuvaraya, who sat stroking Karikalan's body, looked up at Kandamaran. Sambuvaraya's eyes went to the bed curtains which moved: a figure emerged from behind the screen. Surprise and fear flashed across Sambuvaraya's face when he recognized his daughter, Manimekalai. He asked, "Manimekalai, what are you doing here?"

"*Appa*, I was here all this time. He's innocent. Tell my brother not to harm him."

Kandamaran laughed mockingly. "Father, see how he has corrupted Manimekalai's heart."

Manimekalai stood her ground. "He's innocent."

Kandamaran burned with anger and embarrassment. "Shut up, Manimekalai! Who asked you to come here? Go to the other women. You're mad! Why are you speaking up for this murderer?"

"Because he's not a murderer."

Kandamaran laughed angrily. "If he's not the murderer, then who killed the prince? Was it you?"

To everyone's shock, Manimekalai declared, "Yes, I killed him. I killed him with this sword."

Kandamaran leaped to Manimekalai and examined the sword in her hand. "Father, she does not even have the strength to lift the sword: how could she kill the prince with it? And even if she killed him, would she have the strength to pull it out of his body? Look at its edge: it's clean. She's saying this to save Vandhiya Devan. This wretch has cast a spell on her."

Devan face showed his amazement and grief. "Kandamaran, you're right: I'm the murderer. Your sister is trying to save me with her lies." He turned to Manimekalai. "Lady, thank you. I'll never forget your sisterly affection. Now, obey your brother and go to the women …"

Kandamaran's fury exploded. "Have I sunk so low that I need you to support me? Is she my sister or yours? I'll kill you with the very sword your dear sister has in her hand!" Kandamaran raised the sword and leaped on Devan.

Fire!

SAMBUVARAYA JUMPED UP and held his son's hand. "You fool! What are you doing?"

"Father, what's wrong in killing this traitor?"

"You and I and our entire clan will be annihilated! If you kill him, we'll be accused of killing him and the prince."

"Who would dare to accuse us?" Kandamaran asked.

"You idiot! Is this the time to display your courage? It's because I listened to you that we are in this mess. You're the one who invited Lord Ambalavan and the other chieftains here; you're the one who arranged for Prince Madurandaka to come here secretly; you're the one who brought Aditya Karikalan here from Kanchipuram. Aiyo! Malayaman is here with his army! What will I tell him?" Sambuvaraya beat his head with his hands again.

Kandamaran's eyes filled. "Father, I'll make amends. Tell me what you want me to do."

"Drag this girl to the women's quarters. If she blabbers, gag her and tie her up. Or lock her in the secret chamber."

Manimekalai trembled at her father's rage. She also realized that Devan was in no immediate danger. "Forgive me, father. There's no need for Kandamaran to touch me. I'll go to mother at once." She hurried away, with Kandamaran behind her.

Sambuvaraya ordered his men, "Tie him tightly to the leg of the bed."

Devan let the men tie him to the bed. "Sir, the real murderers have escaped through the secret tunnel. I have seen them; if you release me, I'll come with you and help you to catch them. I promise you I won't try to escape."

"Rascal! In that case, what were you doing when the prince was killed? Enjoying the show?"

"Sir, the murderers came here suddenly while Lady Nandini and Prince Karikalan were talking. Just as I was about to attack them, a terrifying Kalamukha caught me by my neck and strangled me. I lost consciousness. When I came to my senses, I found the prince dead."

They heard the angry roar of thousands of voices from outside the palace.

Sambuvaraya listened intently and turned to Devan. "Very well; stay here for a while with your friend, the prince. I'll see what's happening and come back to hear what you have to say." Sambuvaraya and his men left, locking the room door behind them.

Darkness again engulfed the room. Devan's heart was heavy. *How will the emperor bear his son's death? He was so eager to see his son. The roar outside must be Malayaman's men. Have they heard of Karikalan's death? Are they going to attack the palace? Sambuvaraya will try to save his fort by accusing me of killing the prince. But, even if Malayaman believes him, he'll vent his fury on Kadambur Palace. He knows about the conspirators' meeting here ...*

Devan knew that Malayaman adored his grandson. He was capable of annihilating Sambuvaraya and his family when he heard of Karikalan's death. *Kandamaran's a good man, but his friendship has changed to hatred. It's all Nandini's fault, but her life too is a tragedy. Why blame her? Cruel destiny is to blame. Destiny made Manimekalai fall in love with me. She's willing to save my life by confessing to the murder: can there be greater love than this?*

Devan laughed to himself. *I should first worry about myself! I can't prove I'm not the murderer. Ravidasan and his gang have escaped with Nandini and no one's interested in chasing them ... even if they're caught, I'll probably be accused of being a part of their gang. What's the punishment for killing a prince? It must be something so terrible that no one will even dream of committing the same crime. Princess Kundavai and Prince Arulmozli will believe I killed their brother: what punishment could be greater than that!?*

Devan did not know how much time had passed. Suddenly, he noticed some tendrils of smoke in the room, closely followed by a bright light. He looked around and saw smoke and fire coming from the Hunters' Hall. *Did Ravidasan set the hall on fire after entering the tunnel? ... or could it be the lamp Manimekalai and I dropped in the passage?*

The smoke and heat increased; Devan saw the flames through the gaps in the wall. The fire would soon spread to the room. Devan stared at the fire in fascination. *The prince and I will burn on the same funeral pyre.* He jolted out of his trance. *I won't die without proving my innocence to Princess Kundavai and Prince Arulmozli ... and I won't let Prince Karikalan go without his parents performing his last rites. I could not save his life, but I'll save his body and give it to his grandfather. I'll hunt down his murderers ...*

Devan examined the rope which tied him. His hands were tied in front and the rope then went around his body and bound him to the bed. Devan tried to free his hands with his teeth but failed. He tried to jerk his body out of the rope and failed again. But the bed moved. Inch by inch, Devan pulled the bed to the Hunters' Hall's entrance. Each time he pulled the bed, the rope tightened around him and his body shrieked in pain. He gritted his teeth and kept pulling. When he finally made it to the door, he held his hands to the fire burning in the gap between the door and the wall. The rope caught fire and the knots snapped. Devan quickly untied the rest of the rope. Before he could finish, the curtains caught fire and smoke filled the room. Devan felt as if his body was on fire; his eyes watered and his sight dimmed; he could barely open his eyes.

Devan crawled on his knees and groped his way around the room. After what seemed ages, his hands touched the corpse. Devan lifted the body on his shoulders and went to the room's main door. He pushed it with one hand, kicked it with his legs and banged his body against it: the door did not budge. Devan shouted, "Fire! Open the door!" There was no response.

What a fool I am! I must go through the Music Room—how much time I have wasted! I hope the fire has not spread to that room by now. The room was now a furnace and smoke made visibility impossible. As Devan went in the probable direction of the Music Room, he stumbled over something which rolled away with a clang. *It's the twisted-blade dagger. I'll take it. There's something mysterious about it. And it will come in handy if I meet an enemy.* Devan picked up the knife. A spark from the burning bed fell on his shoulder. He brushed it away and ran to the

Music Room, holding Karikalan's body firmly on his shoulder with one hand. He laid the corpse on the ground and ran up the steps to open the door to the terrace. The fire had entered the Music Room: if he had delayed even a few more minutes, this way too would have been blocked. Devan threw Karikalan's corpse on the terrace and climbed out, half dead himself. After the smoke and fire, the cool breeze invited him to rest. *No, I must not waste a minute. God alone knows when this entire building may collapse ...*

Devan lifted Karikalan's body on to his shoulder once again and made his way up terraces and across balconies. But how could he climb down from the palace terrace to the open courtyard and climb the fort walls carrying Karikalan? He was already exhausted ....

Only then did Devan pay attention to the chaos around the fort. *Malayaman's men are battering down the front gate and scaling the walls. What will his soldiers do if they see me carrying Karikalan? They'll probably think I killed him and cut me to pieces! I must not be seen until I find Malayaman and give him his grandson's body ... then let whatever comes, come.*

Devan hid in the shadows and made his way stealthily across the terraces. He finally reached the spot where he had spied on the chieftains' meeting. As he looked around for a way to get down, he noticed a ladder against the wall; a man stood waiting by the ladder. *Who can it be? Who's he waiting for? I need the ladder at any cost.* The commotion at the gate increased and the man went to see what was happening. Devan grabbed the opportunity and quickly climbed down the ladder into the courtyard. He had just stepped from the bottom rung to the ground when the man came back.

"*Swami,* how long you have been!" the man complained from a distance.

Devan recognized Idumbankari and also guessed who Idumbankari was waiting for.

Idumbankari came closer and exclaimed, "You rascal, it's you! Who are you carrying?"

"Yes, my man: it's me. I'm the Kalamukha *swami's* disciple. He sent me ahead with Kali's sacrifice. He's coming behind me and wants you to wait by the ladder. Look, he asked me to show you this knife as a mark of recognition." Devan held out the twisted-blade dagger.

Idumbankari was a little suspicious. "How come you didn't tell me this earlier? Why is the *swami* taking so long? How will we escape from here? Malayaman's men have surrounded the fort and many have come in."

"So what? A crowd will make it easier for us to slip away. The *swami* will find a way. Stay here until he comes and tell him I'm waiting in the garden." Without waiting for a reply, Devan hurried away. Once out of sight, he walked quickly to the terrace above the entrance gate.

Malayaman's Grief

WHEN SAMBUVARAYA REACHED the front gate, he took Kandamaran aside and said, "Son, our clan is in great danger. You must do as I tell you."

Kandamaran replied, "Father, it's my foolishness which has landed us in danger. I promise to do whatever you say."

"Take the secret passage which begins from under my bed. It will join the passage from the Hunters' Hall when it crosses the fort walls. You are the last of our clan. Go and hide in the Kolli Hills. You must come back only after I send word that Madurandaka has become emperor."

"Forgive me, father: I'm ready to die for you … but, I will not hide!"

Sambuvaraya thought a while. "You will not run and hide? Good! I'll give you a brave task. Take the secret passage out and go straight to Thanjavur. Tell Lord Ambalavan what has happened. If he's not there, go to Kalaanthaka and Madurandaka. Tell them our plan has succeeded in an unexpected way. Karikalan is dead and this is the right time to make Madurandaka king. Only Malayaman and Velir stand in our way: we must destroy them."

"What do I say if they ask me how Karikalan died?"

"Tell them that Vandhiya Devan killed him. Another crucial matter: Vandhiya Devan met Prince Arulmozli in Sri Lanka and Princess Kundavai in Pazlayarai; the prince is now on his way to Thanjavur with a massive crowd of supporters. We must spread the rumor that Prince Arulmozli used Vandhiya Devan to kill Karikalan so that he can become the next emperor and that Princess Kundavai is a part of this plot. Make sure to tell the Pazluvur brothers and Madurandaka this."

"Father, this could be true!"

"Maybe. But we must find out why Lady Nandini disappeared. Vandhiya Devan accuses her and her Pandian accomplices of the murder."

"Of course, he'll try to shift the blame to someone else. Father, everything's clear to me now. Princess Kundavai always hated Lady Nandini: she arranged things so that Karikalan dies and Lady Nandini is disgraced. The chief minister must be a part of this conspiracy. They sent Vandhiya Devan here. Aiyo! We have been fooled by them."

"Stop crying over spilt milk. Leave at once. The Pazluvur brothers must know about Karikalan's death before anyone else, including Sundara Chola. You know the underground passage into Thanjavur Fort, right?"

"Yes, I know it." He paused. "I'm worried about Manimekalai."

"Don't worry, I know how to change her mind. How strange destiny is! We planned for Manimekalai to marry Madurandaka; we later decided she must marry Karikalan. Now, Karikalan's dead, we'll go back to our original plan: she'll marry Madurandaka. Thank goodness Manimekalai did not love Karikalan."

"But father, it now looks like she loves that wretch, Vandhiya Devan."

"Manimekalai is not old enough to know her own mind; I'll take care of her. Come, come! I'll take you to the secret passage. Don't delay even a second on the way: get a horse and ride to Thanjavur as fast as you can." Sambuvaraya picked up a lamp and they entered the secret passage and hurried along it. When they had crossed the fort walls, Sambuvaraya hugged his son and blessed him. "Do you want the lamp?" he asked.

"No, father. I know this way well. I can find my way blindfolded."

Once his son was out of sight, Sambuvaraya turned back. He stopped at the Hunters' Hall and listened: there was no sound. He heaved a sigh and came to a decision. He trimmed the lamp so that it burned its brightest, placed it deliberately in a particular position and hurried away.

Sambuvaraya went to the front rooms of the palace and spoke to the women. "We are in great danger. Be prepared to leave the palace at any minute. Be brave: you may have to live in the forest and hills for several days. Collect your clothes and ornaments and come to the courtyard. I will have no sobs or lamentations or muttering, understand?"

Sambuvaraya then walked towards the terrace above the front gate to see what the commotion was about. Before he could get there, the entrance gate crashed open and Malayaman's men charged into the fort, knocking down the Kadambur guards. They were joined by Malayaman's soldiers who had jumped over the fort walls. Sambuvaraya was alarmed. *Does Malayaman already know that Karikalan is dead? Anyway, he has to know at some point. I only need to delay him for half an hour; by then, my plan will work out …*

Sambuvaraya stood majestically in the center of the open courtyard between the fort's gate and the palace entrance. A sword glinted in his hand. Eight soldiers stood behind him, armed with spears and lighted torches. Malayaman and Parthibendran followed the company which had broken down the gate. Parthibendran pointed to Sambuvaraya and they walked to him.

Malayaman said, "Sambuvaraya, why are you standing here sword in hand? What are your intentions?"

"I ask you the same question: what are your intentions? Why have you forced your way in?"

"Sambuvaraya, where's Aditya Karikalan? Where's my grandson?"

"How would I know? He does exactly what he wants. Parthibendran knows this."

Malayaman roared, "Sambuvaraya, you rascal! Don't try to fool me with your excuses. Hand over Karikalan to me. Otherwise, I'll raze this fort and palace to the ground!"

"Parthibendran, has the old man gone mad? Who am I to hand over the prince to him? Have I imprisoned Karikalan?"

Parthibendran was conciliatory. "Stay calm, Sambuvaraya. The old man has reason to be angry. Read this message."

Parthibendran handed over a palm-leaf manuscript to Sambuvaraya who read it by the light of a torch. *Prince Karikalan's life is in danger: come with your army and save him!* Sambuvaraya broke into a sweat and shuddered. "What treachery is this? Who sent this message?"

"What does it matter who sent it? Bring Aditya Karikalan here at once, or take me to him. Or shall I ask my men to search for him?" asked Malayaman.

Parthibendran said, "*Thatha*, come with me, I'll take you," and looked in the direction of Nandini's rooms. "Aiyo!" Parthibendran shouted. "Look!"

Everyone turned in that direction: a fire was raging and a pall of smoke hung over the rooms. "Fire! Fire!" the cry rose from thousands of throats.

Parthibendran recovered from his shock and said, "Sambuvaraya, I did not believe that message, but now I know there's some treachery going on here." He turned to Malayaman. "*Thatha*, arrest these men— I'll go and look for Karikalan."

Sambuvaraya gained courage from the fire. "You are the traitors! You forced your way into my fort and set fire to my palace. You are to blame if anything happens to the prince."

Parthibendran ignored him and ran. The palace women came to the open courtyard. Their faces showed fear but not a whimper came from their lips. Some of them noticed the fire in the rear portion of the palace and pointed to it.

Manimekalai saw the fire, shouted, "Aiyo! Fire! He's there!" and charged in that direction. Sambuvaraya stopped Manimekalai and slapped her. Manimekalai, her father's adored daughter, had never been beaten in all her life. Shocked, she froze and stared at Sambuvaraya.

Sambuvaraya calmed down. "You foolish girl! Have you forgotten what I said?" He pointed: "Look, there's no need for you to panic ..."

Vandhiya Devan staggered towards them with Karikalan's corpse over his shoulder. Malayaman stared as Devan came closer. His aged body trembled; his heart raced; he tried to speak but was tongue-tied. Devan looked straight at Malayaman and walked up to him. "Sir, here's Prince Karikalan, the great warrior who beheaded Veerapandian. I could not bring him to you alive. I bring you only his body which I saved from the fire. Please take your grandson. He was killed by fate and by treachery." Devan gently laid Karikalan's dead body on the ground and collapsed.

Malayaman sat beside his grandson's corpse. He examined the

brave face; his body trembled and he wailed, "Aiyo!!" Malayaman beat himself on his head and chest with his iron hand and lamented over his memories: how he had celebrated Karikalan's birth; how he had carried Karikalan in his lap and on his shoulders as a child; how he had taught him to fight with sword and spear; how he had shone as a warrior from the age of sixteen ...

"Aiyo! Why didn't you die a hero's death on the battlefield? Why did you have to die by Sambuvaraya's treachery? I'm the one who sent you here; I thought I was old and you needed new friends; I thought if you married his daughter, Sambuvaraya would support you; I sent you to your death; I killed you!!" Malayaman repeatedly beat his head. He recovered from his grief and roared, "Sambuvaraya, you rogue! Tell me the truth: how did the prince die? No one could have defeated him face to face. How many men did you use? How did they ambush him?"

The furious Sambuvaraya shouted, "Old man, I know just as much as you do. Ask the man who carried his corpse here. What's the use of asking me?"

"You villain! He was your guest: who will believe you had nothing to do with it? Very well, you can tell Emperor Sundara Chola this when he questions you. Men, arrest Sambuvaraya and raze his fort and palace to the ground!"

Parthibendran came running to say, "Sir, the fire has done our work for us—look!"

Malayaman saw that the fire had spread to the entire palace; tongues of greedy flame reached skywards and engulfed terraces and rooms and turrets. He rose to his feet. "Yes, the fire has done our work. Come, Parthibendran. For three long years, Emperor Sundara Chola waited to see his eldest son; my daughter, Vanamadevi, sent me countless messages asking me to bring her son to Thanjavur ... let them both at least see his corpse. Let them mourn their son. Let the emperor punish these wicked men."

The Banks of the Kollidam Again

SEMBIYAN MADEVI WAS on her way back to Thanjavur after consulting the young saint, Naraiyur Nambi. Azlvarkkadian, walking beside the palanquin, asked, "Mother, did your meeting go well?"

"My mind is clear, Thirumalai. If there's no other way to stop Madurandaka from becoming king, I must reveal the truth. This is Nambi's advice and I agree with him."

"The chief minister expected this. It's now more urgent than ever to resolve this issue. There's dreadful news, mother. Prince Karikalan died in Kadambur: they say he was murdered. We don't know who killed him, or how. His body is coming to Thanjavur in a procession. Malayaman has arrested Sambuvaraya and his family. Only his son, Kandamaran, escaped."

"Thirumalai, what dreadful news! This is the catastrophe predicted by the comet. How will the emperor bear this? Only the compassionate Lord Shiva can save the Cholas."

"The chieftains will fight each other and there'll be a blood bath. While civil war rages, our enemies will grab the opportunity to invade us."

"Thirumalai, why do you say the chieftains will fight each other?"

"You know the reason, mother. Some chieftains will want your son, Madurandaka, as the next emperor; others will insist on Prince Arulmozli. Velir has laid siege to Thanjavur; Malayaman is on his way here with his army; the Pazluvur brothers' supporters are mobilizing their own armies. Chola warriors will kill each other. The chief minister fears the great empire built by generations of Chola kings will shatter in our times. Even he can't find a way to stop this."

"Thirumalai, Madurandaka will not ascend the Tiger Throne. I'll see to that and keep my promise to my husband. There's no chance of civil war." She paused. "I don't believe Sambuvaraya would have dared to kill the crown prince while he was his guest. What does Sambuvaraya have to say?"

"Mother, Vandhiya Devan was found near the prince's dead body. So, Sambuvaraya insists he's the murderer and circumstances are against Vandhiya Devan. When you pass Kudanthai, break the news to Princess Kundavai before she hears it casually from others. It will be best if you take her with you to Thanjavur."

"Aiyo! Poor Kundavai! What shall I tell her? She believed in Vandhiya Devan ... she'll be shattered."

"Tell her not to worry if Vandhiya Devan is accused of the murder; tell her I'll somehow find the real murderer and bring him here."

"Aren't you coming with me, Thirumalai?"

"Mother, I want to unravel the mystery surrounding Prince Karikalan's death. I saw one of the Pandian conspirators on my way to the temple."

"Why didn't you follow him at once?"

"I heard about Prince Karikalan's death only later. I know where these conspirators usually meet. I'll go there."

"Go, Thirumalai. May god grant you success on your mission," Sembiyan Madevi said.

The Rock Cave

FROM THE KOLLIDAM'S southern bank, Azlvarkkadian made his way west. The flood water had ebbed. He reached Thirupurambayam, entered the forest and carefully walked to the war memorial. Although the storm had felled many trees, there was enough cover for him to hide.

He recognized the woman and three men standing by the entrance: Rakamma, Idumbankari, Soman Sambavan and Kiramavithan. Idumbankari was saying something which excited the others.

Azlvarkkadian heard Sambavan say, "Very well. Let's go to the foothills of the Pachai Hills; it's a two-day journey."

As Azlvarkkadian turned to leave before them, he was shocked to find a dagger pointing at his chest: Poonkuzlali held the dagger. They smiled at each other in surprised recognition. Once the conspirators were gone, Azlvarkkadian asked, "Poonkuzlali, what are you doing here?"

"I'm here to take revenge. I followed the wretch who killed my aunt and caught up with him now. I was shocked to see my sister-in-law here with two other men. And then, you came in my way. If you're willing to help, we can follow them and I'll kill my aunt's murderer."

"Are you talking about poor Lady Mandakini? Why did he kill her?"

"He tried to kill the emperor and my aunt threw herself in the path of his spear."

"Your aunt sacrificed her life to save the emperor! How did this happen? Tell me the details."

"Is this the time for it? Those men will escape."

"Poonkuzlali, I know where they are going and can guess who they are meeting there. Let's go there. Let me learn all I need to know from them, then you can take your revenge."

"Let's go," said Poonkuzlali. "I'll tell you everything that happened in Thanjavur as we walk."

After traveling for days and nights, they reached the foothills of the Pachai Hills. There was no sign of the gang in the thick forest. Their spirits fell at the thought that all their travel was for nothing. Suddenly, an owl hooted and another voice echoed the call. Azlvarkkadian beamed and signaled to Poonkuzlali to follow him silently. They came to a clearing with about eight people; some were cooking and others were talking eagerly. Ravidasan was one of the men there. He pointed to a rock cave some distance away and said something.

Azlvarkkadian said, "Poonkuzlali, the person I'm looking for is probably in that cave. I'm going there. You must keep watch; if any of these men come there, give me a warning."

"I can't hoot like an owl," she said. "I'll call like a cuckoo."

Azlvarkkadian peeped into the cave through the large holes made for light and ventilation. He was shocked at the sight which met his eyes. Ambalavan was there dressed in the tiger skin of a Kalamukha. A garland of skulls lay beside him. His pale face suggested that he had lost a lot of blood. He was struggling to sit up after having just regained consciousness. His startled, wild eyes looked as if they had woken from a nightmare.

Nandini was beside him, with disordered dress and ornaments and uncombed hair. Yet, her extraordinary beauty shone brighter than ever.

Her voice brimmed with love and pity. She held out a clay bowl to him. "Lord, drink this gruel."

Ambalavan turned to her with a sweet smile. "Nandini, is it you? Where are we? Have you nursed me and brought me back from death's door? I felt your delicate hand touching my chest: for three years, you refused to touch me ... has your heart finally melted? Give me the gruel: it will taste like divine nectar to me." As Ambalavan took the bowl from her, a sudden change came over him. He shouted, "You demon! How dare you touch me? Did you try to stab me in the chest with your dagger? Is this gruel or poison?" Ambalavan dashed the bowl on the wall where it shattered and fell to the ground.

Let me Go

NANDINI WAS UNRUFFLED by Ambalavan's outburst. For three years, the brave old man had danced to her tune like a puppet on a string. Now, the string had snapped, the puppet had come to life and was thinking for itself. Nandini was not surprised and anyway, the puppet had served its purpose. Nandini's voice was choked with emotion. "Please let me tell you a few things before I leave you forever. Yes, I'm a demon. You found me orphaned in the forest, took me to your palace, forced royalty to respect me and ignored people's curses and insults; you even antagonized the brother you loved more than life itself. But I cheated you for three years: I used your palace for my own purpose, associated with conspirators and bewitched and used young men like Kandamaran and Parthibendran. But in one thing alone, I never betrayed you: from the day you married me, I have been faithful to you ... I have never disgraced your ancient clan of brave warriors."

"What greater disgrace can there be? With this hand ... with my own hand .... you wretch! Where's that sword you had? Cut off my hand with it!"

"Lord, I couldn't even use the sword to take revenge on a person I had sworn to kill for years. Just as I was going mad at the thought that I had let my opportunity slip, you came to my aid ..."

"You she-devil! How dare you say I came to your aid? If I had known this would happen, I would never have come there. Why didn't I drown in the Kollidam!?"

"Lord, you were so bewitched by my beauty that I even considered using you to fulfill my oath. But I did not wish to disgrace your clan: that's why I sent you to Thanjavur. But destiny sent you back to Kadambur at the right time. If your only intention was to save Karikalan, you would have come to Kadambur openly. But because you suspected me of being unfaithful to you, you disguised yourself and came to the palace through the secret passage."

"Nandini, stop tormenting me. Kill me with your sword: I don't have the strength to stop you. Or poison my gruel."

"Lord, I know you can't forgive me. But in our next lives, I'll make amends for my treachery. I will marry you and be a true wife to you. This will be my prayer as long as I live."

Ambalavan was touched. "Nandini, go away at once. If you go on like this, I'll lose my mind. I'll fail to do my duty. Enough of driving me mad. Go!"

"Lord, I did not have the heart to leave you without saying goodbye. You fell unconscious outside Kadambur fort. My men wanted to leave you, but I insisted they carry you here—we have traveled non-stop for three days. My men again wanted to leave you here and go on. I insisted I would stay with you until you regained consciousness. You were justified in trying to kill me, but destiny willed otherwise. You accused me of trying to poison you: for three days, I have spooned water into your mouth and given you life. I can't repay you for making me live like a queen for three years, but I'm grateful that I had the opportunity to serve you for three days. Let me go."

"Nandini, just go! The longer you delay, my mind will waver."

"Yes, you may again decide to kill me. Why did you come disguised?"

"I did not come in disguise through the secret passage because I suspected your chastity. I was afraid that if I stood before you as Lord Ambalavan you would speak to me and I would not be able to kill you. I planned to kill you as you stood stunned and speechless at the sudden appearance of a Kalamukha. I frightened a Kadambur servant, Idumbankari, and took his knife from him. There was another reason for my disguise: I did not want it said that the old man killed his young wife because of jealousy. As you said, destiny played its own game and changed all my plans. Tell me one thing before you go: if I had not intervened, what would have happened?"

"I was waiting to tell you that. When you left for Thanjavur, I promised you your clan would not be disgraced in any way. I made great efforts to keep my promise. I planned to use Kandamaran, Manimekalai or Vandhiya Devan to kill Karikalan. Above all, I had great confidence in Manimekalai. This was my plan: I would get Vandhiya Devan to hide; Karikalan would try to kill him; Manimekalai would kill Karikalan; Vandhiya Devan would take the blame for the murder; I would take revenge on Kundavai through this. But there was no need for all that— Karikalan killed himself."

"No, Nandini! Are you trying to fool me?"

"Lord, if you had not thrown Idumbankari's knife then, the prince would have killed himself with the sword."

"Yes, if I had hesitated for just a second, I would not have committed this great crime. Instead, I would have suspected you. Nandini, no one can defy destiny. You and I can't live as husband and wife in this life. But I'll never forget what you said about being my wife in our next lives: they are the sweetest words I have ever heard. Go! But before you go, give me some gruel or at least some water."

"Very well, sir." Nandini went to get gruel from the stove.

Azlvarkkadian had learnt all that he needed to know. He stealthily moved away from the cave. *It's dangerous to hang around here. Let me go and think what to do next ...*

Azlvarkkadian in Danger

AZLVARKKADIAN AND POONKUZLALI sat under a tree. "Girl, my work is over. Shall we go?"

"If your work's done, go. My aunt's killer is here. An eye for an eye, a tooth for a tooth!"

"Poonkuzlali, who are we to punish the guilty? Leave it to god."

"I have my doubts as to whether god exists and whether he punishes sinners."

"Leave god aside. Punishing the guilty is the duty of the emperor and his officials."

"Vaishnava, that wretch killed a dumb woman who never hurt a soul and suffered much in life. This happened before the emperor, the queen and the commander, but they let him escape."

"Didn't they try to catch Soman Sambavan?"

"The emperor who had rejected my aunt all her life, wept with her on his lap; the others stood there like statues. Lord Kalaanthaka came with me, but he had to go back."

"Why?"

"When we entered the tunnel, we heard a moan in the dark. The commander leaped on a man who was there and shouted, 'Here's the assassin!' A voice cried, 'No, I'm not an assassin!' Lord Kalaanthaka recognized the voice and was stunned: it was Prince Madurandaka, his precious son-in-law. 'What are you doing here?' he asked. The prince replied, 'I came to check if the treasure was safe.' 'My god!' the commander cried. 'If anyone sees you here, they'll suspect you of killing the emperor.' 'Is the emperor dead?' eagerly asked the prince. 'Foolish man! Come with me before anyone sees you.' Lord Kalaanthaka dragged Madurandaka away. I followed the murderer on my own. Are you telling me to leave now without taking revenge?"

"Girl, if you had been born a man, you would have ruled a vast empire. Tell me, if a person tried to kill someone but ended up killing someone else by mistake, is he a murderer?"

"What's the confusion? The killer is guilty of murder."

"Take Soman Sambavan: he aimed his spear at the emperor, but the emperor's alive; your aunt threw herself in the way and died—that's suicide. How can Sambavan be accused of murder?"

"You have a very strange sense of justice."

"Poonkuzlali, one of the two people in that cave unintentionally killed Aditya Karikalan. He threw his knife at another person, but the knife killed the prince. Is he a murderer?"

"Don't confuse me. Who's in the cave?"

Azlvarkkadian shouted, "The Chancellor of the Chola empire, the leader of the chieftains, Lady Nandini's husband ... Lord Ambalavan is in that cave!"

At his shout, Ravidasan, Parameswaran, Sambavan and the rest of the gang turned and charged towards them. Poonkuzlali quickly moved aside.

Ravidasan raised his heavy stick and shouted, "Aniruddha's spy! We have been hunting you for three years. You are finally trapped!!"

Azlvarkkadian shouted even louder, "My dear fellow, we are all Lord Vishnu's children. Listen to me: leave your petty gods and surrender to Vishnu. He'll forgive your sins and give you refuge at his lotus feet. Come, Ravidasan, sing with me ..." Azlvarkkadian burst into a hymn.

Ravidasan roared with laughter. "Enough of your stories. Let's see whether your Vishnu saves you." Ravidasan raised his cudgel.

As Poonkuzlali took her dagger from her waist to rush to Azlvarkkadian's aid, she saw a woman with uncombed hair coming to them from the cave. For a second, Poonkuzlali was shocked. *It's my aunt.* Then her mind cleared and she realized that it must be Nandini.

By then, Nandini was at Azlvarkkadian's side. She blocked Ravidasan's hand with her own and said, "Don't harm my brother. Ravidasan, if I'm truly your queen, drop your cudgel."

Azlvarkkadian said, "Thank you, sister. But these men can't harm me. Vishnu will save me."

Ravidasan laughed mockingly. "How will he save you?"

Azlvarkkadian declared confidently, "Sorcerer, do you see that distant Ayyanar temple? By Vishnu's grace, the three clay horses standing before the temple will come alive; three warriors armed with spears will ride here, arrest you and save me."

Everyone turned in the direction he pointed to ... they could not believe their eyes. They saw the three clay horses come alive and gallop towards them; their riders were armed warriors. Behind them rode a company of soldiers.

Nandini Disappears

RAVIDASAN WAS THE first to recover from his shock. "Lady, how many times have I warned you this imposter is a spy? Come! Before his men are here, let's climb the hills."

Azlvarkkadian said, "Nandini, don't go. Haven't you suffered enough with these wicked men?"

Nandini replied, "Thirumalai, I've been asking you for years to take me to my mother. If you now promise to take me to her, I'll come with you; otherwise, I'll go with them."

Ravidasan interrupted. "I'll take you, come!"

Azlvarkkadian said angrily, "Yes, he'll take you to your mother in the land of the dead. Nandini, one of these wicked men killed your mother."

Ravidasan was furious. "Lies! Lies!"

Nandini's eyes blazed. "Thirumalai, is this true? Is my mother dead? Can I never see her?"

"One of these men, Soman Sambavan, killed your mother. Poonkuzlali, tell her."

"Yes, I saw it with my own eyes. I followed the murderer here to take revenge on him."

Nandini laughed like a madwoman. "You came to take revenge? I swore to take revenge and look at the mess I'm in!" She turned to Ravidasan. "Traitor! How could you do this?"

"My queen, Sambavan threw his spear at the emperor. That dumb madwoman threw herself in its way and died: it was her destiny. Are you coming with us or not? The horses are almost here."

Ignoring him, Nandini sat down and covered her eyes with her hands, weeping and laughing wildly.

Ravidasan shouted to his men, "Run! Hide in the hills. The queen's useless." Saying, "Take this for your treachery!" Ravidasan hit Azlvarkkadian on the head with his cudgel and ran away.

"Narayana!" Azlvarkkadian said, rubbing his head.

The men ran into the cave. Soon, they were seen standing by a waterfall above the cave. At the same time, the riders reached the foothills;

the huge boulders along the way had delayed them. Kalaanthaka and Kandamaran came first. Behind them rode Chendan Amudhan who was tied to his horse. Kandamaran and Kalaanthaka jumped off their horses and saw Nandini weeping. Kandamaran went to her and tried to say something, but he was speechless.

Kalaanthaka turned to Azlvarkkadian. "Vaishnava, what are you doing here?"

"Commander, I too came in search of Lord Ambalavan: he's in that cave. Even death fears your brother. That's why those murderers could not harm him." Azlvarkkadian pointed to Ravidasan and his men at the summit of the hill.

"Who are they? Why do you call them murderers?"

Azlvarkkadian said, "They are the sorcerer Ravidasan and his gang, a part of Veerapandian's bodyguards. The wretches attempted to kill the emperor and killed Prince Aditya Karikalan."

"Lies!" shouted Kandamaran. "Vandhiya Devan killed the prince. He's trying to save his friend."

"Fool! Shut up!" Kalaanthaka shouted and turned to Azlvarkkadian. "Did they also try to kill the chancellor? How did he escape?"

"He escaped with Lady Nandini's help," replied Azlvarkkadian.

"Why is she weeping?"

"She just heard of her mother's death. Can't we discuss all this later? Aren't you going to catch those murderers?"

Kalaanthaka hit his forehead with his hand. "Yes. Last time, I lost my mind and let the man who tried to kill the emperor escape."

"He did not escape: he's also there on the hill."

Kalaanthaka gave orders to his men who ran up the hill. As they neared the waterfall, huge boulders rolled down on them. The soldiers dodged the rocks but a few men were crushed.

"Do you know how they climbed there?" Kalaanthaka asked.

"There must be a secret passage from the cave. Let's see." Azlvarkkadian led the way.

Kalaanthaka and Kandamaran followed him. A tall, dignified figure stumbled out of the cave and stared at the approaching men. It took Kalaanthaka a few minutes to recognize his pale, wounded brother. "*Anna!*" Kalaanthaka cried and rushed to embrace Ambalavan.

Ambalavan's eyes filled with tears as he muttered weakly, "*Thambi*, I ignored your warnings and am ruined." Azlvarkkadian and Kandamaran went towards the cave. Ambalavan blocked them and asked, "Where are you going?"

"Those murderers, Ravidasan and his gang, entered this cave ..."

"They are not murderers," Ambalavan said.

"See? Didn't I tell you Vandhiya Devan is the murderer?" Kandamaran said triumphantly.

Ambalavan stared at him. "How did this stupid young man come here?"

"*Anna*, Kandamaran is the one who brought news of Aditya Karikalan's death."

"Is that so?" Ambalavan said with no enthusiasm. "How are things in Thanjavur?

"*Anna*, there's much to tell. You are weak; why don't you sit?"

Ambalavan sat at the cave entrance.

Azlvarkkadian said, "Sir, if you move aside, we can see whether there's a way to the summit from inside. Ravidasan and his men went up through the cave."

Ambalavan shook his head. "My dear fellow, there's no use going into the cave. Those men rolled down boulders and blocked the cave entrance. I was almost crushed by a rock. Go! Both of you go and find another way up the hill." As Azlvarkkadian and Kandamaran went away, Ambalavan's eyes fell on Poonkuzlali and Amudhan. "Who are they? Why are they here?"

"That's Poonkuzlali, Kodikkarai Vidangar's daughter. She followed her aunt's murderer here. Chendan Amudhan came in search of her. We were able to find you because he showed us the way," Kalaanthaka explained. He then told Ambalavan about the attempt on the emperor's life, Mandakini's sacrifice, Sundara Chola's miraculous recovery of the use of his legs, Velir's siege of Thanjavur Fort and Arulmozli coming there disguised as a mahout. He paused. "*Anna*, Prince Arulmozli has extraordinary charisma. When I stood before him, my heart melted; I instinctively folded my hands in respect. That's why people go mad over him."

"Enough! I know all this. I never believed he had drowned at sea."

Kalaanthaka said, "Luckily the dumb madwoman died to save the emperor. If the emperor had died, our clan would have been disgraced ..."

"As if it has not been disgraced ..." Ambalavan muttered softly. "Go on."

"I followed Poonkuzlali into the vault and found Prince Madurandaka hiding in the darkness."

"What was he doing there?"

"He did not give me a satisfactory answer. I was afraid if anyone saw him, they would suspect him of being the murderer."

"Maybe he is ..." Ambalavan said.

"No, that naïve man is incapable of it. And I saw the assassin with my own eyes. Madurandaka was reluctant to leave the vault. I persuaded him to come with me to his palace and left him there under guard. By then the rumor that the emperor had been assassinated had spread like wildfire. The general ordered his men to attack the fort. By the time I got to the entrance, Velir's men had broken down the gate and scaled the walls: fourteen thousand soldiers were inside. We were only about two thousand, but our men fought bravely. I gathered them and charged out of the fort, cutting my way through the general's men. I sent word to him that if he harmed the Pazluvur family or Prince Madurandaka, I would wipe out the Kodumbalur clan. I rushed to Kadambur, expecting to find you there. I met Kandamaran galloping towards Thanjavur. Both of us were stunned to know that you were not in Thanjavur or Kadambur. Sambuvaraya sent word that Vandhiya Devan had murdered Karikalan and now was the time to make Madurandaka king; he urged us to gather our supporters and prepare for war. I agreed with him and thought you would soon return with an army. I halted our force at Thirupurambayam and sent riders with messages to all the chieftains who support us asking them to raise armies and hurry there at the earliest. *Anna*, don't worry: we'll wipe out Velir and Malayaman; we'll put Prince Madurandaka on the Tiger Throne!" Kalaanthaka roared enthusiastically.

But Ambalavan's attention was elsewhere. "Brother, who's that sobbing there with her hands covering her face?"

"*Anna*, that's Lady Nandini. Please forgive me for criticizing her. I now know it was Lady Nandini who saved you from being killed by the sorcerer and his gang. Is that true?"

"Yes," said Ambalavan. "She saved my life. If it wasn't for her, you would not have seen me alive and the world would not have known the truth."

"I myself did not know about Lady Nandini's matchless virtue—how would the world know?"

Ignoring this, Ambalavan said, "Why is she still here? Hasn't she gone with those men?"

"How could she leave you?"

"Leave that aside. How did you know we were here?"

"We camped at Thirupurambayam. Kandamaran was patrolling the riverbank and caught Amudhan trying to get into a boat. He brought him to me, suspecting him of being a spy. Kandamaran was still angry with Amudhan for helping Vandhiya Devan. When Amudhan heard that Poonkuzlali was going after some murderers alone, he followed her. She sent him away, but he continued to follow her without her knowledge. He overheard some conspirators talking at the Thirupurambayam war memorial and realized that they had caught you and were taking you to the Pachai Hills. He decided to go there, knowing that Poonkuzlali and Azlvarkkadian were also headed there. On hearing this, Kandamaran and I set out with fifty soldiers. Amudhan insisted on coming with us and we tied him to a horse and brought him along. We found you. *Anna*, let's go. I'll arrange for you to be carried carefully. By now, a huge army will have gathered at Thirupurambayam. We can take back Thanjavur Fort in an hour."

"Yes, we might as well go back to Thanjavur at once," said Ambalavan. He walked slowly towards Nandini who sat sobbing on a rock. She jumped up on hearing Ambalavan clear his throat and looked around wildly.

Azlvarkkadian, who stood closest to her, said gently, "Nandini, come with me. We'll leave this country and go on a pilgrimage to the holy temples in the north. We'll spend our lives happily, singing the *Azlvars*' hymns. I'll give up my official work and come with you."

Eyes brimming with tears, Nandini went to him. "Thirumalai, in spite of my betrayal, your love for me is constant—Lord Vishnu will bless you abundantly."

Ambalavan reached Nandini. Nandini prostrated herself at his feet; she stood and looked at him once before turning away abruptly. Her eyes fell on the horses Kalaanthaka and his men had ridden there. She ran to the horses, jumped on the nearest one and pulled on the reins: the horse broke into a gallop. The stunned onlookers came to their senses and rushed to stop her.

"Stop!" roared Ambalavan.

Everyone turned to him and froze. Ambalavan's eyes were on Nandini. The horse, flying like the wind, turned a corner and disappeared from view. Nandini disappeared with it.

You are Not My Son

ADITYA KARIKALAN'S FUNERAL procession moved along the banks of the Ponni towards Thanjavur. Lakhs of people followed it, talking about Karikalan's courage and valor. The procession was an ocean by the time it reached Thanjavur, where the citizens and soldiers joined it. Aniruddha decided against letting the crowd into the fort and advised the grief-stricken emperor and his family to go out and receive the funeral procession.

The crowd broke into cries of lamentation at the sight of Sundara Chola. Karikalan's body was placed outside the fort for the people to pay their last respects. They came in waves and wept over him. But there was no sign of Madurandaka and the Pazluvur brothers. Rumors buzzed in the air: *Karikalan was killed because of Madurandaka and the power-hungry chieftains … the Pazluvur brothers and their supporters are mustering an army …*

The crowd did not disperse even after the funeral rites were concluded and Sundara Chola and his family returned to the fort. Angry shouts of 'Down with Madurandaka!' and 'Down with the Pazluvur brothers!' filled the air and grew louder with the hours. A section of the crowd forced open the gates and surged into the fort. They headed to the Pazluvur palace and shouted, 'Down with the Pazluvur brothers!' Aniruddha ordered the *Velakkara Padai* to disperse the mob. Meanwhile another rumor took wing: *Madurandaka is hiding in Aniruddha's house.* The mob surrounded the chief minister's house shouting, 'Where's that coward, Madurandaka?' 'Send Madurandaka out!'

Madurandaka was indeed in Aniruddha's house. He shivered in fear and said, "Chief Minister, please send me out of the fort somehow. Let me out through the secret passage: I'll join my supporters. If you do this, I'll make you my chief minister when I ascend the Tiger Throne ..."

Aniruddha said, "Why talk about the throne when Sundara Chola is alive?"

"Didn't you see his face when he came back after performing his son's last rites? He was as pale as a ghost. I was watching him from the terrace: he won't live long. Arulmozli or I must become the next emperor. Sundara Chola favors me—why are you and my mother against me?"

"Prince, the queen must have a good reason. And what about the people? Can you hear them?"

The mob was now shouting, 'Long live Prince Arulmozli!' as Arulmozli rode past them on a majestic horse. The crowd followed him and the street outside Aniruddha's house was soon deserted. Madurandaka's jealous eyes followed Arulmozli. *What strange power does he have?*

Aniruddha asked, "Prince, what were you doing in the treasury vault?"

"I was depressed when Arulmozli came disguised as a mahout and did not want to be in the fort with him. Lord Ambalavan had earlier showed me the secret passage; I was wandering in the garden wondering whether to use it when a man came out of the tunnel. He came to me and said, 'Prince, Lord Ambalavan and Kandamaran asked me to take you to them at once. They have mustered a huge army to support your claim to the Tiger Throne.' I was suspicious and asked, 'Why have they not come here to face the general's forces?' He said, 'Prince, there's a mystery surrounding your birth. No one dares to tell you, but I will.' I said, 'In that case, come: let's go at once.' He replied, 'I have some news for the chief minister. I'll be back. Hide in the treasury vault and wait for me.' I waited for him in the vault. Chief minister, did you meet him? What do you think is the mystery surrounding my birth?"

"Prince, only your mother has the right to discuss that with you. I can't tell you."

Again, there was a commotion in the street. Aniruddha looked out. "Here's your mother."

Sembiyan Madevi's face was filled with sorrow. She sat in silence, her head bowed. A hush descended on the house and the street. She looked up at Madurandaka and said, "My child, listen to me: there's no greater hardship than wearing a crown. The kingdom of god is greater than any earthly kingdom. Come, let's go on a pilgrimage to Mount Kailash ..."

"You are at the right age to make the pilgrimage to Mount Kailash: not me! Through Shiva's grace, the throne is now within my reach. Why should I let it go?" Madurandaka asked.

"My dear boy, did you hear the mob? The people believe you and the Pazluvur brothers are responsible for Karikalan's death. Do you think they'll accept you as the emperor?"

"Mother, the people will forget all this once I sit on the Tiger Throne. Arulmozli's dear friend, Vandhiya Devan, is responsible for Karikalan's death. Arulmozli arranged to kill his brother so that he could ascend the throne. See what happens to Arulmozli once the people know this!"

Sembiyan Madevi's eyes blazed in fury. "You wretch! Arulmozli is the very embodiment of compassion. If you speak ill of him again, you'll burn in hell!"

"You monster! You curse your own son and bless his enemy. You can't be my mother."

"Your stubbornness forces me to tell you this: I am not your mother ... you are not my son."

Madurandaka said softly, "My hunch was correct." He turned to Sembiyan Madevi. "If you are not my mother, tell me: who's my mother?"

The queen looked at Aniruddha. "Sir, tell him. Please don't make me speak of my own shame."

Aniruddha chided Madurandaka: "Prince, you have hurt the mother who cared for you from the time you were a baby." He paused. "But you must learn the truth at some point ..."

When Sembiyan Madevi was newly married, she longed for a child who would one day rule the Chola empire. She became pregnant. On one of her temple visits, she saw a dumb pregnant woman wandering about alone. The queen brought the woman to the palace and let her live in a hut in the palace garden. When she heard that the woman had a younger sister in Thanjavur who was also dumb, the queen arranged for her to come and live with her pregnant sister.

At the time of Sembiyan Madevi's delivery, her husband was away. She delivered a child and Aniruddha came to congratulate her. Sembiyan Madevi burst into tears: her baby boy lay as lifeless as a log beside her. She sobbed, 'Sir, what will I tell my husband when he comes back?'

Unable to bear her grief, Aniruddha suggested a plan. The dumb woman had just delivered twins: a boy and a girl. Aniruddha went to her and signaled that if she left her babies there, they would grow up in the palace. At first, she refused to give up her babies. A few hours later, she abandoned them and ran away. Aniruddha asked the younger sister to take the baby boy to Sembiyan Madevi. He gave her the lifeless baby and instructed her to secretly bury it. Aniruddha took the baby girl with him and later sent her to the Pandian country through Azlvarkkadian.

Sembiyan Madevi was haunted by guilt at this exchange of babies. One day, she confessed to her husband. That great man said, 'So what? Whoever gave birth to it, the baby is Lord Shiva's gift to us. Bring him up as your own son. But we must never, for any reason, let him ascend the Tiger Throne: that would be a betrayal of our clan. We will raise him to be a Shiva devotee who prefers the kingdom of god to the kingdom of men. If I'm not alive, you must stand firm and protect the Chola dynasty.'

Aniruddha concluded his story. "Madurandaka, you are not Gandara Aditya's and Sembiyan Madevi's son. Your mother was a wandering orphan. The queen lavished more love and care on you than she would on her own son. Now obey her: it's for your own good."

How Unlucky I Am!

MADURANDAKA WAS STUNNED for a while. Then he jumped up: "Chief minister, this is your work. I know you want to make Arulmozli emperor. Kundavai and Arulmozli forced you to say lies and corrupt my mother's pure heart."

Aniruddha spoke calmly. "Prince, if I hated you so much, I would have left you under the tree in the storm. Do you know what Prince Arulmozli is doing now? He's talking to the soldiers and the people, trying to convince them that you are the rightful heir to the Tiger Throne."

"In that case, Arulmozli does not know the truth about my birth ..."

"No one knows," Aniruddha assured him.

"Why tell anyone? The emperor has gifted you only ten acres of land in a village. I'll give you the entire Pandian country as a reward for your silence."

"Sir, you don't need to buy my silence. I'll obey your mother: talk to her," Aniruddha replied.

Madurandaka looked beseechingly at the mother who had raised him.

"My child," Sembiyan Madevi said. "Everything Aniruddha said is true. He has sworn an oath of loyalty to the Chola dynasty. Yet, he has guarded my secret even from Sundara Chola. If I agree to let you ascend the Tiger Throne, he'll keep quiet."

"Yes, my queen. I'll keep your secret, but I won't serve the throne with falsehood in my heart. I'll resign my post and spend my days serving Lord Vishnu."

"There's no need for that. Madurandaka won't ascend the Tiger Throne. He won't defy me: he'll renounce his right to the throne. Do you agree, my son?"

"Mother, you are the only one standing in my way. Even if I'm not your son, you cared for me as your own child for twenty years. Why are you doing this? What harm have I done to you?"

"My child, you have not harmed me in any way. I would have taken my secret to the grave, but I must keep my promise to my husband. I must not let a child who does not belong to the Chola clan sit on the Tiger Throne. My heart broke when I told you, 'You are not my son.' I was confused; it was Nambi who showed me my duty and the path of righteousness. He said, 'Give all your personal wealth to your son. But the kingdom is a different matter. It's a sin to deprive another of his rightful claim to the throne. Tell your son and the emperor the truth.'"

Madurandaka fell at the queen's feet. "Mother, I'll do whatever you want. But please don't tell anyone I'm not your son. If the truth comes out, I'll die of shame!"

The queen wept as she raised him up and seated him beside her. "My son, promise me you won't harm the Chola dynasty or listen to anyone's wicked advice. The Council of Ministers meets in three days. If you publicly renounce the Tiger Throne and announce your support for Arulmozli, Aniruddha and I will never reveal this secret."

Madurandaka leaned his forehead on his hands. *How unlucky I am: in less than an hour, I have lost my parents, my clan and the throne. All the chieftains who swore to support me will abandon me.* "Mother, I'm confused—give me two days to think about this."

"My child, either you publicly renounce your claim to the Tiger Throne or I'll publicly announce the truth of your birth. What is there to think about?"

Aniruddha intervened. "Lady, there's no harm in giving him two days' time to think calmly."

Madurandaka asked excitedly, "Mother, does anyone else know about this?"

Sembiyan Madevi looked at him in surprise. "Three other people know the truth. The first is your father, who is now dead. The second is your mother. She was killed two days ago in Sundara Chola's palace. I considered telling you the truth so that you could pay your last respects to her but I didn't have the heart to cause you pain."

"Even if you had told me the truth, I would not have gone near her. I think of only you as my mother. The third person who knows the truth is the other dumb sister. Who's she?"

"Vani lives with her son in a garden on the outskirts of the city. She can't reveal the secret as she was born deaf and dumb. Mother and son supply garlands to the temple. I'm their sponsor."

"Ahah! I know them both. The son's name is Chendan Amudhan: he helped the spy, Vandhiya Devan, escape from the fort. Does Amudhan know the secret?"

"No, my son. His mother promised me to tell no one. Only the chief minister, Vani and I know the truth. There's no need for you to worry."

Madurandaka thought, *If these two die, the truth will die with them. I'm not obliged to Aniruddha in any way and she's not my mother: why should I care about them? Who's the man in the palace garden who said that he would tell me the truth about my birth? He tried to kill Sundara Chola but killed the mute woman instead. And they say that mute woman is my mother. In that case, who's my father? Maybe .... maybe .... maybe I'm Sundara Chola's son! Maybe this wicked old woman and this Brahmin are trying to cheat me. How can I discover the truth?*

"My son, think clearly and take a decision. I have cared for you like a mother for twenty-two years: I will not misguide you. Give up this earthly kingdom and work for eternal salvation."

Arulmozli unexpectedly entered the room. He went straight to the queen, paid her his respects and said, "Mother, as you just said, I'm ready to give up my right to the Tiger Throne. Bless me and let me let me devote myself to Lord Shiva."

The queen and Aniruddha looked at each other in amazement.

"I dispersed the crowd and came back here to discuss our next course of action with the chief minister. Your voice was loud and Prince Madurandaka was shouting: I overheard a part of your conversation. You said only three people know this secret: you're wrong. My sister and I also know the truth. Lady Mandakini told me the truth through her paintings in Sri Lanka. I told my sister and we decided that Prince Madurandaka must ascend the Tiger Throne. You raised him as your son and his mother saved my life many times: he has every right to be emperor. I swear on your sacred feet that I renounce all claims to the Tiger Throne!"

The three people in the room with him were stunned. Aniruddha recovered first and said, "Prince, your words deserve to be engraved in the annals of history. But we have to consult the emperor and the chieftains. We have to consider the consequences if the truth comes out later. We have three days before the Council of Ministers meets. Let's think calmly ..."

Kundavai's Troubles

KUNDAVAI WAS HEART-BROKEN at her beloved brother's death. Aditya Karikalan had ignored her warnings and gone to Kadambur Palace. For some reason, Nandini, whom Kundavai believed was their sister, hated Karikalan. If she had killed him, the Cholas were doomed. No one knew what had happened to Nandini. Even now, two days after Karikalan's death, Kundavai's heart melted at the thought of Karikalan's brave face.

He dreamt of great conquests, but his body burnt to ashes in half an hour and mingled with the soil of the Chola country. Thousands of brave Chola warriors will rise from that soil; they'll conquer the world with the triumphant cry, 'Spear of Victory! Spear of Valor!' They'll ensure that the glory of the Cholas lives forever. Arulmozhi will make all Karikalan's dreams come true. But how many obstacles stand in the way! The chieftains are split into factions and who knows what disaster they are heading for? My father is immersed in sorrow; he refuses to talk to anyone ...

As if all this was not enough, Kundavai was deeply troubled by Vandhiya Devan languishing in the dungeon. *How can I interfere in this matter? How shameful if I'm accused of being more concerned about a stranger than about my own brother! Parthibendran says that Vandhiya Devan was caught red-handed by Sambuvaraya and Kandamaran at the scene of the murder. This may be true ... he promised not to leave Karikalan's side. He must have tried to prevent the murder and failed. How do I find out the truth? I can't meet him in the dungeon or have him brought here. No one will dare say anything about me and even if they do, I don't care. But some people are trying to link Arulmozhi to Karikalan's murder. I must not give them grounds to spread rumor. Goddess Durga, why are you flooding me with sorrow?*

Kundavai had not slept a wink after hearing of Karikalan's death and

Devan's supposed involvement in it. She considered and rejected many plans. She even refused to talk to her beloved Vanathi who dogged her like a silent shadow.

Vanathi now came to her: "*Akka*, a woman wants to see you: she's in tears and looks pitiful."

"Who's she? What does she want?"

"You may not like this, *akka*. She's Manimekalai, Sambuvaraya's daughter. His family is under house arrest in Lord Kalaanthaka's mansion. She crept away and insists she will speak only to you. She looks so miserable even your heart will melt."

"Are you accusing me of being stone-hearted?" Kundavai asked angrily.

Vanathi retorted, "Would you leave Vandhiya Devan in the dungeon otherwise?"

"Okay, okay. Bring her here."

Manimekalai's Request

MANIMEKALAI LOOKED AROUND wildly like a madwoman as she walked in. Her eyes and face were swollen by crying, but Kundavai did not pity her. Kundavai believed that all the present tragedies could be traced back to the conspirators' midnight meeting in this girl's house. She was furious that her brother's murder had also taken place at Kadambur. But her interest was aroused when she recalled that this girl's brother and Vandhiya Devan were close friends.

Is this the sister Kandamaran wanted Vandhiya Devan to marry? Is she here to plead for her father and brother? Did she fall in love with Karikalan? Is she out of her mind with grief that he's dead? Or ... or ... is she in love with Vandhiya Devan? He would definitely have rejected her: is she here to take revenge on him by accusing him of the murder?

Kundavai stared at Manimekalai who bowed her head with tears streaming from her eyes. "Girl, I should be the one crying: your brother's alive; it's my brother who was murdered in your palace. Our women do not shed tears over the death of our brave warriors."

Manimekalai looked up. "Lady, I would not cry if my brother died a warrior's death on the battlefield. But your brother …" she hesitated and broke into sobs again.

My suspicion is right: the poor thing loved Karikalan. I must console her. "Girl, be strong. Are you sad that it happened in your house? What could you have done? Your elders are responsible …"

"Lady, the fault is mine. That's why I can't control my grief. When I think I killed that brave hero with my knife, I feel my heart will break …"

The startled Kundavai asked, "What nonsense! Are you mad?"

"I'm not mad … I'm the wretch who killed the prince. I came to confess and be punished."

"Chi! Do you expect me to believe my brave brother was killed by a woman? Are you trying to save your father and brother with this story?"

"Why should I try to save them? They were ready to sacrifice me and force me into marriage. First, they said, 'Marry Prince Madurandaka.' Then they brought Aditya Karikalan there and said, 'You must marry him; you'll become a queen.'"

"Girl, countless princesses vied for my brother's hand. Do you think it's such a dreadful thing to marry into the Chola dynasty?"

"Lady, I don't have any sisters. I'll consider you my own sister and tell you…"

Kundavai cut her off. "You say you killed my brother: how can you be my sister?"

"I have that right: your brother Karikalan called me his sister. He even said that to me in writing. My heart aches to think it was I who killed him …" Manimekalai sobbed.

Kundavai said softly to Vanathi, "Poor thing! She's mad. Why did you bring her here? What if she goes wild suddenly?"

Vanathi replied, "I'm also worried, *akka*. Please talk to her kindly and send her away."

"Girl, it's all destiny's handiwork. Think of me as your sister. What do you have to say?"

"*Akka*, you're a woman and so you'll understand: men never understand such things. Suppose a woman loves a man; suppose that man is unarmed and another man comes to kill him with a sword; if that woman truly loves him, will she stand by quietly?"

Kundavai thought of Mandakini and her eyes filled with tears. "No, she'll throw herself between them and sacrifice her life for her lover."

Manimekalai said, "Ah, how I wish someone had given me such advice! I listened to that wretch, Nandini, and destroyed myself. I killed the great man who thought of me as his sister and promised to arrange my marriage to my beloved."

Kundavai whispered to Vanathi, "Her frenzy is rising!" She turned to Manimekalai. "Girl, don't cry. Tell me what happened or come back later."

"No, no, I'll tell you now. My brother, Kandamaran, often spoke of his friend; a few months ago, this friend came to Kadambur; one look at him, and my heart said, 'This is my beloved.'"

Kundavai's voice shook a little. "Who's the lucky man who stole your heart?"

"My love stole his luck and he's now in the dungeon. The Pazluvur women told me the dungeon is terrible and no one who goes in comes out alive."

"Nonsense! Vanathi and I went there a few weeks ago."

"Lady, can I go there? Can I see him once?"

"You haven't told me who he is," Kundavai pointed out.

"His name is Vandhiya Devan."

Vanathi intervened. "Why are you concerned about him? Who's he to you?"

Manimekalai cried, "What right do you have to question me?" She immediately calmed down. "You are Lady Vanathi; your uncle commands the fort. I'll fall at your feet … ask the general to free Vandhiya Devan and put me in the dungeon instead. I'm the one who killed Prince Karikalan. When I have confessed to the crime, how can you accuse another man?" She turned to Kundavai. "Lady, I beg you, if the general refuses to give me justice, take me to the emperor."

Kundavai's mind was in a turmoil. While she had hesitated to visit Devan in the dungeon, this girl was willing to take his place there. *Is she saying lies to save her lover? Or did she really kill Karikalan under Nandini's evil influence? No, this girl's not capable of murder. No one will*

believe her. But I can clear the mystery surrounding Karikalan's death
with this girl's help.

"Manimekalai, I applaud your courage, but no one will believe
you. Your father and brother say that Vandhiya Devan was caught
by Karikalan's dead body. And I sent Vandhiya Devan to guard the
prince. Vandhiya Devan should have saved Karikalan even at the cost
of his own life. Even if he is innocent of killing Karikalan, he must be
punished for failing in his duty."

"Lady, he did not fail in his duty in any way. Here's the proof in your
brother's own writing." Manimekalai took a palm leaf from her waist.

Kundavai eagerly took the letter addressed to her. Karikalan had
obviously written it himself to keep it confidential.

'My dearest sister, three years ago, I killed an enemy who had
surrendered. He, and the woman who begged for his life, torture me
and give me no peace. I have not slept for years. Today, I saw the comet
fall. Something from my body flew away with it and now, I'm just an
empty shell. Let this bad omen end with me. May Lord Shiva keep
father and Arulmozli from harm.

As children, we shared many dreams about the Chola empire. I
could not make them come true, but my brother will. He was born to
the rule the world. Vandhiya Devan will stand by his side.

Sister, if anything happens to me, it's because of my own stubbornness.
Vandhiya Devan is not to blame. He tried his level best to stop me from
coming to Kadambur. Now, he sticks to me like my shadow. But can he
save me from my own destiny?

Hypnotized by the cobra's dance, some creatures voluntarily go before
the snake to be killed ... I'm going to Nandini like that. You warn me she's
our sister: I can't believe it. But there's something mysterious about her.
I'm determined to find the truth. Whatever happens, Vandhiya Devan is
blameless. Parthibendran and Kandamaran have fallen under Nandini's
spell; Vandhiya Devan is the only one she can't charm. I wonder how
to reward him. There's a lively young girl here whom I love like a sister.
If Vandhiya Devan marries Manimekalai, it will be a fitting reward for
him. I don't know whether you'll agree to that.

My dear sister, I'm giving this letter to Manimekalai: luckily, she
can't read. Do as you want with her. You are the wisest in our family. I

disobeyed you and I'm suffering the consequences. May Arulmozli be guided by you and take the Chola empire to great heights!'

The letter stopped there. Tears streamed from Kundavai's eyes and she quickly wiped her face. "Girl, how did you get this palm leaf?"

"Lady, the prince gave it to me himself. Nandini told me the prince was wicked. So, I first thought it was a love letter and decided to burn it. But I was curious to know what he had written and asked my friend, Chandramathi, to read it to me. My heart aches to think I killed the brave man who called me his sister. Lady, punish me for this wicked murder!"

Kundavai was convinced that she was lying to save Devan. But the letter was real: it was enough to save Devan from the dungeon and prove he was innocent. *If only this girl keeps her mouth shut.* "Manimekalai, Karikalan loved you as a sister: why would you kill him?"

"If I had read the letter earlier, I would not have killed him. That evil Nandini kept telling me the prince hated Vandhiya Devan and would kill him. So, when Karikalan raised the sword and shouted, 'I'll kill Vandhiya Devan!' I believed him. I took my dagger ..."

"Girl, stop it! You are humiliating my dead brother. Think: will Vandhiya Devan let you take the blame for the murder? He'll say, 'I killed the prince.' You know the punishment for murdering a prince— they'll impale him at the crossroads ..."

Manimekalai howled, "*Akka*, you must save him!"

Obstacle to Freedom

JUST THEN, THEY heard the roar of a crowd outside the palace.

Vanathi went to the palace entrance and rushed back in excitement. "*Akka*, he's coming!"

"Who's 'he?'" Kundavai teased.

"He—your brother!"

"Take this girl away." As Vanathi hesitated, Kundavai said, "Go quickly. He won't go without seeing you. I'll send for you."

Vanathi left with Manimekalai and Arulmozli came in.

"*Thambi,* you have brought a noisy crowd to the palace gates. Father will suffer."

"*Akka,* I'm trying to persuade the people and the army to accept Madurandaka as the next king. Velir and Malayaman are the main obstacles to this. You must talk to them."

"I have tried, but they are stubborn. We must find some other way."

"Tell Velir that Vanathi has sworn that she'll never sit on the throne: he'll become less enthusiastic about making me emperor."

"I already told him. He said, 'Are you asking me to destroy an empire because of one girl's foolishness? If not Vanathi, there are a hundred princesses in Bharath willing to marry Arulmozli or to die for him!' He glared at Vanathi and made her tremble."

Arulmozli laughed. "Good thing she didn't faint." He looked around. "I have sent Vanathi on an errand."

"*Akka,* our guess is correct: I was at Aniruddha's house and overheard Sembiyan Madevi tell Madurandaka, 'You are not my son.' You should have seen our uncle's beautiful face change into a demon's mask! Luckily, I walked in and told her that whether Madurandaka was born to her or not, he was the rightful heir to the throne."

"*Thambi,* why didn't you tell her Madurandaka has a right to the Tiger Throne because he's Sundara Chola's son? Are you afraid this will humiliate our father?"

"*Akka,* Aniruddha says the twins, Madurandaka and Nandini, were born two years after father returned from Sri Lanka. So, they can't be our siblings."

"Arulmozli, in spite of this, are you willing to let Madurandaka be the next emperor?"

"Yes. Madurandaka is Lady Mandakini's son and Sembiyan Madevi's adopted son. I'm not interested in being king and Vanathi will not sit on the throne ..."

"Maybe the astrologers are right and the kingship will come to you even if you don't want it. It may be your destiny. In this letter, Karikalan hopes you will fulfill all his dreams. When I read it ..." Kundavai's eyes filled and her voice quavered.

Arulmozli read the letter with tears flowing down his cheeks.

Kundavai said, "*Thambi,* Madurandaka and Nandini don't belong to the Chola dynasty. Even if I'm devoted to Lady Mandakini and Sembiyan Madevi, I can't accept an outsider on the Tiger Throne. Madurandaka must not be king."

"*Akka*, I just promised Sembiyan Madevi, Aniruddha and Madurandaka that I will not be king. I said the same thing to thousands of people and soldiers. How can I break my word?"

"Goddess Durga must show us the way. I don't know what advice to give you …"

"Who gave you this letter, *akka*? Why didn't you tell me about it earlier?"

Kundavai, waiting for a chance to bring up Vandhiya Devan's name, said, "Sambuvaraya's daughter, Manimekalai, just brought it. Question her yourself. I don't know how much we can trust her." Kundavai called out to Vanathi who walked in with a weeping Manimekalai.

Arulmozli said, "My sister, thank you for bringing us our brother's last letter."

Before he could say more, Manimekalai fell at his feet and sobbed her heart out. "Prince, I'm the wretch who killed your brother: put me in the dungeon and let him go!"

Arulmozli turned to Kundavai in surprise. "Is she mad? Who's in the dungeon?"

"She'll probably go mad soon if Vandhiya Devan is not freed from the dungeon. Have you forgotten the messenger I sent to you?" Kundavai asked reproachfully.

In truth, Arulmozli had forgotten Devan as he had been preoccupied with Karikalan's death and with Madurandaka. He now exclaimed, "What? My dear friend, Vandhiya Devan, is in the dungeon? Who sent him there?"

Kundavai told him everything she had heard from Manimekalai.

"What nonsense! Who dares accuse Vandhiya Devan of being the murderer? I know how devoted he was to my brother. Everything else can wait: let me first release Vandhiya Devan from the dungeon. Console that girl." Arulmozli hurried to the door to find Malayaman and Velir there. The general blocked the door with his spear while Malayaman planted his sword on the ground. Arulmozli asked in irritation, "General, what's the meaning of this?"

Velir said, "Sir, you must not visit the dungeon: we'll arrest you if we have to."

"General, have you forgotten who I am … or have you forgotten yourself?" Arulmozli cried.

"I'm the commander of Thanjavur Fort; that makes me the guardian of the dungeon. You are the emperor's son, but you don't have the authority to release a man accused of murder. Only the emperor or his anointed heir has that right. You say you will not ascend the Tiger Throne: so, only the emperor has the right to release anyone from the dungeon."

Malayaman added, "My child, he's right. The emperor has appointed him commander of Thanjavur Fort. You do not have the right to release anyone from the dungeon."

Arulmozli was speechless. The room was silent except for Manimekalai's sobs.

Vanathi's Idea

KUNDAVAI STEPPED FORWARD to say, "*Thatha*, uncle: Arulmozli will not defy you."

Velir said, "Lady, if the prince agrees to ascend the Tiger Throne, we can all submit to his authority. The emperor longs to spend his last days in peace at Karikalan's golden palace."

"Uncle, I was telling Arulmozli the same thing when this girl appealed to him. The prince was moved by her story and decided to release Vandhiya Devan from the dungeon."

"Who's this girl? Why is she sobbing?" Velir asked.

"Don't you recognize her? She's Sambuvaraya's daughter, Manimekalai."

"Oh! She must be crying over her father," Malayaman said. "Girl, don't worry. The emperor has ordered your father's release. Parthibendran has gone to bring him from the dungeon."

"*Thatha*, she's worried about Vandhiya Devan. She insists she killed Karikalan and asks that Vandhiya Devan be released from the dungeon."

Velir pointed to his forehead with his finger and whispered, "The girl is mad."

"Sir," Arulmozli said. "We are wasting time talking. I'll go to the emperor right now and get his permission to release Vandhiya Devan. Then none of you can object."

"Prince, Parthibendran has convinced the emperor that Vandhiya Devan joined Nandini and Veerapandian's bodyguards in their conspiracy and killed Karikalan."

"In that case, I'll go to Parthibendran and demand proof for his accusations."

"You can't see him now. The emperor ordered him to release Sambuvaraya and then go to meet the Pazluvur brothers and their supporters. He has invited them here to resolve the succession issue amicably and declared that he agrees to make Madurandaka his heir." Velir paused. "If you go to the emperor, it will lead to serious trouble. Yesterday, two men went among our soldiers saying that Prince Arulmozli, wanting to become emperor, sent Vandhiya Devan to kill Prince Karikalan."

"My god!" Kundavai cried. "How cruel!"

"Our soldiers ducked them in the river. I happened to pass that way and rescued them and ..."

Arulmozli interrupted. "No one will believe such nonsense."

"They may not believe it today, prince. But the same rumor will come up again: this time a few people will believe it and ..."

"Commander, are you telling me to leave my dearest friend in the dungeon fearing a rumor which may spread in the future?" Arulmozli asked angrily.

"If you get involved in Vandhiya Devan's release today, some people will believe the rumor tomorrow itself. Your father will come to hear of it: think how hurt he will be."

Arulmozli's face fell. He turned to Kundavai. "*Akka*, what do you say?"

Kundavai's face reflected her grief. "Uncle, who's responsible for spreading this rumor?"

"I took the two rumormongers aside and cajoled and threatened them. They confessed that it was Kandamaran who asked them to spread this rumor," Velir said.

Manimekalai said, "I'm ashamed of my brother; Lady Nandini has made him evil. I'm the one who killed Karikalan. Imprison me ... let him go!!" she burst out in anger and sorrow.

Kundavai stroked her face affectionately. "Manimekalai, no one will believe you. You'll only complicate matters. Be calm: we'll find a way out of this." Kundavai turned to Velir. "Uncle, Arulmozli and I agree that releasing Vandhiya Devan now will cause trouble. We must first find the real murderer. I'll consult the chief minister about this. Thirumalai has gone after Veerapandian's bodyguards and will bring us information. We also have no news of Lord Ambalavan and Lady Nandini. If we find them, we'll know the truth. Meanwhile, I'll question Manimekalai as to what happened at Kadambur. Make arrangements for Vandhiya Devan's comfortable stay in the dungeon: it's clear that he's innocent."

Vanathi intervened to say, "*Akka*, why don't we all go to the dungeon and see Vandhiya Devan? We can take Manimekalai with us."

"It's a good idea," Velir said. "Vandhiya Devan was with Karikalan when the prince died. We may find the truth by questioning him."

They immediately went to the dungeon. The Mint was deserted and only a few guards were at their stations. The company crossed the caged tigers, climbed down to the dungeon and came to the cell in which Devan was imprisoned ... he was not there.

They saw Pinakapani, the Pazlayarai doctor's son, fettered to the wall brackets with chains. On seeing them, Pinakapani cried piteously, "Aiyo! Free me! Free me!"

Pinakapani's Feat

PINAKAPANI WAS AMBITIOUS and determined to reach an important position in the kingdom. But he had not met with much success. When Aniruddha sent him to Kodikkarai, Pinakapani was confident that he would make it big. *If I succeed in this mission, the chief minister will help me become powerful. Then I can deal with Vandhiya Devan and that arrogant Poonkuzlali.*

Building castles in the air, Pinakapani went to Kodikkarai. He wormed his way into Rakamma's confidence and fooled her into believing that he was a member of the Pandian gang. With her help, Pinakapani trapped Mandakini and brought her to Thanjavur Fort. During the journey, Pinakapani was obsessed with discovering the secrets surrounding Mandakini. He recalled the ramblings of the madman who was with him when he spent a day in the dungeon. He now suspected that the man had been saying the truth.

Pinakapani was badly hurt when Mandakini's palanquin narrowly missed being crushed by a fallen tree. He could meet Aniruddha only after he recovered. By then, Mandakini had died for the emperor, Karikalan was murdered, the city buzzed with talk of the succession, Velir became the Fort Commander, the Pazluvur brothers and their allies were mustering an army and civil war threatened to break out at any time. The busy chief minister rewarded him for his work and dismissed him abruptly. But when Pinakapani mentioned the madman in the dungeon, he caught Aniruddha's attention. Aniruddha listened eagerly when Pinakapani said that the madman claimed to know where the Pandian dynasty crown jewels were hidden in Sri Lanka.

Generations of Chola kings had tried to find these crown jewels and failed. Some new claimant to the Pandian throne kept popping up, like the little boy whom Azlvarkkadian had seen crowned in the Thirupurambayam forest. The Pandian country would merge with the Chola kingdom once and for all only when the Chola emperor was enthroned in Madurai, wearing the ancient crown and necklace of the Pandians. Aniruddha instructed every Chola general who went to war in Sri Lanka to find the heirlooms, but none had succeeded. The chief minister was now excited to hear that a prisoner in the dungeon had information about them.

Pinakapani also told Aniruddha that the madman knew a secret which proved that one of the contenders to the Tiger Throne was not born into the Chola dynasty. Hearing this, Aniruddha decided to question the madman himself. He changed his mind when he realized that his visit to the dungeon would definitely arouse curiosity and lead to uncomfortable questions. Aniruddha decided to use Pinakapani instead. He gave him his signet ring and instructed him to go to the dungeon and question the madman.

Pinakapani went to see the madman. Delighted to see Devan in the adjoining cell, he stood there mocking him. Devan ignored Pinakapani who cursed him and went to the next cell. Pinakapani realized that the prisoner was not really mad. The man remained silent and refused to answer any questions. He insisted, "First get orders for my release. Then I'll tell you."

Pinakapani went back to Aniruddha and told him the man would not talk without seeing his release orders. Aniruddha decided to bring the prisoner to his house and question him himself. Velir had no objections to releasing a madman whom Kalaanthaka had imprisoned years ago and gave orders in writing for the madman's release.

Pinakapani returned proudly to the dungeon with the order. He told Devan that the release order was for him. When Devan believed him and began to thank him, Pinakapani laughed and said, "Your release will come when they impale you on a stake at the crossroads."

Pinakapani then went to the madman's cell and freed him from his iron chains. Pinakapani wanted to know the man's secrets before he took him to Aniruddha's house. He showed the man the release order and said, "Will you now tell me your secrets?"

Suddenly, stones crashed down from the nearby wall and Pinakapani saw Devan standing behind him. He reached for his dagger but Devan leaped on him, caught him by the neck and knocked the dagger out of his hand. As the two men grappled and rolled on the floor, the madman took the iron chain attached to the wall, threw it around Pinakapani's neck and pulled it.

The Madman

FOR THE FIRST part of the journey from Kadambur to Thanjavur, Vandhiya Devan was unconscious. He was tied and thrown into a wooden cart. During his few minutes of consciousness, he suffered agonies from the effects of the fire and smoke. He had nightmares: Veerapandian's severed head screamed, 'You blocked my revenge!' ... dressed beautifully, Nandini tried to charm him ... Nandini appeared like a witch, laughing hysterically ... a dark figure shadowed Karikalan ...a demon caught Devan and strangled him ... Ravidasan threw him into a fire ... Kandamaran shouted, 'Traitor!' ... Parthibendran mocked, 'When will you marry Princess Kundavai?' ... Chendan Amudhan ran to rescue him from the fire ... Pinakapani beat Amudhan on his head with a cudgel ... Devan shouted, 'Water! Water!' ... his throat was dry ... his swollen tongue stuck to his palate ... Manimekalai poured nectar into his mouth from a golden cup ... Poonkuzlali pointed to her lovers, the marsh lights ... they surrounded him ... he closed his eyes in fear ... they carried him to the sand dunes and rolled him down ...

The startled Devan woke up and saw torch bearing soldiers lifting him into a boat on some river; darkness engulfed him again. Suddenly, he heard a great roar and a mighty wave rolled over him. He came fully to his senses and opened his eyes. Thanjavur Fort was in the distance. His cart was surrounded by weeping people. Karikalan's funeral procession had reached Thanjavur. The crowd went its way while a few soldiers escorted Sambuvaraya and Devan into the fort.

Karikalan's last rites are being performed. I'm his closest friend but there's no room for me with the mourners. I did my best. Although I couldn't save his life, I saved his corpse from the fire so that the people can honor him. Now, I'm accused of murdering him and they are taking me to the dungeon. Prince Arulmozli and Princess Kundavai will release me and praise me for all I did. But will they remember me while they are grieving over Karikalan's death? Will they believe I'm not the murderer? Will they still love me?

They went through the deserted Mint. The Pazluvur men had been replaced by Velir's soldiers who stared at them and whispered, 'That's Sambuvaraya ... and that's Vandhiya Devan, the wicked man who killed the prince!' The caged tigers made Devan recall that the Chola kings were renowned for their justice. But by the time they descended the steps and the soldiers locked him in a cell and left, Devan's confidence vanished completely.

Steeped in sorrow, Devan sat listlessly in his cell. *I'll never be released: only my corpse will leave this place. Kalaanthaka is suspicious of me and Parthibendran hates me. The Pazluvur brothers will see that Sambuvaraya is released soon, but no one will bother about me. Will I have a fair trial? Maybe I can convince them I'm innocent. No, they won't want the truth about Nandini and Ravidasan to come out. They'll leave me to die in the dungeon or condemn me without a trial and impale me at the crossroads. My god! With what enthusiasm I first came to Thanjavur! What dreams I had! I was free as a bird; now I'm locked in a dark dungeon. I can't stay here ... I'll find a way to end my life ...*

Someone in the adjoining cell cleared his throat and began to sing in a dreadful voice. Devan recognized the hymn that Chendan Amudhan had once sung so sweetly. "Who are you, my man? Please be merciful and stop singing."

"I'm the madman," came the reply. "Don't you like my song?"

"My dear madman, I love it!"

"Maybe you'll love it more after I stop singing it?"

"You don't seem mad. Who taught you this song?"

"A young man was in your cell for a few days. He sang this song constantly and I picked it up."

Devan realized that the man was talking about Chendan Amudhan. *What a good man Amudhan is, and such a dear friend!* "Do you know him?" Devan asked.

"He's Chendan Amudhan. He's supposed to be some mute woman's son. But if people only knew who he really is ...the world will turn upside-down!"

"Who is he?"

"I'll only tell the Chola emperor. Is Sundara Chola still the emperor?"

"Yes. Why do you doubt that?"

"Some days ago, the old guards were replaced by new ones and they closed the Mint. I overheard them say that Lord Kalaanthaka has run away from the fort and Velir has taken over."

"Really?" Devan asked in surprise. *The general may believe me and release me ... no ... how can he release someone accused of murdering Karikalan?*

The madman cleared his throat. "*Thambi,* why are you silent? Shall I sing again?"

"No, no! If Amudhan is not the dumb woman's child, I was wondering who he could be."

"Let's talk about something else."

"Okay. Why does everyone call you a madman?"

"I tell everyone I know where the Pandian crown jewels are hidden. So, they say I'm mad."

"It's they who are mad. I believe you, but I can't help you in any way."

"Everyone who stayed in your cell was released in a few days. Some doctor's son called Pinakapani was there; Lady Nandini took him away. Then Chendan Amudhan was there; Princess Kundavai and Lady Vanathi arranged his release."

Devan sighed. "No princess or lady will come to release me."

"In that case, I'll free you."

"Now you really sound like a madman."

"Trust me."

"What choice do I have? I trust you."

"Wait until the guards leave after giving us our dinner tonight."

The Scratching of Rats

ONCE THE LAST guard left, Vandhiya Devan waited eagerly to see what the madman would do. He heard rats scratching at the wall. Devan could face tigers and lions but he was terrified of cats and rats. Worrying that he would have to share his cell with rats that night, Devan called out, "Madman, are you asleep?" There was no reply, but the soft scratching of rats continued. Shortly afterwards, stones fell from the wall and a hole appeared in it.

The madman's voice came through the hole: "My dear man, are you asleep?"

"No, I was waiting for you ... what's this?"

"This is six months' work. And before that, it took me another six months to free my hands from the chains." In a short time, he widened the opening and came to Devan's cell.

"Why have you gone to so much difficulty over this? This hole is useless. You should have made an opening in the outer wall."

"There's no outer wall," the madman explained. "The only exit is through the caged tigers. But this cell is sometimes empty and left unlocked. I calculated that it would be easier to escape through this cell than from mine."

"I came here only today. How can you trust me not to expose you to the guards?"

"I know who to trust and who not to trust by their voices. I trust Amudhan; I don't trust Pinakapani; I trust you. Moreover, this is the right time to escape."

"Why?"

"I told you the guards are new. I overheard two of them talking today. 'What do we do if the tigers pounce on us when we open their cages?' one man asked. 'We die!' the other man replied. From this, it's clear they won't open the cages tonight. I plan to attack these new guards and escape. Anyway, I prefer trying to escape to just waiting here to die."

"I agree," said Devan.

"Your help will make things easier. You're not like me: you have just come in and look strong. We'll overpower the guards, tie them up and take their keys."

"Good idea. When do we start?"

"Wait a while. I'll tell you when the time's right."

"I'm also exhausted. It will be better if we wait for a couple of days."

The madman asked Devan to give him news of the outside world. On hearing of Karikalan's death, the madman asked, "Who's to be the next crown prince?"

"The chieftains are divided between Madurandaka and Arulmozhi."

"What does the emperor say?"

"He wants to avoid civil war and so he supports Madurandaka."

"In that case, it's essential we escape as soon as possible."

He then told Devan how he had discovered where the Pandian

crown jewels were hidden. Devan again asked him about the secret regarding the Chola dynasty.

"I'll tell you that if we escape with our lives. If I die, the secret must die with me."

Devan was stunned by Pinakapani's sudden appearance the first time. He was worried he would ruin their plans. Devan and the madman did not trust Pinakapani. They agreed that Pinakapani had come there with some evil intention; they swore that they would leave the dungeon only together.

They were prepared when Pinakapani came back. While Pinakapani showed the madman the signet ring and tried to get him to reveal the secret, Devan quietly went into the madman's cell through the hole in the wall. In normal circumstances, Devan would have made short work of Pinakapani. But his wounds from the fire were not completely healed and his throat was still raw from the Kalamukha's iron grip. The madman threw the chain around Pinakapani's neck and pulled him to the ground. The two men chained Pinakapani tightly to the wall.

Devan said, "Pinakapani, thanks for your help. I advise you to stick to medicine from now. Why do you want to be a spy and get into unnecessary trouble?"

Pinakapani was too stunned to reply, but his eyes blazed with rage. They took the signet ring from Pinakapani and Devan took his turban and wound it around his own head. They came out of the cell and locked it behind them. They crept slowly up the dungeon steps. They hesitated when they heard the tigers growl: had the guards let the tigers loose after all? Devan and the madman peeped into the room. There was only one guard in the room. He stood staring at the cage with the growling tigers. *What if he sets the tigers on us? Pinakapani is shouting ... I should have gagged him. Will the guard hear him and become suspicious?*

Freedom

VANDHIYA DEVAN HESITATED at the door. He considered jumping on the guard but he saw two more guards standing at the other door.

Even if we overpower this guard, we'll have to deal with the guards stationed at every door from here. Shall I open the tigers' cage? We'll have a chance to escape in the confusion …

Devan was startled to hear the guard say, "Oh! So, you think you can escape?" A tiger growled. "Shut up!" the guard threatened. Realizing that the guard was talking to the tiger, Devan laughed. The guard turned to them. "Watch your back, my dear fellow. This tiger is trying its tricks, but it won't work against a lion like me." The guard twirled his majestic moustache.

Devan said, "As long as it's in a cage, a tiger is a mouse. How can it play tricks?"

"Away with you, sir. The chief minister's men are waiting for you at the entrance. Go quickly." The guard turned to shout in the direction of the dungeon, "Madman, shut up down there!"

Devan gripped the madman's trembling hand and dragged him along with him. They crossed the guard, who heard Pinakapani's shouts and muttered, "You want to be freed? If they free all of you, I'll be out of a job."

Devan's heart raced. They had fooled the guards in the dark dungeon. But could they get away with their impersonation outside? *Nothing ventured, nothing gained. Luckily this madman is a clever fellow.* A plan formed in Devan's mind. As they walked down a long passage, Devan whispered to his companion, "Are you going to the chief minister's house or coming with me?"

"If I go there, I'll be back in the dungeon. I'll come with you. Where are you going?"

"If god is merciful, we'll go to Sri Lanka. Call me Pinakapani in front of the chief minister's men. What's your real name?"

"Oh, that! I'm Karuthiruman."

"Karuthiruman, when we are in the streets, I'll touch your shoulder: you must be ready to run. Can you run fast?"

"Oh, yes! Even King Mahinda of Lanka can't beat me."

Devan laughed. They crossed the Mint and came out. To Devan's relief, only two of Aniruddha's men waited there. One of the men was stout; he seemed familiar but Devan could not remember where he had seen him before. "You are the chief minister's men," Devan said.

"What, *thambi*," one man said. "Have you forgotten us already?"

Karuthiruman intervened. "My dear Pinakapani, I'm afraid to go to the chief minister's house. What if he sends me back to the dungeon?"

The man assured him, "No, but don't try to escape: they'll send us to the dungeon."

They set off with the fat man going ahead and the other man walking behind Devan and Karuthiruman. The streets were deserted. The fort's residents had dispersed after Karikalan's funeral and Velir's men stood guard outside the fort preventing anyone from entering. Devan looked intently in both directions as he walked. *It will be very easy to slip away from these two men, but how do we escape getting caught again?* Devan's heart raced as they crossed Ambalavan's palace. *We'll come to the alley leading to the back of the house. With its twists and turns and overhanging branches, it's the ideal place to make a run for it. We can climb over the wall into Lord Ambalavan's garden, hide among the trees and leave the fort through the treasury vault. I can't think of any other escape route.*

Just as Devan reached out to touch Karuthiruman's shoulder, he saw a company of soldiers riding towards them, armed with spears. Aniruddha's men stood aside at the entrance to the alley. They kept Devan and Karuthiruman behind them, screening them from view. The company quickly went past them. Spearmen rode in front; Malayaman, Velir and Arulmozli followed on majestic horses.

How near the prince is ... and yet so far away, Devan thought sadly. For a split second, Devan considered running to Arulmozli but decided against it. *How can he forgive a man accused of murdering his brother? Or be his friend? He'll be disgusted to see me. And who knows what Malayaman and the general will do?*

Devan turned to the palanquins following the riders. His heart raced: it was Kundavai, Vanathi and Manimekalai. Once, Devan would not have hesitated to ask any of the women for help. *But now, I'm suspected of murdering Karikalan. I'm glad they have taken the innocent Manimekalai under their wings. Has she told them what happened at Kadambur? Is she insisting, 'I'm the murderer?' No, if she did that, they would not be so kind to her ...*

The company went past. Aniruddha's men said, "Come," and went ahead.

Now's the time! Devan touched Karuthiruman's shoulder and dashed into the alley with Karuthiruman running behind him. They heard the guards chasing them. After a while, Karuthiruman said, "One man has fallen back: only one is chasing us."

Devan signaled to Karuthiruman to continue running. They came to the overhanging branch. Devan swung himself up the wall and pulled Karuthiruman after him. Together, they broke the branch. They waited until the guard ran up and dropped the branch on him. Without waiting to see whether the branch had hit him, they jumped into the garden, hid in the thickets and looked at the wall. No one came after them.

"We made it!" Devan said.

"But how do we get out of the fort?"

"There's a way: be patient." Devan stopped when they were near the palace. The former bustle was missing, but there were a few people going about their work. It would be safer to enter the vault after dark. Devan sat on a log and beckoned Karuthiruman to sit beside him. "We must wait until dark. You can tell me your story now."

"I already told you … I can't tell you."

"In that case, I won't take you outside the fort with me."

"How will you know whether I'm telling the truth? What if I fool you?"

"Truth or lies … tell me. We have time to kill."

Karuthiruman began his fantastic story.

Karuthiruman's Story

KARUTHIRUMAN WAS FROM Thopputhurai, a fishing village near Kodikkarai. He made his living ferrying passengers to Sri Lanka. About twenty-five years ago, as he was coming home from Lanka, he was caught in a storm and struggled to bring his boat to the shore. When he was near the Kodikkarai lighthouse, he saw a woman floating in the stormy sea. Pitying her, he lifted her into the boat. She was unconscious and he didn't know whether she was dead or alive. The wind pushed his boat ashore near Thirumaraikadu. As he anxiously watched the woman, some important men came riding by on horses. The woman did not respond to them.

'She is deaf and dumb from birth,' one of the men said. Their leader took Karuthiruman aside and asked him to take the woman to Sri Lanka and leave her on one of the islands there. He promised to reward Karuthiruman handsomely for this. Karuthiruman agreed and took the money. When the storm abated, he rowed the woman across the strait. Halfway across, he saw a man clinging to a log and drifting on the waves. Karuthiruman pulled the exhausted man into his boat. At first, the woman was terrified of the stranger; then she ignored him. Karuthiruman took them both to Boodha island near Lanka. There was an old man on the island who said that the deaf-mute was his daughter: now, she did not recognize even him.

The man Karuthiruman had rescued from the sea gave him a palm leaf and asked him to take it to the Sri Lankan king. Karuthiruman guessed the man must be someone very important. When he delivered the message to the Sri Lankan king, Karuthiruman learnt the man he had rescued was none other than the Pandian king. The exhausted Karuthiruman stayed back while the Lankan king sent a company which escorted the Pandian king to the palace a few days later.

The two kings then went to the Rohanna mountains in the south. The Pandian king liked Karuthiruman and took him along with them. The Lankan king took them to a valley which was difficult to access. In that valley was a cave filled with treasure. The Lankan king opened a golden chest and showed the Pandian king a glittering crown and a long necklace of precious gems. Karuthiruman understood from the kings' conversation that these were the Pandian dynasty's crown jewels. The Lankan king urged the Pandian king to take them, but the latter refused. He insisted that when he had annihilated the Cholas and was crowned in Madurai, the Lankan king should come to Madurai and present the crown jewels to him before the world.

The Pandian king gave Karuthiruman as many gold coins as he could carry and asked him to make comfortable arrangements for the mute woman and then join him in the Pandian country. The father and daughter were not on Boodha Island. Karuthiruman went to

Kodikkarai in search of them. He found the deaf-mute there, but she did not recognize him. He learnt from her family that Mandakini's father had fallen ill and had brought her here to his brother-in-law, the lighthouse keeper, before dying. At first, Mandakini did not remember any of her relatives. One day, she accidently fell into the sea and when she was rescued, she had regained her memory.

When Mandakini realized that she was pregnant, she was steeped in sorrow. She spent most of her time at the Kuzlagar temple and ignored Karuthiruman. Karuthiruman met Mandakini's younger sister, Vani, while he was at Kodikkarai; she was also a deaf-mute. Taking pity on Vani, he decided to marry her. But first he had to go and see the Pandian king. At this time, Queen Sembiyan Madevi visited the Kuzlagar temple. She took pity on the pregnant Mandakini and took her to Pazlayarai with her. Vani also went with them.

Karuthiruman went to the Pandian country and heard that the king was on the battlefield. He followed him there and the king gave him another message for the Sri Lankan king. He also asked him to try to bring Mandakini back with him when he returned.

After his trip to Lanka, Karuthiruman went to Pazlayarai. He could not forget Vani and was eager to see her. As he walked along the bank of the Arasalar near Pazlayarai, he saw a woman digging a hole. He heard the faint cry of an infant coming from a cloth bundle beside her. *That evil woman is burying a child alive*, he thought in revulsion. Karuthiruman went to the woman … it was Vani.

"*Thambi*, just think how I felt! I can't tell you more: it's meant only for the ears of the royal family. If only I had stayed away from Pazlayarai that day, I could have avoided much trouble."

Devan teased, "Let's go and meet some members of the royal family."

Devan took Karuthiruman to the vault. The door was locked, but Devan pressed the secret door within the larger door and it opened. They went in, closed the door behind them and walked through mounds of treasure. Devan pocketed some gold coins. He walked along the underground passage and opened the secret door in the fort wall. There were no guards there. He peeped out: the Vadavar was in flood; far in the distance he saw the light of torches. Once he was sure that the place was deserted, they came out, shutting the door behind them.

As Devan wondered how to cross the river, he saw a boat caught in the roots of a tree which had crashed into the water.

A Bad Omen

VANDHIYA DEVAN EXULTED, *Lady Luck is with me! Karuthiruman is a boat man by profession. We can ride the flood halfway to Kodikkarai.* "Look, Karuthiruman, a boat is waiting for us. We'll be halfway to Kodikkarai before dawn. Not even riders can catch up with us after that."

Karuthiruman looked around suspiciously; he thought he saw something move in the thicket near the fort wall. He threw a stone into the thicket—a cat jumped out and got into the boat.

Devan laughed and threw a stone into the boat; the cat jumped out of the boat and dashed across them. Devan took two steps back. "I'm scared of cats. I get goosebumps if a cat jumps on me."

Karuthiruman said, "I'm scared when a cat crosses my path: it's a bad omen."

"To hell with omens!" Devan said and dragged Karuthiruman to the river.

Devan climbed into the boat. Just as Karuthiruman freed one corner of the boat from the tree roots, four men armed with spears came running and jumped into the boat. Two of the men pushed Devan to the bottom of the boat and tied him to the planks. The other two men stood by Karuthiruman, spears at the ready. Devan recognized the leader of this gang as the stout man who had led them from the dungeon. Devan was amazed that he had had the foresight to wait for them at the door to the secret passage. *He's no ordinary soldier; he's a remarkable spy. Who is he? Where have I seen him before?*

The man spoke to Karuthiruman: "My dear fellow, you are seeing the light of day after years in the dungeon. Why did you listen to this rascal and run? If you obey me, you won't be harmed."

"Sir, I ruined my chances by listening to this fool. I'll do whatever you say. Please don't send me back to the dungeon!"

"The chief minister wants to question you. If you are truthful, he'll reward you handsomely and send you on your way. Where were you off to?"

"To Sri Lanka."

"Wonderful! Did you think you could fool the chief minister, break the general's security cordon and go so far? But this thug will give you such advice." He paused. "Only one of my men knows to row a boat and he's a novice. We managed to come here as we were going with the current. Now, you must row against the current: row us across the river and then along the bank to the fort's northern gate."

"Why don't we row across the river and then walk to the gate? It's hard work rowing against the current."

"If we walk along the river, this ruffian will be up to his tricks. We'll go by boat."

Karuthiruman and another man pushed the boat into the water.

The stout guard came to Devan and said, "My dear fellow, don't try any of your tricks."

"Sir, you seem to know me well," Devan replied.

"Don't I? I saw you come out of the dungeon after leaving Pinakapani in your place."

Devan cried in mock amazement, "You're smarter than me! I thought no one noticed what happened in the dungeon."

"*Thambi*, no corner of this kingdom escapes the chief minister's eyes and ears. Pinakapani is a fool: that's why the chief minister sent me after him."

"The chief minister's eyes and ears are indeed amazing! It looks like he knew that I would come this way. In that case, he must also know that I'm innocent."

"That's got nothing to do with the chief minister. It's the emperor's responsibility to judge you; it's Velir's responsibility to punish you for breaking out of the dungeon."

"Sir, where are you taking me?"

"To Velir who's waiting at the northern gate. Parthibendran is coming with Lord Ambalavan and the other chieftains. Lord Ambalavan will know the truth about Prince Karikalan's murder. There'll be a trial before the emperor. You can prove your innocence then."

Ambalavan and Parthibendran will blame me. How can I look the emperor and Prince Arulmozli in the face? How can I prove my innocence? "Sir, please let me go. I'm innocent. I was Prince Karikalan's closest friend. Circumstances have brought me here. The chief minister ordered you to bring the madman to him. Take him and let me go," Devan said pitifully.

"What will you give me if I let you go?"

Devan remembered the gold coins in his waistband. "I'll fill your hands with gold coins."

"Really? Gold coins? Let's see," said the guard.

"Loosen my ropes; the gold is in my waistband."

"Don't try your tricks again," the guard said and bent to loosen his bonds. Devan examined the guard's face intently as he took out the coins from his waistband. The guard said, "*Thambi*, there are now three accusations against you: murder, breaking out of prison and theft. You can be impaled for any one of these crimes."

"Sir, I have served the Chola dynasty in many ways: I carried messages and tried to save Karikalan's life, risking my own. I have a right to these coins. I took them for my expenses."

"Even if Lord Shiva proves to be greater than Lord Vishnu, I'll never be bought by gold."

Devan gave Karuthiruman a sidelong glance and saw that he was alert and was waiting for Devan's signal. Devan slipped his hands out of the loosened ropes and pulled the fat guard's moustache and turban which came away in his hands: it was Azlvarkkadian. "You Vaishnava imposter! It's you!"

As Azlvarkkadian tried to save his moustache and turban, the gold coins in his hands scattered. Devan freed himself from the ropes in a split second, pushed Azlvarkkadian down and used the ropes to tie him to the cross planks. He unsheathed his sword from his waistband. At the same time, Karuthiruman pushed one of the guards into the river. The other two guards cautiously approached them. When Devan raised his sword, one guard threw himself into the river. Karuthiruman knocked down the last man with an oar and they tied him also to the cross planks. The two guards who had fallen into the river swam to the shore.

Devan went to Azlvarkkadian. "Look here, you have often saved my life. I don't want to kill you, but you must help me."

"My dear fellow, untie me and tell me how I can help you."

"You can stay tied. If you tell me where I can get two horses, we'll get out on the shore and let you drift in the boat. When the current pushes you to the shore, you can use your wits to escape."

"Do you know Lady Vani's house?"

"Who's Lady Vani?"

"The deaf-mute woman; Chendan Amudhan's mother."

Karuthiruman came closer to Azlvarkkadian and listened eagerly.

"Yes, I know the house: it's in a garden," Devan said.

"There are two horses there. One is mine, which I left tied there; the other is Amudhan's. Poor Amudhan! He doesn't know how to ride a horse and the horse threw him. Already weakened by fever, he's now seriously ill. It will be a miracle if he lives. Anyway, he doesn't need the horse."

Devan was worried. "Who's looking after him?"

"His mother and Poonkuzlali."

Karuthiruman asked, "Which mother? Does Sembiyan Madevi know Amudhan's ill?"

Azlvarkkadian frowned. "Sembiyan Madevi is their benefactor. But the royal family is mourning Karikalan's death. Why should they bother about Amudhan?"

Devan turned to Karuthiruman. "What do you say? Shall we see Amudhan and his mother before we go?" Karuthiruman nodded his agreement. "In that case, row to the shore." He turned to Azlvarkkadian. "Vaishnava, watch out! If this is one of your tricks, come what may, I'll kill you and send you to Mount Kailash."

"*Thambi*, I beg you: if you must kill me, send me to Lord Vishnu at Vaikundam."

Amudhan's Worry

A DOCTOR FROM Sundara Chola's hospital examined Chendan Amudhan. Before he left, Poonkuzlali took the doctor aside and asked, "How is he? Will he live?"

"He was already weakened by the fever; he then made a long voyage and fell off his horse. But more than all this, he carries a burden in his heart. This is blocking his recovery."

Poonkuzlali went to Amudhan. "The doctor says something's troubling you: what is it?"

"I'm worried that I'll recover soon."

"What? I'm praying for your speedy recovery and you say you're afraid you'll recover?"

"If I recover, you'll go away, Poonkuzlali."

Poonkuzlali's eyes filled with tears and she smiled. "Amudhan, my heart melts at your love. I don't want to leave you but I can't stay. I have sworn an oath: I'll marry a prince or I'll remain a virgin."

"Yes, you love Prince Arulmozli ... but is that a reasonable expectation?"

"I love Prince Arulmozli like anyone else in the Chola kingdom; Lady Vanathi is the one born to marry him. When I teased her, she took an oath not to sit on the throne ..."

"She belongs to a noble family and she took an oath not to sit on the throne. You are a boat girl and you took an oath to marry only a prince."

"Amudhan, my aunt loved a prince and her life became a tragedy. I want to live the life she let slip from her hands: what's wrong with that? Who says only those born into royalty can be kings? Men from ordinary families like ours have founded empires with their courage. You too swear an oath that somewhere in Bharath or some land across the seas, you will create an empire. I'll stay by your side always."

"I hate war; I can't hurt any living being. I don't want crowns and thrones; I want to celebrate Lord Shiva and his devotees. We don't suit each other. Poonkuzlali, it's useless asking you to stay here. Go, don't wait for me to recover."

They fell silent at the sound of footsteps at the door.

The Engagement

TO AMUDHAN'S SURPRISE, Poonkuzlali opened the door slightly, looked out, closed and locked the door and came back to him. *Has she changed her mind, or will she go on preaching about courage and founding empires? Poonkuzlali and I will never get along* ... Poonkuzlali looked into his eyes. Amudhan's heart raced. "Why did you lock the door? Who's there? Maybe it's mother."

"Whoever it is, they can wait. Who will dare to interrupt the king and queen?"

Amudhan stammered, "King? ... Who's the king?"

"You: you're the king and I'm the queen. Amudhan, your love is worth a million palaces and royal privileges. If you can't follow my path, I'll follow yours. I'll marry you ..."

Amudhan was ecstatic. "Poonkuzlali, am I dreaming? Did I hear you right?"

"I'll tell you again—I'll marry you. I thought my aunt should have been a queen by right and I dreamt of being one. My dreams died when she was murdered. I realized that people in palaces suffer and that rowing a boat in the sea is better than living in a palace. Amudhan, when you are better, we'll go to Kodikkarai. We'll worship Lord Kuzlagar in his forest shrine; we'll sail the sea; we'll go to the beautiful islands near Lanka; we'll be king and queen there. What do you say?"

"Just one thing: when can we leave for Kodikkarai?"

She laughed. "As soon as you have recovered."

"I have recovered, Poonkuzlali. I'll show you I can walk ..." Amudhan tried to get up.

Poonkuzlali pushed him back gently and said, "No, be patient for a day ..."

Someone knocked softly on the door. Poonkuzlali opened the door and was amazed to see Sembiyan Madevi and Madurandaka.

Poonkuzlali bowed and said, "Welcome, lady."

"How's your cousin? Where's Vani?" Sembiyan Madevi asked as she entered the hut.

Madurandaka stayed outside but his angry eyes stared eagerly into the hut.

Amudhan stood on seeing the queen. "Lady, you are the first to hear our good news and bless us. Even my mother does not know: Poonkuzlali has agreed to marry me. You must conduct our wedding. We'll live in Kodikkarai and serve the Kuzlagar temple."

The queen's eyes filled with tears. As Amudhan and Poonkuzlali fell at her feet, she blessed them in a trembling voice: "My children, may your married life be filled with happiness."

Vani came in. Sembiyan Madevi told her that she had come to visit Amudhan as he was ill and that she was delighted to hear that he and Poonkuzlali were to marry. Vani's face reflected her surprise and joy. The queen spent some time talking to Amudhan and Poonkuzlali and then left.

As the queen and Madurandaka walked towards the palanquins, the queen stopped under a tree and looked around to see if they were alone. "Madurandaka, the child I carried in my womb and gave birth to is Chendan Amudhan. When he was eight days old, he lay in his cradle without breathing and I thought he was dead. I adopted you and asked Vani to bury him. When Vani came back after five years with a boy, I knew the truth. But I did not abandon you or bring Amudhan to the palace. 'It's god's will,' I said and raised you as my own son. For this, give me a boon: renounce the Tiger Throne. I don't even object to you being crowned king, but I'm terrified that your children will be born deaf-mutes."

Madurandaka went pale. He had a daughter who was two years old but was yet to speak a word.

The queen looked at the stunned Madurandaka and said, "Come, my child, let's go. Think clearly and tell me your decision tomorrow."

Madurandaka stammered, "There's nothing to decide. You go on. I'll just say a few words to the son who should have grown up in the palace instead of me."

"Very well. When you come back, make sure you close the palanquin screens. If the general's men see you, they may boo and hiss at you."

The queen left without noticing the hatred and fury in Madurandaka's eyes.

The Dagger Flies

MADURANDAKA WAS ROOTED to the spot: should he go to the hut or return to the fort? He walked to his palanquin and took something from it. He then gave his escort instructions. They left, carrying the palanquin, and the light of the torch disappeared with them.

Madurandaka walked towards the hut. As he passed the tree where he had conversed with his mother, a man jumped out from behind its trunk, startling him: it was Karuthiruman. With his disheveled appearance, he still looked like a madman. Madurandaka raised the lance which he had taken from his palanquin.

Karuthiruman held his arm and said, "Sir, I'm your friend."

Madurandaka laughed softly; his voice showed his anger and grief. "When the whole world is abandoning me, you come as a friend."

"I can help you in a way no one else in the world can."

"How? Tell me quickly: it's getting late."

"To go back to the palace where you have no right to be?" Karuthiruman stared at Madurandaka.

Madurandaka was stunned. "Rascal! What do you know? Tell me …" he raised his lance again.

"Sir, keep your lance for your enemies. I overheard you and the queen talking under this tree."

"Ahah! You eavesdropped on our secret. That's why you had the nerve to stop me …"

"I already knew your secret. The queen told you she's not your mother and Gandara Aditya's not your father. She told you who your mother is, but did she tell you who your father is?"

Madurandaka stared at him. "Do you know who he is?"

"Yes, I know."

For a second, Madurandaka feared that this madman would claim to be his father. He asked in revulsion and anger, "How do you know? Who are you?"

Madurandaka's face cleared when Karuthiruman said, "I'm your father's servant." Karuthiruman then whispered into his ear, "Your father is …"

Madurandaka's head whirled. He gripped Karuthiruman's hand to stop himself from falling. "Is this true? Am I really a prince?"

"Sir, many years ago, I came to tell you this truth. I was waiting for a chance to meet you alone. But Lord Kalaanthaka found me in the palace garden and sent me to the dungeon. I escaped only today with the help of a young man, Vandhiya Devan."

"I've heard of him: he's the man accused of murdering Karikalan, right?"

"Yes, sir. But he's innocent."

"Who cares about that? Where's he now?"

"He's hiding behind that hedge some distance away. He's waiting there with two horses for our departure. I don't care: I got the unexpected chance to meet you."

"When did you come here?"

"Just a while ago. We came for the horses. I was seeing Vani after many years and stood talking to her in sign language. Suddenly, you and your adopted mother came to the hut. Vandhiya Devan ran to hide behind the hedge while Vani and I talked a little longer. Then she went into the hut and I waited here for the chance of meeting you."

"Right, what do you plan to do now?"

"Sir, will you go back to Thanjavur after knowing who you are? Remember, some people know you are not a Chola prince. Aniruddha knows; his spy, Azlvarkkadian, knows; someday ..."

"I don't want to go back to the palace. What do you suggest?"

"There are two horses behind that hedge. Pretend to go to the hut and come to the hedge. While I distract Vandhiya Devan, kill him with your lance. We'll ride to Kodikkarai and go to Sri Lanka. The Lankan king is the traditional ally of the Pandian kings and is the Chola dynasty's archenemy. I know the Lankan king well; I also know where the Pandian crown jewels are. What do you say? It's getting late and Vandhiya Devan will soon come searching for me."

Madurandaka thought over this, building many castles in the air. "Must I kill him?"

"If you are hesitant, give me your lance."

"I need it for something else. Vandhiya Devan's a brave warrior; let's take him with us."

"We can take him, but where's the third horse?"

"We can easily get a horse: remember I'm still Prince Madurandaka." He laughed angrily. "Tell Vandhiya Devan to be patient. I'll have a word with that hut-dweller and hurry back."

Karuthiruman went in search of Devan. It was pitch dark; now and then, a lighted torch from the king's highway nearby shed a dim light on the garden. Karuthiruman found two majestic Arabian steeds tied to the hedge but Devan was not there. He called out softly, but there was no reply. *Good riddance to him!* Karuthiruman thought in relief.

When Devan and Karuthiruman came to the garden, it was pitch dark: the only light came from a small lamp burning in the hut. Vani, who had gone to get water from the lotus pond, was startled to see two men coming towards her in the dark. She smiled when she recognized Devan and nodded her head in welcome. She was stunned to see Karuthiruman who reassured her in sign language. Leaving them there, Devan went to the hut just as someone shut its door. He peeped through the window and was relieved to find Amudhan talking happily to Poonkuzlali with a radiant face instead of being on his deathbed. As he debated whether to interrupt them to say goodbye, Sembiyan Madevi and her escort arrived.

Devan immediately left the hut and jumped over the hedge. He saw the horses and was relieved that Azlvarkkadian had not fooled him. He waited for Karuthiruman. The queen and her escort left, but there was no sign of Karuthiruman. Losing patience, Devan jumped back over the fence and saw Karuthiruman and Madurandaka talking under a tree. Not wanting to be seen by Madurandaka, the suspicious Devan eavesdropped on them, hearing a part of their conversation. He followed Madurandaka stealthily as he walked to the hut.

Madurandaka hesitated at the door when he heard laughter from inside. Whether the laughter made him change his mind or whether he lost courage, Madurandaka turned away and made his way towards the hedge. As Devan jumped to hide behind a tree, he saw a dim figure standing at the hut's rear window, holding a dagger. The figure stared through the window and aimed the dagger. At the same time, Devan heard the sound of horses' hooves. Devan hesitated for a split second. If the horses left, it would be impossible for him to escape. But if he went after the horses, he could not stop that dark figure. *Forget the horses; I must do my duty.* Devan crept towards the figure. He heard a woman's terrified scream from inside the hut. Throwing caution to the winds, he charged towards the figure which turned at the sound of his running footsteps and hurled the dagger at him. The dagger pierced Devan's breast and he collapsed. Without a backward glance, the dark figure ran away.

Pinakapani's Treachery

ARULMOZLI'S COMPANY FOUND Pinakapani chained to the wall of the cell shouting, "Aiyo! The murderer has escaped! The madman has escaped!" Pinakapani quickly gave them a gist of what had happened in the dungeon. He was eager to search for the escaped prisoners, but the others secretly applauded Devan's brilliance and were glad that he had escaped.

Velir was at the dungeon entrance. When he heard about the prisoners, he was not worried. He knew that Arulmozli and Kundavai respected Devan and were convinced of his innocence. The general laughed in appreciation and said, "Vandhiya Devan is a clever young man! Once before, in Sri Lanka, he escaped from his cell in the same way."

Pinakapani intervened angrily to ask, "Sir, mustn't we start a manhunt? The murderer knows the secret passage: he may escape through that."

Velir roared, "Fool! Do you presume to advise me? You're the one responsible for their escape—maybe you're their accomplice. Throw this man back into the dungeon!"

Pinakapani trembled. "Sir! I swear I had nothing to do with them. The chief minister sent me."

Arulmozli said, "Yes, he's the chief minister's man; let Aniruddha question and punish him."

Velir ordered his men to escort Pinakapani to Aniruddha. Aniruddha too was not worried by the prisoners' escape. When Aniruddha sent a spy on a mission, he usually sent another man behind him as back-up. He was confident that Azlvarkkadian would catch the prisoners or at least come back with news of them. He also felt that it would save much trouble if the prisoners escaped.

Pinakapani said, "Sir, give me four men and I'll bring back the prisoners."

Aniruddha shouted, "You fool, you have ruined everything! I sent you to the dungeon instead of going there myself because I did not want to draw attention to the madman. Now, everyone knows about him. Do you want to draw more attention to this matter? Enough! Don't let me see you again. And if I hear you have opened your mouth about this, I'll see you impaled."

Pinakapani hung his head and left Aniruddha's house. All his anger was focused on Devan. *I'm in disgrace because of Vandhiya Devan. Never mind if the madman escapes; I'll find Vandhiya Devan and take revenge on him ...he's my enemy.* Pinakapani was sure that Devan would use the secret passage to escape from the fort. He calculated that the passage must end at some point in the fort walls. *I'll walk along the fort's outer wall. I may catch them red-handed ...*

Pinakapani walked along the wall, examining the stones. When he saw the general's men on their rounds, he jumped into the thickets. He was shocked to see two other men hiding in the bushes a little way from him. One man held a sword which glinted when the patrol's torchlight fell on it through the thicket. When the patrol passed, the two men crept out and went in the opposite direction.

Pinakapani went on his way and then stopped. *Were those two men Vandhiya Devan and the madman? But they are going towards the fort entrance ... Vandhiya Devan's smart; he'll have something up his sleeve.* Pinakapani turned and went after the men. He did not want to confront them, as one of them had a sword. *This is not the time to get into a quarrel with strangers. I must first make sure who those men are. I have my dagger; I'll throw it on Devan and kill him ...*

Pinakapani looked towards the northern gate for a moment. It was crowded with palanquins and torch bearers: some very important person was either leaving or entering the fort. When he turned back, the men had vanished. *My god! Where are those men? Have they taken a short cut? Would they dare to take the highway?* Pinakapani remembered that Chendan Amudhan's hut was near the highway and that Devan had hidden there once before. *Yes, those two men must be Vandhiya Devan and the madman ... they have gone to Amudhan's hut.*

Pinakapani went to Amudhan's hut, struggling to find his way there in the darkness. He was shocked to find palanquins and guards there, but the company soon left. Pinakapani looked around and saw the heads of two horses above the hedge. His curiosity was aroused and he crept towards the hut. He saw two men talking under a tree. *There they are! How come they have horses ready for their escape? Maybe someone in the royal family is helping them ... it may be a plot to see the madman's secret does not come out.*

Pinakapani hid behind a tree and looked at the two men: one was undoubtedly the madman, but the other was not Devan. A crown on his head; a yellow silk cloak on his shoulders; pearl chains around his neck; bracelets on his wrists ... *It's Madurandaka! But what's the connection between the prince and the madman? To hell with that! Where's Vandhiya Devan? He must be the man with the sword. Is he waiting for the madman with the horses? Madurandaka must be helping them. Did Madurandaka goad Vandhiya Devan to kill Karikalan? God! If all this is true ... if I can prove it ...* Pinakapani's twisted mind worked overtime. *Better to check the horses. If Vandhiya Devan is there alone, I can stab him with my dagger. Then I can catch the madman and frighten him into telling the truth ...*

The madman and the prince were standing opposite the hedge where the horses were tied. Pinakapani could not cross them without being seen. He decided to get to the hedge from the back of the hut. When Pinakapani reached the back, he heard Amudhan and Poonkuzlali. Pinakapani had desired Poonkuzlali from the time he first saw her in Kodikkarai. It was because of her that he hated Devan. When he went to bring Mandakini from Kodikkarai, he learnt about Poonkuzlali's friendship with Amudhan and began to hate Amudhan too.

Through the small rear window, Pinakapani saw Amudhan and Poonkuzlali talking happily. He overheard their plans of getting married and living in Kodikkarai. Their laughter fanned the flames of his jealousy. He blazed with hatred for Amudhan. He couldn't bear the thought of this mute woman's son winning Poonkuzlali. He forgot all about Devan and the madman. *I must first kill this hymn-singing Amudhan ... everything else can wait.* Pinakapani stood at the window and aimed his dagger at Amudhan. Poonkuzlali happened to look up and saw the hand with the dagger: she shrieked. Amudhan turned towards the window, making a perfect target. As Pinakapani raised his hand to throw the dagger, he heard footsteps behind him. He turned to see a man running towards him. He could not identify the man in the dark. *Whoever it is, he has guessed my plan and is coming to catch me.* Pinakapani hurled his dagger at the running man who fell. At the same time, he heard the sound of horses galloping away. *Vandhiya Devan and the madman are riding away ... in that case, the man I stabbed must be Madurandaka!* Pinakapani panicked. He heard cries from the hut and the sound of the door opening ... he ran for his life.

A few seconds later, Poonkuzlali and Amudhan came out with a lamp. They found Devan lying in a pool of blood and gently carried him inside. To their relief, he was still alive. Vani immediately treated him with her herbal medicines.

Tell Me the Truth

AZLVARKKADIAN'S BOAT DRIFTED on the river for a while and was then washed to the shore. The two soldiers struggled through the flood and reached the boat. Azlvarkkadian instructed the three men to hide, while he stayed on the boat, pretending to be tied.

In truth, Azlvarkkadian wanted Devan and the madman to escape. He instinctively knew that it was what Aniruddha wanted. Aniruddha and Azlvarkkadian were sure that Devan was innocent. But if he was tried, some awkward truths about the past would become public knowledge and hurt important people. If Devan was found guilty, Arulmozli would lose a good friend and the Chola kingdom would lose a brave warrior and shrewd strategist. Aniruddha was also aware of Kundavai's feelings for Devan and Manimekalai's open regard for him. After weighing all this, Aniruddha decided to help Devan escape.

Azlvarkkadian was confident that Devan and the madman would ride this way on the horses they found in Amudhan's garden. If they went along the bank of the Vadavar, they would cover half the distance to Kodikkarai. Azlvarkkadian planned to stop them and give Devan some news before sending him on his way. He waited, but there was no sign of the men. *I guessed wrong: they have taken another route or something has happened.* Just as he was about to climb out of the boat, he heard horses' hooves. He immediately lay down again and pretended to be tied.

When the horses were near, Azlvarkkadian shouted, "Hello! Who's that? Stop! Untie me!"

The first horse did not stop: Azlvarkkadian saw that the rider was Karuthiruman. So, when the second horse passed him, he shouted, "Vandhiya Devan! Stop!" The second horse too did not stop. Azlvarkkadian looked at the rider and was stunned. *There's something wrong with my eyes, or my brain is addled …*

The two horses stopped some distance away and one horse trotted back—it was Karuthiruman. He jumped off the horse and came to the boat. "Are you still tied to the boat? You helped us: in return, I'll untie you before I go. But don't try any of your tricks with me."

As Karuthiruman bent over the boat, Azlvarkkadian leaped to the shore, caught him by the neck and knocked him down. Caught unawares, Karuthiruman lay stunned on the ground. "Aiyo! Let me go. Is this my reward for trying to help you? Look, your friend, Vandhiya Devan, is waiting there. What will he think if he sees this? He'll kill you. Let me go."

"Rascal! How boldly you lie! Who's on that horse? Tell me the truth and I'll let you go. Or you'll die."

"It's not Vandhiya Devan: it's Prince Madurandaka. Let me go. I'll ask him to give you any reward you want."

"The reward can wait. Where's Vandhiya Devan?"

"He went towards the hut in the garden and I didn't see him after that."

"Where are you going?"

"To Sri Lanka."

"Why's Prince Madurandaka going there with you?"

"How do I know? Ask him yourself."

Azlvarkkadian squeezed Karuthiruman's chest. "Tell me the truth: whose son is Madurandaka?"

"What a question! Sembiyan Madevi's ... no, no! Don't crush my chest. I'll die. He's the mute Mandakini's son."

"The truth if you want to live: who's Madurandaka's father?"

Karuthiruman whispered his answer.

"Good! You have saved your life. Now, one last question: whose son is Chendan Amudhan? He's Sembiyan Madevi's and Gandara Aditya's son, isn't he?"

"Yes, but he's alive only because of me. The deaf-mute, Vani, thought he was dead and was going to bury him. I heard the baby cry and saved it. Spare my life at least for that."

"In truth, I'm letting you go only because of that." Azlvarkkadian got off his chest.

Karuthiruman charged to the horse and jumped on it. The two horses galloped away into the darkness and rain.

Aiyo! Ghost!

AZLVARKKADIAN CALLED HIS men and walked towards the fort's northern gate. He had not asked for their help in dealing with Karuthiruman as he did not want them to learn the secrets. When they were halfway there, a man came running wildly towards them. He bumped into Azlvarkkadian in the dark; Azlvarkkadian caught him and refused to let him go. He peered into his face and exclaimed, "You rascal, Pinakapani! Why are you running as if devils are chasing you?"

"Oh, it's you, Vaishnava! Tell me, did you happen to see two horses go by?"

"Yes, what's that to you?"

"If only you knew who was on those horses! Didn't you recognize even one of them?"

"One of them looked like Vandhiya Devan, but I decided it couldn't be him. Isn't Vandhiya Devan in the dungeon?"

"You wretch! He and another madman tied me up and escaped."

"My goodness! What were you doing while they tied you? And why were you in the dungeon?"

"The chief minister sent me. But there's no time for all that. You are also the chief minister's man, right? Come with me: we'll catch them and bring them back."

"What's it to us? Let them go."

"If everyone is like you, the Chola kingdom will go to the dogs! Don't you know that Vandhiya Devan murdered Prince Karikalan? And a short while ago, he killed another man with a dagger outside Chendan Amudhan's hut."

"God help us! Who was that man?"

"I didn't see who is was. You don't have to come with me, but move aside. Let me go."

"Pinakapani, you are the biggest fool in the world! They are fleeing for their lives on horseback. How can you chase them on foot and bring them back? What's it to me? Go!"

"You are right; that's why I asked you to come with me. But you refuse."

"What can I do? I tried to stop them and got beaten for my pains; my body still aches. I'm not used to fighting. Maybe if you .... what's this? There's blood on your hand."

"They attacked and wounded me in the dungeon: the evil demons!"

"And yet, you are ready to go behind those demons on foot by yourself. If I were you, I would go to someone in authority, ask for five or six mounted warriors and hunt down those men. Of course, I would arm myself with a sword and spear before I climbed on my horse."

Pinakapani thought about this. He was terrified that the man he had stabbed outside Amudhan's hut was Madurandaka. But, as Azlvarkkadian said, it was useless to go on foot after the riders. *If the man I stabbed is Madurandaka, I must see that Vandhiya Devan is blamed for that too. After all, a man who killed one prince is capable of killing another ... and the punishment is the same.* Pinakapani convinced himself that Devan had killed both the princes.

"Vaishnava, take me to someone in authority and ask them to give me some mounted soldiers. I don't know how to deal with important people. I tried telling the general and the chief minister that we should chase and catch these men, but both of them called me a fool and scolded me."

"They don't have confidence in you. You let the prisoners escape from the dungeon. How will they trust you to catch them and bring them back?"

"I tried to catch the prisoners on my own. Anyway, they have to go to Kodikkarai. I have people there to help me and I know all Vandhiya Devan's hideouts there. But it will be better to go with men and horses. Will you help me?"

They reached the main northern entrance. In the light of the torches, they saw Malayaman, Velir, and Aniruddha standing there. A little distance away on the highway, elephants with howdahs waited, followed by ranks of horsemen and foot soldiers.

"Our master is here on some important mission; this is not the right time to disturb him. On this side, I see the Pazluvur brothers, Sambuvaraya, Kandamaran and Parthibendran: let's tell them. They are the ones who will be most eager to catch Vandhiya Devan."

The heralds came ahead, announcing the glory and lineage of the chieftains; drums beat a tattoo and conches blew. Kalaanthaka, Kandamaran and Parthibendran led the procession, riding majestic white horses. They were followed by Ambalavan and Sambuvaraya seated in the howdah of a huge elephant. Behind them came the other chieftains, on horses and elephants. A hundred soldiers, armed with swords and spears, marched behind.

Kalaanthaka saw Azlvarkkadian and stopped his horse. "Vaishnava, is there any important message from the chief minister?"

Azlvarkkadian said, "Commander, the chief minister did not give me any message for you; he'll tell you himself. But there's important news: Vandhiya Devan has escaped from the dungeon."

"There's a conspiracy here!" exclaimed Parthibendran. "Someone must have helped him."

"Did he vanish by magic?" mocked Kalaanthaka. "And even if he escaped, where can he go? He has to be inside the fort."

Azlvarkkadian replied, "That's what the general says. The chief minister ordered me to go around the fort as a precaution. He's worried the Kadambur clan may be in danger ..."

"I'm glad at least one person is concerned about us," Kandamaran said.

Parthibendran was suspicious. "Vaishnava, tell me the truth: are you trying to stop him from escaping or helping him get away?"

"Sir, we can't argue now. The doctor's son, Pinakapani, says he saw Vandhiya Devan and Karuthiruman riding down this road. I also saw two fugitives gallop past."

"Pinakapani, is this true?" Kalaanthaka asked.

"Sir, I swear it's the truth! Give me a horse and four soldiers: I'll bring back the fugitives."

Parthibendran said, "Let's send men. I have to take you to the emperor, or I would ride after them myself. Catching Vandhiya Devan is crucial."

Kandamaran intervened. "I'll go with him. I'll bring Vandhiya Devan back, dead or alive!"

Kalaanthaka agreed and said he would inform Sambuvaraya. Kandamaran and Pinakapani, accompanied by four soldiers, galloped like the wind along the northern bank of the Vadavar.

Madurandaka was not a skilled horseman; Karuthiruman was an accomplished rider but had no stamina after years in the dungeon. But they were both filled with new energy and rode on through the night. They stopped after midnight by a bamboo bridge. Karuthiruman was sure that they would be followed. He planned to confuse their pursuers by crossing over to the southern bank and going back to the Kodikkarai road after travelling some distance. Doubting that Madurandaka could cross the flooded river on horseback, he decided to let Madurandaka use the bridge while he took both their horses across the river.

The two men rested under a tree before crossing the river. The flood water roared past them and the croaking of frogs filled the night air. Madurandaka, used to soft mattresses and couches, was exhausted and frightened. Sensing this, Karuthiruman encouraged him. He told him that the Lankan king, Mahinda, was a traditional ally of the Pandians and that once Madurandaka reached him, all his troubles would end. Mahinda would crown Madurandaka Pandian emperor with the ancient crown jewels. The Chola empire would be destroyed by civil war. The Pazluvur brothers and Sambuvaraya would be accused of murdering Karikalan; Velir and Malayaman would be accused of killing Madurandaka; Arulmozli would be suspected of being an accomplice and this would wipe out his popularity with the public. Seizing his opportunity, Mahinda would invade the Pandian country and capture Madurai. He would hold a second public coronation for Madurandaka there. He would confer the title, 'Destroyer of the Cholas,' on Madurandaka. Madurandaka's heart burst with pride and he was filled with enthusiasm. He heard drums beat a tattoo of victory; he heard thousands of people cry, 'Long live the Pandian Emperor!' 'Long live the Destroyer of the Cholas!'

Madurandaka's sweet dreams were shattered by the sound of galloping horses. They saw torches in the distance. Karuthiruman had not expected their pursuers to be so fast. He jumped up in a panic and cried, "Prince, get on your horse. We must cross the river before they are here!" Karuthiruman was on his horse in an instant; seeing Madurandaka struggle to mount his horse, he said, "Sir, cross the river by the bridge: I'll bring your horse across."

"Nonsense! Do you think I'm a coward? If I cannot cross this river on horseback, how will I cross the sea to Lanka? How will I win the Pandian kingdom and throne?" Madurandaka boasted and slowly climbed on to his horse. As the two horses entered the river, Madurandaka's horse suddenly went down on its knees near the shore.

"Aiyo!" screamed Karuthiruman.

Luckily, the horse recovered and stepped into the river.

Madurandaka was terrified but put on a bold front. "That's nothing: why were you so scared?" Madurandaka's horse may have hurt its knees when it fell; it was slower than the other horse and was almost washed away by the flood. Madurandaka had a hard time taking it to the opposite bank. Meanwhile, the sound of horses' hooves came closer and closer.

Karuthiruman kept stopping and waiting for the prince to catch up. He then had an idea. Telling Madurandaka to keep going, Karuthiruman quickly reached the opposite bank. He jumped off his horse and crossed the bamboo bridge back to the northern bank. He used Madurandaka's dagger to hurriedly cut the ropes which hung from the bridge. He knotted the pieces into one long rope; he tied one end to the bridge and the other to a tree on the opposite side of the road. In the darkness, the riders galloping down the road would not notice the rope stretched across their path. Karuthiruman considered running back across the bridge to his horse on the opposite bank; he changed his mind, quickly climbed a tree and hid among the branches.

Madurandaka's horse was almost across the river: it needed just a few minutes to make it to the bank. The riders galloped down the road and reached the tree. The two leading horses charged against the rope … they tripped and rolled over. Karuthiruman automatically burst into laughter.

One of the riders who had fallen off his horse screamed, "Aiyo! Ghost!"

It's Pinakapani, Karuthiruman thought. *What a pity he didn't break his neck when he fell.*

The other rider took the fall in his stride and jumped up at once: it was Kandamaran.

Madurandaka Disappears

EVEN AS HE rose, Kandamaran was ready with his spear. He was sure that the rider who had almost reached the opposite bank was Vandhiya Devan. He hated Devan and believed that he had betrayed their friendship. He blamed him for his family's disgrace. Devan had spread the news of the conspirators' secret meeting at Kadambur Palace. He was an accomplice of Veerapandian's bodyguards, whether at Nandini's instigation or because he profited from it in some way. *I was also bewitched by Nandini, but I would never commit such crimes.* Above all, Kandamaran was furious with Devan for corrupting his beloved sister's pure heart. *I dreamed of making Manimekalai an empress and that evil wretch made her publicly declare, 'I killed Karikalan!' It doesn't matter if I can't catch him alive: I'll at least have the satisfaction of killing him. My horse is down and unlikely to survive; same goes for Pinakapani's horse. Devan has almost reached the opposite bank … the other soldiers will take a few minutes to get here; even then it will be impossible to catch Devan once he gallops away.* All this flashed through Kandamaran's mind in an instant. He stood, planted his feet firmly on the ground, took aim and threw his spear with all his might.

The spear whizzed through the air and struck Madurandaka. Madurandaka screamed and fell into the river; his horse struggled to the shore. Karuthiruman, caught unawares by the speed of these events, shuddered on his tree. He had calculated that the front riders would be crushed by their fall or at least be too stunned to react. Karuthiruman recovered and jumped down from the tree with a loud yell and knocked down Kandamaran; as he turned to run, Pinakapani, now aware that it was no ghost but Karuthiruman, tried to stop him. Karuthiruman vented all his pent-up anger on Pinakapani: he stabbed him with his knife, threw him aside and charged for the bridge. The soldiers reached there and saw a man running across the bamboo bridge. Unaware of what had just happened, they stopped and waited.

Kandamaran shouted, "Catch that man!"

The four men jumped off their horses and went after Karuthiruman. Kandamaran recovered from his fall and ran behind them. The wounded Pinakapani, filled with rage, followed the others on to the bridge. But after taking a few steps, Pinakapani's strength vanished; his vision went blank; his head whirled; he stumbled and fell into the river. The men ahead of him did not notice him fall. The poor doctor's son, who had built so many castles in the air, died of greed. His dreams were washed away by the floodwater which also became his grave.

Karuthiruman stopped and turned back when he was three-fourths of the way across the bridge. He saw that the soldiers had just stepped on the bridge. He quickly took his knife and slashed at the ropes which held the bamboo bridge together. He stamped on the underlying beams and broke them as he ran. Once he was across, he cut the ropes which tied the bridge to the tree roots, lifted up the end of the bridge and heaved it into the river—a third of the bridge collapsed and was washed away by the water.

The soldiers pelting across the bridge did not notice the broken section; they fell into the flood and fought their way up to the surface. Only Kandamaran, bringing up the rear, escaped. Kandamaran signaled to the men to swim to the opposite bank. Two of the soldiers obeyed while the other two fought against the tide, clung to the remnants of the broken bridge and climbed on to it. Kandamaran scolded them but realized that it was no use asking them to jump into the river again. He instructed them to make a raft with the broken bamboo, clung on to it with the two men and drifted to the opposite shore. The two soldiers who had swum across met them and said that a short while ago, the man who had cut the bridge had disappeared into the darkness and that they had heard two horses galloping away. They had waited there as it was impossible to pursue them on foot.

But Kandamaran was not ready to give up. He decided that the man in the tree had to be the madman. With his own eyes, Kandamaran had seen Devan hit by his spear and fall headlong into the flood, but he would be satisfied only when he saw Devan's corpse. *Maybe I can take his dead body to Thanjavur. Devan's escape proves his guilt. My family's honor will be restored.* Kandamaran made his way downstream along the riverbank, followed by the four soldiers. They searched to see whether Devan's corpse had been washed ashore. It was no easy task in the dark but Kandamaran went on. After covering a long distance, they heard the roar of a waterfall. They reached a weir across the river where the water collected before it gathered force and fell to a lower level where it swirled and roared away.

If Devan's corpse reaches this weir, it will take several days to surface. It may never come up ... it's no use searching further. Just then, Kandamaran saw a dark object swirl above the foaming white water of the weir before it was washed down the waterfall. *There goes his body. May god forgive him for his sins. I can forget about him. Let me go to Thanjavur and get on with my life.*

We Have Not Helped Anyone

ONCE THE CHIEFTAINS' procession had passed them, Azlvarkkadian gathered his men and made his way to Chendan Amudhan's garden. He came across Madurandaka's palanquin and its bearers some distance away, partially concealed behind a tree. The bearers told him that

Madurandaka had ordered them to wait there for him. Azlvarkkadian whispered orders to his men to search the garden thoroughly while he crept to the hut and stood at the door. He placed his ear against the locked door and listened. He heard Poonkuzlali's and Amudhan's worried voices; he also heard the sound of a man in his death throes. One of his men hurried to him with some objects. By the dim light filtering through the door, Azlvarkkadian saw Madurandaka's crown, silk cloak, pearl necklace and other ornaments. Satisfied, he whispered, "Call off the search and bring everyone here. Stay armed and ready for anything." Azlvarkkadian knocked on the door. When there was no reply, he banged harder.

"Who's there? What do you want?" Poonkuzlali asked.

"My dear girl, it's me, Thirumalai. Please open the door: it's urgent."

Poonkuzlali came to the door. "My cousin's ill. Why are you disturbing him?"

"Ocean Princess, open the door or I'll break it down!"

"Vaishnava, do you have the courage to do that?" Poonkuzlali threw open the door, her beautiful eyes flashing fire. She was stunned to see the men standing behind Azlvarkkadian. Controlling her anger, she said, "Sir, what's happening? Who are these men?"

"They are with me on the king's business; anyone who obstructs us will be punished."

Poonkuzlali sneered. "I don't know what business the king has in this poor hut. I can't wait to go to Kodikkarai and get away from all this! My cousin's ill and his condition will worsen if he sees your men. You can come in by yourself if you must."

Azlvarkkadian entered the hut and shut and locked the door behind him. "Poonkuzlali, why are you in a hurry to go to Kodikkarai? Don't you want to marry a prince and sit on a throne?"

"Sir, I don't want to go anywhere near a throne. I have decided to marry my cousin, Chendan Amudhan. Once Amudhan is better, we're going to Kodikkarai."

"Who knows? If you are destined to wear a crown, it will happen whether you want it or not."

"Enough of your mockery. Why are you here?"

"My dear girl, why did you help a man who broke out of the dungeon escape?"

Poonkuzlali feigned innocence. "What? We have not helped anyone."

"Vandhiya Devan and a madman escaped from the dungeon today. They were seen here. Two men rode away from here on horseback. There's a pool of blood near the hut and signs of people coming and going. It's clear you have helped the fugitives. The chief minister sent me because of the regard he has for you. The general's men would have arrested you at once."

"We are grateful to you and the chief minister. Amudhan will recover in two days and we'll go to Kodikkarai and never set foot in Thanjavur again. Until then, you must help us and see that the king's men don't disturb us."

"I'll help you, but you must tell me the truth."

"Vaishnava, I swear we have not helped anyone escape from here."

"Ahah! In that case, Vandhiya Devan is still in this hut …"

They heard a pitiful moan of pain from under Amudhan's cot.

Prince for a Day

"SO, THAT'S HOW things are!" Azlvarkkadian moved towards the cot.

Poonkuzlali drew her dagger and stood in his way. "Vaishnava, if you take another step forward, I'll send you to your Vishnu at Vaikundam!"

Amudhan rose from his cot. "Poonkuzlali, enough! Put away your dagger. No good comes from lies. Let's tell the Vaishnava the truth; after all, he too is Vandhiya Devan's friend."

Devan was hidden under the cot, behind cloth curtains. The men laid him gently on the bed. Devan's moan of pain was the only sign of life in him. Azlvarkkadian and Amudhan held his hands and legs as Vani and Poonkuzlali spread hot herbal paste over his wound.

Devan's eyes opened with the agony and he saw Azlvarkkadian. "Vaishnava, you betrayed me! You sent me here and sent an assassin after me." He sank back into unconsciousness.

Azlvarkkadian's face reflected his sorrow at this accusation but Poonkuzlali smiled. "Vaishnava, I don't know why you sent him here:

but if he had not come at the right time, I would have become a widow before I became a wife."

Azlvarkkadian and Amudhan exclaimed, "What? What?"

"Yes," Poonkuzlali turned to Amudhan. "I didn't tell you. A man stood outside aiming a dagger at you—Vandhiya Devan threw himself in the way and saved you."

Amudhan's eyes filled. "Aiyo! Is my friend dying because of me?!"

Azlvarkkadian said, "My dear girl, Vandhiya Devan coming here and saving Amudhan's life is nothing short of a miracle. You will live happily with your husband for many long years ... but who would want to kill this good man? Did you recognize the killer?"

"Of course! It was that wretch, Pinakapani. Sir, tell us how we can save Vandhiya Devan. Amudhan and I will be forever grateful to you."

"Lady, it's not that simple," Azlvarkkadian said, "Soldiers are combing the kingdom for the fugitives. They'll be here soon. I don't know how I'll manage the four men standing outside."

"Your respect for me keeps growing," commented Poonkuzlali. "Yesterday, I was 'the boat girl;' a while ago, I became 'my dear girl;' now I'm 'Lady.' Soon you'll call me 'Princess!'"

"If you want to save Vandhiya Devan, your to-be husband must become prince for a day. If he's a prince, then aren't you a princess? But first, look at this ..." Azlvarkkadian opened the bundle he carried and showed them Madurandaka's crown, cloak and ornaments.

"These belong to Madurandaka," Amudhan said. "He was wearing them when he came here."

"Where did you get these things from?" Poonkuzlali asked.

"They were found near the garden hedge. While I was walking along the Vadavar, the two horses I left here galloped past me. The madman who blabbers about the Pandian crown jewels was riding one of the horses and the other rider was Prince Madurandaka."

"How strange! Why should Madurandaka leave behind his ornaments?"

"I don't know. I planned to get the chief minister to send men after him but I was afraid something terrible would happen by the time he's brought back to Thanjavur."

"Like what?"

"The Pazluvur brothers and their allied chieftains have arrived; the emperor has commanded that the succession issue must be settled peacefully. But before the Pazluvur brothers agree to talks, they will ask, 'Where's Madurandaka?' If Madurandaka's missing, they'll accuse Velir of killing him in order to make Prince Arulmozli king. Even if the general denies this, he has no proof. There will be civil war and the Chola empire will break up."

"Let's go to Kodikkarai before that happens." said Poonkuzlali.

"Lady, that's not possible."

"Then, what do you suggest?"

"Let Amudhan wear this crown and these ornaments. I'll bring the elephant which Prince Arulmozli rode into the fort. Let Amudhan ride the elephant. I'll arrange for my men to walk beside the elephant shouting, 'Long live Madurandaka!' Madurandaka's palanquin is nearby; we will put Vandhiya Devan in it and close the curtains. Lady, you must walk beside the palanquin ... leave the rest to me."

"What a mad scheme!" Amudhan exclaimed.

"As if no one can identify him if he wears this crown," said Poonkuzlali.

"Who can identify someone riding an elephant at night? They will look closely at him only if they are suspicious. I'll be with you and it's my responsibility to take you all safely to the chief minister's house. There's no other way to save Vandhiya Devan."

After much argument, Poonkuzlali and Amudhan agreed to go along with Azlvarkkadian.

A Sword for a Sword

AS VELIR, MALAYAMAN and Aniruddha waited in the courtyard just beyond the fort gate, the Pazluvur contingent was obliged to dismount and walk to them. Kalaanthaka told his peers that this was a deliberate tactic and asked them to let him do the talking.

As the chieftains approached them, Velir said, "Welcome. May your arrival bring good fortune to the Chola kingdom and the Chola dynasty."

Kalaanthaka replied, "Yes sir, and may your departure also bring good fortune."

Velir's eyes reddened. "Sir, my brother gave his life for the Cholas in Sri Lanka; I have just returned from the battlefield myself. We are not in the habit of staying safely behind fort walls and guarding the women's quarters and the treasury vaults."

Aniruddha intervened. "My lords, for generations, each of your clans has sacrificed lives and worked for the glory of the Cholas. Now and always, the Cholas need your united service. Emperor Sundara Chola has set aside his grief over the death of his beloved son to bring you together. I beg you, please do not hurt the bereaved emperor with your quarrels."

These words touched everyone there; they realized this was not the time for personal grievances.

Kalaanthaka said, "Chief minister, when can we meet the emperor? Can we see him tonight? We are eager to hear directly from him what he wants."

"Commander, you are all aware that the emperor's suffering increases at night. He also wishes to consult Sembiyan Madevi and make a last attempt to change her mind: you know what I'm referring to. So, the emperor will meet you tomorrow. He has ordered the general to make comfortable arrangements for those of you who do not have residences in the fort."

Kalaanthaka again spoke up. "Chief minister, we are used to camping in the open on the battlefield. If we are to meet the emperor tomorrow, why must we enter the fort today?"

"Maybe the commander is afraid to spend the night in the fort," said Velir.

"I do not know the meaning of fear!" Kalaanthaka retorted. "Maybe the general who ran away from the Sri Lankan battlefield knows the meaning."

It looks like these two can't be stopped from fighting and killing each other! Ambalavan cleared his throat and came forward. Everyone gave way respectfully. "*Thambi*, the general belongs to a clan which keeps its word. He assures us of our safety: why not stay in the fort?"

"*Anna*, our swords and thirty thousand soldiers are enough for our safety. I'm the commander of Thanjavur Fort and I'll agree to stay in the fort only if it's under my control again."

Velir addressed Ambalavan. "Sir, if the emperor so commands, I'm ready for that."

"Did he capture the fort at the emperor's command?" Kalaanthaka sneered.

"No, I captured the fort with my sword!" countered Velir.

"I'll take it back with my sword!" said Kalaanthaka and prepared to draw his sword.

Ambalavan stopped him. "*Thambi,* this is not the time to fight. We are here at the emperor's invitation. You left our women and Prince Madurandaka here because you trusted this man."

"I now doubt whether I did the right thing. If Madurandaka has been harmed in any way, I'll annihilate the Kodumbalur clan!" Kalaanthaka roared.

A short while before, Aniruddha had seen Azlvarkkadian signaling to him and had gone to hear what he had to say. He came back now in time to hear Kalaanthaka's words. Aniruddha said, "Commander, no harm will come to Prince Madurandaka. Sembiyan Madevi and he went to visit Chendan Amudhan outside the fort ...."

Kalaanthaka interrupted: "Chief minister, you are not the only one with a network of efficient spies—only the queen came back. Why has Madurandaka not returned to the fort?"

Aniruddha beamed as cheers of "Long live Prince Madurandaka!" came from the entrance. Everyone turned eagerly in that direction. 'Madurandaka,' wearing his crown and ornaments, entered the fort on an elephant; a screened palanquin came along with his escort.

"Commander, Prince Madurandaka was a little delayed. Chendan Amudhan fell off his horse and was seriously injured. The queen asked the prince to bring Amudhan back in his palanquin. So, the prince is on the elephant. Very soon, he may have to ride an elephant after his coronation: maybe he's practicing," said Aniruddha.

The Fort's Security

KALAANTHAKA LOOKED AT the elephant and the palanquin and said, "Strange! The prince is traveling in such grand style… he's usually shy and travels in a screened palanquin."

"He must get over his shyness one day or another; after all, he'll soon be emperor," said Aniruddha.

"Has it been decided to crown Madurandaka? Who decided?"

"The emperor of course," replied Aniruddha. "As soon as we all meet the emperor and agree …"

"If the emperor has decided, why does he need our agreement? It is Velir and his men who must agree. It's strange to see the prince so openly enter the fort guarded by Velir's men." Kalaanthaka took a few steps towards the elephant and then turned back. He addressed Ambalavan. "*Anna*, I don't object to you staying in the fort. But I can't find the heart to enter a fort which I commanded until recently while it's under someone else's control. Meet the emperor and find out what he wants. I'll stay with our army outside the walls. Kandamaran has gone in search of Vandhiya Devan. I must find out how Vandhiya Devan escaped from the dungeon and who helped him. Forgive me: all of you go into the fort."

Ambalavan roared, "General, this fool's brain is addled. To hell with him! Come, let's go."

But, the next day, Sundara Chola insisted on Kalaanthaka's presence. "My dear chieftains, I have confidence in you all. But above all, I trust Lord Kalaanthaka."

Ambalavan said, "Emperor, my brother will honor any decision taken by me."

"Chancellor, he has attended every meeting of the Council before this and we have never taken a decision without his consent. Why is he not here now?" Sundara Chola asked.

There was silence.

Ambalavan cleared his throat. "Sir, Thanjavur Fort has been under Kalaanthaka's authority for many years; it is now under the general's control; so, my brother refuses to enter the fort. What can we do about his stubbornness?"

"We can give him justice," Sundara Chola said. "The Cholas' glory is founded on justice. The general was wrong to wrest control of the fort from Lord Kalaanthaka. Mourning my beloved son's death, I failed in my duty to Kalaanthaka." He turned to Velir. "General, hand over control of the fort to Lord Kalaanthaka again."

Velir's face turned to stone.

Malayaman intervened. "Sir, Lord Kalaanthaka failed in his duty as Fort Commander. An assassin entered the fort and threw a spear at you. It was left to some mute woman to save your life. What was the use of battalions of soldiers and an armory filled with weapons? Was it wrong of the general to take over of the fort?"

"Uncle, who can stand against destiny? Who can we blame? In spite of all your efforts, could you save your beloved grandson?" Sundara Chola asked sadly.

"We must investigate Karikalan's death. The truth must be found," Malayaman insisted.

Velir said, "As Lord Ambalavan is now here, we can begin the investigation."

Parthibendran intervened. "Before we begin the investigation, we need to know how the accused, Vandhiya Devan, escaped from the dungeon. Who was responsible for it?"

"Yes, I heard about this," Sundara Chola said. "General, how did Vandhiya Devan escape?"

"Lord, I accept responsibility for this," Aniruddha said. "He escaped because of a small mistake I made. But I also accept the responsibility of bringing him back and delivering him to you ... if I fail in this, you can punish me suitably."

"My friend, Kandamaran, has gone after Vandhiya Devan," Parthibendran said.

Two women were present it the room: Vanamadevi and Kundavai. Only Aniruddha noted the change in Kundavai's expression at Parthibendran's words.

Aniruddha turned to Parthibendran. "Kandamaran is a clever young man. But he could not save Prince Karikalan who was a guest in his own palace. Can he catch Vandhiya Devan? I doubt it." Aniruddha noted that Kundavai had caught the meaning of his last words.

"I also heard that Kandamaran and Vandhiya Devan are close friends," added Velir.

"That's an old story," Sambuvaraya said. "No on in our clan will have anything to do with a man who betrayed the Cholas."

"Why are we discussing this now?" Sundara Chola asked. "The chief minister accepts responsibility for Vandhiya Devan; the general will hand over the fort to Lord Kalaanthaka."

"If that is the emperor's command, I'm ready to obey." Velir's tone reflected his anger.

"Uncle," Sundara Chola said. "You are older and wiser than me. Can I presume to command you? I only expressed my opinion. Shall we hear what the others have to say?"

"I'm against this," Malayaman declared firmly. "Lord Kalaanthaka failed in his duty."

"What does the chief minister say?" Sundara Chola asked.

Aniruddha advised, "Changing the fort's security arrangements now will cause problems. We are here to discuss the succession issue. We can come back to other matters after that."

"We cannot take any decisions without Lord Kalaanthaka," Sundara Chola insisted. "Chancellor, what do you say?"

"Malayaman is right: my brother failed in his duty," Ambalavan said.

The others, familiar with his affection for his younger brother, were amazed at his words. They were even more surprised at the emperor's reply.

"Chancellor, Lord Kalaanthaka did not fail in his duty. It is you and I who are to blame for ignoring his warnings. Hear me, all of you: Lord Kalaanthaka warned me that Veerapandian's bodyguards had penetrated the fort. He urged me to strengthen the security around the palace and the women's quarters. He insisted the secret passage between the chancellor's palace and mine be blocked and a cordon of guards be placed between our two palaces. In spite of his devotion to his brother, he complained his brother was being fooled and he suspected Lord Ambalavan's palace was being used by the conspirators. He advised me to move Lord Ambalavan to another palace and to shift the treasure to a different vault. I ignored all these warnings …"

Ambalavan cleared his throat. "Emperor, I'll tell everyone what you, in your mercy, have not said. In my old age, I was bewitched by Nandini. My brother warned me about her and told me a sorcerer who visited her was the leader of Veerapandian's bodyguards. Bewitched by Nandini, I ignored him. Yet, he failed in his duty. He should have hunted down that wretch and her accomplices and killed them. If I had stopped him, he should have killed me too."

His listeners broke into goosebumps at his ringing tones. The indescribable pain in his voice tugged at their heartstrings.

Sundara Chola said, "Chancellor, your brother tried to do his duty, but I stopped him. I ordered him not to come to me with rumors about you or your wife. I refused to move you from your palace and let my bodyguards occupy it. I asked him whether it was worth living in fear. My diseased mind and body made me tired of living. Lord Ambalavan, you and your brother are in no way responsible for any evil which has befallen me and my family. I brought it upon myself."

At these words, tears streamed down Ambalavan's cheeks.

Sundara Chola continued. "The very first time Vandhiya Devan came here, Kalaanthaka warned me about him. He told me Vandhiya Devan spoke secretly with Lady Nandini when she was travelling by palanquin near Thanjavur Fort. He suspected Vandhiya Devan of being a part of the Pandian conspiracy as he entered the fort using the Pazluvur signet ring and escaped through the secret passage. I did not take him seriously. The wise Aniruddha and my beloved daughter, Kundavai, were also fooled by Vandhiya Devan. They sent important messages through him ..."

Aniruddha intervened. "Emperor, the princess is not easily fooled. She gave Vandhiya Devan a message but asked me to keep an eye on him. I sent Azlvarkkadian to follow him ..."

"Let's assume both of you were not fooled by him. Isn't it a fact that he and another man escaped from the dungeon? Such a thing would never have happened under Kalaanthaka's watch. So, general, have Lord Kalaanthaka brought here and hand over command of the fort to him."

"As you wish, lord. Do I have your permission to leave?" Velir's voice was now calm. Sundara Chola's love and support for the Pazluvur brothers, along with his obvious forbearance and friendship, had stunned the general and melted his heart.

"Yes, you may all leave. Once Lord Kalaanthaka joins us, we'll discuss other matters. I also need time to discuss the succession with Sembiyan Madevi."

As they rose to leave, Parthibendran spoke up. "Lord, I wish to remind the chief minister that he has taken on the responsibility of catching Vandhiya Devan, who betrayed his friend and his country. Even if others forget, I will not. Karikalan's murderer must be found and punished."

Ambalavan cleared his throat like an aged lion. He started to speak and then changed his mind. He walked out silently and the others followed him.

That very evening, Kalaanthaka took over Thanjavur Fort once more. Except a few soldiers, Velir's army was sent out of the fort and Kalaanthaka's men again took up station at the gates. This change had an unfortunate consequence: the Kodumbalur men and the Pazluvur men often clashed. One side shouted, 'Long live Prince Arulmozli!' and the other, 'Long live Prince Madurandaka!' These shouts spread through the kingdom, with the people also taking sides. In the next three days, a flood of fury swept through the Chola kingdom. Arguments led to fist-fights and then to cudgels; it looked like sticks would soon be exchanged for swords and spears.

My Son

SUNDARA CHOLA MET Sembiyan Madevi at the door and asked her to sit beside him on his throne.

"Emperor, I'm glad to see your health has improved: may you live long to rule the world!"

"Mother, I'm pleased I can walk. I owe it to a deaf-mute woman's love. But must I live after losing my brave son? Why couldn't I die before him?"

"The loss of a son is the cruelest of all suffering, but who knows the workings of destiny?"

"If I know the truth behind my son's death, I'll find some peace."

"Why torment yourself over the past? What will you gain by finding out how and why he died?"

"Without knowing the truth, I suspect everyone. People are even accusing Lord Ambalavan who is the Cholas' strongest pillar of support."

"Why don't you ask him for the truth?"

"I don't have the courage to question him. He's somehow involved in it and is heartbroken. Until he speaks up on his own, who will dare to ask him?"

"Is there no other way to find out the truth?"

"I thought Vandhiya Devan would tell me the truth, but he has escaped from the dungeon."

Kundavai, who had remained silent all this while, said, "Father, hasn't the chief minister said he will somehow bring that warrior to you?"

"My child, the chief minister does not always fulfill such responsibilities. Kandamaran is rash and obsessed with his family's honor. I'm worried that he's following Vandhiya Devan."

"Forget the past; look to the future," Sembiyan Madevi advised.

"Mother, please advise me as to the future," Sundara Chola replied.

"Emperor, when you have many wise ministers, why do you need a foolish woman's advice?"

"Women can be wise and bring good fortune to their families. Their stubbornness can also destroy their families. Mother, will you destroy our family?"

Sembiyan Madevi jumped as if scorched by fire. "What do you mean?" Her eyes filled.

"Mother, forgive me for my harsh words. I'm heartbroken to be alive when my eldest son is dead. But I have an even greater sorrow: what if the empire founded by my ancestors shatters under my rule? For some reason, the Pazluvur brothers and their supporters disliked Karikalan and worked to make Madurandaka my heir. There's nothing wrong in this: Madurandaka is in all ways worthy of being my successor. In truth, I should not have become king. I bowed to the wishes of my elders and am now paying the price for that: my son is dead. Enough! I can't see the empire die before my eyes. I need your help for this."

Sembiyan Madevi wiped away her tears. "Emperor, you were

crowned according to the wishes of three generations of Chola kings. My husband devoted his energy to Lord Shiva's service and the empire shrunk during his reign. Under you, the empire expanded and its enemies were annihilated. You made your son the crown prince. Now, you want me to agree to let my son succeed you. Even if I agree, will the people agree? You want to prevent civil war and the breaking up the empire … won't both happen if you make my son king?"

"Yes, mother. That's why I hesitated. I planned to convince everyone to accept Karikalan but fate intervened and Karikalan died. Madurandaka is older than Arulmozli; crowning Arulmozli is against justice and the principles of our dynasty. Mother, help me! Give me your consent to make Madurandaka king. I'll make Velir and Malayaman agree. Save the Chola empire."

"Lord, don't ask for my consent: I won't go against my husband's wishes. But I will no longer interfere in affairs of state. Ask Madurandaka what he wants and make your decision."

"I need your help for that too. Where's Madurandaka?"

Sembiyan Madevi's voice choked. "Lord, I have been asking the same question for the past three days. Summon the commander and ask him where my son is."

"Lord Kalaanthaka accuses you and Aniruddha of conspiring to hide him. I'll send for both of them."

Kundavai gave orders to the guards at the door and Kalaanthaka and Aniruddha were soon there.

"Commander," Sundara Chola said. "The queen asks me the same question you asked: 'Where is Madurandaka?' Tell us what you know— speak openly."

Kalaanthaka said, "I know the queen, for some reason, does not want her son to ascend the Tiger Throne. I also know the queen loves her son dearly, but some questions must be asked. Three days ago, the queen and Madurandaka visited Chendan Amudhan, but the queen alone returned to the fort. Later, a procession led by an elephant and a palanquin entered the fort. The chief minister pointed to it and said Madurandaka was on the elephant but I was rather suspicious. Madurandaka usually stays in my palace. The next day, I heard he had not come there at all. I searched the entire fort but there's no sign of him. How could he vanish from the fort? I fear the queen and the chief minister gave Madurandaka some alarming news and convinced him to flee from this kingdom. If I'm wrong, I beg the queen's forgiveness."

Sembiyan Madevi's voice quavered. "Commander, I swear on Lord Shiva's feet I have not discussed my son with the chief minister recently or conspired with him. Madurandaka and I visited Chendan Amudhan that evening. When I left, Madurandaka said he would follow me a little later. I have not seen him after that. I have been looking for him for three days."

"I accept the queen's explanation," Kalaanthaka said. "Let the chief minister explain the mystery of Madurandaka's disappearance."

Aniruddha said, "My emperor, the son conceived in this lady's womb spent the last three days in my palace. He's now waiting at the door to see you and his mother."

Aniruddha went to the door and clapped his hands. Azlvarkkadian entered, letting Chendan Amudhan walk ahead of him.

Kalaanthaka was furious. "Is there no limit to the chief minister's mockery?"

But Sembiyan Madevi's face was radiant with love. She held out her hands and said, "My son!"

Amudhan's eyes brimmed with tears. "Mother, have you at last found the heart to send for me?" He went to Sembiyan Madevi who embraced him with tears streaming down her face.

Mother and Son Reunited

WHEN CHENDAN AMUDHAN was five, Sembiyan Madevi saw Vani after many years. The queen instinctively felt a great love for Amudhan whom she assumed to be Vani's child. She noted the fear and hesitation on Vani's face but as Vani could only communicate through sign language, she did not learn much from her. The queen arranged a comfortable living for her. Sembiyan Madevi's love for Amudhan increased as she saw him grow in knowledge, discipline and devotion to Lord Shiva.

One day, a thought came to her, filling her with pain and happiness and a vague fear. She sent for Vani, told her that she wanted to build a memorial for her dead son and asked her to show her the place where he was buried. When the queen insisted, Vani finally told her the truth. She said that a man called Karuthiruman heard the baby cry while she was about to bury it; afraid of what the queen would say if she took the baby back to her, Vani went to Thirumaraikadu with Karuthiruman. When Karuthiruman left her after some years, Vani came back to Pazlayarai.

Sembiyan Madevi wept tears of joy. She longed to embrace her son but controlled her instincts. *What does it matter whether he lives in a palace or a hut? The comforts of this fleeting life are illusions. It's god's will that a mute woman's son lives in a palace and that a queen's son lives in a hut. If I try to change this, there will be many complications. My adopted son will suffer.*

Her deep faith in god helped her, but she often thought of Amudhan with a mother's yearning. She kept her love hidden in her heart over the years. At the same time, Sembiyan Madevi's resolve not to let her adopted son, Madurandaka, ascend the Tiger Throne grew stronger.

Now, at Aniruddha's words, her love for her son burst its constraints and flooded her heart and mind, making her cry out, 'My son!' Suddenly, she recalled Amudhan's words: 'Mother, have you at last found the heart to send for me?' *Does he know the truth? Has he kept it a secret all these years?* She asked in a voice choked with emotion: "My son, did you know I'm your real mother? Were you angry with me? Is that why you never brought it up?"

"Mother, I have known for some time that you are my real mother. I tried to be worthy of you and decided to come to you even if you did not send for me. I was only waiting for the succession issue to be settled. Because I did not want to hurt you, I was ready to give up Poonkuzlali. Luckily, she changed her mind about marrying a prince. I longed for the day you would call me, 'Son.' This is enough for me. Let no one outside this room know the truth … it will cause too much confusion in the kingdom."

All this while, Sundara Chola, Kalaanthaka and Kundavai were frozen in shock.

Kundavai recovered first and said, "Father, now we know why grandmother was so adamant Madurandaka should not be king."

Sundara Chola replied, "Yes, dear, but now, she can't object to her son ascending the Tiger Throne."

Sembiyan Madevi said, "Emperor, as my son said, let's keep this truth to ourselves. He has not claimed his right to the throne."

"Yes, lord," Amudhan added. "The kingdom faces many problems already: let's not add to them." He turned to the door. Poonkuzlali came in and stood with him. The couple prostrated themselves at Sembiyan Madevi's and Sundara Chola's feet. Amudhan said, "Bless us and let us go to Kodikkarai."

Aniruddha intervened. "Lord, let's not make a decision now. Let them remain in my house until we have news of Madurandaka. Until then, let this secret stay in this room."

"Arulmozli must be told," Kundavai said.

"No, no! Please don't tell him," Amudhan pleaded.

Finally, Sundara Chola decided, "Mother, you have been reunited with your son after all these years. I will not send him away at once. Stay here for a few days, either in my palace or with Aniruddha. We'll think about sending them to Kodikkarai after the succession issue has been settled. Until then, no one other than those in this room must know the truth."

Vanathi's Secret

ARULMOZLI WAS TROUBLED by the increasing agitation in the kingdom. He was also upset that Madurandaka was missing. *Malayaman and Velir are determined to make me king. It looks like Aniruddha is also in league with them. What if they have conspired to hide Madurandaka somewhere ... or even to kill him? They blame the Pazluvur brothers and Sambuvaraya for Karikalan's death. Maybe they have taken revenge on them through Madurandaka. Public opinion is fickle: tomorrow the people may accuse me of killing Madurandaka for the throne. They may even blame me for Karikalan's death ... god save me!*

He had even lost confidence in his beloved sister, Kundavai. He suspected her of doing something behind his back. Why, even Vanathi, the love of his life, was being secretive. *I will not put up with Vanathi's behavior.*

Arulmozli saw Vanathi look around furtively and steal away. He followed her stealthily. She crossed the palace's upper terraces and courtyards, reached the lower terrace and walked along a secret passage between two high walls. Certain that she was going to the place where Madurandaka was hidden, Arulmozli followed her, his anger mounting. Finally, Vanathi entered a room and was about to lock the door. Arulmozli leaped forward and planted one foot across the threshold. He gripped her hand and cried angrily, "Vanathi, who's hidden in this room?"

Vanathi smiled broadly. "Sir, my deceit has succeeded. If I had called you, you would not have come with me. Look who's in the room!"

Arulmozli, expecting to see Madurandaka, was amazed and delighted to find Vandhiya Devan lying in a bed there.

Devan sat up on seeing Arulmozli. "Sir, welcome. I've been expecting you for the past two days. Please save me from these women!"

Arulmozli sat beside him on the bed. "My friend, how did you end up here? I thought you would have made it to Sri Lanka; I planned to join you there in a few days."

"I'm supposed to be in Sri Lanka, searching for the Pandian crown jewels. I tried to stop Pinakapani from killing Chendan Amudhan and fell unconscious when Pinakapani threw his dagger at me. When I opened my eyes, I found myself here. Please help me escape or I'll be falsely accused of murdering Karikalan."

Vanathi intervened. "Sir, he'll be blamed only if he runs away. Princess Kundavai wants him to stay hidden here until the truth comes out."

"She's right: if you run away, you'll be blamed and it will also reflect on me. It's best to tell the world the truth. Tell me what happened at Kadambur."

Devan told Arulmozli all he knew, but he could not unravel the mystery of Karikalan's death.

I Will be King

VANDHIYA DEVAN CONCLUDED with, "Sir, there's one man who can prove my innocence: Lord Ambalavan. I believe he was the man who strangled me and knocked me down when I was hiding in the Music Room. Suspecting Nandini's fidelity, the old man disguised himself as a Kalamukha and came there. Idumbankari, who belongs to that cult, must have shown him the secret passage. But Lord Ambalavan dislikes me and will not volunteer the truth. He probably rejoices over my predicament. So, please allow me to escape. If I can, I'll find the Pandian crown jewels in Sri Lanka. Or kill me with your sword right now—don't let me be impaled at the crossroads for killing your brother who showered me with affection. Or ask Lady Vanathi to poison me: she and your sister brought me back from death's door."

Arulmozli was deep in thought. He jumped up abruptly and said, "I have made up my mind: I'll bow to the will of the people and the soldiers and ascend the Tiger Throne. Do you know why? To declare your innocence and release you."

Vanathi said excitedly, "How I wish Princess Kundavai was here to hear you!"

Devan wiped away his tears. "Sir, if you change your mind because of an orphan like me, the Chola kingdom will be blessed. Prince Madurandaka is not worthy to be king. Is a man who travels secretly in a woman's screened palanquin and participates in conspiracies fit to rule an empire? Is it just for such a coward to sit on the throne of heroes such as Vijayalaya Chola? No wonder the people refuse to accept it."

"Yes," said Arulmozli. "I'll stop searching for him. I will be king!"

Kundavai walked in and heard his words. "*Thambi*, have you forgotten Vanathi's oath not to sit on the throne? I can't see you crowned with another woman by your side."

"*Akka*," said Arulmozli. "Can the Chola kingdom stay without a king just for your friend's sake? Our father insists on going to Kanchipuram to spend his last days in peace and Madurandaka has vanished. We have no other choice—I must be crowned king. Don't you know the country is in a turmoil over the succession? How long can this go on?"

"*Thambi*, I came running here with good news. Prince Madurandaka has been found. Even if he refuses the crown, we must insist and make him king."

Arulmozli hid his surprise and asked, "Where was he hiding? How was he found?"

"*Thambi*, Sembiyan Madevi's son is the true heir to the Tiger Throne. The kingship is his by right. Forget about being king. Listen to this miracle: four days ago, an assassin threw his dagger at Prince Madurandaka. If he had succeeded, there would have been another untimely death in our family. Do you know the brave warrior who risked his own life to save the prince?" Kundavai turned her beautiful eyes to Vandhiya Devan.

Devan was shaken to the core by the love, respect and gratitude he saw in those eyes.

Arulmozli was amazed. "*Akka*, I don't understand: my friend didn't say a word about this ..."

"Your friend does not know how much the Chola dynasty is indebted to him."

"*Akka*, you are talking in riddles. How did Vandhiya Devan save Prince Madurandaka? Where's Madurandaka now?" asked Arulmozli.

"He'll be here in a few minutes," Kundavai said. "I sent for him when I heard you were here. Let him tell you himself, or let Poonkuzlali, who saw it all, tell you. I think I hear them ..."

Chendan Amudhan, Poonkuzlali, Aniruddha and Azlvarkkadian walked in. Amudhan wore a prince's crown, silk cloak and ornaments. The people in the room looked at him in surprise.

Arulmozli said, "*Akka*, didn't you say Prince Madurandaka is coming? I don't see him."

"*Thambi*, the man before you is the true son of Sembiyan Madevi and Gandara Aditya. All these years, he lived as Chendan Amudhan. He's the one the assassin tried to kill four days ago. Vandhiya Devan saved his life and Thirumalai brought him into the fort. This is the true Prince Madurandaka. He lived in a hut all these years, but we saw the Cholas' traits in him: he helped Vandhiya Devan escape; Poonkuzlali and he brought Arulmozli from Kodikkarai to Nagapattinam; he rode to the Pachai Hills. Today, Sembiyan Madevi revealed the truth. On this happy day, I welcome him into our family. This occasion deserves to be honored, but we are forced to keep the truth a secret. So, we'll celebrate it within our circle. Whenever my beloved brother leaves or returns from a voyage, it's my custom to anoint his forehead with holy ash and vermilion. And so …"

Kundavai anointed Amudhan's forehead with holy ash and vermilion.

Aniruddha blessed him. "Long live the Chola prince, Madurandaka Uthama!"

"Long may he live!" echoed Azlvarkkadian.

At first, Arulmozli was suspicious: *Is this some trick?* But as Kundavai went on, he realized that she spoke from the depths of her heart. He was also carried away by the flood of her emotion. He hugged Amudhan, wept and said, "I have always loved you and wished you were my brother: it must have been your blood which drew me to you."

Devan added, "I had a sneaking suspicion that the blood of a courageous warrior clan flowed in Amudhan's veins. There's one thing which gives me even more satisfaction than Amudhan becoming king: Poonkuzlali is to be queen! Her dreams have come true."

Amudhan turned to Arulmozli. "Overnight, you are all giving me the respect due to a prince. But after twenty-two years in a hut, I can't suddenly see myself as royalty. When I was locked in the dungeon for helping Vandhiya Devan escape, the man in the adjoining cell said, 'The mute woman's child is in the palace; the queen's child is in the hut.' Something clicked: I thought of the affection Sembiyan Madevi showered on me and guessed the truth. I longed for the day she would call me her son. I got my wish today and there's nothing more I want."

Aniruddha said, "Prince, this is not about what you want: it's about justice and tradition."

Amudhan said, "I have made up my mind. When Poonkuzlali insisted she would marry only a prince, I was tempted to tell her I was a prince with a right to the Tiger Throne. But I disciplined myself and prayed I would never covet the throne. I was ready to sacrifice Poonkuzlali, my greatest love, for this. Luckily, Poonkuzlali gave up her unworthy desire and agreed to marry a poor Shiva devotee like me."

Poonkuzlali intervened. "Sir, why do you call it an 'unworthy desire?'

I'm worthy of being an empress, but I agree to live with you weaving flower garlands and rowing a boat."

"Well said, Poonkuzlali!" Kundavai applauded. "Doesn't the *Thirukkural* say, 'All men are equal by birth?' There's no need for you to give up your wish." She turned to Amudhan. "Renouncing the throne shows your detachment and is a credit to you. But now, all of us, from the emperor to the chief minister, ask you to ascend the throne. Why do you refuse?"

"Lady, what about the people? I have lived among them and know them well. The majority of people in this kingdom shout, 'Crown Prince Arulmozli!' Can I swim against this tide? Even if I wanted to, can I rule this empire? Everyone hates the man you call the 'former Madurandaka.' Must I bear the brunt of all that hatred? No, don't do this to me!" Amudhan pleaded.

Arulmozli raised his head majestically. "Enough! I told Vandhiya Devan I'll be king. I stand by that. We won't discuss the succession any further."

Disastrous Consequences

SUNDARA CHOLA SAT on the throne in Thanjavur palace's Council Chamber. He was flanked by the important women of the royal family, including Sembiyan Madevi, Vanamadevi, Kundavai and Vanathi. The hesitant Poonkuzlali stood a little away from them. The ministers, commanders and nobles stood respectfully before Sundara Chola. The Pazluvur brothers, Malayaman, Velir, Parthibendran, Aniruddha and Arulmozli were present. Azlvarkkadian stood behind Aniruddha.

Sundara Chola inspected the hall. "I don't see Sambuvaraya ..."

"His son just arrived; they'll be here soon," said Parthibendran.

"Oh! Is Kandamaran back? Has he caught the fugitives?"

"Lord, the madman escaped but Kandamaran killed Vandhiya Devan."

Ambalavan cleared his throat. Everyone turned expectantly towards him but he remained silent.

Sundara Chola said, "I don't know what else my mistake will lead to! I have summoned those who matter most to me and my family. Chief minister, you know my mind. Please speak on my behalf to those assembled here."

Aniruddha faced the gathering. "You are all aware of the emperor's grief. He recently lost his brave son; the prince's death remains a mystery. The emperor did not see his son for three years and ignored the prince's request to stay with him at his golden palace in Kanchipuram. This is the reason: the emperor was in Thanjavur Fort, commanded by Lord Kalaanthaka and the kingdom was buzzing with rumors. In this situation, if the emperor moved from Thanjavur, it would be said that he did not trust the Pazluvur brothers. I'll tell you what the emperor is reluctant to mention: he was broken in body and spirit because you, the Cholas' pillars of support, quarreled among yourselves. Your courage and resolve helped build this glorious empire. Because of your united strength, we recovered Thondaimandalam, annexed the Pandian kingdom and planted the Tiger Flag in Sri Lanka."

Aniruddha continued. "But things have changed in recent years. For some reason, you no longer see eye to eye; you are split into two factions. None of you came out openly about this, but the emperor guessed it is the succession issue which is at the root of your enmity. He decided to settle this matter peacefully after consulting you all and leave for Kanchipuram. He decided to make Gandara Aditya's son the king. He was confident Aditya Karikalan would agree to this and sent for him." He paused. "The emperor was delighted about Karikalan's visit to Kadambur. He thought if Karikalan married Sambuvaraya's daughter, you would all be united once more and the matter of the succession would be easily settled. I thought the same—so did many of you. Lord Malayaman let Karikalan go to Kadambur because he too agreed. But all our hopes were dashed when Karikalan died in Kadambur Palace."

"We must know how that happened," Malayaman said. "Other things can wait."

"Yes, it's pointless to talk about other matters without settling that," echoed Velir.

Aniruddha said, "The emperor prefers not to dig up the past."

Velir declared, "Chola justice is world renowned. Even if a penniless orphan is murdered in this kingdom, his death is investigated and the person responsible is punished. How can we not investigate the murder of the crown prince?"

Sundara Chola sighed. "Uncle, I grieve over my son's death, but I'm against an investigation. I'm certain no one here is responsible. My son's death is a punishment for my sins. Let's not look for further reasons."

"Lord, if you take this stand, it will give the impression that you are trying to shield the murderer. The people are already accusing different men of the crime. The truth must be brought to light. Whoever the murderer is, he must be punished," insisted Kalaanthaka.

"Hear, hear!" applauded Parthibendran. "That's what justice demands. If we do not conduct an impartial trial, the people will lose confidence in our judicial system."

"My elders, why are we wasting time arguing? The guilty person has been punished: I killed Vandhiya Devan, the wicked man who murdered Karikalan and ruined my sister's life, with my spear. What more is there to investigate?" Kandamaran had come in during Aniruddha's speech.

Ambalavan muttered, "Fool! What a son Sambuvaraya has!"

Aniruddha asked, "Kandamaran, did you see Vandhiya Devan when you threw your spear at him? After all, it was night."

"Chief minister, you have always doubted my words. Just because it was night, it doesn't mean I couldn't identify him."

"He's also a warrior. Didn't he fight with you?"

"And you also doubt my courage. I appeal to the emperor: one of the fugitives was the madman; he tried to stop me while the second man made for the opposite shore. I threw my spear at that man and killed him. He has to be Vandhiya Devan."

"Didn't you bring the dead man's corpse?"

"If I knew you would doubt me, I would have searched further along the flooded Vadavar," Kandamaran said. "But I would have missed this council."

"Yes," Kalaanthaka was sarcastic. "If you had missed the council, it would have been a great blow to us all."

Velir asked, "Why are you so interested in capturing Vandhiya Devan?"

"Must you ask me that? The murder took place in my house; if the murderer is caught, no one will suspect my father and me."

Sundara Chola intervened. "My boy, I do not suspect you or your father. Don't I know your father's devotion and loyalty to me? Leave that aside: where's Sambuvaraya?"

"Emperor, it falls on me to tell you about our family's shame. My sister, Manimekalai, heard me telling my father I had killed Vandhiya Devan ... she tried to kill me with her dagger. My father is trying to calm her. He sent a message that he will agree to any decision taken by this council."

Malayaman asked, "Wasn't your sister insisting like a madwoman, 'I killed Karikalan?'"

"Yes, she was trying to save Vandhiya Thevan by taking the blame for his crime. Now she has gone completely mad. It's a tragedy for our family."

"Kandamaran, how are you so sure Vandhiya Devan killed Karikalan?" Aniruddha asked. "Did you see it with your own eyes or did someone who saw it tell you about it?"

"Sir, does one need a mirror to see a wound on one's palm? Vandhiya Devan was the only one near Karikalan's corpse and his guilt was written on his face. What was he doing in Lady Nandini's room? If he was not guilty, why did he escape from the dungeon?" Kandamaran retorted.

Parthibendran spoke up. "I would like to remind this council that the chief minister took on the responsibility of bringing Vandhiya Devan here."

"It's true I accepted the responsibility," Aniruddha said. "But I did not expect Kandamaran to appoint himself judge, deliver a verdict of 'guilty,' and execute the punishment himself. Vandhiya Devan too comes from an ancient clan of warriors; his ancestors once ruled a large kingdom; they had marriage alliances with the Cholas. If a chieftain is accused of murder, it's the emperor who must sit in judgement on him."

Parthibendran came to Kandamaran's defense. "Sir, it's understood that an escaped prisoner can be captured dead or alive."

"But Kandamaran has not captured Vandhiya Devan dead or alive," pointed out Aniruddha. "He has left him in the Vadavar."

All eyes now turned to Sambuvaraya who walked into the room. His face reflected his grief.

Kandamaran went to him and asked in a whisper, "Is Manimekalai better?"

Sambuvaraya's voice was loud and stern. "She's the same. I left your mother to guard her."

Sundara Chola suggested, "Sir, go to your daughter; we can resume our council tomorrow."

"No, lord. It's no use my staying with her. Only one thing can help her: Vandhiya Devan coming back to life."

His listeners were silenced by his pain and bitterness.

Aniruddha continued. "Sir, we are discussing the unfortunate events which took place in your palace. We all understand your pain at the prince being murdered under your roof. The emperor does not hold you responsible in any way. But the truth must be revealed to stop the rumors flying through the kingdom. That is the council's opinion. Do you have anything to say? Kandamaran insists Vandhiya Devan is the murderer: what do you say?"

Sambuvaraya hesitated and looked around. His eyes fell on Kandamaran. "Yes, this fool said the same thing that day. I didn't believe him then and I don't believe him now. I took his advice and invited Prince Karikalan to Kadambur. All this misfortune is the result of that. I and my family have been disgraced forever."

Malayaman was sympathetic. "Sambuvaraya, calm yourself: what has happened has happened. You invited my grandson to your palace with good intentions. No one here blames you for Karikalan's murder. That's why we want to find the truth. You must help us."

"How can I help you?" Sambuvaraya asked. "My son says one thing; my daughter says another. I don't believe either of them. I don't know the truth—I'm groping in the dark. Lord Ambalavan is the one who can help you discover the truth: ask him. He's the root cause of everything. He brought Prince Madurandaka secretly to Kadambur and suggested my daughter marries the prince ... from then, my family has been dogged by misfortune. I hear that Prince Madurandaka himself has vanished. Lord Ambalavan brought Lady Nandini there and arranged for the prince to come from Kanchipuram. He left them both in my palace and went away. Ask him why he went ... ask him where his wife is ..."

Sundara Chola intervened. "Enough! This is why I did not want to dig into the past. Do you want to cause more enmity? You are not responsible for what happened in your palace: that's why I ordered your immediate release from the dungeon. My son's death is punishment for my past sins. You owe me no explanation ... the same goes for Lord Ambalavan."

Ambalavan cleared his throat. "My king, I could not save Aditya Karikalan. As I failed in my duty to protect the Cholas, I must fulfill my oath to cut off my own head. Before that, I must reveal the truth; otherwise, doubts and accusations will multiply."

There was pin-drop silence in the room and the listeners' hearts melted.

Sundara Chola was flustered. "Uncle, think! Why do you want to talk about the past? The dead will not come back to life. You would never intentionally harm the Cholas ..."

"Sir, I must talk about the past. I must tell you how I was ready to betray the Cholas. Durga, the patron goddess of your clan and mine, stopped me. Please be compassionate and listen to me."

Realizing that he could not stop Ambalavan, Sundara Chola sat back on his throne.

Ambalavan made a clean breast of everything that took place over the last three years: he met Nandini on the roadside and lusted after her; he ignored Kalaanthaka's warnings; at her instigation, he conspired to make Madurandaka king; he took Madurandaka to Kadambur Palace in Nandini's screened palanquin and held a midnight meeting with his fellow conspirators; he became suspicious about Nandini because of Vandhiya Devan, but his mind went blank whenever Nandini was with him; finally, he overheard the Pandian conspirators' plans; he hurried back to Kadambur; on the way, he disguised himself as a Kalamukha; with Idumbankari's support, he used the secret passage to reach the women's quarters; he hid in the Music Room; he overheard the conversation between Nandini and Karikalan; in his excitement, he faltered—by then the prince had dropped down dead; the lamp went out as he leaped to hold the prince; he was surrounded and attacked by many men; he lost consciousness; when he came to, he found himself in a cave in the Pachai Hills.

"Lord," Ambalavan said. "I'm guilty of betraying the Cholas. I let the Pandian conspirators use my palace and let them take treasure from our vault to finance their plots. They planned to kill you and your two sons. A deaf-mute woman gave her life to save you and Prince Arulmozli was saved by an elephant, but I failed to save Aditya Karikalan. From beginning to end, I'm the cause of his death." He paused. "I will now fulfill the vow I took before Goddess Durga ..." Ambalavan drew his sword and raised it ...

Everyone was frozen in shock. But Arulmozli, who had quietly inched his way to Ambalavan's side, leaped forward and gripped Ambalavan's sword hand.

"Sir," Arulmozli said. "Wait! By tradition, it is someone from the Pazluvur clan who crowns the Chola emperor. It's you who must crown me: after that, you may do as you like."

The Vadavar Changes its Course

EVERY MAN IN that room believed in his heart that Arulmozli was worthy of ascending the Tiger Throne and was the rightful heir. They were aware of his charisma and public popularity. But for reasons of their own, no one had openly announced his support for Arulmozli. Now that Arulmozli himself had come forward and staked his claim to the throne, everyone was delighted –and relieved that it had not fallen on them to voice their opinion.

Ambalavan was moved to tears by Arulmozli's gesture. He controlled his feelings and said, "Prince Arulmozli, I wanted to ask you to be king but kept quiet because I had betrayed the Cholas and no longer had the right to advice you. Gandara Aditya insisted that Sundara Chola's sons were to succeed their father to the Tiger Throne. We treacherously plotted to make Madurandaka king: what a disaster that would have been! Prince, you are your father's rightful heir and the one worthy of wearing the Chola crown. When you were a child, I carried you on my shoulders and celebrated the auspicious lines on your palms, telling you, 'You will rule the earth!' Over the last three years, lust made me a traitor. I'm not worthy of placing the crown on your head. I must kill myself and atone for my sins."

The Council Chamber echoed with cries of, "No! No!"

Sundara Chola said in an emotion-filled voice, "What's all this? You have not betrayed the Cholas. Thinking of making my cousin the emperor was not a betrayal. My cousin has a stronger claim to the throne than my son. Even now, if you'll let me speak my mind ..."

Aniruddha interrupted him. "Lord, the country echoes with cries of, 'Make Prince Arulmozli king!' Gandara Aditya's son is also determined about this and now, Prince Arulmozli has taken the same stand. It's useless to discuss this any further."

"I'll never agree to anything else," Chendan Amudhan insisted.

"My son is right: there's no need for further discussion," Sembiyan Madevi added.

Sundara Chola said, "Mother, no one can defy you. God's will be done! But Lord Ambalavan did not betray the Cholas: he must not take his own life."

Ambalavan cleared his throat. "Lord, if I had succeeded in my conspiracy, it would have been a disaster for the Cholas. I wanted to die without revealing this secret; I did not want to hurt my brother, Kalaanthaka, who holds the welfare of the Cholas above all else. But now, I'll harden my heart and tell you the truth: the man we thought was Gandara Aditya's son is actually the son of King Veerapandian, the Cholas' arch-enemy."

"Aiyo!" "No!" "Impossible!" rang through the room.

"You will find this hard to believe. I would not have believed it myself if I had not heard it with my own ears. The woman who bewitched me, the woman I married three years ago ... she's Veerapandian's daughter. I heard her tell Karikalan this. She came to Pazluvur Palace only to wait for the opportunity to avenge her father's death. That wicked woman and her accomplices planned to kill Karikalan and make Veerapandian's son king. By Goddess Durga's grace, this disaster was averted. Durga sent Vandhiya Devan to open my eyes. There's more I need to know from him, but that idiot, Kandamaran, killed him and threw him into the flood."

While the others stood stunned and speechless, Kandamaran spoke up. "Anyway, Vandhiya Devan was the murderers' accomplice: so, I was right to kill him."

Ambalavan turned angrily on him, but Aniruddha intervened. "Sir, he says he killed Vandhiya Devan—but how does he know for sure?"

Parthibendran was sarcastic. "Maybe we'll know the truth if the Vadavar changes its course and brings us Vandhiya Devan's corpse."

The next instant, Vandhiya Devan walked into the room: his clothes were soaking wet and water dripped on the floor. With his horror-struck expression and disheveled appearance, he looked like the reanimated corpse of a drowned man.

Aniruddha cried, "The Vadavar has changed its course and brought us Vandhiya Devan!"

Devan was depressed after the others left. He who dreamt of impressing the world with his courage, hated being an object of pity. He found this cell in the women's quarters crueler than the dungeon. Through Arulmozli's intercession, he might be absolved from the accusation of murder and escape punishment, but suspicions would linger. They would all look down on him as a tainted man. Kundavai would feel pity and compassion for him, but nothing more. He could not dream of marrying her. And who knew how long Arulmozli's affection would last?

If only I had galloped away on a horse from Amudhan's house! By now, I would be in Kodikkarai, or even in Sri Lanka. Who were the two riders? One was Karuthiruman—who was the second man? Could it have been the former Madurandaka? Yes, there's some significance in their escaping together. How surprised everyone will be if they know the truth about Madurandaka. If they reach Lanka safely, what will happen? Madurandaka will recover the Pandian crown jewels which are his by right. With Mahinda's help, he'll fight to recover his kingdom. I'm the only one who can stop him. What's the point of living in hiding like this?

Deep in thought, Devan paced the room. He stopped often to look out from the window. He was in a corner room in the upper floor of the palace. The Vadavar flowed along the palace's outer wall which, at this point, was also the outer wall of the fort. If he jumped out of the window, he would fall into the river. Or, he could carefully climb down the wall. Maybe there was a way to the river from the ground floor for the women to bathe ....

Suddenly, something caught Devan's attention: a woman with uncombed hair was running wildly around the garden of the adjoining palace. *That's Lord Ambalavan's palace garden. Who's that girl? My god! It's Manimekalai! What's wrong with her? Why is she running like a madwoman?* Two old women ran behind Manimekalai, trying to catch her. But Manimekalai left them far behind. She reached the fort wall and swung herself up by a low-hanging tree branch. *Aiyo! What's she doing? Is that a dagger glinting in her hand? Oh my god! She's jumped headlong into the river ...*

Devan climbed out of the window and plunged into the river. He surfaced, gasped for breath and looked around. Near him was a pavilion with steps to the river; a door connected this pavilion to the palace's women's quarters. Manimekalai had jumped into the flood a little distance from him. Luckily, the current was flowing against Devan and would soon carry Manimekalai to him. Devan struggled to the shore and walked quickly towards her.

Ah, there's Manimekalai! Is she alive or is that her corpse floating in the river? Aiyo! Must I again suffer the agony of carrying the dead body of a loved one in my arms? How much she loves me! Let this innocent girl live ... I'll visit every temple in this kingdom and give thanks. He leaped into the flood, lifted Manimekalai into his arms and carried her to the pavilion.

Devan, who had recently been at death's door, was weakened further by the shock of his sudden leap into the river. He panted under the weight of Manimekalai's drenched body. Unable to walk any further, Devan laid her on the wide top step of the pavilion. She was still alive, but she needed help urgently. Devan saw the door leading into the palace. Using all his remaining strength, he dashed against the door. Luckily the inner bolt shifted and the door opened. He ran down narrow passages which widened into terraces and courtyards. "Anybody here?" Devan shouted as he ran. "A girl's life is in danger!"

Two soldiers standing guard at the entrance to a large hall tried to stop him. Devan pushed them aside and ran in, only to stop short at the sight of the emperor seated on a throne with people gathered before him. Devan recovered at the sight of Poonkuzlali and cried, "Ocean Princess, help! Manimekalai has jumped into the river: come save her at once."

The Mighty Tree Falls

VANDHIYA DEVAN ENTERED the Council Chamber through the door from the women's quarters. Poonkuzlali, who stood a little behind the other women, turned at a sound and was shocked to see the drenched and disheveled Devan walk in. Along with Kundavai and Vanathi, she listened to Devan's account of what had happened to Manimekalai. The three women hurried through the door he had used, guessing from his drenched clothes that he had come from the river pavilion.

Devan's words were not clearly heard by the others in the room. Most of them only heard him say, 'Help!' Kandamaran and Parthibendran did not hear anything. They first thought that the strange figure which had walked in from the women's quarters was Devan's ghost: it was commonly believed that the spirits of those who died untimely deaths haunted the world. This belief was reinforced by Devan's drenched figure appearing just when Aniruddha announced, 'The Vadavar has changed its course!' But they snapped out of their trance when two soldiers came running and caught Devan.

"Lord, pardon us," one of the soldiers said. "This madman came running from the river gate. We couldn't stop him."

As they tried to drag Devan away, Parthiban burned with rage. *Why does he refuse to die? Obviously, he has barged in here by accident. This time, I won't let him get away.* Forgetting that he was in the emperor's court, Parthibendran leaped forward, gripped Devan by the shoulder and cried, "He's not a madman, he's the traitor who killed Karikalan!" He gestured to the soldiers to move back. Kandamaran caught Devan by the other shoulder. The two men dragged Devan before the emperor on his throne.

Sundara Chola looked Devan up and down. "Are you accusing this innocent-looking man of murder? I can't believe it. Isn't he the man who brought me a message from Karikalan?"

"Yes, sir. He's the man who brought the message; he's also the man who spoke secretly with Nandini in her screened palanquin outside Thanjavur Fort; he's the one who later escaped from the fort and now from the dungeon," Kalaanthaka said.

"He's the one who stabbed me in the back before he escaped," added Kandamaran.

Aniruddha spoke up. "Why, my dear fellow! And isn't this the man you said you had killed?"

"How was I to know you would help this murderer and bring him back to life?" Kandamaran retorted.

Arulmozli had remained silent. He was angry with Devan, assuming that he had tried to escape by jumping into the river and had landed up in this mess because of his poor swimming skills. At Kandamaran's words, Arulmozli walked forward majestically and stood by Devan. "Father, Vandhiya Devan is my dearest friend. He saved my life in Lanka and in the sea. I'm glad he's alive. Anyone who accuses him, accuses me too!" Arulmozli's tone silenced the room.

Aniruddha broke the silence. "Prince, please think. The man whom Kandamaran claims to have killed with his spear has somehow survived and landed up here. He has already been accused. Wouldn't it be better if he was questioned?"

Parthibendran said, "Sir, you are the next Chola emperor. You have the right to punish or pardon anyone. But is it fair to do away with a trial? It will only give rise to useless speculation."

Kandamaran said, "Our prince must also consider another point: we must not give further cause for the rumor that Prince Arulmozli used Vandhiya Devan to kill his brother, Prince Karikalan."

In the stunned silence, Sambuvaraya walked up to his son and gave him a resounding slap across his face. "Fool! You'll destroy our ancient clan. Have you no sense of time and place?"

Kandamaran glared at his father and his lips twitched in fury. Before he could say or do anything, Ambalavan stepped forward and held Sambuvaraya. Ambalavan cleared his throat. "Sambuvaraya, your son has made up for his foolishness by doing the Cholas a great favor.

When you know the truth, you'll be proud to be his father. Patience!" Ambalavan took Sambuvaraya firmly by the hand and led him a little distance away from the others.

Aniruddha said, "Sir, please allow my disciple, Thirumalai, to say a few words."

Azlvarkkadian stepped forward. "Lords, Vandhiya Devan did not escape on horseback. He was seriously wounded while saving our new Prince Madurandaka from an assassin. I brought him into the fort in a screened palanquin. It's impossible for Kandamaran to have thrown his spear at him."

"I guessed the same," Ambalavan said. "Sambuvaraya, forgive your son: the man he killed has to be Veerapandian's son. After all, the former Madurandaka went missing on that evening, isn't it? He has to be the man who tried to escape."

Ambalavan continued before his listeners could recover from their shock. "Emperor, please listen to my last words. The comet vanished after working its evil: the brave Aditya Karikalan died. But fortune will shine on the Chola empire your ancestors and mine gave their lives for; it will endure for ages; it will grow in size and strength. The Cholas have evaded a great disaster, mainly because of Vandhiya Devan. It was he who opened my eyes which were veiled by lust. He happened to come to Kadambur Palace on the night of our secret meeting. On that day, he made me ashamed of being involved in something which I had to hide from a young man. Then, my brother told me Vandhiya Devan had spoken to Nandini outside Thanjavur Fort and she had helped him escape from the fort. This sowed the seed of suspicion in my heart. I began to think about the things happening around me and their cause. Finally, by Goddess Durga's grace, I overheard the Pandian conspirators. After that, your beloved daughter, Kundavai, confused me: she said Nandini was her sister and begged me not to harm her. I feared Kundavai too had been fooled."

Ambalavan continued. "To my disgrace, I let Nandini sow the seeds of greed and betrayal in my heart: she urged me to become emperor. The Kalamukha's, who had selected me to be their leader, fanned the flames of my ambition. They suggested that after crowning Madurandaka, I should push him aside and make myself emperor. I disguised myself as a Kalamukha and went to Kadambur. One of the Kalamukhas, Idumbankari, was a servant in Kadambur Palace; he was also an accomplice of the Pandian conspirators. I frightened him and learned that, at that time, the Pandians were waiting in the Hunters' Hall, Karikalan was in Nandini's room and Vandhiya Devan and Manimekalai were hiding there. I was hungry to know the truth about Nandini. Coming to know about the secret passage to the Music Room which adjoined Nandini's room, I hid there. I heard the truth about Nandini from her own mouth. I saw that Karikalan was an honorable man. I understood how Nandini and her Pandian accomplices had hatched their wicked plot to avenge Veerapandian's death. I tried to foil their plans, but I could not defeat destiny. It was my fate to see Karikalan fall down dead before my eyes …"

Ambalavan covered his eyes with his hands and sobbed: the sound was like stormy waves crashing on the shore. No one dared say a word; his listeners' hearts melted at the old man's grief.

Ambalavan controlled his sobs and looked around. "Karikalan was destined to die, but, at the same time, by Durga's grace, Prince Arulmozli's wisdom triumphed over destiny. My lord, my dear friends, crown Arulmozli emperor: this kingdom will reach great heights under him."

Aniruddha replied, "Sir, your wish will come true. Prince Arulmozli himself has agreed to ascend the Tiger Throne. But you have not told us how Karikalan died."

Ambalavan's voice shook. "Why do you want to know? What does it matter whose hand wielded the knife? It was truly a quirk of fate."

"If the truth is not revealed, Vandhiya Devan stands accused of murder and may be punished," Aniruddha pointed out.

"Who accuses him?" Ambalavan asked.

"Kandamaran and Parthibendran."

"Idiots!" scolded Ambalavan. "Kandamaran and Parthibendran, on what basis do you accuse this young man of murdering Karikalan?"

Aniruddha replied. "He was hiding in Nandini's room at that time. Manimekalai was also there and claims to have killed Karikalan. This is incredible as there was no blood on her knife. It's clear she's trying to shield Vandhiya Devan—she may have seen Vandhiya Devan kill Karikalan from his hiding place."

"If Manimekalai did not kill Karikalan, how could Vandhiya Devan have killed him? What weapon did he use?"

"He used this sharp, twisted-blade dagger stained with dry blood." Parthibendran displayed the dagger he had picked up and kept carefully when Devan lost consciousness.

Ambalavan went up to him and took the dagger from him. He examined it intently and murmured, "This is Idumbankari's dagger. Kandamaran and Parthibendran, like me, you two also fell under Nandini's spell; only Vandhiya Devan was immune to her charms. He did not throw this knife ... he did not kill Karikalan."

Aniruddha asked, "How can you be so sure about that?"

"Because I know who threw the dagger and killed Karikalan," Ambalavan declared.

"Who? Who killed him?"

"Yes, I must tell you. This young man was hiding in the Music Room when I climbed down into the room. I did not want him to see me and sound the alarm so, I crept up behind him and strangled him. He fell unconscious and there's no way he could have seen who killed Karikalan. I'm the one who borrowed this dagger from Idumbankari; I'm the one who threw it ... with the hand which has crowned Chola emperors. But I did not throw the dagger at Karikalan: I threw it at Nandini; I threw it at that witch who bewitched me and made me a traitor .... but I missed my mark and killed Karikalan instead!"

Cries of shock and lamentation filled the room.

"I have ruined hundred years of service to the Cholas. I don't know how I'll remove this stain on my family's honor."

"*Anna*, I'll redeem our family's honor!" Kalaanthaka roared and walked up to his brother, knife in hand. "We have both sworn an oath to take revenge on anyone who betrays the Cholas. I'll kill you right now and wipe out our family's shame." Kalaanthaka raised his knife.

"Stop! No bloodshed here!" cried Sundara Chola.

Arulmozli and Aniruddha leaped forward and held Kalaanthaka's hand.

Ambalavan said, "*Thambi*, I won't burden you with the task of redeeming our family's honor. I won't let you become the man who killed his own brother. I'll fulfill my oath to Durga myself!" Ambalavan raised the twisted-blade dagger he had taken from Parthibendran …

Everyone was caught unawares as Ambalavan had earlier sheathed his sword and no one had expected him to use the dagger. Arulmozli leaped forward with a cry of, "No!" but he was too late: Ambalavan crashed to the ground like a mighty tree. The room filled with shouts as some rushed to the fallen Ambalavan and others ran to Sundara Chola who lay back on his throne with closed eyes.

The Council Chamber emptied.

That night, as Ambalavan battled for his life, a steady stream of visitors came to his palace. Sundara Chola, Aniruddha, Arulmozli and Kundavai were among them. The four concealed themselves in the room where Ambalavan lay. A little later, Kalaanthaka came in with Azlvarkkadian and sat before Ambalavan.

Ambalavan's fading eyes fell on Azlvarkkadian. "Vaishnava, what are you doing here?"

"I bring news from my adopted sister, Nandini," Azlvarkkadian replied. "Nandini asked me to thank you for taking the blame for killing Karikalan and shielding her. She says she will eternally remember your love for her."

"Ah! Let her keep her illusions and be happy. Although she betrayed and harmed me, I can't forget her. Who knows, she may come looking for me in my next birth." Ambalavan's deathly pale face became animated. "I must tell someone the truth. The knife I threw did not strike the prince: he had already fallen. I took the blame not only to shield Nandini but for a more important reason. Come closer, I'll tell you. Your friend, Vandhiya Devan, is an extraordinary man: the Cholas are indebted to him and Princess Kundavai loves him. I hated the princess for no reason … I atoned for this by taking the blame for the murder and killing myself. If I did not do this, someone or the other would keep casting doubts on Vandhiya Devan. Now, no one will dare say a word against him. Vaishnava, tell the princess I'm sorry for hating her."

Ambalavan panted. Azlvarkkadian's heart melted while tears streamed down Kundavai's face. "Vaishnava, one more thing: tell Aniruddha we must recover the Pandian crown jewels. Vandhiya Devan is the best man for this task. Go with him. Bring the heirlooms and crown Prince Arulmozli in Madurai, understand? And I have a request for Arulmozli: don't blame my brother for my sins. Tell him there can be no greater friend to the Cholas than Kalaanthaka. Goddess Durga! I have fulfilled my oath ... I'm coming ... bless the Cholas!"

Ambalavan's voice weakened and finally faded. The heroic old man was dead.

Parting of Friends

ARULMOZLI, VANDHIYA DEVAN, Kandamaran and Parthibendran galloped to the Kollidam and dismounted at the ferry.

"Kandamaran," Arulmozli teased. "Are you still angry with your old friend?"

"Sir, I only regret my own foolishness. Vandhiya Devan forgave me for having wronged him and offered to be my friend again. How can I ever repay him for saving my sister from the river? If only I had let Manimekalai marry him in the beginning, she would not be mad now."

Arulmozli said, "It's just the shock of falling into the river: given time, her mind will clear."

"Her mind is clear in every other way—the only two people she does not recognize are Vandhiya Devan and me. My heart breaks when I think how much she once loved me. She cries, 'Aiyo! I killed my beloved brother with my own hand!'"

"But why does she say that? After all, you're alive."

"And I wish I was dead," Kandamaran said sadly. "She believes that I killed Vandhiya Devan and that she killed me in revenge. Sometimes she laments over me; sometimes she cries over him. I can't convince her I'm her brother ... and if she sees Vandhiya Devan, she asks, 'Who are you? Have you seen Vandhiya Devan?'"

Arulmozli noticed the tears in Devan's eyes.

Parthibendran said, "What a pity Manimekalai will never know that Vandhiya Devan is now a king,"

Kandamaran looked questioningly at Arulmozli who smiled. "The emperor has decided to return Vallam to your friend and make him its king. He has also decided to create a kingdom from the area adjoining Vallam and make you its king. You'll be neighbors; you must not let anything spoil your friendship."

"The emperor's mercy is boundless! Does this mean I don't have to go back to Kadambur?"

"Kadambur will bring back painful memories. Build a new palace on the northern bank of the Palar. Once your sister has recovered, she can join you there," said Arulmozli.

"I don't think Manimekalai will come back to us. Sembiyan Madevi plans to take her along on her pilgrimage. Manimekalai is very fond of the queen. She has gone to Thiruvaiyaru with her today."

"Yes, they have gone as a group with the newly married Chendan Amudhan and Poonkuzlali."

"What a simple wedding that was!" Parthibendran exclaimed.

"My coronation too will be a simple affair," said Arulmozli.

Kandamaran complained, "There's talk in Thanjavur that your coronation will be held in January, but you are sending me and Parthibendran north at this time. Vandhiya Devan is lucky …"

"Nothing of the sort," Arulmozli said. "I'll soon be sending Vandhiya Devan to Sri Lanka. My friends, believe me, my coronation won't take place without you."

"When the date is fixed, send a fast rider to us with a message and we'll return immediately."

"The Chola empire must reach new heights in our time: our victorious armies must plant the Tiger Flag on the banks of the Ganga and across the sea in Srivijaya. We must capture the Western Ghats and the Lakshadweep islands. Sri Lanka must be ours. We must build temples greater than the ones there. Generations to come must be awed by our legacy. Friends, I'll make my dreams come true with your help. Parthibendran, you are the supreme commander of our northern forces. Our enemies are waiting to exploit my brother's death: our army must stand like an iron fort on the northern bank of the Pennai. Make the necessary arrangements, leave Kandamaran there as commander and go to Kanchipuram to prepare the golden palace for my father."

Kandamaran's eyes filled with tears. "Sir, I have not yet proved myself on the battlefield, but you have appointed me commander ... am I worthy of your confidence?"

"My friend, by god's grace I have the gift of discerning the best man for a task. I have made Vandhiya Devan commander of our Sri Lankan army. I have full confidence in both of you."

"Yes, it's a good idea to keep one of them in the north and the other in the south for some time," Parthibendran smiled. "If they are together somewhere without you, they may fight again."

"That will never happen!" Kandamaran protested.

Without a word, Devan held out his arms and embraced Kandamaran; the friends shed tears. Parthibendran and Kandamaran climbed into a boat and set out, while Arulmozli and Devan turned their horses back towards Thanjavur.

A Meeting on the Road

SUNDARA CHOLA GRIEVED over the deaths of Karikalan, Mandakini and Ambalavan. But he was consoled by the fact that the succession was settled with the chieftains and the people supporting Arulmozli. The emperor decided to hold Arulmozli's coronation as a simple affair in mid-January and spend the rest of his life in Karikalan's golden palace in Kanchipuram. The news that Arulmozli would soon be crowned spread like wildfire through the kingdom. To stop the people from making a big celebration out of it, Arulmozli decided to avoid the public until the coronation. Devan and he now stayed away from the highway and rode along the Kudamurutti, taking in the beauty of the Chola kingdom's rivers, groves and fields.

Arulmozli said, "My friend, can there be a more beautiful land than this in the whole world?"

"Sir, I wonder whether you are sending me to Lanka to make me a commander or to exile me from the Chola kingdom. Nowadays, you have one thing in mind but say something else. Your coronation is scheduled for mid-January, but you told Parthibendran and Kandamaran, 'I won't hold my coronation without you.'"

Arulmozli smiled. "After becoming your friend, I have learnt spells and tricks."

"You are a past master at that! What can be more magical than the charm you whispered into the elephant's ear? Who can match the mahout disguise with which you tricked the world?"

"My friend, don't you want to go to Lanka?"

"Who says so?" Devan replied. "The further away I am from kings, the better. If I'm far away, I won't lose the friendship of kings."

"You're going to be disappointed … I plan to join you in Sri Lanka. I plan to take you with me to the islands across the seas. My only regret is we can't take Poonkuzlali with us."

"Sir, you leant spells and tricks from me and I learnt to speak the truth from you. Can I now be frank with you?"

"Of course."

"You are taking the Chola kingdom from my friend, Chendan Amudhan. This can be justified: you have public support. But if you take Poonkuzlali from him, there can be no greater betrayal than that. Please remember she's now Madurandaka's wife."

Arulmozli laughed. "You will make me out to be a villain! You are right to talk on your friend's behalf, but what about Poonkuzlali? Did she marry Madurandaka wholeheartedly?"

"No one can force Poonkuzlali to do something against her wishes. I was lucky to see the deep love Poonkuzlali has for Amudhan. I have seen such love only in one other woman."

"And who is that?"

"Lady Vanathi, of course. Who else?" Devan replied.

"You heartless demon! A girl came forward to give her life for you and went mad. Doesn't her love mean anything to you?" Arulmozli demanded angrily.

Devan was silent. Then, "Sir, you are twisting the facts. I pity Manimekalai and grieve for her. But it was her brother, Kandamaran, who made her mad, not I. Anyway, both of us are now dead to her: so, what's the point of talking about it?"

Arulmozli began, "I'm sorry for losing my temper …" and paused. "My sister thinks if you stay away for some time, Manimekalai may recognize you."

"Now I know Princess Kundavai is more eager than you to send me far away." Devan pointed ahead. "There comes the very person we are talking about."

The two friends had reached the highway. A palanquin escorted by soldiers came towards them. In it were Kundavai and Vanathi. On seeing the two riders, the women's eyes widened in surprise and their faces glowed with happiness.

The Earth's Lover

ARULMOZLI RODE UP to the palanquin. Vandhiya Devan reined in his horse a little distance away and declared, "I must be careful: the princess's wicked palanquin may bang into my poor horse!" This was the same place where, six months ago, he had banged into Nandini's palanquin and said, 'the palanquin banged into my horse.'

Kundavai controlled her laughter. "*Thambi,* you must be discussing some good news: both your faces are so happy."

"Yes, *akka*. But it won't make your friend, Vanathi, happy. My wedding day is coming, isn't it? We were glad to see the woman I love and am going to marry; we were discussing her beauty."

Both the women's faces fell. Vanathi bowed her head.

Kundavai was furious. "Aren't you ashamed to talk like this? What pleasure do you get out of hurting this girl? Which girl did you see? What's her name? Where's she from?"

Devan intervened. "Lady, we were admiring the Chola kingdom. The prince will soon be crowned king of this beautiful land: he's referring to his love for his country."

"Ahah!" said Kundavai. "My brother did not talk in riddles before; he must have picked it up from you."

Arulmozli laughed. "My friend, you deserve this. Didn't I tell you I learnt tricks and intrigue from you? See, my sister feels the same."

"Brother and sister are ganging up to make false accusations against me," Devan replied.

"*Thambi*," said Kundavai. "I have not yet released him from his duty: there are some things he must do for me in Lanka."

Arulmozli smiled. "Don't ever release him, *akka*. I'm okay with you giving him a life sentence."

"I'll see you before I leave, lady," Devan said.

"You must come to Pazlayarai. We are going to join Sembiyan Madevi and the others at the Thiruvaiyaru temple and from there, we're going straight to Pazlayarai."

"What?!" exclaimed Arulmozli. "Aren't you staying for my coronation?"

"What do Vanathi and I have to do with your coronation?"

"There will be no coronation without you!" Arulmozli declared.

"Why not? The astrologer who fixed the date is a renowned man," Kundavai pointed out.

"*Akka*, I do not believe in astrology and horoscopes," Arulmozli said. "Every day on which one does one's duty is an auspicious day; idle days are bad days."

"May all the days of your life be such auspicious days, *thambi*," Kundavai blessed him.

"*Akka*, you're encouraging Vanathi to be obstinate. She thinks if she refuses to sit beside me on the Tiger Throne the world will come to a standstill. Don't blame me if some other woman takes her place."

"I have never blamed him for anything," Vanathi retorted.

"Vanathi, those who are hungry to rule are deaf to everything else," Kundavai said.

"Don't forget you are the one who made me hungry to rule," Arulmozli pointed out. "Even you, a woman, often said you loved this land so much, you would never marry and leave it."

"You were deaf to my words then. You said there are many more beautiful lands in the world. It is this Vallam warrior who has fueled your hunger for the throne."

"My god!" exclaimed Devan. "Must I be blamed for this too?!"

Kundavai turned to Arulmozli. "*Thambi*, it's getting late. We'll be on our way." She signaled to the palanquin bearers and the company set off.

Arulmozli looked after the palanquin for some time and then continued towards Thanjavur. After a while, he turned to Devan and said, "My friend, I don't think the women are going to the temple. The Kudanthai astrologer has moved to a place near Thiruvaiyaru after the flood washed away his house. They are going to see him."

"Sir, you seem to be better than the astrologer at making predictions." laughed Devan.

A Child Will Be Born

ARULMOZLI WAS RIGHT. Kundavai and Vanathi left the palanquin and escort at the Thiruvaiyaru palace and told the guards that they were going to the temple to join Sembiyan Madevi and her family. Taking just one soldier with them, they went to the Kudanthai astrologer's house on the outskirts of the town.

Kundavai had reason to be happy: Sundara Chola's health had improved and Arulmozli was to finally ascend the Tiger Throne. Yet, she was troubled. Kundavai wavered between belief and doubt about astrology but whenever she was worried, she was drawn towards the astrologer.

As they crossed the threshold, the astrologer hurried into the room, alerted by the sound of their anklets. "Welcome, my ladies," he said. "My hut is blessed by your presence."

Kundavai sighed. "I feel like first asking whether there's any truth in astrology."

"What do I say to that? For those who believe, astrology is true; for others it's a lie."

Kundavai said, "Astrology let me down. You did not predict my brother's death."

"Even if I had known, could I have said it openly? I would have been accused of being an accomplice of the Pandian conspirators. In the case of royalty, we can only make general predictions: the planetary alignment is bad ... there's danger ..."

"Even if you had predicted his death, you could not have prevented it."

"How could I? Only god can change the dictates of destiny."

"In that case, what's the point of astrology?"

"How can you say this? How will a poor man like me earn a living?" Kundavai burst into laughter and Vanathi smiled.

The astrologer continued. "You are judging me by what I left unsaid: judge me by what I said. Didn't I read Prince Arulmozli's horoscope? And now, the date of his coronation approaches."

"Lady Vanathi's stupid stubbornness has taken the joy out of the occasion for me. Do you remember her oath?"

"What oath? So many disasters happened that day, I don't remember anything clearly."

"Just because Poonkuzlali said something out of jealousy, Vanathi swore she would never sit on the throne as long as she lived .... as if one can sit on a throne after one is dead!" Kundavai said sarcastically. "Do you remember what you said about her?"

"The Ponni carried away my collection of royal horoscopes, but Lady Vanathi's horoscope is engraved in my mind. I see the lines of her palm ... the man who marries her will be marrying the Goddess of Wealth and the Earth Goddess in one. Her son will plant the flag of victory wherever he goes ..." The astrologer suddenly sat up straight and spoke like one possessed. "On this very day in the near future, a child will be born who will take the Chola empire to glorious new heights. I may not be alive to see this, but you will live long and rejoice over it."

The Chinese Merchants

KUNDAVAI WAS NOT completely convinced by the astrologer's predictions; Vanathi, on the other hand, was angry. "*Akka*, this man is an expert in flattery. Let's go."

"Lady, my words will come true one day. At that time, don't forget this poor man."

Kundavai said, "She rejoices in her heart, but she's furious because she thoughtlessly took an oath."

Velir had met Kundavai the previous day and said, "Lady, I'm leaving for Kodumbalur. Can I take my niece, Vanathi, with me?"

The startled Kundavai asked, "Uncle, what's the hurry? Aren't you staying for the coronation?"

"I'll be back for the coronation. By god's grace, Prince Arulmozli has agreed to ascend the throne and the chieftains all agree. There's no need for my army. Feeding and housing the men is a drain on the Thanjavur merchant guilds. So, I must go and disperse my men."

"But why must you take my friend, Vanathi?"

"Lady, we chieftains met yesterday and came to a decision. Your great-grandfather, Emperor Paranthaka, married six women, one from each of the important clans. Because of this, there was no rivalry among the chieftains during his reign. Your grandfather too had many wives. But your father married only your mother, Malayaman's daughter. This has led to jealousy and conflict among us. We have decided that all future Chola kings must marry several women from different clans. We plan to place our request before Prince Arulmozli after his coronation. If I leave Vanathi behind now, the other chieftains will think I'm working against the consensus."

Kundavai controlled her anger. "Uncle, have you forgotten you once asked me to be both mother and father to your orphaned niece? I can't part with her. If you want, I'll take Vanathi with me to Pazlayarai. We won't even attend the coronation. Let's not talk about marriage now. Tell Arulmozli about it after the coronation and we'll see how it goes."

Velir agreed and left. Kundavai had come to consult the astrologer about Arulmozli's marriage.

Vanathi was immersed in her own thoughts. *How I wish he was a mahout, or an ordinary warrior. It's because he's a prince that people see me as a schemer who wants to be empress …*

A cry came from the door: "Silks! Chinese silks!"

The astrologer's disciple came in and said, "*Swami*, two Chinese men are here to see you. Shall I tell them to come back tomorrow?"

"No," said Kundavai. "Let them come; we're leaving."

As Kundavai and Vanathi left, they saw an elephant with two Chinese merchants and sacks on its back. The merchants were discussing something with the mahout who stood on the ground. The women did not pay much attention; they summoned their guard and went back to the palace.

Are They Spies?

THE THIRUVAIYARU TEMPLE festival was held that evening. Elephants, camels and huge bulls led the procession, carrying drums. They were followed by flag bearers holding ensigns with holy symbols; behind them walked musicians and dancers; then came the gods in their temple cars; singers brought up the rear. Crowds of people thronged the procession.

Kundavai, Vanathi and Poonkuzlali watched the procession from the palace terrace. They saw an elephant; the two Chinese merchants on its back often got down and mingled with the crowd.

Are they really merchants? Kundavai wondered. *Or are they foreign spies?* News of the recent chaos and conflict in the Chola kingdom had spread. Maybe some enemy kings had sent their spies, disguised as Chinese merchants, to gather information.

Hearing Kundavai and Vanathi discussing this, Poonkuzlali said, "Lady, these merchants were at the temple entrance this morning. I asked them to come to the palace in case you were interested in buying Chinese silk. They will probably come—you can ask them your doubts in person."

Sembiyan Madevi and Madurandaka returned from the procession and joined the women on the terrace. Madurandaka and Poonkuzlali moved their listeners to tears with a *Thevaram* hymn and Sembiyan Madevi then narrated some incidents from Saint Appar's life.

A guard came to say, "Two Chinese merchants are at the gate. They insist on seeing the ladies."

The indignant Kundavai said, "What insolence! Send them away."

Poonkuzlali intervened. "Lady, pardon me. I asked them to come."

"In that case, let them in," Kundavai said.

The two merchants came with their cloth sacks.

Coronation Gifts

THE CHINESE MEN wore large turbans and had thick beards and mustaches. Their features were vague in the dim light of the torches on the terrace. It was difficult to even guess their ages. Kundavai's suspicions increased. She instructed the guard, "This light is too dim to see the silks–bring a large torch."

"I'll go and send a good lamp," Madurandaka said and left with Sembiyan Madevi.

Kundavai turned to the merchants. "What's the hurry? Couldn't you show us your silks in the morning? Why come here at night?"

One merchant said, "Pardon us, princess. We have been in Thanjavur for several days but could not meet you. Our ship leaves from Nagapattinam in two days. That's why we are in a hurry."

Although his voice was rather strange, they were amazed by his fluent Tamil. "Chinese merchant," Kundavai said. "You speak Tamil very well."

"I have been doing business in the Chola country for some time," the man replied. "I like Tamil and Tamil Nadu."

"Then why are you in such a hurry to leave? Why don't you stay until the coronation?"

"If we miss this ship, we don't know when the next one will come. There are very few ships sailing from Nagapattinam these days. Sea routes are no longer safe. Ferocious Arab fighters roam the seas. They lie in wait along the coast; when they see a merchant vessel, they pounce on it, kill everyone on board and plunder the cargo. Now, ships are forced to sail in convoys of ten and twenty. We can't afford to miss our ship. Ladies, be kind and look at our silks." The two men began to untie their sacks of merchandise.

Kundavai stopped them. "There's no point in displaying your silks to us now. We can't judge their quality in the dark. And we have not brought money to pay for the silks."

The first merchant jumped up and folded his hands. "Lady, we would never take money from you. We have brought these silks as our coronation gifts."

"You have come to the wrong place," Kundavai declared. "None of us here is going to be crowned. It's Prince Arulmozli who's to be crowned. Find him and give him your gifts."

The merchant said, "Lady, we're in the right place. They say if one wishes to gain Prince Arulmozli's favor, one must first please Princess Kundavai."

The women laughed at this. "Where did you hear this?" Kundavai asked.

The second merchant spoke for the first time. "It's true, ladies. During the procession, people said, 'Crowning Prince Arulmozli is equal to crowning Princess Kundavai. From now, the Chola kingdom will be ruled by a woman, and it will prosper.'" The women laughed again.

The merchant said, "Please accept our gifts and pass on our request to Prince Arulmozli."

"What request?" Kundavai demanded. "What do you want from the prince?"

"Lady, during Emperor Paranthaka's reign, the only thing to fear on a sea voyage was a storm. Chola merchants traded cargo in many ports on their way to China. Chinese merchants too sailed safely to the Chola country. Now, there's no guarantee these silks will get back to China. We'd rather give them to you than have them snatched from us by Arab pirates."

Kundavai's beautiful dark eyes danced in excitement. "Do you believe Prince Arulmozli will make the seas safe? Do you think his fame will reach the island nations across the seas?"

"Both Chola and Chinese merchants believe in Prince Arulmozli. In fact, an astrologer we saw this morning said the prince would build huge fleets of ships, destroy the pirates and make the sea routes safe again. But for this to happen, the Chola princesses must not stand in his way."

"So, what else did the astrologer say about us?" Kundavai asked.

The first merchant replied, "He said that you had just visited him and that both of you would soon be married. If you will not accept the silks as coronation gifts, take them as your wedding gifts."

Vanathi said, "*Akka*, these Chinese merchants are troublemakers. Send them away."

"Patience, Vanathi," Kundavai said. "Let's see how far these troublemakers go." She turned to the merchants. "Were you the ones who came to the astrologer's house on an elephant?"

"Yes, lady. And the astrologer correctly predicted that we would meet you again. If his predictions about Lady Vanathi also come true, all our troubles will be over."

Vanathi again said, "*Akka*, send them away."

"And were you also the ones in the procession? You mingled with the crowd often."

"Yes, lady. We wanted to hear what the people had to say about the coming coronation."

"And what did they say? Are they happy Prince Arulmozli is to be crowned?"

"No, lady. The only thing they talked about was Prince Madurandaka's devotion to god."

"Good! Poonkuzlali, did you hear that?" Kundavai asked. "What else did they say about him?"

"They praised him: though he has a claim to the Tiger Throne, he says, 'I will not be king.' They say Prince Madurandaka loved and married a boat girl and insisted she be made empress. So, the chieftains withdrew their support for him and said, 'In that case, Prince Arulmozli will be king.' If that boat girl happens to be here, we would like to present her too with a gift of silks."

Poonkuzlali said, "Lady, these men are indeed troublemakers. Send them away."

"My dear lady," the merchant said. "Are you that lucky woman? What the people say is right!"

Poonkuzlali's face broke into a smile. "What do they say?"

"One man said, 'Prince Madurandaka sacrificed the kingdom for Lady Poonkuzlali.' Another man replied, 'Even if I had nine kingdoms, I would sacrifice them all for Lady Poonkuzlali.' I agreed with him."

Poonkuzlali pretended to be angry. "*Akka*, this man must be punished for his insolence."

Madurandaka heard this as he came back to the terrace. "Why should he be punished? I agree with what he said, Poonkuzlali."

Poonkuzlali said, "One can agree with a real merchant, not with an imposter," and pulled the merchant's turban. The turban fell down along with the man's mustache and beard ... Vandhiya Devan stood before them.

Devan cried, "Sir, help!" and ran to hug the other merchant whose turban and beard also came off. A smiling Arulmozli stood there.

The women had a good laugh.

Poonkuzlali said, "I had my doubts when I saw them outside the temple: that's why I invited them here."

"I too recognized my friend," Madurandaka added. "That's why I left them here and went away."

"Vanathi, only you and I foolishly fell for these men's disguises. And what good did your disguise do?" Kundavai challenged the men.

"We moved anonymously in the crowd and felt the pulse of public opinion," Arulmozli said.

Kundavai asked eagerly, "And what did you hear, *thambi*?"

"The people want to see the Chola empire regain the glory it enjoyed under Emperor Paranthaka. We came across two Chinese merchants at the Thanjavur fort entrance. We bought their silks, disguised ourselves and came back here. The merchants told us about the Arabian pirates; we have experienced these pirates' cruelty first-hand. Come what may, my friend and I will go to Sri Lanka after the coronation. Once our work there is done, we plan to go to the countries across the sea. I don't know whether we'll come back alive or die as martyrs on the battlefield. We came to ask you to stay with us until we leave and to send us off with your blessings."

Kundavai's eyes filled with tears.

Poonkuzlali said in a choked voice, "I don't know why men have to go to war. Why can't men love each other and live happily in peace?"

"My daughter," Sembiyan Madevi said. "As long as the world exists, there will be war. Those who are born to uphold righteousness must fight."

Her listeners were amazed to hear this from the devout, peaceful queen.

The Battle Between Good and Evil

MADURANDAKA TURNED TO his mother. "*Amma,* there are many men in the world who feel a day without war is a day wasted. Vandhiya Devan and Prince Arulmozli belong to this group. On the other hand, you believe a day without prayer is a day wasted. How can you approve of war?"

"My children, Lord Shiva and Goddess Durga battled and triumphed over demons," Sembiyan Madevi pointed out. "Lord Vishnu took ten avatars to kill the wicked. From the day of creation, the battle between good and evil continues. I'm glad you are eager to hear these things."

"Yes, even Vandhiya Devan's eyes, which keep darting around, are now fixed on you," Arulmozli said.

The women giggled at this. They had noticed Devan's eyes wandering often to Kundavai's face.

"My children," the queen continued. "It's your duty to destroy the pirates and safeguard the life and livelihood of Tamil merchants."

"We will do our duty, mother," Devan declared firmly.

"Arulmozli," the queen said. "You must be prepared to die on the battlefield. But you must also take precautions to ensure the continuity of the Chola dynasty. Karikalan died without getting married; you are the only one left. So, before you set out on your conquest, you must marry and ensure our dynasty lives on through your heir. Celebrate your marriage along with your coronation. You are lucky to get a wife like Vanathi: the mangalasutra you tie around her neck will be your shield in battle."

"Mother, I'm ready to get married. It's Vanathi who insists, 'I have taken an oath: I will not sit on the throne,'" Arulmozli complained.

Poonkuzlali laughed. "Lady Vanathi wants Prince Arulmozli to beg her a little." The others laughed with her, but Vanathi burst into sobs.

Kundavai said, "Foolish girl, why are you sobbing like this?" and led her from the terrace.

Daydreams

THE NEXT MORNING, Arulmozli went to see Kundavai. "*Akka*, must you go to Pazlayarai?"

"Why don't you come to Pazlayarai with us?"

"No, I have to meet Azlvarkkadian in Uraiyur on an important matter."

"You have changed; you don't respect me anymore."

"*Akka*, I'm going to become emperor. Can't I do as I please at least now?"

"Do as you please," Kundavai retorted. "As long as you don't expect me to obey you."

"Just come for the coronation. After that, you can do as you want."

"That's up to Vanathi. If she wants to attend it, I'll come with her. Otherwise, I'll stay away."

"Where's she, *akka*?"

"She's gone to the Ponni to pray that you come to your senses. I have never seen a crueler man than you. She sobbed all night. Go and see her before you leave."

"If she does not understand what's in my heart, what else can she do but sob? Do you want me to marry such a girl and suffer all my life?"

Arulmozli hurried to the river. Vanathi sat on the ghat, throwing flowers into the water. He sat quietly on the step behind her. Vanathi sensed his presence and froze. Arulmozli was silent for a while. Then, "Vanathi, are you daydreaming?"

"Yes, I'm daydreaming. When I first met you, I thought you were a mahout. I dreamed of us riding together on an elephant. I dreamed I was an ordinary boat girl ..."

"I know, Vanathi—you're jealous of Poonkuzlali."

"Yes, I envy Poonkuzlali. She has got her heart's desire. She and her beloved are going to Kodikkarai to row their boat, serve the Kuzlagar temple and live happily. Sir, punish me in any way, but don't make Poonkuzlali laugh at me."

Arulmozli recalled the previous night. "Just wait, Vanathi. Poonkuzlali laughed at you yesterday; the day will come when you laugh at her."

"I don't want to laugh at anyone. I only want to see you smile. Your face is radiant when you talk to other people, but when you look at me, you frown. I'm scared to even look at you."

"Vanathi, other people don't rob my peace of mind. My sister said you did not sleep last night: I have not slept for days. When I lie on the palace terrace and look up at the sky, I see your eyes in the stars; I hear your laughter in the rustling leaves; I feel your petal-soft touch in the gentle breeze. I frown at you because I'm afraid you'll stand in the way of my ambition."

"Sir, I'll never stand in your way."

"Can anyone stop the dark thunder clouds carried by the eastern gales? My body throbs with excitement; my mind races; millions of trumpets and war drums pull me like magnets. No one can stand in my way, Vanathi, but you can ruin my peace of mind by trying."

"I'll never do that. If I can't help you, who are born to rule the world, I will at least leave you in peace. That's why I refuse to sit beside you on the Tiger Throne. All I want is a small place in your heart."

"You have already made a place for yourself in my heart. Are you sure you don't want to be empress of the great Chola empire? Don't you want to wear the dazzling, jeweled crown?"

"No. It will weigh me down and smother me. Give me a different gift: I'll weave a garland of flowers; before you go on your campaign, garland me with it and make me yours forever."

"I bought a garland of precious stones from the Chinese merchants as your coronation gift."

"Why should you give me a gift for your coronation?"

"Okay, I'll give it to someone else. Vanathi, let's make an agreement: I'll garland you as you want; in return, each time I come home after planting the Tiger Flag on foreign soil, you must wait for me with a flower garland of victory."

"I'll weave hundreds of garlands and wait for you, along with the entire Chola kingdom."

The Stunned Poet

EXCITEMENT MOUNTED AS the people celebrated Arulmozli's ascension to the Tiger Throne. Except for a close circle, no one knew about Chendan Amudhan being the real Madurandaka. The former Madurandaka had rarely been seen in public and so the people did not notice the change in identity. There was some talk about Poonkuzlali: some said that she was Kalaanthaka's daughter; others said that she was a boat girl. The people accepted the marriage, as it was normal for princes to take several wives. Madurandaka was respected for his devotion and for giving up his claim to the throne because of Poonkuzlali. It was rumored that Arulmozli planned to give him an important position in the government.

Two days before the coronation, people flocked to Thanjavur. The gates of the fort were left open and the public had free access. Arrangements were made for the people's comfortable stay outside the fort walls. The Kodumbalur and Pazluvur soldiers forgot their former enmity and joined the king's bodyguards in happy camaraderie. Thanjavur Fort and the city wore a festive look and the citizen's houses filled with guests.

The day of the coronation dawned in a splash of golden sunlight. People gathered at the entrance to the Coronation Hall, eager to see the crowned Arulmozli ride the royal elephant through the city streets. The royal family entered the hall through a private entrance. Sundara Chola and Vanamadevi came first, followed by Sembiyan Madevi, Madurandaka, Poonkuzlali, Kundavai and Vanathi. Aniruddha, Kalaanthaka, Velir, Malayaman, Sambuvaraya and the other chieftains, officials, merchant association leaders, temple priests, poets and artists waded through the crowd at the front entrance. Finally, Arulmozli and

Vandhiya Devan rode up to the hall in a golden, lotus-shaped, open chariot. Cheers filled the air.

The hereditary Chola crown, garland of gems, sword and scepter were carried around the hall on an ornamental platter and blessed by those present. The Court Poet recited the glorious history of the Chola kings, beginning with Emperor Sibi of the Surya dynasty. Other poets and priests waited to speak their praises and blessings. Kalaanthaka stood ready to crown Arulmozli.

A stranger pushed his way through the crowd, entered the hall and went to Kalaanthaka. Devan recognized Azlvarkkadian in disguise and signaled to Arulmozli. Azlvarkkadian whispered to Kalaanthaka and the commander became anxious. He hesitated and then took Azlvarkkadian to an empty corner of the hall.

Arulmozli, who stood with folded hands listening to the Court Poet, now interrupted him. "Sir, you recite the glory of my ancestors. But what have I done to be worthy of this ancient crown? Can you recite my achievements?"

The stunned poet was silent.

"Sir, it's not your fault. I have not yet achieved anything that can be celebrated in verse."

The Coronation

ARULMOZLI CONTINUED. "SIR, if I have the right to wear the crown of my illustrious forefathers, surely Prince Madurandaka, Emperor Gandara Aditya's son, is equally entitled to it?"

The poet could only manage a nod. Everyone turned to Madurandaka, who sat quietly beside Sundara Chola, and looked at him with new eyes. Madurandaka bowed his head.

Meanwhile, Azlvarkkadian had troubling news for Kalaanthaka. On Arulmozli's orders, the disguised Azlvarkkadian had mingled with the people. He saw Rakamma outside the Coronation Hall and followed her to Kalaanthaka's palace where he lost her in the crowd. He waited, watching the entrance. He saw two women come out from the palace;

the second woman carried a child on her hip and partially concealed her face with a scarf. Azlvarkkadian guessed that she was Kalaanthaka's daughter. He wondered whether to stop them or see where they went. He decided to follow them until he was sure of the woman's identity.

Rakamma noticed him following them and shouted, "Aiyo! This man is stalking us women!"

Immediately, a threatening crowd surrounded Azlvarkkadian. By the time he had convinced them he was just another man who had come to watch the coronation, the women had disappeared. Guessing that they would try to leave the fort, Azlvarkkadian ran to the fort entrance; in the distance, he saw a woman and a child climb into a screened palanquin, escorted by four riders. They set off quickly. As Azlvarkkadian went after them, a huge crowd surged forward and carried him back into the fort. He hurried to the Coronation Hall to give Kalaanthaka this news.

Kalaanthaka was already worried about his daughter, the former Madurandaka's wife. Alarmed at Azlvarkkadian's news, he asked him to inform Sundara Chola and Aniruddha about this and hurried home to find out the truth.

Arulmozli had kept an eye on Kalaanthaka even as he was talking to the Court Poet. The prince now turned to Sundara Chola and said in a majestic voice: "Father, I am a descendent of Sibi Chola who gave his own flesh to save a dove; I am a descendent of Manu Neethi Chola who awarded his own son the death sentence for killing a calf. My ancestors are as renowned for their justice as for their valor. Coming from such a clan, can I claim a position which rightfully belongs to another? As the Court Poet recited their glory, I saw my ancestors; I heard them ask, 'Is this throne rightfully yours? Have you earned the right to it?' I summoned up my courage and replied, 'With your blessings, I'll take the Chola empire to great heights; I'll awe the world with my achievements; I'll earn your praise.' They smiled and blessed me."

Arulmozli's speech electrified his listeners. Cries of, "Spear of Valor!" "Spear of Victory!" filled the hall.

Arulmozli continued. "Father, during your grandfather's time, this brave battle cry of the Cholas was heard far and wide and our enemies trembled at the sound. Our warriors sailed the seas in hundreds of ships to ensure our trade flourished. After your illness, this brave cry faded and our enemies have grown powerful. The Pandians are determined to crown a king and sow chaos; Lanka's Mahinda is mustering an army; Veerapandian's bodyguards murdered Prince Karikalan; the Cheras have built up a huge elephant brigade and navy; a new breed of savage Arabs is terrorizing the oceans. These Arabs have now allied with the Cheras and Kalinga to destroy our fleet. We must expand our navy to safeguard our maritime trade. We must build thousands of ships and train our sailors. We must enroll soldiers who can fight the pirates. We must capture the islands in the east and establish permanent posts there. Father, I have promised our ancestors to achieve all this. I need the approval and blessing of all the elders here."

Again, cries of, "Spear of Victory!" "Spear of Valor!" filled the hall.

"Father, you all approve of my plans and give me your blessings. But if I'm to succeed in my endeavor, I must have peace of mind. I must not do anything my ancestors would disapprove of; I must not grab something which rightfully belongs to another. If I go against our clan's code of honor, I will be tormented by guilt. How can I triumph against our enemies? How can I be confident that righteousness is on my side? How can I have the energy and resolve to achieve anything?"

Madurandaka raised his bowed head and prepared to speak. At a signal from Arulmozli, Devan went to stand beside Madurandaka.

Devan said, "Look, Poonkuzlali is laughing at you."

Madurandaka turned towards Poonkuzlali; her complete attention was focused on Arulmozli who now held the ancient Chola crown in his hands.

Arulmozli said, "Father, Lord Kalaanthaka is delayed, but we must conduct the coronation ceremony within the auspicious hour. You have chosen to give me this hereditary crown with the approval of everyone, from the ministers and commanders to the soldiers and the common people. This crown now belongs to me. I am entitled to do as I want with it. There is someone here who is more worthy of the crown that I am: he is my senior in age; although he has the strongest claim to the Tiger Throne, he renounced his right and came here prepared to rejoice at my coronation; he saved my life; he saved my dearest friend's life; he saved the Cholas from disaster. I have done nothing to match his achievements. And so, I crown Gandara Aditya's son, Madurandaka, emperor …"

Arulmozli walked up to Madurandaka and placed the crown on his head. Devan stood behind Madurandaka with a firm hand on his shoulder but Madurandaka was too stunned to react.

Arulmozli cried, "Long live Emperor Uthama Chola!"

Devan shouted, "Long live Emperor Uthama Chola!"

The amazed audience found its voice and cried, "Long live Emperor Uthama Chola!"

The news of Madurandaka's coronation spread like wildfire through Thanjavur. Devan and Azlvarkkadian had arranged for men to shout, "Long live Emperor Uthama Chola!" These men also spread the news that Arulmozli had handed over the kingdom to Madurandaka while he built a large navy and sailed to destroy the Arab pirates. These new developments were accepted at once by some while others were incredulous. But soon, millions of voices joined in cheering the new emperor.

The newly crowned Uthama Chola sat in a golden howdah on a caparisoned elephant and was taken in a procession through Thanjavur. The mahout was none other than Arulmozli. While the people shouted, "Long live Uthama Chola!" it was Arulmozli's valor and sacrifice which captured their hearts. At the sight of Madurandaka and Arulmozli together on the elephant, the people danced and sang, hugged each other and scattered flowers on the streets.

It was dusk by the time the royal procession returned to the palace. Flowers showered down on them from the terrace. A sweet voice called, "Mahout! Mahout!" Arulmozli looked up to see a radiant Vanathi.

Springtime

ONE AND A half months after the coronation of Uthama Chola, Vandhiya Devan rode to Pazlayarai, taking in the sweet scents and sights of spring. Kundavai and Vanathi welcomed him at the palace entrance. Kundavai asked him to rest after his long journey before meeting her in the palace garden. Devan quickly bathed and ate and hurried to the garden where Kundavai waited. Both their hearts fluttered with excitement and hope.

"Sir, I heard you were not completely successful in your mission," Kundavai said. "Is this true?"

Devan sighed. "I have never been completely successful in any mission."

"You saved King Uthama Chola's life: we have not forgotten that. The king wanted to make you chancellor in Lord Ambalavan's place ..."

"Thank god, I escaped!"

"Why do you say that? The chancellor is more powerful than the chief minister and the general. Even the emperor can't do anything without the chancellor's approval."

"Lady, I once happened to hide in Lord Ambalavan's vault. In the glow of the gold coins, I saw a spider's web and a human skeleton. I decided never to set foot in the vault again."

Kundavai smiled. "There's no need for you to enter the treasury. Arulmozli has decided to sell the gold to build a navy. He has the emperor's permission for this."

"My only regret is I was not present when Prince Arulmozli married Lady Vanathi. Why such a hurry?"

"They were not in in hurry, but I insisted the marriage must take place before my parents left for Kanchipuram. Velir was also satisfied. We were all shocked when Arulmozli suddenly crowned Madurandaka. You two friends kept your secret well."

"Lady, I assumed he would confide in you."

"Until recently, Arulmozli never made a decision without consulting me ...he has changed now because of your friendship. He has learned to pretend and has mastered tricks and stratagems."

"Lady, don't blame me without cause. The coronation drama was entirely conceived by him. He said that, for once in his life, he wanted to do something without your advice and earn your approval. Are you pleased with him?"

"Nothing could please me more. Thank you for helping him."

"I thought you were waiting eagerly for Prince Arulmozli to ascend the throne ..."

"I admit I once wanted that but, after Vanathi's oath, I changed my mind. And if Arulmozli became king immediately after Karikalan's death, what impression would people get?"

"Prince Arulmozli declared his intention to become king to stop me from being accused of murder. Luckily, Lord Ambalavan saved me."

"Poor old man! The Chola kingdom seems empty without him."

"It's sad to think his younger brother has followed him."

"Aiyo! Is Lord Kalaanthaka dead? Has it been confirmed?"

"When I left him, he was alive. But how can anyone survive a fall from such a height? He must be dead by now. I'm in agony when I think I'm partly responsible for his death."

"Sir, tell me the details. On the day of the coronation, you and Arulmozli conspired to send Lord Kalaanthaka from the hall. What happened after that?"

Devan narrated the series of events involved in Madurandaka's coronation.

Arulmozli judged that if Madurandaka's coronation was announced openly, it would lead to trouble: Velir and Malayaman would oppose it; Ambalavan's supporters would insist on fulfilling his wish to crown Arulmozli; Kalaanthaka would object to making a boat girl empress; Sembiyan Madevi, Madurandaka and Poonkuzlali would protest; Sundara Chola might hesitate to go against their wishes.

Arulmozli decided to keep his plan a secret. He identified the men who would oppose Madurandaka's coronation either out of affection for him or jealousy for Madurandaka and gave them tasks which took them far away from Thanjavur. He confided only in Devan and the two of them carefully laid their plans. Arulmozli sent Kandamaran, Parthibendran and Velir from Thanjavur, but Kalaanthaka could not be dealt with so easily. It was the Pazluvur clan's privilege to crown the Chola kings and Kalaanthaka would never agree to crown Madurandaka. If Kalaanthaka refused, it would be seen as a bad omen and other complications would follow. Just as they were wondering what to do about Kalaanthaka, Azlvarkkadian came with some strange news.

With Aniruddha's approval, Arulmozli had sent Azlvarkkadian to discover the whereabouts of Ravidasan and his gang, along with Nandini and the little boy who had been crowned in the Thirupurambayam forest. Azlvarkkadian was also asked to find out whether Karuthiruman was with them and whether the former Madurandaka had died from Kandamaran's spear or survived and joined the conspirators. To their surprise, Azlvarkkadian was back in a few days.

Azlvarkkadian had spotted Rakamma near the Kolli Hills. He had followed her in disguise, hoping that she would lead him to the conspirators. To his surprise, Rakamma headed for Thanjavur and mingled with the crowd coming for the coronation. Azlvarkkadian was alarmed when she surveyed the area around Kalaanthaka's palace and reported this to Arulmozli and Devan. They considered arresting her but decided that it would be better to keep her under observation to find out why she was there. They guessed that she had brought a message for Kalaanthaka's daughter. They decided to use this to get Kalaanthaka to leave the hall during the coronation.

Kalaanthaka left the hall with Azlvarkkadian and went straight to his palace. He was shocked to find his daughter missing. Before he could return to the hall, cries of, "Long live Emperor Uthama Chola!" filled the air. He realized that there was nothing more he could do in the hall. Taking a few trusted men with him, Kalaanthaka went to find his daughter. He fumed at the thought of his daughter having anything to do with the Cholas' arch-enemy. *I would rather kill her with my own hands!*

That night, Azlvarkkadian met Arulmozli and Devan. The three of them were aware of Ravidasan's cunning; the short-tempered, rash Kalaanthaka would be no match for him. If the gang caught him, his life would be in danger. Kalaanthaka was also capable of getting into a rage and killing his beloved daughter. They decided that Devan and Azlvarkkadian must immediately go to Kalaanthaka's rescue.

As Kalaanthaka went after his daughter and her abductors, Devan and Azlvarkkadian followed his tracks. They realized that the Pandian conspirators were deliberately laying false trails and diversions for Kalaanthaka. They covered a long distance and finally reached the foothills of the Annamalai mountains. From here, the going was very difficult. The forest was dense. The roar of wild animals was heard everywhere. It was difficult to ride through the thickets; at the same time, they feared to leave their horses in case wild animals preyed on them.

Finally, the friends came to dense jungle where it was almost impossible to ride a horse. They stopped when they heard a horse whinny. They followed the sound and found a Pazluvur man guarding Kalaanthaka's horses. He told them that Kalaanthaka and three of his men had dismounted and continued on foot from there. The friends left their horses with the man and walked on. They went through dark forest where the sunlight did not penetrate and then climbed a thickly forested hill on a narrow trail with no visibility.

They came to an open space where a waterfall plunged straight down from a high cliff. The cliff wall was so steep, there was no way to go any further. Devan and Azlvarkkadian assumed that Kalaanthaka and his men had been killed by wild animals. They decided to refresh themselves with a bath in the waterfall, rest a while and go back.

Suddenly, they saw two men fighting on the cliff where the waterfall began: it was Kalaanthaka and the former Madurandaka. To their amazement, the cowardly Madurandaka was wielding his sword with a skill that matched his father-in-law's. Kalaanthaka was on the defensive … slowly, he gave way to Madurandaka and backed closer and closer to the edge of the cliff.

Devan and Azlvarkkadian shouted their warnings but it was useless: their voices were drowned by the roar of the waterfall. They were forced to watch helplessly as Kalaanthaka inched further back, lost his footing and plummeted down the steep cliff. His enemy, the former Madurandaka, peered over the cliff edge and disappeared.

No one could survive a fall from such a great height. However, the two friends decided to try to at least recover his body. They ran to the deep pool into which the waterfall crashed and dashed against the rocks. There was no sign of Kalaanthaka's body. They guessed that his body had sunk to the bottom of the pool and were relieved that he had not fallen and shattered on the rocks. As expected, the water currents soon pushed the body to the surface. The two friends dived into the pool and pulled the body to the shore. Without much hope, they gave Kalaanthaka first aid. To their surprise, he gasped and opened his eyes. He managed to tell them what had happened.

After much difficulty, Kalaanthaka had reached the summit of the hill. He found his daughter there in a crowd of about hundred people.

Ravidasan invited Kalaanthaka to join them. He told Kalaanthaka that his son-in-law was the rightful heir to the Pandian throne; the Cheras and King Mahinda of Sri Lanka had come forward to support him. Kalaanthaka accused them of being conspirators and asked them to give him his daughter.

"If your daughter wants to go with you, you may take her," Ravidasan said.

Kalaanthaka turned to his daughter who said, "Father, I'll share my husband's fate, whatever it may be. I won't come with you."

"I'll kill you! I won't leave you with these men." Kalaanthaka raised his sword.

The former Madurandaka charged out of hiding and cried, "What right do you have to kill my wife?"

To Kalaanthaka's surprise, Madurandaka started a swordfight. *How can I kill my own son-in-law and make my daughter a widow?* His reluctance weakened his fighting skills and he was forced backwards over the cliff.

Kalaanthaka said, "I'm dying; leave me here and hurry back to Thanjavur. The Chola army must go on the offensive against the Cheras and the Sri Lankans. Take Prince Arulmozli to Madurai and crown him 'Emperor Chola Pandian.' If you don't do this, the Pandian kingdom will again become independent. Go at once!"

The friends did not have the heart to abandon the dying man. They decided that Devan, the faster rider, would carry the news to Thanjavur, while Azlvarkkadian stayed with Kalaanthaka.

Golden Showers

WHEN VANDHIYA DEVAN stopped, Kundavai said, "Sir, your story is hard to believe. I know you are a master at spinning tales. You stop often, look up and down, stare and then pick up the thread of your story: this makes me more suspicious."

"Lady, I sometimes happen to look into your black eyes. I don't know what strange magic there is in them: it makes me speechless. I have to collect myself and continue ..."

Kundavai's cheeks dimpled and her eyes sparkled with laughter. "Sir, there's no strange black magic in my eyes. But whether my eyes are open or closed, whether you stand before me or not, your image is always reflected in my eyes. What do you think is the reason for this?"

Devan's flesh rose in goosebumps and his voice shook. "I don't know, lady."

"I'll tell you: you are the one with magic; even Nandini's hard heart melted for you."

"Your sweet words thrilled me. Why do you talk about that venomous cobra in the same breath?"

"I used to think of Nandini as a cobra; now I pity her."

"Don't let your compassion make you forget that she's the daughter of the Cholas' arch-enemy. See what happened when Veerapandian's son grew up in the Chola family. Isn't that enough? What would have happened if Nandini too had grown up here and married Karikalan?!"

"The Cholas and the Pandians would have buried their enmity and become one clan. But is it true that Nandini's Veerapandian's daughter?"

"Both Lord Ambalavan and I heard Nandini tell Karikalan this. It was this which roused Lord Ambalavan's fury and caused Karikalan's death."

"Think ... maybe she said this just to complete her revenge on Karikalan. When she tried to save Veerapandian's life, she called him her lover: which daughter would call her father her lover?"

"Lady, Karikalan was in a frenzy at that time. Who knows what she said and what he interpreted it as? Karikalan believed her when she claimed to be Veerapandian's daughter. Maybe Nandini herself learnt this truth only later ..."

"You must have heard what the madman said when Azlvarkkadian threatened him."

"Of course. He claimed to be the father of Nandini and her brother."

"Maybe that's true ..."

"If that's the case, lies sometimes make one strong. I was amazed to see how the former Madurandaka's fighting skills have improved after he heard that he was Veerapandian's son. Who would believe that the man who hid in a screened palanquin and trembled at the very mention of the Pazluvur brothers would dare to have a sword fight with the iron-fisted Kalaanthaka … and best him? But Azlvarkkadian will confirm my story."

"Sir, can you meet Nandini?"

"Why should I meet that demon?"

"Don't talk like that about her. Some day or the other, I'll meet her. I'll discover the truth about her father. Whoever her father may be, her mother is Lady Mandakini: that's reason enough for me to love her. There's another reason too …"

"What's that?"

"Nandini was fond of you. She gave you her signet ring and helped you escape from Thanjavur Fort. She saved your life when Ravidasan had you in his clutches in the Kolli Hills."

"All her scheming was to make me the scapegoat for Karikalan's murder."

"Don't you realize why she did that? She loved you."

"Oh my god!!"

"Men are sometimes blind. That poor woman did not love Veerapandian or Karikalan or Ambalavan: all she wanted from them was to be made queen …"

"I know that. There's no room for love in her hard heart."

"But she knew true love when she met you. She was ready to do anything for your love."

"She was also ready to make me take the blame for the prince's murder."

"Why? She wanted to stop you from having any relationship with the Chola family."

"For that she need not have planned to have me impaled at the crossroads: she could have killed me with her sword."

"If you were really sentenced to be impaled, Ravidasan and his gang would have rescued you. You may have become a part of the company gathered in Annamalai now."

"God save me from such a catastrophe! Ravidasan is a brilliant strategist. He has created two heirs to the Pandian throne. First, he crowned a little child Parangusan Nedunchezlian Pandian in the forest on the shore of the Kollidam. Now, he has added Amarabujangan Nedunchezlian."

"Who's that?"

"Who else but our former Madurandaka? When Lord Kalaanthaka fell off the cliff, the shout, 'Long live Amarabujangan Nedunchezlian Pandian,' drowned the roar of the waterfall."

"What's the advantage of having two claimants to the throne?"

"If anything happens to one, they will still have the other. I suppose they'll send one to Lanka and the other to the Cheras to gather support for their cause."

"Uthama Chola will not find it easy to rule the Chola empire in these dangerous times."

"Uthama Chola will focus on helping his mother serve god and his temples. It's your brother, Arulmozli, who will guard the Chola empire."

"That's true. But Arulmozli lacks experience and the Cholas' two pillars of support, the Pazluvur brothers, are no more. Lord Ambalavan is dead and, from what you say, Lord Kalaanthaka will not survive his fall."

"Even if he lives, he'll be of no use to the kingdom: he's heartbroken over his daughter."

"The same goes for Sambuvaraya. Malayaman is old and broken in spirit because one grandson died and the other was not crowned emperor. Velir can't forgive us for fooling him into believing that Arulmozli was to be crowned. He has withdrawn from affairs of state and gone to Kodumbalur to do service to the temples. The chieftains involved in the Kadambur conspiracy feel humiliated by the failure of their plans. Sir, Arulmozli needs true, wise friends with strong shoulders and sword arms."

"Thank goodness he has Parthibendran."

"I'm not sure Parthibendran will support Arulmozli. He's angry that he was sent away before Madurandaka was crowned. He also resents you being Arulmozli's close friend."

"He has cause to be angry: he has done much for the Cholas while I'm a newcomer. If you want, I'll ask his forgiveness."

"That will only add fuel to the fire."

"Parthibendran is a mighty warrior. Is there no other way to pacify him?"

"Parthibendran could not tolerate the idea of a flower seller suddenly ascending the throne or a boat girl becoming queen. He requested my father to make him independent king of the former Pallava territory with the right to issue royal proclamations …."

"Ah! How's that possible? It will cut the Chola kingdom into pieces."

"My father agreed to it. But the Pallava prince did not stop with that. I believe a Pallava princess once married a Chola prince. Quoting that as a precedent, he asked to marry Sundara Chola's daughter."

Devan turned away to hide the grief in his eyes. Kundavai smiled and deliberately remained silent. After a while, Devan asked, "What did the emperor say?"

"How could the emperor say anything? It was up to his daughter; he asked his daughter …"

"And what did the emperor's daughter say?"

"She said she did not want to marry Parthibendran. She said she would never marry and leave the land through which the Ponni flows."

Devan looked at Kundavai's face as if he was seeing it for the first time. "Is that the only reason?"

Lightning flashed … waves collided … heaven descended on earth …

With a mischievous smile Kundavai said, "What can I say about a man who can't read a woman's heart and expects her to spell it out to him in words? How can such a man read the cunning minds of the Cholas' enemies?"

Devan glanced up and down again. "Lady, if a young man without a family or even a hut to his name, makes the same request as Parthibendran who hails from the ancient Pallava clan … what would the emperor say?"

"Whatever he may think, he will ask his daughter and then reply accordingly."

"And what will the emperor's daughter say?"

"Why don't you just ask the emperor? You'll know the answer at once."

"How can a young man without family or wealth dare to ask the emperor for his daughter's hand in marriage?"

"What has made this warrior from Vallam so modest? I remember you singing the praises of your ancestors and lineage when I first met you ..."

"Your brother's friendship makes me hate using ancestry as a claim to fame. He says, 'When my forebears issued proclamations, they began with the Surya dynasty and listed every king in their line. I'll change this tradition: all records in my reign will list only my achievements.' I agree. I won't ask for your hand based on the achievements of my ancestors. Prince Arulmozli and I will make the Tiger Flag fly from the Vindhya in the north to Trincomalee in the south; from Lakshadweep in the west to Srivijaya in the east. Once we fulfill a part of our goal, I'll go to the emperor and say, 'Let me garland your daughter with my victories.' I'll recover the Pandian crown jewels, lay them at your feet and say, 'If I'm worthy of you, let's get married.'"

"If my father arranged a swayamvara for me and invited all the princes in this vast land, I would search among them for one man: the young man who escaped from Thanjavur Fort, reached Pazlayarai, crossed the lake by boat, entered the palace garden and met me there. I would garland him."

Devan heard music; colorful butterflies danced among the blossoming trees; the skies showered him with gold. He jumped up with his hand on his sword. "Your words give me new energy to achieve my goals!"

"Please remember one thing: you'll face danger; you'll fight many battles; your enemies will try to kill you by treachery. If anything happens to you, a Chola princess will become a widow before becoming a wife."

"Nothing will happen to me. When my ship is lost at sea, you will be my guiding Pole Star and I'll find my way to you. When storms threaten to dash my ship against the rocky coast at night, you will be the lighthouse which leads me safely to the shore. Lady, wherever I may go in this vast world, I promise I'll come back and marry you."

Kundavai gazed at his face. Just then, Vanathi came running. "*Akka*, there's an urgent message for him from Kandamaran."

The Flower Wilts

VANDHIYA DEVAN TOOK the message from Vanathi saying, "Princess, do you remember me?"

"Sir, how can I ever forget all the help you have given me and my husband?"

"Is that why you got married without me?"

Vanathi smiled mischievously. "If you were present, who knows what tricks you would have played? The wedding might have turned out like the coronation."

The women noticed the worry on Devan's face.

"What news from Kandamaran?" Kundavai asked.

"Read it," Devan said, passing the palm leaf to her.

The message read: 'My dear friend, please forgive me for all the wrongs I have done you and come at once to see my sister, Manimekalai, one last time.'

"In a way, this is good news. It means that Manimekalai has been found," Kundavai remarked.

"What? Where did Manimekalai go?" Devan asked in surprise.

"Haven't you heard anything about Manimekalai?"

"No. I was planning to ask you about her."

"Sembiyan Madevi pleaded to keep Manimekalai with her, but Sambuvaraya insisted that Kandamaran would be away on border patrol and that he wanted to have at least his daughter with him. He was on his way to build a new palace on the northern bank of the Palar. He set up camp that night near Veeranam and Manimekalai was missing the next morning. We feared she had thrown herself into the lake and drowned. We heard a search was on for her. Kandamaran's message suggests she has been found."

"What's the use of me seeing her?" Devan wondered. "She won't recognize me. But I wonder what Kandamaran means by 'one last time.' Is he going to forbid me from seeing her again? Or is he going to enroll her in a Buddhist monastery?"

"You'll know everything at the end of one day's travel," Kundavai pointed out.

It took Devan a day to go from Pazlayarai to Veeranam, but it seemed an age. His mind seethed with memories. When he first took this road, his head was filled with dreams. Many of them had come true. Prince Arulmozli was his close friend; Princess Kundavai loved him; he was the commander-in-chief of the Chola army in Sri Lanka. All this was because he happened to spend a night at Kadambur Palace and learn about the chieftains' conspiracy. How many momentous events the last eight months had brought! Some people believed in the alignment of the stars and planets, but there was definitely some unknown force which directed human lives. Was it this force which man called, 'God'? How else could he have survived so many dangers? Who sent his way the men and women who had helped him out of each tricky situation? Devan's heart melted at the thought of all those who had helped him.

Even if Kandamaran later became my enemy, can I forget his help? Azlvarkkadian stood by me many times; even that enchantress Nandini helped me. Princess Kundavai's concern for me is amazing. And can I ever forget Poonkuzlali's help? She's worthy of being queen. And what about Chendan Amudhan? I can repay my debts to them only by serving the Cholas all my life. And Lord Ambalavan: what a great man he was! His confession saved me. But, above all, what about Manimekalai? Why did she love me so much? Why did she go mad? That fool, Kandamaran— Manimekalai must have fallen in love with me when he praised me constantly ...

When Kandamaran told Devan, 'Forget my sister; she is to marry someone important,' Devan had obeyed. Meeting Kundavai had helped him to do this. But Manimekalai had kept him in her heart. *Manimekalai is as innocent and mischievous as a child ... her heart is pure. It's best she thinks I'm dead. Her mind will clear and she'll marry a brave young man and live happily. Am I fooling myself? Am I responsible for her condition? What does Kandamaran mean by, 'one last time'? Maybe she's dying!*

Devan's horse was as fast as his thoughts and he soon reached the Kollidam. Fortunately, the river was not in flood and he did not need a boat. Devan rode across the river by keeping to the shallows. He saw the charred remains of Kadambur Palace in the distance. He rode on to Veeranam where he met Kandamaran's men. They said that their master was waiting for him in a boat on the shore of the lake.

Why is Kandamaran waiting by the lake? Devan wondered as he rode on. He carefully guided his horse up the steep bank of the lake and looked down: the clear water was pooled in the middle of the lake; lilies and lotuses covered the surface. Devan saw the waiting boat and quickly made his way to it.

Kandamaran helped him on board and said tearfully, "My friend, thank you for coming so quickly. If you had delayed, you may not have seen Manimekalai alive."

Devan's resolute heart, which had got him through many dangers and helped him achieve so much, melted at these words. Tears flowed down his cheeks. "Kandamaran, is Manimekalai's life in danger? How? It's only her mind which is affected, and that too only where you and I are concerned ..."

"Friend, her mind is now clear, but I can't say how much longer she'll live. I pray she stays alive until she sees you."

Kandamaran was in Kanchipuram renovating the golden palace for the emperor's stay when he heard that Manimekalai was missing. He rushed to Veeranam. His father was mad with grief and could only say, 'She went to bed at night in the camp; she was missing in the morning.' He learnt that men had been sent to search for her in Pazlayarai and around Kadambur Palace. Kandamaran feared that she had jumped into the lake or was wandering in the nearby forest. For four days, he searched along the shore of the lake. He crisscrossed the lake in a boat and also searched the forest. His search yielded no results.

Kandamaran then remembered the bathing pavilion on the island near the lake's western shore. Nandini and Manimekalai had met Karikalan and Devan there on the day of the hunting expedition. It was impossible for Manimekalai to have made her way there alone without a boat as wild animals roamed the forest along that shore. Anyway, Kandamaran rowed himself there. At first the pavilion seemed empty. He stood on the ghat and sighed, thinking of all his lost dreams. He was stunned to hear a sigh echoing his own. He ran to the other side of the pavilion and found Manimekalai lying on the steps. She was shrunken and emaciated. Her sari was in tatters and her body was covered with scratches.

At first, Kandamaran thought she was dead. She must have starved and wandered in the forest for days before finally collapsing and dying on the pavilion steps. Kandamaran's heart ached as he took his sister's body in his lap and wept over it. He suddenly remembered the sigh: he quickly sprinkled water on her face and poured a little into her mouth; he rubbed her body to warm it.

Manimekalai's eyes opened and she whispered, "*Anna*, is it you? I knew I would see you and him in heaven. Where's he?"

Kandamaran controlled his sobs and reassured her, "He's coming, my dear."

He understood that Manimekalai thought that she had died and gone to heaven. He did what he could for his sister and sent an urgent message to Devan.

"My friend," Kandamaran said. "Manimekalai does not have long to live. It's her longing to see you which keeps her alive. She thinks we're all in heaven: don't contradict her. You must also hide your grief and talk to her cheerfully."

Their boat reached the pavilion and Devan heard Manimekalai singing and playing her *yazl*: it was the love song she had performed for him and Karikalan. Devan sat on the steps, waited until the song ended and then went to her. As soon as she saw him, Manimekalai pushed away her *yazl* and tried to stand. Her wasted legs gave way; Devan rushed to her and caught her before she fell. He gently lowered her to the ground, sat beside her and placed her head in his lap.

Manimekalai looked up at him as if to assure herself that it was Devan and that she was lying in his lap. She murmured, "My brother said the truth: this is heaven."

Devan replied, "Yes, Manimekalai. This is heaven. I'm really here."

Unable to control his grief, Devan sobbed over her. Manimekalai's face shone with an inner light. She whispered something, but Devan could not catch her sweet words. But when the heart speaks, who needs words? Soon, Manimekalai's lips fell silent; her eyes closed; her face dimmed and became calm. A soft breeze caressed Manimekalai and her life left her body.

Where did her life go? Did it merge with the wind or with the songs of the birds? Did it reach the lotus feet of the god who creates and ends all life? Or did it merge with the heart of Vandhiya Devan who sat frozen like a statue with tears streaming from his eyes? Who knows? But one thing is sure: Manimekalai lived forever in Devan's heart. From that minute, Devan's laughter and mischief, his daring and high spirits were tempered with a new maturity, compassion and kindness. Devan went on to achieve much and earned renown and glory. Wherever he went and whatever he did, Manimekalai was with him.

Epilogue

Vandhiya Devan marries **Kundavai** and they are respected and loved throughout the Chola kingdom.

Kalaanthaka, the Iron Man, survives his fall and goes on to serve the Cholas for many years.

Azlvarkkadian continues his espionage, tracking Nandini and the Pandian conspirators.

Arulmozli and Vandhiya Devan build a huge navy, defeat the pirates and make the island nations in the eastern seas a part of the Chola kingdom. When **Uthama Chola** dies fifteen years after being crowned, Arulmozli ascends the throne as Raja Raja Chola and rules for many years.

The former **Madurandaka,** with the help of the Sri Lankan and Chera kings, wins the Pandian kingdom and rules as Amarabujangan Nedunchezlian. He is later defeated by Raja Raja Chola and dies on the battlefield.

The young boy crowned in the Thirupurambayam forest claims the Pandian throne and conspires to win it. He is killed by Rajendra Chola.

Nandini dies after Amarabujangan Nedunchezlian's death. Before that, she meets Raja Raja Chola and gives him the details of her birth and Karikalan's death.

The Kudanthai astrologer's predictions come true. **Vanathi's son** becomes the renowned Emperor Rajendra Chola. Vanathi keeps her oath, as she dies before Arulmozli ascends the throne. It is Ulagamadevi who sits on the throne beside Raja Raja Chola.

Ravidasan and his accomplices are captured and punished by Raja Raja Chola after Nandini's death. Their property is confiscated.

Sundara Chola lives in the golden palace in Kanchipuram for three years. When he dies, **Vanamadevi** enters his funeral pyre.

Parthibendran, furious at Kundavai's rejection, tries to establish an independent Pallava kingdom in Kanchipuram. He fails and dies without heirs.

Kandamaran builds a new palace on the bank of the Palar and serves the Cholas. His Sambuvaraya clan earns much glory and wealth.

Glossary

Aadi Perukku	festival celebrated on the 18th day of the Tamil month of Aadi
amma	mother
Andal	a poet-saint and the only woman among the twelve *Azlvars*
anna	elder brother
Azlvars	twelve poet-saints devoted to Lord Vishnu (5th to 10th CE)
appa	father
Aravan	village deity and patron god of transgenders in Tamil Nadu
devi	goddess, lady or honorific for a wife
kamandalam	water pot carried by ascetics
kangan	ornamental bracelet worn by men
Kuravai Koothu	folk art performance with song and dance
Nayanmars	the sixty-three Tamil Shaiva saints (3rd to 8th CE)
rudraksha	prayer beads from stone fruit
Sambandar	Shaiva poet-saint and child prodigy
Shaiva	Shiva devotee
Shivoham	a mantra meaning, 'I am Shiva.'
swami	god, holy man or honorific for a husband
thambi	younger brother
thatha	grandfather
Thevaram	works of the Shaiva saint-poets, Sambandar, Appar and Sundarar

Thirukkural	Tamil text of verses by Valluvar (300 BC to 5 CE)
udukkai	hourglass-shaped drum
Vaikundam	abode of Lord Vishnu
Vaishnava	Vishnu devotee

JAICO PUBLISHING HOUSE

Elevate Your Life. Transform Your World.

ESTABLISHED IN 1946, Jaico Publishing House is home to world-transforming authors such as Sri Sri Paramahansa Yogananda, Osho, the Dalai Lama, Sri Sri Ravi Shankar, Sadhguru, Robin Sharma, Deepak Chopra, Jack Canfield, Eknath Easwaran, Devdutt Pattanaik, Khushwant Singh, John Maxwell, Brian Tracy, and Stephen Hawking.

Our late founder Mr. Jaman Shah first established Jaico as a book distribution company. Sensing that independence was around the corner, he aptly named his company Jaico ('Jai' means victory in Hindi). In order to service the significant demand for affordable books in a developing nation, Mr. Shah initiated Jaico's own publications. Jaico was India's first publisher of paperback books in the English language.

While self-help, religion and philosophy, mind/body/spirit, and business titles form the cornerstone of our non-fiction list, we publish an exciting range of travel, current affairs, biography, and popular science books as well. Our renewed focus on popular fiction is evident in our new titles by a host of fresh young talent from India and abroad. Jaico's recently established translations division translates selected English content into nine regional languages.

Jaico distributes its own titles. With its headquarters in Mumbai, Jaico has branches in Ahmedabad, Bangalore, Chennai, Delhi, Hyderabad, and Kolkata.

SINCE 1946

CPSIA information can be obtained
at www.ICGtesting.com
Printed in the USA
BVHW041205020922
646135BV00002B/60